SHIP OF MAGIC

BANTAM BOOKS BY ROBIN HOBB

THE FARSEER: ASSASSIN'S APPRENTICE

THE FARSEER: ROYAL ASSASSIN

THE FARSEER: ASSASSIN'S QUEST

THE LIVESHIP TRADERS: SHIP OF MAGIC

SHIP OF MAGIC

THE LIVESHIP TRADERS: BOOK I

ROBIN HOBB

BANTAM BOOKS

NEW YORK   TORONTO   LONDON   SYDNEY   AUCKLAND

SHIP OF MAGIC

A Bantam Spectra Book / March 1998

SPECTRA and the portrayal of a boxed "s" are trademarks of Bantam Books, a
division of Bantam Doubleday Dell Publishing Group, Inc.

Book design by Lisa Stokes

Cover art copyright © 1998 by Stephen Youll.

ISBN 0-553-10324-5

PRINTED IN THE UNITED STATES OF AMERICA

THIS ONE IS FOR

The *Devil's Paw*
The *Totem*
The *E J Bruce*
The *Free Lunch*
The *Labrador* (Scales! Scales!)
The (aptly named) *Massacre Bay*
The *Faithful* (Gummi Bears Ahoy!)
The *Entrance Point*
The *Cape St. John*
The *American Patriot* (and Cap'n Wookie)
The *Lesbian Warmonger*
The *Anita J* and the *Marcy J*
The *Tarpon*
The *Capelin*
The *Dolphin*
The (not very) *Good News Bay*
And even the *Chicken Little*

But especially for *Rain Lady*, wherever she may be now.

ACKNOWLEDGMENTS

The author would like to thank Gale Zimmerman of Software Alternatives, Tacoma, Washington, for rendering swift and compassionate aid in stamping out the computer virus that nearly ate this book.

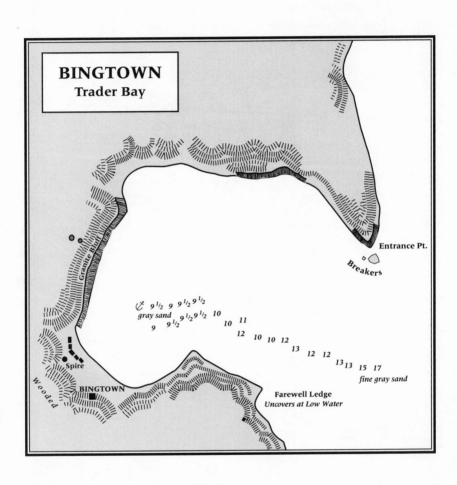

BINGTOWN
Trader Bay

Entrance Pt.

Breakers

Granite Bluff

$9^{1}/_{2}$ 9 $9^{1}/_{2}$ $9^{1}/_{2}$
gray sand 10
9 $9^{1}/_{2}$ $9^{1}/_{2}$ $9^{1}/_{2}$ 10 11
12 10 10 12
13
12 12
13 13 15 17
fine gray sand

Spire

Wooded

BINGTOWN

Farewell Ledge
Uncovers at Low Water

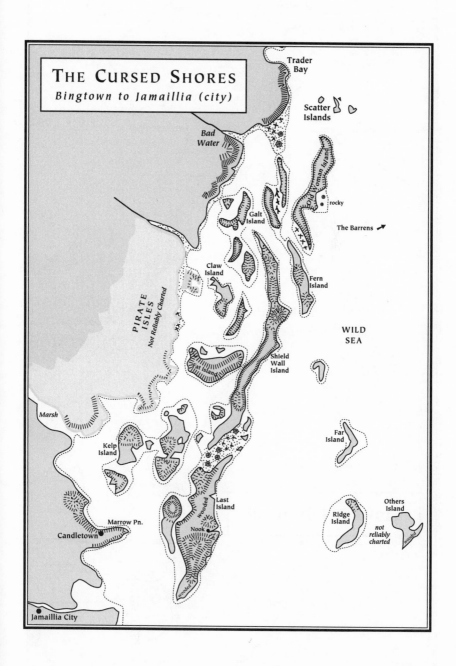

THE CURSED SHORES
Bingtown to Jamaillia (city)

Trader Bay

Scatter Islands

Bad Water

Old Woman Island

rocky

Galt Island

The Barrens →

Claw Island

Fern Island

PIRATE ISLES
Not Reliably Charted

WILD SEA

Shield Wall Island

Ear Island

Far Island

Marsh

Kelp Island

Others Island

not reliably charted

Ridge Island

wooded

Last Island

Marrow Pn.

Nook

Candletown

wooded

Jamaillia City

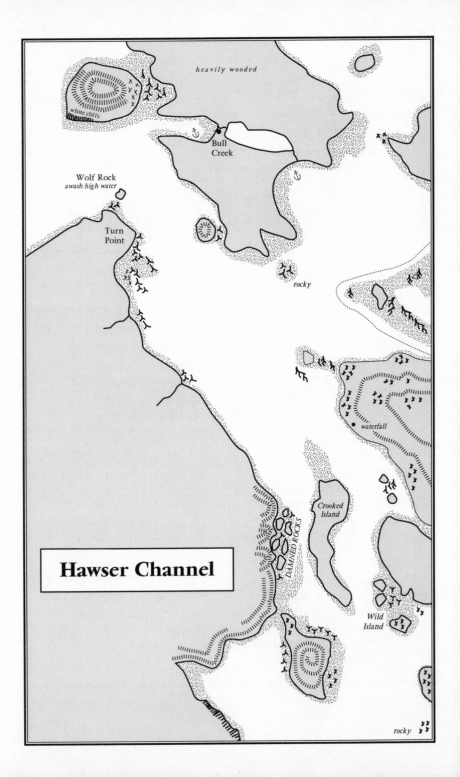

heavily wooded

white cliffs

Bull
Creek

Wolf Rock
awash high water

Turn
Point

rocky

waterfall

*Crooked
Island*

DAMNED ROCKS

*Wild
Island*

Hawser Channel

rocky

THE TANGLE

MAULKIN ABRUPTLY HEAVED HIMSELF OUT OF HIS WALLOW WITH A WILD THRASH THAT LEFT THE ATMOsphere hanging thick with particles. Shreds of his shed skin floated with the sand and muck like the dangling remnants of dreams when one awakes. He moved his long sinuous body through a lazy loop, rubbing against himself to rub off the last scraps of outgrown hide. As the bottom muck started to once more settle, he gazed about at the two dozen other serpents who lay basking in the pleasantly scratchy sediments. He shook his great maned head and then stretched the vast muscle of his length. "Time," he bugled in his deep-throated voice. "The time has come."

They all looked up at him from the sea-bottom, their great eyes of green and gold and copper unwinking. Shreever spoke for them all when she asked, "Why? The water is warm here, the feeding easy. In a hundred years, winter has never come. Why must we leave now?"

Maulkin performed another lazy twining of himself. His newly bared scales shone brilliantly in the filtered blue sunlight. His preening burnished the golden false-eyes that ran his full length, declaring him one of those with ancient sight. Maulkin could recall things, things from the time before all this time. His perceptions were not clear, nor always consistent. Like many of those caught twixt times, with knowledge of both lives, he was often unfocused and incoherent. He shook his mane until his paralyzing poison made a pale cloud about his face. He gulped his own toxin in, breathed it out through his gills in a show of truth-vow. "Because it is time now!" he said urgently. He sped suddenly away from them all, shooting up to the surface, rising straighter and faster than the bubbles. Far above them all he broke the ceiling and leaped out briefly into the great Lack before he dove again. He swam about them in frantic circles, wordless in his urgency.

"Some of the other tangles have already gone," Shreever said thoughtfully. "Not all of them, not even most. But enough to notice they are missing when we rise into the Lack to sing. Perhaps it is time."

Sessurea settled deeper into the muck. "And perhaps it is not," he said lazily. "I think we should wait until Aubren's tangle goes. Aubren is . . . steadier than Maulkin."

Beside him, Shreever abruptly heaved herself out of the muck. The gleaming scarlet of her new skin was startling. Rags of maroon still hung from her. She nipped a great hank of it free and gulped it down before she spoke. "Perhaps you should join Aubren's tangle, if you misdoubt Maulkin's words. I, for one, will follow him north. Better to go too soon than too late. Better to go early, perhaps, than to come with scores of other tangles and have to vie for feeding." She moved lithely through a knot made of her own body, rubbing the last fragments of old hide free. She shook her own mane, then threw back her head. Her shrill trumpeting disturbed the water. "I come, Maulkin! I follow you!" She moved up to join their still circling leader in his twining dance overhead.

One at a time, the other great serpents heaved their long bodies free of clinging muck and outgrown skin. All, even Sessurea, rose from the depths to circle in the warm water just below the ceiling of the Plenty, joining in the tangle's dance. They would go north, back to the waters from whence they had come, in the long ago time that so few now remembered.

MIDSUMMER

CHAPTER ONE

OF PRIESTS AND PIRATES

KENNIT WALKED THE TIDELINE, HEEDLESS OF THE SALT WAVES THAT WASHED AROUND HIS BOOTS AS THEY licked the sandy beach clean of his tracks. He kept his eyes on the straggling line of seaweed, shells and snags of driftwood that marked the water's highest reach. The tide was just turning now, the waves falling ever shorter in their pleading grasp upon the land. As the salt water retreated down the black sand, it would bare the worn molars of shale and tangles of kelp that now hid beneath the waves.

On the other side of Others Island, his two-masted ship was anchored in Deception Cove. He had brought the *Marietta* in to anchor there as the morning winds had blown the last of the storm clean of the sky. The tide had still been rising then, the fanged rocks of the notorious cove grudgingly receding beneath frothy green lace. The ship's gig had scraped over and between the barnacled rocks to put him and Gankis ashore on a tiny crescent of black sand beach that disappeared completely when storm winds drove the waves up past the high tide marks. Above, slate cliffs loomed, and evergreens so dark they were nearly black leaned precariously out in defiance of the prevailing winds.

Even to Kennit's iron nerves, it was like stepping into some creature's half-open mouth.

They'd left Opal, the ship's boy, with the gig to protect it from the bizarre mishaps that so often befell unguarded craft in Deception Cove. Much to the boy's unease, Kennit had commanded Gankis to come with him, leaving the boy and boat alone. At Kennit's last sight, the boy had been perched in the beached boat. His eyes had alternated between fearful glances over his shoulder at the forested cliff-tops and staring anxiously out to where the *Marietta* strained against her anchors, yearning to join the racing current that swept past the mouth of the cove.

The hazards of visiting this island were legendary. It was not just the hostility of the "best" anchorage on the island, nor the odd accidents known to befall ships and visitors. The whole of the island was enshrouded in the peculiar magic of the Others. Kennit had felt it tugging at him as he and Gankis followed the path that led from Deception Cove to the Treasure Beach. For a path seldom used, its black gravel was miraculously clean of fallen leaves or intruding plant life. About them the trees dripped the second-hand rain of last night's storm onto fern fronds already burdened with crystal drops. The air was cool and alive. Brightly hued flowers, always growing at least a man's length from the path, challenged the dimness of the shaded forest floor. Their scents drifted alluringly on the morning air as if beckoning the men to leave off their quest and explore their world. Less wholesome in appearance were the orange fungi that stairstepped up the trunks of many of the trees. The shocking brilliance of their color spoke to Kennit of parasitic hungers. A spider's web, hung like the ferns with fine droplets of shining water, stretched across their path, forcing them to duck under it. The spider that sat at the edges of its strands was as orange as the fungi, and nearly as big as a baby's fist. A green tree-frog was enmeshed and struggling in the web's sticky strands, but the spider appeared disinterested. Gankis made a small sound of dismay as he crouched to go beneath it.

This path led right through the midst of the Others' realm. Here was where the nebulous boundaries of their territory could be crossed by a man, did he dare to leave the well-marked path allotted to humans and step off into the forest to seek them. In ancient times, so the tales told, heroes came here, not to follow the path but to leave it deliberately, to beard the Others in their dens, and seek the wisdom of their cave-imprisoned goddess, or demand gifts such as cloaks of invisibility and swords that ran with flames and could shear through any shield. Bards that had dared to come this way had returned to their homelands with voices that could shatter a man's ears with their power, or melt the heart of any listener with their skill. All knew the ancient tale of Kaven Ravenlock, who visited the Others for half a hundred years and returned as if but a day had passed for him, but with hair the color of gold and eyes like red coals and true songs that told of the future in twisted rhymes. Kennit snorted softly to himself. All knew such ancient tales, but if any man had ventured to leave this path in Kennit's lifetime, he had told no other man about it. Perhaps he had never returned to brag of it. The pirate dismissed it from his mind. He had not come to the island to leave the path, but to follow it to its very end. And all knew what waited there as well.

Kennit had followed the gravel path that snaked through the forested hills of the island's interior until its winding descent spilled them out onto a coarsely grassed tableland that framed the wide curve of an open beach. This was the opposite shore of the tiny island. Legend foretold that any ship that anchored here had only the netherworld as its next port of call. Kennit had found no record of any ship that had dared challenge that rumor. If any had, its boldness had gone to hell with it.

The sky was a clean brisk blue scoured clean of clouds by last night's storm. The long curve of the rock and sand beach was broken only by a freshwater stream that cut its way through the high grassy bank backing the beach. The stream meandered over the sand to be engulfed in the sea. In the distance, higher cliffs of black shale rose, enclosing the far end of the crescent beach. One toothy tower of shale stood independent of the island, jutting out crookedly from the island with a small stretch of beach between it and its mother-cliff. The gap in the cliff framed a blue slice of sky and restless sea.

"It was a fair bit of wind and surf we had last night, sir. Some folk say that the best place to walk the Treasure Beach is on the grassy dunes up there . . . they say that in a good bit of storm, the waves throw things up there, fragile things you might expect to be smashed to bits on the rocks and such, but they land on the sedge up there, just as gentle as you please." Gankis panted out the words as he trotted at Kennit's heels. He had to stretch his stride to keep up with the tall pirate. "An uncle of mine—that is to say, actually he was married to my aunt, to my mother's sister—he said he knew a man found a little wooden box up there, shiny black and all painted with flowers. Inside was a little glass statue of a woman with butterfly's wings. But not transparent glass, no, the colors of the wings were swirled right in the glass they were." Gankis stopped in his account and half-stooped his head as he glanced cautiously at his master. "Would you want to know what the Other said it meant?" he inquired carefully.

Kennit paused to nudge the toe of his boot against a wrinkle in the wet sand. A glint of gold rewarded him. He stooped casually to hook his finger under a fine gold chain. As he drew it up, a locket popped out of its sandy grave. He wiped the locket down the front of his fine linen trousers, and then nimbly worked the tiny catch. The gold halves popped open. Saltwater had penetrated the edges of the locket, but the portrait of a young woman still smiled up at him, her eyes both merry and shyly rebuking. Kennit merely grunted at his find and put it in the pocket of his brocaded waistcoat.

"Cap'n, you know they won't let you keep that. No one keeps anything from the Treasure Beach," Gankis pointed out gingerly.

"Don't they?" Kennit queried in return. He put a twist of amusement in his voice, to watch Gankis puzzle over whether it was self-mockery or a threat. Gankis shifted his weight surreptitiously, to put his face out of reach of his captain's fist.

"S'what they all say, sir," he replied hesitantly. "That no one takes home what they find on the Treasure Beach. I know for sure my uncle's friend didn't. After the Other looked at what he'd found and told his fortune from it, he followed the Other down the beach to this rock cliff. Probably that one." Gankis lifted an arm to point at the distant shale cliffs. "And in the face of it there were thousands of little holes, little what-you-call-'ems. . . ."

"Alcoves," Kennit supplied in an almost dreamy voice. "I call them alcoves, Gankis. As would you, if you could speak your own mother tongue."

"Yessir. Alcoves. And in each was a treasure, 'cept for those that were empty. And the Other let him walk along the cliff wall and look at all the treasures, and there was stuff there such as he'd never even imagined. China teacups done all in fancy rosebuds and gold wine cups rimmed with jewels and little wooden toys all painted bright and, oh, a hundred things such as you can't imagine, each in an alcove. Sir. And then he found an alcove the right size and shape, and he put the butterfly lady in it. He told my uncle that nothing ever felt quite so right to him as setting that little treasure into that nook. And then he left it there, and left the island and went home."

Kennit cleared his throat. The single noise conveyed more of contempt and disdain than most men could have fitted into an entire stream of abuse. Gankis looked aside and down from it. "It was him that said it, sir, not me." He tugged at the waist of his worn trousers.

Almost reluctantly he added, "The man is a bit in the dream world. Gives a seventh of all that comes his way to Sa's temple, and both his eldest children besides. Such a man don't think as we do, sir."

"When you think at all, Gankis," the captain concluded for him. He lifted his pale eyes to look far up the tide line, squinting slightly as the morning sun dazzled off the moving waves. "Take yourself up to your sedgy cliffs, Gankis, and walk along them. Bring me whatever you find there."

"Yessir." The older pirate trudged away. He gave one rueful backward glance at his young captain. Then he clambered agilely up the short bank to the deeply grassed tableland that fronted on the beach. He began to walk a parallel course, his eyes scanning the bank ahead of him. Almost immediately, he spotted something. He sprinted toward it, then lifted an object that flashed in the morning sunlight. He raised it up to the light and gazed at it, his seamed face lit with awe. "Sir, sir, you should see what I've found!"

"I might be able to, did you bring it here to me as you were commanded," Kennit observed irritably.

Like a dog called to heel, Gankis made his way back to the captain. His brown eyes shone with a youthful sparkle, and he clutched the treasure in both hands as he leaped nimbly down the man-height drop to the beach. His low shoes kicked up sand as he ran. A brief frown creased Kennit's brow as he watched Gankis advancing towards him. Although the old sailor was prone to fawn on him, he was no more inclined to share booty than any other man of his trade. Kennit had not truly expected Gankis willingly to bring to him anything he found on the grassy bank; in fact he had been rather anticipating divesting the man of his trove at the end of their stroll. To have Gankis hastening toward him, his face beaming as if he were a country yokel bringing his beloved milkmaid a posy, was positively unsettling.

Nevertheless Kennit retained his customary sardonic smile, not allowing his face to betray his thoughts. It was a carefully rehearsed posture that suggested the languid grace of a hunting cat. It was not just that his greater height allowed him to look down on the seaman. By capturing his face in a pose of amusement, he suggested to his followers that they were incapable of surprising him. He wished his crew to believe that he could anticipate not only their every move, but their thoughts, too. A crew that believed that of their captain was less likely to become mutinous; and if they did, no one would wish to be the first to act.

And so he kept his poise as Gankis raced across the sand to him. Moreover, he did not immediately snatch the treasure away from him, but allowed the man to hold it out to him while he, Kennit, gazed down at it in amusement.

From the instant he saw it, it took all of Kennit's control not to snatch at it. Never had he seen such a cunningly wrought bauble. It was a bubble of glass, an absolutely perfect sphere. The surface was not marred with so much as a scratch. The glass itself had a very faint blue cast to it, but the tint did not obscure the wonder within. Three tiny figurines, garbed in motley with painted faces, were fixed to a tiny stage and somehow linked to one another so that when Gankis shifted the ball in his hands, it sent them off into a series of actions. One pirouetted on his toes, while the next did a series of flips over a bar. The third bobbed his head in time to their actions, as if all three heard and responded to a merry tune trapped inside the ball with them.

Kennit allowed Gankis to demonstrate it for him twice. Then, without a word, he extended a long-fingered hand towards him gracefully, and the sailor set the treasure in his palm. Kennit held his bemused smile firmly as he first lifted the ball to the sunlight, and then set the tumblers within to dancing for himself. The ball did not quite fill his hand. "A child's plaything," he surmised loftily.

"If the child were the richest prince in the world," Gankis dared to observe. "It's too fragile a thing to give a kid to play with, sir. All it would take would be dropping it once. . . ."

"Yet it seems to have survived bobbing about in the waves of a storm, and then being flung up on a beach," Kennit pointed out with measured good nature.

"That's true, sir, that's true, but then this is the Treasure Beach. Almost everything cast up here is whole, from what I've heard tell. It's part of the magic of this place."

"Magic." Kennit permitted himself a slightly wider smile as he placed the orb in the roomy pocket of his indigo jacket. "So you believe it is magic that sweeps such trinkets up on this shore, do you?"

"What else, Captain? By all rights, that should have been smashed to bits, or at least scoured by the sands. Yet it looks as if it just come out of a jeweler's shop."

Kennit shook his head sadly. "Magic? No, Gankis, no more magic than the rip-tides in the Orte Shallows, or the Spice Current that speeds sailing ships on their journeys to the islands and taunts them all the way back. It's but a trick of wind and current and tides. No more than that. The same trick that promises that any ship that tries to anchor off this side of the island will find herself beached and broken before the next tide."

"Yessir," Gankis agreed dutifully, but without conviction. His traitorous eyes strayed to the pocket where Captain Kennit had stowed the glass ball. Kennit's smile might have deepened fractionally.

"Well? Don't loiter here. Get back up there and walk the bank and see what else you find."

"Yessir," Gankis conceded, and with one final regretful glance at the pocket, the older man turned and hastened back to the bank. Kennit slipped his hand into his pocket and caressed the smooth cold glass there. He resumed his stroll down the beach. Overhead, gulls followed his example, sliding slowly down the wind as they searched the retreating waves for tidbits. He did not hasten, but kept in mind that on the other side of the island, his ship was awaiting him in treacherous waters. He'd walk the whole length of the beach, as tradition decreed, but he had no intention of lingering after he had heard the sooth-saying of an Other. Nor did he have any intention of leaving whatever treasure he found. A true smile tugged at the corner of his mouth.

As he strolled, he took his hand from his pocket and absently touched his opposite wrist. Concealed by the lacy cuff of his white silk shirt was a fine double thong of black leather. It bound a small wooden trinket tightly to his wrist. The ornament was a carved face, pierced at the brow and lower jaw so the face would be snugged firmly against his wrist, exactly over his pulse point. At one time, the face had been painted black, but most of that was worn away now. The features still stood out distinctly: a tiny mocking face, carved with exquisite care. Its visage was twin to his own. It had cost him an inordinate amount of coin to commission it. Not everyone who could carve wizardwood would, even if they had the balls to steal some.

Kennit remembered well the artisan who had worked the tiny face for him. He'd sat for long hours in the man's studio, washed in the cool morning light as the artist painstakingly worked the iron-hard wood to reflect Kennit's features. They had not spoken. The artist could not. The pirate did not. The carver had needed absolute silence for his concentration, for he worked not only wood but a spell that would bind the charm to protect the wearer from enchantments. Kennit had had nothing to say to him anyway. The pirate had paid him an exorbitant advance months before, and waited until the artist had sent him a messenger to say that he had obtained some of the precious and jealously guarded wood. Kennit had been outraged when the artist had demanded still more money before he would begin the carving and spell-setting, but Kennit had only smiled his small sardonic smile, and put coins and jewels and silver and gold links on the artist's scales until the man had nodded that his price had been met. Like many in

Bingtown's illicit trades, he had long ago sacrificed his own tongue to ensure his client's privacy. While Kennit was not convinced of the efficacy of such a mutilation, he appreciated the sentiment it implied. So when the artist was finished and had personally bound the ornament to Kennit's wrist, the man had only been able to nod vehemently his extreme satisfaction with his own skill as he touched the wood with avid fingertips.

Afterwards Kennit had killed him. It was the only sensible thing to do, and Kennit was an eminently sensible man. He had taken back the extra fee the man had demanded. Kennit could not abide a man who would not honor his original bargain. But that had not been the reason he'd killed him. He'd killed him for the sake of keeping the secret. If men knew that Captain Kennit wore a charm to ward off enchantments, why, then they would believe that he feared them. He could not let his crew believe that he feared anything. His good luck was legendary. All the men who followed him believed in it, most more strongly than Kennit himself did. It was why they followed him. They must not ever think that he feared anything could threaten that luck.

In the year since he had killed the artist, he had wondered if killing him had somehow harmed the charm, for it had not quickened. When he had originally asked the carver how long it would take for the little face to come to life, the man had shrugged eloquently, and indicated with much hand fluttering that neither he nor anyone else could predict such a thing. For a year Kennit had waited for the charm to quicken, to be sure that its spell was completely activated. But there had come a time when he could not wait any longer. He had known, on an instinctive level, that it was time for him to visit the Treasure Beach and see what fortune the ocean would wash up for him. He could wait no longer for the charm to awaken; he'd decided to take his chances. He'd have to once more trust his good luck to protect him, as it always had. It had protected him the day he'd had to kill the artist, hadn't it? The man had turned unexpectedly, just in time to see Kennit drawing his blade. Kennit was convinced that if the man had had a tongue in his head, his scream would have been much louder.

Kennit set the artist firmly out of his mind. This was no time to be thinking of him. He hadn't come to the Treasure Beach to dwell on the past, but to find treasure to secure his future. He fixed his eyes on the undulating tideline and followed it down the beach. He ignored the glistening shells, the crab claws and tangles of uprooted seaweed and driftwood large and small. His pale blue eyes searched for jetsam and wreckage only. He did not have to go far to be rewarded. In a small battered wooden chest, he found a set of teacups. He did not think men had made them nor used them. There were twelve of them and they were made of hollowed-out ends of birds' bones. Tiny blue pictures had been painted on them, the lines so fine that it looked as if the brush had been a single hair. The cups were well used. The blue pictures were faded beyond recognition of their original form and the carved bone handles were worn thin with use. He tucked the small case in the crook of his arm and walked on.

He strode along under the sun and against the wind, his fine boots leaving clean tracks in the wet sand. Occasionally he lifted his gaze, casually, to scan the entire beach. He did not let his expectations show on his face. When he let his gaze drop to the sand, he discovered a tiny cedar box. Salt water had warped the wood. To open it he had to strike it on a rock like a nut. Inside were fingernails. They were fashioned of rich mother-of-pearl. Minute clamps would affix them on top of an ordinary nail and in the tip of each one was a tiny hollow, perhaps to store poison. There were twelve of them. Kennit put them into his other pocket. They rattled and clicked together as he walked.

It did not distress him that what he had found was obviously neither of human make nor designed for human use. Although he had earlier mocked Gankis' belief in the magic of the beach, all knew that more than one ocean's waves brushed these rocky shores. Ships foolish enough to anchor anywhere off of this island during a squall were likely to disappear entirely, leaving not even a splinter of wreckage. Old sailors said they had been swept clean out of this world and into the seas of another one. Kennit did not doubt it. He glanced at the sky, but it remained clean and blue. The wind was crisp, but he had faith the weather would hold so that he could walk the Treasure Beach and then hike back across the island to where his ship waited at anchor in Deception Cove. He trusted his luck to hold.

His most unsettling discovery came next. It was a bag made of red and blue leather stitched together, half buried in the wet sand. The leather was stout, the bag meant to last. Salt water had soaked and stained it, bleeding the colors into one another. The brine had seized up the brass buckles that had secured it and stiffened the leather straps that went through them. He used his knife to rip open a seam. Inside was a litter of kittens, perfectly formed with long claws and iridescent patches behind their ears. They were dead, all six of them. Quelling his distaste, he picked up the smallest. He turned the limp body over in his hands. It was blue-furred, a deep periwinkle blue with pink-lidded eyes. Small. The runt, most likely. It was sodden and cold and disgusting. A ruby earring like a fat tick decorated one of the wet ears. He longed to simply drop it. Ridiculous. He plucked the earring free and dropped it in his pocket. Then, moved by an impulse he did not understand, he returned the small blue bodies to the bag and left it beside the tideline. Kennit walked on.

Awe flowed through him with his blood. Tree. Bark and sap, the scent of the wood and the leaves fluttering overhead. Tree. But also the soil and the water, the air and the light, all was coming and going through the being known as tree. He moved with them, sliding in and out of an existence of bark and leaf and root, air and water.

"Wintrow."

The boy lifted his eyes slowly from the tree before him. With an effort of will, he focused his gaze on the smiling face of the young priest. Berandol nodded in encouragement. Wintrow closed his eyes for an instant, held his breath, and pulled himself free of his task. When he opened his eyes, he took a sudden breath as if breaking clear of deep water. Dappling light, sweet water, soft wind all faded abruptly. He was in the monastery work room, a cool hall walled and floored with stone. His bare feet were chill against the floor. There were a dozen other slab tables in the big room. At three others, boys like himself worked slowly, their dreamlike movements indicative of their tranced state. One wove a basket and two others shaped clay with wet gray hands.

He looked down at the pieces of gleaming glass and lead on the table before him. The beauty of the stained-glass image he had pieced together astonished even him, yet it still could not touch the wonder of having been the tree. He touched it with his fingers, tracing the trunk and the graceful branches. Caressing the image was like touching his own body; he knew it that well. Behind him he heard the soft intake of Berandol's breath. In his state of still-heightened awareness, he could feel the priest's awe flowing with his own, and for a time they stood quietly, glorying together in the wonder of Sa.

"Wintrow," the priest repeated softly. He reached out and traced with a finger the tiny dragon that peered from the tree's upper branches, then touched the glistening curve of a serpent's body, all but hidden in the twisting roots. He put a hand on the boy's shoulders and turned him gently away from his worktable. As he steered him from the workroom, he rebuked him gently. "You are too young to sustain such a state for the whole morning. You must learn to pace yourself."

Wintrow lifted his hands to knuckle at eyes that were suddenly sandy. "I've been in there all morning?" he asked dazedly. "It did not seem like it, Berandol."

"I am sure it did not. Yet I am sure the weariness you feel now will convince you it is so. One must be careful, Wintrow. Tomorrow, ask a watcher to stir you at mid-morning. Talent such as you possess is too precious to allow you to burn it out."

"I do ache, now," Wintrow conceded. He ran his hand over his brow, pushing fine black hair from his eyes and smiled. "But the tree was worth it, Berandol."

Berandol nodded slowly. "In more ways than one. The sale of such a window will yield enough coin to re-roof the novitiates' hall. If Mother Dellity can bring herself to let the monastery part with such a thing of wonder." He hesitated a moment, then added, "I see they appeared again. The dragon and the serpent. You still have no idea. . . ." he let his voice trail away questioningly.

"I do not even have a recollection of putting them there," Wintrow said.

"Well." There was no trace of judgment in Berandol's voice. Only patience.

For a time they walked in companionable silence through the cool stone hallways of the monastery. Slowly Wintrow's senses lost their edge and faded to a normal level. He could no longer taste the scents of the salts trapped in the stone walls, nor hear the minute settling of the ancient blocks of stone. The rough brown bure of his novice robes became bearable against his skin. By the time they reached the great wooden door and stepped out into the monastery gardens, he was safely back in his body. He felt groggy as if he had just awakened from a long sleep, yet as bone weary as if he had hoed potatoes all day. He walked silently beside Berandol as monastery custom dictated. They passed others, some men and women robed in the green of full priesthood and others dressed in white as acolytes. Greetings were exchanged as nods.

As they neared the tool shed, he felt a sudden unsettling certainty that they were going there and that he would spend the rest of the afternoon working in the sunny garden. Any other time, it might have been a pleasant thing to look forward to, but his recent efforts in the dim work room had left his eyes sensitive to light. Berandol glanced back at his lagging step.

"Wintrow," he chided softly. "Refuse the anxiety. When you borrow trouble against what might be, you neglect the moment you have now to enjoy. The man who worries about what will next be happening to him loses this moment in dread of the next, and poisons the

next with pre-judgment." Berandol's voice took on an edge of hardness. "You indulge in pre-judgment too often. If you are refused the
priesthood, it will most likely be for that."

Wintrow's eyes flashed to Berandol's in horror. For a moment
stark desolation dominated his face. Then he saw the trap. His face
broke into a grin, and Berandol's answered it when the boy said, "But
if I fret about it, I shall have pre-judged myself to failure."

Berandol gave the slender boy a good-natured shove with his
elbow. "Exactly. Ah, you grow and learn so fast. I was much older
than you, twenty at least, before I learned to apply that Contradiction
to daily life."

Wintrow shrugged sheepishly. "I was meditating on it last night
before I fell asleep. 'One must plan for the future and anticipate the
future without fearing the future.' The Twenty-Seventh Contradiction of Sa."

"Thirteen years old is very young to have reached the Twenty-
Seventh Contradiction," Berandol observed.

"What one are you on?" Wintrow asked artlessly.

"The Thirty-Third. The same one I've been on for the last two
years."

Wintrow gave a small shrug of his shoulders. "I haven't studied
that far yet." They walked in the shade of apple trees, under leaves
hanging limp in the heat of the day. Ripening fruit weighted the
boughs. At the other end of the orchard, acolytes moved in patterns
through the trees, bearing buckets of water from the stream.

" 'A priest should not presume to judge unless he can judge as Sa
does; with absolute justice and absolute mercy.' " Berandol shook his
head. "I confess, I do not see how that is possible."

The boy's eyes were already turned inward, with only the slightest
line to his brow. "As long as you believe it is impossible, you close
your mind to understanding it." His voice seemed far away. "Unless,
of course, that is what we are meant to discover. That as priests we
cannot judge, for we have not the absolute mercy and absolute justice
to do so. Perhaps we are only meant to forgive and give solace."

Berandol shook his head. "In the space of a few moments, you
slice through as much of the knot as I had done in six months. But
then I look about me, and I see many priests who do judge. The
Wanderers of our order do little except resolve differences for folk. So
they must have somehow mastered the Thirty-Third Contradiction."

The boy looked up at him curiously. He opened his mouth to
speak and then blushed and shut it again.

Berandol glanced down at his charge. "Whatever it is, go ahead and say it. I will not rebuke you."

"The problem is, I was about to rebuke you," Wintrow confessed. The boy's face brightened as he added, "But I stopped myself before I did."

"And you were going to say to me?" Berandol pressed. When the boy shook his head, his tutor laughed aloud. "Come, Wintrow, having asked you to speak your thought, do you think I would be so unfair as to take offense at your words? What was in your mind?"

"I was going to tell you that you should govern your behavior by the precepts of Sa, not by what you see others doing." The boy spoke forthrightly, but then lowered his eyes. "I know it is not my place to remind you of that."

Berandol looked too deep in thought to have taken offense. "But if I follow the precept alone, and my heart tells me it is impossible for a man to judge as Sa does, with absolute justice and absolute mercy, then I must conclude . . ." His words slowed as if the thought came reluctantly. "I must conclude that either the Wanderers have much greater spiritual depth than I. Or that they have no more right to judge than I do." His eyes wandered among the apple trees. "Could it be that an entire branch of our order exists without righteousness? Is not it disloyal even to think such a thing?" His troubled glance came back to the boy at his side.

Wintrow smiled serenely. "If a man's thoughts follow the precepts of Sa, they cannot go astray."

"I shall have to think more on this," Berandol concluded with a sigh. He gave Wintrow a look of genuine fondness. "I bless the day you were given me as student, though in truth I often wonder who is student and who is teacher here. I shall miss you."

Sudden alarm filled Wintrow's eyes. "Miss me? Are you leaving, have you been called to duty so soon?"

"Not I. I should have given you this news better, but as always your words have led my thoughts far from their starting point. I am not leaving, but you. It was why I came to find you today, to bid you pack, for you are called home. Your grandmother and mother have sent word that they fear your grandfather is dying. They would have you near at such a time." At the look of devastation on the boy's face, Berandol added, "I am sorry to have told you so bluntly. You so seldom speak of your family. I did not realize you were close to your grandfather."

"I am not," Wintrow simply admitted. "Truth to tell, I scarcely know him. When I was small, he was always at sea. At the times when he was home, he always terrified me. Not with cruelty, but with . . . power. Everything about him seemed too large for the room, from his voice to his beard. Even when I was small and overheard other folk talking about him, it was as if they spoke of a legend or a hero. I don't recall that I ever called him Grandpa, nor even Grandfather. When he came home, he'd blow through the house like the North Wind and mostly I took shelter from his presence rather than enjoyed it. When I was dragged out before him, all I can recall was that he found fault with my growth. 'Why is the boy so puny?' he'd demand. 'He looks just like my boys, but half the size! Don't you feed him meat? Doesn't he eat well?' Then he would pull me near and feel my arm, as if I were being fattened for the table. I always felt ashamed of my size, then, as if it were a fault. Since I was given over to the priesthood, I have seen even less of him, but my impression of him has not changed. Still, it is not my grandfather I dread, nor even keeping his death watch. It's going home, Berandol. It is so . . . noisy."

Berandol grimaced in sympathy.

"I don't believe I even learned to think until I came here," Wintrow continued. "There, it was too noisy and too busy. I never had time to think. From the time Nana rousted us out of bed in the morning until we were bathed, gowned and dumped back in bed at night, we were in motion. Being dressed and taken on outings, having lessons and meals, visiting friends, being dressed differently and having more meals . . . it was endless. You know, when I first got here, I didn't leave my cell for the first two days. Without Nana or Grandma or Mother chasing me about, I had no idea what to do with myself. And for so long, my sister and I had been a unit. 'The children' need their nap, 'the children' need their lunch. I felt I'd lost half my body when they separated us."

Berandol was grinning in appreciation. "So that is what it is like, to be a Vestrit. I'd always wondered how the children of the Old Traders of Bingtown lived. For me, it was very different, and yet much the same. We were swineherds, my family. I had no nanny or outings, but there were always chores aplenty to keep one busy. Looking back, we spent most of our time simply surviving. Stretching out the food, fixing things long past fixing by anyone else's standards, caring for the swine . . . I think the pigs received better care than anyone else. There was never even a thought of giving up a child for the priesthood. Then my mother became ill, and my father made a promise that if she lived, he would dedicate one of his children to Sa. So when she lived, they sent me off. I was the runt of the litter, so to speak. The youngest surviving child, and with a stunted arm. It was a sacrifice for them, I am sure, but not as great as giving up one of my strapping older brothers."

"A stunted arm?" Wintrow asked in surprise.

"It was. I'd fallen on it when I was small, and it was a long time healing, and when it did heal, it was never as strong as it should have been. But the priests cured me. They put me with the watering crew on the orchard, and the priest in charge of us gave me mismatched buckets. He made me carry the heavier one with my weaker arm. I thought he was a madman at first; my parents had always taught me to use my stronger arm for everything. It was my earliest introduction to Sa's precepts."

Wintrow frowned to himself for a moment, then grinned. " 'For the weakest has but to try his strength to find it, and then he shall be strong.' "

"Exactly." The priest gestured at the long low building before them. The acolyte's cells had been their destination. "The messenger was delayed getting here. You will have to pack swiftly and set out right away if you are to reach port before your ship sails. It's a long walk."

"A ship!" The desolation that had faded briefly from Wintrow's face flooded back. "I hadn't thought of that. I hate traveling by sea. But when one must go from Jamaillia to Bingtown, there is no other choice." His frowned deepened. "Walk to port? Didn't they arrange a man and a horse for me?"

"Do you so quickly revive to the comforts of wealth, Wintrow?" Berandol chided him. When the boy hung his head, abashed, he went on, "No, the message said that a friend had offered you passage across and the family had been glad to accept it." More gently he added, "I suspect that money is not so plentiful for your family as it once was. The Northern War has hurt many of the trading families, both in the goods that never came down the Buck River and those that never were sold there." More pensively, he went on, "And our young Satrap does not favor Bingtown as his father and grandfathers did. They seemed to feel that those brave enough to settle the Cursed Shores should share generously in the treasures they found there. But not young Cosgo. It is said that he feels they have reaped the reward of their risk-taking long enough, that the Shores are well settled and whatever curse was once there is now dispersed. He has not only sent them new taxes but has parceled out new grants of land near Bingtown to some of his favorites." Berandol shook his head. "He breaks the word of his ancestor, and causes hardship for folk who have always kept their word with him. No good can come of this."

"I know. I should be grateful I am not afoot all the way. But it is hard, Berandol, to accept a journey to a destination I dread, let alone by ship. I shall be miserable the whole way."

"Sea-sick?" Berandol asked in some surprise. "I did not think it afflicted those of seafaring stock."

"The right weather can sour any man's stomach, but no, that is not it. It's the noise and the rushing about and the crowded conditions. The smell. And the sailors. Good enough men in their own way but . . ." the boy shrugged. "Not like us. They haven't the time to talk about the things we speak of here, Berandol. And if they did, their thoughts would likely be as basic as that of the youngest acolyte. They live as animals do, and reason as animals. I shall feel as if I am living among beasts. Through no faults of their own," he added at seeing the young priest frown.

Berandol took a breath as if to launch into speech, then reconsidered it. After a moment, he said thoughtfully, "It has been two years since you have visited your parents' home, Wintrow. Two years since you last were out of the monastery and about working folk. Look and listen well, and when you come back to us, tell me if you still agree with what you have just said. I charge you to remember this, for I shall."

"I shall, Berandol," the youth promised sincerely. "And I shall miss you."

"Probably, but not for some days, for I am to escort you on your journey down to the port. Come. Let's go and pack."

Long before Kennit reached the end of the beach, he was aware of the Other watching him. He had expected this, yet it intrigued him, for he had often heard they were creatures of the dawn and the dusk, seldom moving about while the sun was still in the sky. A lesser man might have been afraid, but a lesser man would not have possessed Kennit's luck. Or his skill with a sword. He continued his leisurely stroll down the beach, all the while gathering plunder. He feigned unawareness of the creature watching him, yet he was eerily certain that it knew of his deceit. A game within a game, he told himself, and smiled secretly.

He was immensely irritated when, a few moments later, Gankis came lolloping down the beach to wheeze out the news that there was an Other up there watching him.

"I know," he told the old sailor with asperity. An instant later he had regained control of his voice and features. In a kindly tone, he explained, "And it knows that we know it is watching us. That being so, I suggest you ignore it, as I do, and finish searching your bank. Have you found anything else of note?"

"A few things," Gankis admitted, not pleased. Kennit straightened and waited. The sailor dug into the capacious pockets of his worn coat. "There's this," he said as he reluctantly drew an object of brightly painted wood from his pocket. It was an arrangement of disks and rods with circular holes in some of the disks.

Kennit found it incomprehensible. "A child's toy of some kind," he deemed it. He raised his eyebrow at Gankis and waited.

"And this," the seaman conceded. He took a rose bud from his pocket. Kennit took it from him carefully, wary of the thorns. He had actually believed it real until the moment that he held it and found the stem stiff and unyielding. He hefted it in his hand; it was as light as a real rose would be. He turned it, trying to decide what it was made from: he concluded it was nothing he had ever seen before. Even more mysterious than its structure was its fragrance, as warm and spicy as if it were a full-blown rose from a summer garden. Kennit raised one eyebrow at Gankis as he fastened the rose to the lapel of his jacket. The barbed thorns held it securely. Kennit watched Gankis' lips fold tight, but the seaman dared no words.

Kennit glanced at the sun, and then at the ebbing waves. It would take them over an hour to walk back to the other side of the island. He could not stay much longer without risking his ship on the rocks exposed by the retreating tide. A rare moment of indecision clouded his thoughts. He had not come to the Treasure Beach for treasure alone; he had come instead seeking the oracle of the Other, confident that the Other would choose to speak to him. He needed the confirmation of the oracle; was not that why he had brought Gankis with him to witness? Gankis was one of the few men aboard his ship who did not routinely embroider his own adventures. He knew that not only his own crew members but any pirate at Divvytown would accept Gankis' account as true. Besides. If the oracle that Gankis witnessed did not suit Kennit's purposes, he'd be an easy man to kill.

Once again he considered the amount of time left to him. A prudent man would stop his search of the beach now, confront the Other, and then hasten back to his ship. Prudent men never trusted their luck. But Kennit had long ago decided that a man had to trust his luck in order for it to grow. It was a personal belief, one he had discovered for himself and saw no reason to share with anyone else. He had never achieved any major triumph without taking a chance and trusting his luck. Perhaps the day he became prudent and cautious, his luck would take insult and desert him. He smirked to himself as he concluded that would be the one chance he would not take. He would never trust to luck that his luck would not desert him.

This convolution of logic pleased him. He continued his leisurely search of the tideline. As he neared the toothy rocks that marked the end of the crescent beach, every one of his senses prickled with awareness of the Other. The smell of it was alluringly sweet, and then abruptly it became rancidly rotten when the wind changed and brought it stronger. The scent was so strong it became a taste in the back of his throat, one that almost gagged him. But it was not just the smell of the beast; Kennit could feel its presence against his skin. His ears popped and he felt its breathing as a pressure on his eyeballs and on the skin of his throat. He did not think he perspired, yet his face suddenly felt greasy with sweat, as if the wind had carried some substance from the Other's skin and pasted it onto his. Kennit fought distaste that bordered on nausea. He refused to let that weakness show.

Instead he drew himself up to his full height and unobtrusively straightened his waistcoat. The wind stirred both the plumes on his hat and the gleaming black locks of his hair. Generally speaking, he cut a fine figure, and drew a great deal of power from knowing that both men and women were impressed by him. He was tall, but muscled proportionately. The tailoring of his coat showed off the breadth of his shoulders and chest and the flatness of his belly. His face pleased him, too. He felt he was a handsome man. He had a high brow, a firm jaw and a straight nose over finely drawn lips. His beard was fashionably pointed, the ends of his mustache meticulously waxed. His only feature that displeased him were his eyes: they were his mother's eyes, pale and watery and blue. When he encountered their stare in a looking-glass, she looked out of them at him, distressed and teary at his dissolute ways. They seemed to him the vacuous eyes of an idiot, out of place in his tanned face. In another man, folk would have said he had mild blue eyes, inquiring eyes. Kennit strove to cultivate a cold blue stare, but knew his eyes were too pale even for that. He augmented the effort with a slight curl of his lip as he let his eyes come to rest on the waiting Other.

It seemed little impressed. It returned his stare from a height near equal to his own. It was oddly reassuring to find how accurate the legends were. The webbed fingers and toes, the obvious flexibility of the limbs, the flat fish eyes in their cartilaginous sockets, even the supple scaled skin that covered the creature were all as Kennit had expected. Its blunt, bald head was mis-shapen, neither that of a human nor a fish. The hinge of its jaw was under its ear holes, anchoring a mouth large enough to engulf a man's head. Its thin lips could not conceal the rows of tiny sharp teeth. Its shoulders seemed to slump forward, but the posture suggested brute strength rather than slovenliness. It wore a garment somewhat like a cloak, of a pale azure, and the weave was so fine that it had no more texture than a flower petal. It draped the Other in a way that suggested the fluidity of water. Yes, all was as he had read of it. What he had not expected was the attraction he felt. Some trick of the wind had lied to his nose. This creature's scent was like a summer garden, the air of its breath the subtle bouquet of a rare wine. All wisdom resided in those unreadable eyes. He suddenly longed to distinguish himself before it and be deemed worthy of its regard. He wanted to impress it with his goodness and intelligence. He longed for it to think well of him.

He heard the slight crunch of Gankis' footfalls on the sand behind him. For an instant, the Other's attention wavered. The flat eyes slid away from contemplating Kennit and in that moment the glamour was broken. Kennit almost startled. Then he crossed his arms on his chest so that the wizardwood face pressed into his flesh securely. Quickened or not, it had seemed to work, holding off the creature's enchantment. And now that he was aware of the Other's intent, he could hold his will firm against such manipulation. Even when its eyes darted back to lock with Kennit's gaze, he could see the Other for what it was: a cold and squamous creature of the deep. It seemed to sense it had lost its hold on him, for when it filled the air pouches behind its jaws and belched its words at him, Kennit sensed a trace of sarcasm.

"Welcome, pilgrim. The sea has well rewarded your search, I see. Will you make a goodwill offering, and hear the oracle speak the significance of your finds?"

Its voice creaked like unoiled hinges as it wheezed and gasped words at him. A part of Kennit admired the effort it must have taken for it to learn to shape human words, but the harder side of him dismissed it as a servile act. Here was this creature, foreign in every way to his humanity. He stood before it, on its own territory, and yet it waited upon him, speaking in his tongue, begging alms in exchange for its prophecies. Yet if it recognized him as superior, why was there sarcasm in its voice?

Kennit dismissed the question from his mind. He reached for his purse, and took from it the two gold bits that were the customary offering. Despite his earlier dissembling with Gankis, he had researched exactly what he might expect. Good luck works best when it is not surprised. So he was unruffled when the Other extended a stiff, grayish tongue to receive the coins, and he did not shrink from placing them there. The creature jerked its tongue back into its maw. If it did aught with the gold other than swallow it, Kennit could not tell. That done, the Other gave a stiff sort of bow, and then smoothed a fan of sand to receive the objects Kennit had gathered.

Kennit took his time in spreading them out before it. He set down first the glass ball with the tumblers within it. Beside it he placed the rose, and then he carefully arranged the twelve fingernails around it. At the end of the arc he placed the small chest with the tiny cups in it. A handful of small crystal spheres he nested in a hollow. He had gathered them on the final stretch of beach. Beside them he set his final find, a copper feather that seemed to weigh little more than a real one. He gave a nod that he was finished and stepped back slightly. With an apologetic glance at his captain, Gankis shyly placed the painted wooden toy to one side of the arc. Then he, too, stood back. The Other looked for a time at the fan of treasures before it. Then it lifted its oddly flat eyes to meet Kennit's blue stare. It finally spoke. "This is *all* you found?" The emphasis was unmistakable.

Kennit made a tiny movement of his shoulders and head, a movement that might mean yes or no, or nothing at all. He did not speak. Gankis shifted his feet about uncomfortably. The Other refilled its air sacs noisily.

"That which the ocean washes up here is not for the keeping of men. The water brings it here because here is where the water wishes it to be. Do not set yourself against the will of the water, for no wise creature does that. No human is permitted to keep what he finds upon the Treasure Beach."

"Does it belong to the Other, then?" Kennit asked calmly.

Despite the difference in species, it was still easy for Kennit to see he had disconcerted the Other. It took a moment to recover, then answered gravely, "What the ocean washes up upon the Treasure Beach belongs always to the ocean. We are but caretakers here."

Kennit's smile stretched his lips tight and thin. "Well then, you need have no concern. I'm Captain Kennit, and I'm not the only one who will tell you that all the ocean is mine to rove. So all that belongs to the ocean is mine as well. You've had your gold, now speak your prophecy, and take no more care for that which does not belong to you."

Beside him Gankis gasped audibly, but the Other gave no sign of reacting to these words. Instead it bowed its head gravely, inclining its neckless body toward him, almost as if compelled to acknowledge Kennit as its master. Then it lifted its head and its fish eyes found Kennit's soul as unerringly as a finger on a chart. When it spoke there was a deeper note to its voice, as if the words were blown up from deep inside it.

"So plain this telling that even one of your spawn could read it. You take that which is not yours, Captain Kennit, and claim it as your own. No matter how much falls into your hands, you are never sated. Those that follow you must be content with what you have cast off as gew-gaws and toys, while you take what you perceive as most valuable and keep it for yourself." The creature's eyes darted briefly to lock with Gankis' goggling stare. "In his evaluations, you are both deceived, and both made the poorer."

Kennit did not care at all for the direction of this sooth-saying. "My gold has bought me the right to ask one question, has it not?" he demanded boldly.

The Other's jaw dropped open wide—not in astonishment, but perhaps as a sort of threat. The rows of teeth were indeed impressive. Then it snapped shut. The thin lips barely stirred as it belched out its answer. "Yesss."

"Shall I succeed in what I aspire?"

The Other's air sacs pulsed speculatively. "You do not wish to make your question more specific?"

"Do the omens need me to be more specific?" Kennit asked with tolerance.

The Other glanced down at the array of objects again: the rose, the cups, the nails, the tumblers inside the ball, the feather, the crystal spheres. "You will succeed in your heart's desire," it said succinctly. A smile began to dawn on Kennit's face but faded as the creature continued, his tone growing more ominous. "That which you are most driven to do, you will accomplish. That task, that feat, that deed which haunts your dreams will blossom in your hands."

"Enough," Kennit growled, suddenly hasty. He abandoned any thought of asking for an audience with their goddess. This was as far as he wished to press their sooth-saying. He stooped to retrieve the prizes on the sand, but the creature suddenly fanned out its long-fingered webbed hands and spread them protectively above the treasures. A drop of venom welled greenly to the tip of each digit.

"The treasures, of course, will remain on the Treasure Beach. I will see to their placement."

"Why, thank you," Kennit said, his voice melodic with sincerity. He straightened slowly, but as the creature relaxed its guard, he suddenly stepped forward, planting his foot firmly on the glass ball with the tumblers inside. It gave way with a tinkle like wind chimes. Gankis cried out as if Kennit had slain his first-born and even the Other recoiled at the wanton destructiveness. "A pity," Kennit observed as he turned away. "But if I cannot possess it, why should anyone?"

Wisely, he forbore a similar treatment for the rose. He suspected its delicate beauty was created from some material that would not give way to his boot's pressure. He did not wish to lose his dignity by attempting to destroy it and failing. The other objects had small value in his regard; the Other could do whatever it wished with such flotsam. He turned and strode away.

Behind him he heard the Other hiss its wrath. It took a long breath, then intoned, "The heel that destroys that which belongs to the sea shall be claimed in turn by the sea." Its toothy jaws shut with a snap, biting off this last prophecy. Gankis immediately moved to flank Kennit. That one would always prefer the known danger to the unknown. Half a dozen strides down the beach, Kennit halted and turned. He called back to where the Other still crouched over the treasures. "Oh, yes, there was one other omen that perhaps you might wish to consider. But methinks the ocean washed it to you, not me, and thus I left it where it was. It is well-known, I believe, that the Others have no love for cats?" Actually, their fear and awe of anything feline was almost as legendary as their ability to sooth-say. The Other did not deign to reply, but Kennit had the satisfaction of seeing its air sacs puff with alarm.

"You'll find them up the beach. A whole litter of kits for you, with very pretty blue coats. They were in a leather bag. Seven or eight of the pretty little creatures. Most of them looked a bit poorly after their dip in the ocean, but no doubt those I let out will fare well. Do remember they belong, not to you, but the ocean. I'm sure you'll treat them kindly."

The Other made a peculiar sound, almost a whistle. "Take them!" it begged. "Take them away, all of them. Please!"

"Take away from the Treasure Beach that which the ocean saw fit to bring here? I would not dream of it," Kennit assured him with vast sincerity. He did not laugh, nor even smile as he turned away from its evident distress. He did find himself humming the tune to a rather bawdy song currently popular in Divvytown. The length of his stride was such that Gankis was soon puffing again as he trotted along beside him.

"Sir?" Gankis gasped. "A question if I might, Captain Kennit?"

"You may ask it," Kennit granted him graciously. He half expected the man to ask him to slow down. That he would refuse. They must make all haste back to the ship if they were to work her out to sea before the rocks emerged from the retreating tide.

"What is it that you'll succeed in doing?"

Kennit opened his mouth, almost tempted to tell the man. But no. He had schemed this too carefully, staged it all in his mind too often. He'd wait until they were underway and Gankis had had plenty of time to tell all the crew his version of events on the island. He doubted that would take long. The old hand was garrulous, and after their absence the men would be eaten with curiosity about their visit to the island. Once they had the wind in their sails and were fairly back on their way to Divvytown, then he'd call all hands up on deck. His imagination began to carry him, and he pictured the moon shining down on him as he spoke to the men gathered below him in the waist. His pale blue eyes kindled with the glow of his own imaginings.

They traversed the beach much faster than they had when they were seeking treasure. In a short time they were climbing the steep trail that led up from the shore and through the wooded interior of the island. He kept well concealed from Gankis the anxiety he felt for the *Marietta*. The tides in the cove both rose and fell with an extremity that paid no attention to the phases of the moon. A ship believed to be safely anchored in the cove might abruptly find her hull grinding against rocks that surely had not been there at the last low tide. Kennit would take no chances with his *Marietta*; they'd be well away from this sorcerous place before the tide could strand her.

Away from the wind of the beach and in the shelter of the trees, the day was still and golden. The warmth of the slanting sunlight through the open-branched trees combined with the rising scents of the forest loam to make the day enticingly sleepy. Kennit felt his stride slowing as the peace of the golden place seeped into him. Earlier, when the branches had been dripping with the aftermath of the storm's rain, the forest had been uninviting, a dank wet place full of brambles and slapping branches. Now he knew with unflagging certainty that the forest was a place of marvels. It had treasures and secrets every bit as tantalizing as those the Treasure Beach had offered.

His urgency to reach the *Marietta* peeled away from him and was discarded. He found himself standing still in the middle of the pebbled pathway. Today he would explore the island. To him would be opened the wonder-filled fey places of the Other, where a man might pass a hundred years in a single sublime night. Soon he would know and master it all. But for now it was enough to stand still and breathe

the golden air of this place. Nothing intruded on his pleasure, save Gankis. The man persisted in chattering warnings about the tide and the *Marietta*. The more Kennit ignored him, the more he pelted him with questions. "Why have we stopped here, Captain Kennit? Sir? Are you feeling well, sir?" He waved a dismissive hand at the man, but the old tar paid it no attention. He cast about for some errand that would take the noisy, smelly man from his presence. As he groped in his pockets, his hand encountered the locket and chain. He smiled slyly to himself as he drew it out.

He interrupted whatever it was Gankis was blithering about. "Ah, this will never do. See what I've accidentally carried off from their beach. Be a good lad now, and run this back to the beach for me. Give it to the Other and see it puts it safely away."

Gankis gaped at him. "There isn't time. Leave it here, sir! We've got to get back to the ship, before she's on the rocks or they have to leave without us. There won't be another tide that will let her back into Deception Cove for a month. And no man survives a night on this island."

The man was beginning to get on his nerves. His loud voice had frightened off a tiny green bird that had been on the point of alighting nearby. "Go, I told you. Go!" He put whips and fetters into his voice, and was relieved when the old sea-dog snatched the locket from his hand and dashed back the way they had come.

Once he was out of sight, Kennit grinned widely to himself. He hastened up the path into the island's hilly interior. He'd put some distance between himself and where he'd left Gankis, and then he'd leave the trail. Gankis would never find him, he'd be forced to leave without him, and then all the wonders of the Others' island would be his.

"Not quite. You would be theirs."

It was his own voice speaking, in a tiny whisper so soft that even Kennit's keen ears barely heard it. He moistened his lips and looked about himself. The words had shivered through him like a sudden awakening. He'd been about to do something. What?

"You were about to put yourself into their hands. Power flows both ways on this path. The magic encourages you to stay upon it, but it cannot be worked to appeal to a human without also working to repel the Other. The magic that keeps their world safe from you also protects you as long as you do not stray from the path. If they persuade you to leave the path, you'll be well within their reach. Not a wise move."

He lifted his wrist to a level with his eyes. His own miniature face grinned mockingly back at him. With the charm's quickening, the wood had taken on colors. The carved ringlets were as black as his own, the face as weathered, and the eyes as deceptively weak a blue. "I had begun to think you a bad bargain," Kennit said to the charm.

The face gave a snort of disdain. "If I am a bad bargain to you, you are as much a one to me," it pointed out. "I was beginning to think myself strapped to the wrist of a gullible fool, doomed to almost immediate destruction. But you seem to have shaken the effect of the spell. Or rather, I have cloven it from you."

"What spell?" Kennit demanded.

The charm's lip curled in a disdainful smile. "The reverse of the one you felt on the way here. All succumb to it that tread this path. The magic of the Other is so strong that one cannot pass through their lands without feeling it and being drawn toward it. So they settle upon this path a spell of procrastination. One knows that their lands beckon, but one puts off visiting them until tomorrow. Always tomorrow. And hence, never. But your little threat about the kittens has unsettled them a bit. You they would lure from the path, and use as a tool to be rid of the cats."

Kennit permitted himself a small smile of satisfaction. "They did not foresee I might have a charm that would make me proof against their magic."

The charm prissed its mouth. "I but made you aware of the spell. Awareness of any spell is the strongest charm against it. Of myself, I have no magic to fling back at them, or use to deaden their own." The face's blue eyes shifted back and forth. "And we may yet both meet our destruction if you stand about here talking to me. The tide retreats. Soon the mate must choose between abandoning you here or letting the *Marietta* be devoured by the rocks. Best you hasten for Deception Cove."

"Gankis!" Kennit exclaimed in dismay. He cursed, but began to run. Useless to go back for the man. He'd have to abandon him. And he'd given him the golden locket as well! What a fool he'd been, to be so gulled by the Others' magic. Well, he'd lost his witness and the souvenir he'd intended to carry off with him. He'd be damned if he'd lose his life or his ship as well. His long legs stretched as he pelted down the winding path. The golden sunlight that had earlier seemed so appealing was suddenly only a very hot afternoon that seemed to withhold the very air from his straining lungs.

A thinning of the trees ahead alerted him that he was nearly to the cove. Instants later, he heard the drumming of Gankis' feet on the path behind him, and was shocked when the sailor passed him without hesitation. Kennit had a brief glimpse of his lined face contorted with terror, and then he saw the sailor's worn boots flinging up gravel from the path as he ran ahead. Kennit had thought he could not run any faster, but he suddenly put on a burst of speed that carried him out of the sheltering trees and onto the beach.

He heard Gankis crying out to the ship's boy to wait, wait. The lad had evidently decided to give up on his captain's return, for he had pushed and dragged the gig out over the seaweed and barnacle-coated rocks to the retreating edge of the water. A cry went up from the anchored ship at the sight of Kennit and Gankis emerging onto the beach. On the afterdeck, a sailor waved at them frantically to hurry. The *Marietta* was in grave circumstances. The retreating tide had left her almost aground. Straining sailors were already laboring at the anchor windlass. As Kennit watched, the *Marietta* gave a tiny sideways list and then slid from atop a bared rock as a wave briefly lifted her clear. His heart stood still in his chest. Next to himself, he treasured his ship above all other things.

His boots slipped on squidgy kelp and crushed barnacles as he scrambled down the rocky shore after the boy and gig. Gankis was ahead of him. No orders were necessary as all three seized the gunwales of the gig and ran her out into the retreating waves. They were soaked before the last one scrambled inside her. Gankis and the boy seized the oars and set them in place while Kennit took his place in the stern. The *Marietta*'s anchor was rising, festooned with seaweed. Oars battled with sails as the distance between the two craft grew smaller. Then the gig was alongside, the tackles lowered and hooked, and but a few moments later Kennit was astride his own deck. The mate was at the wheel, and the instant he saw his captain safely aboard, Sorcor swung the wheel and bellowed the orders that would give the ship her head. Wind filled the *Marietta*'s sails, and flung her out against the incoming tide into the racing current that would buffet her, but carry her away from the bared teeth of Deception Cove.

A glance about the deck showed Kennit that all was in order. The ship's boy cowered when the captain's eyes swept over him. Kennit merely looked at him, and the boy knew his disobedience would not be forgotten nor overlooked. A pity. The boy had had a sweet smooth back; tomorrow that would no longer be so. Tomorrow would be soon enough to deal with him. Let him look forward to it for a time, and savor the stripes his cowardice had bought him. With no more than a nod to the mate, Kennit sought his own quarters. Despite the near mishap, his heart thundered with triumph. He had bested the Others at their own game. His luck had held, as it always had; the costly charm on his wrist had quickened and proved its value. And best of all, he had the oracle of the Others themselves to give the cloak of prophecy to his ambitions. He would be the first King of the Pirate Isles.

LIVESHIPS

THE SERPENT FLOWED THROUGH THE WATER, EFFORT-
LESSLY RIDING THE WAKE OF THE SHIP. ITS SCALED
body shone like a dolphin's, but more iridescently blue.
The head it lifted clear of the water was wickedly quilled
with dangling barbels like those on a ratfish. Its deep blue
eyes met Brashen's and widened in expectation like a
woman's when she flirts. Then the maw of the creature
opened wide, brilliantly scarlet and lined with row upon
row of inward slanting teeth. It gaped open, big enough to
take in a standing man. The dangling barbs stood up suddenly around the serpent's head, a lion's mane of poisonous
darts. The scarlet mouth came darting towards him to engulf him.

Darkness surrounded Brashen, and the cold carrion
stench of the creature's mouth. He flung himself away
wildly with an incoherent cry. His hands met wood, and
with the touch of it, relief flooded him. Nightmare. He
drew a shuddering breath. He listened to the familiar
sounds; the creaking of the *Vivacia*'s timbers, the breathing
of other sleeping men and the slapping of the water against
the hull. Overhead, he could hear the barefoot patter of

someone springing to answer a command. All was familiar, all was safe. He took a deep breath of air thick with the scent of tarry timbers, the stink of men living long in close quarters, and beneath it all, faint as a woman's perfume, the spicy smells of their cargo. He stretched, pushing his shoulders and feet against the cramped confines of his wooden bunk, and then settled back into his blanket. It was hours yet to his watch. If he didn't sleep now, he'd regret it later.

He closed his eyes to the dimness of the forecastle, but after a few moments, he opened them again. Brashen could sense his dream lurking just beneath the surface of sleep, waiting to reclaim him and drag him down. He cursed softly under his breath. He needed to get some sleep, but there'd be no rest in it if all he did was drop back down into the depths of the serpent dream.

The recurrent dream was now almost more real to him than the memory. It came to trouble him at odd times, usually when he was facing some major decision. At such times it reared up from the depths of his sleep to fasten its long teeth into his soul and try to pull him under. It little mattered that he was a full-grown man now. It mattered not at all that he was as good a sailor as any he'd ever shipped with, and better than nine-tenths of them. When the dream seized on him he was dragged back to his boyhood, back to a time when all, even himself, had rightly despised him.

He tried to decide what was troubling him most. His captain despised him. Yes, that was true, but it didn't make him any less a seaman. He'd been mate on this ship under Captain Vestrit and had well proved his worth to that man. When Vestrit had taken ill, Brashen had dared to hope the *Vivacia* would be put into his hands to captain. Instead the old Trader had turned it over to his son-in-law Kyle Haven. Well, family was family, and Brashen could accept what had been done. Then Captain Haven had exercised his option of choosing his own first mate, and it hadn't been Brashen Trell. Still the demotion was no fault of his own, and every sailor in the ship—no, every sailor in Bingtown itself—had known that. No shame to it; Kyle had simply wanted his own man. Brashen had thought it over and decided he'd rather serve as second mate on the *Vivacia* than first on any other vessel. It had been his own decision and he could fault no one else for it. Even after they had left the docks and Captain Haven had belatedly decided that he wanted a familiar man as second, and Brashen could move down yet another notch, he had gritted his teeth and obeyed his captain. But despite his years with the *Vivacia* and his gratitude to Ephron Vestrit, he suspected this would be the last time he shipped on her.

Captain Haven had made it clear to him that he neither welcomed nor respected Brashen as a member of his crew. During this last leg of the journey, nothing he did pleased the captain. If he saw a task that needed doing and put men to work on it, he was told he'd overstepped his authority. If he did only the duties that were precisely assigned to him, he was told he was a lazy lackwit. With each passing day, Bingtown grew nearer, but Haven grew more abrasive as well. Brashen was thinking that when they tied up in their home port, if Vestrit wasn't ready to step back on as captain again, Brashen would step off the *Vivacia*'s decks for the last time. It gave him a pang, but he reminded himself there were other ships, some of them fine ones, and Brashen had a name now as a good hand. It wasn't like it had been when he'd first sailed and he'd had to take any berth he could get on any ship. Back then, surviving a voyage had been his highest priority. That first ship out, that first voyage and his nightmare were all tied together in his mind.

He had been fourteen the first time he'd seen a sea serpent. It was ten long years ago now, and he had been as green as the grass stains on a tumble's skirts. He'd been less than three weeks aboard his first ship, a wallowing Chalcedean sow called the *Spray*. Even in the best of water she moved like a pregnant woman pushing a barrow, and in a following sea no one could predict where the deck would be from one moment to the next. So he'd been seasick, and sore, both from the unaccustomed work and from a well-earned drubbing from the mate the night before. Sore in spirit, too, for in the dark that slimy Farsey had come to crouch by him as he slept in the forepeak, offering him words of sympathy for his bruises and then a sudden hand groping under his blanket. He'd rebuffed Farsey, but not without humiliation. The tubby sailor had a lot of muscle underneath his lard, and his hands had been all over Brashen even as the boy had punched and pummeled and writhed away from him. None of the other hands sleeping in the forepeak had so much as stirred in their blankets, let alone offered to aid him. He was not popular with the other sailors, for his body was too unscarred and his language too elevated for their tastes. "Schoolboy" they called him, not guessing how that stung. They knew they couldn't trust him to know his business, let alone do it, and a man like that aboard a ship is a man who gets other men killed.

So when he fled the forepeak and Farsey, he went to the afterdeck to sit huddled in his blanket and sniffle a bit to himself. The school and masters and endless lessons that had seemed so intolerable now beckoned to him like a siren, recalling him to soft beds and hot meals and hours that belonged to him alone. Here on the *Spray*, if he was seen to be idle, he caught the end of a rope. Even now, if the mate came across him, he'd either be ordered back below or put to work. He knew he should try to sleep. Instead he stared out over the oily water heaving in their wake and felt an answering unrest in his own belly. He'd have puked again, if there had been anything left to retch up. He leaned his forehead on the railing and tried to find one breath of air that did not taste of either the tarry ship or the salt water that surrounded it.

It was while he was looking at the shining black water rolling so effortlessly away from the ship that it occurred to him he had one other option. It had never presented itself to him before. Now it beckoned to him, simple and logical. Slip into the water. A few minutes of discomfort, and then it would all be over. He'd never have to answer to anyone again, or feel the snap of a rope against his ribs. He'd never have to feel ashamed or frustrated or stupid again. Best of all, the decision would only take an instant, and then it would be done. There'd be no agonizing over it, not even a prayer of undoing it. One moment of decisiveness would be all he'd have to find.

He stood up. He leaned over the railing, searching within himself for that one moment of strength to seize control of his own fate. But as he took that one great breath to find the will to tumble over the rail, he saw it. It slipped along, silent as time, its great sinuous body concealed in the smooth curve of water that was the wake of the ship. The wall of its body perfectly mimicked the arch of the moving water: but for the betraying moonlight showing him a momentary flank of glistening scales, Brashen would never have known the creature was there.

His breath froze in his chest, catching hard and hurting him. He wanted to shout out what he'd seen, bring the second watch running back to confirm it. Back then, sightings of serpents were rare, and many a landsman still claimed they were no more than sea-tales. But he also knew what the sailors said about the big serpents. A man who sees one sees his own death. With sudden certainty, Brashen knew that if anyone else knew he'd seen one, it would be taken as an ill omen for the entire ship. There'd be only one way to purge such bad luck. He'd fall from a yard when someone else didn't quite hold the flapping canvas down tightly enough, he'd tumble down an open hatch and break his neck, or he'd just quietly disappear some night during a long dull watch.

Despite the fact that he'd been toying with the notion of suicide but a moment before, he was suddenly sure he didn't want to die. Not by his own hand, not by anyone else's. He wanted to live out this thrice-damned voyage, get back to shore and somehow get his life back. He'd go to his father, he'd grovel and beg as he'd never groveled and begged before. They'd take him back. Perhaps they wouldn't take him back as heir to the Trell family fortune, but he didn't care. Let Cerwin have it, Brashen would be more than satisfied with the portion of a younger son. He'd stop his gambling, he'd stop his drinking, he'd give up cindin. Whatever his father and grandfather demanded, he'd do. He was suddenly gripping life as tightly as his blistered hands gripped the rail, watching the scaled cylinder of flesh slide along effortlessly in the wake of the ship.

Then came what had been worst. What was still worst, in his dreams. The serpent had known its defeat. Somehow, it had sensed he would not fall prey to its guile, and with a shudder as jolting as Farsey's hand on his crotch, he knew that the impulse had not been his own, but the serpent's suggestion. With a casual twist, the serpent slid from the cover of the ship's wake, to expose its full sinuous body to his view. It was half the length of the *Spray* and gleamed with scintillant colors. It moved without effort, almost as if the ship drew it through the water. Its head was not the flat wedge shape of a land serpent but full and arched, the brow curved like a horse's, with immense eyes set to either side. Toxic barbels dangled below its jaws.

Then the creature rolled to one side in the water, baring its paler belly scales, to stare up at Brashen with one great eye. That glance was what had enervated him and sent him scrabbling away from the railing and fleeing back to the forepeak. It was still what woke him twitching from his nightmares. Immense as they had been, browless and lashless, there had still been something horribly human in the round blue eye that gazed up at him so mockingly.

Althea longed for a fresh-water bath. As she toiled up the companionway to the deck, every muscle in her body ached, and her head pounded from the thick air of the aft hold. At least her task was done. She'd go to her stateroom, wash with a wet towel, change her clothes and perhaps even nap for a bit. And then she'd go to confront Kyle. She'd put it off long enough, and the longer she waited, the more uncomfortable she became. She'd get it over with and then damn well live with whatever it brought down on her.

"Mistress Althea." She had no more than gained the deck before Mild confronted her. "Cap'n requires you." The ship's boy grinned at her, half-apologetic, half-relishing being the bearer of such tidings.

"Very well, Mild," she said quietly. Very well, her thoughts echoed to herself. No wash, no clean clothes and no nap before the confrontation. Very well. She took a moment to smooth her hair back from her face and to tuck her blouse back into her trousers. Prior to her task, they had been her cleanest work clothes. Now the coarse cotton of the blouse stuck to her back and neck with her own sweat, while the trousers were smudged with oakum and tar from working in the close quarters of the hold. She knew her face was dirty, too. Well. She hoped Kyle would enjoy his advantage. She stooped down as if to re-fasten her shoe, but instead placed her hand flat on the wood of the deck. For an instant she closed her eyes and let the strength of the *Vivacia* flow through her palm. "Oh, ship," she whispered as softly as if she prayed. "Help me stand up to him." Then she stood, her resolve firm once more.

As she crossed the twilit deck to the captain's quarters, not an eye would meet hers. Every hand was suddenly very busy or simply looking off in another direction. She refused to glance back to see if they watched after her. Instead she kept her shoulders squared and her head up as she marched to her doom.

She rapped sharply at the door of the captain's quarters and waited for his gruff reply. When it came she entered, and then stood still, letting her eyes adjust to the yellow lantern light. In that instant, she felt a sudden wash of homesickness. The intense longing was not for any shoreside house, but rather for this room as it once had been. Memories dizzied her. Her father's oilskins had hung on that hook, and the smell of his favorite rum had flavored the air. Her own hammock he had rigged in that corner when he had first allowed her to start living aboard the *Vivacia*, that he might better watch over her. She knew a moment of anger as her eyes took in Kyle's clutter overlaying the familiar hominess of these quarters. A nail in his boot had left a pattern of scars across the polished floorboards. Ephron Vestrit had never left charts out, and would never have tolerated the soiled shirt flung across the chair back. He did not approve of an untidy deck anywhere on his ship, and that included his own quarters. His son-in-law Kyle apparently did not share those values.

Althea pointedly stepped over a discarded pair of trousers to stand before the captain at his table. Kyle let her stand there for a few moments while he continued to peruse some notation on the chart. A notation in her father's own precise hand, Althea noticed, and took strength from that even as her anger burned at the thought that he had access to the family's charts. A Trader family's charts were among their most guarded possessions. How else could one safeguard one's swiftest routes through the Inside Passage, and one's trading ports in lesser-known villages? Still, her father had entrusted these charts to Kyle; it was not up to her to question his decision.

Kyle continued to ignore her, but she refused to rise to his bait. She stood silent and patient, but did not let his apparent disinterest fluster her. After a time he lifted his eyes to regard her. Their blueness was as unlike her father's steady black eyes as his unruly blond hair was unlike her father's smooth black queue. Once more she wondered with distaste what had ever possessed her older sister to desire such a man. His Chalcedean blood showed in his ways as much as in his body. She tried to keep her disdain from showing on her face, but her control was wearing thin. She'd been too long at sea with this man.

This last voyage had been interminable. Kyle had muddled what should have been a simple two-month turnaround trip along Chalced's coast into a five-month trading trek full of unnecessary stops and marginally profitable trade runs. She was convinced all of it was an effort on his part to show her father what a sly trader he could be. For herself, she had not been impressed. At Tusk he had stopped and taken on pickled sea-duck eggs, always an uncertain cargo, and barely made dock in Brigtown in time to sell them off before they went rotten. In Brigtown, he'd taken on bales of cotton, not just enough to fill the empty space in the holds but enough to make a partial deck load as well. Althea had had to bite her tongue and watch her crew take their chances as they scrambled over and around the heavy bales, and then they'd had a late gale that had soaked and most likely ruined the portion of the load on deck. She hadn't even asked him what the profit had been, if any, when he'd stopped to auction it off in Dursay. Dursay had been their last port. The wine casks had yet again been shifted about to allow for a whim cargo. Now, in addition to the wines and brandies that had comprised their original cargo, the hold was stuffed with crates of comfer nuts. Kyle had held forth endlessly on the good price they'd bring, both for the fragrant oil from their kernels for soap and the lovely yellow dye that could be made from their husks. Althea thought that if he crowed once more about the extra profit this would wring from the voyage, she'd throttle him. But self-congratulation was not in the gaze he turned on her. It was cold as seawater, lit with tiny glints of anger.

He neither smiled nor bid her be seated. Instead he simply demanded. "What were you doing in the aft hold?"

Someone had run to the captain and tattled. She kept her voice steady. "I re-stowed the cargo."

"You did."

It was a statement, almost an accusation. But it was not a question, so she did not need to make any answer. Instead, she stood very straight under that piercing gaze. She knew he expected her to babble out explanations and excuses, as Keffria would have. But she was not her sister, nor his wife. He suddenly slammed his palm down on the table before him, and though the sudden impact made her flinch, she still did not speak. She watched him waiting for her to say something, and then felt an odd sense of victory when his temper snapped.

"Did you presume to tell the men to change how that cargo was stowed?"

She spoke very softly, very calmly. "No. I did not. I did the work myself. My father has taught me that aboard a ship, one must see what needs doing, and do it. That is what I have done. I arranged the casks as father would have had them done, were he here. Those casks are now as every shipment of wine has been stowed since I was ten years old, bung up and bilge free, fore and aft, ends wedged off in the wings. They are secure, and if they have not already been spoiled by jostling, they will be marketable when we get to Bingtown."

His cheeks grew pink. Althea wondered how Keffria could stand a man whose cheeks turned pink when he was angry. She braced herself. When Kyle spoke, his voice was not raised, but the longing to shout the words was clear in his clipped accent.

"Your father is not here, Althea. That is precisely the point. I am the master of this vessel, and I gave commands as to how I wanted that cargo stowed. Yet again you have gone behind my back and counter-manded those orders. I can't have this interference between me and my crew. You sow discord."

She spoke quietly. "I acted on my own, by myself. I gave the crew no orders at all, nor did I even speak of what I intended to do. I have done nothing to come between you and the crew." She clamped her jaws shut before she could say more. She would not tell him that what stood between him and his crew was his own lack of expertise. The sailors who would have gone to their deaths willingly for her father now spoke openly in the forecastle of finding another vessel when next they shipped out. Kyle was in danger of destroying the hand-picked crew that her father had spent the last decade assembling.

Kyle looked furious that she would contradict him. "It is enough that you went against my orders. That is all it takes to challenge my authority. Your bad example on this ship makes the crew restless. Then I am forced to clamp down the discipline. You should be ashamed for what you bring down on them. But no. You don't care one whit for that. You're above the captain. Althea Vestrit is probably above almighty Sa! You've shown the entire crew your complete disregard for my orders. Were you truly a sailor, I'd make an example of you, one that would prove my orders are the only orders on this ship. But you're nothing but a spoiled merchant's brat. I'll treat you as such, and spare the flesh of your back. But only until you cross me again. Take this warning to heart, girl. I am captain of this vessel, and my word on this ship is law."

Althea did not speak, but neither did she look aside. She met his gaze levelly and kept as much expression off her face as she could. The pink spread to Kyle's forehead. He took a breath and reached for control. He speared her with his eyes. "And what are you, Althea?"

She had not expected such a question. Accusations and rebukes she could deal with silently. But in asking her a question, he demanded an answer, and she knew it would be construed as open defiance. So be it. "I am the owner of this vessel," she said with as much dignity as she could muster.

"Wrong!" This time he did shout. But in an instant he had mastered himself. He leaned forward on the table and near spat the words at her. "You are the daughter of the owner. And even were you the owner, it wouldn't make a whit of difference. It's not the owner who commands the ship, it's the captain. You're not the captain, you're not the mate. You aren't even a proper sailor. All you do is take a stateroom to yourself that should be the second mate's, and do only the chores it suits you to do. The owner of this vessel is Ephron Vestrit, your father. He is the one who gave the *Vivacia* over to my command. If you cannot respect me for who I am, then respect your father's choice to captain his ship."

"But for my age, he would have made me captain. I know the *Vivacia*. I should be her captain."

As soon as the words were out of her mouth, Althea regretted them. It was all the opening he had needed, this voicing of what they both knew was true.

"Wrong again. You should be at home, married off to some fancy boy as spoiled as yourself. You haven't the faintest idea of how to captain a vessel. You believe that because your father has allowed you to play at sailoring you know how to command a vessel. You've come to believe you're destined to captain your father's ship. You're wrong. You're father only brought you aboard because he had no sons of his own. He as much as told me so, when Wintrow was born. Were not the *Vivacia* a liveship, requiring a family member aboard, I'd never have tolerated your pretenses for a moment. But bear this in mind. A member of the Vestrit family is all this ship requires; it needn't be you.

If this ship demands a Vestrit aboard her, then she can bear one that has Haven for a surname. My sons share as much of your sister's blood as mine, they're as much Vestrit as Haven. And the next time this ship leaves Bingtown, one of my boys will take your place on her. You'll be left ashore."

Althea could feel she had gone white. The man had no idea what he was saying to her, had no idea of the depth of his threat. It only proved he had no true concept of what a liveship was. He should have never been allowed authority over the *Vivacia*. If only her father had been well, he would have seen that.

Something of both her despair and defiance must have shown in her face, for Kyle Haven's mouth grew tauter. She wondered if he fought down a smile as he added, "You are confined to your quarters for the remainder of this voyage. And now you are dismissed."

She stood her ground. As well have it out then, now that the lines were drawn. "You have declared that I am not even a sailor aboard this vessel. Very well, then. If that is so, then I am not yours to command. And I have no idea why you fancy that you will command the *Vivacia* on her next voyage. When we return to Bingtown, I have every expectation that my father will have recovered his health and will resume his command. And hold it, until such time as ship and command are both mine."

He fixed her with a flat stare. "Do you really think so, Althea?"

She puffed up with hatred, believing for an instant that he mocked her faith that her father would recover. But he went on, "Your father's a good captain. And when he hears what you've been up to, countermanding my orders, sowing discord among the men, making mock of me behind my back—"

"Making mock of you?" Althea demanded.

Kyle gave a snort of disdain. "Do you think you can get drunk and witless and throw wild words about Dursay town and not have them come back to me? It only shows what a fool you are."

Althea raced frantically through her scrabbled memories of Dursay. She had got drunk, yes, but only once, and she remembered vaguely that she'd bemoaned her situation to some shipmates. Who? The faces blurred in her memory, but she knew it had been Brashen who'd rebuked her, daring to tell her to shut her hatch and keep private problems private. She did not recall just what she'd said, but now she had a fair idea of who had tattled.

"So. What tales did Brashen carry back to you?" she asked in as calm a voice as she could muster. God of fishes, what had she said? If it had to do with family business, and Kyle carried that tale home . . .

"It wasn't Brashen. But it confirms my opinion of him that he'd sit and listen to you mouth such dirt. There's another just like you, a Trader boy trying to play at sailor. I've no idea why your father ever indulged him on this ship, unless he hoped to make him a match for you. Well, if I have my way, I'll leave him on land in Bingtown, too, so you can still enjoy one another's company there. He's likely the closest you'll get to a man for yourself; best anchor him down while you can."

Kyle leaned back in his chair. He seemed to enjoy Althea's shocked silence at his inferences. When he spoke again, his voice was low and satisfied. "Well, little sister, it seems you do not enjoy it when I bandy such words about. So perhaps you can understand how I took it when the ship's carpenter came back, a bit the worse for grog, talking loudly of how you'd told him I only married your sister because I hoped to get my hands on the family ship, because the likes of me would never have the chance at commanding a liveship otherwise." His calm voice suddenly was gritty with fury.

She recognized her own words. Oh, she'd been drunker than she thought, to voice those thoughts out loud. Coward or liar, she challenged herself. She had either to step up and claim those words, pretend disdain of them, or lie and claim she'd never said them. Well, regardless of what Kyle might say of her, she was Ephron Vestrit's daughter. She found her courage.

"That's true. I said it, and it's true. So. How does the truth make mock of you?"

Kyle stood suddenly and came around the table. He was a big man. Even as Althea began to retreat, the force of his slap sent her staggering. She caught at a bulkhead and forced herself to stand. He was very pale as he walked back to his chair and sat down. Too far. They'd both gone too far, as she had always feared they would. Had he feared it, too? He seemed to be shaking as badly as she was.

"That wasn't for me," he said huskily. "That was for your sister. Drunk as a soldier, in a public tavern, and you as much as call her a whore. Do you realize that? Do you truly think she'd need to buy a man with the bribe of a liveship to command? She's a woman that any man would be proud to claim, even if she came with not a copper to her name. Unlike you. You they'll have to buy a husband for, and you'd better hope to the gods that your family fortunes do better, for they'd have to dower you with half the town before any decent man would look at you. Get to your quarters before my temper truly runs away with me. Now!"

She tried to turn and walk away with dignity, but Kyle stood up and came from behind the table, to place a broad hand on her back and propel her toward the door. As she left the Captain's quarters, shutting the door firmly behind her, she observed Mild diligently sanding some splintering from a railing nearby. The lad had ears like a fox; he'd have heard everything. Well, she'd neither done nor said anything she was ashamed of. She doubted Kyle could say the same. She kept her head up as she made her way aft to the small stateroom that had been hers since she was twelve years old. As she shut the door behind her, the full measure of Kyle's threat to move her off the ship came to her.

This was home. He couldn't force her out of her home. Could he?

She'd loved this room since she was a child, and never would forget that thrill of ownership that came to her the first time she'd walked in and tossed her sea-bag up onto the bunk. That was close to seven years ago, and it had been home and safety ever since. Now she clambered up onto that same bunk and lay curled there, her face to the bulkhead. Her cheek stung, but she would not put her hand to it. He'd struck her. Let it bruise and darken. Maybe when she got home, her sister and her parents would look at it and perceive what sort of vermin they had welcomed into their family when they'd wedded Keffria to Kyle Haven. He was not even Trader stock. He was a mongrel, part Chalcedean and part wharf-rat. But for marrying her sister, he'd have nothing now. Nothing. He was a piece of dung and she would not cry because he was not worth her tears, only her anger. Only her anger.

After a few moments, the beating of her heart calmed. Her hand wandered idly over the pieced comforter that Nana had made for her. After a moment she twisted to stare out the porthole on the other side of the room. Limitless gray sea at the bottom, vast sky in the upper third. It was her favorite view of the world, always constant yet always changing. Her eyes wandered from the view to her room. The small desk securely bolted to the bulkhead, with its tiny railing to contain papers during weather. Her book shelf and scroll rack were beside it, her books securely fenced against even the roughest weather. She even had a small chart table that would fold down, and a selection of charts, for her father had insisted she learn to navigate, even to take her own bearings. Her instruments for that were within a small cushioned case that clipped securely to the wall. Her sea clothes hung on their hooks. The only decoration in the room was a small painting of the *Vivacia* that she had commissioned herself. Jared Pappas had done it, and that alone would have made it a valuable painting, but it was the subject matter that endeared it to Althea. In the painting, the

Vivacia's sails were bellied full of wind and her bow was cutting the waves cleanly.

Althea reached overhead, to press her hands against the exposed timbers of *Vivacia*'s body. She could feel the near-life of the ship thrumming through them. It was not just the vibration of the wood as the ship cut the water, it was not even the thud of the sailors' feet on the decks or their gull cries as they sang out in response to the mate's commands. It was the life of the *Vivacia* herself, so close to waking.

The *Vivacia* was a liveship. Sixty-three years ago, her keel had been laid, and that long true timber had been wizardwood. The wood of her figurehead was also wizardwood, harvested from the same great tree, as was the planking of her hull. Great-grandma Vestrit had commissioned her, had signed away the lien against the family's holdings that her father Ephron was still paying off. That was back when women could still do such things without creating a scandal, back before the stupid Chalcedean custom of showing one's wealth by keeping one's women idle had taken hold in Bingtown. Great-grandma, Father was fond of saying, had never let other folk's opinions come between her and her ship. Great-grandma had sailed the *Vivacia* for thirty-five years, past her seventieth birthday. One hot summer day she had simply sat down on the foredeck, said, "That'll do, boys," and died.

Grandpa had taken over the ship next. Althea could vaguely remember him. He'd been a black bull of a man, his voice always full of the roar of the sea even when he was at home. He'd died fourteen years ago, on the deck of the *Vivacia*. He'd been sixty-two, and Althea herself but a little girl of four. But she had stood beside his litter with the rest of the Vestrit family and witnessed his death, and even then felt the faint quiver that ran through the *Vivacia* at his passing. She had known that that shiver was both regret and welcome; the *Vivacia* would miss her bold captain, but she welcomed the flowing of his anma into her timbers. His death put her one life closer to awakening.

And now there only remained her father's death to complete the quickening. As always, Althea felt a rush of conflicting emotions when she considered it. The thought of her father dying filled her with dread and horror. It would devastate her for her father to be gone. And if he died before she reached her majority, and authority over her fell to her mother and Kyle . . . she hastily pushed the thought away, rapping her knuckles against the wood of the *Vivacia* to ward off the ill luck of thinking of such a bad thing.

Yet she could not deny how she anticipated the quickening of the *Vivacia*. How many hours had she spent, stretched out on the bowsprit as close to the figurehead as she could get as they plowed through the seas, and stared at the carved wooden lids that covered the *Vivacia*'s eyes? She was not wood and paint like the figurehead of any ordinary ship. She was wizardwood. She was painted for now, yes, but at the moment of Ephron Vestrit's death aboard her decks, the painted locks of her tumbling hair would be not gilt but curling gold, and her high-boned cheeks would lose their rouge of paint and glow pink with her own life. She'd have green eyes. Althea knew it. Of course, everyone said that no one could truly know what color a liveship's eyes would be until those eyes were opened by the deaths of three generations. But Althea knew. The *Vivacia* would have eyes as green as sea lettuce. Even now, thinking of how it would be when those great emerald eyes opened, Althea had to smile.

The smile faded as she recalled Kyle's words. It was plain what he hoped to do. Put her off the ship and bring one of his sons aboard. And when her father did die, Kyle would try to keep command of the *Vivacia*, would keep his boy aboard as his token Vestrit to keep the ship happy. It had to be an empty threat. Neither boy was suited: the one too young, the other given to the priests. Althea had nothing against her nephews, but even if Selden were not too young to live aboard ship, he had the soul of a farmer. As for Wintrow, Keffria had given him over to the priests years ago. Wintrow cared nothing for the *Vivacia*, knew nothing of ships; her sister Keffria had seen to that. And he was destined to be a priest. Kyle had never been much enthused about that, but last time Althea had seen the boy, it was plain that he'd make a good priest. Small and spindly, always staring off into the distance, smiling vaguely, thoughts full of Sa: that was Wintrow.

Not that Kyle would care where the boy's heart was, or even about backing out on dedicating his eldest son to Sa. His children by Keffria were no more than tools to him, the blood he'd claim in order to gain control of the liveship. Well, he'd shown his hand a bit too plainly this time. When they got back to port, she'd see to it that her father knew exactly what Kyle had planned, and how badly he'd treated her. Perhaps then her father would reconsider his decision that Althea was too young to captain the ship. Let Kyle go and find some dead chunk of wood to push about the seas, and give the *Vivacia* back into Althea's care where she would be safe and respected. Through the palms of her hands, she was sure she felt a response from the ship. The *Vivacia* was hers, no matter what plots Kyle might make. He'd never have her.

She shifted again in her bunk. She'd outgrown it. She should have the ship's carpenter come in and redo the room. If she put her bunk on the bulkhead, below the porthole, she could have an extra hand of length to it. Not much, but even a bit would help. Her desk could come over against this wall. . . . Then she frowned to herself, recalling how the carpenter had betrayed her. Well, she'd never liked the man, and he'd never cared for her. She should have guessed he'd be the one to make mischief between her and Kyle with his tale telling.

And she should have known also that it wasn't Brashen. He wasn't a man to go about behind another's back, no matter what Kyle might think of him. No, Brashen had told her, to her face and quite rudely, that she was a childish little troublemaker and he'd thank her to stay away from his watch. As she mulled on it, that night in the tavern came clearer in her head. He'd chewed her out as if she were a green hand, telling her she ought not criticize the captain's decisions to the crew, nor talk out her family business in public. She'd known what to say to that. "Not everyone feels ashamed to speak of their family, Brashen Trell." That was all she'd had to say. Then she'd risen from the table and stalked away.

Let him sit there and choke on that, she'd told herself. She knew Brashen's history, and she'd wager half the crew did, even if they daren't talk about it to his face. Her father had rescued him when he was on the very threshold of the debtor's gaol. The only route out of there for him would have been an indentureship, for all knew his own family had had their fill of his wastrel ways. And all knew what lay down the road from an enforced indentureship. He'd probably have ended up in Chalced, a face full of slave tattoos, were it not for Ephron Vestrit. And yet he had dared to speak to her like that. He thought entirely too much of himself, did Brashen Trell. Most Trells did. At the Trader's Harvest Ball last year, his younger brother had presumed to ask her to dance twice with him. Even if Cerwin was the Trell heir now, he should not be so bold. She half smiled as she thought of his face when she'd coolly declined. His polite acceptance of her refusal had been correct, but all his training had not been enough to keep the flush from his face. Cerwin had prettier manners than Brashen, but he was slender as a boy, with none of Brashen's muscle. On the other hand, the younger Trell had been smart enough not to throw away both family name and fortune. Brashen hadn't.

Althea pushed him from her mind. She felt a twinge that Kyle was going to let him go at the end of the voyage, but she would not be especially sad to see him go. Her father's feelings on that matter would be another thing. He'd always made something of a pet of Brashen, at least on shore. Most of the other Trader families had stopped receiving Brashen when the Trells disinherited him. But Ephron Vestrit had shrugged and said, "Heir or not, he's a good seaman. Any sailor of my crew who isn't fit to call at my door isn't fit to be on my decks." Not that Brashen came often to the house, or ever sat at table with them. And on the ship her father and Brashen were strictly master and man. It was probably only to her that her father had spoken admiringly of the boy's gumption in picking himself up and making something of himself. But she'd say nothing to Kyle on that score. Let him make yet one more mistake for her father to see. Let her father see just how many changes Kyle would make on the *Vivacia* if he were not checked.

She was strongly tempted to go out on deck, simply to challenge Kyle's order to her. What could he do? Order a deckhand to put her back in her quarters? There wasn't a hand on this ship that would dare lay hands on her, and not just because she was Althea Vestrit. Most of them liked and respected her, and that had been a thing she'd earned for herself, not bought with her name. Despite what Kyle said, she knew this ship better than any sailor aboard it now. She knew it as only a child who has grown up aboard a ship could; she knew the places in the holds where no grown man could have fit himself; she had climbed masts and swung on rigging as other children climbed trees. Even if she did not stand a regular watch, she knew the work of every hand aboard and could do it. She could not splice as fast as their best rigger, but she could make a neat strong splice, and cut and sew canvas as well as any deckhand. She had divined this was her father's intention in bringing her aboard; to learn the ship and every sailor's task of running her. Kyle might despise her as a mere daughter of her family, but she had no fear that her father thought her any less than the three sons the family had lost to the Blood Plague. She was not a substitute for a son; she was to be Ephron Vestrit's heir.

She knew she could defy Kyle's order and nothing would befall her. But like as not he'd take it out on the hands, punishing them when they did not leap to obey his order to confine her to quarters. She would not let that happen to them. This was her quarrel with Kyle; she'd settle it herself. Because despite what he'd said, she did not care just for herself. The *Vivacia* deserved a good crew, and save for Kyle, her father had chosen every hand well. He paid good money, more than the going rate, to keep able and willing hands aboard. Althea would not give Kyle an excuse to discharge any of them. She felt again a pang of guilt that she'd been part of that fate coming down on Brashen.

She tried to push thoughts of him aside, but he refused to budge. In her mind's eye, he stood before her, arms crossed on his chest, looking down at her from his superior height as he so often did. Lips flat in disapproval of her, brown eyes narrowed to slits, with even the bristle of his beard betraying his annoyance. Good deckhand he might be, and a promising mate, but for all of that, the man had an attitude. He'd thrown over the Trell name, but not the family's aristocratic ways. She could respect that he'd worked his way up the decks to his position of mate; still, she found it irritating that he moved and spoke as if command were his birthright. Perhaps it had been once, but when he'd thrown that over, he should have discarded his prideful ways along with the name.

She rolled suddenly from her bunk, landing lightly on the deck. She crossed to her sea chest and flung the lid open. Here were things that could sweep all these unpleasant thoughts from her mind. The trinkets she had brought for Selden and Malta now faintly annoyed her. She'd spent good coins on these gifts for her niece and nephew. Fond as she was of both children, right now she could only see them as Kyle's children and her threatened replacements. She set aside the elaborately dressed doll she'd chosen for Malta and put the brightly painted top for Selden with it. Beneath were the bolts of silk from Tusk. The silver-gray was for her mother, the mauve for Keffria. Below them was the bolt of green she had chosen for herself.

She stroked it with the back of her hand. Lovely, liquid fabric. She took out the cream-colored lace she had chosen for trim. As soon as she got to Bingtown, she planned to take it to the Street of the Tailors. She'd have Mistress Violet sew her a gown for the Summer Ball. Her services were expensive, but silk this fine merited a skillful dressmaker. Althea wanted a gown that would show off her long waist and round hips, and perhaps attract a dance partner more manly than Brashen's little brother. Not too tight in the waist, she decided; the dancing at the Summer Ball was the lively sort, and she wished to be able to breathe. Ample skirts that would move with the complex steps of the dances, she decided, but not so full they got in the way. The cream lace would frame her modest cleavage and perhaps make it look more ample. She'd wear her dark hair swept up this year, and use her silver clasps to hold it. Her hair was as coarse as her father's, but its rich color and thickness more than made up for that. Perhaps her mother would finally allow her to wear the silver beads her grandmother had left her. Nominally, they were Althea's, but her mother seemed jealous of parting with her guardianship of them, and often cited their rarity and value as reasons they should not be worn casually. They'd go well with the silver earrings she'd bought in Brigtown.

She stood and shook out the silk, and held it up against her. The looking-glass in the room was small. She could see no more than how her tanned face looked above the green silk draped over her shoulder. She smoothed the silk, only for her rough hands to snag on it. She shook her head at that. She'd have to pumice them every day once she was home to work the callus off them. She loved working the *Vivacia* and feeling the ship respond to the sailors' tasks, but it did take a heavy toll on her hands and skin, not to mention the bruising her legs took. It was her mother's second biggest objection to her sailing with her father, that it absolutely ruined her appearance at social events. Her main objection was that Althea should have been home sharing the tasks of managing the house and lands. Her heart sank as she wondered if her mother would finally win her way. She let the silk slither from her hands and reached overhead, to touch the heavy timbers that supported the *Vivacia*'s decks.

"Oh, ship, they can't separate us now. Not after all these years, not when you're so close to quickening. No one has the right to take that from us." She whispered the words knowing that she need not speak aloud at all. She and the ship were linked that closely. She would have sworn she felt a shivering of response from the *Vivacia*. "This bond between us is something my father intended as well; it is why he brought me aboard when I was so young, that we might come to adulthood already knowing one another." There was a second tiny shivering of the ship's timbers, so faint another might not have noticed it. But Althea knew the *Vivacia* too well to be deceived. She closed her eyes and poured herself forth into her ship, all her fears and anger and hopes. And in turn she felt the soft stirring of the *Vivacia*'s as yet unawakened spirit, answering her soothingly.

In years to come, after the *Vivacia* had quickened, she would be the one the ship preferred to speak to; it would be her hand on the wheel that the *Vivacia* answered most promptly. Althea knew the ship would run willingly before the wind for her, and would battle adverse seas with all her heart. Together they would seek out trade ports and goods that not even the traders of Bingtown could match, wonders beyond even those of the Rain Wild folk. And when she died, it would be her own son or daughter that stepped up to the helm, not one of Kyle's get. This she promised to both herself and the ship. Althea wiped her tears on the back of her hand and then stooped to gather the silk from the floor.

He was dozing on the sand. Dozing. That was the word the humans had always used, but he had never agreed that what he did was similar to the sleep they indulged in. He did not think a liveship could sleep. No. Even that escape was denied him. Instead, he could go somewhere else in his mind, and immerse himself so deeply in that past moment that the deadly boredom of the present retreated. There was one place in his past that he used most frequently for that. He was not entirely sure what it was he was recalling. Ever since his log books had been taken from him, his memory had begun to stretch and grow thin. There were growing gaps in it now, places where he could not make the events of one year connect to those of another. Sometimes he thought perhaps he should be grateful for that.

So as he dozed in the sun, what he chose to recall was satiation and warmth. The gentle scratching of the sand beneath his hull translated into an elusively similar sensation that refused to be completely called to his mind. He did not try very hard. It was enough to cling to an ancient memory of feeling replete and satisfied and warm.

The men's voices stirred him from that. "This is it? This has been here for, what did you say? Thirty years?" An accent flavored the words. Jamaillian, Paragon thought to himself. And from the capital, Jamaillia City itself. Those from the south provinces swallowed their end consonants. This he recalled without knowing the source of the knowledge.

"This is it," another voice replied. The second voice was older.

"This has not been here thirty years," the younger voice asserted. "A ship pulled out and left on a beach for thirty years would be worm-holed and barnacled over."

"Unless it's made from wizardwood," responded the older voice. "Liveships don't rot, Mingsley. Nor do barnacles or tubeworms find them appetizing. That is but one of the reasons the ships are so expensive, and so desirable. They endure for generations, with little of the hull maintenance an ordinary ship requires. Out on the seas, they take care of themselves. They'll yell to a steersman if they see hazards in their paths. Some of them near sail themselves. What other vessel can warn you that a cargo has shifted, or that you've overloaded them? A wizardwood ship on the sea is a wonder to behold! What other vessel . . ."

"Sure. So tell me again why this one was hauled out and abandoned?" The younger voice sounded extremely skeptical. Mingsley did not trust his older guide, that much was certain.

Paragon could almost hear the older man shrug. "You know what a superstitious lot sailors are. This ship has a reputation for bad luck. Very bad luck. I might as well tell you, because if I don't someone else will. He's killed a lot of men, the *Paragon* has. Including the owner and his son."

"Um." Mingsley mused. "Well, if I buy it, I wouldn't be buying it as a ship. I wouldn't expect to pay a ship's price for it, either. Quite honestly, it's the wood I want. I've heard a lot of strange things about it, and not just that the liveships quicken and then move and speak. I've seen that down in the harbor. Not that a newcomer like me is very welcome on the North wall where the liveships tie up. But I've seen them move and heard them speak. Seems to me, if you can make a figurehead do that, you could do it with a smaller carving of the same wood. Do you know how much they'd pay for something like that in Jamaillia City? A moving, speaking carving?"

"I've no idea," the older man demurred.

The young man gave a snort of sarcastic laughter. "Of course you don't! It's never occurred to you, has it? Come on, man, be honest with me. Why hasn't this ever been done before?"

"I don't know." The older man spoke too hastily to be believable.

"Right," Mingsley replied skeptically. "All the years Bingtown has existed on the Cursed Shores, and no one has thought of marketing wizardwood anywhere except to the residents of Bingtown. And then only as ships. What's the real catch? Does it have to be this big before it can quicken? Does it have to be immersed in salt water a certain amount of time? What?"

"It's just . . . never been done. Bingtown is an odd place, Mingsley. We have our own traditions, our own folklore, our own superstitions. When our ancestors left Jamaillia all those years ago and came to try to colonize the Cursed Shores, well . . . most came because they had no other options left. Some were criminals, some had shamed or ruined their family names, some were very unpopular with the Satrap himself. It was almost an exiling. They were told that if they survived, each family could claim two hundred leffers of land and would be granted amnesty for their past. He also promised us we would be left in peace, with trade monopoly over whatever goods we found worth trading. In return for the Satrap granting them this, they ceded to him a fifty percent tax on their profits. For years, this bargain worked well."

"And now it no longer does." Mingsley laughed mockingly. "How could anyone believe that such a bargain would last forever? Satraps are human. And Satrap Cosgo finds the contents of his coffers too small for the habits of pleasure he acquired while waiting for his father to die. Chalcedean pleasure herbs are not cheap, and once the habit has been acquired, well, lesser herbs simply do not compare. And so he sold, to me and my friends, new trading and land grants for Bingtown and the Cursed Shores. And we have come and been very poorly welcomed by you all. You act as if we will snatch the bread from your mouths, when all know that business but begets more business. Why, look at us here. This ship has been rotting here for thirty years, or so you say, of no use to its owners or anyone else. But if I buy, the owner will get a nice price, I don't doubt you will work yourself a nice commission and I will have a quantity of this mysterious wizardwood." Mingsley paused and Paragon could hear the silence that his companion allowed to grow.

After a moment, Mingsley continued discontentedly, "But I will admit I am disappointed. I thought you said the ship had quickened. I thought it would speak to us. You did not mention it had been vandalized. Did that kill it?"

"The *Paragon* speaks only when it pleases him. I don't doubt he's heard every word we said."

"Hmf. Is that true, ship? Have you heard every word we've said?"

Paragon saw no reason to reply. After a time, he heard the younger man make an expression of disgust. His footsteps began a slow circuit of the ship, while his heavier, slower companion followed.

After a time, Mingsley spoke again. "Well, my friend, I'm afraid this substantially lowers what I shall offer for the ship. My first estimate to you was based on the concept that I could cut the figurehead free of the ship, take it to Jamaillia City, and sell the quickened wood for a goodly sum. Or more likely, I would end up 'gifting' it to the Satrap for some extensive land grants. But as it is . . . wizardwood or not, it's a singularly ugly bit of carving. What possessed someone to chop the face up so badly? I wonder if an artisan could reshape it into something more pleasing?"

"Perhaps," his companion conceded uneasily. "I do not know that that would be wise. I had assumed you were interested in the *Paragon* as he is, not as a source of wizardwood. Though you must recall, as I warned you, I have not yet approached the Ludlucks with the idea of selling him. I did not wish to broach the idea unless I was sure you were interested."

"Come, Davad, you cannot believe me so naive as that. What is 'he,' besides a beached hulk? The owners will probably be glad to be rid of him. Were this ship seaworthy, it would hardly be chained to the beach like this."

"Well." A long pause. "I do not think even the Ludlucks would be moved to sell him, if he is to be chopped into bits." An intake of breath. "Mingsley, I caution you not to do this. To buy the ship and re-fit it is one thing. What you are speaking of is something else entirely. None of the Old Traders would deal with you if you did such a thing. As for me, I would be ruined entirely."

"Then you must be discreet about that when you make my offer. As I have been discreet about buying this hulk." Mingsley sounded condescending. "I know the Bingtown Traders have many odd superstitions. And I have no wish to flout them. If my offer is accepted, I will float the ship and tow it off before I dismantle it. Out of sight, out of mind, as the saying is. Does that satisfy you?"

"I suppose it must," the man muttered discontentedly. "I suppose it must."

"Oh, don't be so glum. Come. Let us go back to town, and I shall buy you dinner. At Souska's. Now that's a handsome offer, you must admit, for I know the prices there, and I've seen you eat." The younger man laughed appreciatively at his own humor. The older man did not join in. "And then this evening you will call on the Ludluck family and 'discreetly' present my offer. It's all to everyone's good. Money for the Ludlucks, a commission for you, a large supply of rare wood for my backers. Show me the ill fortune in that, Davad."

"I cannot," the older man said quietly. "But I fear you will find it for yourself. Whether he speaks or not, this ship is quickened, and he has a mind of his own. Try to chop him into bits, and I am sure he will not be silent for long."

The younger man laughed merrily. "You but do this to pique my interest, Davad. I know you do. Come. Let's back to town. And Souska's. Some of my backers would very much like to meet you."

"You promised to be discreet!" the older man objected.

"Oh, I have been, I assure you. But you cannot expect men to advance me money on my word alone. They want to know what they are buying, and from whom. But they are discreet men, one and all, I promise you."

Paragon listened for a long time to their retreating footsteps. Eventually the small sounds of men were swallowed by the more pervasive sounds of the waves and the gulls' cries.

"Chopped into bits." Paragon tried the phrase out loud. "Well, it does not sound pleasant. On the other hand, it would at least be more interesting than laying here. And it might kill me. It might."

The prospect pleased him. He let his thoughts drift again, toying with this new idea. He had nothing else to occupy his mind.

CHAPTER THREE

EPHRON VESTRIT

EPHRON VESTRIT WAS DYING. RONICA LOOKED AT HER HUSBAND'S DIMINISHED FACE AND IMPRESSED THE thought on her mind. Ephron Vestrit was dying. She felt a wave of anger, followed by one of annoyance with him. How could he do this to her? How could he die now and leave her to handle everything by herself?

Somewhere beneath the tides of those superficial emotions she knew the cold deep current of her grief sought to pull her down and drown her. She fought savagely to be free of it, fought to keep feeling only the anger and irritation. Later, she told herself. Later, when I have pulled through this and have done all the things I must do, then I will stop and feel. Later.

For now she folded her lips tight in exasperation. She dipped a cloth in the warm balsam-scented water, and gently wiped first his face and then his lax hands. He stirred lightly under her ministrations, but did not waken. She had not expected him to. She'd given him the poppy syrup twice today already, to try to keep the pain at bay. Perhaps for now, the pain had no control over him. She hoped so.

She wiped gently at his beard again. That clumsy Rache

had let him dribble broth all over himself again. It was as if the woman just didn't care to do things properly. Ronica supposed she should just send her back to Davad Restart; she hated to, for the woman was young and intelligent. Surely she did not deserve to end up as a slave.

Davad had simply brought the woman to her house one day. Ronica had assumed she was a relative or guest of Davad, for when she was not staring sorrowfully at nothing, her genteel diction and manners had suggested she was well-born. Ronica had been shocked when Davad had bluntly offered the woman to her as a servant, saying he dared not keep her in his own household. He'd never fully explained that statement, and Rache refused to say anything at all on the topic. Ronica supposed that if she sent Rache back to Davad, he would shrug and send her on to Chalced to be sold as a slave. While she remained in Bingtown, she was nominally an indentured servant. She still had a chance to regain a life of her own, if she would but try. Instead Rache was simply refusing to adapt to her changed status. She obeyed the orders she was given, but not with anything like grace or goodwill.

In fact, as the weeks passed, it seemed to Ronica that Rache had become more and more grudging in her duties. Yesterday Ronica had asked her to take charge of Selden for the day, and the woman had looked stricken. Her grandson was only seven, but the woman seemed to have a strange aversion to him. She had shaken her head, fiercely and mutely, her eyes lowered, until Ronica had ordered her off to the kitchen instead. Perhaps she was seeing how far she could push her new mistress before Ronica ordered her punished. Well, she'd find that Ronica Vestrit was not the kind of woman who ordered her servants beaten or their rations reduced. If Rache could not find it within herself to accept living comfortably in a well-appointed house with relatively light duties and a gentle mistress, well, then, she would have to go back to Davad, and eventually take her place on the block and see what fate dealt her next. That was all there was to it. A shame, for the woman had promise.

A shame, too, that despite Davad's kindness in offering Rache's services to her, the Old Trader was perilously close to becoming a slave dealer. She had never thought to see one of the old family lines enticed into such a scurrilous trade. Ronica shook her head, and put both Rache and Davad out of her mind. She had other, more important things to think of beside Rache's sour temperament and Davad's dabbling in semi-legal professions.

After all, Ephron was dying.

The knowledge jabbed at her again. It was like a splinter in the foot that one could not find and dig out. That little knife of knowing stabbed into her at every step.

Ephron was dying. Her big bold husband, her dashing and handsome young sea-captain, the strong father of her children, the mate of her body was suddenly this collapsed flesh that sweated and moaned and whimpered like a child. When they had first been married, her two hands could not span the muscled right arm of her groom. Now that arm was no more than a stick of bone clothed in slack flesh. She looked down into his face. It had lost the weathering of the sea and wind; it was almost the color of the linen he lay on. His hair was black as ever, but the sheen had fled it, leaving it dull when it was not matted with sweat. No. It was hard to find any trace of the Ephron she had known and loved for thirty-six years.

She set aside her basin and cloth. She knew she should leave him to sleep. It was all she could do for him anymore. Keep him clean, dose him against pain and then leave him to sleep. She thought bitterly of all the plans they had made together, conspiring until dawn as they sprawled together on their big bed, the stifling blankets thrown aside, the windows flung open to the cool night breeze.

"When the girls are grown," he'd promised her, "wedded and bedded, with lives of their own, then, my lass, we'll take up our own life again. I've a mind to carry you off with me to the Perfume Isles. Would you fancy that? Twelvemonth of clean salt air and naught to do but be the captain's lady? And then, when we get there, why, we shall not hurry to take on a cargo. We shall go together, into the Green Mountains. I know a chieftain there who's often invited me to come and see his village. We could ride those funny little donkeys of theirs, right up to the very edge of the sky, and . . ."

"I'd rather stay home with you," she'd always said then. "I'd rather keep you at home here with me for a full year, have you beside me to see a full turning of the seasons with me. We could go to our holdings in the hills for spring; you've never seen it, when the trees are covered with red and orange blossoms, with not a leaf to be seen on one of them. And once, just once, I'd like to have you suffer alongside me during the mafe harvest. Up every morning before dawn, rousing the workers, getting them out to pick the ripe beans before the sun can touch them and shrivel them. Thirty-six years we've been married, and never once have you had to help me with that. Come to think of it, in all the years we've been married, you've never been home for the blooming of our wedding tree. You've never seen the pink buds swell and then open, so full of fragrance."

"Oh, there will be time enough for that. Time enough for posies and land work, when the girls are grown and the debts paid."

"And when they are, I'll have a year of you, all to myself," she'd threatened him. And always he'd promised her, "A whole year of me. You'll probably be heartily sick of me before it's done. You'll be begging me to go back to sea and leave you to sleep nights in peace."

Ronica bowed her face into her hands. She'd had her year of him at home; woeful gods, but what a way to gain her wish. She'd had a fall of him coughing and fractious, feverish and red-eyed, lying in their bed all day and staring out the window at the sea whenever he was well enough to sit. "He'd best be taking care of them," he'd growled whenever the sky showed a dark cloud, and Ronica had known that his thoughts were always with Althea and the *Vivacia*. He'd been so reluctant to turn the ship over to Kyle. He'd wanted to give it to Brashen, an untried boy. It had taken Ronica weeks of arguing with him to make him see how that would look to the town. Kyle was his own son-in-law, and had proved himself as captain on three other ships. If he'd passed him over to put Brashen in charge of the *Vivacia*, it would have been a slap in the face to his daughter's husband, to say nothing of his family. Even though the Havens were not Bingtown Traders, they were an old family in Bingtown nonetheless. And the way the Vestrit fortunes were faring lately, they could afford to offend no one. So last autumn she'd persuaded him to entrust his precious *Vivacia* to Kyle and take a trip off, to strengthen his lungs again.

As winter had darkened their skies and whitened the streets, he'd stopped coughing. She had thought he was getting better, except that he couldn't seem to *do* anything. At first, when he walked the length of the house, he'd lost his breath. Soon he was stopping to breathe between their bedroom and the parlor. By the time spring came, he could not cover the distance unless he leaned on her arm.

He'd finally been home for the blooming of their wedding tree. As the year warmed, the tree had budded. There had been a few weeks when, if Ephron was not getting better, at least he got no worse. She sat by his lounge and sewed or did the accounts while he did scrimshaw or made rope mats for the doorsteps. They had spoken of the future and he had fretted about his ship and daughter. The only times they had disagreed had been over Althea. But there was nothing new about that. They'd been disagreeing about her for as long as they'd had her.

Ephron had never been able to admit that he spoiled their youngest child. The Blood Plague had carried off their boys, one by one, back in that hellish disease year. Even now, close to twenty years later, Ronica felt the squeeze in her chest when she thought of it. Three sons, three bright little boys, taken in less than a week. Keffria had barely come through it alive. Ronica had thought it would drive them both mad, to see the tree of their family stripped of every male flower. Instead, Ephron had suddenly turned his attention and hopes to the babe that had sheltered inside her womb. Attentive as he had never been during her other pregnancies, he had even tied up the ship for an extra two weeks to be sure of being home when the child was born.

When the babe had been a girl, Ronica had expected Ephron to be bitter. Instead, he had given all his attention to his young daughter, as if somehow his will could make a man of her. He had encouraged her wildness and stubbornness until Ronica despaired of her. Ephron had always denied it was anything other than high spirits. He refused her nothing, and when Althea one day demanded to go with him on his next voyage, Ephron had even consented to that. It had been a short trip, and Ronica had met the ship at the docks, convinced she would get back a girl who had had more than enough of the rough living conditions on the ship. Instead she'd seen a wild monkey up the rigging, her black hair cut back to no more than a brush, barefoot and bare-armed. Ever since then, she had sailed with her father. And now she sailed without him.

They'd had words about that, too. It had taken all her words and his pain atop them to convince him that he should stay home for a time. Ronica had assumed that, of course, Althea would stay home, too. What business had she aboard a ship without her father? When she had suggested as much to Ephron, he had been aghast.

"Our family live ship leave port without one of our blood aboard her? Do you know the kind of ill luck you'd be inviting, woman?"

"The *Vivacia* has not quickened yet. Surely Kyle, our marriage-kin, should be sufficient. He has been Keffria's husband for close on fifteen years! Let Althea stay home for a time. It would do her hair and skin a world of good, and give her a chance to be seen about town. She is of an age to marry, Ephron, or at least to be courted. But to be courted, she must first be seen. She appears but once or twice a year, a Spring Ball one year, a Harvest Gathering the next. Folk scarcely recognize her on the street. And when the young men of the Trader families do see her, she is in trousers and jacket with her hair queued down her back and her skin like a tanned hide. It is scarcely a suitable way to present her if we wish her to marry well."

"Marry well? Let her marry happy instead, as we did. Look at Keffria and Kyle. Remember how the talk raced through the town when I let an upstart sea-captain with Chalcedean blood start courting my eldest? But I knew he was a man, and she knew what was in her heart, and they've been happy enough. Look at their children, healthy as gulls. No, Ronica, if Althea has to be kept on a leash and primped and powdered to catch a man's eyes, then he's not the kind of man I want sniffing after her anyway. Let her be seen by a man who admires her spirit and strength. Soon enough she'll have to settle down, to be lady, wife and mother. I doubt she'll find that kind of monotony to her taste much. So let's allow the lass a life while she can have one." Having delivered this statement, Ephron had leaned back on his cushions, panting.

And Ronica, because he was so ill, had swallowed her ire that he could so disparage the life that she led, and thrust down the jealousy she felt for her own daughter's freedom and careless ways. Nor had she mentioned that the way the family fortunes were going, there might be a need for Althea to marry well. Sourly Ronica now mused that if they tamed the girl down, perhaps they could wed her off to one of their creditors, preferably a generous one who would forgive the family's debt as a wedding gift. Ronica shook her head slowly. No. In his own subtle way, Ephron had taken the argument right to her weakest position. She had married Ephron because she'd fallen in love with him. Just as Keffria had succumbed to Kyle's blond charms. And despite all the family faced, she hoped that when Althea married, she would love the man. She looked with heartsick fondness on the man she still loved.

Afternoon sunlight pouring in the window was making Ephron frown in his sleep. Ronica got up quietly to draw a curtain across the window. She no longer enjoyed that view. Once it had been a great pleasure to look out that window and see the sturdy trunk and branches of their marriage tree. Now it stood stark and leafless in the midst of the summer garden, bare as any skeleton. She felt a shiver up her back as she drew the curtain across the sight.

He had so looked forward to seeing their tree in bloom. But that spring the bud blight that had always spared the tree struck it full force. The flowers browned and fell soddenly to the earth. Not a one opened for them, and the scent of the rotting petals was like funeral herbs. Neither of them spoke of it as an omen. Neither of them had ever been religious folk. But shortly after that, Ephron had begun to cough again. Weak little bird coughs that brought up nothing, until the day he had wiped his mouth and nose, and then frowned at the scarlet tracings of blood on the napkin.

It had been the longest summer of her life. The hot days were a torment to him. He'd declared that breathing the heavy humid air was no better than breathing his own blood, and then coughed up stringy clots as if to prove his point. The flesh had fallen from his body, and he'd had neither the appetite nor the will to take in sustenance. Still, they did not speak of his death. It hovered over the whole house, more oppressive than the humid summer air; Ronica would not give it any more substance by speaking of it.

She moved silently, carefully picking up a small table and setting it close to her bedside chair. She brought back to it her accounting ledgers, her ink and pen, and a handful of receipts to be entered. She bent to her work, frowning as she did so. The entries she made in her small, precise hand did nothing to cheer her. Somehow it was more depressing now that she knew Ephron would insist on looking over the book the next time he awoke. For years he had taken almost no interest in the running of the farms and orchards and other holdings. "I leave them in your competent hands, my dear," he would tell her whenever she tried to present her worries to him. "I'll take care of the ship and see she pays herself off in my lifetime. To you I entrust the rest."

It had been both heady and frightening to have her husband trust her so. It was not that unusual for wives to manage the wealth they brought with them as dowries, and many of the women in time quietly handled substantially more than that, but when Ephron Vestrit openly turned over the directing of almost all his holdings to his young wife, it near scandalized Bingtown. It was no longer the fashion for women to take a hand in the financial end of things; it smacked of their old pioneer life to revert to such a custom. The old Bingtown Traders had always been known for their innovative ways, but as they prospered, it had become a symbol of wealth to keep one's womenfolk free of such tasks. Now it was seen as both plebeian and foolish to so entrust a Trader's fortune to a woman.

Ronica had known that it was not just his fortune Ephron had put in her hands, but his reputation as well. She had vowed to be worthy of that trust. For more than thirty years their holdings had prospered. There had been bad harvests, grain blights, frosts both early and late to contend with, but always a good fruit crop had balanced out the grain not doing well, or the sheep had prospered when the orchards suffered. Had they not had the heavy debt from constructing the *Vivacia* to pay off, they would have been wealthy folk. Even as it had been, they'd been comfortable, and in some years a bit more than that.

Not so the last five years. In that time they had slipped from comfortable to well-off, and then to what Ronica had come to think of as anxious. The money went out almost as swiftly as it came in, and always it seemed she was asking a creditor to wait a day or a week until she could pay him. Over and over she had gone to Ephron to beg his advice. He had demurred to her, telling her to sell off what was not profitable to shore up what was. But that was the problem. Most of the farms and orchards were doing as well as they ever had in producing. But there were cheap slave-grown grain and fruit from Chalced to compete with, and the damned Red Ship wars to the north destroying trade there and the thrice-damned pirates to the south. Shipments sent forth never arrived at their destinations, and expected profits did not return. She feared constantly for the safety of her husband and daughter always out at sea, but Ephron seemed to class pirates with stormy weather; they were simply among the hazards a good sea-captain had to face. He might come home from his own voyages and tell her unnerving tales of running from sinister ships, but all his stories had happy endings. No pirate vessel could hope to run down a liveship. When she had tried to tell him of how severely the war and the pirates were affecting the rest of the family fortunes, he would laugh good-naturedly and tell her that he and the *Vivacia* would but work all the harder until things came right. Back then he had not been interested in seeing her account books nor in hearing the grim tidings of the other merchants and traders. Ronica recalled with frustration that he had seemed able to see only that his own voyages were success-ful, and that the trees bore fruit and the grain ripened in their fields as it always had. He'd take a brisk trip out to one of the holdings, give a cursory glance to their accounts and take himself and Althea back to sea, leaving Ronica to cope.

Only once had she ever been bold enough to suggest to him that perhaps they might have to return to trading up the Rain Wild River. They had the rights, and the contacts, and the liveship. In the days of his grandmother and father, that had been the principal source of their trade goods. But ever since the Blood Plague days, he had re-fused to go up the Rain Wild River. There was no concrete evidence that the sickness had come from the Rain Wilds. Besides, who could say where a sickness came from? There was no sense in blaming themselves, and in cutting themselves off from the most profitable part of their trade. But Ephron had only shaken his head, and made her promise never to suggest it again. He had nothing against the Rain Wild Traders, and he did not deny their trade goods were exotic and beautiful. But he had taken it into his head that one could not traffic in magic, even peripherally, without paying a price. He would, he'd told her, rather that they be poor than risk it.

First she'd had to let the apple orchards go, and with them the tiny winery that had been her pride. The grape arbors had been sold off as well, and that had been hard for her. She had acquired them when she and Ephron were but newlyweds, her first new venture, and it had been her joy to see them prosper. Still, she would have been a fool to keep them at the price that had been offered. It had been enough to keep their other holdings afloat for a year. And so it continued. As war and the pirates tightened the financial noose on Bingtown, she'd had to surrender one venture after another to keep the others afloat. It shamed her. She had been a Carrock and, like the Vestrits, the Carrocks were one of the original Bingtown Trader families. It did nothing for her fears to see the other old families foundering as hungry young merchants moved into Bingtown, buying up old holdings and changing the ways things had always been done. They'd brought the slave-trade to Bingtown, at first as merchandise on their way to the Chalced States, but lately it seemed that the flow of slaves that passed through Bingtown surpassed every other trade. But the slaves didn't flow through anymore. More and more of the fields and orchards were being worked with slaves now. Oh, the landowners claimed they were indentured servants, but all knew that such "servants" were routinely sent on to Chalced and sold as slaves if they proved unwilling workers. More than a few of them wore slave tattoos on their faces. It was yet another Chalcedean custom that seemed to have gained popularity in Jamaillia and was now beginning to be accepted in Bingtown as well. It was these "New Traders," Ronica thought bitterly. They might have come to Bingtown from Jamaillia City, but the baggage they brought with them seemed directly imported from Chalced.

Ostensibly, it was still against the law in Bingtown to keep slaves except as transient trade goods, but that did not seem to bother the New Traders. A few bribes at the Tax Docks, and the Satrap's treasury agents became very gullible, more than willing to believe that folk with tattooed faces and chained in coffles were indentured servants, not slaves at all. The slaves would have gained nothing by speaking the truth of their situation. The Old Traders' Council had complained in vain. Now even a few of the old families had begun to flout the slavery law. Traders like Davad Restart, she thought bitterly. She supposed Davad had to do as he did to stay afloat in these hard times. Had not he as much as said so to her last month, when she had been worrying aloud about her wheat fields? He'd all but suggested she cut her costs by working the fields with slaves. He'd even implied he could arrange it all for her, for a small slice of the profits. Ronica did not like to think of how sorely she'd been tempted to take that advice.

She was writing the last dreary entry into her account books when the rustle of Rache's skirts broke her attention. She lifted her eyes to the servant girl. Ronica was so weary of the mixture of anger and sorrow she always saw in Rache's face. It was as if the woman expected her to do something to mend her life for her. Couldn't she see that Ronica had all she could cope with between her dying husband and tottering finances? Ronica knew that Davad had meant well when he'd insisted on sending Rache over to help her, but sometimes she just wished the woman would disappear. There was no gracious way to be rid of her, however, and no matter how irritated Ronica became with her, she could never quite bring herself to send her back to Davad. Ephron had always disapproved of slavery. Ronica thought it was something that most slaves had brought on themselves, but somehow it seemed disrespectful to Ephron to condemn this woman to slavery when she had helped care for him as he was dying. No matter how poorly she had helped.

"Well?" she asked tartly of Rache when she just stood there.

"Davad is here to see you, lady," Rache mumbled.

"Trader Restart, you mean?" Ronica corrected her.

Rache bobbed her head in silent acknowledgment. Ronica set her teeth, then gave it up. "I'll see him in the sitting room," she instructed Rache, and then followed the girl's sullen eyes to where Davad already stood in the door.

As always he was immaculately groomed, and as always everything about his clothes was subtly wrong. His leggings bagged slightly at the knees, and the embroidered doublet he wore was laced just tightly enough that he had spoiled the lines of it: it made his modest belly seem a bulging pot. He had oiled his dark hair into ringlets, but most of the curl had fallen from them so it hung in greasy locks. Even if the curl had stayed, it was a style more suited to a much younger man.

Somewhere Ronica found the aplomb to smile back at him as she set down her pen and shut her account book. She hoped the ink was dry. She started to rise, but Davad motioned her to stay as she was. Another small gesture from him sent Rache scurrying from the room as Davad advanced to Ephron's bedside.

"How is he?" Davad asked, softening his deep voice.

"As you see," Ronica replied quietly. She set aside her irritation at his calm assumption of welcome in her husband's sickroom. She also put aside her embarrassment that he had caught her at her totting up, with ink on the side of her hand and her brow wrinkled from staring at her own finely penned numbers. Davad meant well, she was sure. How he had managed to grow up in one of Bingtown's old Trader families and still have such a hazy idea of good manners, she would never know. Without invitation, he drew up a chair to sit on the other side of Ephron's bed. Ronica winced as he dragged it across the floor, but Ephron did not stir. When the portly Trader was settled, he gestured at her accounting books.

"And how do they go?" he asked familiarly.

"No better nor worse than any other Trader's these days, I am sure." She evaded his prying. "War, blight and pirates trouble all of us. All we can do is to persevere and wait for better days. And how are you today, Davad?" She tried to recall him to his manners.

He put a splay-fingered hand on his belly meaningfully. "I have been better. I have just come from Fullerjon's table; his cook has an abominable hand with the spices, and Fullerjon has not the tongue to tell it." He leaned back in his chair and heaved a martyred sigh. "But one must be polite, and eat what is offered, I suppose."

Ronica stifled her irritation. She gestured toward the door. "We could take our conversation to the terrace. A glass of buttermilk might help to settle your indigestion as well." She made as if to rise, but Davad did not budge.

"No, no, thank you all the same. I've but come on a brief errand. A glass of wine would be welcome, however. You and Ephron always did keep the best cellars in town."

"I do not wish Ephron disturbed," she said bluntly.

"Oh, I'll take care to speak softly. Though, to be frank, I would rather bring this offer to him than to his wife. Do you expect him to wake soon?"

"No." Ronica heard the edge in her voice, and coughed slightly, as if it had been the result of a dry throat. "But if you wish to tell me the terms of whatever offer you bring, I shall present it to Ephron as soon as he awakens." She pretended to have forgotten his request for wine. It was petty, but she had learned to take her small satisfactions where she could.

"Certainly, certainly. All Bingtown knows you hold his purse-strings. And his trust, I might add, of course." He nodded jovially at her as if this were a high compliment.

"The offer?" Ronica pushed.

"From Fullerjon, of course. I believe it was his sole purpose in inviting me to share his table this noon, if you can credit that. The little upstart seems to think I have nothing better to do than act as his

SHIP OF MAGIC

61

go-between with the better families in town. Did I not think that you and Ephron could benefit from his offer just now, I'd have told him as much. As things stand, I did not want to alienate him, you understand. He's no more than a greedy little merchant, but . . ." He shrugged his shoulders eloquently. "One can scarce do business in Bingtown these days without them."

"And his offer was?" Ronica prompted.

"Ah yes. Your bottom lands. He wishes to buy them." He espied the platter of small biscuits and fruits that she kept at Ephron's bedside and helped himself to a biscuit.

Ronica was shocked. "Those are part of the original grant lands of the Vestrit family. Satrap Esclepius himself granted those lands."

"Ah, well, you and I know the significance of such things, but newcomers such as Fullerjon . . ." Davad began placatingly.

"Also understand. The granting of those lands was what made the Vestrit family a Trader family. They were part of the Satrap's agreement with the Traders. Two hundred leffers of good land, to any family willing to go north and settle on the Cursed Shores, to brave the dangers of life near Rain Wild River. There were few enough willing to in those days. All know that strangeness flows down the Rain Wild River as swiftly as the waters. Those bottom lands and a share in the monopoly on the trade goods of the Rain Wild River are what make the Vestrits a Trader family. Can you seriously think any Trader family would sell off their grant lands?" She was angry now.

"You needn't give me a history lesson, Ronica Vestrit." Davad rebuked her mildly. He helped himself to another biscuit. "Need I remind you that my family came here in the same expedition? The Restarts are as much Traders as the Vestrits. I know what those lands mean."

"Then how can you even bring such an offer here?" she demanded hotly.

"Because half of Bingtown knows how desperate things have become for you. Look here, woman. You haven't the capital to hire the workers to farm those lands properly. Fullerjon does. And buying them would increase his land ownership to the point where he'd be qualified to petition for a seat on the Bingtown Council. Between the two of us, I think that's all he's really after anyway. It needn't be your bottom lands, though that is what he'd like. Offer him something else; he'll probably buy it from you." Davad leaned back with a dissatisfied look on his face. "Sell him the wheat fields. You can't work them properly anyway."

"And he can gain a seat on the Bingtown Council. So he can vote to bring slaves to Bingtown. And work the lands I've sold him with slaves and sell the grain he grows cheaper than I can compete with. Or you, for that matter, or any other honest Trader. Davad Restart, use your mind. This offer not only asks me to betray the Vestrit family, but all of us. We've enough greedy little merchants on the Bingtown Council already. The Old Trader Council is barely able to keep them in check. I shan't be the one to sell land and a council seat to another latecomer upstart."

Davad started to speak, then visibly controlled himself. He folded his small hands on his lap. "It's going to happen, Ronica." She heard true regret in his voice. "The days of the Old Traders are fading. The wars and the pirates bit into us too deeply. And now that the wars are mostly over, these merchants have come, swarming over us like fleas on a dying rabbit. They'll suck us dry. We need their money in order to recover, so they force us to sell cheap what cost us so dear in blood and children." For a moment his voice faltered. Ronica suddenly recalled that the year of the Blood Plague had carried off all his children as well as left him a widower. He had never remarried.

"It's going to happen, Ronica," he repeated. "And those of us who survive will be the ones who have learned to adapt. When our families first settled Bingtown, they were poor and hungry and oh so adaptable. We've lost that. We've become what we fled. Fat and traditionalist and desperate to hang on to our monopolies. The only reason we despise the new merchants who have started moving in is that they remind us so much of ourselves. Or rather of our great-great-grandparents, and the tales we've heard of them."

For a moment, Ronica almost felt inclined to agree with him. Then she felt a rush of anger. "They are nothing like the original Traders! They were wolves, these are eye-picking carrion birds! When the first Carrock set foot on this shore, he risked everything. He sold all he had for his ship-share, and mortgaged half of whatever he might gain for the next twenty years to the Satrap. And for what? For a grant of land and a guarantee of a share in the monopoly. What land? Why, whatever acreage he could claim. What monopoly? Why, on whatever goods he might discover that would be worth trading in. And where was this wonderful bargain granted to him? On a stretch of coast that for hundreds of years had been known as the Cursed Shores, a place where even the gods themselves did not claim dominion. And what did they find here? Diseases unknown before, strangeness that drove men mad overnight, and the doom that half our children are born not quite human."

Davad suddenly went pale and made shushing motions with his

hands. But Ronica was relentless. "Do you know what it does to a woman, Davad, to carry something inside her for nine months, not knowing if it's the child and heir they've been praying for, or if it's a malformed monster that her husband must strangle with his own hands? Or something in between? You must know what it does to a man. As I recall, your Dorill was pregnant three times yet you only had two children."

"And the Blood Plague carried them all off," Davad admitted brokenly. He suddenly lowered his face into his hands and Ronica was sorry, sorry for all she had said, and sorry for this pathetic shell of a man who had no wife to tell him to relace his tunic and scold the tailor for badly fitting trousers. She was sorry for all of them, born in Bingtown to die in Bingtown, and in between to carry on the curse-plagued bargain their forebears had struck. Perhaps the worst part of that bargain was that one and all, they had come to love Bingtown and the surrounding green hills and valleys. Verdant as a jungle, soil black and rich in the hand, crystal water in the streams, and abundant game in the forests, it offered them wealth beyond the dreams of the sea-weary and draggled immigrants who had first been brave enough to anchor in the Bingtown harbor. In the end, the real contract had been made, not with the Satrap who nominally claimed these shores, but with the land itself. Beauty and fertility balanced with disease and death.

And something more, she admitted to herself. There was something in calling oneself a Bingtown Trader, in not only braving all the strangeness that came down the Rain Wild River, but claiming it for one's own. The first Traders had tried to establish their settlement at the mouth of the Rain Wild River itself. They had built their homes on the river's edge, using the roots of the stilt-trees as foundations for their cottages, and stringing bridges from home to home. The rising and falling river had rushed by beneath their floors and the wild storm winds had rocked their tree houses at night. Sometimes the very earth itself would heave and tremble, and then the river might suddenly run milky white and deadly, for a day or a month.

For two years the settlers had abided there, despite insects and fevers and the swift river that devoured anything that fell into it. Yet it had not been those hardships, but the strangeness that had finally driven them away. The little company of Traders had been pushed south by death and disease and the odd panics that might strike a woman as she kneaded the bread, the furies of self-destruction that could come on a man gathering wood and send him leaping into the river. Of 307 households that had been the original Traders, sixty-two families had survived that first three years. Even now, from Bingtown to the mouth of the Rain Wild River there stretched a trail of abandoned townsites that marked the path of their attempts at settlement. Finally, here in Bingtown, on the shores of Trader Bay, they had found a tolerable distance from the Rain Wild River and all that flowed down it. Of those families that had chosen to remain as settlers on the Rain Wild River, the less said the better. The Rain Wild Traders were kin and a necessary part of all Bingtown was. She acknowledged that. Still.

"Davad?" She reached across Ephron to touch their old friend's arm gently. "I'm sorry. I spoke too roughly, of things better left unmentioned."

"It's all right," he lied into his hands. He lifted a pale face to meet her eyes. "What we Traders do not speak of amongst ourselves is common talk among these newcomers. Have not you noticed how few bring their wives and daughters with them? They do not come here to settle. They will buy land, yes, and sit on the Council and wring wealth out of Bingtown, but in between they will sail back to Jamaillia. That is where they will wed and keep their wives, where their children will be born, that is where they will go to spend their aging years and send but a son or two here to manage things." He snorted disdainfully. "The Three-Ships Immigrants I could respect. They came here, and when we honestly told them what price this sanctuary would cost them, they still stayed. But this wave of newcomers arrive hoping only to reap the harvest we have watered with our blood."

"The Satrap is as much to blame as they are," Ronica agreed. "He has broken the word that was given to us by Esclepius, his forebear. It was sworn to us that he would make no more grants of land to newcomers, save that our Council approved it. The Three-Ships Immigrants came with empty hands, but willing backs, and they have become a part of us. But this latest wave come clutching land grants and claim their leffers with no regard for who or what they harm. Felco Treeves claimed his land on the hillsides above Trader Drur's beer valley, and put cattle to graze on it. Now Drur's springs that flowed so clear are yellow as cow's piss, and his beer is scarcely drinkable. And when Trudo Fells came, he claimed as his own the forest where all had been free to cut firewood and oak for furniture, and . . ."

"I know, I know it all," Davad cut in wearily. "Ronica, there is naught but bitterness in chewing these thoughts again. And there is no good in pretending that things will go back to how they once were. They will not. This is but the first wave of change. We can either ride over the wave or be swamped by it. Don't you think the Satrap will sell other grants of lands, once it is seen that these newcomers prosper? More will come. The only way to deal with them is to adapt to them. Learn from them, if we must—and take up their ways where we must."

"Aye." Ephron's voice was like a rusted hinge breaking free. "We can learn to like slavery so well that we do not care when our grandchildren may become slaves because of a year's debts mounting too high. And as for the sea serpents that the slaveships lure into our waters, chumming them along with the bodies they throw overboard, well, we can welcome them right into Trader Bay and never need the boneyard again."

It was a long speech for a sick man. He stopped to breathe. At the first sign of his wakening, Ronica had arisen to fetch the poppy milk. She drew the stopper from the heavy brown bottle, but Ephron slowly shook his head. "Not yet," he told her. He breathed for a moment before he repeated, "Not just yet." He turned his weary gaze to Davad, whose tactless dismay at Ephron's weakness was writ large on his face. Ephron gave a feeble cough.

Davad bent his face into an attempt at a smile. "It's good to see you awake, Ephron. I hope our conversation didn't disturb you."

For a moment or two Ephron just stared at the man. Then, with the casual rudeness of the truly ill, he ignored him. His dull eyes focused on his wife. "Any word of the *Vivacia*?" he asked. He asked the question as a starving man might ask for food.

Ronica shook her head reluctantly as she set the poppy milk down. "But she should not be much longer. We have had word from the monastery that Wintrow is on his way home to us." She offered these last words brightly, but Ephron only turned his head slowly against the pillow.

"What will he do? Look solemn and beg an offering for his monastery before he leaves? I gave up on that boy when his mother sacrificed him to Sa." Ephron closed his eyes and breathed for a time. He did not open his eyes before he spoke again. "Damn that Kyle. He should have been back weeks ago . . . unless he's taken her to the bottom, and Althea, too. I knew I should have put the ship in Brashen's hands. Kyle's a good enough captain, but it takes Trader blood to truly feel the ways of a liveship."

Ronica felt the blush rise in her cheeks. It shamed her to have her husband speak so of their son-in-law in Davad's presence. "Are you hungry, Ephron? Or thirsty?" she asked to change the subject.

"Neither." He coughed. "I'm dying. And I'd like my damn ship here so I can die on her decks and quicken her, so my whole damn life won't have been for nothing. That's not much to ask for, is it? That the dream that I was born to fulfill should be played out as I've always planned it?" He took a ragged breath. "The poppy, Ronica. The poppy now."

She measured the syrupy medicine into a spoon. She held it to Ephron's mouth and he swallowed it with no complaint. Afterwards he took a breath and motioned at his water jug. He drank from the cup in small sips, then lay back against his pillows with a wheezing sigh. Already the lines on his forehead were loosening, his mouth getting slacker. His eyes wandered to Davad, but it was not to him he spoke.

"Don't sell anything, my love. Bide your time as best you can. Let me but die on the decks of my ship, and I'll see the *Vivacia* serves you well. She and I will cut the waves as no ship ever has before, swift and true. You'll lack for nothing, Ronica. I promise you. Just stay your course, and all will go well."

His voice was winding down, going deeper and slower on each word. She held her own breath as he took another gulp of air. "Hold your course," he repeated, but she did not think he spoke to her. Perhaps the poppy had already carried his dreaming mind back to the deck of his beloved ship.

She felt the hated tears rising and fought them back. They struggled against her determination, choking her until the pain in her throat almost stopped her breath. She gave a sideways glance at Davad. He hadn't the courtesy to turn his stare away, but at least he had the grace to be uncomfortable. "His ship," she found herself saying bitterly. "Always his damn ship; that was all he ever cared about." She wondered why she would rather that Davad believed she cried over that instead of Ephron's death. She sniffed, horribly loud, then gave in and found her handkerchief and wiped her eyes.

"I should be going," Davad realized belatedly.

"Must you?" Ronica heard herself replying reflexively. She found the discipline appropriate to her position. "Thank you so much for dropping in. Let me at least walk you to the door," she added, before Davad could change his mind about leaving.

She rose and tugged a light cover up over Ephron. He muttered something about the topsail. Davad took her arm as they left the sickroom, and she forced herself to tolerate that courtesy. She blinked as she left the dimness of the sickroom behind her. She had always been proud of her bright and airy home; now the clear sunlight that flooded in the generous windows seemed harsh and glaring. She averted her eyes from the atrium as they passed it. Once it had been her pride and joy; now, bereft of her attentions, it was a desolate wasteland of browning vines and sprawling, straggling plant life. She tried to promise herself that after Ephron was finished dying, she'd have time to attend to it once again, but suddenly that thought seemed vile and traitorous, as if she were hoping her husband would soon die so she could take care of her garden.

"You are quiet," Davad observed bluntly. In truth, she had forgotten him despite his arm linked with hers.

Before she could formulate a polite apology, he added gruffly, "But as I recall, when Dorill died, there was really nothing left to talk about to anyone." He turned to her as they reached the great white door and surprised her by taking both her hands in his. "If there is anything I can do . . . and I truly mean anything . . . will you let me know?"

His hands were damp and sweaty, his breath smelled of his over-spiced lunch, but the worst part was the absolute sincerity in his eyes. She knew he was her friend, but at the moment all she could see was what she might become. When Dorill had been alive, Davad had been a powerful man in Bingtown, a sharp Trader, well-dressed and prosperous, hosting balls at his great house, flourishing not only in his businesses but socially. Now his great house was only a collection of dusty, ill-kempt rooms presided over by unsupervised and dishonest servants. Ronica knew that she and Ephron were one of the few couples that still included Davad when they issued invitations to balls or dinners. When Ephron was gone, would she be like Davad, a social left-over, a widow too old to court and too young to seat in a quiet corner? Her fear came out as a sudden bitterness.

"Anything, Davad? Well, you could always pay off my debts, harvest my fields, and find a suitable husband for Althea." She heard her own words in a sort of horror and watched Davad's eyes widen so far that they almost bulged at her. Abruptly she pulled her hands free of his moist clasp. "I'm sorry, Davad," she said sincerely. "I don't know what possessed me to . . ."

"Never mind," he interrupted her hastily. "You're talking to the man who burned his wife's portrait, simply so I wouldn't have to look at what I couldn't see. At times like these, one says and does things that . . . never mind, Ronica. And I did, truly, mean anything. I'm your friend, and I'll see what I can do to help you."

He turned and hurried away from her, down a white stone walkway to where his saddle horse waited. Ronica stood watching as he mounted the beast awkwardly. He lifted one hand in farewell and she waved in return. She watched him ride off down the drive. Then she lifted her eyes to look out over Bingtown. For the first time since Ephron had been taken ill, she truly looked at the town. It had changed. Her own home, like many of the Old Trader homes, was on a gentle hill above the harbor basin. Through the trees below, she could catch glimpses of the cobbled streets and white stone buildings of Bingtown, and beyond them the blue of Trader Bay. She could not see the Great Market from here, but she trusted it bustled on with the same trust she gave to the rising of the sun. The broad paved streets of it echoed the gentle horseshoe curve of the bay. Open and airy was the Great Market, planned out as carefully as any nobleman's estate. Clumps of trees shaded small gardens where tables and chairs beckoned the weary buyer to relax for a time before arising to go forth and purchase more. One hundred and twenty shops with tall windows and wide doors welcomed trade from near and far. On a sunny day like today, the brightly dyed awnings would be spread over the walkways to lure strollers closer to the merchants' doors with their shade.

Ronica smiled to herself. Her mother and grandmother had always told her, proudly, that Bingtown did not look like a city hacked out of a wilderness on this chill and remote coast, but like any proper city in the Satrap's dominion. The streets were straight and clean, offal and slops relegated to the alleys and drains behind the shops. Even those areas were regularly cleaned. When one left the Great Market and strolled away from the Lesser Marts, the city still presented a polished and civilized face. The houses of white stone shone in the sunlight. Orange and lemon trees flavored the air with their fragrance, even if they did grow in tubs and have to be taken in every winter. Bingtown was the gem of the Cursed Shores, the farthest jewel of the Satrap's cities, but still one of the brightest. Or so Ronica had always been told.

She reflected in a moment's bitterness that she would never know, now, if her mother and grandmother had spoken truly. Once, Ephron had promised her that someday they would make a pilgrimage to holy Jamaillia City, and visit Sa's groves and see the gleaming palace of the Satrap himself. Another dream turned to dust. She pulled her mind away from such thoughts and gazed out again over Bingtown. All there looked as it always had; a few more ships anchored in the harbor, a few more folk hastening through the streets, but that was to be expected. Bingtown had been growing, just as it had been growing all her life.

It was when she lifted her eyes to gaze out over the surrounding hills that she realized how much things had changed. Hammersmith

Hill, where the oaks had always stood tall and green, now showed a bald pate. She gazed at it in a sort of awe. She had heard that one of the newcomers had claimed land there and was going to use slaves to log it. But never before had she seen a hill so completely stripped of forest. The heat of the day beat down mercilessly on the naked hill; what greenery remained looked scorched and sagging.

Hammersmith Hill was the most shocking change, but it was by no means the only one. To the east, someone had cleared space on a hillside and was building a house. No, Ronica corrected herself, a mansion. It was not just the size of the building that jolted her, but the number of workers employed in its construction. They swarmed over the building site like white-coated ants in the heat of the mid-day sun. Even as she watched, the timber framework for a wall was hoisted into place and secured. Off to the west, a new road cut an arrow-straight path into the hills. She could only glimpse segments of it through the trees, but it was wide and well-traveled. Uneasiness rose in her. Perhaps Davad had been more correct than she had suspected. Perhaps the changes that had come to Bingtown were more significant than a mere swelling of population. And if he were right about that, then he might also be correct in saying that the only way to survive this wave of new traders would be to emulate them.

She turned away from Bingtown and her uncomfortable thoughts. She had no time to think of such things now. It was all she could do to live with her own disaster and fears. Bingtown would have to take care of itself.

CHAPTER FOUR

DIVVYTOWN

KENNIT MOISTENED HIS KERCHIEF IN LEMON OIL AND SMOOTHED IT OVER HIS BEARD AND MUSTACHE. HE regarded himself in the gilt-framed mirror over his washbasin. The oil gave an added sheen to his facial hair, but it was not that effect he had sought. The fragrance of the oil was still not sufficient to keep the stench of Divvytown from his nostrils. Coming to Divvytown was, he reflected, rather like being towed to dock in the musk and stench of a slave's armpit.

He left his quarters and emerged onto the deck. The outside air was as sultry and humid as within, and the stink more powerful. He looked with distaste at the nearing shores of Divvytown. This pirate's sanctuary had been well chosen. To find it, one not only had to know the way, but to be a consummate master of bringing a ship up an inland waterway. The limpid river that led to this lagoon looked no more promising than a dozen others that threaded their way through the multiple islands of the Shifting Shore to the true sea, but this one had a deep if narrow channel that a sailing ship could navigate, and a placid lagoon sheltered from even the wildest storms for anchorage.

At one time, no doubt, it had been a beautiful place. Now mossy docks and piers poked out from every piece of firm land. The lush greenery that cloaked and overhung the river banks had been sheared back to bare mud. There was neither sufficient flow of water nor stirring of breeze to disperse the sewage and smoke of the clustering huts and hovels and stores of the pirate city. Eventually the rains of winter would come, to flush both city and lagoon briefly clean, but on a hot still summer day, the Divvytown lagoon harbor had all the beckoning charm of an unemptied chamber pot.

To anchor here for more than a few days at a stretch invited moss and rot to the hull of a ship; to drink the water from all but a few wells gave a man the flux—and, if he were unlucky, the fever as well. Yet as Kennit stood looking down over the deck of his ship, he saw his crew working well and willingly. Even those in the boats towing the *Marietta* into harbor pulled away heartily, for to their noses, this stench was the sweet smell of both home and pay. By tradition, their trove would be divvied out on deck as soon as the *Marietta* was tied up. In a few hours, they'd be up to their navels in whores and beer.

Aye, and before sun-up tomorrow, most of their hard-won loot would have passed into the hands of the soft innkeepers and whore-masters and merchants of Divvytown. Kennit shook his head pityingly and dabbed once more at his mustache with his lemon-scented hand-kerchief. He permitted himself a small smile. At least this time, in addition to sowing their plunder throughout the town, his crew would spread the seeds of Kennit's ambition. Before sun-up tomorrow, he'd wager that half of Divvytown would have heard the tale of Captain Kennit's sooth-saying at the Others' Island. He intended to be excep-tionally generous with his men this day when it came to divvy-time. He would not flaunt it, but he'd take no more than a double crew-share this time. He wanted the pockets of his crew to be heavy with their pay; he wanted all Divvytown to remark and remember that the men of his ship seemed always to come to port with well-laden purses. Let them mark it up to the luck and largesse of their captain. Let them wonder if a bit of that luck and largesse might not benefit all of Divvytown in time.

The mate came to stand respectfully beside him as he leaned on the rail.

"Sorcor, do you see that bit of a bluff there? A tower there would command a long view of the river, and a ballista or two beneath it could defend it from any ship that ever discovered our channel. Not only could Divvytown be warned well ahead of any attack, but it could defend itself. What do you think?"

Sorcor bit his lip but otherwise contained himself. Every time they put into port here, Kennit made this same proposal to him. Each time the seasoned mate answered the same. "Could there be found enough stone in this bog, a tower might be built, and rocks hauled up to throw. I suppose it might be done, sir. But who would pay for it, and who would oversee it? Divvytown would never stop quarreling long enough to build and man such a defense."

"If Divvytown had a strong enough ruler, he could accomplish it. It would be only one of the many things he could accomplish."

Sorcor glanced cautiously at his captain. This was new territory for their discussion. "Divvytown is a town of free men. We have no ruler."

"That is true," Kennit agreed. Experimentally, he added, "And that is why we are ruled instead by the greed of merchants and whoremasters. Look about you. We risk our lives for our gains, every sailor of us. Yet by the time we weigh anchor again, where will our gold be? Not in our own pockets. And what will a man have to show for it? Naught but an aching head, unless he has the ill luck to catch the crabs in a bagnio as well. The more a man has to spend in Divvytown, why then the more the beer or the bread or the women cost.

"But you are right. What Divvytown needs is not a ruler, but a leader. A man who can stir men to rule themselves, who can waken them so that they open their eyes and see what they could have." Kennit let his gaze move back out to the men who bowed their backs to the oars as the ship's boats towed the *Marietta* into dock. Nothing in his relaxed stance could indicate to Sorcor that this was a carefully rehearsed speech. Kennit thought well of his first mate. He was not only a good seaman, but an intelligent man despite his limited education. If Kennit could sway him with his words, then perhaps others would begin to listen as well.

He ventured to shift his eyes to Sorcor's face. A frown furrowed the mate's tanned brow. It pulled at the shiny scar that was the remains of his slave tattoo. When he spoke, it was after laborious thought. "We be free men here. That wasn't always true. More than half of them who have come here were slaves, or going to be slaves. Many wear a tattoo still, or the scar where a slave tattoo was. And the rest, well, the rest would have to face a noose or a lash, or maybe both if they went back to wherever they come from. A few nights back, you spoke of a king for us pirates. You're not the first to speak of it, and it seems the more merchants we get here, the more they talk up such ideas. Mayors and councils and kings and guards. But we had enough of that where we come from, and for most of us, it's why we're here instead of there. Not a one of us wants any man telling us what we can or can't do. We get enough of that on shipboard. Begging your pardon, sir."

"No offense taken, Sorcor. But you might consider that anarchy is but disorganized oppression." Kennit watched Sorcor's face carefully. The moment of puzzlement told him that his selection of words had been wrong. Obviously, he was going to need more practice at this persuasion. He smiled genially, "Or so some would say. I have both more faith in my fellow men, and a greater appreciation for simpler words. What do we have in Divvytown now? Why, a succession of bullies. Do you remember when Podee and his gang were going about breaking heads and taking pouches? It was almost accepted that if a sailor did not go ashore with his ship-mates, he'd be beaten and robbed before midnight. And that if he did, the best he could expect was a brawl with Podee's gang. If three ships' companies hadn't turned on Podee and his men at once, it would still be going on. Right now, there's at least three taverns where a man stepping into a dim chamber is as likely to get a stick behind his ear as the whore he paid for. But no one does anything. It's only the business of the man who gets clubbed and robbed." Kennit stole a glance at Sorcor. The mate's brow was furrowed, but he was nodding to himself. With an odd little thrill, Kennit realized that the man on the wheel was paying as much attention to their words as to holding the ship steady. At any other time, Kennit would have rebuked him. Now he felt a small triumph. But Sorcor noticed it at the same moment his captain did.

"Hey, you, 'ware there! You're to hold the ship steady, not be listening in on your betters!"

Sorcor sprang to the man with a look that threatened a blow. The sailor screwed up his face to accept it but did not wince nor budge from his post. Kennit left Sorcor berating him for being a lazy idiot and strolled forward. Beneath his boots, the decks were white as sand and stone could make them. Everywhere he cast his eyes he found precision and industry. Every hand was engaged at a task, and every bit of gear that was not in immediate use was carefully stowed. Kennit nodded to himself. Such had not been the case when he had first come on board the *Marietta* five years ago. Then she had been as slatternly a tub as any in the pirate fleet. And the captain that welcomed him aboard with a curse and an ill-aimed blow had been as indistinguishable from his greasy, scurvy crew as any mongrel in a street pack.

But that had been why Kennit had chosen the *Marietta* to ship aboard. Her lines were lovely beneath the debris of years of neglect and the badly patched canvas on her yards. And the captain was ripe for overthrow. Any ship's master who had not even the leadership to let his mate do his cursing and brawling for him was a man whose reign was ending. It took Kennit seventeen months to overthrow the captain, and an additional four months to see his mate over the side as well. By the time he stepped up to command the *Marietta*, his fellow sailors were clamoring eagerly to follow him. He chose Sorcor with care, and all but courted the man to make him his loyal subordinate. Once they had taken command, he and Sorcor took the vessel out on the open seas, far from sight of land. There they culled the crew as a gambler discards worthless cards at a table. As the only men capable of reading a chart or setting a course, they were almost immune from mutiny, yet Kennit never let Sorcor's strictness cross the line into abuse. Kennit believed that most men were happiest under a firm hand. If that hand also supplied cleanliness and the security of knowing one's place, the men would be only the more content. Those that could be made into decent sailors were. They sailed to the limits of the ship's biscuits and the stars he and Sorcor knew.

By the time he and Sorcor brought the *Marietta* into a port so distant that not even Sorcor knew the language, the *Marietta* had the guise of a prim little merchant vessel, and a crew who scrambled at a glance from either captain or mate. There Kennit spent his long-hoarded crew-shares to refit his ship as best he could. When the *Marietta* left that shore, it was to indulge in a month of precision piracy such as the little ports on that coast had never faced before. The *Marietta* returned to Divvytown heavy with exotic goods and oddly stamped coins. Those of the crew that returned with him were as wealthy as they had ever been, and loyal as dogs. In a single voyage, Kennit had gained a ship, a reputation and his fortune.

Yet even as he stepped down onto the docks of Divvytown, thinking he had realized his life's ambition, all his joy in his accomplishment peeled away from him like dead skin from a burn. He watched his crew strut up the docks, dressed in silk as if they were lords, their swag bags heavy with coins and ivory and curiously wrought jewelry. He knew then that they were but sailors, and their plunder would be engulfed in Divvytown's maw in a matter of hours. And suddenly the immaculately clean decks and neatly sewn sails and crisp paint on the *Marietta* seemed as brief and shallow a triumph as his crew's wealth. He rebuffed Sorcor's companionship, and instead spent their week in port drinking in the dimness of his cabin. He had never expected to be so disheartened by success. He felt cheated.

It took him months to recover. He moved through that time in a numb blackness, bewildered by the hopelessness that had settled on him. Some distant part of himself recognized then how well he had chosen in Sorcor. The mate carried on as if nothing were amiss, and never once inquired into the captain's state of mind. If the crew sensed something was odd, there was no evidence of it. Kennit was of the philosophy that on a well-run ship, the captain need never speak directly to the crew, but should only make his wishes known to the mate and trust him to see them carried out. That habit served him well in those despairing days. He had not felt himself again until the morning that Sorcor had rapped on his door to announce that they had a fine fat merchant vessel in sight, and did the Captain wish him to pursue her?

They not only pursued her, but grappled and boarded her, securing for themselves a fine cargo of wine and perfumes. Kennit left Sorcor in charge of the *Marietta*'s deck while he himself led the crew onto the merchant vessel. Up to that time, he had viewed battle and killing as one of the untidy aspects of his chosen career. For the first time that day, his heart caught fire with battle fury. Over and again he slew his anger and disappointment, until to his shock there was suddenly no one left to oppose him. He turned from the last body that had fallen at his feet to find his men gathered in knots on the deck, staring at him in a sort of fascination. He heard not so much as a whispered remark, but the combination of horror and admiration in their eyes told him much. He thought he had won his crew to him with discipline, but that was the day when they actually gave him their hearts. They would not speak familiarly with him nor ever regard him with fondness. But when they went forth to drink and carouse through Divvytown, they would brag of his strict shipboard discipline that marked them as men of endurance, and his savagery with a sword that marked them as a ship to be feared.

From that time on, they expected their captain to lead their forays. The first time he held them back and accepted a captain's surrender of their ship, the crew had been somewhat disgruntled, until he shared out amongst them the greater crew-shares from the ransom of the ship and cargo. Then it had been all right; the satisfaction of greed can make most things right with a pirate crew.

In the intervening years, he secured his little empire. He cultivated in Chalced both merchants in the seedier ports that would buy unusual cargoes with no questions asked, and lesser Chalcedean lords who did not scruple to act as go-betweens in the ransoming of ships, cargoes and crews. One got far more from them for pirated cargo than one did in Divvytown or Skullsport. In recent months he had begun to fantasize that these Chalcedean lordlings could help him gain recognition of the pirate isles as a legitimate domain, once he had convinced the inhabitants to accept him as their ruler. He once again tallied up what he had to offer both sides. For the pirates, legitimacy, with no threat of a noose to haunt them. Open trade with other ports. Once he unified the pirate isles and towns, they could act together to put an end to the slavers raiding their towns. He worried briefly that that would not be enough for them, but then pushed that thought aside. For the merchants of Chalced and the traders of Bingtown, the benefits were clearer. Safe use of the inside passage up the coast to Bingtown, Chalced and the lands beyond. It would not be free, of course. Nothing could be free. But it would be safe. A smile ghosted across his lips. They'd like that change.

He was broken from his reverie by the flurry of activity as the deck crew hastened to throw and secure lines. The hands turned to with a will, positioning the heavy hemp camels that would prevent the *Marietta* from grinding against the dock. Kennit stood silent and aloof, listening to Sorcor bark the necessary orders. All about him, the ship was made tidy and secure. He neither moved nor spoke until all the hands were mustered in the waist below him, restlessly awaiting the division of the loot. When Sorcor mounted the deck to stand beside him, Kennit gave him a brief nod, then turned to his men.

"I make to you the same offer I have made the last three times we've made port. Those of you who choose may take your shares as allotted and carry them off to trade and peddle as best you can. Those of you with patience and good sense can take a draw against your share, and allow the mate and me to dispose of our cargo more profitably. Those who choose to do so can return to the ship the day after tomorrow to take their remaining share of those profits." He looked out over the faces of his men. Some met his eyes and some glanced at their fellows. All shuffled restlessly as children. The town and rum and women awaited them. He cleared his throat. "Those of you who have had the patience to allow me to sell their cargo for them can tell you that the coin they received as their shares was greater than if they had tried to barter on their own. A wine merchant will pay more for our whole shipment of brandy than you will get for a single keg you bargain away to an innkeeper. The bales of silk, sold as a lot to a trader, will fetch far more than you can trade a single bolt to a whore for."

He paused. Below him, men fidgeted and shifted impatiently. Kennit clenched his jaws. Time and time again, he had proven to them all that his way was more profitable. They knew it, any man of them would admit it, but the moment they were tied to the dock, all good sense deserted them. He permitted himself a brief sigh of exasperation, then turned to Sorcor. "The tally of our gains, Mate Sorcor."

Sorcor was ready with it. Sorcor was always ready with everything. He held up the scroll and unfurled it as if reading from it, but Kennit knew he had actually memorized what they had taken. The man could not even read his own name, but if you asked him what each crew share should be from forty bales of silk, he could tell you in an instant. The men murmured appreciatively amongst themselves as the tally was read aloud. The pimps and freegirls who had gathered on the dock to await his crewmen catcalled and whistled, with some of the freegirls already calling out offers on their wares. The men shifted about like tethered beasts, eyes darting from Sorcor and his scroll to all the pleasures that awaited them on the dock and up the muddy roads. When Sorcor finished, he had to roar twice for silence before Kennit would speak. When he did, his voice was deliberately soft.

"Those of you wishing to take a draw against your crew share of what our goods will bring may line up outside my cabin to see me one at a time. You others may meet with Sorcor."

He turned and descended the ways to his cabin. He'd found it best to let Sorcor deal with the others. They would simply have to accept the mate's assessment of what one-third of a bale of silk was worth in terms of two-fifths of a keg of brandy or a half measure of cindin. If they hadn't the patience to wait to get their shares as coin, they'd have to accept whatever equivalent Sorcor thought fair. So far, he'd heard no grumbling against the mate's division of the loot. Either, like Kennit, they did not question his honesty among his shipmates, or they simply did not dare to bring their grumbling to the captain's door. Either was fine with Kennit.

The line of men that came to receive a coin advance against their crew shares was disappointingly short. Kennit gave each of them five selders. It was, he judged, enough to keep them in women, drink, and food for an evening, and a decent bed in an inn, if they did not decide to return to the ship to sleep. As soon as they had their money, they left the ship. Kennit emerged onto the deck in time to see the last man jump down onto the crowded dock. It reminded him of throwing bloody meat into shark waters. The folk on the dock churned and swarmed around the last seaman, the freegirls proffering their wares even as the pimps shouted over their heads that a wealthy young tar like him could afford better, could afford a woman in a bed all night, yes, and a bottle of rum on the table beside it. With less determination, apprentices hawked fresh bread and sweets and ripe fruit. The young pirate grinned, enjoying their avidity. He seemed to have forgotten that as soon as they'd shaken the last coin from his pocket, they'd be as happy to leave him in a gutter or alley.

Kennit turned aside from the bluster and noise. Sorcor was already finished with his divvying. He was standing on the high deck by the tiller, looking out over the town. Kennit frowned slightly. The mate must have known in advance which men wanted their shares as goods, and have already calculated what he would give them. Then his brow smoothed. It was more efficient that way, and that was ever Sorcor's way. Kennit offered him a pouch heavy with coin, and the mate took it wordlessly. After a moment, he rolled his shoulders and turned to face his captain. "So, Sorcor. Are you coming with me to change our cargo to gold?"

Sorcor took an embarrassed step sideways. "If the captain doesn't mind, I'd sooner have a bit of time to myself first."

Kennit concealed his disappointment. "It's all one to me," he lied. Then he said quietly, "I've a mind to turn off those men who always insist on taking their shares as raw goods. The more I have to sell in bulk, the better price I can get. What think you?"

Sorcor swallowed. Then he cleared his throat. "It is their right, sir. To take their crew shares as goods if they choose. That's the way it's always been done in Divvytown." He paused to scratch at a scarred cheek. Kennit knew he had weighed his words before speaking when he went on, "They're good men, sir. Good sailors, true shipmates, and not a one shirks whether the work is with a sail needle or a sword. But they didn't become pirates to live under another man's rules, no matter how good for them that rule might be." With difficulty he met Kennit's eyes and added, "No man becomes a pirate because he wants to be ruled by another."

His certainty increased as he added, "And we'd pay hell's own wages to try and replace them. They're seasoned hands, not scrapings from a brothel floor. The kind of man you'd get, if you went about asking for men who'd let you sell their prizes for them, wouldn't have the spines to act on their own. They'd be the kind as would stand back while you cleared another ship's deck, and only cross when the victory was assured." Sorcor shook his head, more to himself than to his captain. "You've won these men over to you, sir. They'll follow you. But you'd not be wise to try to force them to give up their wills to you. All this talk of kings and leaders make them uneasy. You can't force a man to fight well for you. . . ." Sorcor's voice trailed off and he glanced suddenly up at Kennit as if recalling to whom he spoke.

A sudden icy anger seethed through Kennit. "No doubt that's so, Sorcor. See that a good watch is kept aboard, for I won't be back this night. I leave you in charge."

With no more than that, Kennit turned and left him. He didn't glance back to read the expression on the mate's face. He'd essentially confined him to the ship for the night, for the agreement between them was that one of them would always sleep aboard when the ship was in port. Well, let him mutter. Sorcor had just crippled all the dreams that Kennit had been entertaining for the last few months. As he strode across his decks, Kennit wondered bitterly how he could be such a fool as to dream at all. This was as much as he'd ever be: the captain of a ship full of wastrels who could see no farther than their own cocks.

He jumped easily from the deck to the docks. At once the crowd of vendors surged toward him, but a single scowl sent them shrinking back. At least he still had that much of a reputation in Divvytown. The thought only soured him further. They gave way as he pushed past them. A reputation in Divvytown. Why, that was at least as good as admiring oneself in a piss-puddle. So he was captain of a ship. For how long? For as long as the curs under him believed in his fist and his sword. Ten years from now, there'd be a man bigger or faster or sneakier, and then Kennit could look forward to being one of the gray-faced beggars that slunk about the alleys robbing drunks, and stood outside taverns begging for leavings.

His anger grew in him like a poison in his blood. He knew he'd be the wiser to find a place to be alone until this black mood left him, but his sudden hatred for himself and his world was such that he did not care what was wiser. He detested the sticky black mud of the streets and byways, he despised the dumped slops he stepped around, he loathed the stench and noise of Divvytown. He wished he could avenge himself on his world and on his own stupidity by destroying it all. He knew it was no time to go bargaining. He didn't care. The brokers in Divvytown added such a large cut for themselves that it was scarcely worth his time to deal with them. They'd done far better when they'd disposed of their goods in Chalced. All the prizes they'd taken between Chalced and home he was practically giving to these vultures. In his reckless temper he let the silk go for half what it was worth, but when the trader tried to get as good a bargain on the brandy and cindin, he uncovered Kennit's icy wrath, and ended up paying more than their worth to keep Kennit from taking the entire cargo elsewhere. The bargain was sealed with a nod, for Kennit disdained even to shake hands with the man. The gold would be paid tomorrow when the broker sent his longshoremen to off-load the cargo. Kennit left the trader's parlor without another word.

Outside a summer's dusk had fallen. The raucous noise from the taverns had increased, while the shrilling of insects and frogs from the surrounding swamps and the brackish swale provided a background chorus. The cooling of the day seemed to free a new regiment of odors to assault Kennit's nose. The greasy mud of the streets sucked noisily at his boots as he strode along. He stayed well to the middle of the street, away from the dimmer alley mouths and the predators that would lurk there. Most of them were desperate enough to attack any man who came within reach. As if recalling a forgotten appointment, it came to Kennit that he was hungry and thirsty. And tired. And sad.

The tide of his anger had retreated, leaving him stranded in weariness and misery. Hopelessly, he tried to discover who was at fault for his situation. It did not please him to decide that the fault, as always, was his own. There was no one else to blame, there was no one else to punish. No matter how he seared the faults from himself, another always arose to take its place.

His feet had carried him to Bettel's bagnio. Light leaked past the shutters on the low windows. Music sounded faintly from within, and the edged soprano of a woman singing. There were perhaps a dozen buildings in Divvytown that were more than one story high. Bettel's was one of them. White paint, tiny balconies, and a red-tiled roof; it looked as if someone had plucked up a Chalcedean brothel and plopped it down in the mud of Divvytown. Pots of flowers on the steps struggled to perfume the air, while two copper and brass lanterns gleamed invitingly on either side of the green-and-gilt door. The two bravos on watch smirked at him knowingly. Abruptly he hated them, so big and so stupid, making a living by their muscle alone. They thought it would always be enough; he knew better. He longed to seize them by the throats and smash their grinning faces together, to feel their skulls impact against each other and give way, bone to bone. He longed to feel their windpipes crumple beneath his fingers, to hear their last breaths whistle in and out of their crushed throats.

Kennit smiled at them slowly. They stared back at him, their smirks changing to uncomfortable sneers. Finally they gave way to him, almost cringing as they stepped clear of the door that he might pass.

The doors of the bagnio swung shut behind him, shutting out the mud and the stench of Divvytown. Here he stood in a carpeted foyer in muted yellow lamplight. Bettel's familiar perfume rode the air, and the smoky tang of burnt cindin. The singing and the soft drumming that accompanied it were louder here. A serving boy stood before him and gestured mutely at his muddy boots. At a slight nod from Kennit, he sprang forward with his brush to wipe the worst of the mud from his boots and then follow it up with a careful wiping with a rag. Next he poured cool water into a basin and offered it to Kennit. Kennit took the cloth draped over the boy's arm and wiped the day's sweat and dust from his face and hands. The boy glanced up at Kennit wordlessly when he was done, and the pirate captain was moved to bestow a pat upon his shaven pate. The boy grinned at him and scuttled across the room to open the second door for him.

As the white door swung open slowly, the singing became louder. A blond woman sat cross-legged on the floor, accompanying herself on three small drums as she sang some ditty about her brave love gone off to sea. Kennit hardly spared her a glance. She and her sentimental crooning were not what he sought here. Before he could even think of becoming impatient, Bettel had risen from her cushioned throne to take his arm gently. "Kennit!" she cried aloud in sweet disapproval. "So you have finally come, you naughty man! The *Marietta* tied up hours ago! Whatever has taken you so long to get here?" She had hennaed her black hair this month and her perfume hung about her as heavily as her jewels. Her breasts surged against her dress like seas threatening to swamp the gunwales of a boat.

He ignored her scolding. He knew the attention was supposed to flatter him, and knowing that made Bettel's whole routine irritating. Of course she remembered him. He paid her to remember him. He glanced over her head, scanning the tastefully furnished room and the handful of well-made women and men who lounged on the cushioned chairs and divans. Two of the women smiled at him. They were new. None of the others met his eyes. He gave his attention back to Bettel and interrupted her flow of complimentary prattle.

"I don't see Etta."

Bettel made a moue of disapproval at him. "Well, do you suppose you're the only one who favors her? She could not wait forever upon you. If you choose to come late, Master Kennit, then you must . . ."

"Fetch her and send her to the topmost chamber. Wait. Have her bathe first, while I am eating. Send me up a good meal, with fresh bread. Neither fish nor pork. The rest I leave to you. And the wine,

Bettel. I have a palate. Do not send me the decomposing grape you served me with last time, or this house shall lose my patronage entirely."

"Master Kennit, do you suppose I shall simply rap on a chamber door and tell one of my other patrons that Etta is required elsewhere? Do you suppose your money spends better than anyone else's? If you come late, then you must choose from . . ."

He paid her no mind, but ascended the curving staircase in the corner of the room. For a moment he paused on the second floor. The sounds reminded him of a wall full of rats. He gave a snort of disgust. He opened a door to a dim staircase and went up yet another flight of steps. Here, under the eaves, was a chamber that shared no walls with any other. It had a window that looked out over the lagoon. Habit made him cross first to that vantage point. The *Marietta* rode quietly beside the dock, a single lantern shining on her deck. All was well there.

He turned back to the room as a servant tapped at the door. "Enter," he said gruffly. The man who came in looked the worse for wear. The scar of many a brawl showed on his wide face, but he moved with quiet grace as he laid a fire in the small fireplace at the opposite end of the room. He kindled two branches of candles for Kennit. Their warm light made him aware how dark the summer night outside had become. He stepped away from the window and sat down by the fireplace in a cushioned chair. The evening needed no more warmth, but something in him sought the sweet fragrance of the resinous wood and the dancing light of the flames.

A second tap announced two more servants. One set out a tray of food upon a snowy cloth on a small table, while the other presented him with a bowl and an ewer of steaming water, well-scented with lavender. That much, at least, Bettel had remembered of his tastes, he thought, and felt flattered in spite of himself. He washed his face and hands again, and gestured the servants out of the room before he sat down to his meal.

Food did not have to be very good to compare favorably with ship-board fare, but this meal was excellent. The meat was tender in a rich dark gravy, the bread was warmly fresh-baked, and the compote of spiced fruit that accompanied the meal was a pleasant counterpoint to the meat. The wine was not exceptional, but it was more than adequate. Kennit took his time with his food. He seldom indulged in physical pleasures except when he was bitter of spirit. Then he savored his small efforts at comforting himself. The diversions he allowed himself now reminded him somewhat of how his mother would pamper him when he was ill. He gave a snort of disdain at his own thought and pushed it aside with his plate. He poured himself a second glass of wine, kicked his boots out towards the fire and leaned back in his chair. He stared into the flames and thought carefully of nothing.

A tap at the door heralded the dessert. "Enter," Kennit said listlessly. The brief distraction of the meal had faded, and the pit of depression that now yawned before him was bottomless. Useless, it was, all of it. Useless and temporary.

"I've brought you warm apple tart and sweet fresh cream," Etta said quietly.

He turned only his head to regard her. "That's nice," he said tonelessly. He watched her come towards him. Straight and sleek, he thought. She wore only a white shift. She was near as tall as he was, long-limbed and limber as a willow wand. He leaned back and crossed his arms on his chest as she set the white china plate and dessert before him. The cinnamon-and-apple scent of it mingled with the honeysuckle of her skin. She straightened and he considered her for a moment. Her dark eyes met his dispassionately. Her mouth betrayed nothing.

He suddenly wanted her.

"Take that off and go and lie on the bed. Open the bedding to the linen first."

She obeyed him without hesitation. It was a pleasure to watch her as she moved to his commands, folding the bedding back to bare the white sheets, and then standing, reaching down to the hem of her shift to lift it up and over her head. She placed it carefully upon the lowboy at the foot of the bed. Kennit watched her move, her long flat flanks, the slight roundness of her belly, the modest swells of her breasts. Her hair was short and sleek, cut off square like a boy's. Even the planes of her face were long and flat. She did not look at him as she meticulously arranged herself upon the sheets, nor did she speak as she awaited him.

He stood and began to unbutton his shirt. "Are you clean?" he asked her callously.

"As clean as soap and hot water can make me," she replied. She lay so still. He wondered if she dreaded him.

"Do you fear me?" he asked her, and then realized that was a different question.

"Sometimes," she answered him. Her voice was either controlled or indifferent. His coat he hung on the bedpost. His shirt and folded trousers joined her shift on the lowboy. It pleased him to make her wait while he carefully removed his clothing and set it aside. Delayed pleasure, he thought to himself, like the warm tart and cream upon the fireside tray. That, too, awaited him.

He sat on the bed beside her, and ran his hands down her smoothness. There was a slight chill upon her skin. She did not speak nor move. She had learned, over the years, what he demanded. He paid for his satisfaction. He did not want her encouragement or enthusiasm, he did not need her approval. This was for his pleasure, not hers. He watched her face as he sleeked a hand down her. Her eyes did not seek his. She studied the ceiling above as he explored the planes of her flesh.

There was only one flaw to her smoothness. In her navel, small as an apple pip, was a tiny white skull. The little charm of wizardwood was attached to a fine silver wire that pierced her navel. Half her wages went to Bettel for the renting of the token. Early in his acquaintance with her, she had told him that it kept away both disease and pregnancy. It had been the first time he had heard of using wizardwood for charms. It had led to the face on his wrist. Such thoughts made him recall that the face had neither moved nor spoken since they had left the waters of the Others' Island. Another waste of his time and money, another token that marked him as a fool. He gritted his teeth. Etta flinched minutely. He realized he had gripped her hip and squeezed it nigh to bruising. He released it and ran his hand down her thigh. Forget it. Think only of this.

When he was ready, he opened her thighs and mounted her. A dozen strokes and he emptied himself into her. All tension, all anger, all frustration ebbed away. For a time he lay upon her, resting, and then he had her again, leisurely. This time her arms came up around him to hold him, this time her hips rose to meet his, and he knew she found her own release. He did not begrudge that pleasure to her, as long as it did not interfere with his own. He surprised himself when he kissed her afterwards. She lay carefully still as he did so. He thought about it as he got off her. Kiss the whore. Well, he could if he wished; he paid to do whatever he wished with her. All the same, he would not wonder where else her whore's mouth had been this night.

There was a silk robe in the drawer of the lowboy. He took it out and put it on, then crossed the room to his dessert. Etta remained in the bed, where she belonged. He was two bites into the apple tart when she spoke. "When you were late, I feared you were not coming."

He cut another forkful of the tart. Crisp flaky crust and tender spiced fruit within. He scooped up cream with it, and chewed it slowly. After he had swallowed, he asked her, "Do you imagine I care what you fear, or think?"

Her eyes almost met his. "I think you would care if I were not here now. As I cared when you were not here before."

He finished another bite of the tart. "This is a stupid conversation. I do not care to continue it."

"Aye," she said, and he did not know if she were accepting his command, or agreeing with him. It didn't matter. She was silent as he finished the tart. He poured another glass of the wine and leaned back with it. His mind roved back over the last few weeks, assessing all he had done. He'd been a fool, he decided. He should have put off going to the Others' Island, and when he'd had the Other's oracle, he'd been a fool to spout off his ambitions to his crew. Idiot. Dolt. By now he was the laughing-stock of Divvytown. He could imagine their mockery in the taverns and inns. 'King of the Pirates,' they'd say. 'As if we want or need a king. As if we'd have him as king, if we did want or need one.' And they'd laugh.

Shame rose up to engulf him. He'd humiliated himself yet again, and as always it was his own fault. He was stupid, stupid, stupid, and his only hope of surviving was in not letting anyone else know how stupid he was. He sat twisting his ring on his finger and staring into the fire. He glanced once at the wizardwood charm strapped to his wrist. His own sardonic smile mocked him. Had it ever moved at all, or had it only been another trick of the Others' magic? Going to the Others' Island at all had been a mistake. No doubt his crew were talking that up as well, their captain seeking an oracle as if he were a barren woman or a god-struck fanatic. Why did his highest hopes always have to turn to his deepest humiliations?

"Shall I come and rub your shoulders, Kennit?"

He turned to glare at her. Who did she think she was, to interrupt his thoughts?

"Why do you think I'd welcome that?" he demanded coldly.

Her voice had no inflection as she observed, "You looked troubled. Weary and tense."

"You think you can know those things by looking at me, whore?"

Her dark eyes dared to meet his. "A woman knows these things by looking at a man when she has looked at him often over three years." She rose and came to stand behind him, naked still. She set her long narrow hands to his shoulders and worked at his muscles through the thin silk of the robe. It felt so good. For a time he sat still and tolerated her touch on him. But then she began to speak as she kneaded at his knotted muscles.

"I miss you when you are gone on these longer voyages. I wonder if you are all right. Sometimes I wonder if you are coming back at all. After all, what ties you to Divvytown? I know you care little for me. Only that I be here and behave as you wish me to. I think Bettel only keeps me on because of your preference for me. I am not . . . what most men would wish for. Do you see how important that makes you in my life? Without you, Bettel would turn me out of the house and I'd have to work as a freegirl. But you come here, and you ask for me by my name, and you take the finest chamber in the house for our use, and always pay in true gold. Do you know what the others here call me? Kennit's whore." She gave a brief snort of bitter laughter. "Once I would have been shamed by that. Now I like the sound of it."

"Why are you talking?" Kennit's voice cut her musings as harshly as a blunt knife. "Do you think I pay to hear you talk?"

It was a question. She knew she was allowed to answer. "No," she replied in a low voice. "But I think that with the gold you pay Bettel, I could rent a small house for us. I would keep it tidy and clean. It would always be there for you to come home to, and I would always be ready and clean for you. I vow there would never be the smell of another man upon me."

"And you think I would like that?" he scoffed.

"I do not know," she said quietly. "I know that I would like that. That's all."

"I care not at all what you would like or not like," he told her. He reached back to lift her hands from his shoulders. The fire had heated her skin. He rose from the chair and turned to face her. He ran a hand over her bared skin, fascinated for a time with the feel of the fire-warmed flesh. It roused him again. But when he lifted his eyes to her face, he was shocked to find tears on her cheeks. It was intolerable.

"Go back to the bed," he commanded her in disgust, and she went, obedient as ever. He stood facing the fire, recalling sleek skin under his fingers and wanting to use her again, but dismayed at the thought of her wet face and teary eyes. This was not why he bought a whore. He bought a whore to avoid all this. Damn it, he had paid. He did not look at the bed as he commanded her suddenly, "Lie on your belly. Face down."

He heard her shift in the sheets. He went to her quickly across the darkened room. He mounted her that way, face down like a boy, but he took her as a woman. Let no one, not even a whore, say that Kennit did not know the difference between the two.

He knew he was not unduly rough, but still she wept, even after he rolled off her. Somehow the near-noiseless weeping of the woman beside him troubled him. The disturbance he felt at it combined with his earlier shame and self-disgust. What was the matter with her? He paid her, didn't he? What right did she have to expect any more than that from him? She was, after all, just a whore. It was the deal they had made.

Abruptly he rose and began pulling on his clothes. After a time, her weeping stopped. She turned over suddenly in the bedding. "Please," she whispered hoarsely. "Please don't go. I'm sorry I displeased you. I'll be still now. I promise."

The hopelessness in her voice rang against the hopelessness in his heart, steel against steel. He should kill her. He should just kill her rather than let her say such words to him. Instead, he thrust his hand into his coat pocket. "Here, this is for you," he said, groping for some small coin to give her. Money would remind them both of why they were here together in this room. But fate had betrayed him, for there was nothing in his pocket. He'd left the ship in that much haste. He'd have to go back to the *Marietta* to get money to pay Bettel. It was all damnably embarrassing. He knew the whore was looking at him, waiting. What could be more humiliating than to stand penniless before the whore one had already used?

But there, in the smallest corner of his pocket he felt something, something tiny that jabbed him under the fingernail. He picked it loose in annoyance, a thorn or a stray pebble, and drew forth instead the tiny jeweled earring from the blue kitten's ear. The ruby winked at him. He had never cared for rubies. It would do for Etta. "Here," he said, pushing it into her hand. He added, "Don't leave the room. Keep it until tomorrow night. I'll be back." He left the room before she could speak. It irked him, for he suspected Bettel would demand a small king's ransom for keeping both room and girl occupied a full night and a day besides. Well, let her demand, he knew what he'd pay. And it would keep him from having to admit to Bettel that he had not the money to pay her tonight. At least he could avoid that shame.

He rattled down the stairs and out the door. "I want the room and girl kept for me, as they are," he informed Bettel as he passed. Another time, he might almost have enjoyed the look of consternation that brought to her face. He was well down the street before he felt his purse thudding against his left pocket. Ridiculous. He never kept it there. He thought of going back and paying Bettel off right now, but decided against it. He'd only look like a fool if he went back now saying he'd changed his mind. A fool. The word burned in his mind.

He lengthened his stride to try and escape his own thoughts. He needed to be out and moving just now. As he strode down the mud-sticky street, a tiny voice spoke at his wrist. "That was likely the only bit of treasure ever carried off from the Others' Island, and you gave it to a whore."

"So?" he demanded, bringing the small face up to his own to stare into it.

"So perhaps you do have both luck and wisdom." The tiny face smirked at him. "Perhaps."

"What mean you by that?"

But the wizardwood charm did not speak again that evening, not even when he flicked his forefinger against its face. The carved features remained as still and hard as stone.

He went to Ivro's parlor. He did not know he was going there until he stood outside the door. It was dark within. It was far later than he'd thought. He kicked at the door until first Ivro's son, and then Ivro, yelled at him to stop.

"It's Kennit," he said into the darkness. "I want another tattoo."

A feeble light was kindled inside the house. After a moment, Ivro jerked the door open. "Why should I waste my time?" the small craftsman demanded furiously. "Take your trade elsewhere, to a dolt with some needles and ash who doesn't give a damn about his work. Then when you have it burned off the next day, you won't have destroyed anything worth having." He spat, narrowly missing Kennit's boots. "I'm an artist, not a whore."

Kennit found himself holding the man by his throat, on his toes, as he shook him back and forth. "I paid, damn you!" he heard himself shouting. "I paid for it and I did what I wanted with it. Understand?"

He found his control as abruptly as he had lost it. Breathing hard, he set the artist back on his own feet. "Understand," he growled more softly. He saw hatred in the man's eyes, but also fear. He would do it. He'd do it for the heavy gold that clinked in the purse Kennit showed him. Artists and whores, gold always bought them. An artist was no more than a whore who had been well-paid.

"Come in, then," Ivro invited him in a deadly soft voice. With a shivering up his back, Kennit knew the small man would give him pain as well as art. Ivro would see that his tiny needles were as painful as he could make them. But there was enough of the artist in him that Kennit knew his tattoo would also be as perfect as Ivro could contrive it. Pain and perfection. It was the only path to redemption he knew. And if ever he needed to make reparation to his luck, it was tonight. Kennit followed the man into his parlor, and unbuttoned his shirt as Ivro lit branch after branch of candles. He folded his shirt carefully and sat down on the low stool with both his shirt and his jacket across his lap. Pain and perfection. He felt a terrible anticipation of release as Ivro moved about the room, setting up candles on tables and pulling supplies closer.

"Where and what?" Ivro demanded. His voice was as callous as Kennit's when he spoke to a whore.

"The nape of my neck," Kennit said softly. "And an Other."

"Another what?" Ivro asked testily. He was already drawing up a table beside them. Tiny pots of brilliant inks were arrayed upon it in precise rows. He placed a taller stool behind Kennit's and sat upon it.

"An Other," Kennit repeated. "Like from the Others' Island. You know what I mean."

"I do," Ivro said harshly. "It's a bad-luck tattoo, and I'm more than happy to drill it into you, you son of a bitch." His fingertips walked lightly over Kennit's skin, measuring. In Jamaillia, an owner could stab his mark into a man's face. Even if a slave won his freedom later, it was forever illegal to deface the marks of his servitude. But in the Pirate Isles, that same man could put whatever art he wanted anywhere he wanted on his body. Some former slaves, like Sorcor, preferred a burn scar. Others had artists like Ivro rework their old slave tattoos into new symbols of their freedom. Ivro's fingers prodded the two scars that already adorned Kennit's back. "Why'd you have them burned off? I worked hours on those tattoos, and you paid well for them. Didn't you like them?" Then, "Drop your head forward. Your shadow's in my way."

"I liked them fine," Kennit muttered. He felt the first stab of a needle into his taut flesh. Goose flesh stood up on his arms and he felt his scalp twitch with the pain. More softly, he added to himself, "I liked the burns even better."

"You're a mad man," Ivro observed, but his voice was distracted. Kennit was nothing to him anymore, not a man, not an enemy. Only a canvas for his passionate work. The tiny needle drilled in, over and over. His skin twitched with pain. He heard Ivro expel a tiny breath of satisfaction.

It was the only way, he thought to himself. The only way to expunge the bad luck. Going to the Others' Island had been a bad decision, and now he had to pay for it. A thousand jabs of the needle, and the stinging freshness of the new tattoo for a day. Then the cleansing agony of the hot iron to burn the mistake away and make it as if it had never happened. To keep the good luck strong, Kennit told himself as he knotted his hands into fists. Behind him, Ivro was humming to himself, enjoying both his work and his revenge.

CHAPTER FIVE

BINGTOWN

SEVENTEEN DAYS. ALTHEA LOOKED OUT THE TINY PORT-
HOLE OF HER STATEROOM, AND WATCHED BINGTOWN
draw nearer. The bared masts of caravels and carracks forested the docks that lined the placid bay. Smaller vessels
plied busily between anchored ships and the shore. Home.

She had spent seventeen days within this chamber, leaving only when it was necessary, and then during the watches
when Kyle was asleep. The first few days had been spent in
seething fury and occasional tears as she railed against the
injustice. Childishly, she had vowed to endure the restric-
tion he had put upon her simply so she could complain of it
to her father at journey's end. "Look what you made me
do!" she said to herself, and smiled minutely. It was the old
shout from when she was small and she would quarrel with
Keffria. The semi-deliberate breaking of a dish or vase, the
dumping of a bucket of water, the tearing of a dress: Look
what you made me do! Keffria had screeched it at an annoying small sister as often as Althea had shrieked it up at an
older oppressor.

That was only how her withdrawal had begun. She had
by turns sulked or raged, thinking of all she would say if

Kyle dared come to her door, either to be sure she was obeying him or to say he had repented his command. While waiting for that, she read all her books and scrolls again, and even laid out the silk and considered making a start at dressmaking herself. But her sewing skills were more suited to canvas than silk, and the fabric was too fine to take a chance on botching the job. Instead she mended all her ship-board clothes. But even that task ran out, and she had found she hated the empty, idle time that stretched before her. One evening, irritated at the confines of her too-small bunk, she had flung her bedding to the floor and sprawled on it as she read yet again Deldom's *Journal of a Trader*. She fell asleep there. And dreamed.

Often as a girl, she would catnap on the decks of the *Vivacia*, or spend an evening stretched out on the deck of her father's quarters reading his books. Dozing off always brought her vivid dreams and semi-waking fancies. As she had grown, her father chided her for such behavior, and saw that she had chores enough that she would have no time for napping on deck. In recalling her old dreams, she put them down to a child's vivid imaginings. But that night, on the deck of her own stateroom, the color and detail of her childhood dreams came back to her. The dream was too vivid to dismiss as the product of her own mind.

She dreamed of her great-grandma, a woman she had never known, but in her dream she knew Talley as well as she knew herself. Talley Vestrit strode the decks, shouting orders at the sailors who floundered through a tangle of canvas, lines and splintered wood in the midst of the great storm. In an instant, sudden as remembering, Althea knew what had happened. A great sea had taken off the mast and the mate, and Captain Vestrit herself had joined her crew to bring order and sanity back with her confident bellows. She was nothing like her portrait; here was no woman sitting docilely in a chair, attired primly in black wool and white lace, a stern-faced husband standing at her shoulder. Althea had always known that her great-grandma had commissioned the building of the *Vivacia*. In that dream, however, she was not just the woman who had gone to the money lenders and the ship builders; she was suddenly a woman who had loved the sea and ships and had boldly determined the course of her family's descendants with her decision to possess a liveship. Oh, to have lived in such a time, when a woman could wield such authority.

The dream was brief and stark, like the image etched in one's vision by a lightning flash, yet when Althea woke with her cheek and palms pressed to the wooden deck, she had no doubt of her vision. There had been too many details too swiftly impressed upon her. In the dream the *Vivacia* had carried a fore-and-aft rig, or what remained of one after the storm's fury. Althea had never seen her so fitted. She instantly grasped the advantages of such a rigging, and for the interval of the dream, shared her great-grandma's belief in it.

It was dizzying to awaken and find herself Althea, so completely immersed in Talley had she been. Hours later, she was still able to shut her eyes and recall the night of the storm, Talley's true memory shuffled in with hers like a foreign card in a deck. It had come to her from the *Vivacia*; there could be no other way.

That night, she had deliberately composed herself to sleep on the deck of her stateroom. The oiled and polished planks were not comfortable, yet she put no blanket or cushion between herself and them. The *Vivacia* rewarded her trust. Althea had spent an afternoon with her grandfather as he carefully negotiated one of the narrower channels in the Perfume Isles. She saw over his shoulder the sightings he took of the jutting rocks, witnessed him putting out a boat and men to pull them the more swiftly through a place passable only at a certain tide. It was his secret, and it had led to the Vestrit monopoly on a certain tree sap that dried into richly fragrant droplets. No one had been up that channel to trade with the villages there since her grandfather's death. Like any Captain, he took to his death more than he could ever pass on to his descendants. He had made no chart. But the lost knowledge was not lost, but stored in the *Vivacia*, and would awaken with her when she quickened. Even now, Althea was certain that she could take the ship up that channel, so completely had its secrets been passed on to her.

Night after night, Althea sprawled upon the wooden deck and dreamed with her ship. Even by day, she lay there, her cheek pressed firmly to the plank, musing on her future. She became attuned to the *Vivacia*, from the shuddering of her wooden body as she strained through a sudden change in course, to the peaceful sounds the wood made when the wind drove her on a steady and true course. The shouts of the sailors, the light thunder of their feet on her decks were only slightly more significant than the cries of the gulls who sometimes alighted on her. At such times it seemed to Althea that she became the ship, aware of the small men who clambered up her masts only as a great whale might be aware of the barnacles that clung upon it.

There was so much more to the ship than the folk that worked her. Althea had no human words to express the fine differences she now sensed in wind and current. There was pleasure in working with a good steersman, and annoyance in the one who was always making minute and unnecessary adjustments, but it was a surface thing compared to what went on between the ship and the water. This concept that the life of a ship might be larger than what went on between her and her captain was a major revelation to Althea. In the space of a handful of nights, her whole concept of what a ship was underwent a sea-change.

Instead of an enforced confinement to her quarters, the days she spent closeted in her room became an all-involving experience. She recalled well a day when she had opened her door to find it blazing morning rather than the soft evening she had expected. The cook had been so bold as to take her by the shoulder and shake her when she had drifted off into a daydream in the galley on one of her visits for food. Later she had been annoyed by an incessant tapping at her door. When she opened it, she had found not Kyle, but Brashen standing outside it. He looked uncomfortable at questioning her but still demanded to know if all was well with her.

"Certainly. I'm fine," she replied and tried to shut the door on him. He stiff-armed it ajar.

"You don't look fine. The cook told me you looked like you'd lost half a stone of weight and I'm inclined to agree. Althea, I don't know what went on with Captain Kyle, but the health of the crew is still part of my duty."

She looked at his knit brow and dark troubled eyes and saw only an interruption. "I'm not part of the crew," she heard herself saying. "That is what happened between Captain Kyle and myself. And the health of a mere passenger is not your concern. Leave me be." She pushed at the door.

"The health of Ephron Vestrit's daughter is my concern, then. I dare to call him friend as well as captain. Althea. Look at yourself. You've not brushed your hair in days, I'd say. And several of the men have said that when they have seen you on deck, you drift like a ghost with eyes as empty as the space between the stars." He actually looked worried. Well he might. The slightest things could set off a crew that had endured too long under too strict a captain. A bewitched woman wandering about the decks might precipitate them into anything. Still, there was nothing she could do about it.

"Sailors and their superstitions," she scoffed, but could not find much strength to put into her voice. "Leave it, Brashen. I'm fine." She pushed again at the door, and this time he let her close it in his face. She'd wager that Kyle knew nothing of that visit. She had once more arranged herself on the deck and, closing her eyes, sunk into communion with the ship. She felt Brashen standing outside the door for a few moments longer, and then sensed him hastening away, back to his proper tasks. By then Althea had already dismissed him and was considering instead the water purling past her bow as the pure wind drove her slicing forward.

Days later, the *Vivacia* tasted the waters of home, recognized the current that gently swept her towards Trader Bay and welcomed the sheltered waters of the bay itself. When Kyle ordered out two boats to draw the *Vivacia* into anchorage, Althea found herself rousing. She rose to peer out through the glass. "Home," she told herself, and "Father." She felt an answering thrum of anticipation from the *Vivacia* herself.

She turned away from the porthole and opened her sea chest. In the bottom were her port clothes, items of "proper" apparel to wear from the docks to her home. It was a concession both she and her father had made to her mother years ago. When Captain Vestrit walked about town, he was always resplendent in blue trousers and coat over a thick white shirt, heavy with lace. It was fitting. He was Old Trader, and a captain of note. Althea would not have minded such garb for herself, but her mother insisted that regardless of how she dressed aboard ship, in port and in town she must wear skirts. If nothing else, it set her apart from the serving folk of the town. Always her mother would add that, to look at her hair and skin and hands, no one would ever think her a lady, let alone a daughter of an Old Trader family. Yet it had not been her mother's nagging but a quiet word from her father that had convinced her to comply. "Don't shame your ship," he had told her quietly. That was all that was needed.

So, amidst the bustle of the crew setting the anchor and making the *Vivacia* ship-shape for her rest in port, Althea fetched warm water from the galley kettle and bathed herself in her stateroom. She donned her port clothes: petticoat and overskirts, blouse and vest and lacy shawl and a ridiculous lace snood to confine her hair. Atop it all went a straw hat annoyingly adorned with feathers. It was when she was sashing her skirts and lacing her vest that she realized Brashen had been right. Her clothing hung on her like a scarecrow's rags. Her looking-glass showed dark circles under her eyes, and her cheeks were almost hollow. The dove-gray of her garments and the pale blue trim made her look even more sickly. Even her hands had lost flesh, the bones of her wrist and fingers standing out. Oddly, it did not trouble her. It had been no different, she told herself, from the fasting and isolation that one might do to seek Sa's guidance. Only instead of Sa, it had been the very spirit of the liveship that had possessed her. It had been worth it. She was almost grateful to Kyle for bringing it about. Almost.

She emerged from her room onto the deck, blinking in the bright afternoon sunlight that bounced off the placid harbor waters. She lifted her eyes and surveyed the walls of the harbor basin. Bingtown spread out along the shores like the brightly colored wares in her marketplace. The smell of land drenched Althea. The tax docks were busy, as always. Ships coming into Bingtown had always to report there first, that the Satrap's tax agents might inspect and tax the incoming cargoes as they were unloaded. The *Vivacia* would have to await her turn; it looked as if the *Goldendown* were nearly ready to leave. They'd take that slip, then, as soon as it was clear.

Instinctively her eyes sought her home: she could see one corner of the white walls of the house; the rest was obscured by shade trees. She frowned for a moment at the changes she saw on the surrounding hills, but then dismissed them. Land and town had little to do with her. Her impatience and her worry about her father's health mingled with a strange reluctance to leave the *Vivacia*. The captain's gig had not yet been lowered over the side; by tradition, she would ride ashore in that. She did not relish the thought of seeing Kyle again, let alone sharing a boat ride with him. But somehow it did not seem as significant a displeasure as it would have a week or two ago. She knew now that he could never part her from the *Vivacia*. She was bonded to the ship; the ship herself would not tolerate being sailed without her. Kyle was an irritation in her life, but his threats no longer had any weight. Once she had spoken to her father, he would see what had happened. He'd be angry with her about what she had said of Kyle's reasons for marrying Keffria. Recalling her own words now made even Althea wince. Her father would be angry with her and she would deserve it. But she knew him too well to fear that he would separate her from the *Vivacia* now.

She found herself on the foredeck, leaning far out on the bowsprit to look at the figurehead. The carved eyes were still closed, but it did not matter. Althea had shared her dreams.

"Don't slip."

"Small fear of that," Althea replied to Brashen without turning.

"Not usually. But as pale as you looked, I feared you'd get giddy and just go over the side."

"No." She hadn't even glanced at him. She wished he would go away. When next he spoke, his voice had become more formal.

"Mistress Althea. Have you baggage you wish taken ashore?"

"Just the small chest inside the door of my stateroom." It held the silk and small gifts for her family. She'd seen to its packing days ago.

Brashen cleared his throat awkwardly. He did not walk away. She turned to him in some irritation. "What?"

"The captain has ordered me to assist you in any way necessary to remove your possessions from the, uh, officer's stateroom." Brashen stood very straight and his eyes looked past her shoulder. For the first time in months, she truly saw him. What had it cost him to step down from first mate to sailor, simply to remain aboard this ship? She'd taken the brunt of Kyle's tongue only once; she'd lost count of the times that either he or his first mate had taken Brashen to task. Yet here he was still, given a distasteful order whose wisdom he doubted, and doing his best to carry it out as a proper ship's officer.

She spoke more to herself than to Brashen when she said, "No doubt he gets a great deal of pleasure from assigning this duty to you."

He didn't reply. The muscles in his jaws bunched a notch tighter, but he held his tongue. Even now, he would not speak out against his captain's orders. He was hopeless.

"Just the small chest, Brashen."

He drew up a breath as if it had the weight of an anchor. "Mistress Althea. I am ordered to see your possessions removed from that cabin."

She looked away from him. She was suddenly horribly weary of Kyle's posturing. Let him think he had his way for now; her father would soon put it all right.

"Then follow your order, Brashen. I shan't hold it against you."

He stood as if stricken. "You don't want to do the packing up yourself?" He was too shocked even to add "Mistress Althea."

She gave him the ghost of a smile. "I've seen you stow cargo. I'll warrant you'll do a tidy job of it."

For a moment longer he stood at her elbow, as if hoping for reprieve. She ignored him. After a time she heard him turn and pad lightly away across the deck. She went back to her consideration of the *Vivacia*'s visage. She gripped the railing tightly and vowed fiercely to the ship never to give her up.

"Gig's waiting on you, Mistress Althea."

The note in the man's voice implied that he had spoken to her before, possibly more than once. She straightened herself and reluctantly put her dreams aside. "I'm coming," she told him spiritlessly, and followed him.

She rode into town in the gig, facing Kyle but seated as far from him as possible. No one spoke to her. Other than necessary commands, no one spoke at all. Several times she caught uneasy glances from the sailors at the oars. Grig, ever a bold sort, ventured a wink and a grin. She tried to smile at him in return, but it was as if she could not quite recall how. A great stillness seemed to have found her as soon as she left the ship; a sort of waiting of the soul, to see what would befall her next.

The few times her eyes did meet Kyle's, the look on his face puzzled her. At their first encounter, he looked almost horror-struck. A second glance showed his face deeply thoughtful, but the last time she caught him looking at her was the most chilling. For he nodded at her and smiled fondly and encouragingly. It was the same look he would have bestowed on his daughter Malta if she had learned her lessons particularly well. She turned expressionlessly away from it and gazed out over the placid waters of Trader Bay.

The small rowing vessel nosed into a dock. Althea submitted to being assisted up to the dock as if she were an invalid; such was the nuisance of full skirts and shawls and hats that obscured one's vision. She gained the dock, and for an instant Grig annoyed her by holding on to her for longer than was strictly necessary. She drew herself free of his arm and glanced at him, expecting to find mischief in his eyes. Instead she saw concern, and it deepened a moment later when a wave of giddiness made her catch at his arm. "I just need to get my land-legs again," she excused herself, and once more stepped clear of him.

Kyle had sent word ahead of them and an open two-wheeled shimshay waited for them. The skinny boy who drove it abandoned the shady seat to them. "No bags?" he cawed.

Althea just shook her head. "No bags, driver. Take us up to the Vestrit House. It's on the Traders' Circle."

The half-naked boy nodded and offered her his hand as she clambered up onto the seat. Once Kyle had joined her there, the boy leaped nimbly to the nag's back and clicked his tongue at her. Her shod hooves rang on the wooden planks of the dock.

Althea stared straight ahead as the shimshay left the docks for the cobbled streets of Bingtown, and offered no conversation. Bad enough that she had to sit next to Kyle. She would not annoy herself by conversing with him. The hustle and bustle of folk and cart traffic, the shouts of bargaining, the smells of the streetfront restaurants and tea shops seemed oddly distant to her. When she and her father had docked, it had been usual that her mother would be waiting to greet them. They would have left the docks on foot, her mother rattling off an account of all that had happened since they had left port. Like as not they would have stopped at one of the tea shops for fresh, warm sweet buns and cold tea before strolling the rest of the way home. Althea sighed.

"Althea? Are you all right?" Kyle intruded.

"As well as I could expect, thank you," she replied stiffly.

He fidgeted, and then cleared his throat as if he were getting ready to say more. She was saved by the boy pulling in the horse right in front of home. He was by the side of the shimshay, offering his hand to her before Kyle could even stir. She smiled at him as she stepped down and he grinned back at her. A moment later the door of the house flew open and Keffria rushed out, crying, "Oh, Kyle, Kyle, I'm so glad you're home. Everything is just awful!" Seldon and Malta were at their mother's heels as she flew forwards to embrace her husband. Another boy followed them awkwardly. He looked oddly familiar: probably a visiting cousin or some such.

"Nice to see you, too, Keffria," Althea muttered sarcastically, and headed for the door.

Inside the manor, it was cool and shady. Althea stood a moment, gratefully letting her eyes adjust. A woman she did not recognize appeared with a basin of scented water and a towel and began to offer her the welcome of the house. Althea waved her away. "No, thank you. I'm Althea, I live here. Where is my father? In his sitting room?"

She thought she saw a brief flash of sympathy in the woman's eyes. "It has been many days since he was well enough to enjoy that room, Mistress Althea. He is in his bedchamber and your mother is with him."

Althea's shoes rang on the tiled floors as she raced down the hallway. Before she reached the door, her mother appeared in the entry, a worried frown creasing her forehead. "What is going on?" she demanded, and then, as she recognized Althea, she cried out in relief. "Oh, you are back! And Kyle?"

"He's outside. Is Father still ill? It has been months, I thought surely he would have . . ."

"Your father is dying, Althea," her mother said.

As Althea recoiled from her bluntness, she saw the dullness in her mother's eyes. There were lines in her face that had not been there, a heaviness to her mouth and a curl in her shoulders that Althea did not recall. Even as her own heart near stilled with the shock of it, she recognized that her mother's words were not cruel, but hopeless. She had given her the news quickly, as if by doing so she could save her the slow pain of realization.

"Oh, mother," she said, and moved towards her, but her mother flapped her hands at her in refusal. Althea stopped instantly. Ronica

Vestrit had never been one for tearful embraces and weeping on shoulders. She might be bowed by her sorrow, but she had not surrendered to it.

"Go and see your father," she told Althea. "He's been asking for you, near hourly. I must speak to Kyle. There are arrangements to be made, and not much time, I fear. Go in to him, now. Go." She gave Althea two quick pats on the arm and then hastened past her. Althea heard the pattering of her shoes and the rustling of her skirts as she hurried away down the hall. Althea glanced once after her and then pushed open the door of her father's bedchamber.

This was not a familiar room to her. As a small child, it had been forbidden to her. When her father had been home from voyages, he and her mother had spent time there together, and Althea had resented the mornings when she was not allowed to intrude on their rest. When she had grown old enough to understand why her parents might value their time alone together on his brief visits home, she had willingly avoided the room. Still, she recalled the room as a large, bright chamber with tall windows, furnished sumptuously with exotic furniture and fabrics from many voyages. The white walls had displayed feather fans and shell masks, beaded tapestries and hammered copper landscapes. The bed had a headboard of carved teak, and in winter the thick mattress was always mounded with feather comforters and fur throws. During the summers there had been vases of flowers by the bedside and cool cotton sheets scented with roses.

The door opened onto dimness. Attar of roses had been vanquished by the thick sour odor of the sickroom and the stinging scent of medicines. The windows were closed, the curtains drawn against the day's brightness. Althea moved uncertainly into the room as her eyes adjusted to the darkness. "Papa?" she asked hesitantly of the still, mounded bed. There was no reply.

She went to a window and pushed back the heavy brocaded curtains to admit the slanting afternoon light. A corner of the light fell on the bed, lighting a fleshless yellow hand resting atop the covers. It reminded her of the gaunt curled talons of a dead bird. She crossed the room to the bedside chair and took what she knew was her mother's post there. Despite her love for her father, she felt a moment's revulsion as she took that limp hand in her own. Muscle and callus had fled that hand. She leaned forward to look into his face. "Papa?" she asked again.

He was already dead. Or so she thought from that first look into his face. Then she heard the rasp of an in-drawn breath. "Althea," he breathed out in a voice that rattled with mucus. His gummy eyelids pried themselves open. The sharp black glance was gone. These eyes were sunken and bloodshot, the whites yellowed. It took him a moment to find her. He gazed at her and she desperately tried to smooth the horror from her face.

"Papa, I'm home," she told him with false brightness, as if that could make some difference to him.

His hand twitched feebly in hers, then his eyes slid shut again. "I'm dying," he told her in despair and anger.

"Oh, Papa, no, you'll get better, you'll . . ."

"Shut up." It was no more than a whisper, but the command came from both her captain and her father. "Only one thing that matters. Get me to Vivacia. Got to die on her decks. Got to."

"I know," she said. The pain that had just started unfolding in her heart was suddenly stilled. There was no time for it, just now. "I'll get things ready."

"Right now," he warned her. His whisper sounded gurgly, drowning. A wave of despair washed over her, but she righted herself.

"I won't fail you," she promised him. His hand twitched again, and fell free of hers. "I'll go right now."

As she stood he choked, then managed to gag out, "Althea!"

She halted where she stood. He strangled for a bit, then gasped in a breath. "Keffria and her children. They're not like you." He took another frantic breath. "I had to provide for them. I had to." He fought for more breath for speaking, but could not find any.

"Of course you did. You provided well for all of us. Don't worry about that now. Everything is going to be fine. I promise."

She had left the room and was halfway down the hall before she heard what she had said to him. What had she meant by that promise? That she would make sure he died on the liveship he had commanded so long! It was an odd definition of fine. Then, with unshakable certainty, she knew that when her time came to die, if she could die on the *Vivacia*'s decks, everything would be fine for her, too. She rubbed at her face, feeling as if she were just waking up. Her cheeks were wet. She was weeping. No time for that, just now. No time to feel, no time to weep.

As she hurried out the door into the blinding sunlight, she all but ran into a knot of people clustered there. She blinked for a moment, and they suddenly resolved into her mother and Kyle and Keffria and the children. They stared at her in silence. For a moment she returned that stricken gaze. Then, "I'm going down to get the ship ready," she told them all. "Give me an hour. Then bring Papa down."

Kyle frowned darkly and made as if to speak, but before he could her mother nodded and dully said, "Do so." Her voice closed down on the words, and Althea watched her struggle to speak through a throat gone tight with grief. "Hurry," she managed at last, and Althea nodded. She set off on foot down the drive. In the time it took a runner to get to town and send a shimshay back for her, she could be almost to the ship.

"At least send a servant with her!" she heard Kyle exclaim angrily behind her, and more softly her mother replied, "No. Let her go, let her go. There's no time to be concerned about appearances now. I know. Come help me prepare a litter for him."

By the time she reached the docks, her dress was drenched in sweat. She cursed the fate that made her a woman doomed to wear such attire. An instant later she was thanking the same Sa she had been rebuking, for a space had opened up on the tax docks, and the *Vivacia* was being edged into place there. She waited impatiently, and then hiked up her skirts and leaped from the dock to her decks even as the ship was being tied up.

Gantry, Kyle's first mate, stood on the foredeck, hands on hips. He started at the sight of her. He'd recently been in some kind of a tussle. The side of his face had swelled and just begun to purple. She dismissed it from her mind; it was the mate's job to keep the crew in line and the first day back in port could be a contentious one. Liberty was so close, and shore and deck crews did not always mingle well. But the scowl he wore seemed to be directed at her. "Mistress Althea. What do you here?" He sounded outraged.

At any other time, she'd have afforded the time to be offended at his tone. But now she simply said, "My father is dying. I've come to prepare the ship to receive him."

He looked no less hostile, but there was deference in his tone as he asked, "What do you wish done?"

She lifted her hands to her temples. When her grandfather had died, what had been done? It had been so long ago, but she was supposed to know about these things. She took a deep calming breath, then crouched down suddenly to set her hand flat atop the deck. Vivacia. So soon to quicken. "We need to set up a pavilion on deck. Over there. Canvas is fine, and set it so the breezes can cool him."

"What's wrong with putting him in his cabin?" Gantry demanded.

"That's not how it's done," Althea said tersely. "He needs to be out here, on the deck, with nothing between him and the ship. There must be room for all the family to witness. Set up some plank benches for those who keep the death watch."

"I've got a ship to unload," Gantry declared abruptly. "Some of the cargo is perishable. It's got to be taken off. How is my crew to get that done, and set up this pavilion and work around a deck full of folk?" This he demanded of her, in full view and hearing of the entire crew. There was something of challenge in his tone.

Althea stared at him, wondering what possessed the man to argue with her just now. Couldn't he see how important this was? No, probably not. He was one of Kyle's choosing; he knew nothing of the quickening of a liveship. Almost as if her father stood at her shoulder, she heard her voice mouth the familiar command he'd always given Brashen in difficult times. She straightened her spine.

"Cope," she ordered him succinctly. She glanced about the deck. Sailors had paused in their tasks to follow this interchange. In some faces she saw sympathy and understanding, in others only the avidity with which men watch a battle of wills. She put a touch of snarl in her voice. "If you can't deal with it, put Brashen in charge. He'd find it no challenge." She started to turn away, then turned back. "In fact, that's the best solution. Put Brashen in change of the setting up for Captain Vestrit. He's his first mate, that's fitting. You see to the unloading of your captain's cargo."

"On board, there can be but one captain," Gantry observed. He looked aside as if not truly speaking to her, but she chose to reply anyway.

"That's correct, sailor. And when Captain Vestrit is aboard, there is but one captain. I doubt you'll find many men on board to question that." She swung her eyes away from him to the ship's carpenter. As much as she currently disliked the man, his loyalty to her father had always been absolute. She caught his glance and addressed him. "Assist Brashen in any way he requires. Be quick. My father will arrive here soon. If this is the last time he sets foot on board, I'd like him to see the *Vivacia* ship-shape and the crew busy."

This simple appeal was all she needed. Sudden understanding swept over his face, and the look he gave to the rest of the crew quickly spread the realization. This was real, this was urgent. The man they had served under, some for over two decades, was coming here to die. He'd often bragged that his was the best hand-picked crew to sail out of Bingtown; Sa knew he paid them better than they'd have made on any other vessel.

"I'll find Brashen," the carpenter assured her and strode off with purpose in his walk. Gantry took a breath as if to call him back. Instead, he paused for just an instant, and then began barking out orders for the continued unloading of the ship. He turned just enough that Althea was not in his direct line of sight. He had dismissed her. She had a reflex of anger before she recalled she had no time for his petty insolence just now. Her father was dying.

She went to the sailmaker to order out a length of clean canvas. When she came back up on deck, Brashen was there talking with the ship's carpenter. He was gesticulating at the rigging as they discussed how they'd hang the canvas. When he turned to glance at her, she saw a swollen knot above his left eye. So it was he whom the mate had tangled with. Well, whatever it had been, it had been sorted out in the usual way.

There was little more for her to do except stand about and watch. She'd given Brashen command of the situation and he'd accepted it. One thing she had learned from her father: once you put a man in charge of something, you didn't ride him while he did the task. Nor did she wish Gantry to grumble that she stood about and got in the way. With nowhere else to gracefully go, she went to her cabin.

It had been stripped, save for the painting of the *Vivacia*. The sight of the empty shelves near wrenched her heart from her chest. All her possessions had been neatly and tightly stowed in several open crates in the room. Planking, nails, and a hammer were on the deck. This, then, had been the task Brashen had been called away from. She sat down on the ticking mattress on her bunk and stared at the crates. Some industrious creature inside her wanted to crouch down and hammer the planks into place. Defiance bid her unpack her things and put them in their rightful places. She was caught between these things, and did nothing for a time.

Then with a shocking suddenness, grief throttled her. Her sobs could not come up, she couldn't even take a breath for the tightness in her throat. Her need to cry was a terrible squeezing pain that literally suffocated her. She sat on her bunk, mouth open and strangling. When she finally got a breath of air into her lungs, she could only sob. Tears streamed down her face, and she had no handkerchief, nothing but her sleeve or her skirts, and what kind of a terrible heartless person was she that she could even think of handkerchiefs at a time like this? She leaned her head into her hands and finally allowed herself simply to weep.

They moved off, clucking and muttering to one another like a flock of chickens. Wintrow was forced to trail after them. He didn't know what else to do. He had been in Bingtown for five days now, and still had no idea why they had summoned him home. His grandfather was dying; of course he knew that, but he could scarcely see what they expected him to do about it, or even how they expected him to react.

Dying, the old man was even more daunting than he had been in life. When Wintrow had been a boy, it had been the sheer force of the man's life-strength that had cowed him. Now it was the blackness of dwindling death that seeped out from him and emptied its darkness into the room. On the ship home, Wintrow had made a strong resolve that he would get to know something of his grandfather before the old man died. But it was too late for that. In these last weeks, all that Ephron Vestrit possessed of himself had been focused into keeping a grip on life. He had held on grimly to every breath, and it was not for the sake of his grandson's presence. No. He awaited only the return of his ship.

Not that Wintrow had had much time with his grandfather. When he had first arrived, his mother had scarcely given him time to wash the dust of travel from his face and hands before she ushered him in and presented him. Disoriented after his sea voyage and the rattling trip through the hot and bustling city streets, he had barely been able to grasp that this short, dark-haired woman was the Mama he had once looked up to. The room she hurried him into had been curtained against the day's heat and light. Inside was a woman in a chair beside a bed. The room smelled sour and close, and it was all he could do to stand still when the woman rose and embraced him. She clutched at his arm as soon as his mother released her grip on him, and pulled him towards the bedside.

"Ephron," she had said quietly. "Ephron, Wintrow is here."

And in the bed, a shape stirred and coughed and then mumbled what might have been an acknowledgment. He stood there, shackled by his grandmother's grip on his wrist, and only belatedly offered a "Hello, Grandfather. I've come home to visit."

If the old man had heard him at all, he hadn't bothered with a reply. After a few moments, his grandfather had coughed again and then queried hoarsely, "Ship?"

"No. Not yet," his grandmother replied gently.

They all stood there a while longer, he, his mother and grandmother. Then, when the old man made no more movements and took no further notice of them, his grandmother said, "I think he wants to rest now, Wintrow. I'll send for you later when he's feeling a bit better."

That time had not come. Now his father was home, and the news of Ephron Vestrit's imminent death seemed to be all his mind could grasp. He had glanced at Wintrow over his mother's shoulder as he embraced her. His eyes widened briefly and he nodded at his eldest son, but then his mother Keffria began to pour out her torrent of bad news and all its complications. Wintrow stood apart, like a stranger, as first his sister Malta and then his younger brother Selden welcomed their father with a hug. At last there had been a pause in Keffria's lament, and he stepped forward, to first bow and then grip hands with his father.

"So. My son the priest," his father greeted him, and Wintrow could still not decide if there had been a breath of derision in those words. The next did not surprise him. "Your little sister is taller than you are. And why are you wearing a robe like a woman?"

"Kyle!" his mother rebuked her husband, but he turned away from Wintrow without awaiting a reply.

Now, following his aunt's departure, he trailed into the house behind them. The adults were already discussing the best ways of moving Ephron down to the ship, and what must be taken or brought down later. The children, Malta and Selden, followed, trying vainly to ask a string of questions of their mother and continually being shushed by their grandmother. And Wintrow trailed after all, feeling neither adult nor child, nor truly a part of this emotional carnival.

On the journey here, he had realized he did not know what to expect. And ever since he had arrived, that feeling had increased. For the first day, most of his conversations had been with his mother, and had consisted of either her exclamations over how thin he was, or fond remembrances and reminiscing that inevitably began with, "I don't suppose you remember this, but . . ."

Malta, once so close to him as to seem almost his shadow, now resented him for coming home and claiming any of their mother's attention. She did not speak to him but about him, making stinging observations when their mother was out of earshot, ostensibly to the servants or Selden. It did not help that at twelve she was taller than he was, and already looking more like a woman than he did a man. No one would have suspected he was the elder. Selden, scarcely more than a baby when he had left, now dismissed him as a visiting relative, one scarcely worth getting to know, as he would doubtless soon be leaving. Wintrow fervently hoped Selden was right. He knew it was not worthy to long for his grandfather to die and simply get it over with so he could return to his monastery and his life, but he also knew that to deny the thought would only be another sort of lie.

They all halted in a cluster outside the dying man's room. Here they lowered their voices, as if discussing secrets, as if his death must not be mentioned aloud. It made no sense to Wintrow. Surely this was what the old man had been longing for. He forced himself to focus on what was being said.

"I think it best to say nothing at all about any of it," his grandmother was saying to his father. She had hold of the door knob but was not turning it. She almost appeared to be barring him from the room. From his father's furrowed brow, it was plain that Kyle Haven did not agree with his mother-in-law. But Mother had hold of his arm and was looking up at him beseechingly and nodding like a toy.

"It would only upset him," she interjected.

"And to no purpose," his grandmother went on, as if they shared a mind. "It has taken me weeks to talk him around to our way of seeing things. He has agreed, but grudgingly. Any complaints now would but re-open the discussion. And when he is weary and in pain, he can be surprisingly stubborn."

She paused and both women looked up at his father as if commanding his assent. He did not even nod. At last he conceded, resentfully, "I shall not bring it up immediately. Let us get him down to the ship first. That is the most important thing."

"Exactly," Grandmother Vestrit agreed, and finally opened the door. They entered. But when Malta and Selden tried to follow, she stepped briskly to block them. "You children run and have Nana pack a change of clothes for you. Malta, you dash down to Cook and tell her that she'll need to pack a food hamper for us to take, and then make arrangements for meals to be sent down to us." His grandmother was silent when she looked at Wintrow, as if momentarily puzzled as to what to do with him. Then she nodded at him briskly. "Wintrow, you'll need a change of clothes as well. We'll be living aboard the ship now until . . . Oh, dear."

Color suddenly fled from her face. Bleak realization flooded it. Wintrow had seen that look before. Many a time had he gone out with the healers when they were summoned, and many a time there was little or nothing their herbs and tonics and touches could do for the dying. At those times, it was what he could do for the grieving survivors that mattered most. Her hands rose like talons to clutch at the neck of her gown and her mouth contorted as if with pain. He felt a welling of genuine sympathy for the woman. "Oh, Grandmother," he sighed and reached towards her. But as he stepped forward to embrace her and with a touch draw off some of her grief, she stepped back. She patted at him with hands that all but pushed him away. "No, no, I'm fine, dear. Don't let Grandma upset you. You just go get your things so you're ready to go when we are."

Then she shut the door in his face. For a time he stood staring at it in disbelief. When he did step back from it, he found Malta and Selden regarding him. "So," he said dully. Then, in a desperation he did not quite understand himself, he reached after some feeling of kinship with his siblings. He met their gazes openly. "Our grandfather is dying," he said solemnly.

"He's been doing it all summer," Malta replied disdainfully. She shook her head over Wintrow's witlessness, then dismissed him by turning away. "Come, Selden. I'll ask Nana to pack your things." Without a glance, she led the boy off and left Wintrow standing there.

Briefly, he tried to tell himself he should not feel hurt. His parents had not meant to diminish him by their exclusion of him and his sister was under the stress of grief. Then he recognized the lie and turned to embrace what he felt and thus understand it. His mother and grandmother were pre-occupied. His father and his sister had both deliberately attempted to wound him, and he had let them succeed. But these things that had happened, and these feelings he now experienced, were not faults to be conquered. He could not deny the feelings, nor should he try to change them. "Accept and grow," he reminded himself, and felt the pain ease. Wintrow went to pack a change of clothes.

Brashen stared down at Althea in disbelief. This was the last thing he needed today, he thought inanely, and then hung on to the anger in that thought to keep the panic from his mind. He pushed the door shut and then knelt on the floor by Althea. He had entered her cabin when she had completely refused to answer his raps and then his loud knocking on her door. When he had angrily thrust the unlocked door open and strode in, he expected her to hiss and spit at him. Instead he found her sprawled on the floor of her cabin, looking for all the world like one of the fainting heroines in a penny-theater play. Except instead of falling gracefully with her hands to cushion her face, Althea lay with her hands almost clutching at the deck, as if she strove to dig her fingers into it.

She was breathing. He hesitated, then shook her shoulder gently. "Mistress," he began gently, then, in annoyance, "Althea. Wake up!"

She moaned softly but did not stir. He glared at her. He should yell for the ship's doctor, except he shared her feelings about having anyone make a fuss. He knew she would rather not be seen like this. At least, that had been true of the old Althea. This fainting and sprawling on the deck was as unlike her as her moping in the cabin had been on the long voyage home. Nor did he like her paleness and the bony look to her face. He glanced about the stripped cabin, then scooped her up and deposited her on the bare mattress on the bunk. "Althea?" he demanded again, and this time her eyelids twitched, then opened.

"When the wind fills your sails, you can cut the water like a hot knife through butter," she told him with a gentle smile. Her eyes were distant, transfigured, as they looked into his. He almost smiled back at her, drawn into the sudden intimacy of her soft words. Then he caught himself.

"Did you faint?" he asked her bluntly.

Abruptly her eyes snapped into wariness. "I . . . no, not exactly. I just couldn't stand . . ." She let her words trail off as she pushed herself up from the bed. She staggered a step, but even as he reached for her arm she steadied herself against a bulkhead. She gazed at the wall as if it presented some perfect view. "Have you readied a place for him?" she asked huskily.

He nodded. She nodded in unison with him, and he made bold to say, "Althea. I grieve with you. He was very important to me."

"He's not dead yet," she snapped. She smeared her hands over her face and pushed her hair back. Then, as if she thought that restored her bedraggled appearance, she stalked past him, out the cabin door. After a moment he followed her. Typical Althea. She had no concept that any other person beside herself truly existed. She had dismissed his pain at what was happening as if he had offered the words out of idle courtesy. He wondered if she had ever stopped to think at all what her father's death meant to him or to any of the crew. Captain Vestrit was as open-handed and fair a man as skippered a ship out of Bingtown. He wondered if Althea had any idea how rare it was for a captain to actually care about the well-being of his crew. No. Of course she couldn't. She'd never shipped aboard a boat where the rations were weevily bread and sticky salt pork almost turned poison. She'd never seen a man near beaten to death by the mate's fists simply because he hadn't moved fast enough to a command. True enough that Captain Vestrit never tolerated slackness in any man, but he'd simply be rid of him at the next port of call; he'd never resorted to brutality. And he knew his men. They weren't whoever happened to be standing about on the docks when he needed a crew, they were men he had trained and tried and knew to their cores.

These men had known their Captain, too, and had believed in him. Brashen knew of some who had turned down higher positions on other vessels simply to remain with Vestrit. Some of the sailors, by Bingtown standards, were too old to work a deck, but Ephron had kept them on for the experience of their years, and chosen carefully the young, strong sailors he put alongside to learn from them. He had entrusted his ship to them, and they had entrusted their future to him. Now that the *Vivacia* was about to become hers, he hoped to Sa she'd have the morals and the sense to keep them on and do right by them. A lot of the older hands had no home save the *Vivacia*.

Brashen was one of them.

CHAPTER SIX

THE QUICKENING OF THE VIVACIA

THEY BROUGHT HIM ABOARD ON A LITTER. THAT WAS WHAT MADE BRASHEN'S HEART CLENCH AND SUDDEN tears burn his eyes. In the moment that he beheld the limp form beneath the linen sheet, he grasped the full truth. His captain was coming back aboard to die. His secret hope that Ephron Vestrit was not truly that badly off, that somehow the sea air and the deck of his own ship would miraculously revive him was only a silly child's dream.

He stood back respectfully as Kyle supervised the men who carried his father-in-law up the gangplank. They set his litter under the canopy Brashen had improvised from canvas. Althea, as pale as if she were carved of ivory, stood there to receive him. The family trailed after him like lost sheep, to take up places around Ephron Vestrit's litter as if they were guests and he were a laden table. His wife and elder daughter looked both panicky and devastated. The children, including an older boy, looked mostly confused. Kyle stood back from them all, a look of disapproval on his face as if he were studying a poorly repaired sail or a badly loaded cargo. After a few minutes, Althea seemed to break loose of her stupor. She left quietly, returning with a pitcher of water and a cup. She knelt on the deck beside her father and offered him a drink.

In the first hint of motion that Brashen had seen from him, Ephron turned his head and managed to sip some water. Then, with a vague motion of one skeletal hand, he reminded them that he must be lifted from the pallet and placed on the deck of his ship. Brashen found himself starting forward to that gesture, as he had so often sprung to obey his captain. He was briefly aware of Kyle's scowl before he crouched by Captain Vestrit's pallet.

"If I may, sir," he said softly, and waited for the half nod of both recognition and permission that he was given. Althea was suddenly beside him, slipping her arms under her father's bony legs as Brashen himself took the bulk of the old man's weight. Not that there was much weight to him, or even that he was all that old, Brashen reminded himself as he eased the emaciated body down to the bare planks of the deck. Instead of frowning at the hardness of the deck, the captain sighed as if some great pain had suddenly eased. His eyes flicked open and found Althea. A trace of their old spark was there as he quietly commanded her, "Althea. The figurehead peg."

Her eyes widened for an instant in a sort of horror. Then she squared her shoulders and rose to obey him. Pinched white lines formed around her mouth as she left her father's side. Instinctively Brashen began to withdraw. Captain Vestrit would not have asked for the figurehead's peg if he had not felt death was very near. This was a time for him to be alone with his family. But as Brashen drew back, he felt his wrist suddenly seized in a surprisingly tight grip. The captain's long fingers dug into the flesh of his arm, and drew him back, closer. The smell of death was strong on him, but Brashen did not flinch as he lowered his head to catch his words.

"Go with her, son. She'll need your help. Stand by her through this." His voice was a hoarse whisper.

Brashen nodded that he understood, and Captain Vestrit released him. But as Brashen rocked back onto his heels to stand, the dying man spoke again. "You've been a good sailor, Brashen." He now spoke clearly and surprisingly loudly, as if he desired not just his family, but everyone to hear his words. He dragged in a breath. "I've no complaint against you nor your work." Another breath. "Could I but live to sail again, you'd be my choice for first mate." His voice failed on the last words, coming out as a wheeze. His eyes left Brashen's face suddenly, to turn unerringly to where Kyle stood and glowered. He struggled, then drew in a whistling breath. "But I shan't sail again. The *Vivacia* will never again be mine." His lips were going blue. He found no more air, struggle as he might. His hand knotted in a fist, made a sudden violent gesture that would have been meaningless to any other. But Brashen leaped to his feet and dashed forward to find Althea and hurry her back to him.

The secret of the figurehead peg was not a widely known one. Ephron had entrusted it to Brashen shortly after he had made him first mate. Concealed in the tumbling locks of the figurehead's hair was a catch that would release a long smooth peg of the silky gray wood that comprised her. It was not a necessity, but it was believed that if the dying person grasped this peg as his life departed, more of his wisdom and essence would be imparted to the ship. Ephron had shown it to Brashen and illustrated how it worked, so that if some ship's disaster felled him, Brashen might bring him the peg in his last moments. It was a duty Brashen had fervently hoped never to perform.

He found Althea dangling all but upside down from the bowsprit as she tried to tug the peg loose from its setting. Without a word he followed her out, grasped her around the hips and lowered her to where she might reach it more easily. "Thanks," she grunted as she pulled it free. He effortlessly lifted her and set her back on her feet on the deck. She raced back to her father, the precious peg clutched tightly in her fist. Brashen was right behind her.

They were not a moment too soon. Ephron Vestrit's death was not to be a pleasant one. Instead of closing his eyes and going in peace, he fought it as he had fought everything in life that opposed him. Althea offered him the peg and he gripped it as if it would save him. "Drowning," he strangled out. "Drowning on a dry deck."

For a time the strange tableau held. Althea and her father gripped either end of the peg. Tears ran freely down her ravaged face. Her hair, gone wild about her face, clung to her damp cheeks. Her eyes were wide open, focused and caring as she stared down into the depths of her father's mirroring black eyes. She knew there was nothing she could do for him, but she did not flinch away.

Ephron's free hand scrabbled against the deck as if trying to find a grip on the smoothly sanded planks. He managed to draw in another choking, gurgling breath. A bloody froth was beginning to form at the corners of his mouth. Other family members clustered around them. The older sister clung tightly to her mother, wordless in grief, but the mother spoke in a low voice into her hair as she embraced her. The girl child wept, caught in a sort of terror, and clutched at her confused smaller brother. The older grandson stood back and apart from his family, face pale and set as one who endures pain. Kyle stood, arms crossed on his chest, at the dying man's feet. Brashen had no idea what thoughts passed behind that still countenance. A second circle had also formed, at a respectful distance outside the canopy. The still-faced crew had gathered, hats in hands, to witness their captain's passing.

"Althea!" the captain's wife called out suddenly to her daughter. At the same time she thrust her older daughter forward, towards their father. "You must," she said in an odd, low voice. "You know you must." There was an odd purposefulness to her voice, as if she forced herself to some very unpleasant duty. The look on the older daughter's face—Keffria, that was her name—seemed to combine shame with defiance. Keffria dropped to her knees suddenly beside her sister. She reached out a pale, trembling hand. Brashen thought she would touch her father. Instead she resolutely grasped the peg between Althea's hand and her father's. Even as Keffria made her unmistakable claim to the ship by grasping the peg above Althea's hand, her mother affirmed it for her.

"Althea. Let go the peg. The ship is your sister's, by right of her birth order. And by your father's will." The mother's voice shook as she said the words, but she said them clearly.

Althea looked up in disbelief, her eyes tracing up the arm from the hand that gripped the peg to her sister's face. "Keffria?" she asked in confusion. "You can't mean it!"

Uncertainty spread over the older woman's face. She glanced up at the mother. "She does!" Ronica Vestrit declared, almost savagely. "It's how it has to be, Althea. It's how it must be, for all our sakes."

"Papa?" Althea asked brokenly.

Her father's dark eyes had never left her face. His mouth opened, moved, and he spoke a last phrase. ". . . let go. . . ."

Brashen had once worked on a ship where the mate was a bit too free with his marlinespike. Mostly he used it to bludgeon fellows from behind, sailors he felt were not paying sufficient attention to their tasks. More than once, Brashen had been an unwilling witness to the look on a man's face as the tool connected with the back of his skull. He knew the look a man wore at that moment when pain registered as unconsciousness. That was how Althea looked at the uttering of her father's words. Her grip on the peg laxed, her hand fell away from it to clutch instead at her father's thin arm. That she held to, as a sailor clings to wreckage in a storm-tossed sea. She did not look again at her mother or her sister. She only gripped her father's arm as he gaped and gasped like a fish out of water.

"Papa," she whispered again. His back arched, his chest swelling high with his effort to find air. He rolled his head, turning his face to find hers before he suddenly collapsed back to the deck. The long fight was over. The light of life and struggle suddenly left his eyes. His body settled bonelessly against the deck as if he were melting into the wood. His hand fell from the peg. As her sister Keffria stood, Althea collapsed forward. She put her head on her father's chest and wailed shamelessly and hopelessly.

She did not see what Brashen saw. Keffria stood and surrendered the peg to her waiting husband. In disbelief, Brashen watched Kyle accept it. He walked away from them all, carrying the precious peg as if he truly had a right to it. For an instant, Brashen nearly followed him. Then he decided it was something he'd just as soon not witness. Peg or no, the ship would quicken. Brashen thought he already felt a difference about her; the use of a peg would only hasten the process. But the promise he had given his captain now had a different shade of meaning for him.

"Go with her, son. She'll need your help. Stand by her through this." Captain Vestrit had not been speaking about the peg, or his death. Brashen's heart sank as he tried to decide exactly what he had promised to do.

When Althea felt hands grip her shoulders, she tugged away from them. She didn't care who it was. In the space of a few moments, she had lost her father and the *Vivacia*. It would have been simpler to lose her life. She still could not grasp either fact. It was not fair, she thought inanely. Only one unthinkable thing should happen at a time. If the events had only happened one at a time, she could have thought of a way to deal with them. But whenever she tried to think of her father's death, at the moment of realizing it, the loss of the ship would suddenly loom up in her mind. Yet she could not think about that, not here by her father's dead body. For then she would have to wonder how this father she had worshipped could have betrayed her so completely. As devastating as her pain was, she feared even to consider her anger. If she let her anger take her over, it might completely consume her, leaving nothing but blowing ash.

The hands came back, settling on her bowed shoulders and grasping them firmly. "Go away, Brashen," she said with no strength. But she no longer had the will to shrug his grip away. The warmth and steadiness of his hands on her shoulders were too much like her father's steady clasp. Sometimes her father would come up on deck while she was on wheel watch. He could move as silently as a ghost when he wanted to; his whole crew knew that, and knew, too, that one could never know when he would silently appear, never interfering in a man's work but checking the task with a knowing eye. She would be standing at the wheel, both hands on it and holding a steady course, and she wouldn't even know he was there until she felt the firm, approving grip of his hands on her shoulders. Then he might drift off, or he might stand beside her and have a pipe while he watched the night and the water and his daughter steering his ship through both.

Somehow that memory gave her strength. The sharp edges of her grief settled into a dull, throbbing lump of pain. She straightened up, squaring her shoulders. She didn't understand anything; not how he could have died and left her, and certainly not how he could have taken her ship from her and given it to her sister. "But, you know, there were a lot of times when he barked orders, and I couldn't fathom the sense of them. But if I simply jumped up and obeyed, it always came right. It always came right."

She turned, expecting to confront Brashen. Instead it was Wintrow who stood behind. It surprised her, and that made her almost angry. Who was he, to touch her so familiarly, let alone to give her a pale ghost of her father's smile and say quietly, "I am sure it will be so again, Aunt Althea. For it is not only your father's will that we accept tragedy and disappointment in our lives, but Sa's will also. If we endure what he sends us cheerfully, it never fails that he will reward us."

"Stuff it," she snarled in a low and savage voice. How dare he puke out platitudes at her just now, this son of Kyle's that stood to gain all she had lost! No doubt he could endure that fate quite easily. The look of shock on his boy's face almost made her laugh out loud. His hands dropped clear of her and he took a step backwards.

"Althea!" her mother gasped in shock and rebuke.

Althea dragged her sleeve across her wet face and returned her mother's glare. "Don't think I don't know whose idea it was that Keffria inherit the ship," she warned her heatedly.

"Oh, Althea!" Keffria cried out, and the pain in her voice sounded almost real. The grief and dismay on her sister's face nearly melted her. Once they had been so close. . . .

But then Kyle strode into their midst, announcing angrily, "Something's wrong. The peg won't go into the figurehead."

Everyone turned to stare at him. The impatient irritation in his voice was too much at odds with the pathetic body stretched on the deck before them. For a moment the silence held, then even Kyle had the grace to look abashed. He stood holding the silver-gray peg and glancing about as if his eyes could find nowhere to rest. Althea took a long shuddering breath, but before she could speak, she heard Brashen's voice, dripping sarcasm.

"Perhaps you do not know that only a blood-family member may quicken a liveship?"

It was as if he stood in an open field in a storm and called the lightning down on himself. Anger convulsed Kyle's face, and he went redder than Althea had ever seen him.

"What gives you the right to speak here, dog? I'll see you off this ship!"

"That you will," Brashen affirmed calmly. "But not before I've done my last duty to my captain. He spoke clearly enough, for a dying man. 'Stand by her through this,' he said to me. I do not doubt that you heard him. And I shall. Give the peg to Althea. The quickening of the ship at least belongs to her."

He never knows when to shut up. That had always been her father's strongest criticism of his young first mate, but when he had said it, an awed admiration had always crept into his voice. Althea had never understood it before. Now she did. He stood there, ragged as any deckhand was at the end of a long voyage, and spoke back to the man who had commanded the ship and likely would again. He heard himself publicly dismissed, and did not even flinch. She knew Kyle would never concede to his demand; she did not even let her heart yearn for it. But in making that demand, he suddenly gave her a glimpse of what her father had seen in him.

Kyle stood glowering. His eyes went around the circle of mourners, but Althea knew he was just as aware of the outer circle of crewmembers, and even of the folk who had come down to the docks to see a liveship quicken. In the end, he decided to ignore Brashen's words.

"Wintrow!" he commanded in a voice that snapped like a lash. "Take the peg and quicken the ship."

All eyes swung to the boy. His face blanched and his eyes became huge. His mouth shook and then he firmed his lips. He took a deep breath. "It is not my right."

He did not speak loudly, but his young voice carried well.

"Damn it, are you not as much Vestrit as Haven? It is your right, the ship shall be yours some day. Take the peg and quicken it."

The boy looked at him without comprehension. When he spoke, his voice teetered and then cracked high on the words. "I was given to be a priest of Sa. A priest can own nothing."

A vein began to pound in Kyle's temple. "Sa be damned. Your mother gave you, not I. And I hereby take you back. Now take this peg and quicken the ship!" As he spoke, he had stepped forward, to seize his eldest by the shoulder. The boy tried not to cower away from him, but his distress was plain. Even Keffria and Ronica looked shocked by Kyle's blasphemy, as well they might.

Althea's grief seemed to have stepped back from her, leaving her numbed but oddly sensitized. She watched these strangers who shouted and squabbled with one another while an unburied man slowly stiffened at their feet. A great clarity seemed to have come into her mind. She knew, with abrupt certainty, that Keffria had known nothing of Kyle's intentions regarding Wintrow. The boy obviously had not; the shock on his face was too great as he stood staring in confusion at the silky-gray peg his father thrust into his hands.

"Now!" Kyle commanded, and as if the boy were five instead of on the brink of manhood, he turned him and propelled him down the deck. The others drifted after him like wreckage bobbing in a ship's wake. Althea watched them go. Then she crouched down, to clasp in her own her father's cooling hand. "I am glad you are not here to see this," she told him gently. She tried unsuccessfully, to close the lids of his staring eyes. After several attempts, she gave up and left him staring up at the canvas canopy.

"Althea. Get up."

"Why?" She did not even turn to Brashen's command.

"Because . . ." He paused, fumbling, then went on, "because they can take the ownership of the ship from you, but that does not excuse you from what you owe the ship. Your father asked me to help you through this. He would not want the *Vivacia* to quicken and see only strangers' faces."

"Kyle will be there," she said dully. The hurt was coming back. Brashen's blunt words had wakened it again.

"She will not know him. He is not the blood of her family. Come."

She looked down at the still body. Death was working swiftly, sinking her father's features into lines and planes he had never worn in life. "I don't want to leave him here alone."

"Althea. That's not the Captain, it's just his body. He's gone. But the *Vivacia* is still here. Come. You know you have to do this; do it well." He leaned down, putting his face near her ear. "Head up, girl. The crew is watching."

She rose reluctantly to his last words. She looked down at her father's sagging face and tried to meet his eyes one last time. But he was looking past her now, looking into the infinite. She squared her shoulders and held up her head. Very well, then.

Brashen offered his arm, as if he were escorting her into Bingtown's Presentation Ball. Without thinking, she placed her hand lightly on his forearm as she had been schooled and allowed him to guide her to the bow of the ship. Something about the formality of his walking her there restored her. As she drew near and overheard Kyle's savagely low tones of anger, it touched a spark off in her as if it were flint against steel. He was berating Wintrow.

"It's simple, boy. There's the hole, there's the peg, here's the catch. Push the catch to one side and shove the peg in the hole and release the catch. That's all. I'll hold on to you. You needn't fear that you'll fall into the bay, if that's what's cowing you."

The boy's voice rose in reply, too high still, but gentle, not weak. "Father. I did not say I could not. I said I would not. I do not feel it is my right, nor proper as a servant of Sa, for me to make this claim." Only a slight tremor at the end of this speech revealed how difficult it was for the boy to keep his aplomb.

"You'll do as I damn well tell you," Kyle growled. Althea saw his hand lift in the familiar threat of a blow, and heard Keffria gasp out, "Oh, Kyle, no!"

In two strides, Althea was suddenly between Kyle and the boy. "This is not a fitting way for any of us to behave on the day of my father's death. Nor is it a proper way to treat the *Vivacia*. Peg or no, she is quickening. Would you have her awaken to quarreling voices and discord?"

And Kyle's answer betrayed his total ignorance of all a liveship was. "I'd have it awaken, in any way it can be managed."

Althea took breath for an angry retort, but then heard Brashen's whisper of awe. "Oh, look at her!"

All eyes swung to the figurehead. From the foredeck, Althea could not see that much of her face, but she could see the paint flaking away from the wizardwood carving. The locks of hair shone raven under the peeling gilt paint, and the sanded flesh had begun to flush pink. The silken fine grain of the wizardwood still remained, and always would, nor would the wood ever be as soft and yielding as human flesh. Yet it was unmistakable that life now pulsed throught the figurehead, and to Althea's heightened awareness, the entire ship rode differently on the quiet waves of the harbor. She felt as she imagined a mother must feel the first time she beholds the life that has grown within her.

"Give me the peg," she heard herself say quietly. "I'll quicken the ship."

"Why?" Kyle asked suspiciously, but Ronica intervened.

"Give her the peg, Kyle," she commanded him quietly. "She'll do it because she loves the *Vivacia*."

Later Althea would recall her mother's words, and they would rouse hate in her to a white-hot heat. Her mother had known all she felt, and still she had taken the ship from her. But at that moment, she only knew that it pained her to see the *Vivacia* caught between wood and life, suspended so uncomfortably. She could see the distrust on Kyle's face as he grudgingly offered her the peg. What did he think she would do, throw it overboard? She took it from him and bellied out on the bowsprit to reach the figurehead. She was just a trifle short of being able to reach it safely. She hitched herself forward another notch, teetering dangerously in her awkward skirts, and still could not quite reach.

"Brashen," she said, neither asking nor commanding. She did not even glance back at him, but only stayed as she was until she felt his hands clasp her waist just above her hips. He eased her down to where she could rest one hand on Vivacia's hair. The paint flaked away from the coiling lock at her touch. The feel of the hair against her hand was strange. It gave way to her touch, but the carved locks were all of a piece rather than individual hairs. She knew a moment of unease. Then her awareness of the *Vivacia* flooded through her, heightened as never before. It was like warmth, yet it was not a sensation of the skin. Nor was it the heat of whiskey in one's gut. This flowed with her blood and breath throughout her body.

"Althea?" Brashen's voice sounded strained. She came back to herself, wondered how long she had been dangling near upside down. In a sleepy way she realized she had entrusted her entire weight to Brashen's grip as she hung there. The peg was in her hand still. She sighed, and became aware of blood pounding in her face. With one hand she pushed the catch to one side; with the other she slid the peg in smoothly. When she released the catch, it seemed to vanish as if it had never been. The peg was now a permanent part of the figurehead.

"What is taking so long?" Kyle's voice demanded.

"It's done," Althea breathed. She doubted if anyone but Brashen heard her. But as his grip on her tightened and he began to pull her up, Vivacia suddenly turned to her. She reached up, her strong hands catching hold of Althea's own. Her green eyes met Althea's.

"I had the strangest dream," she said engagingly. Then she smiled at Althea, a grin that was at once impish and merry. "Thank you so for waking me."

"You're welcome," Althea breathed. "Oh, you are more beautiful than I imagined you would be."

"Thank you," the ship replied with the serious artlessness of a child. She let go of Althea's hands to brush flecks of paint from her hair and skin as if they were fallen leaves. Brashen drew Althea abruptly back up onto the deck and set her on her feet with a thump. He was very red in the face, and Althea was suddenly aware of Kyle speaking in a low, vicious voice.

". . . and you are off this deck forever, Trell. Right now."

"That's right. I am." Somehow the timbre of Brashen's voice took Kyle's dismissal of him and made it his own disdainful parting. "Farewell, Althea." Courtesy was back in his voice when he spoke to her. As if he were departing from some social occasion, he next turned and took formal leave of her mother. His calm seemed to rattle the woman, for though her lips moved, she spoke no farewell. But Brashen turned and walked away lightly across the deck, as if absolutely nothing had happened. Before Althea could recover from that, Kyle turned on her.

"Are you out of your mind? What is wrong with you, letting him touch you like that?"

She squeezed her eyes shut, then opened them again. "Like what?" she asked dazedly. She leaned on the railing to look down at Vivacia. The figurehead twisted about to smile up at her. It was a bemused smile, the smile of a person not quite awake on a lovely summer morning. Althea smiled sadly back at her.

"You know very well what I speak of! His hands were all over you. Bad enough that you look like a dusty slattern, but then to let a deckhand manhandle you while you dangle all but upside down . . ."

"I had to put the peg in. It was the only way I could reach." She looked away from Kyle's face, mottled red with his anger, to her mother and sister. "The ship is quickened," she announced softly but formally. "The liveship *Vivacia* is now aware."

And my father is dead. She did not speak the words aloud, but the reality of them cut her again, deeper and sharper. It seemed to her that each time she thought she had grasped the fact of his death, a few moments later it struck her again even harder.

"What are people going to think of her?" Kyle was demanding of Keffria in an undertone. The two younger children stared at her openly, while the older boy, Wintrow, looked aside from them all as if even being near them made him acutely uncomfortable. Althea felt she could not grasp all that was happening around her. Too much had occurred, too fast. Kyle attempting to put her off the ship, her father's death, the quickening of the ship, his dismissal of Brashen, and now his anger at her for simply doing a thing that had needed doing. It all seemed too much for her to deal with, but at the same time she felt a terrible void. She groped inside herself, trying to discover what she had forgotten or neglected.

"Althea?"

It was Vivacia, calling up to her anxiously. She leaned over the railing to look down at her, almost sighing.

"Yes?"

"I know your name. Althea."

"Yes. Thank you, Vivacia." And in that moment, she knew what the void was. It was all she had expected to feel, the joy and wonder at the ship's quickening. The moment, so long awaited, had come and gone. Vivacia was awakened. And save for the first flush of triumph, she felt nothing of what she had expected to feel. The price had been too high.

The instant her mind held the thought, she wished she could unthink it. It was the ultimate in betrayal, to stand on this deck, not so far from her father's body, and think that the cost had been too high, that the liveship was not worth the death of her father, let alone the death of her grandfather and great-grandma. And it was not a fair thought. She knew that. Ship or no, they all would have died. Vivacia was not the cause of their deaths, but rather the sum total of their legacies. In her, they lived on. Something inside her eased a bit. She leaned over the side, trying to think of something coherent and welcoming to say to this new being. "My father would have been very proud of you," she managed at last.

The simple words woke her grief again. She wanted to put her head down on her arms and sob, but would not allow herself to, lest she alarm the ship.

"He would have been proud of you, also. He knew this would be difficult for you."

The ship's voice had changed. In moments, it had gone from high and girlish to the rich, throaty voice of a grown woman. When Althea looked down into her face, she saw more understanding than she could bear. This time she did not try to stop the tears that flowed down her cheeks. "I just don't understand it," she said brokenly to the ship. Then she swung her gaze back to her family, who like her lined the railing and looked down at Vivacia's face.

"I don't understand it," she said more loudly, although her thickened voice was not more clear. "Why did he do this? Why, after all the years, did he give Vivacia to Keffria and leave me with nothing?"

She spoke her words to her mother's stern anguish, but it was

Kyle who dared to speak. "Maybe he wanted her to be in responsible hands. Maybe he wanted to entrust her to someone who had shown he could be reliable and steady and care for someone besides herself."

"I'm not talking to you!" Althea shrieked at him. "Can't you just shut up?" She knew she sounded childish and hysterical and she hated it. But there had just been too much to take today. She had no control left. If he spoke to her again, she would fly at him and claw him to shreds.

"Be quiet, Kyle," her mother bade him firmly. "Althea. Compose yourself. This is neither the time nor the place. We will discuss this later, at home, in private. In fact, I need to discuss it with you. I want you to understand your father's intentions. But for now there is his body to dispose of, and the formal presentation of the ship. The Traders and other liveships must be notified of his death, and boats hired to bring them out to witness his burial at sea. And . . . Althea? Althea, come back here, right now!"

She had not realized she was striding away until she came to the gangplank and started down it. Somehow she had marched right past her father's body and not even seen it. She did then what she would regret the rest of her life. She walked away from Vivacia. She did not accompany her on her maiden voyage to witness the sinking of her father's body in the waters beyond the harbor. She did not think she could stand to watch his feet bound to the spare anchor and his body swathed in canvas before it was tilted over the side. Ever after, she would wish she had been there, to bid him farewell one final time.

But at that moment, she only knew she could not abide the sight of Kyle for one more moment, let alone her mother's reasonable tones as she spoke horrible words. She did not look back to see the dismay on the faces of the crew nor how Keffria clung to Kyle's arm to keep him from charging after her to drag her back. At that moment, she knew she could not bear to see Vivacia untied from the dock with Kyle in command of her. She hoped the ship would understand. No. She knew the ship would understand. She had always hated the thought of Kyle commanding the family ship. Now that Vivacia was quickened and aware, she hated it even more. It was worse than leaving a child in the control of a person you despised, but she also knew there was absolutely nothing she could do about it. At least not now.

The ship's agent had a tiny office right on the docks. He had been somewhat taken aback to find Brashen leaning on his counter, his sea-bag slung over one shoulder.

"Yes?" he asked in his polished, businesslike way.

Brashen thought to himself that the man reminded him of a well-educated chipmunk. It was something about the way his beard whiskered his cheeks, and how he sat up so suddenly straight in his chair before he spoke. "I've come for my pay," he said quietly.

The man turned to a shelf, considered several books there before taking down a fat ledger. "I'd heard that Captain Vestrit had been brought down to his ship," he observed carefully as he opened the book flat and ran his finger down a line of names. He looked up and met Brashen's eyes. "You've been with him for a long time. I'd think you want to stay with him to the end."

"I did," Brashen said briefly. "My captain is dead. The *Vivacia* is Captain Haven's ship now, and we've little liking for one another. I've been cashiered." He found he could keep his voice as low and pleasant as the chipmunk's.

The agent looked up with a frown. "But surely his daughter will take it over now? For years, he's been grooming her. The younger one, Althea Vestrit?"

Brashen gave a brief snort. "You're not the only one surprised that isn't to be so. Including Mistress Vestrit herself, to her shock and grief." Then, feeling abruptly that he had said too much about another's pain, he added, "I've just come for my pay, sir, not to gossip about my betters. Please pay no mind to an angry man's words."

"Well said, and I shall not," the agent assured him. He straightened from a money box to set three short stacks of coins on the counter before Brashen. Brashen looked at it. It was substantially less than what he'd pulled down when he was first mate under Captain Vestrit. Well, that was how it was.

He suddenly realized there was one other thing he should ask for. "I'll need a ship's ticket, too," he added slowly. He'd never thought he'd have to ask for one from the *Vivacia*. In fact, several years ago, he had thrown away his old ones, convinced he'd never again have to show anyone proof of his capability. Now he wished he'd kept them. They were simple things, tags of leather embossed with the ship's stamp and scored with the sailor's name and sometimes his position, to show he'd satisfactorily performed his duties. A handful of ship's tickets would have made it a lot easier to get another position. But even one from a liveship would carry substantial weight in Bingtown.

"You have to get that from the captain or mate," the ship's agent pointed out.

"Hmf. Small chance of that." Brashen abruptly felt robbed. All his years of good service to the ship, and these stacks of coins were all he had to show for them.

The agent cleared his throat suddenly. "It's well known to me, at least, that Captain Vestrit thought highly of you and your work. If you need a recommendation, feel free to refer them to this office. Nyle Hashett. I'll see they get an honest word from me."

"Thank you, sir," Brashen said humbly. It was not a ship's ticket, but it was something. He took a moment to stow the coins—a few in his purse, some in his boot and the rest in the kerchief bound tight to his neck. No sense in letting one pickpocket have them all. Then he shouldered his sea-bag with a grunt and left the office. He had a mental list of what he needed to do. First, find a room at a cheap rooming house. Before this, he'd lived aboard the *Vivacia* even when she was in port. Now everything he owned was in the bag on his back. Next he'd go to a banker. Captain Vestrit had urged him, often enough, to set aside a few coins each trip. He'd never got around to it. When he'd sailed with Vestrit, his future had seemed assured. Now he abruptly wished he'd taken that advice much sooner. Well, he'd start now, as he could not start sooner, and remember this hard lesson well.

And then? Well, then he'd allow himself one good night in port before he set himself to looking for a new berth. Some fresh meat and new baked bread, and a night of beer and good companionship at the harbor taverns. Sa knew he'd earned a bit of pleasure for himself on this voyage. He intended to take this night and enjoy it. Tomorrow was soon enough to worry about the rest of his life. He felt a moment's shame at anticipating pleasure while his captain lay dead. But Kyle would never allow him back aboard to pay his last respects. The best he could do for Captain Vestrit's memory was not to be yet another discordant element at his funeral. Let him go to the bottom from a peaceful deck. Tonight Brashen would drink to his memory with every mug he raised. Let that be his own private tribute to the man. Resolutely he turned towards town.

But as he stepped out of the shady offices of the ship's agent, he spotted Althea storming down the gangplank. He watched her come down the docks, striding along so that her skirts trailed out behind her like shredded sails in a gale. Her face was tear-streaked, her hair disheveled and her eyes hot-black with an anger that was almost frightening. Heads turned to watch her go by. Brashen groaned to himself, then settled his sea-bag more firmly on his shoulder. He'd promised he'd watch over her. With a heartfelt sigh, he followed her.

CHAPTER SEVEN

LOYALTIES

I T TOOK THE REST OF THE DAY TO BURY HIS GRANDFA-
THER. RUNNERS WERE SENT THROUGHOUT THE TOWN
to advise friends and neighbors, and his death services were
cried aloud in the public markets and on the dock. Wintrow
had been surprised at the number of folk who came, and
how swiftly they gathered. Merchants and sea captains, Old
Traders and tradesmen forsook the business of the day and
converged on the dock and ship. Those closest to the family
were welcomed aboard Vivacia, while others followed on
the vessels of friends. Every liveship currently in the harbor
followed Vivacia as she carried her former master out to
where he would be surrendered to the sea.

Wintrow was uncomfortable throughout the whole ceremony. He could not sort out what he felt about any of it. It
stirred his pride that so many turned out to honor his
grandfather, but it seemed uncouth that so many of them
offered first their condolences and then their congratula-
tions on the quickening of the ship. As many who stopped
by the body to pay their final respects also stepped forward
to the bow of the ship, to greet Vivacia and wish her well.
That was where his grandmother stood, not by the body of

her dead husband, and only his grandmother seemed to notice his unease. At one point she quietly told him that he had been too long away from Bingtown and its customs. That they congratulated her on the ship did not diminish one whit the grief they felt that Ephron had died. It was simply not the way of Bingtown folk to dwell on the tragic. Why, if the founders of Bingtown had dwelt on their tragedies, they would have drowned in their own tears. He nodded to her explanations, but kept his own private counsels as to what he thought of that.

He hated standing on the deck next to his grandfather's body, hated the proximity of the other great-sailed ships as they left the harbor together to do homage to his grandfather's burial at sea. It all seemed overly complicated, not to mention dangerous, to have all these ships sail forth, and then drop anchor in a great circle so folk might crowd along their railings and watch Ephron Vestrit's canvas-wrapped corpse slide off a plank and slip beneath the moving waves.

Afterwards there was some totally incomprehensible ceremony in which Vivacia was presented formally to the other individual liveships. His grandmother had presided quite solemnly. She stood on the fore-deck and loudly introduced Vivacia to each ship as it was sailed across her bow. Wintrow stood alongside his scowling father, and wondered at both the smile on the old woman's face and the tears that coursed down it. Clearly, something had been lost when he was born a Haven. Even his mother had looked on glowingly, her younger two children standing at her side and waving to each ship in turn.

But that had been the larger scope of the ceremonies. Aboard Vivacia, there had been another sort of ritual entirely. Kyle possessed himself of the ship. Even to Wintrow's untrained eyes that was plain. He barked out orders to men decades his senior and cursed them roundly if he thought they did not scamper quickly enough to his will. More than once, he loudly observed to his first mate that he had some changes in mind to make in the way this ship was run. The first time he said those words, something like a grimace of pain crossed Ronica Vestrit's features. Observing her quietly the rest of the afternoon, it had seemed to Wintrow that the old woman grew graver and graver as the day passed, as if her sorrow for her husband's death took root in her and grew with each passing hour.

He found little to say to anyone and they said even less to him. His mother was occupied with keeping a sharp watch on little Selden, and preventing Malta from even exchanging glances with any of the younger deckhands. His grandmother mostly stood on the foredeck and stared out over the bow. If she spoke at all, it was to the figurehead, and quietly. The very thought of that put a shiver up Wintrow's spine. There was nothing natural about the life that animated that carved artifact, nothing at all of Sa's true spirit in her. While he sensed no evil about her, neither did he sense anything of good. He was glad he had not been the one to insert the peg in her, and avoided the foredeck.

It was only on the trip home that his father seemed to recall he had an elder son. In a sense, it was his own fault. He heard the mate bark an incomprehensible order at two of the men. In trying to step quickly out of their way, he blundered backwards into the path of a third man he had not even seen. They both went down, Wintrow hard enough to knock the wind out of his lungs. In a moment the hand had sprung back to his feet and dashed on to his duties. Wintrow stood up more slowly, rubbing an elbow and gradually remembering how to breathe. When he finally managed to straighten up, he found himself face to face with his father.

"Look at you," his father growled, and in some puzzlement Wintrow glanced down at himself, wondering if he had dirt on his clothes. His father gave him a light shove on the shoulder.

"I don't mean your priest's robes, I mean *you*. Look at you! A man's years and a boy's body, and the wits of a landsman. You can't even get out of your own way, let alone another man's. Here. Torg. Here! Take him and put him to doing something so he's out of the way at least."

Torg was the second mate. He was a brawny man if not tall, with short blond hair and pale gray eyes. His eyebrows were white; it struck Wintrow that his face looked bald, it was composed of so many pale things. Torg's notion of keeping him out of the way was to put him below, coiling lines and hanging chain in the chain locker. The coils that were already there looked just fine to Wintrow, but Torg gruffly told him to coil them up tidy, and not be slack about it. It sounded easier than it was to do, for once disturbed, the coils tangled themselves alarmingly, and seemed reluctant to lay flat again. The thick coarse ropes soon reddened his hands and the coils were much heavier than he had expected them to be. The close air of the chain locker and the lack of any light save a lantern's combined to make him feel queasy. Nevertheless, he kept at it for what seemed like hours. Finally it was Malta who was sent to find him, telling him with some asperity that they were dockside and tied up, if he'd care to come ashore now. It took every fragment of self-control he had to remind himself that he should behave as a future priest of Sa, not an annoyed elder brother.

Silently he set down the coil of rope he'd been working on. Every piece of rope he'd touched looked less, not more, orderly than when he'd began. Well, Torg could re-coil them as he wished, or push the task off on some poor sailor. Wintrow had known it was busy work from the start, though why his father had wished to humiliate and irritate him, he could not fathom. Perhaps it had something to do with his refusal to push in the peg that quickened the ship. His father had said some wild words then. Well, it was over now. His grandfather was dead and consigned to the sea, the family had made plain they wished no comfort from him, and he would go home as soon as he decently could. Tomorrow morning, he decided, would not be too soon.

He went up on deck and joined his family as they thanked and bid farewell to those mourners who had accompanied them on board the ship. Not a few said their good-byes to the living figurehead as well. The summer dusk was venturing into true night as the last person left. The family stood a bit longer, silent and exhausted, while Kyle gave orders to the mate for the unloading to proceed at earliest daybreak. Then Kyle came to tell the family it was time to go home. Kyle took his mother's arm, and Wintrow his grandmother's. He was silently grateful that there would be a coach awaiting them; he was not sure the old woman could have managed the uphill walk through the dark cobbled streets.

But as they turned to leave the foredeck, the figurehead spoke up suddenly. "Are you going?" she asked anxiously. "Right now?"

"I'll be back at first light," Kyle told her. He spoke as if a deckhand had questioned his judgment.

"Are all of you going?" the ship asked again. Wintrow was not sure what he responded to. Perhaps it was the note of panic in her voice.

"You'll be all right," he told her gently. "You're safe, tied up to the docks here. There's nothing to fear."

"I don't want to be alone." The complaint was a child's, but the voice was that of an uncertain young woman. "Where's Althea? Why isn't she here? She wouldn't leave me all alone."

"The mate will sleep aboard, as will half the crew. You won't be alone," Kyle replied testily. Wintrow could remember that tone from his own childhood. His heart went out to the ship despite his better judgment.

"It's not the same!" she cried out, even as he heard himself offer, "I could stay aboard if she wished it. For this night, at least."

His father scowled as if he had countermanded his order, but his grandmother squeezed his arm gently and gave him a smile. "Blood will tell," she said softly.

"The boy can't stay," Kyle announced. "I need to speak to him tonight."

"Tonight?" Keffria asked incredulously. "Oh, Kyle, not tonight. Not anything more tonight. We are all too weary and full of sorrow."

"I had thought we might all sit down together tonight, and discuss the future," his father pointed out ponderously. "Weary and sorrowful we may be, but tomorrow will not wait."

"Whether tomorrow will wait or not, I shall," his grandmother cut across the argument. There was a shadow of imperiousness in her voice, and for a moment, he recalled more vividly the woman he had known as a child. Even as his father drew breath to speak, she added, "And if Wintrow would sleep aboard and give comfort to Vivacia as best he can, I would take it as a personal favor." She turned to the figurehead and added, "I shall need him to escort me to the coach first, though. Will you be all right alone for just a few moments, Vivacia?"

He had been vaguely aware of how anxiously the ship had been following their conversation. Now a beaming smile broke out over the carved features. "I am certain I shall be just fine, Ronica. Just fine." She shifted her glance to Wintrow, her gaze diving into his eyes so deeply that it startled him. "When you come back on board, would you sleep up here, on the foredeck, where I can see you?"

He glanced uncertainly at his father. They seemed to be the only two aware that he had not yet given his permission for this. Wintrow decided to be diplomatic. "If my father permits it," he concurred cautiously. He still had to look up to his father to meet his eyes, but he forced himself to do it and not to look away.

His father scowled still but Wintrow thought he also saw grudging respect in the man's eyes. "I permit it," he said at last, making it clear to everyone that he regarded this decision as his. He looked his son up and down. "When you come on board, report to Torg. He'll see you get a blanket." Kyle glanced from the boy to the waiting second mate, who nodded at the order.

His mother sighed out, as if she had been holding her breath. "Well, if that's settled, then let's go home." Her voice broke unexpectedly on that last word, and fresh tears spilled down her cheeks. "Oh, my father," she said softly, as if rebuking the dead man. Kyle patted her hand where it rested on his arm and escorted her from the ship. Wintrow followed more slowly with his grandmother. His younger siblings scrambled impatiently past them and hurried ahead to the carriage.

His grandmother moved so slowly, he thought she was excessively weary until she began speaking. Then he realized she had deliberately delayed to have a moment of privacy with him. Her voice was lowered, pitched for his ears alone.

"It all seemed strange and foreign to you earlier today, Wintrow. Yet just now, you spoke as a Vestrit, and I believe I saw your grandfather in your face. The ship reaches for you."

"Grandmother, I fear I have no idea what you are talking about," he confessed quietly.

"Don't you?" She halted their slow stroll and he turned to face her. Small but straight, she looked up into his face. "You say you don't, but I see otherwise," she said after a moment. "If you did not already know it yourself, in your heart, you could not have spoken up for the ship the way you did. You'll come to it, Wintrow. You'll come round to it in time, no fear."

He felt a tightening of foreboding. He wished he were going home with them tonight, and that he could sit down with his father and mother and speak plainly. Obviously they had discussed him. He did not know what they had been talking about, but he felt threatened by it. Then he sternly reminded himself to avoid pre-judgment. His grandmother said no more and he assisted her down the gang-plank and then handed her up into the waiting carriage. All the others were already within.

"Thank you, Wintrow," she told him gravely, and "You're welcome," he replied, but uncomfortably, for he suspected she thanked him for more than walking her to the carriage. He wondered briefly whether he would truly welcome giving her whatever it was she assumed. He stood alone as the driver chupped to his horses and drove them off, their hooves thudding hollowly on the wooden planks of the docks. After they had gone, he lingered for a time, seeking the quiet of the night.

In truth, it was not quiet at all. Neither Bingtown proper nor the docks ever truly slept. Across the curve of the harbor, he could see the lights and hear the distant sounds of the night market. A trick of the wind brought him a brief gust of music, pipes and wrist-bells. A wedding, perhaps, with dancing. Closer to hand, the tarry torches bracketed to the dock supports provided widely spaced circles of fitful light. The waves sloshed rhythmically against the pilings beneath the docks, and the tethered boats rubbed and creaked in their slips. They were like great wooden animals, he thought, and then a shiver walked up his spine as he recalled the liveship's awareness. Neither animal nor wooden ship, he realized, but some unholy mix and wondered how he could have volunteered to spend the night aboard her.

As he walked down the docks to where Vivacia was tied, the dancing torch-light and moving water combined to confuse his vision and make every step uncertain. By the time he reached the ship, the weariness of the day had caught up with him.

"Oh, there you are!"

He startled at the ship's greeting, then recovered. "I told you I would come back," he reminded her. It seemed strange to stand on the docks and look up at her. The torchlight moved strangely over her, for though her features were human, the light reflected from her skin as it did from wood. From this vantage, it was markedly more obvious that she was substantially larger than life. Her ample bared breasts were more obvious from this point of view as well. Wintrow found himself avoiding looking at them, and thus uncomfortable about meeting her eyes as well. A wooden ship, he tried to remind himself. She's a wooden ship. But in the gloom as she smiled down on him, she seemed more like a young woman leaning alluringly from a window. It was ridiculous.

"Aren't you coming aboard?" she asked him, smiling.

"Of course," he replied. "I'll be with you in a moment."

As he mounted the gang-plank, and then groped his way forward on the darkened deck, he again wondered at himself. Liveships, so far as he knew, were unique to Bingtown. His instruction as a priest of Sa had never touched upon them. Yet there were certain magics he had been warned of as running counter to the holiness of all life. He ran through them in his head: the magics that deprived something of life in order to bring life to something else, the magics that deprived something of life in order to enhance one's own power, the magics that brought misery to another's life in order to enhance one's own or another's life. . . . None of them seemed to apply exactly to whatever it was that wakened life in a liveship. His grandfather would have died whether the ship existed or not. He decided that one could not say his grandfather had been deprived of life in order to quicken the ship. At about the time he resolved that, he stumbled over a coil of rope. In trying to catch himself, his feet tangled in the hem of his brown novice's robe and he fell, sprawling full length on the deck.

Somewhere, someone brayed out a laugh. Perhaps it was not at him. Perhaps somewhere on the shadowed deck, sailors kept watch together and told humorous stories to pass the time. Perhaps. His face still flushed, and he suppressed anger at the possible ridicule. Foolishness, he told himself. Foolish to be angered if a man was dull-witted enough to find his stumbling humorous, and even more foolish to be angry when he could not be certain that was the case at all. It had simply been too long a day. He got carefully to his feet and groped his way to the foredeck.

A single coarse blanket had been left in a heap there. It smelt of whoever had used it last, and was either badly woven or stiffened in spots with filth. He let it drop back to the deck. For a moment he considered making do with it; the summer night was not that cold, he might not need a blanket at all. Let the insult go by; he'd not be dealing with any of them after tomorrow. Then he stooped to snatch the blanket up from the deck. This was not the misfortune of an early fall of hail or a flooding river, a happenstance of nature to be weathered stoically. This was the cruelty of men, and a priest of Sa was not expected silently to accept it, regardless of whether that cruelty was inflicted on himself or on others.

He squared his shoulders. He knew how they saw him. The captain's son, a boy, a runt, sent off to live in a monastery, to be raised to believe in goodness and kindness. He knew there were many who saw that as a weakness, who saw the priests and priestesses of Sa as sexless ninnies who spent their lives wandering about prating that the world could be a beautiful peaceful place. Wintrow had seen the other side of a priest's life. He had tended priests brought back to the monastery, priests maimed by the cruelty they had fought against, or dying of the plagues they had contracted when they nursed other victims. A clear voice and a steady eye, he counseled himself. He draped the offending blanket over one arm and picked his way carefully towards the afterdeck where a single night-lantern was burning.

Three men sat in the circle of dim light, a scatter of gaming pegs on the deck. Wintrow smelled the harsh edge of cheap spirits, and frowned to himself. The tiny flame of outrage inside him flared brighter. As if possessed by his grandfather's anma, he stepped boldly into the circle of their lantern. Throwing the blanket to the deck, he asked bluntly, "And when did the night watch on board this ship begin drinking on duty?"

There was a general recoil from his direction until the three saw who had spoken.

"It's the boy-priest," one sneered, and sank back down into his sprawl.

Again the flash of anger ignited in him. "It's also Wintrow Haven of Vestrit lineage, and on board this ship, the watch neither drinks nor games. The watch watches!"

All three men lumbered to their feet. They towered over him and all were brawnier, with the hard muscles of grown men. One had the grace to look shamed, but the other two were the worse for drink and unrepentant.

"Watches what?" a black-bearded fellow demanded insolently. "Watches while Kyle takes over the old man's ship, and replaces her crew with his cronies? Watches while all the years we worked, and worked damn loyal, go over the side and mean naught?"

The second man took up the first's litany. "Shall we watch while a Haven steals the ship that should be run by a Vestrit? Althea might be a snotty little vixen, but she's Vestrit to the bone. Should be her that has this ship, woman or no."

A thousand possible replies raced through Wintrow's mind. He chose as he thought best. "None of that has anything to do with drinking on watch. It's a poor way to honor Ephron Vestrit's memory."

The last statement seemed to have more effect on them than anything else he had said. The shame-faced man stepped forwards. "I'm the one that's been assigned the watch, and I ain't been drinking. They was just keeping me company and talking."

Wintrow could think of nothing to say to that, so he only nodded gravely. Then his eyes fell on the discarded blanket and he recalled his original mission. "Where's the second mate? Torg?"

The black-bearded man gave a snort of disdain. "He's too busy moving his gear into Althea's cabin to pay attention to anything else."

Wintrow gave a short nod to that and let it pass without comment. He did not address any particular man as he added to the night, "I do not think I should have been able to board Vivacia unchallenged, even in our home port."

The watchman looked at him oddly. "The ship's quickened now. She'd be swift to sing out if any stranger tried to board her."

"Are you sure she knows she is to do that if a stranger comes aboard?"

The incredulous look on the watch man's face grew. "How could she not know? What Captain Vestrit and his father and his grandmother knew of shipboard life, she knows." He looked aside and shook his head slightly as he added, "I thought all Vestrits would know that about a liveship."

"Thank you," Wintrow said, ignoring the last bit of the man's comment. "I'll be seeking Torg now. Carry on."

He stooped and swept up the discarded blanket. He walked carefully as he left the dim circle of light, letting his eyes adjust to the deepening darkness. He found the door to Althea's cabin standing ajar, light spilling out onto the deck. Those of her boxes that had not already been carted off were stacked unceremoniously to one side. The mate was engaged in judiciously arranging his own possessions.

Wintrow rapped loudly on the opened door, and tried not to take pleasure in the way Torg started almost guiltily.

"What?" the man demanded, rounding on him.

"My father said to see you to get a blanket," Wintrow stated quietly.

"Looks to me like you've got one," Torg observed. He could not quite hide the glint of his amusement. "Or does the priest-boy think it's not good enough for him?"

Wintrow let the offending blanket drop to the deck. "This won't do," he said quietly. "It's filthy. I've no objection to worn, or patched, but no man should willingly endure filth."

Torg scarcely gave it a glance. "If it's filthy, then wash it." He made a show of returning to his stowing of his goods.

Wintrow refused to be cowed. "I should not need to point out that there is no time for the blanket to dry," he observed blandly. "I am simply asking you to do as my father commanded. I've come aboard for the night, and I need a blanket."

"I've done as your father commanded, and you have one." The cruel amusement in Torg's voice was less veiled now. Wintrow found himself responding to that rather than to the man's words.

"Why does it amuse you to be discourteous?" he asked Torg, his curiosity genuine. "How could it be more trouble to you to provide me with a clean blanket than to give me a filthy rag and force me to beg for what I need?"

The honesty of the question caught the mate off-guard. He stared at Wintrow, speechless. Like many casually cruel men, he had never truly considered why he behaved as he did. It was sufficient for him that he could. Quite likely, he had been a bully from his childhood days, and would be until he was disposed of in a canvas shroud. For the first time, Wintrow took physical stock of the man. All his fate was writ large upon him. He had small round eyes, blue as a white pig's. The skin underneath the roundness of his chin had already began to sag into a pouch. The kerchief knotted about his neck was anciently soiled, and the collar of his blue-and-white-striped shirt showed an interior band of brown. It was not the dirt and sweat of honest toil, but the grime of slothfulness. The man did not care to keep himself tidy. It already showed in the way his possessions were strewn about the cabin. In a fortnight, it would be a reeking sty of unwashed garments and scattered food scraps.

In that instant, Wintrow decided to give over the argument. He'd sleep in his clothes on the deck and be uncomfortable, but he would survive it. He judged there was no point to further bickering with this man; he'd never grasp just how distasteful Wintrow found the soiled blanket, nor how insulting. Wintrow rebuked himself for not looking more closely at the man before; it might have saved them both a lot of useless chafing.

"Never mind," he said casually and abruptly. He turned away. He blinked his eyes a few times to let them adjust and then began to pick his way forward. He heard the mate come to the door of the cabin to stare after him.

"Puppy will probably complain to his daddy, I don't doubt," Torg called mockingly after him. "But I think he'll find his father expects a man to be tougher than to snivel over a few spots on a blanket."

Perhaps, Wintrow conceded, that was true. He wouldn't bother complaining to his father to find out. Pointless to complain about one night's discomfort. His silence seemed to bother Torg.

"You think you'll get me in trouble with your whining, don't you? Well, you won't! I know your father better than that."

Wintrow didn't even bother to reply to the man's threatening taunt. At the moment of deciding not to argue further, he had given up all emotional investment in the situation. He had withdrawn his anma into himself as he had been taught to do, divesting it of his anger and offense as he did so. It was not that these emotions were unworthy or inappropriate; it was simply that they were wasted upon the man. He swept his mind clean of reactions to the filthy blanket. By the time he reached the foredeck, he had regained not just calmness, but wholeness.

He leaned against the rail and looked out across the water. There were other ships anchored out in the harbor. Lights shone yellow from these vessels. He looked them over. His own ignorance surprised him. The ships were foreign objects to him, the son of many generations of traders and sailors. Most of them were trading vessels, interspersed with a few fishing or slaughter ships. The traders were transom-sterned for the most part, with aftercastles that sometimes reached almost to the mainmasts. Two or three masts reached toward the rising moon from each vessel.

Along the shore, the night market was in full blossom of sound and light. Now that the heat of the day was past, open cook fires flared in the night as the drippings of meat sizzled into them. An errant breeze brought the scent of the spiced meat and even the baking bread in the outdoor ovens. Sound, too, ventured boldly over the water in isolated snippets, a high laugh, a burst of song, a shriek. The moving waters caught the lights of the market and the ships and made of them rippling streamers of reflection. "Yet there is a peace to all of it," Wintrow said aloud.

"Because it is all as it should be," Vivacia rejoined. Her voice was a woman's timbre. It had the same velvety darkness as the night, with the same tinge of smoke. Warm pleasure welled up in Wintrow at the sound of it, and pure gladness. It took him a moment to wonder at his reaction.

"What are you?" he asked her in quiet awe. "When I am away from you, I think I should fear you, or at least suspect you. Yet now I am aboard, and when I hear your voice, it is like . . . like I imagine being in love would be."

"Truly?" Vivacia demanded, and did not hide the thrill of pleasure in her own voice. "Then your feelings are like to my own. I have been awakening for so long . . . for years, for all the life of your father and his father, ever since your great-great-grandmother gave herself into my keeping. Then today, when finally I could stir, could open my eyes to the world again, could taste and smell and hear you all with my own senses, then I knew trepidation. Who are you, I wonder, you creatures of flesh and blood and bone, born in your own bodies and doomed to perish when that flesh fails? And when I wonder those things, I fear, for you are so foreign to me, I cannot know what you will do to me. Yet when one of you is near, I feel you are woven of the same strand as I, that we are but extensions of a segmented life, and that together we complete one another. I feel a joy in your presence, because I feel my own life wax greater when we are close to one another."

Wintrow leaned on the rail, as motionlessly silent as if he were listening to a blessed poet. She was not looking at him; she did not need to look at him to see him. Like him, she gazed out across the harbor to the festive lights of the night market. Even our eyes behold the same sight, he thought, and his smile widened. There had been a few occasions when words had so reached into him and settled their truth in him like roots in rich earth. Some of the very best teachers in the monastery could wake this awe in him, when they spoke in simple words a truth that had swum unvoiced inside him. When her words had faded into the warmth of the summer night, he replied.

"So may a harp string, struck strongly, awaken its twin, or a pure high note of a voice set crystal to shimmering as you have wakened truth in me." He laughed aloud, surprising himself, for it felt as if a bird, long caged in his chest, had taken sudden flight. "What you say is so simple, only that we complement one another. I can think of no reason why your words should so move me. But they do. They do."

"Something is happening, here, tonight. I feel it."

"As do I. But I don't know what it is."

"You mean you have no name for it," she corrected him. "We both cannot help but know what this is. We grow. We become."

Wintrow found himself smiling into the night. "We become what?" he asked of her.

She turned to face him, the chiseled planes of her wooden face catching the reflected gleam of the distant lights. She smiled up at him, lips parting to reveal her perfect teeth. "We become us," she said simply. "Us, as we were meant to be."

Althea had never known that misery could achieve perfection. Only now, as she sat staring at her emptied glass, did she grasp how completely wrong her world had become. Things had been bad before, things had been flawed, but it was only today that she had made one stupid decision after another until everything was as completely wrong as it could possibly be. She shook her head at her own idiocy. As she fingered the last coins from her flattened pouch, and then held up her glass to be refilled, she reviewed her decisions. She had conceded when she should have fought, fought when she should have conceded. But the worst, the absolute worst, had been leaving the ship. When she had walked off Vivacia before her father's body had even been consigned to the waves, she had been worse than stupid and wrong. She had been traitorous. False to everything that had ever been important to her.

She shook her head at herself. How could she have done it? She had not only stalked off leaving her father unburied, but leaving her ship to Kyle's mercy. He had no understanding of her, no real grasp of what a liveship was or what she required. Despair gripped her heart and squeezed. After all the years of waiting, she had abandoned Vivacia on this most crucial day. What was the matter with her? Where had her mind been, where had her heart been to have put her own feelings before that of the ship? What would her father have said to that? Had not he always told her, "The ship first, and all else will follow."

The tavern-keeper appeared suddenly, to take her coin, ogle it closely, and then re-fill her glass. He said something to her, his voice unctuous with false solicitude. She waved him away with the re-filled glass and nearly spilled its contents. Hastily she drank it down lest she waste it.

She opened her eyes wide as if that would clear her head and looked around her. It seemed wrong that the folk in this tavern shared none of her misery. To all appearances, this slice of Bingtown had not even noticed the departure of Ephron Vestrit. Here they were having the same conversations that they'd been having for the past two years: the newcomers were ruining Bingtown; the Satrap's delegate was not only overstepping his authority in inventing taxes, but was taking bribes to ignore slave ships right in the harbor; the Chalcedeans were demanding of the Satrap that Bingtown drop their water taxes, and the Satrap would probably concede for the sake of the pleasure herbs Chalced sent him so freely. The same old woes, Althea thought to herself, but damn few in Bingtown would stand up and do anything about any of it.

The last time she had gone to the Old Traders' Council with her father, he had stood up and told them to simply outlaw it all. "Bingtown is our town," he'd told them determinedly. "Not the Satrap's. We should all contribute toward our own patrol ship, and simply deny slave ships access to our harbor. Turn the Chalcedean grain boats back, too, if they don't want to pay a tax to water and provision here. Let them re-supply elsewhere, perhaps in one of the pirate towns, and see if they're better treated there."

A roar of consternation had greeted his words, composed of both shock and approval, but when it came to the vote, the council had failed to take action. "Wait a year or two," her father had told Althea as they left. "That's how long it takes for an idea to take root here. Even tonight, most of them know that I'm right. They just don't want to face what needs to be done, that there must be confrontations if Bingtown is to remain Bingtown and not become southern Chalced. Sa's sweat, the damn Chalcedeans are already challenging our northern border. If we ignore it, they'll creep in here in other ways: face-tattooed slaves working Bingtown fields, women married off at twelve, all the rest of their corruption. If we let it happen, it will destroy us. And all the Old Traders know that, in their hearts. In a year or two, I'll bring this up again, and they'll suddenly all agree with me. You'll see."

But he wouldn't. Her father was gone forever now. Bingtown was a poorer, weaker town than it had been, and it didn't even know it.

Her eyes brimmed with tears once more. Yet again, she wiped them on the cuff of her sleeve. Both cuffs were sodden, and she did not doubt that her face and her hair were a wreck. Keffria and her mother would be scandalized to see her now. Well, let them be scandalized. If she was a disgrace, they were worse. She had acted on impulse, going on this drunk, but they had planned and plotted, not just against her but ultimately against the family ship. For they must realize what it meant for them to turn Vivacia over to Kyle, to a man not even blood-related to her. A tiny cold trickle of doubt suddenly edged through her. But her mother was not born a Vestrit. She had married into the family, just as Kyle had. Perhaps, like him, she had no real feelings for the ship. No. No, it could not be so, not after so many years with her father. Althea sternly forbade the thought to have any truth in it. They must know, both of them, what Vivacia was to their family. And surely all of this was only some strange and awful, but temporary, revenge upon her. For what, she was not sure; perhaps for loving her father more than she had loved anyone else in the family.

Tears welled afresh. It didn't matter, none of it mattered. They would have to change their minds, they would have to give the ship back to her. Even, she told herself sternly, even if it meant she had to serve under Kyle as captain. As much as she hated the thought, she suddenly embraced it. Yes. That was all they wanted. Some assurance that the ship's business would be conducted as he and they saw fit. Well, at this point, she cared nothing for any of that. He could traffic in pickled eggs and dyeing nuts as much as he wished, as long as she could be aboard Vivacia and be a part of her.

Althea sat up suddenly. She heaved a huge sigh of relief, as if she had suddenly resolved something. Yet nothing had changed, she told herself. A moment later, she denied that as well. For something had changed, and drastically. She had found that she was much more willing to abase herself than she had believed, that she would do virtually anything to remain aboard Vivacia. Anything.

She glanced about herself and gave a soft groan of dismay. She'd had too much to drink, and wept too much. Her head was throbbing and she was not even sure which of Bingtown's sailor dives she was in. One of the most sordid, that was for certain. A man had passed out and slid from his seat to the floor. That was not that unusual, but usually there was someone to drag them out of the way. Kinder inn-keepers left them snoring by the door, while the more heartless simply tumbled them out into the alleys or streets for the crimpers to find. It was rumored that some tavern-keepers even trafficked with the crimpers, but Althea had always doubted that. Not in Bingtown. Other seaports, yes, she was certain of that, but not Bingtown.

She rose unsteadily. The lace of her skirts snagged against the rough wood of the table leg. She pulled it free, heedless of how it tore and dangled. This dress she would never wear again anyway; let it tatter itself to rags tonight, she did not care. She gave a final sniff and rubbed her palms over her weary eyes. Home and to bed. Tomorrow, somehow, she would face all of it and deal with all of it. But not tonight. Sweet Sa, not tonight, let everyone be asleep when she reached home, she prayed.

She headed for the door, but had to step over the sodden sailor on the floor. The wooden floor seemed to lurch under her, or perhaps she did not quite have her land-legs back. She took a bigger stride to compensate, nearly fell, and recovered herself only when she grabbed at the door post. She heard someone laugh at her, but would not sacrifice her dignity to turn and see who. Instead, she dragged the door open and stepped out into the night.

The darkness and the cool were both disorienting and welcome. She halted a moment on the wooden walkway outside the tavern and took several deep breaths. On the third one, she thought suddenly that she might be sick. She grasped at the railing and stood still, breathing more shallowly and staring with wide eyes until the street stopped swinging. The door behind her scraped open again and disgorged another patron. She turned warily to have him in view. In the dimness, it took a moment for her to recognize him. Then, "Brashen," she greeted him.

"Althea," he replied wearily. Unwillingly he asked, "Are you all right?"

For a moment she stood in the street looking at him. Then, "I want to go back to Vivacia." The moment she impulsively spoke the thought, she knew it was something she had to do. "I have to see the ship tonight. I have to speak to her, to explain why I left her today."

"Tomorrow," Brashen suggested. "When you've slept and you're sober. You don't want her to see you like this, do you?" She heard the note of cunning in his voice as he added, "Surely she would be no more pleased than your father would."

"No. She'd understand. We know one another that well. She'd understand anything I did."

"Then she'd also understand if you came in the morning, clean and sober." Brashen pointed out reasonably. He sounded very tired. After a moment's silence, he proffered her his arm. "Come on. I'll walk you home."

CHAPTER EIGHT

NIGHT CONVERSATIONS

HER MOTHER BROKE DOWN AS SOON AS THEY WERE IN-SIDE THE DOOR, HER KNEES SIMPLY FOLDING. KYLE stood shaking his head, so Keffria saw her mother to bed. The bedroom she had so long shared with her husband had become a chamber of sickness and dying. Rather than put her mother on the cot where she had kept watch so many nights, Keffria ordered Rache to make a guest room ready for her. She sat with her until the bed was ready and the serving woman settled her impassive mother into it. Then she went to check on Selden. He was crying. He had wanted his mother, and Malta had told him she was busy, too busy for a crying baby. Then she had left him sitting on the edge of his bed, without so much as calling a servant to see to him. For an instant Keffria was angry with her daughter; then she reminded herself that Malta was little more than a child herself. It was not reasonable to expect a twelve-year-old to care for her seven-year-old brother after a day such as they had just had.

So she soothed the boy and helped him into his night-robe and stayed by him until his eyes sagged shut. When she finally left him to seek her own bed, she was sure that every other soul in the household was already asleep. The dancing light of the candle as she trod the familiar halls put her in mind of spooks and spirits. She suddenly wondered if the anma of her father might not still linger in the chambers where he had suffered so long. A shiver walked up her spine, standing up the hair on the back of her neck. A moment later she reproached herself. Her father's anma was one with the ship now. And even if it were lingering here, surely her own father would bear her no ill will. Still, she was glad to slip soundlessly into the chamber where Kyle had already gone to bed. She blew out the candle lest she disturb him and undressed in the darkness, letting her garments fall as they might. She found the nightgown Nana had laid out for her and slipped into its coolness. Then finally, finally, her own bed. She turned back the blanket and linen and eased in beside her slumbering husband.

He opened his arms to welcome her in. He had not slept without her, but had waited for her here. Despite how long the day had been, despite how weary and sorrowful she was, that gladdened her. Keffria felt as if Kyle's touch cut through knots of pain that had been strangling her for days. For a time he simply held her close. He stroked her hair and rubbed her neck until she relaxed in his arms. Then he made love to her, simply and gently, without words as moonlight spilled into their bedroom from the high windows. This summer night's moon was bright enough to lend almost colors to all it touched; the cream-colored sheets on the bed, Kyle's hair like ivory, his skin two shades of dull gold where sun had and had not touched it. Afterwards, as she curved her body against his and rested her head on his shoulder, all was silence for a time. She listened to the beating of his heart and the movement of air through his chest and was glad of it, and of his warmth.

Then she suddenly felt selfish and thoughtless, that she could possess all this and enjoy it, on the very night of the day when her mother lost her father, and with him all possibility of physical closeness and this kind of sharing. Lax and warm from their lovemaking, it suddenly seemed too terrible a loss to exist in any world. She did not move away from Kyle, but closer as her throat closed painfully and a single hot tear slid across her cheek to drip onto his bare shoulder. He reached up to touch it, and then her face.

"Don't," he told her gently. "Don't. There have been enough tears today, and enough mourning. Let it all go, for now. Don't let there be anything or anyone in this bed save we two."

She caught a breath. "I'll try. But my mother's loss . . . I just truly realized what she lost. All this." Her free hand charted the length of him, from shoulder to thigh, before he caught it up and brought it to his mouth for a kiss.

"I know. I thought of that, too, as I was touching you. Wondered if there would be a time I didn't come back to you, what you would do. . . ."

"Don't even speak such an idea!" she begged him. She put her palm to his jaw and turned his face to hers in the moonlight. "I still don't know that it was right," she suddenly declared in an altered tone. "I know we talked about it, that we all agreed it would be for the best, that it would protect everyone. But the look on her face when I put my hand on the peg . . . and then the way she just stormed off. I never would have believed Althea would do that, just leave the funeral that way. I thought she loved him more than that. . . ."

"Umh." Kyle considered. "I hadn't expected it either. I thought she loved the ship more than that, if not her father. I expected a real battle with her, and was just as glad when she gave in easily. I was sure the whole funeral ceremony would be one bitter scene after another with her. At least she spared us that. Thought I confess I'm uneasy as to where she is right now. A girl should be at home on the night of her father's death, not out gallivanting around a wild port like Bingtown." He paused, then added almost cautiously, "You know I can't let her get away with it. She has to be rebuked; someone has to take a hand with her before she ruins herself entirely."

"Papa always said that Althea ran best under a light hand," Keffria ventured. "That she had to have room to make her own mistakes, as it seemed they were the only things she could learn from."

Kyle gave a snort of disgust. "Forgive me, my love, but I think he said it to excuse himself from taking a father's stand with her. She's spoiled. She's been indulged for as long as I've known her, and it shows. She constantly assumes she's going to get her own way. It's made her selfish and thoughtless of others. But it's not too late for her. Finding out that was more of a shock to me than you can imagine. On the way home, when I lost my temper and ordered her into her cabin for the remainder of the voyage, I never dreamed she'd heed me. I was angry and barked out the words to get her out of my sight before I could really lose my temper with her. But she obeyed me. And I think she finally had time to do a lot of thinking in that time alone. You saw how she was when we landed. Quiet and repentant. She dressed like a lady when we left the ship, or as closely as she knows how to."

He paused for a moment. He shook his head, tangling his blond hair against the pillow. "I was amazed. I kept waiting for her to try to start up the quarrel again. And then I realized, this was what she has been looking for all along. Someone to draw a line. Someone to finally take charge of her and make her behave as she knows she should. All this time, I think she was just seeing how far she could go before someone took in her sails and dropped anchor." He cleared his throat. "I respected your father. You know I did. But when it came to Althea, he was . . . blind. He never forbade her anything, never really told her 'no' and enforced it. When I stepped in and did that, well, the difference was amazing. Of course, when she got off the ship and I was no longer in charge, then she started to get a bit wild again." He shrugged. For a time there was silence as he and Keffria considered her sister and her strange ways.

Kyle took a deep breath and sighed it out heavily. "I used to think there was no hope for her. That she'd only bring us sorrow and come to a bad end herself. But today, when she finally saw all of us united in what was best for the family, she didn't truly oppose us. Deep inside, she knows what is right. The ship must be worked for the good of the whole family. You are eldest: it's only right and just that you inherit the family's real wealth. Besides, you've children to provide for, and the ship will let us do that. Who has Althea to provide for? Why, only herself, and I think we can trust ourselves to see that she doesn't go hungry or naked or roofless. But if the situation were reversed and the ship had been given over to her, she would have sailed the *Vivacia* out of the harbor without a backward glance, and like as not she'd have that ne'er-do-well Brashen as the captain on her."

He stretched slightly, but not enough to dislodge her. His arm came around her, held her close. "No, Keffria, I don't think you need to question that what we did today was for the best. We know we'll provide for Althea, and get your mother out of her financial tangle as well. Could you say for certain that Althea would take care of your mother, let alone us and our children? I think that toward the end even your father saw the wisdom of bequeathing the ship to you, hard as he found it to hurt his little favorite's feelings."

Keffria heaved a sigh and settled closer against him. Every word he said made sense. That was one of the reasons she had married him; his ability to think things through so carefully and logically had made her feel so safe. That was one thing she had been certain of when she wed; that she did not want to live her life tied to a man as impulsive and fanciful as her father had been. She had seen what it had done to her mother, how it had aged her far beyond her years. Other Trader matrons lived sedate lives of ease, tending their rose gardens and grandbabies, while her own mother had each day arisen to face a man's load of decisions and work. It was not just the accounts and the laborious working-out of agreements with fellow Traders. Often as not her mother had been out on the fields on horseback, checking for herself that what her overseers said was true.

Ever since Keffria could remember, she had hated the season of the mafe harvest. When she was tiny, all she had known was that it meant her mother was already gone when she awakened, and that she might see her for an hour before bedtime, or not at all that day. As she grew older, there had been a few years when her mother had insistently dragged her along to the hot fields and the long rows of prickly dark green bushes heavy with ripening beans. She had forced her to learn how the beans were harvested, what the pests that plagued them looked like, and which diseased bushes must be pulled up immediately and burned and which must be painstakingly doused with a strong tea made from leaf mold and horse manure. Keffria had hated it. As soon as she was old enough to be concerned with her hair and skin, she had rebelled and refused to be tormented any longer. That, she recalled, was the same year that she resolved she would never marry a man who would go to sea and leave her with such burdens. She would find a man willing to fulfill a man's role, to take care of her and keep her safe and defend their door from all troubles and worries. "And then I went and married a sailor," she said aloud. The fondness in her voice made it a compliment.

"Um?" The sleepy question came from deep within his chest. She set a hand on its paleness in the moonlight, enjoyed the contrast of her olive skin against his whiteness.

"I just wish you weren't gone so much," she said softly. "Now that papa is dead, you're the man of our family. If you're not around . . ."

"I know," he said quietly. "I've thought of that, I've worried about that. Why else do you think I must insist I take Wintrow on the ship with me? It's time he stepped forward as a man of this family, and took on his share of the responsibilities."

"But . . . his priesthood," Keffria objected in a tiny voice. It was very hard for her to disagree with her husband, but in this one area, he had always before let her have her way. She could scarcely grasp that he might change his mind now.

"You know I never approved of that nonsense," he said quietly as if in answer to her thought. "Offering our first-born son to the service of Sa . . . that's a fine thing for the rich folk of Jamaillia to do. Shows off their wealth, that they can offer up the labor of a son and think nothing of it. That's not the case with us, dear. But I knew you wanted it, and I tried to let you have it. We sent the boy off to the monastery. And if your father had lived for another handful of years, they could have kept him. But he didn't. Selden's too young to sail. The plain and simple truth of it is that this family needs Wintrow a lot more than some monastery in Jamaillia. Sa provides, you always say. Well, look at it this way. He provided us with a son, thirteen years ago. And now we need him."

"But we promised him," she said in a small voice. Inside her was a sort of agony. It had meant so much to her that Wintrow was a priest, offered up to Sa. Not all boys who were offered were accepted. Some were returned to their parents with the thanks of the monastery, but a polite letter explaining their sons were not truly suitable for the priesthood. Wintrow had not been returned. No, he had been cherished from the very beginning, advancing swiftly to his novice's brown robe, transferred from the outlying monastery at Kall to Kelpiton monastery on the Marrow peninsula. The priests did not often send reports, but those she had received had been glowing. She kept them, tied with the gilt ribbons that had originally bound them, in the corner of her clothing chest.

"You promised him," Kyle pointed out. "Not I. Here. Let me up." He disentangled himself from her arms and bedding to rise. His body was like carved ivory in the moonlight. He groped at the foot of the bed for his night robe and then dragged it on over his head.

"Where are you going?" she asked quietly. She knew her comment had displeased him, but he had never quitted her bed to sleep elsewhere before.

He knew her so well. As if sensing her worry, he reached down to smooth her hair back from her face. "I'll be back. I'm just going to go check Althea's room, and see if she's in yet." He shook his head. "I can't believe her foolishness. I hope she doesn't make a spectacle of herself in Bingtown tonight. When she has a few drinks, she's capable of saying almost anything. Scandal is the last thing we need right now. The family must be seen as stable and united until we get these financial problems under control. Any wild talk from Althea, and we could find our creditors panicking, thinking they should get what they can out of us while we've got it. Ah, well. We've had enough worries and grief for tonight. Try to go to sleep. I'll be back in a few moments either way."

For a long moment, Brashen feared she was going to refuse his offer of escort. Althea wove slightly on her feet as she blearily appraised him. He returned her gaze evenly. Sa, she was a sight! Her hair had come loose and sprawled across her brow and shoulders. Her face was smeared with the day's dust and her own tears. Only her dress marked her as a woman of quality, and its disheveled condition made it look like someone else's cast off. Right now, he thought sourly, she looked more like a doxie looking for a tumble than the proud daughter of a Bingtown Trader family. If she attempted to walk home alone, anything might befall her in the wildness of the night market.

But in another moment she sighed loudly. "Aye," she said, and with another heavy sigh she took his offered arm. She leaned on him heavily, and he was glad he had jettisoned his sea-bag earlier in the day. The tavern-keeper holding it for him knew him well, and he had parted with several small coins to ensure its safety. He did not like to think of how much more coin he had spent following her from tavern to tavern. More than he had meant to, true, but not as much as he would have ordinarily spent on a night out on the town. He was still almost sober, he reflected. This had been the most depressing first night back in home port that he had ever spent. Well, it was nearly over. All he had to do was get her safely home, and then the few hours between the stars and dawn would be his to spend as he wished.

He looked up and down the street. It was ill lit with widely spaced torches and all but deserted at this hour. Those who were still capable of drinking were within the taverns, and everyone else in this quarter would be passed out somewhere. Nevertheless, there would be a few rogues who'd lurk down this way, hoping for a drunken sailor's last coin. He'd be wise to go carefully, especially with Althea in tow.

"This way," he told her and attempted to lead her at a brisk pace, but she almost immediately stumbled. "Are you that drunk?" he asked her in annoyance before he could curb his tongue.

"Yes," she admitted with a small belch. She stooped so abruptly that he thought she was going to fold up on the boardwalk. Instead she tore off first one and then another heeled-and-ribboned shoe. "And these damn things don't help a bit." She stood and flung them both out into the dark street. Straightening, she turned back to him and took his arm firmly. "Now let's go."

She made her way much better barefoot, he had to admit. He grinned at himself in the darkness. Even after all the years of doing for himself, there was still some of the strait-laced Trell in him. He'd felt a shudder of horror at the impropriety of a Trader's daughter going barefoot through the town. Well, given the rest of her condition, he doubted it would be the first thing anyone noticed. Not that he intended to troll her through the market as she was; he'd keep to the lesser-traveled streets and hope they met no one who could recognize them in the darkness. That much he owed to the memory of Ephron Vestrit.

But as they came to an intersection, she tugged at his arm and tried to turn toward the bright streets of the night market. "I'm hungry," she announced, and she sounded both surprised and annoyed, as if it were his fault.

"Too bad. I'm broke," he lied succinctly and tried to draw her away.

She stared at him suspiciously. "You drank all your pay that fast? Sa's ass, man, I knew you were a sot in port, but I didn't think even you could go through coin that fast."

"I spent it on whores," he embellished irritably.

She appraised him in the flickering torch light. "Yes. You would," she confirmed to herself. She shook her head. "Nothing you wouldn't do, is there, Brashen Trell?"

"Not much," he agreed coldly, resolute on ending the conversation. Once more he tugged at her arm but she still resisted.

"Lots of places there will give me credit. Come on. I'll buy for you, too." She had gone from judgmental to effusive in one breath.

He decided on a direct tack. "Althea. You're drunk and a mess. You're in no condition to be seen in any public place. Come on. I'm taking you home."

The resistance went out of her and he led her docilely along the semi-dark street. They were in an area of smaller shops here, some of an unsavory nature, others incapable of paying the high rent of a night market location. Dim lanterns shone outside those that were still open for business: tattoo parlors, incense and drug shops, and those that sated the more unusual cravings of the flesh. He was glad that trade was paltry tonight. Just when he thought that the night's trials were over for him, Althea drew a long shuddering breath. He realized she was weeping, all but silently.

"What's wrong?" he asked her wearily.

"Now that my father's dead, no one will ever be proud of me again." She shook her head blindly, and then blotted her eyes on her sleeve. Her voice was choked when she spoke. "With him, it was what I could do. With all of them, it's how I look, or what others think of me."

"You've had too much to drink," he said quietly. He had meant the words to sound comforting, to mean that such things would only bother her when she was drunk and her defenses were down. Instead they came out sounding like another condemnation. But she only bowed her head to it and followed him docilely, so he let it be. He was certainly having no luck at making her feel better, and honestly he was not sure that he wanted to make her feel better, or had any responsibility to do so. So her family had condemned her. Could she speak to him and forget how completely cast out from his kin he was? Only a few weeks ago, she had thrown that in his face. It wasn't fair of her to expect sympathy now that the tables were turned.

They had walked some way in silence when she spoke again. "Brashen," she said quietly in a serious voice. "I'm going to get my ship back."

He made a noncommittal noise. There was no sense in telling her he believed there was absolutely no chance of that.

"Did you hear what I said?" she demanded.

"Yes. I heard you."

"Well. Aren't you going to say anything?"

He gave a short, bitter laugh. "When you get your ship back, I expect to be first mate again."

"Done," she replied grandiosely.

Brashen snorted. "If I knew it were that easy, I'd have demanded to be captain."

"No. No, I'm going to be the captain. But you can be the mate. Vivacia likes you. When I am captain, I'm only going to have people we like aboard her."

"Thank you," he said awkwardly. He had never believed that Althea liked him. In a strange way, it touched him. The captain's daughter had liked him after all.

"What?" she asked him drunkenly.

"Nothing," he told her. "Nothing at all."

They turned into the street of the Rain Wild River merchants. Here the stores were more ornate, and all but one or two were closed for the evening. The exotic and expensive merchandise they dealt in was for the very wealthy, not the wild and reckless youth that were the main customers of the night market. The tall glass windows were shuttered for the night, and hired guards, heavily armed, loitered purposefully near the various shops. More than one glowered at the pair as they made their way down the boardwalks. The wares behind the shuttered windows were tinged with the magic of the Rain Wilds. It had always seemed to Brashen that there was a shimmer of something both shivery and sweet on this street. It prickled the hair on the back of his neck at the same time that it closed his throat with awe. Even in the night, with the mysterious goods of the forbidding river trade hidden from sight, the aura of magic simmered silvery-cold in the night air. He wondered if Althea felt it and nearly asked her, save that the question seemed both too serious and too trivial to utter aloud.

The silence between them had grown until Althea's hand on his arm was an uncomfortable closeness. When he spoke again, it was to dispel that more than from any need. "Well, she's come up in the world quite swiftly," he observed aloud as they passed Amber's shop. He nodded toward a storefront on the corner of Rain Wild Street, where Amber herself sat in the window behind an expensive set of Yicca glass panes. They were as clear as water, and set in elaborately carved and gilded frames. They made the woman in the window look like a framed piece of art. The woven chair she lounged in was of white wickerwork. She wore a long brown gown that hung simply from her shoulders; it more cloaked than enhanced her slight form. Her shop windows were neither shuttered nor barred; no guards lurked outside. Perhaps Amber trusted to her own strange presence to deter thieves. A single dish lamp burned on the floor beside her with a mellow yellow light. The rich brown of her draped gown pointed up the gold of her skin and hair and eyes. Her bare feet peeped from the bottom of her long skirts. She watched the street with a cat's wide unblinking stare.

Althea halted to return that stare. She swayed slightly on her feet and without thinking Brashen put his arm around her shoulders to steady her. "What is she selling?" Althea wondered out loud. Brashen winced, certain that the woman beyond the glass had heard her words, but Amber's expression neither changed nor faltered from her emotionless regard of the disheveled girl in the street. Althea screwed her eyes tight shut, then opened them wide as if that would change the view. "She looks as if she's all carved of wood. Golden maple."

The woman behind the glass could hear her words, for Brashen saw a small smile begin to form on her sculpted lips. But when Althea added plaintively, "She reminds me of my ship. Lovely Vivacia, with all the colors of life over the silk grain of wizardwood," Amber's face abruptly changed to an expression of extreme distaste. Not quite sure of why that patrician disdain so alarmed him, Brashen nonetheless seized Althea by the elbow and firmly hurried her past the window and on down the dimly lit street.

At the next intersection, he allowed her to slow down. She was limping by then, and he recalled her bare feet and the rough wood of the boardwalk. She said not a word of that, but only asked again, "What does she sell there? She's not one of the Bingtown Traders who have Rain Wild River trade; only liveship families can trade up the Rain Wild River. So who is she and why does she have a shop on Rain Wild Street?"

Brashen shrugged. "She was new here, about two years ago. Had a tiny little shop off the Odds and Bodkins Square. She made wooden beads and sold them. Nothing else. Just very pretty wooden beads. A lot of people bought them for their children to string. Then, last year, she moved to a better location and started selling, well, jewelry. Only it's all made of wood."

"Wooden jewelry?" Althea scoffed. She sounded much more herself and Brashen suspected the walk was sobering her up. Good. Maybe she'd have the sense to tidy herself up before walking barefoot into her father's house.

"That's what I thought, too, until I saw it. I had never known a crafter could find so much in wood. She works with the odd little knotty bits, and brings out faces and animals and exotic flowers. Sometimes she inlays pieces. But it's as much the wood she chooses as the skill with which she does it. She has an uncanny eye, to see what she does in a bit of wood."

"So. Does she work wizardwood, then?" Althea asked boldly.

"Fa!" Brashen exclaimed in disgust. "She might be new, but she knows our ways well enough to know that would not be tolerated! No, she only uses ordinary wood. Cherry and oak and I don't know, all different colors and grains . . ."

"There's a lot more that work wizardwood in Bingtown than would like to own up to it," Althea observed darkly. She scratched at her belly. "It's a dirty little trade, but if you want a carved bit and have the coin, you can get it."

Her suddenly ominous tone made Brashen uneasy. He tried to lighten the conversation. "Well, isn't that what all the world says of Bingtown? That if a man can imagine a thing, he can find it for sale here?"

She smiled crookedly at him. "And you've heard the rejoinder to that, haven't you? That no man can truly imagine being happy, and that's why happiness isn't for sale here."

The sudden bleakness of her mood left him at a loss for words. The silence that followed seemed in tune with the cooling of the summer night. As they left the streets of the merchants and tradesmen behind and followed the winding roads into the residential sections of Bingtown, the night grew darker around them. Lanterns were more widely spaced and set far back from the road. Barking dogs threatened them from fenced or hedged yards. The roads here were rougher, the only walkways were of gravel, and when Brashen thought of Althea's bare feet, he winced sympathetically. But she herself said nothing of it.

In the silence and darkness, his grief for his fallen captain found space to grow in him. More than once he blinked away the sting of tears. Gone. Captain Vestrit was gone, and with him Brashen's second chance at life. He should have taken better advantage of all the Old Trader offered him while he was alive. He should never have assumed that the helping hand the man had extended him would always be available. Well, now he'd have to make his own third chance. He glanced over at the girl who still depended on his arm. She'd have to make her own way, too, now. Either that, or accept the fate her family parceled out to her. He suspected they'd find a younger son of a Trader family willing to wed her despite her risqué reputation. Maybe even his own little brother. He didn't think Cerwin would be any match for Althea's willfulness, but the Trell fortunes would mingle well with those of the Vestrits. He wondered how Althea's adventurousness would stand up to Cerwin's hide-bound traditionalism. He smiled grimly to himself, and wondered who he'd pity more.

He'd been to the Vestrits' home before, but always it had been by daylight, with some bit of ship's business to take to the Captain. The walk to Althea's home seemed much longer in the night. They left even the distant sounds of the night market behind them. They passed hedges with night-blooming flowers perfuming the air. An almost eerie peace descended over Brashen. Today had seen an end to so many things. Once more he was cut loose and drifting, with only himself to rely on. No obligations tomorrow, no schedules. No crews to supervise, no cargo to unload. Only himself to feed. Was that bad, really?

The Vestrit mansion was set well back from the public road. The gardens and grounds hosted insects and frogs, all trilling in the summer night. They provided the only sound other than the crunching of his boots as they walked up the stone drive. It was when he stood before the white stone of the entryway, before the familiar door where he had sometimes awaited admittance on ship's business, that he suddenly felt grief once more clutch at his throat. Never again, he supposed. This would be the last time he'd stand before this door. After a moment, he noticed that Althea had not let go of his arm. Here, clear of the narrow streets and shops, the moonlight could find her. Her bare feet were dirty, her gown draggled. Her hair had come loose of the lace thing she'd bound it in; at least, half of it had. She suddenly released his arm, stood up straight, and heaved a great sigh.

"Thank you for seeing me home," she said, her voice as level and formal as if he had escorted her home in a carriage after a Trader festival.

"You're welcome," he said quietly. As if the words had awakened in the rough sailor the genteel boy his mother had once schooled, he bowed deeply to her. He very nearly lifted her hand to his lips, but the sight of his own battered shoes and the tattering edges of his rough cotton trousers recalled to him who he was now. "You'll be all right?" he half asked, and half told, her.

"I suppose," she said vaguely. She turned away from him and set her hand on the latch, only to have the door violently jerked open before her.

Kyle filled the door. He was in his night robe and barefoot and his pale hair stood up in tousled tufts on his head, but his fury was such that there was nothing ridiculous about him. "What goes on here?" he demanded. He had pitched his voice low, as if for secrecy, but the force of his emotions gave them the same strength as a bellow. Instinctively, Brashen straightened up before the man he had served as captain. Althea initially recoiled in shock from him, but recovered quickly.

"None of your damn business," she declared and tried to walk past him into the house. He caught her by the upper arm and spun her about. "Damn you," she cried out, and made no effort to keep her voice low. "Get your hands off me!"

Kyle ignored that, instead giving her a shake that snapped her smaller body about like the weight on the end of a lash. "This family is my business!" he growled. "This family's reputation and good name is my business, just as it should be yours. Look at yourself. Barefoot, looking and smelling like a drunken slut, and here's a rogue sniffing after you like he'd go after some cheap whore. . . . Is that why you brought him here, to your own family home? How could you? On the night of your father's death, how could you shame us all like this?"

Althea had bared her teeth like a vixen at his wild accusations. She clawed at the hand that gripped her so firmly. "I've done nothing!" she cried wildly, the drink all too plain in her voice. "I've done nothing to be ashamed of! You're the one who should be ashamed. You thief! You've stolen my ship from me! You've stolen my ship!"

Brashen stood transfixed by horror. This was the last thing he wanted to get mixed up in. No matter what he did, it was going to be wrong in someone's eyes. But worst was to stand still and do nothing at all. So. Be damned for a ram as deeply as a lamb. "Cap'n. Kyle. Let her go, she did nothing except to get a bit drunk. Given what she's been through today, I think that's to be expected. Let her go, man, you're hurting her!"

He hadn't lifted a hand, had given no sign that he intended to attack Kyle at all, but Kyle abruptly threw Althea aside and advanced on the sailor. "That might be what you expect, but it's not what we expect." Behind Kyle, down the darkened hallway, Brashen caught a glimpse of a light being kindled, and heard a woman's voice raised questioningly. Kyle made a grab for Brashen's shirt front, but Brashen stepped backwards. Behind him, Althea had staggered to her feet. She was crying, hopeless as a lost child. She clung to the door frame, the sweep of her hair hiding her bowed face, and wept. Kyle ranted on. "Yes, you'd expect her to get drunk, wouldn't you, you scurvy dog? And followed her hoping for more than that. I've seen you watching her on the ship, and I know what you had in mind. Couldn't wait for her father's body to settle to come sniffing after her, could you?"

Kyle was stalking forward towards him, and Brashen found himself giving ground. Physically, he was no more afraid of Kyle than he was of any man larger than himself, but Kyle carried more than the weight of his fists as he advanced. He had all the advantage of Old Trader family line to fall back on. If he killed Brashen right here, few would question any account he might give of the event. So he told himself it was not cowardice, but savvy that made him back up, lifting his hands placatingly and saying, "It was nothing like that. I was just seeing her safely home. That's all."

Kyle swung, and Brashen sidestepped it easily. The one swing was all he needed to gauge the man. Captain Haven was slow. And he overstepped his balance. And while the man was bigger, and had a longer reach and might even be stronger, Brashen knew he could take him, and without too much difficulty.

In his brief moment of wondering if he'd have to fight him a woman's voice sounded from the door. "Kyle! Brashen!" Despite the age and grief in her voice, or perhaps because of it, Ronica Vestrit sounded as if she were a mother rebuking two unruly children. "Stop this! Stop this right now!" The old woman, her hair braided back for sleep, clung to the door frame. "What is going on? I demand to know what is happening here."

"This son of a pig—" Kyle began, but Althea's low, even voice cut through his outrage. Her voice was hoarse from weeping, but other than that it was very controlled.

"I was distraught. I had too much to drink. I ran into Brashen Trell in a tavern and he insisted on seeing me home. And that is all that happened or was going to happen, before Kyle stormed out here and began calling people names." Althea lifted her head suddenly and glared at Kyle, daring him to contradict her.

"That's true," Brashen added just as Kyle complained, "But look at her, just look at her!"

He never could decide who Ronica Vestrit believed. Something of the steel she was known for showed in her as she simply said, "Kyle and Althea. Go to bed. Brashen, go home. I'm too tired and heartsick to deal with any of this just now." When Kyle opened his mouth to protest she added compromisingly, "Tomorrow is soon enough, Kyle. If we wake the servants, they'll tattle this scandal all through the market. I don't doubt that more than one is listening at a door right now. So let's put an end to this now. Keep family business inside the walls. That was what Ephron always said." She turned to face Brashen. "Good night, young man," she dismissed him, and he was only too happy to flee. He did not even say good-bye or good-night, but walked briskly away into the night. When he heard the heavy door shut firmly, he felt it had closed on a chapter of his life.

He strode back toward the harbor basin and Bingtown proper. As he wended his way down, he heard the first cautious calls of the dawn birds. He lifted his eyes to the east, to a horizon that was starting to be tinged with light, and felt suddenly weary. He thought of the cramped bunk awaiting him on Vivacia, and suddenly realized the truth of the day. No bunk awaited him anywhere. He considered paying for a room at an inn, someplace with soft beds and clean quilts and warm wash water in the mornings. He made a face between a snarl and a grin. That would deplete his coin rapidly. Maybe tonight, when he could take a full night's advantage of the bed, he'd pay for one. But the most sleep he was going to get this morning was a few hours before the light and noise and heat of the day had him up again. He wouldn't spend coin for a bed he'd hardly use.

Long habit had led him toward the harbor. He shook his head at himself and turned his steps toward Wield Road, out of town and down to the rocky beaches where the poorest fishermen pulled up their small boats. Paragon would put him up for the day and be glad of the company. Afternoon would be soon enough to recover his sea-bag and begin to look for work and lodgings. For now, he'd take a few hours rest for himself, well away from both Vestrits and Havens.

Maulkin halted where he was. His jaws gaped wide and closed repeatedly as he tasted this new atmosphere. The tangle settled wearily into the soft muck, grateful for this brief respite from his dogged pace. Shreever watched their leader with something like fondness as he sampled the brine of this Plenty. His ruff stood up around his throat, half-challenging, half-questioning. A few of the other serpents rumbled at his attitude, shifting their coils uneasily.

"There is no challenger here," observed Sessurea. "He feints with bubbles."

"No," Shreever asserted quietly. "Memories. He fights to capture them. He has told me. They shine before his mind like a great school of capelin, confounding the eye with its multitude. Like a wise fisher, he must gape and lunge into the midst, trusting that when his jaws close there will be substance in his grasp."

"Silt, most likely," Sessurea said softly.

Shreever stood her ruff up at him, and he swiftly turned aside from her, to nose at his own tail as if grooming. She herself stretched, preening showily to demonstrate she did not fear him. "Tubeworms," she observed as if to herself, "are always content with a stationary view."

The others, she knew, were beginning to question Maulkin's leadership. She did not. It was true that of late his thoughts seemed even more unfocused than usual. True, also, that he trumpeted strangely in his dreams during the brief rests he allowed them, and that he spoke to himself more often than he did to his followers.

But the very things that unnerved the others were the signs that convinced Shreever that Maulkin was guiding them true. The farther north they had followed him, the more certain she became that he was truly one of those who carried the old memories. She watched him now. His great copper eyes were shielded by his milky eyelids as he danced the full length of his body through a knot, stroking himself over and over until his golden false-eyes glowed. Some of the others watched disdainfully, as if they believed Maulkin stimulated his senses simply for the pleasure of it. Shreever watched him hungrily. If the rest of the tangle had not been so intently watching him, she might even have dared to join him, to wrap his length with her own and try to share the memories he was seeking.

Instead, she discreetly drew more brine into her own half-opened jaws and then let it escape slowly over her gills. She tasted the strangeness of this new brine. It carried foreign salts that near stung with their intensity. She tasted, too, the salts of Maulkin's body as he twisted strenuously against himself. The lids of her own eyes rose, cloaking her vision. For an instant, she dreamed, and in the dream the Lack was the Plenty and she soared freely within it.

Before she could control herself, she threw back her head and trumpeted triumphantly. "The way is clear!" she called, and then came to awareness of her own cry. The others were watching her now with the same tension with which they regarded Maulkin. She sleeked her ruff back to her throat in confusion. Maulkin sheered towards her and suddenly wrapped her firmly in the full length of his body. His ruff stood out in wild aggression, welling toxins that both stunned and intoxicated her. He gripped her with immense strength, daubing his musk against her scales, deluging her senses with the half-grasped memories that lured him on. Then he freed her abruptly and whipped his body clear of hers. Slowly, limply, she settled to the bottom, gulping to breathe.

"She shares," Maulkin declared to his followers. "She sees and is anointed with my memories. With our memories. Come, Shreever, arise and follow me. The time of the gathering is nigh. Follow me to rebirth."

CHAPTER NINE

A CHANGE OF FORTUNES

THE CRUNCHING OF SHOD FEET ON THE SANDY ROCKS BROUGHT HIM TO ALERTNESS. DESPITE HIS YEARS OF blindness, he lifted his head and turned his eyes towards the sound. Whoever was coming was silent save for the footsteps. It was not a child: children walked more lightly and besides, they usually came in groups, to run past him shouting insults at him and dares to one another. They had thrown rocks at him, until he learned not to dodge them. When he endured them stoically, they soon became bored and went off to find small crabs or starfish to torture instead. Besides, the rocks did not hurt that much, and most of them did not even hit. Most of them.

He kept his arms crossed over his scarred chest, but it took an act of will to do so. When one fears a blow and cannot know from what quarter it will come, it is hard not to try to guard one's face, even when all that is left of that face is a mouth and nose and the splintered wreckage that a hatchet has made of the eyes.

The last high tide had nearly reached him. Sometimes he dreamed of a gigantic storm, one that would come to lift him from the rocks and sand and carry him back out to sea.

Even better would be one that almost lifted him, one that would slam and crash him against the rocks, break him up into planks and beams and oakum, and scatter him wherever the waves and winds pushed him. He wondered if that would bring him oblivion, or if he would live on as a carved chunk of wizardwood, bobbing forever on the tides. Sometimes such thoughts could deepen his madness. Sometimes, as he lay on the beach, listing to starboard, he could feel the screw worms and barnacles eating into his wood, boring in and chewing deep, but never into his keel nor any of the wizardwood planking. No. That was the beauty of wizardwood; it was impervious to the assault of the sea. The beauty and the eternal condemnation.

He knew of only one liveship that had died. Tinester had perished in a fire that spread swiftly through his cargo holds full of barrels of oil and dry hides, consuming him in a matter of hours. A matter of hours of the ship screaming and begging for help. The tide had been out. Even when the blaze holed him and he sank, salt water pouring onto his internal flames, he could not sink deeply enough to douse the deck fires. His wizardwood self had burned slowly, with black greasy smoke that poured up from him into the blue sky over the harbor, but he had burned. Maybe that was the only possible peace for a liveship. Flames and a slow burning. He wondered that the children had never thought of that. Why did they fling stones when they could have set fire to his decaying hulk a long time ago? Should he suggest it to them some-time?

The footsteps were closer now. They halted. Feet grinding sand grittily against underlying stone. "Hey, Paragon." A man's voice, friendly, reassuring. It took him a moment and then he had it.

"Brashen. It's been a time."

"Over a year," the man admitted easily. "Maybe two." He came closer, and a moment later Paragon felt a warm human hand brush the point of his elbow. He unfolded his arms and reached down his right hand. He felt Brashen's small hand attempt to grasp his own.

"A year. A full turning of the seasons. That's a long time for you folk, isn't it?"

"Oh, I don't know." The man sighed. "It was a lot longer when I was a kid. Now each passing year seems shorter than the one before." He paused. "So. How have you been?"

Paragon grinned through his beard. "Now there's a question. Answer it yourself. I'm the same as I have been for the past, what, thirty of your years? At least that many, I think. Passing time has little meaning for me." It was his turn to pause. Then he asked, "So. What brings you out to see an old derelict like me?"

The man had the grace to sound embarrassed. "The usual. I need a place to sleep. A safe place."

"And you've never heard that just about the worst luck that can be found will be found aboard a ship like me." It was an old conversation between them. But they had not had it in a while, and so Paragon found it comforting to lead Brashen once more through its measures.

Brashen gave a bark of laughter. He gave a final squeeze to Paragon's hand before releasing it. "You know me, old ship. I've already got about the worst luck that anyone could hunt up. I doubt that I'll find worse aboard you. And at least I can sleep sound, knowing I've a friend watching over me. Permission to come aboard?"

"Come aboard and welcome. But watch your step. Bound to be a bit more rot than the last time you sheltered here."

He heard Brashen circle him, heard his leap and then a moment later felt the man hauling himself up and over the old railing. Strange, so strange to feel a man walk his decks after such a long time. Not that Brashen strode them easily. Hauled out as he was on the sand, the *Paragon*'s decks sloped precipitously. Brashen more clambered than walked as he crossed the deck to the forecastle door. "No more rot than the last time I was here," the man observed aloud, almost cheerily. "And there was damn little then. It's almost spooky how sound you are after all the weathering you must take."

"Spooky," Paragon agreed, and tried not to sound glum about it. "No one's been aboard since the last time you were here, so I fancy you'll find all within as you left it. Save for a bit more damp."

He could hear and feel the man moving about inside the forecastle, and then into the captain's quarters. His raised voice reached Paragon's ears. "Hey! My hammock is still here. Still sound, too. I'd forgotten all about it. You remember, the one I made last time I was here."

"Yes. I remember," Paragon called back. He smiled a rare smile of remembered pleasure. Brashen had kindled a small fire on the sand, and drunkenly instructed the ship in the ways of weaving. His hands, so much larger than a man's, had proven a challenge to Brashen as he tried to teach the blind ship the necessary knots by touch alone. "Didn't no one ever teach you anything before?" Brashen had demanded with drunken indignance as Paragon had fumbled his way through the simple motions.

"No. No one. At least, nothing like this. When I was young, I saw it done, but no one ever offered me a chance to try it for myself," Paragon had answered. He wondered how many times since then he had dragged out the memory to pass the long night hours, how many times he had held his empty hands up before him and woven imaginary lines into the simple webbing of a hammock. It was one way to keep the deeper madness at bay.

Within the captain's quarters, he knew Brashen had kicked his shoes off. They slid down into a corner, the same corner that everything slid into. But the hammock was secured to hooks that Brashen had mounted, and so it hung level as the man grunted and clambered his way into it. Paragon could feel it give with his weight, but the hooks held. It was as Brashen had said: surprisingly little new rot. As if Brashen could sense how hungry the ship was for companionship, he roused himself enough to call, "I'm really tired, Paragon. Let me sleep a few hours and then I'll tell you all my adventures since the last time I saw you. My misadventures, too."

"I can wait. Get some sleep," the ship told him affably. He wasn't sure if Brashen heard him or not. It didn't matter.

He felt the man shift in the hammock and then settle more comfortably. After that there was almost silence. The ship could sense his breathing. It was not much for company, but it was more than Paragon had had for many a month. He folded his arms more comfortably across his bare chest, and focused on the sound of Brashen breathing.

Kennit faced Sorcor across the white linen cloth on the captain's table. The mate wore a new shirt of red-and-white striped silk, and garish earrings: mermaids with tiny pearls in their navels and green glass eyes. Sorcor's scarred face looked painfully scrubbed above his beard and his hair was sleeked back from his brow with an oil that was probably supposed to be aromatic. To Kennit, the scent suggested both fish and musk. But he let nothing of that opinion show on his face. Sorcor was ill at ease enough. Formality always strained the man. Formality plus the captain's disapproval would probably paralyze his mind entirely.

The *Marietta* creaked softly against the dock. Kennit had closed the cabin's small window against the stench of Divvytown, but the noise of night revelry still penetrated in a distant cacophony. There was no crew aboard save for the ship's boy to wait the table and a single man on watch on deck. "That will do," Kennit told the boy abruptly. "Be careful cleaning those. That's pewter, not tin."

The boy left the cabin with his tray of dishes, shutting the door firmly but respectfully behind himself. For a few moments, there was almost silence within the snug chamber as Kennit deliberately considered the man who was not only his right hand on the deck, but his sounding line for the crew's temper.

Kennit leaned back slightly from the table. The white beeswax candles had burned about a third down. He and Sorcor had disposed of a sizable lamb's haunch between them. Sorcor had eaten the most of it; not even formality could curb his appetite when confronted with any food a notch better than swill. Still silent, Kennit leaned forward again, to lift a bottle of wine and refill both their long-stemmed crystal goblets. It was a vintage that Sorcor's palate probably had no appreciation for, but tonight it was not the quality of the wine but the expense of it that he wanted the mate to notice. When both glasses were near brimming, he lifted his and waited for the mate to take up his as well. He leaned forward to gently ring their glasses together. "To better things," he offered softly. With his free hand, he indicated the more recent changes in his chamber.

Sorcor had been dumbfounded when he had first entered. Kennit had always had a taste for quality, but in the past he had restrained it save for pragmatic areas. He had far rather wear small earrings of gold with flawless gemstones than ornate brass gauded with glass. The quality had been in the cut and fabric of his clothing, rather than in a vast amount of ostentatious garments. Not so now. The simplicity of his cabin had given way to glitter and splendor as he had spent every last coin of his last trip's share in Divvytown. Some of the items were not of the very finest quality, but they were the best Divvytown had to offer. And they had had the desired effect upon Sorcor. Beneath the awe in the mate's eyes were the beginnings of a gleam of avarice. Sorcor needed but to be shown to desire.

"To better things," Sorcor echoed him in his bass voice, and they drank together.

"And soon. Very soon," Kennit added as he leaned back against the cushions of his austerely carved oak chair.

Sorcor set down his glass and regarded his captain attentively. "You have something specific in mind," he guessed.

"Only the ends. The means are still to be considered. That's why I invited you to dine with me. That we might consider our next voyage, and what we desire from it."

Sorcor pursed his lips and sucked his teeth speculatively. "I desire what I've always desired from a voyage. Rich booty, and plenty of it. What else is there for a man to want?"

"A lot, dear Sorcor. A very great deal. There is power, and fame. Security in one's riches. Comfort. Homes and families safe from the slaver's whip." The last item had no place at all in Kennit's personal list of desires, but well he knew it was the fantasy of many a sailor. A fantasy he suspected they would find stifling were it ever granted to them. It didn't matter. What he was offering the man was what Sorcor thought he wanted. Kennit would have offered him sugared lice if he had believed they'd be a better bait.

Sorcor affected a clumsy nonchalance. "A man can want such things, of course. But he's only going to have them if he's born to them. A noble or lord or some such. It's never going to be for me, nor even for you, begging your pardon for saying so."

"Ah, but it will be. It will be if we have the spine to reach out and take those things for ourselves. Lords and nobles, you say, and a man has to be born to it, you say. But somewhere, there had to be the first lord. Somewhere back there, there had to be some common man who reached out and took what he wanted, and kept it, too."

Sorcor took another drink of his wine, slugging it down like beer. "I suppose," he conceded. "I suppose those things all had to get started somehow." He set his wine back down on the table and considered his captain. "How?" he finally asked, as if fearing he wouldn't like the answer.

Kennit rolled his shoulders, in a movement gentler than a shrug. "As I have told you. We reach out and take it."

"How?" Sorcor repeated stubbornly.

"How did we get this ship, and this crew? How did I get the ring on my finger, or you the earrings you wear? What we'll be doing is no different than anything we've done before. Except in scale. We'll be setting our goals a bit higher."

Sorcor shifted nervously. When he spoke, his deep voice had gone almost dangerously soft. "What do you have in mind?"

Kennit smiled at him. "It's very simple. All we must do is dare to do something no one has dared do before."

Sorcor frowned. Kennit suspected the wine was reaching his wits. "This is that 'king' stuff you were talking before, isn't it?" Before Kennit could answer, the mate shook his heavy head slowly. "It won't work, Cap'n. Pirates don't want a king."

Kennit forced his smile to remain. He shook his own head in response to his mate's charge. As he did so, he felt the blistered flesh under the linen bandage break anew. The nape of his neck grew wet with fluid. Fitting. Fitting. "No. My dear Sorcor, you took my earlier words much too literally. What do you suppose, that I see myself sitting on a throne, wearing a gold crown covered with jewels while the pirates of Divvytown bend a knee to me? Folly! Sheerest folly! No man could look at Divvytown and imagine such a thing. No. What I see is what I have told you. A man living like a lord, with a fine house and fine things, and knowing he will keep his fine house and fine things, yes and knowing his wife may sleep safely at his side, and his kiddies in their beds as well." He took a measured sip of his wine and replaced the glass on the table. "That is kingdom enough for you and me, eh, Sorcor?"

"Me? Me, too?"

There. It was reaching him at last. Kennit was proposing that Sorcor himself could have these things, not just Kennit. Kennit's smile broadened. "Of course. Of course you, why not you?" He permitted himself a deprecating laugh. "Sorcor, do you think I'd ask you to throw in with me as we have done before, would I ask you to risk everything alongside me, if all I had in mind were improving my own fortunes? Of course not! You're not such a fool. No. What I have in mind is that together we shall reach for this fortune. And not just for ourselves, no. When we are done, all our crew will have benefitted. And if Divvytown and the other pirate isles choose to follow us, they will benefit as well. But no man will be forced to throw in his hand with ours. No. It will be a free alliance of free men. So." He leaned forward across the table to his mate. "What say you?"

Sorcor blinked his eyes and looked aside from his captain's gaze. But when he did so, he must look about the finely appointed room, on the carefully arrayed wealth Kennit had set out just for that reason. There was no spot in the room where the man's eyes could rest without avarice awaking in his heart.

But in the depths of his soul, Sorcor was a more cautious sort than Kennit had given him credit. His dark eyes came back to lock gazes with Kennit's pale ones. "You speak well. And I cannot think of a reason not to say yes. But I know that does not mean there isn't a reason." He put his elbows on the table and leaned on his arms heavily. "Speak plainly. What must we do to bring these things about?"

"Dare," said Kennit briefly. The licking flame of triumph he felt would not let him sit still. He had the man, even if Sorcor himself did not know it yet. He rose to pace the small cabin, wine glass in his hand. "First, we capture their imaginations and their admiration by what we dare to do. We amass wealth, yes, but we do it as no one has before. Look you, Sorcor. I need not show you a chart. All trade that comes from Jamaillia and the Southlands must pass us before it can reach Bingtown, or Chalced and the lands beyond. This is so?"

"Of course." The mate's brow furrowed in his effort to see where this obvious fact might lead. "A ship can't get from Jamaillia to Bingtown, save that they pass the pirate isles. Unless they're fool enough to go Outside and dare the Wild Sea."

Kennit nodded agreement. "So ships and captains have but two choices. They can take the Outside Passage, where storms off the Wild Sea are fiercest and serpents thickest and the way is longest. Or they can risk the Inside Passage, with the tricky channels and currents and us pirates. Correct?"

"Serpents, too," Sorcor insisted on pointing out. "Almost as many serpents haunt the Inside Passage as the Outside now."

"True. That's true. Serpents, too," Kennit acceded easily. "Now. Imagine yourself a merchant skipper facing that choice. And a man comes to you and says, 'Sir, for a fee, I can see you safely through the Inside Passage. I've a pilot who knows the channels and the currents like the back of his hand, and not a pirate will molest you on your way.' What would you say?"

"What about the serpents?" Sorcor demanded.

" 'And the serpents are no worse within the sheltered water of the passage than without, and a ship stands a better chance within them than if she's on the Outside, battling both serpents and storms at once. And perhaps we'll even have an escort ship for you, one full of skilled archers and laden with Baley's Fire, and if serpents attack you, the escort will take them on while you escape.' What would you say, merchant skipper?"

Sorcor narrowed his eyes suspiciously. "I'd say, how much is this going to cost me?"

"Exactly. And I'd name a fat price, but you'd be willing to pay it. Because you'd just add that fat price to your goods at the end of your run. Because you'd know you'd get through safe to sell those goods. Paying a fat price for that assurance is much better than sailing free and taking a big chance you'll lose it all."

"Wouldn't work," Sorcor declared.

"Why not?"

"Because the other pirates would kill you if you gave out the secret ways of our channels. Or they'd let you lead a fat ship in like a lamb to the slaughter, and then they'd fall on you both. Why should they sit back and let you have all the money?"

"Because they'd get a cut of it, one and all. Every ship that came through would have to pay into a treasury and everyone would get a cut of that treasury. Plus, we'd make them promise that there'd be no more raids against us or our towns. Our folk could sleep peaceful at night, knowing that their daddies and brothers would be coming home safe to them, and that there'd be no Satrap's boats coming to burn their towns and take them as slaves." He paused. "Look at us now. We waste our lives chasing their ships. When we do catch one, then it's bloodshed and mayhem, and sometimes for naught. Sometimes the whole ship goes down, cargo and all, or sometimes we battle for hours and what do we get? A hold full of cheap cotton or some such trash. Meanwhile, the Satrap's ships and soldiers are putting into our villages and towns, and rounding up everyone who doesn't flee to be carted off as slaves, in revenge for our pirating. Now look at it my way. Instead of risking our lives to attack every tenth ship that comes through, and perhaps come up with nothing, we'd get a cut of every cargo on every ship that passed through our waters. We'd control it all. At no risk to our lives save what any sailor must face. Meanwhile, our homes and families are safe. The riches we garner, we keep to enjoy."

An idea dawned slowly in Sorcor's eyes. "And we'd say no slavers. We could cut the slaves-trade's throat. No slaveships, no slavers could use the Inland Passage."

Kennit knew a moment's dismay. "But the fattest trade to be fleeced is the slaves-trade ships. They'd be the ones that would pay the most to get through fast and easy, with their cargo alive and healthy still. What percentage of their wares do they get through . . ."

"Men," Sorcor interrupted harshly. "Women and kiddies. Not wares. If you'd ever been inside one of those ship . . . and I don't mean on the deck, I mean inside, chained up in a hold . . . you wouldn't say 'wares.' No. No slavers, Kennit. Slavers made us what we are. If we're going to change that, then we start by doing to them what they done to us. We take their lives away. Besides. It's not just that they're evil. They bring the serpents. The stink of slaveships is what lured the serpents into our channels in the first place. We get rid of the slaveships, maybe the serpents will go, too. Hells, Cap'n, they lure the serpents right into our islands and ways, chumming them along with dead slaves. And they bring disease. They breed sickness in those holds full of poor wretches, sickness we never knew or had before. Every time a slaveship ties up to take on water, they leave disease in their wake. No. No slavers."

"All right, then," Kennit agreed mildly. "No slavers." He'd never suspected Sorcor had an idea in his skull, let alone that he'd felt so passionately about something. A miscalculation. He looked anew at Sorcor. The man might have to be discarded. Not just yet, and perhaps not for some time. But at some point in the future, he might outlive his usefulness. Kennit decided he must keep that in mind, and make no long-range plans based on Sorcor's skills. He smiled at him. "You are right, of course. I am sure there are many of our folk who will agree with you, and can be won over to us with such an idea." He nodded again as if considering it. "Yes. No slavers, then. But all of this, of course, is a way down the wind. Were we to voice such ideas now, no one would listen to us. They'd say that what we suggested was impossible. Or every man would want to try it for himself, competing with every other. It would be ship against ship. We don't want that. So we must keep this idea quiet and private between us, until we've got every pirate in the islands looking up to us and ready to believe what we tell them."

"That's likely so," Sorcor agreed after a moment's pondering. "So. How do we get them to listen to us?"

Finally. The question he had been leading him to ask. Kennit came swiftly back to the table. He forced himself to pause for the drama of the moment. He set his own glass down, and uncorked the bottle. He refilled Sorcor's glass, and added a dollop to his own nearly full glass. "We make them believe we can do the impossible. By doing things all others deem impossible. Such as, say, capturing a liveship and using it as our main vessel."

Sorcor scowled at him. "Kennit, old friend, that's crazy. No wooden ship can capture a liveship. They're too fleet. I've heard tell that the ship herself can scent a passage through a channel, and cry it to her steersman. And that they can feel the luff of the wind, and catch and use a breath of air that wouldn't budge another ship. Besides, even if we did fall upon one and manage to kill off her crew, the ship itself would be no good to us. They'll only sail for their own family members. Anyone else, they turn on. The ship would run herself aground, or onto the rocks, or just turn turtle on us. Look at that death ship, what was his name? The one that went mad and turned on his own family and crew? He rolled and took all hands with him. Not once, but three times, or so I've heard. And the last time they found him, he was floating upside down in the mouth of Bingtown harbor itself. Some say the ghost crew brought him home, others that he came back to show them Traders what he'd done. They dragged him out and beached him, and there he's been ever since. *Pariah*. That was his name. The *Pariah*."

"The *Paragon*," Kennit corrected him with wry amusement. "His name was the *Paragon*, though even his own family have taken to calling him the *Pariah*. Yes, I've heard all the old myths and legends about liveships, Sorcor. But that's what they are. Myths and legends. I believe a liveship could be taken and could be used. And if the heart of the ship could be won over, you'd have a vessel for piracy that no other ship could stand against. It's true, what you say about the currents and winds and liveships. True, also, that they can sense a serpent long before a man can spot him, and cry it out to the archers to be ready. A liveship would be the perfect vessel for piracy. And for charting out new passages through the Pirate Isles, or battling serpents. I'm not saying we should forsake all else and go hunting a liveship. I'm just saying that if one comes our way, instead of saying there's no use in pursing it, let's give it a chase. If we win it, we win it. If not, well, plenty of other ships get away from us. We'll have lost no more than we had before."

"Why a liveship?" Sorcor asked bewilderedly. "I don't get it."

"I . . . want one. That's why."

"Well, then. I'll tell you what I want." For some odd reason, Sorcor thought they were striking a bargain. "I'll go along with it," he conceded grudgingly. "We'll chase liveships when we see them, though I don't see much use to it. Not that I'll admit that to the men. In front of the men, I'll be as hot to go after them as a hound on a scent. But you make me this balance. For every liveship we chase, we go after the next slaver we smell. And we board them, and throw the crew to the serpents, and see the slaves safe back to a town. No offense to your judgment, Cap'n, but I think that if we stop enough slavers and do away with the crews, we'll gain the respect of the others a lot faster than by capturing a liveship."

Kennit did not mask his scowl. "I think you overestimate the righteousness and morality of our fellows here in Divvytown. I think they'd be as likely to think us soft-headed fools to waste our time pursuing slavers only to free the cargo."

Perhaps the fine wine had gone to Sorcor's head faster than a lesser vintage would have. Or perhaps Kennit had unwittingly found the man's one nerve. His deep voice was deadly soft as he pointed out, "You only think so because you've never been chained hand and foot in a stinking hold when you're scarcely more than a lad. You've never had your head gripped in a vise to still you while a tattooist jabs your new master's mark into your face."

The man's eyes glittered, turned inward towards a darkness only his sight could pierce. He drew a slow breath. "And then they put me to work in a tanner's pit, curing hides. They cared nothing for what it did to my own hide. I saw older men there coughing blood from their lungs. No one cared, and I knew it was only a matter of time before I was one of them. One night I killed two men and got away. But where was I to go? North where it's all ice and snow and barbarians? Back south to where my tattoo would mark me as an escaped slave, easy money for anyone who wanted to club me down and return me to my owner? Or should I make for the Cursed Shores, and live like an animal until some demon drained my blood? No. The only thing left to a man like me was the Pirate Isles and a pirate's life. But it's not what I would have chosen, Kennit, given the chance to choose. There's damn few here would have chosen this." His voice wandered off as did his eyes. He stared past Kennit into the dim corner of the room, seeing nothing for a time. Then his gaze snapped suddenly back to Kennit's. "For every liveship we chase, we run down a slaver. That's all I'm asking. I give you a shot at your dream, you allow me one at mine."

"Fair enough," Kennit declared brusquely. He knew when the final bargain had been set out on a table. "Fair enough, then. For every liveship, a slaver."

A coldness welled up in Wintrow. It had filled his belly first and now it flowed out through him. He literally shook with it. He hated how it made his voice waver, as if he were a child on the brink of crying when all he was trying to do was present his case rationally and calmly, as he had been trained. As he had been taught in his beloved monastery. The memory of the cool stone halls where peace flowed with the wind rose up unbidden. He tried to take strength from it. Instead it only unmanned him more. He was not there, he was here, in the family's dining hall. The low table of golden oak polished until it shone, the cushioned benches and lounges that surrounded the table, the paneled walls and the paintings of ships and ancestors all reminded him that he was here, in Bingtown. He cleared his throat and tried to steady his voice as he looked from his mother to his father to his grandmother. They were all seated at the same table, but they were grouped at one end of it, like a panel about to pass judgment on him. As perhaps they were. He took a breath.

"When you sent me off to be a priest, it was not my choice." Again he looked from face to face, trying to find some memory in them of that devastating day. "We stood in this very room. I clung to you, Mother, and promised I'd be good forever, if only you wouldn't send me away. But you told me I had to go. You told me that I was a first-born son, dedicated to Sa from the moment that I drew breath. You said you couldn't break your promise to Sa, and you gave me over to the wandering priest to take me to the monastery at Kells. Don't you remember at all? You stood there, Father, over by that window, on a day so bright that when I looked at you, all I could see was a black shadow against the sunlight. You said not a word that day. Grandmother, you told me to be brave, and gave me a little bundle with a few cakes from the kitchen to keep me on my way."

Again he looked from face to face, seeking some discomfort with what they were doing to him, some trace of guilt that would indicate they knew they were wronging him. His mother was the only one to show any signs of uneasiness. He kept trying to catch her eye, to make her speak her thoughts, but her gaze slid away from him to his father. The man looked as if he were carved of stone.

"I did what you told me to do," he said simply. The words sounded weak, whiny. "I left here and went off with a stranger. The way to the monastery was hard, and when I got there, everything was foreign. But I stayed and I tried. And after a time, it came to be my home, and I realized how correct your decision for me had been." Memories of his first taste of priestly life were bittersweet; the strangeness and then the rightness of it all washed over him yet again. Tears pricked at his eyes as he said, "I love serving Sa. I have learned so much, grown so much, in ways I cannot even express to you. And I know that I'm only at the beginning, that it is all just starting to unfold for me. It's like . . ." He fumbled for a metaphor. "When I was younger, it was like life was a beautiful gift, wrapped in exquisite paper and adorned with ribbons. And I loved it, even though all I knew of it was the outside of the package. But in the last year or so, I've finally started to see there is something even better inside the package. I'm learning to see past the fancy wrappings, to the heart of things. I'm right on the edge. I can't stop now."

"It was wrong," his father conceded suddenly. But even as Wintrow's heart started to soar with relief, the sea-captain went on. "All those years ago, I knew it was wrong to send you away. I stood there and I kept my mouth shut and I let your mother have her way, because it seemed so important to her. And small as Selden was, he was a brave little fellow, and I knew I'd have a son to follow after me."

He rose from his seat at the table and crossed the room, to stare out the window as he had on that morning years ago. Kyle Haven shook his head at himself. "But I should have followed my instincts. I knew it was a bad decision, and so it has proved. The time has come when I, when this family, needs a young son to rise up and take his place on the family ship, and we are not prepared. Selden is still too young. Two years from now, even one perhaps, and I'd take him as a ship's boy." He turned back to face the room. "We brought this on ourselves, all of us. And so all of us will have to endure, without complaining, the pain of correcting that mistake. It means that you women will have to manage on your own here for yet another year. Somehow our creditors must be made to wait, and you must do whatever it takes to wring a profit out of our holdings. Those that cannot be made profitable must be sold to shore up those that can. It means another year of sailing for me, and a hard year, for we will have to sail fast and traffic in that which is most profitable. And for you, Wintrow, it means a single year in which I must teach you all you should have learned in the last five, a single year for you to learn the ways of a man and a sailor." He paced the room as he spoke, ticking off orders and goals on his fingers. Wintrow suddenly knew that this was how he spoke to his mate on board ship, lining out tasks to be done. This was Captain Haven, accustomed to unquestioning obedience, and he was sure to be astonished by what was about to happen.

Wintrow stood, pushing his chair back carefully. "I am going back to the monastery. I have little to pack, and all I can do here I have done. I shall be leaving today." He looked around the table. "I promised Vivacia when I left her this morning that someone would come down to spend the rest of the day with her. I suggest you wake Althea and ask her to go."

His father's face reddened with instant rage. "Sit down and stop talking nonsense," he barked. "You'll do as you're told. That'll be your first lesson to learn."

Wintrow thought the beating of his heart was making his whole body shake. Was he afraid of his own father? Yes. It took all the defiance he could muster to remain standing. He had nothing left to speak with. Yet even as he met his father's glare and did not look away, even as he stood still and silent as the furious man advanced on him, a cool and particular part of himself observed, "yes, but it's only physical fear of physical things." The notion caught up his whole mind in its web, so he paid no attention to his mother crying out and then shrieking, "Oh, Kyle, no, please, please don't, just talk to him, persuade him, don't, oh, please don't!" and his grandmother's voice raised in command, a fierce shout of "This is my home and you will not . . . ."

Then the fist hit the side of his face, making a tremendous crack as it impacted. So fast and so slowly he went down, amazed or ashamed that he had neither lifted a hand to defend himself nor fled, and all the time somewhere a philosophical priest was saying, "physical fear, ah, I see, but is there another kind, and what would have to be done to me to make me feel it?" Then the flagstone floor struck him, hard and cool despite the dawning heat of the day. Losing consciousness felt like he was sinking down into the floor, becoming one with it as he had with the ship, save that the floor thought only of black darkness. So did Wintrow.

CHAPTER TEN

CONFRONTATIONS

KYLE, I WILL NOT HAVE IT!"

HER MOTHER'S VOICE ECHOED CLEARLY DOWN the stone-flagged hall. The strident ring of it made Althea want to hurry her headache off in the other direction, even as the mention of Kyle's name made her want to charge into battle. Caution, she counseled herself. The first thing to do was to find out what kind of weather she was sailing into. She slowed her step as she made her way down the hall to the dining room.

"He's my son. I'll discipline him as I see fit. It may seem harsh right now, but the faster he learns to mind, and mind quickly, the easier it will go for him on the ship. He'll come round, and you'll find he's not much hurt. More shocked than anything else, most likely."

Even Althea could hear the vague note of anxiety in Kyle's voice. That muffled sound, she decided, was her sister weeping. What had he done to little Selden? A terrible dread rose up in her, a desire to flee this messy domestic life and go back to . . . what? The ship? That was no escape any longer. She halted where she stood, until the dizzying misery could pass.

"That was not discipline. It's brawling, and it has no place in my home. Last night, I was willing to make some allowances for you. It had been a horrible day already, and Althea's appearance was shocking. But this, inside my own walls, between blood-kin . . . no. Wintrow's not a child any more, Kyle. Even if he were, a spanking would not have been the answer. He was not throwing a temper tantrum, he was trying to make you see his side of things. One doesn't spank a child for courteously voicing an opinion. Nor does one strike a man for it."

"You don't understand," Kyle said flatly. "In a few days he's going to be living aboard a ship, where opinions don't matter unless they're mine. He won't have time to disagree. He won't even have time to think. On a ship, a hand obeys, at that instant. Wintrow's just had his first lesson in what happens if he doesn't." In a quieter voice he added, "It just may save my son's life someday."

Althea heard the scuff of his boots as he walked. "Come, get up, Keffria. He'll come around in a few minutes, and when he does, I don't want you fussing over him. Don't encourage him in behavior I won't tolerate. If he thinks we're divided on this, he'll only fight it the more. And the more he fights it, the more times he's going to meet the floor."

"I hate this," Keffria said in a small dull voice. "Why does it have to be this way? Why?"

"It doesn't," her mother said flatly. "And it won't. I tell you this plainly, Kyle Haven, I won't tolerate it. This family has never treated one another so, and we are not going to start on the day after Ephron's death. Not in my home." Ronica Vestrit left no room for disagreement.

It was the wrong tone to take with Kyle. Althea could have told her that. Setting herself up directly against him would only bring out the worst in him. It did.

"Fine. As soon as he comes round, I'll take him down to the ship. He can learn his manners there. Actually, that's probably for the best anyway. If he learns a bit of the ship in port, he won't have to scramble so hard when we're under weigh. And I won't have to listen to women argue with every order I give him."

"Aboard my ship or in my home," her mother began, but Kyle cut across her words with words of his own that made Althea both cold and hot with anger.

"Keffria's ship. And mine, as I am her husband. What happens aboard the *Vivacia* is no longer your affair, Ronica. For that matter, I believe by Bingtown laws of inheritance, this house is now hers as well. To run as we see fit."

There was a terrible silence. When Kyle spoke again, there was an offer of apology in his voice. "At least, it could be that way. To the detriment of all of us. I don't propose a splitting of our ways, Ronica. Obviously the family will prosper best if we work together, from a common home toward a common goal. But I cannot do that with my hands tied. You must see it is so. You've done very well, for a woman, all these years. But times are changing, and Ephron should not have left you to cope with everything on your own. As much as I respected the man . . . perhaps because I respected the man, I must learn from his mistakes. I'm not going to just sail off into the sunset and tell Keffria to mind things and manage until I return. I have to make provisions now to be able to stay home and run things. Nor am I going to let Wintrow come aboard the *Vivacia* and behave like some spoiled prince. You've seen what became of Althea: she's willful and thoughtless of others to the point of uselessness. No, worse, to the point of doing damage to the family name and reputation. I'll tell you bluntly, I don't know if you two can draw the lines with her that need to be drawn. Perhaps the simplest thing to do with her would be to marry her off, preferably to a man who does not live in Bingtown. . . ."

Like a ship under full sail, Althea swept around the corner and into the room. "Would you care to mouth your insults to my face, Kyle?"

He was not at all surprised to see her. "I thought I saw your shadow. How long have you been eavesdropping, little sister?"

"Long enough to know that you intend no good for my family or our ship." Althea tried not to be rattled by his calmness. "Who do you think you are, to speak to my mother and sister so, calmly telling them what you plan to do, how you intend to come back and 'run' things?"

"I think I'm the man of this family now," he proclaimed bluntly.

Althea smiled coldly. "You can be the man of this family all you like. But if you think you're keeping my ship, you're mistaken."

Kyle sighed dramatically. "I thought it was only your so-called Rain Wild kin that believed that saying a thing often enough can make it so," he observed sarcastically. "Little sister, you are such a fool. Not only does the common law of Bingtown recognize your sister as sole heir, but it was put into writing and signed by your father himself. Will you oppose even him in this?"

His words disemboweled her. She felt that everything that had ever given her strength had been torn from her. She had almost managed to convince herself that yesterday had been an accident, that her father could never have consciously intended to take the ship from

her. It had only been that he had been in great pain and dying. But to
hear that it was in writing, and sealed by him . . . NO. Her eyes
darted from Kyle to her mother and then back again. "I don't care
what my father was deceived into signing on his deathbed," she said in
a low but furious voice. "I know that Vivacia is mine. Mine in a way
you can never claim her, Kyle. And I tell you now, I will not be
stopped until I have her under my command—"

"Your command!" Kyle gave a great bark of laughter. "You command a ship? You're not even fit to serve aboard a ship. You have this
great conceit about your abilities, this self-deception that you are
some kind of a seaman. You're not! Your father kept you aboard to
keep you from getting into trouble on shore, as near as I can see.
You're not even a good sailor."

Althea opened her mouth to speak, but a groan from Wintrow,
sprawled on the floor, turned all eyes that way. Keffria started forward, but Kyle stopped her with a gesture. Their mother ignored both
his look and his hand, however, to go to the boy. He sat up, obviously
dizzy, holding both hands to the sides of his head. With an effort he
focused his eyes on his grandmother. "Am I all right?" he asked her
dazedly.

"I hope so," she responded gravely. She gave a small sigh. "Althea, would you fetch me a cold, wet cloth?"

"The boy is fine," Kyle proclaimed grumpily, but Althea ignored
him. She stormed off down the hall to fetch her mother a wet rag,
wondering all the time why she did so. She suspected her mother of
having deceived her father, of getting him to sign something he never
intended. So why did she so meekly obey her now? She didn't know,
save that perhaps it was to give herself a moment away from Kyle
before she killed him.

As she went down the hall to the pump room, she wondered what
had become of her world. Never before had there been such doings in
her home. People shouting at one another in her home was strange
enough, but Kyle had knocked his own son cold on the floor. She still
couldn't believe it had happened. These things were too foreign to
her, so shocking she had no idea how to deal with them or even what
to feel. She doused a towel under the cold stream of water she pumped
up, and wrung the cloth out well. A very nervous serving woman was
lurking there in the water room.

"Do you need my help?" the woman all but whispered.

"No. No, everything is under control. Captain Haven just had a
bit of a temper tantrum," Althea heard herself lie calmly. Under control, she thought to herself. It felt far from that to her. Instead she felt

like she was a juggler's club, flying through the air, not knowing what hand would next seize her and fling her into a rhythm. No hand, perhaps. Perhaps she would just go flying off, out of control, never again to be a part of her family's pattern. She smiled bitterly at the ridiculous image, and put the wet cloth into an earthenware bowl before she bore it down the hall to the dining room. When she got there, Wintrow and her mother were seated at a corner of the low table. Wintrow looked pale and shaken, her mother very determined. She held both the boy's hands in her own as she spoke to him earnestly.

Kyle, arms crossed on his chest, stood by the window. His back was to the room, but Althea could sense his indignation. Keffria stood next to him, looking up at him imploringly, but he appeared unaware of her existence.

". . . all in Sa's hands." Her mother spoke earnestly to her nephew. "I believe that He has sent you back to us, and created this bond between you and the ship for a reason. It's meant to be, Wintrow. Can you accept it, as you once accepted the way we sent you off with the priest?"

A bond between Wintrow and her ship. It could not be. Her heart turned to ice in her chest, but strangely her body kept moving and her eyes kept seeing. Wintrow's whole attention was on his grandmother's face. He simply looked at her. His Haven blood showed plain in him, in the set of his chin and the anger in his eyes. Then, as Althea set the bowl and cloth down next to him, she saw the boy take control of himself. In half a dozen breaths, his features relaxed, and for a fleeting instant she glimpsed not only a strong resemblance to her father but to her own image in the looking-glass. It shocked her into silence.

When the lad spoke, his voice was mild and reasoned. "So I've heard people speak a thousand times. It's Sa's will, they say. Bad weather, late storms, stillborn children. Sa's will." He reached for the damp cloth in the bowl, folded it carefully and pressed it against his jaw. The side of his face was already starting to purple, and the boy still looked shaky and unfocused. The edges of his words were soft; Althea guessed it was painful for him to speak. But he did not seem angry, or cowed, or frightened, only intent on reaching his grandmother with his words, as if by winning her to his side he could save his own life. Perhaps he could.

"Weather and storms I am willing to say are his will. Stillborn children, perhaps. Though not when the husband had beaten his wife but the day before . . ." his voice trailed off into some unpleasant memory. Then his eyes came back to his grandmother's face. "I think

Sa gave us our lives, and his will is for us to live them well. He gives us obstacles, yes. . . . I have heard folk rail against his cruelty and loudly ask 'why, why?' But the next day the same folk will take their saws and go out and cut limbs from their fruit trees, and dig up young trees and move them far from where they sprouted. 'They will grow better and yield more,' the orchard workers say. They do not stand by the trees and explain that it is for their own good."

He lifted the cloth from his face and refolded it to find a cooler spot. "My mind wanders," he said unhappily. "Just when I want to speak most clearly to you. Grandmother. I do not think it is Sa's will for me to leave his priesthood and live aboard a ship so that our family may prosper financially. I am not even sure it is your will. I think it is my father's will. To get his way, he proposes breaking a promise, and breaking my heart. Nor am I unaware that this unwelcome 'gift' he thrusts upon me was snatched but yesterday from my Aunt Althea's hands."

For the first time he turned his eyes to Althea. Despite the pain and bruised skin, for an instant her father seemed to look out of those eyes. The same infinite patience cushioning an iron will. This was not some frail, cowering priest boy, but a man's mind in a boy's changing body, she realized in amazement.

"Even your own son recognizes the injustice of what you do," she accused Kyle. "Your snatching Vivacia from me has nothing to do with whether or not you believe I can command her. It is solely a matter of your own greed."

"Greed?" Kyle shouted in disdain. "Greed? Oh, I like that! Greed makes me want to take over a ship so ridiculously in debt, I'll be lucky to pay her off before I die. Greed makes me want to step forward and take responsibility for a household with no concept of wise money management. Althea, if I thought you had any capacity to be useful aboard the *Vivacia*, I'd seize on the chance of making you work for a change. No. More than that. If you could show me but one sign of true seamanship, if you had a single ship's ticket to your belt, I'd make you a gift of the damn ship and all her debts with her. But you're nothing but a spoiled little girl."

"You liar!" Althea cried in infinite disgust.

"By Sa, I swear it's so!" Kyle roared angrily. "If but one reputable captain would vouch for your seamanship, I'd hand the ship over to you tomorrow! But all of Bingtown knows you for what you are. A dabbler and a pretense."

"The ship would vouch for her," Wintrow observed in a wavering voice. He lifted a hand to his forehead, as if to hold his head together.

"If the ship vouched for her, would you do as you've sworn? For by Sa, you've offered that oath, and we all witnessed it. You'd have to live up to it. I cannot believe this quarreling and anger was what my grandfather willed for us. It is so simple for us to restore a balance. If Althea was on board Vivacia, I could go back to my monastery. We could all go back to where we belong. Where we were happy . . ." His voice trailed off as he realized all eyes were on him. His father's look was black with fury, but Ronica Vestrit had lifted her hand to her mouth as if his words had cut her to the quick.

"I've had enough of this whining!" Kyle suddenly exploded. He crossed the room in a few strides, to lean on the table and glare down on his son. "Is this what the priests taught you? To twist things about to get your own way? It shames me that a boy of my own bloodlines could use such tricks on his own grandmother. Stand up!" he barked, and when Wintrow stared up at him wordlessly, bellowed "Stand up!"

The young priest hesitated a moment, and then came to his feet. He opened his mouth to speak, but his father spoke first. "You are thirteen years old, even if you look more like ten and behave like three. Thirteen. By law, in Bingtown, a son's labor belongs to his father until he is fifteen years old. Oppose me and I'll invoke that law. I don't care if you wear a brown robe, I don't care if you grow sacred antlers from your brow. Until you are fifteen, you'll work that ship. Do you understand me?"

Even Althea was shocked at the near-blasphemy of Kyle's words. Wintrow's voice quavered as he replied, but he stood straight. "As a priest of Sa, I am bound only by those civil laws that are just and righteous. You invoke a civil law to break your promise. When you gave me to Sa, you gave my labor to Sa as well. I no longer belong to you." He glanced about, from his mother to his grandmother, then added, almost apologetically, "I am not even truly a member of this family any more. I have been given to Sa."

Ronica stood to block him, but Kyle brushed past her with a force that sent the older woman staggering. With a cry, Keffria sprang to her mother's side. Kyle gripped Wintrow by the front of his robe and shook him until his head whipped back and forth. His words were distorted by rage. "Mine," he roared at the boy. "You are mine. And you'll shut up and do as you're told. Now!" He stilled the boy's body and then hauled him up on his toes. "Get yourself down to that ship. Report to the mate. Tell him you're the new ship's boy, and that's all you are. The ship's boy. Understand?"

Althea had watched in horrified fascination. She was dimly aware that her mother was now holding and trying to comfort a sobbing, near-hysterical Keffria. Two servants, no longer able to restrain their curiosity, were peeping around the corner of the door. Althea knew she should intervene, but all that was happening was so far outside her experience that she could only gape. Kitchen servants gossiped of having squabbles like this at home, or one heard of tradesmen apprenticing their sons against their wills. She'd heard of ship's discipline like this on other vessels. Things like this simply never happened in the homes of Old Trader families. Or if it did, it was never spoken of.

"Do you understand me?" Kyle demanded, as if shouting louder at the boy would make his words more comprehensible. Dazed as he was, Wintrow still managed a nod. Kyle let go of his shirt front. The boy staggered, then caught at the table's edge. He stood, head hanging.

"Now means now!" Kyle barked in angry triumph. His head swiveled to the door and a gaping serving man there. "You! Welf! Stop your gawking and escort my son down to the *Vivacia*. See that he packs and takes everything he came here with, for he'll be living on the ship from now on."

As Welf hastened into the room to take Wintrow's arm and lead him out of the room, Kyle rounded on Althea. His success at bullying his son seemed to have bolstered his courage, for he challenged her with, "Are you wise enough to take a lesson from this, sister?"

Althea kept her voice even and low. "I'd be very surprised if we had not all learned something about you today, Kyle. Chiefly that there is very little you won't do in your ambition to control the Vestrit family."

"Control?" Kyle stared at her incredulously, and then turned to the other two women to see if they were as astonished as he was. But Ronica met his gaze with a black stare, while Keffria sobbed against her shoulder. "Is that what you think this is about? Control?" He shook his head and gave a brittle laugh. "This is about salvage. Damn me, I don't know why I try. You all look at me as if I were a criminal, when all I'm trying to do is keep this family afloat. Keffria! You know what this is about. We've talked about this."

He turned towards his wife. She finally lifted her tear-stained face to meet his gaze, but there was no understanding in her eyes. He shook his head in disbelief. "What am I supposed to do?" he asked of them all. "Our holdings are losing money every day, we've a liveship we're still paying the money lenders for, our creditors are threatening to start confiscating our holdings, and you all seem to think we should genteelly ignore it and take tea together. No, I take that back. Althea seems to think she should hasten our progress toward ruin by keeping the liveship as a toy for herself, while she spends her evenings getting drunk with the local water rats and having a bit of slap and tickle on the side."

"Stop it, Kyle," Ronica warned him in a low voice.

"Stop what? Telling you what you already know but refuse to recognize? Listen to me, all of you, just for a few moments." He paused and took a deep breath, as if trying to set aside his anger and frustration. "I have my children to think of, Selden and Malta. Just like Ephron, I, too, will die someday. And I don't intend for them to inherit naught but a mass of debts and a bad name. Ephron left you no sons to protect you, Ronica, no men to take over the running of the holdings. So I step up, as a dutiful son-in-law, to do what must be done, however painful. I've given it a lot of thought these last few months, and I believe I can get us back on our feet. I've established a number of contacts in Chalced, ready to deal with us. It is not really that unusual a plan: we must work the ship, and work her hard, running the most profitable cargoes as swiftly as we can transport them. In the meanwhile, we must evaluate all our holdings, without sentiment, and keep only those that can actually give us a profit this year. But even more important, we must not panic our creditors. If we sell things off wildly, they will think we are going under, and will close in on us, to get a share of what is left before it is gone. And, quite frankly, if they see Althea out drinking and carousing with lowlifes, as if there is no hope nor pride left in the family, that, too, will have its effect. Blacken your name, Althea, and you blacken my daughter's with yours. Someday I hope to see Malta make a good marriage. She will not ever receive the attention of honorable men if you have established yourself as a drunk and a slattern."

"How dare you—" Althea growled.

"I dare much, for my children. I'll see Wintrow hammered into a man, even if he grows up thinking he hates me for it. I'll see a sturdy financial basis back under this family, even if I have to work that liveship as you never could to do it. If you cared for your own kin even half as much as I do, you'd be straightening yourself up and presenting yourself as a lady and trying to make an acceptable marriage to shore up the family fortunes."

A cold fury now possessed Althea. "So I should whore myself out to the highest bidder, so long as he'll call me wife and offer a good bride price?"

"Better than to the lowest bidder, as you seemed so intent on doing last night." Kyle replied as coldly.

Althea drew breath, swelling like an angry cat, but her mother's cold voice cut across her quarrel with Kyle.

"Enough."

It was a single word, quietly spoken. As if she were setting down an armful of bedding, she moved Keffria to a nearby chair and deposited her in it. Something in the finality of her tone had silenced them all. Even Keffria's sobs were stilled. Her small, dark mother seemed even smaller in her dark mourning garments, but when she imposed herself between Althea and Kyle, they both stepped back. "I am not going to shout," she told them both. "Nor am I going to repeat myself. So I suggest you both pay attention, and commit to memory what I am going to tell you. Althea. I address you first, because I have not had the opportunity to truly speak to you since you landed. Kyle, do not even think of interrupting, not even to agree with me. Now."

She drew a breath and showed an instant of uncertainty. She approached Althea and took both her unresisting hands in hers. "My daughter. I know you feel yourself wronged. You expected to inherit the ship. It was your father's plan for you. He is gone, and though it pains me, I will speak plainly of such things. He always treated you as if you were one of the sons we lost. If your brothers had survived the plague . . . but they did not. But, back when the boys were alive, he always said the land would go to his daughters, the ship to his sons. And although he never said so plainly, after our boys died, I believe that he intended Keffria to inherit the land holdings, and you the ship. But he also intended to live until he was an old man, to see the debt on the ship and the notes against our holdings paid off, and to see you married to a man who would sail the *Vivacia* for you. No. Be quiet!" she said harshly as Althea opened her mouth to object.

"It is hard enough to say these things. If I am interrupted, we shall never get this over with," she went on in a softer voice. She lifted her head up straight and met her daughter's eyes firmly. "If you wish to blame someone for your disappointment, blame me. For when I could no longer deny that your father was dying, I sent for Curtil, our old adviser. And between us, we set on paper what I believed best, and I persuaded your father to set his sign to it. I persuaded him, Althea, I did not deceive him. Even your father finally saw the wisdom of what we had to do. If the family fortunes were divided now, none of us would survive. As Keffria is elder with children to provide for, I did as tradition decreed and made her the sole heir." Ronica Vestrit looked away from Althea's shocked stare to her other daughter. Keffria still sat on the bench, her head on the table, but her weeping was stilled. Kyle moved to set a hand on his wife's shoulder. Althea could not decide if he were comforting her or claiming her. Her mother spoke on. "Keffria knew of her inheritance. She also knows that the document states plainly that she must continue to provide for her sister's maintenance until such time as Althea makes an appropriate marriage, at which time Althea is to be dowered with a goodly sum. So Keffria is bound, not only by blood but by written word, to do well by you."

Althea's gaze of dismay had not changed. "Althea," her mother pleaded. "Please try to see it impartially. I have been as fair as I could. If the ship had been left to you, you would have barely enough to operate her. It takes coin to provision a ship and hire a crew and maintain and refit her, and a profitable voyage might still leave you scrambling to make a payment on the note and still have enough money to sail again. And if you did not show a profit, then what? The note on the ship is secured also with the land holdings. There was no way to sensibly divide the inheritance. It must be used together to pull itself out of debt."

"So I have nothing," Althea said quietly.

"Althea, your sister would never let you lack—" her mother began, but Althea shocked her by blurting out, "I don't care. I don't care, really, if I am a pauper or not. Yes, I dreamed that Vivacia would be mine. Because she is mine, mother, in a way that I cannot make you understand. In the same way that Seddon Dib's carriage horses pull his carriage, but all know their hearts belong to his stable boy. Vivacia's heart is mine, and I am hers. I look forward to no better marriage than that. Keep whatever coin she brings in, let all say she belongs to Keffria. Just let me sail her. That's all I'm asking, mother, Keffria. Just let me sail her and I'll be no trouble to you, I won't dispute your will in all else." Her desperate eyes besought first her mother's face and then the tear-stained visage that Keffria lifted to her. "Please," she breathed, "please."

"No." It was Kyle who spoke. "No. I've already given orders that you are not to be allowed on the ship, and I won't change them. You see how she is," he announced, turning to Ronica and Keffria. "She has not a practical notion in her head. All she wishes is to have her own way, to continue as she always has. She would remain her father's willful daughter, living aboard ship, taking no responsibility beyond playing sailor, and coming home to stroll through the shops, picking out whatever she fancies and have it set to her father's account. Only now it would be her sister's and hence, mine. No, Althea. Your childhood is over with your father's death. It is time you started behaving as befits a daughter of this family."

"I am not talking to you!" Althea flared. "You have no concept of what I am speaking of. To you Vivacia is no more than a ship, even if she speaks aloud to you. To me she is a member of my family, closer to me than a sister. She needs me to be aboard her, and I need to sail her. She would sail for me as she never will for you, with her own heart as the wind."

"Girlish fancies," Kyle scoffed. "Tripe. You walked away from her in anger on the day she was quickened, leaving Wintrow to spend the first night with her. If you'd had all these great feelings for her, you could not have done that. She seems to like him well enough, and he'll be aboard to keep her company or whatever it is. And he'll be learning to work as a true sailor, not mooning about the ship or getting drunk in foreign ports. No, Althea. There's no fitting place aboard the *Vivacia* for you, and I won't have you sowing discord or setting up a rivalry with Wintrow for the ship's favor."

"Mother?" Althea pleaded desperately.

Her mother looked grieved. "Had I not seen you last night, drunk and bedraggled, I would oppose Kyle in this. I would believe he was being far too harsh." She sighed heavily. "But I can't deny what I've seen with my own eyes. Althea, I know you love the *Vivacia*. If your father had lived . . . there's no use in wondering about that, I suppose. Instead, it is time, perhaps, for you to let her go. I have seen that Wintrow has the makings of a good man. He will do well by the ship. Let him. It is time, and more than time that you stepped forward and took your proper place in Bingtown."

"My place is aboard the *Vivacia*," Althea said faintly.

"No," Kyle said, and her mother echoed it with a shake of her head.

"Then I have no place, in this family or in Bingtown." Althea heard herself speak the words in a sort of wonder. She heard the ring of finality in them, and it shocked her. Like a rock dropped into still water, she thought, for she suddenly had a dizzying sense of the words spreading out like a widening ripple, changing every relationship she had, forever altering her days to come. For a moment, she could not take a breath.

"Althea? Althea!"

Her mother's voice rang loud behind her. She was walking down the hallway, and her home was suddenly an unfamiliar place. It had been years, she realized, since she had spent more than a month at one time here. How long had that tapestry hung there, when had those tiles cracked? She didn't know, she hadn't been here, no, she was not really changing anything, she hadn't lived here for years. This had not been her home for years. She was only recognizing the reality, not creating it. With no more than the clothes on her back, she stepped out the front door and into the wider world.

"If she comes home drunk again, I'm going to lock her in her room for a week. Make it plain to her that we won't tolerate her blackening the family name and her reputation in Bingtown." Kyle was sitting next to Keffria on the bench now, his arm about her protectively.

"Kyle. Shut up." Ronica Vestrit heard herself say the words crisply but quietly. It was all falling apart, her family, her home, her dreams of the future. Althea had meant what she had said; Ronica had heard Ephron's voice in her words. Her daughter was not going to turn up on the doorstep tonight, drunk or any other way. She had left. And all that idiot boy Keffria had married could do was play King of the Hill and make up ways to try out his new authority. She sighed heavily. Perhaps that was the only problem she could solve just now. And perhaps solving that would put her on a path to solving the others. "Kyle. I avoided saying this in front of Althea, as she needs no encouragement toward rebelling, but you've been acting like an ass all morning. As you have so tactfully pointed out, there is little I can do to intervene between you and your son. My daughter, Althea is another matter. She is not under your authority, and your efforts to correct her I have found extremely offensive."

She had expected him to look at least apologetic. Instead, his face hardened into affront, and she wondered, not for the first time, if she had completely misjudged this man's common sense when she put the family's fortunes into her elder daughter's hands. His first statement confirmed her worst fears. "I am the man of this family now. How can you say she is not under my authority?"

"She is my daughter, not yours. She is your wife's sister, not yours."

"And she shares a name with you both, and her actions affect that name. If you and Keffria cannot reach her with reasoning, then I will have to restrain her with something stronger. We have no time to coax and cozy them along; Wintrow and Althea both must be made to accept their duties and perform them well."

"When it comes to Althea, you are not the one to decide what her duties are. I am." The iron resolve that had so often served her well at a bargaining table came to Ronica Vestrit's aid now.

"Perhaps you see it so. I do not. You have given control of her maintenance to me. In judging what maintenance she actually needs, I may be able to persuade her to curb her behavior to decent standards."

His voice was so calm and rational, but the sense of his words still stung Ronica.

"When you criticize my daughter's behavior, you criticize the training she received from her parents. While you may not agree with how Ephron and I raised Althea, it is not your place to voice it. Nor did I give Keffria management over Althea's finances as a method to govern her, but solely as a way to determine what the budget could afford to allow her. It is not fitting that sister should govern sister. It is even less fitting that her sister's husband do so. And it was never my intent to force Althea from the *Vivacia* but only to encourage her to discover another life for herself, after she had seen the ship was in good hands."

Ronica sank down on a bench beside the table, shaking her head at how her plans had been twisted awry. "Ephron was right about her. She needs a light hand. She will not be dragged or driven to do what is best for her. Last night, well, she was grieving. And whatever you may think of Brashen, I know Ephron thought highly of him. Perhaps he did no more than see her safely home, a fitting thing for a gentleman to do when confronted with a distressed lady."

"And perhaps they had been drinking tea together all day as well," Kyle noted with heavy sarcasm.

A mistake. A grievous mistake. Ronica looked past Kyle, stared at Keffria until her daughter became aware of her gaze and briefly met it.

"Keffria," her mother said quietly. "You knew my intent with those documents. It would be dishonest of you to take advantage of your sister, to use your inheritance to coerce her to your will. Tell me you will not allow that to happen."

"She has children to think of," Kyle interjected.

"Keffria," her mother repeated, and she could not quite keep a plea out of her voice.

"I—" Keffria's eyes darted from her mother's face to her husband's granite stare. Her breath came fast as a cornered mouse's. "I can't be in the middle like this. I can't!" she cried out in dismay. Her hands rose to tangle desperately over her breast.

"You needn't be," Kyle assured her. "The papers are signed and witnessed. You know what is right is what is best for Althea. You know that neither of us have anything but her own good at heart. Believe in yourself, Keffria. Believe in me, your husband."

Keffria met her mother's disbelieving stare one last time before she looked down at the table's polished surface. Her hands edged along it, smoothed the wood nervously. "I believe in you, Kyle," she whispered. "I do. But I don't want to hurt Althea. I don't want to be cruel to her."

"We won't be," he assured her promptly. "As long as she is not cruel to us. That is fair."

"That . . . seems fair," she said hesitantly. She glanced at her mother seeking assurance, but Ronica's face was set. She had always thought of her elder daughter as the stronger of the two. After all, had not Keffria chosen a life that demanded strength, while Althea had gone off to dangle after her father and play? Keffria had taken a husband, had children, managed her own household and assisted in the running of the larger holdings. Or so it had seemed to Ronica when she had been making out the documents that determined inheritance. Now it seemed to her that Keffria had mostly managed the internal workings of the house, determining menus and shopping lists and managing social occasions. It had left Ronica free to do all the real tasks of running the holdings. Why had she not seen that Keffria was becoming little more than a place-holder, following her mother's directions, obeying her husband, but seldom standing up for herself? Ronica tried to recall the last time that Keffria had suggested a change or initiated an action. She could not think of one.

Why, oh why, did these insights have to come to her now? Sa help her, she had just put all the reins of their lives into Keffria's hands. By Bingtown customs and traditions, when a man died, his property passed to his offspring. Not his wife, his offspring. Oh, Ronica had the right to retain control of the properties she had brought to her marriage to Ephron, but precious little was left of them. With a lurch of her heart, she abruptly realized it was not just her younger daughter who was now at the mercy of what Kyle considered fitting for a woman. It was herself as well.

She glanced quickly at him, willing her face to stillness. She could only pray to Sa that he had not realized that yet. If he did, she might lose everything. Could not she, too, be brought to heel with a financial noose about her neck?

She took a deep breath and found control of her voice. "It does seem fair," Ronica conceded. She must not suddenly be too meek. "We shall see if it turns out that way in reality."

She made a show of sighing, and then rubbing at her eyes as if wearied. "There are so many things to think of now. So many. For now, I shall leave Althea to you. And, as Kyle says, the *Vivacia* must sail as soon as possible. That, I suppose, is a more important thing to turn our minds to. May I inquire as to what ports and cargoes you have chosen for her, and how soon you must leave?" She hoped she did not sound too eager for his departure. Her mind was already racing as to how she could work best in his absence. She could at least make sure that what remained of her own holdings would be passed to Althea upon her own death. Not that she would make mention of that; she had suddenly decided it would be very wise if she did not appear to oppose Kyle. And time alone with Keffria was time in which she could work on her elder daughter.

Kyle seemed content to be diverted with her question. "As you have said, we must sail soon, and not just for our finances. The sooner I get Wintrow away from the distractions of shore life, the faster he will accept his destiny. He has much to learn, and through no fault of his own, he comes to it when he is closer to man than boy. He cannot begin too soon to master it."

He paused just long enough for them to nod. It irked Ronica to do it, as he seemed to imply they had somehow been at fault in the boy's upraising. When he was satisfied of their agreement, Kyle went on, "As to ports and cargoes, well, as we have all agreed, we must trade most swiftly in that which is most profitable." Again he paused for their nods.

"There is but one answer, then," he decided for them all. "I'll take the *Vivacia* south to Jamaillia, to take on the very best we can afford. Then north to Chalced, as swift as we may go."

"The cargo?" Ronica asked faintly. Already her heart was sinking with certainty.

"Slaves, of course. Educated ones. Not pickpockets and thieves and murderers, but those that will be prized in Chalced as tutors and overseers and nannies. Artists and craftsmen. We need to buy up those whose debts have brought them to the block, rather than those condemned to slavery for crimes." He paused, pondering, then shook his head. "They will not be as hardy, of course. So perhaps we should balance the load with a hold full of . . . whatever our purse will afford. War captives and bred slaves and what not. The second mate, Torg, has worked slaveships before and knows many of the auction folk. He should be able to guide us to some bargains."

"Slavery is illegal in Bingtown," Keffria pointed out uncertainly.

Kyle gave a short bark of laughter. "For now. Not for much longer, I suspect. And you need not fear, my dear. I have no intention of stopping in Bingtown with them. It will be a swift straight run down the Inside Passage to Jamaillia City, then north again past Bingtown on to Chalced. No one will bother us."

"Pirates," Keffria pointed out shyly.

"Have never bothered the *Vivacia*. How often have you heard your father brag of how fleet she is, and how nimbly she keeps a channel? Now that she is quickened, she will be even more so. Pirates know that pursuing a liveship is a waste of their time. They'll leave us alone. Try not to trouble yourself with worrying over things I have already pondered. I would not be taking this course if I deemed it risky."

"The cargo itself may be risky to a liveship," Ronica pointed out quietly.

"What do you fear, an uprising of some sort? No. They'll be under the hatches and well secured below for the full trip." Kyle was starting to sound annoyed at their reservations about his plan.

"That could be even worse then." Ronica tried to speak gently, as if she were offering an opinion rather than stating a danger he should plainly see for himself. "Liveships are sensitive creatures, Kyle, and Vivacia is only recently quickened. Just as you would not expose Malta to the . . . discomforts slaves must endure during transport, so, too, the *Vivacia* should be sheltered from them."

Kyle scowled, then his expression softened. "Ronica. I am not unaware of the traditions surrounding liveships. And so far as our finances will allow us, I will respect them. Wintrow will be aboard, and he will be allowed some time each day simply to converse with the ship. He'll be able to reassure her that all is well and that none of this has anything to do with her own well-being. Nor do I intend any unnecessary cruelty. The slaves must be kept confined and controlled, but beyond that, they will experience no harshness. I think you worry needlessly, Ronica. Besides. Even if she is distressed by it, it's only for a time. What harm can come of that?"

"You seem to have considered it well," Ronica tried to put reason in her voice, and replace the anger she felt with a tone of concern. "There are tales, of course, of what a distressed liveship may do. Some, they say, go unwillingly, spilling wind from their sails, running aground where it seems they should float freely, dragging their anchors . . . but all that, no doubt, is nothing that a lively and well-trained crew cannot deal with. In more grave cases, it is said that ill-used ships can go mad. The *Pariah* is but the most famous of them. There are rumors of others, of liveships that went out and never returned, because the ship turned on its owner and crew. . . ."

"And every season there are ordinary ships that go out and do not come back. Storms and pirates are as like to be the cause of a liveship not returning as a ship going mad," Kyle cut in impatiently.

"But with both you and Wintrow aboard, I could lose half my family at a single blow," Keffria wailed suddenly. "Oh, Kyle, do you think this is wise? Papa made money with the *Vivacia*, and never took on illegal cargoes or dangerous ones."

Kyle scowled even more darkly. "Keffria, my dear, your father did not make enough money. That is exactly what we are discussing here. How to avoid his mistakes and make this family financially sound and respectable once more. Another one of his quirky decisions immediately comes to mind, in this light." He met Ronica's eyes suddenly and studied her face as he observed, "If you don't care for the slave trade, we could trade up the Rain Wild River. Certainly that's where the world's most desirable goods come from. Every other liveship trades up the Rain Wild River. Why shouldn't we?"

Ronica met his gaze calmly. "Because years ago Ephron decided that the Vestrit family would no longer do River trade. And we have not. Our trading contacts with the folk of the Wilds are gone now."

"And Ephron is dead now, too. Whatever he feared, I am ready to face it. But give to me the charts of the Rain Wild River, and I'll make contacts of my own," Kyle offered.

"You would die," Ronica said with great certainty.

Kyle snorted. "I doubt that. The Rain Wild River may be a savage one, but I've taken ships up rivers before. So." He paused, then uttered the words. "I'll take those charts now. They are Keffria's by right, you cannot withhold them from us any longer. Then we can all be content. No slaves aboard the *Vivacia*, and a fat trade up the Rain Wild River."

Ronica did not hesitate. She lied. "That might be so, if such charts still existed. But they do not, Kyle. Ephron destroyed all charts of the Rain Wild River years ago, when he decided to sever out trade connections there. He wanted to put an end to the Vestrit family trading up the Rain Wild River. And he did."

Kyle shot to his feet. "I don't believe it!" he snarled. "Ephron was not a fool, and only a fool would destroy charts that valuable. You're keeping them back from us, aren't you? Saving them for precious Althea and whatever you can find to marry her?"

"I don't care to be called a liar," Ronica hissed. That, at least, was truth.

"And I don't care to be treated like a fool!" Kyle raged in return. "No one in this family has ever given me the respect I deserve. I was willing to endure it from old Ephron. He was a man and years my senior. But I will not tolerate it from anyone else under this roof. Once and for all, I want the truth. Why did Ephron sever the family trading contacts up the Rain Wild River, and what will it take for us to recover them?"

Ronica merely looked at him.

"Damn it, woman, can't you see? What is the point of having a liveship if we don't use it to exploit the River trade? Everyone knows that only liveship families can trade up the Rain Wild. We're a liveship Old Trader family, and what has your husband done with that privilege and that debt? He's traded in silks and brandies, as could anyone with a raft and a sail, and watched our debt grow larger every year. Money flows down the Rain Wild River faster than its waters do, and yet you'd have us stand on the banks of it and starve."

"There are worse things than starving, Kyle Haven," Ronica heard herself say.

"Like what?" he demanded.

She could not stop herself. "Like having a greedy fool for a son-in-law. You don't know what you're talking about when you speak of the Rain Wild River."

Kyle gave her an icy smile. "Why don't you give me the charts then, and let me find out? If you're right, you'll be rid of me as a son-in-law. You'll be free to sink all your children and grandchildren into debt."

"No!" Keffria started up with a shriek. "I can't stand this! Don't talk about things like that. Kyle, you mustn't go up the Rain Wild River. Slaves are far better, trade in slaves, and take Wintrow with you if you must, but you mustn't go up the Rain Wild River!" She looked at them both pleadingly. "He would never come back. We both know that. Papa's only just died and now you're talking about letting Kyle get himself killed."

"Keffria. You're over-wrought, and over-reacting to everything." The look Kyle shot Ronica suggested it was her fault for playing upon her daughter's imagination. A tiny spark of anger kindled in Ronica's heart, but she doused it firmly, for her daughter was looking at her husband with eyes full of hurt. Opportunity, she breathed to herself. Opportunity.

"Let me take care of her," she suggested smoothly to Kyle. "I'm sure you have so much to do to ready the ship. Come, Keffria. Let's go to my sitting room. I'll have Rache bring us some tea. In truth, I feel a bit over-wrought myself. Come. Let's leave things to Kyle for a while."

She stood and slipped an arm around Keffria and led her from the room. *Salvage*, she silently whispered to Ephron. *I'll salvage what I can of what you left me, my dear. At least one daughter I shall keep safe by me.*

CHAPTER ELEVEN

CONSEQUENCES AND REFLECTIONS

ND IF I WISHED TO DISPUTE THESE DOCUMENTS?" AL-THEA ASKED SLOWLY. SHE TRIED TO MAKE HER VOICE impartially calm, but inside she was quivering with both anger and hurt.

Curtil scratched reluctantly at what was left of his gray-ing hair. "That is specifically provided for. Anyone who disputes this last testament is automatically excluded from benefitting from it." He shook his head, almost apologeti-cally. "It's a standard thing," he told her gently. "It's not as if your father was thinking specifically of you when we wrote it."

She looked up from her tangled hands and met his eyes firmly. "And you believe this is actually what he wished? That Kyle take over Vivacia, and I be dependent on my sister's charity?"

"Well, I doubt that is how he envisioned it," Curtil said judiciously. He took a sip of his tea. Althea wondered if that were a delaying tactic, to give him time to think. The old man straightened in his chair as if he'd decided something. "But I do believe he knew his own mind. No one deceived him or coerced him. I would never have been a party to that. Your father wished to see your sister as his sole heir. He did not desire to punish you, but rather to safeguard his entire family."

"Well, in both of those desires, he failed," Althea said harshly. Then she lowered her face into her hands, ashamed to have spoken so of her father. Curtil let her be. When she lifted her face some time later, she observed, "You must think me a carrion bird. Yesterday my father died, and today I come quarreling for a share of what was his."

Curtil offered her his handkerchief and she took it gratefully. "No. No, I don't think that. When the mainstay of one's world is taken away, it's only natural to cling to all the rest, to try desperately to keep things as close to the way they were as one can." He shook his head sorrowfully. "But no one can ever go back to yesterday."

"No. I suppose not." She sighed heavily. She considered her last pathetic straw of hope. "Trader Curtil. By Bingtown law, if a man swears an oath to Sa, cannot he be held to that oath as a legal contract?"

Curtil's long brow furrowed. "Well. It depends. If in a fit of anger, in a tavern, I say that by Sa, I'm going to kill so-and-so, well, that's not a legal action in the first place, so . . ."

Althea stopped mincing words. "If Kyle Haven swore before witnesses that if I could produce proof that I was a worthy seaman, he would give Vivacia back to me, if he swore that in Sa's name, could it be enforced?"

"Well, technically, the ship is your sister's property, not his—"

"She has ceded control of it over to him," Althea said impatiently. "Is such an oath legally binding?"

Curtil shrugged. "You'd end up before the Traders' Council, but, yes, I think you'd win. They're conservative, the old customs count for much with them. An oath sworn before Sa would have to be legally honored. You have witnesses to this, at least two?"

Althea leaned back in her chair with a sigh. "One, perhaps, who would speak up for the truth of what I say. The other two . . . I no longer know any more what I could expect of my mother and sister."

Curtil shook his head. "Family disputes such as these are such messy things. I counsel you not to pursue this, Althea. It can only lead to even worse rifts."

"I do not believe that it can get any worse," she observed grimly, before bidding him farewell.

She was her father's daughter. She had gone immediately to Curtil in his offices. The old man had not seemed at all surprised to see her. As soon as she was shown into his chambers, he rose and took down several rolled documents. One after another, he set them before her, and made plain to her just how untenable her position was. She had to give her mother credit for thoroughness; the whole thing was lashed down like storm-weather cargo. Legally, she had nothing. Legally, she was dependent entirely on her sister's goodwill.

Legally. She did not intend that her reality would have anything to do with that kind of legality. She would not live off Keffria's charity, especially not if it meant she would have to dance to Kyle's tunes. No. Let them go on thinking her father had died and left her nothing. They'd be wrong. All he had taught her, all her knowledge of the sailing trade and her observations of his trading were still hers. If she could not make her own way on that, then she deserved to starve. Stoutly she told herself that when the first Vestrit came to Bingtown, he probably knew little more than that, and he had made his own way. She should be able to do as much for herself.

No. More than that. She'd get the damn proof that she was all she said she was, and she'd hold Kyle to his oath. Wintrow, she was sure, would support her. It was his only way out from under his father's thumb. But would her mother or Keffria? Althea considered. She did not think they would willingly do so. On the other hand, she did not think they would speak before the Traders' Council and lie. Her resolve firmed itself. One way or another, she'd stand up to Kyle and claim what was rightfully hers.

The docks were busy. Althea picked her way down to where the *Vivacia* was tied, sidestepping men with barrows, freight wagons drawn by sweating horses, chandlers making deliveries of supplies to outbound ships and merchants hastening to inspect their incoming shipments before taking delivery. Once the hustle of the midday business on the docks would have excited her. Now it weighed her spirits. Abruptly she felt excluded from these lives, set apart and invisible. When she walked the docks dressed as befitted a daughter of a Bingtown Trader, no sailor dared to notice her, let alone call out a cheery greeting to her. It was ironic. She had chosen the simple dark dress and laced sandals that morning as a partial apology to her mother for how badly she had behaved the night before. She had little expected that it would become her sole fortune as she set off on her own into the world.

But as she walked down the docks, her confidence peeled away from her. How was she to employ such knowledge to feed herself? How could she approach any ship's captain or mate, dressed as she was, and convince him that she was an able-bodied sailor? While female sailors were not rare in Bingtown, they were not all that com-

mon either. One frequently saw women working the decks of Six
Duchies ships when they came to Bingtown. Many of the Three-Ships
Immigrants had become fisherfolk, and among them, family ships
were worked by the whole family. So while female sailors were not
unknown in Bingtown, she'd be expected to prove herself just as tough
or tougher than the men she'd have to work alongside. But she
wouldn't even be given the chance to try, dressed as she was. As the
rising heat of the day made her uncomfortably aware of the weight
and breadth of her dark skirts and modest jacket, she longed more and
more for simple canvas trousers and a cotton shirt and vest.

Finally she stood beside the *Vivacia*. She glanced up at the figurehead. To anyone else, it would have appeared that the ship was dozing
in the sun. Althea did not even need to touch her to know that in
actuality, Vivacia's senses and thoughts were turned inward, keeping
track of her own unloading. That job was proceeding apace, with
longshoremen streaming down her gangplanks burdened with the variety of her cargo like ants fleeing a disturbed nest. They paid scant
attention to her; Althea was just another gawker on the docks. She
ventured closer to the *Vivacia* and set a hand to her sun-warmed
planking. "Hello," she said softly.

"Althea." The ship's voice was a warm contralto. She opened her
eyes and smiled down at Althea. Vivacia extended a hand toward
Althea, but lightened as she was, she floated too high for their hands
to reach. Althea had to content herself with the sensations she received through the rough planking her hand rested on. Already her
ship had a much greater sense of self. She could speak to Althea, and
still keep awareness of cargo as it was shifted in her holds. And, Althea
realized with a pang, she was focusing much of her awareness on
Wintrow. The boy was in the chain locker, coiling and stowing lines.
The heat of the tiny enclosed room was oppressive, while the thick
ship's smell all around him made him nauseated. The distress he felt
had spread through the ship as a tension in the planking and a stiffness
to the spars. Here, tied to the dock, that was not so bad, but out in the
open sea a ship had to be able to give with the pressures of the water
and wind.

"He'll be all right," Althea told Vivacia comfortingly, despite the
jealousy she felt over the ship's concern. "It's a hard and boring task
for a green hand, but he'll survive it. Try not to think of his discomfort
right now."

"It's worse than that," the ship confided quietly. "He's all but a
prisoner here. He doesn't want to be aboard, he wants to be a priest.

We started out to be such wonderful friends, and now I think they are making him hate me."

"No one could hate you," Althea assured her, and tried to make her words sound confident. "He does want to be somewhere else; there's no use in my lying to you about that. So what he hates is not being where he wants to be. He couldn't possibly hate you." Steeling herself, as if she plunged her hand into fire, she added, "You can be his strength, you know. Let him know how much you value him, and what a comfort it is to you that he is aboard. As you once did for me." Try as she might, she could not keep her voice from breaking on the last words.

"But I am a ship, not your child," Vivacia replied to Althea's unvoiced thought rather than her words. "You are not giving up a little child with no knowledge of the world. I know in many ways I am naïve still, but I have a wealth of memories and information to draw on. I just need to put them in some sort of order, and see how they relate to who I am now. I know you, Althea. I know you did not abandon me by choice. But you also know me. And you must understand how deeply it hurts me when Wintrow is forced to be aboard me, forced to be my companion and heart's friend when he wishes he were elsewhere. We are drawn to one another, Wintrow and I. But his anger at the situation makes him resist that bond. And it makes me ashamed that I so often reach toward him."

The division within the ship's heart was terrible to feel. Vivacia battled her own need for Wintrow's companionship, forcing herself to stand still in a cold isolation that was gray as fog. Almost Althea could sense it as a terrible place, rain swept and chill and endlessly gray. It appalled her. As Althea searched for comforting words, a man's voice rang out loud and commanding over the ordinary dock yells and thuds. "You. You there! Get away from the ship! Captain's orders, you aren't to come aboard her."

Althea tipped her head back, shielding her eyes against the sun's glare. She stared up at Torg as if she had not recognized his voice. "This, sir, is a public dock," she pointed out calmly.

"Well, this ain't a public ship. So shove off!"

As little as two months ago, Althea would have exploded at him. But the time she had spent secluded with Vivacia and the events of the last three days had changed her. It was not that she was a better-tempered person, she decided detachedly. It was that her anger had learned a terrible patience. What good was wasting words on a petty and tyrannical second mate? He was a little yapping dog. She was a tigress. One did not waste snarls on such a creature. One waited until one could snap his spine with a single blow. He had sealed his fate with his mistreatment of Wintrow. His rudeness to Althea would be redeemed at the same time.

And with a wave of giddiness, Althea realized that while her hand rested on the planking, her thoughts were Vivacia's and Vivacia's were hers. Belatedly she pulled free of the ship, feeling as if she drew her hand out of cold wrist-deep molasses. "No, Vivacia," Althea said quietly. "Do not let my anger become your own. And leave vengeance to me, do not soil yourself with it. You are too big, too beautiful; it is unworthy of you."

"He is unworthy of my deck, then," Vivacia replied in a low, bitter voice. "Why must I tolerate vermin like him while you are put ashore? You cannot tell me it is the Vestrit way to treat kinsmen so."

"No. No, it is not," Althea hastily assured her.

"I said, move on," Torg shouted once more from the deck above her. Althea glanced up at him. He was leaning over the railing, shaking his fist at her. "Move along, or I'll have you moved along!"

"There's really nothing he can do," Althea assured the ship. But even as she spoke, she heard a muffled cry and then a heavy thud from within Vivacia's hold. Someone cursed fluently on the deck, followed by cries for Torg. A young sailor's voice floated up clearly. "The hoist tackle's pulled free of the beam, sir! I'd swear it was set sound enough when we started work."

Torg's head disappeared and Althea heard the sound of his feet running across the deck. The unloading of Vivacia's cargo ground to a halt as half the crew came to gawk at the smashed pallet and crates and the scattered comfer nuts. "That should keep him busy for a time," Vivacia observed sweetly.

"I do have to leave, though," Althea hastily decided. If she stayed, she would have to ask the ship if she had had anything to do with the fallen block and tackle. It was suddenly too chill a secret; she could live with her suspicions more easily than she could live with being a party to such knowledge. "Take care of yourself," she told Vivacia. "And look after Wintrow, too."

"Althea! Will you be back?"

"Of course I will. There are just a few things I need to take care of. But I'll be back to see you again before you sail."

"I can't imagine sailing without you," Vivacia said desolately. The figurehead lifted her eyes to the distant horizon, as if she were already far beyond Bingtown. A stray breeze stirred the heavy locks of her hair.

"It's going to be hard to stand here on the docks and watch you go off into the distance. At least you'll have Wintrow aboard."

"Who hates being with me." The ship abruptly sounded very young again. And very distressed.

"Vivacia. You know I can't stay here. But I will be back. Know that I am working on a way to be with you. It will take me some time, but I will be with you again. Until then, behave yourself."

"I suppose," Vivacia sighed.

"Good. I will see you again soon."

Althea turned and hastened away. Her insincerity had nearly choked her. She wondered if the ship had been fooled at all. She hoped she had, and yet every instinct she had about the *Vivacia* told her that she could not be tricked that easily. She must know how jealous Althea was of Wintrow's place aboard her, she must be able to sense her deep, deep anger at how things had turned out. And yet Althea hoped she did not, hoped that Vivacia had had nothing to do with the fallen hoist, and prayed to Sa fervently that the ship would not attempt to right things on her own.

As she turned to go, she reflected that the ship was both like and unlike what she had expected. She had dreamed of a ship with all the good qualities of a proud and beautiful woman. She had not paused to think that Vivacia had inherited not just her father's experience, but that of her grandfather and great-grandma as well, to say nothing of what Althea herself had added. She feared now that the ship would be just as hammer-headed as any other Vestrit, just as slow to forgive, just as intent on having her own way. *If I were aboard, I could guide her, as my father guided me through my stubborn times. Wintrow will not have the vaguest idea of how to deal with her.* A tiny black thought pushed itself into her mind. *If she kills Kyle, he will have brought it on himself.*

A chill of disgust raced through her that she could even harbor such a thought. She stooped hastily, to rap her knuckles against the wood of the dock, to proof her fate against the *Vivacia* ever doing anything so horrible. As she straightened up, she felt eyes on her. She lifted her gaze to find Amber standing and staring at her. The golden woman was dressed in a long simple robe the color of a ripe acorn, and her hair was bound down her back in a single shining plait. The fabric of the robe fell in pleats from her shoulders to the hem, concealing every line of her body. Her hands were gloved, to conceal the scars and calluses of an artisan's fingers in the guise of a gentlewoman's hands. Amidst the hustle and bustle of the busy dock, she stood still, as unaffected by all of it as if she were enclosed in a glass bubble. For a second her tawny eyes locked with Althea's, and Althea's mouth went dry. There was something other-worldly about her. All around her, folk came and went on their business, but where she stood there was stillness and focus. She wore a necklace of simple wooden beads, gleaming in every tone of brown that wood could be. Even from where she stood, they caught Althea's eyes and she felt drawn to them. She doubted that anyone could look at them and not desire to possess them.

Her eyes darted up to Amber's face. Once more their eyes met. Amber did not smile. She slowly turned her head, first to one side and then to another as if inviting Althea to admire her profile. Instead Althea noticed only her mismatched earrings. She wore several in each ear, but the ones that drew Althea's attention were the twisted serpent of gleaming wood in her left ear and the shining dragon in her right. Each was as long as a man's thumb, and so cunningly carved she almost expected them to twitch with life.

Althea suddenly realized how long she had been staring. Unwillingly she met Amber's gaze again. The woman smiled questioningly at her. When Althea kept her own features perfectly still, the woman's smile faded to a look of disdain. That expression did not change as she set a slender-fingered hand to her flat belly. As if those gloved fingers had touched her own midsection, Althea felt a chill dread spread throughout her. She glanced once more at Amber's face; it now looked set and purposeful. She stared at Althea like an archer fixing his eye on his target. In all the hurrying, busy folk, they were abruptly alone, eyes locked, impervious to the crowd. With an effort as physical as pulling away from a grasping hand, Althea turned and fled up the docks, back towards the Bingtown Market.

She hurried clumsily through the crowded summer market, bumping into folk, knocking against a table full of scarves when she turned to look back over her shoulder. There was no sign of Amber following her. She moved on more purposefully down the walk. Her pounding heart slowed and she became aware of how she was sweating in the afternoon sun. Her encounters with the ship and Amber had left her dry-mouthed and almost shaky. Silly. Ridiculous. All the woman had done was look at her. Where was the threat in that? She had never before been prone to such flights of fancy. Likely it was the stress of the last two days. And she could not recall when she had last eaten a decent meal. Come to think of it, other than beer, she had had almost nothing since the day before yesterday. That was most likely what was wrong with her.

She found a back table in a small street front tea shop, and sat down. She felt limply grateful to be out of the afternoon sun. When the boy came to the table, she ordered wine and smoked fish and melon. After he had bowed and gone, she belatedly wondered if she had enough coin to pay for it. When she had dressed so carefully that morning, she had not given any thought to such things. Her room at home was as immaculately tidy as it always was when she had returned to it after a sea voyage. There had been some coins and notes in the corner of her drawer; these she had scooped and stuffed in her pockets before she tied them on, more out of habit than anything else. Even if there was enough to pay for this simple meal, there was certainly not enough to pay for an inn room somewhere. Unless she wanted to go crawling home with her tail between her legs, she'd better think of what she actually planned to do to get by.

While she was still wrestling with that, the food came. She recklessly called for wax and pressed her signet ring into a blotch on a tally stick. Probably the last time she'd get away with sending the bill to her father's house. If she'd thought of that, she would have let Keffria buy her a more elegant meal. But the melon was crisp and sweet, the fish moistly smoked and the wine was, well, drinkable. She had worse before and would no doubt have worse again. She just had to persevere, and things would get better with time. Things had to get better.

As she was finishing her wine, it came to her in a sudden rush that her father was still dead, and he was going to be dead for the rest of her life. That part of her life was never going to get better. She had almost become accustomed to her grief; this new sense of deep loss jellied her legs. It was a new and painful way to think of it. No matter how long she managed to hang on, Ephron Vestrit wasn't going to come home and straighten it all out. No one was going to make it all right unless she did it herself. She doubted Keffria's ability to manage the family fortunes. Keffria and her mother might have handled things well enough, but Kyle was going to be stirring the pot, too. Leaving herself entirely out of the picture, how bad could things get for the Vestrits?

They could lose everything.

Even Vivacia.

It had never quite happened yet in Bingtown, but the Devouchet family had come close. They had sunk themselves so deeply in debt that the Traders' Council had agreed that their main creditors, Traders Conry and Risch, could take possession of the Devouchet liveship. The eldest son was to have remained aboard the ship as an indentured servant to them until the family debts were paid, but before the settlement had been finalized, that same son had brought the ship into port at Bingtown with a cargo rich enough to satisfy their creditors. The whole town had rejoiced in his triumph, and for a time he had been a sort of hero. Somehow Althea could not see Kyle in that role. No. More likely he would surrender both ship and son to his creditors, and tell Wintrow it was his fault.

With a sigh, she forced her mind back to that which she feared most. What was happening to Vivacia? The ship was but newly quickened; liveship lore claimed that her personality would develop over the next few weeks. All agreed there was really no predicting what temperament a ship might have. A ship might be markedly like its owners, or amazingly different. Althea had glimpsed a ruthlessness in Vivacia that chilled her. In the weeks to come, would that trait become more marked, or would the ship suddenly evince her father's sense of justice and fair play?

Althea thought of the *Kendry*, a notoriously willful ship. He would not tolerate live cargo in his hold and he hated ice. He'd sail south to Jamaillia willingly enough, but sailors declared that working his decks on a trip north to Six Duchies or beyond was like sailing a leaden ship. On the other hand, given a fragrant cargo and a southern destination, the ship would fair sail himself, swift as the wind. So a strong will in a ship was not so terrible a thing.

Unless the ship went mad.

Althea poked at the last bit of fish on her plate. Despite the warmth of the summer day, she felt cold inside. No. Vivacia would never become like Paragon. She could not. She was properly quickened, with ceremony and welcome, after three full lifetimes of sailing had been put into her. All knew that was what ruined the *Paragon*. The greed of the owners had created a mad liveship, and brought death and destruction on their family line.

The *Paragon* had had but one lifetime when Uto Ludluck assumed command. All said that Uto's father Palwick had been a fine Trader and a great captain. Of Uto, the kindest thing that could be said was that he was shrewd and cunning. And willing to gamble. Anxious to pay off the liveship in his lifetime, he had sailed the *Paragon* always overloaded. Few sailors cared to ship aboard him twice, for Uto was a harsh taskmaster, not only with his underlings but with his young son Kerr, the ship's boy. There were rumors that the unquickened ship was difficult to handle, though most blamed it on too much canvas and too little freeboard due to Uto's greed.

The inevitable happened. There came a winter day in the storm season when the *Paragon* was reported as overdue. Setre Ludluck haunted the docks, asking word of every ship that came in, but no one had seen the *Paragon* or had word of her husband and son.

Six months later, the *Paragon* came home. He was found floating in the mouth of the harbor, keel up. At first no one knew who the derelict was; only that from the silver wood it was a liveship. Volunteers in dories towed the ship into the beach and anchored it there until a low tide could ground it and bare the disastrous news it bore. When the retreating waters ebbed away, there lay the *Paragon*. His masts had been sheared away from the ferocity of some killer storm, but the hardest truth was on his deck. Lashed so securely to his deck that no storm or wave could loose it were the remains of his final cargo. And tangled in the cargo net were the fish-eaten remains of Uto Ludluck and his son Kerr. The *Paragon* had brought them home.

But perhaps most horrible of all was that the ship had quickened. The deaths of Uto and Kerr had finished out the count of three lives ended aboard him. As the water slipped away to bare the figurehead, the bearded countenance of the fiercely carved warrior cried out aloud in a boy's voice, "Mother! Mother, I've come home!"

Setre Ludluck had shrieked and then fainted. She was borne away home, and refused ever after to visit the sea wall in the harbor where the righted *Paragon* was eventually docked. The bereft and frightened ship was inconsolable, sobbing and calling for days. At first folk were sympathetic and made efforts to comfort him. The *Kendry* was tied up near him for close to a week, to see if the older ship could not soothe him. Instead the *Kendry* became agitated and difficult and eventually had to be moved. And Paragon wept on. There was something infinitely terrible in that fierce bearded warrior with the muscled arms and hairy chest, who sobbed like a frightened child and begged for his mother. From sympathy, folks' hearts turned to fear, and finally a sort of anger. It was then that Paragon earned a new name for himself: the *Pariah*, the outcast. No ship's crew wanted to tie up alongside him; bad luck, sailors nodded to one another, and left him to himself. The ropes that bound him to the docks grew soft with rot and heavy with barnacles. The *Paragon* himself grew silent, save for unpredictable outbursts of savage cursing and wailing.

When Setre Ludluck died young, ownership of the *Paragon* passed to the family's creditors. To them he was but a stone about their necks, a ship that could not be sailed, taking up an expensive slip in the harbor. In time, several cousins were grudgingly offered a part ownership in the vessel if they could induce the ship to sail. Two brothers, Cable and Sedge, came forward to claim the ship. The competition was fierce, but Cable was the elder by a few minutes. He claimed the prize and vowed he would reclaim the family's liveship. He spent months talking to the *Paragon*, and eventually seemed to have a sort of bond with him. To others, he said the ship was like a frightened child who responded best to coaxing. Those who held the family's debt on the liveship extended Cable credit, muttering somewhat about sending good money after bad, but unable to resist the hope that they might recoup their losses. Cable hired crew and workmen, paying outrageous wages simply to get sailors to approach the inauspicious ship. It took the better part of a year for him to have the *Paragon* refitted and to hire a full crew to sail him. He was roundly congratulated on having salvaged the ship, for in the days before he sailed, the *Paragon* became known as a bashful but courteous ship, given to few words but occasionally smiling so as to melt anyone's heart. On a bright spring day, they left Bingtown. Cable and his crew were never heard from again.

When next the *Paragon* was sighted, he was a wreck of shattered and dangling rigging and tattered canvas. Reports of him reached Bingtown months before he did. He rode low in the water, his decks nearly awash, and no human replied to the hails of other passing ships. Only the figurehead, black-eyed and stone-faced, stared back at those who ventured close enough to see for themselves that no one worked his decks. Back to Bingtown he came, back to the sea wall where he had been tied for so many years. The first and only words he was reputed to have spoken were, "Tell my mother I've come home." Whether that was truth or the stuff of legend, Althea could only guess.

When Sedge had been bold enough to tie up the ship and go aboard, he found no trace of his brother or of any sailor, living or dead. The last entry in the log spoke of fine weather, and the prospect of a good profit on their cargo. Nothing indicated a reason why the crew would have abandoned the ship. In his hold had been a waterlogged cargo of silks and brandy. The creditors had claimed what was salvageable, and left the ship of ill-omen to Sedge. All the town had thought the man was mad when he claimed the *Paragon*, and took notes on his house and lands to refit him.

Sedge had made seventeen successful voyages with the *Paragon*. To those who asked how he had managed it, he replied that he ignored the figurehead, and sailed the ship as if it were no more than wood. For those years, the figurehead of the *Paragon* was indeed a mute thing, glaring balefully on any who glanced his way. His powerful arms were crossed on his muscled chest, his jaws clamped as tightly shut as they had been when he was wood. Whatever secret the ship knew about the fates of Cable and his crew, he kept them to himself. Althea's father had told her that the *Paragon* had been almost accepted in the harbor; that some said that Sedge had broken the string of ill luck that had haunted the ship. Sedge himself bragged of his mastery of the liveship, and fearlessly took his eldest son off to sea with him. Sedge redeemed the note on his house and lands and made a comfortable living for his wife and children. Some of the ship's former creditors began to mumble that they had acted too hastily in signing the ill-omened ship back to him.

But the *Paragon* never returned from Sedge's eighteenth voyage. It was a bad year for storms, and some said that Sedge's fate was no different from what many a mariner suffered that year. Heavily iced rigging can overturn any ship, live or no. Sedge's widow walked the docks and watched the horizon with empty eyes. But it was a full twenty years, and she had remarried and borne more children before the *Paragon* returned.

Once more he came floating hull up, defying wind and tide and current to drift slowly home. This time when the silvery wood of his keel was sighted, folk knew almost at once who he was. There were no volunteers to tow him in, no one was interested in righting him or finding out what had become of his crew. Even to speak of him was deemed ill luck. But when his mast stuck fast in the greasy mud of the harbor and his hulk became a hazard to every ship that came and went, the harbor master ordered his men out. With curses and sweat they dragged him free, and on the highest tide of that month, they winched him as far ashore as they could. The retreating tides left him completely aground. All could see then that it was not just the crew of the *Paragon* that had suffered a harsh fate. For the figurehead itself was mutilated, hacked savagely with hatchet bites between brow and nose. Of the ship's dark and brooding glance, nothing remained but splintered wood. A peculiar star with seven points, livid as a burn scar, marred his chest. It was all the more terrible that his mouth scowled and cursed as savagely as ever, and that the groping hands reached out, promising to rend whoever came in reach of them.

Those bold enough to venture aboard told of a ship stripped to its bare bones. Nothing remained of the men who had sailed him, not a shoe, not a knife, nothing. Even his log books were gone, and deprived of all his memories, the liveship muttered and laughed and cursed to himself, all sense run out of his words like sand out of a shattered hourglass.

So the *Paragon* had remained for all of Althea's lifetime. The *Pariah* or *Goner*, as he was sometimes referred to, was occasionally almost floated by an exceptionally high tide, but the harbor master had ordered him well anchored to the beach cliffs. He would not allow the hulk to break free and wash out to sea where he might become a hazard to other ships. Nominally, the *Pariah* was the property of Amis Ludluck now, but Althea doubted she had ever visited the beached wreckage of the liveship. Like any other mad relative, he was kept in obscurity, spoken of in whispers if spoken of at all. Althea imagined such a fate befalling Vivacia and shuddered.

"More wine?" the serving boy asked pointedly. Althea shook her head hastily, realizing she had lingered far too long at this table. Sitting here and mulling other people's tragedies was not going to make her own life any better. She needed to act. The first thing she should do was tell her mother just how troubled the liveship seemed to be and somehow convince her that Althea must be allowed back on board to sail with her. The second thing she would do, she decided, was cut her own throat before she did anything that might appear as childish whining.

She left the tea shop and wandered the busy market streets. The more she tried to focus her mind on her problems, the more she could not decide which problem to confront first. She needed a place to sleep, food, a prospect of employment for herself. Her beloved ship was in insensitive hands, and she could do nothing to change it. She tried to think of allies she could depend on to help her and could come up with no one. She cursed herself now for not cultivating the company of other Traders' sons and daughters. She had no beau she could turn to, no best friend who would shelter her for a few days. On board the *Vivacia* she had had her father for companionship and serious talk, and the sailors for company and joking. Her days in Bingtown had either been spent at home, reveling in the luxury of a real bed and hot meals of fresh food, or following her father about on business errands. She knew Curtil his advisor, and several money-changers, and a number of merchants who had bought cargo from them over the years. Not one of them was someone she could turn to in her present difficulties.

Nor could she go home without appearing to crawl. And there was no predicting what Kyle would attempt to do if she appeared on the doorstep, even to claim her things. She wouldn't put it past him to try and lock her up in her room like a naughty child. Yet she had a responsibility to the *Vivacia* that didn't stop even if they had declared the ship no longer belonged to her.

She finally salved her conscience by stopping a message runner. For a penny, she got a sheet of coarse paper and a charcoal pencil and the promise of delivery before sundown. She penned a hasty note to her mother, but could find little more to say except that she was concerned for the ship, that Vivacia seemed unhappy and restless. She asked for nothing for herself, only that her mother would visit the *Vivacia* herself and encourage the ship to speak plainly to her and reveal the source of her unhappiness. Knowing it would be seen as overly dramatic, she nevertheless reminded her mother of the *Paragon*'s sad fate, saying she hoped her family's ship would never share it. Then Althea re-read her missive, frowning at how histrionic it seemed. She told herself it was the best she could do, and that her mother was the kind of person who would at least go down and see for herself. She sealed it with a dab of wax and an uneven press from her ring, and sent the lass on her way with it.

That much done, she lifted her head and looked around her. She had wandered into Rain Wild Street. It had always been a favorite section of town for her father and her. After they had conducted their business, they almost always found an excuse to stroll down it arm in arm, delighting in calling each other's attention to new and exotic wares. The last time they had walked here together, they had spent almost an afternoon in a crystal shop. The merchant featured a new kind of wind chimes. The slightest breath stirred them to music, and they played, not randomly, but an elusive and endless tune, too delicate for mortal tongue to hum and lingering oddly in the mind afterward. He had bought her a little cloth bag full of candied violets and rose petals, and a set of earrings shaped like sailfish. She had helped him pick out some perfume gems for her mother's birthday, and had gone with him to the silversmith to have them set in rings. It had been an extravagant day, of wandering in and out of the odd little shops that showcased the wares of the Rain Wild River folk.

It was said that magic flowed with the waters of the Rain Wild River. And certainly the wares that the Rain Wild River families sent into town were marvelously tinged with it. Whatever dark rumors one might hear of those settlers who had chosen to remain in the first settlement on the Rain Wild River, their trade goods reflected only wonder. From the Verga family came trade goods with the scent of antiquity on them: finely woven tapestries depicting folk not quite human, with eyes of lavender or topaz; bits of jewelry made of a metal whose source was unknown, in wondrously strange designs; lovely pottery vases, both aromatic and graceful. The Soffrons marketed pearls in deep shades of orange and amethyst and blue, and vessels of cold glass that never warmed and could be used to chill wine or fruit or sweet cream. From others came Kwazi fruit, whose rind yielded an oil that could numb even a serious wound and whose pulp was an intoxicant with an effect that lingered for days. The toy shops always lured Althea the most strongly: there one could find dolls whose liquid eyes and soft warm skin mimicked that of a real infant, and clockwork toys so finely geared they would run for hours, pillows stuffed with herbs that assured wonderful dreams, and marvelously carved smooth stone that glowed with a cool inner light to keep nightmares at bay. The prices on such things were dear even in Bingtown, and outrageously high once the goods had been shipped to other ports. Even so, price was not the reason why Ephron Vestrit refused to buy such toys, even for the outrageously spoiled granddaughter Malta. When Althea had pressed him about it, he had only shaken his head. "You cannot touch magic and not carry away some of its taint upon you," he had told her darkly. "Our forebears judged the price too high, and left the Rain Wilds to settle Bingtown. And we ourselves do not traffic in Rain Wild goods." When she had pressed him as to what he meant, he had shaken his head and told her that they would discuss it when she was older. But even his misgivings had not stopped him from buying the perfume gems that his wife had so longed for.

When she was older.

Well, no matter how much older she got, that was a discussion they would never have. The bitterness of this broke her out of her pleasant memories and into the dwindling afternoon. She left Rain Wild Street, but not without an apprehensive glance at Amber's shop on the corner. She almost expected to spy the woman standing in the window and staring at her. Instead the window showed only her wares draped artfully on a spread of cloth-of-gold on the lounge. The door to the shop stood invitingly open, and folk were coming and going. So her business prospered. Althea wondered which of the Rain Wild River families she was allied with, and how she had managed it. Unlike most of the other stores, her street sign did not bear a Trader family insignia.

In a quiet alley, Althea untied her pockets and considered their contents. It was as she had expected. She could have a room and a meal tonight, or she could eat frugally for several days on what they held. She thought again of simply going home, but could not bring herself to do it. At least, not while Kyle might be there. Later, after he had sailed, if she had not found work and a place to stay by then, then she might be driven to go home and retrieve at least her clothes and personal jewelry. That much she surely could claim, without loss of pride. But not while Kyle was there. Absolutely not. She dumped the coins and notes into her purse and cinched it tight, wishing she could call back the money she had spent so carelessly on drink the night before. She couldn't, so best to be careful with what remained. She hung the pockets back inside her skirts.

She left the alley and found herself walking purposefully down the street. She needed a place to stay for the night and there was but one that came to mind. She tried not to think of the many times her father had sternly warned her about his company before he finally outright forbade her to visit him. It had been months since she had last spoken to him, but when she was a child, before she began sailing with her father, she had spent many summer afternoons in his company. Although the other children from town had found him both alarming and disgusting, Althea had soon lost her fear of him. She had felt sorry for him, truth to be told. He was frightening, true, but the most frightening part about him was what others had done to him. Once she had grasped that, a tentative friendship had followed.

As the afternoon sun dimmed into a long summer's evening, Althea left Bingtown proper behind her and began to pick her way down the rock-strewn beach to where the beached *Paragon* reposed on the sand.

CHAPTER TWELVE

OF DERELICTS AND SLAVESHIPS

BELOW THE WATER. NOT JUST FOR A BREATH, NOT EN-GULFED IN THE MOMENT OF A WAVE, BUT HANGING upside down below the water, hair flowing with the movement of it, lungs pumping only salt water. *I am drowned and dead*, he thought to himself. *Drowned and dead as I was before.* Before him was only the greenly lit world of fishes and water. He opened his arms to it, let them dangle below his head and move with the waves. He waited to be dead.

But it was all a cheat, as it was always a cheat. All he wanted was to stop, was to cease being, but it was never allowed him. Even here, beneath the water, his decks stilled of battering feet and shouted commands, his holds replete with sea water and silence, there was no peace. Boredom, yes, but no peace. The silver shoals of fish avoided him. They came toward him like phalanxes of sea birds, only to veer away, still in formation, as they sensed the unholy wizardwood of his bones. He moved alone in a world of muted sounds and hazed colors, unbreathing, unsleeping.

Then the serpents came.

They were drawn to him, it seemed, both repulsed and

fascinated by him. They taunted him, peering at him, their toothy maws opening and closing so close to his face and arms. He tried to push them away, but they mobbed him, letting his fists batter at them as frantically as he might, and never showing any sign that they felt his strength as anything greater than a fish's helpless flopping. They spoke about him to one another, submerged trumpeting he almost understood. That was the most frightening thing, that he almost understood them. They looked deep into his eyes, they wrapped his hull in their sinuous embraces, holding him tight in a way that was both threatening and reminiscent of . . . something. It lurked around the last corner of his memory, some vestige of familiarity too frightening to summon to the forefront of his mind. They held him and dragged him down, deeper and deeper, so that the cargo still trapped inside him tore at him in its buoyant drive to be free. And all the while they accused and demanded furiously, as if their anger could force him to understand them.

"Paragon?"

He startled awake, from a dream with vision into the eternal hell of darkness. He tried to open his eyes. Even after all the years, he still tried to open his eyes and see who addressed him. Self-consciously, he lowered his up-reaching arms, crossed them protectively over his scarred chest to conceal the shame there. He almost knew her voice. "Yes?" he asked guardedly.

"It's me. Althea."

"Your father will be very angry if he finds you here. He will roar at you."

"That was a very long time ago, Paragon. I was just a girl then. I've come to see you a number of times since then. Don't you remember?"

"I suppose I do. You do not come often. And your father roaring at us when he found you here with me is what I remember best about you. He called me a 'damnable piece of wreckage,' and 'the worst sort of luck one could have.' "

She sounded almost ashamed as she replied, "Yes. I remember that too, very clearly."

"Probably not as clearly as I. But then, you probably have a greater variety of memories to choose from." He added petulantly, "One does not gather many unique memories, hauled out on a beach."

"I am sure you had a great many adventures in your day," Althea offered.

"Probably. It would be nice if I could remember any of them."

He heard her come closer. From the shifting in the angle of her voice, he judged she had sat down on a rock on the beach. "You used to speak to me of things you remembered. When I was a little girl and came here, you told me all sorts of stories."

"Most of them were lies, most likely. I don't remember. Or maybe I did then, but no longer do. I think I am getting vaguer. Brashen thinks it might be because my log is missing. He says I do not seem to recall as much of my past as I used to."

"Brashen?" A sharp edge of surprise in her voice.

"Another friend," Paragon replied carelessly. It pleased him to shock her with the news he had another friend. Sometimes it irritated him that they expected him to be so pleased to see them, as if they were the only folk he knew. Though they were, they should not have been so confident of it, as if it were impossible a wreck such as he might have made other friends.

"Oh." After a moment, Althea added, "I know him as well. He served on my father's ship."

"Ah, yes. The . . . *Vivacia*. How is she? Has she quickened yet?"

"Yes. Yes, she has. Just two days ago."

"Really? Then it surprises me you are here. I thought you would rather be with your own ship." He had had all the news from Brashen already, but it gave him an odd pleasure to force Althea to speak of it.

"I suppose I would be, if I could," the girl admitted unwillingly. "I miss her so much. I need her so badly just now."

Her honesty caught Paragon off guard. He had accustomed himself to think of people as givers of pain. They could move about so freely and end their lives anytime they chose; it was hard for him to understand that she could feel such a depth of pain as her voice suggested. For a moment, somewhere in the labyrinths of his memory a homesick boy sobbed into his bunk. Paragon snatched his consciousness back from it. "Tell me about it," he suggested to Althea. He did not truly want to hear her woes, but at least it was a way to keep his own at bay.

It surprised him when she complied. She spoke long, of everything, from Kyle Haven's betrayal of her family's trust to her own incomplete grief for her father. As she spoke, he felt the last warmth of the afternoon ebb away and the coolness of night come on. At some time she left her rock to come and lean her back against the silvered planking of his hull. He suspected she did it for the warmth of the day that lingered in his bones, but with the nearness of her body came a greater sharing of her words and feelings. Almost it was like they were kin. Did she know that she reached toward him for understanding as if he were her own liveship? Probably not, he told himself harshly. It was probably just that he reminded her of the *Vivacia* and so she extended her feelings into him. That was all. It was not especially intended for him.

Nothing was especially intended for him.

He forced himself to remember that, and so he could be calm when, after she had been silent for some time, she said, "I have no place to stay tonight. Could I sleep aboard?"

"It's probably a smelly mess in there," he cautioned her. "Oh, my hull is sound enough, still. But one can do little about storm waters, and blown sand and beach lice can find a way into anything."

"Please, Paragon. I won't mind. I'm sure I can find a dry corner to curl up in."

"Very well, then," he conceded, and then hid his smile in his beard as he added, "if you don't mind sharing space with Brashen. He comes back here every night, you know."

"He does?" Startled dismay was in her voice.

"He comes and stays almost every time he makes port here. It's always the same. The first night it's because it's late and he's drunk and he doesn't want to pay a full night's lodging for a few hours sleep and he feels safe here. And he always goes on about how he's going to save his wages and only spend a bit of it this time, so that someday he'll have enough saved up to make something of himself." Paragon paused, savoring Althea's shocked silence. "He never does, of course. Every night he comes stumbling back, his pockets a bit lighter, until it's all gone. And when he has no more to spend on drink, then he goes back and stays on whatever ship will have him until he ships out again."

"Paragon," Althea corrected him gently. "Brashen has worked the *Vivacia* for years now. I think he always used to sleep aboard her when he was in port here."

"Well, but, yes, I suppose, but I meant before that. Before that, and now." Without meaning to, he spoke his next thought aloud. "Time runs together and gets tangled up, when one is blind and alone."

"I suppose it would." She leaned her head back against him and sighed deeply. "Well. I think I shall go in and find a place to curl up, before the light is gone completely."

"Before the light is gone," Paragon repeated slowly. "So. Not completely dark yet."

"No. You know how long evening lingers in summer. But it's probably black as pitch inside, so don't be alarmed if I go stumbling about." She paused awkwardly, then came to stand before him. Canted as he was on the sand, she could reach his hand easily. She patted it, then shook it. "Good night, Paragon. And thank you."

"Good night," he repeated. "Oh. Brashen has been sleeping in the captain's quarters."

"Right. Thank you."

She clambered awkwardly up his side. He heard the whisper of fabric, lots of it. It seemed to encumber her as she traversed his slanting deck and finally fumbled her way down into his cargo hold. She had been more agile as a girl. There had been a summer when she had come to see him nearly every day. Her home was somewhere on the hillside above him; she spoke of walking through the woods behind her home and then climbing down the cliffs to him. That summer she had known him well, playing all sorts of games inside him and around him, pretending he was her ship and she was captain of him, until word of it came to her father's ears. He had followed her one day, and when he found her talking to the cursed ship, he soundly scolded them both and then herded Althea home with a switch. For a long time after that, she had not come to see him. When she did come, it was only for brief visits in early dawn or evening. But for that one summer, she had known him well.

She still seemed to remember something of him, for she made her way through his interior until she came to the aft space where the crew used to hang their hammocks. Odd, how the feel of her inside him could stir such memories to life again. Crenshaw had had red hair and was always complaining about the food. He had died there, the hatchet that ended his life had left a deep scar in the planking as well, his blood had stained the wood. . . .

She curled up against a bulkhead. She'd be cold tonight. His hull might be sound, but that didn't keep the damp out of him. He could feel her, still and small against him, unsleeping. Her eyes were probably open, staring into the blackness.

Time passed. A minute or most of the night. Hard to tell. Brashen came down the beach. Paragon knew his stride and the way he muttered to himself when he'd been drinking. Tonight his voice was dark with worry and Paragon judged he was close to the end of his money. Tomorrow he would rebuke himself long for his stupidity, and then go out to spend the last of his coins. Then he'd have to go to sea again.

Paragon would almost miss him. Having company was interesting and exciting. But also annoying and disturbing. Brashen and Althea made him think about things better left undisturbed.

"Paragon," Brashen greeted him as he drew near. "Permission to come aboard."

"Granted. Althea Vestrit's here."

A silence. Paragon could almost feel him goggling up at him. "She looking for me?" Brashen asked thickly.

"No. Me." It pleased him inordinately to give the man that answer. "Her family has turned her out, and she had nowhere else to go. So she came here."

"Oh." Another pause. "Doesn't surprise me. Well, the sooner she gives up and goes home, the wiser she'll be. Though I imagine it will take her a while to come to that." Brashen yawned hugely. "Does she know I'm living aboard?" A cautious question, one that begged for a negative answer.

"Of course," Paragon answered smoothly. "I told her that you had taken the captain's cabin and that she'd have to make do elsewhere."

"Oh. Well, good for you. Good for you. Good night, then. I'm dead on my feet."

"Good night, Brashen. Sleep well."

A few moments later, Brashen was in the captain's quarters. A few minutes after that, Paragon felt Althea uncurl. She was trying to move quietly, but she could not conceal herself from Paragon. When she finally reached the door of the aftercastle chamber where Brashen had strung his hammock, she paused. She rapped very lightly on the paneled door. "Brash?" she said cautiously.

"What?" he answered readily. He had not been asleep, nor even near sleep. Could he have been waiting? How could he have known she would come to him?

Althea took a deep breath. "Can I talk to you?"

"Can I stop you?" he asked grumpily. It was evidently a familiar response, for Althea was not put off by it. She set her hand to the door handle, then took it away without opening the door. She leaned on the door and spoke close to it.

"Do you have a lantern or a candle?"

"No. Is that what you wanted to talk about?" His tone seemed to be getting brusquer.

"No. It's just that I prefer to see the person I'm talking to."

"Why? You know what I look like."

"You're impossible when you're drunk."

"At least with me, it's only when I'm drunk. You're impossible all the time."

Althea sounded distinctly annoyed now. "I don't know why I'm even trying to talk to you."

"That makes two of us," Brashen added as an aside, as if to himself. Paragon suddenly wondered if they were aware of how clearly he could hear their every word and movement. Did they know he was their unseen audience, or did they truly believe themselves alone? Brashen, at least, he suspected, included him.

Althea sighed heavily. She leaned her head on the paneled door between them. "I have no one else to talk to. And I really need to . . . Look, can I come in? I hate talking through this door."

"The door isn't latched," he told her grudgingly. He didn't move from his hammock.

In the darkness, Althea pushed the door open. She stood in the entry uncertainly for a moment, then groped her way into the room. She followed the wall, bracing herself to keep from falling on the slanted deck. "Where are you?"

"Over here. In a hammock. Best sit down before you fall."

He offered her no more courtesy than that. Althea sat, bracing her feet against the slope of the floor and leaning back against a bulkhead. She took a deep breath. "Brashen, my whole life just fell apart in the last two days. I don't know what to do."

"Go home," he suggested without sympathy. "You know that eventually you'll have to. The longer you put it off, the harder it will be. So do it now."

"That's easy to say, and hard to do. You should understand that. You never went home."

Brashen gave a short, bitter laugh. "Didn't I? I tried. They just threw me out again. Because I had waited too long. So. Now you know you are getting good advice. Go back home while you still can, while a bit of crawling and humble obedience will buy you a place to sleep and food on your plate. Wait too long, let the disgrace set in, let them get used to life without the family troublemaker, and they won't have you back, no matter how you plead and crawl."

Althea was silent for a long time. Then, "That really happened to you?"

"No. I'm making it all up," Brashen replied sourly.

"I'm sorry," Althea said after a time. More resolutely she went on, "But I can't go back. At least, not while Kyle's in port. And even after he's gone, if I do go back, it will only be to get my things."

Brashen shifted in his hammock. "You mean your dresses and trinkets? Precious relics from your childhood? Your favorite pillow?"

"And my jewelry. If I have to, I can always sell that."

Brashen threw himself back in the hammock. "Why bother? You'll find you can't drag all that stuff around with you anyway. As for your jewelry, why not pretend you already got it, sold it piece by painful piece and the money is gone and now you really have to find out how to live your own life? That'll save you time, and any heirloom stuff will at least remain with your family. If Kyle hasn't seen to having it locked up already."

The silence that followed Brashen's bitter suggestion was blacker than the starless darkness that Paragon stared into. When Althea did speak again, her voice was hard with determination.

"I know you're right. I need to do something, not wait around for something to happen. I need to find work. And the only work I know anything about it sailing. And it's my only path to getting back on board Vivacia. But I won't get hired dressed like this. . . ."

Brashen gave a contemptuous snort. "Face it, Althea. You won't get hired no matter how you are dressed. You've got too much stacked up against you. You're a woman, you're Ephron Vestrit's daughter, and Kyle Haven won't be too happy with anyone who hires you, either."

"Why should being Ephron Vestrit's daughter be a mark against me?" Althea's voice was very small. "My father was a good man."

"True. That he was. A very good man." For a moment Brashen's tone gentled. "But what you have to learn is that it isn't easy to stop being a Trader's daughter. Or son. The Bingtown Traders look like as solid an alliance you can imagine, from the outside. But you and I, we came from the inside, and the inside works against us. See, you're a Vestrit. All right. So there are some families that trade with you and profit, and other families that compete with you, and other families that are allied with those who compete with you . . . no one is an enemy, exactly. But when you go looking for work, it's going to be, well, like it was for me. 'Brashen Trell, eh, Kelf Trell's son? Well, why don't you work for your family, boy? Oh, had a falling out? Well, I don't want to get on your father's bad side by hiring you.' Not that they ever come right out and say it, of course, they just look at you and put you off and say, 'come back in four days,' only they aren't in when you come back. And those that don't get along with your family, well, they don't want to hire you, either, cause they like seeing you down in the dirt."

Brashen's voice was winding down, getting deeper and softer and slower. He was talking himself to sleep, Paragon thought, as he often did. He'd probably forgotten that Althea was even there. Paragon was overly familiar with Brashen's long litany of wrongs done him and injustices suffered by him. He was even more familiar with Brashen's caustic self-accusations of idiocy and worthlessness.

"So how did you survive?" Althea asked resentfully.

"Went to where it didn't matter what my name was. First boat I shipped out on was Chalcedean. They didn't care who I was, long as I would work hard and cheap. Meanest set of rotten bastards I ever shipped with. No mercy for a kid, no, not them. Jumped ship in the first harbor we put into. Left that same day, on a different boat. Not much better, but a little. Then we . . ." Brashen's voice trailed off. For a moment Paragon thought he had fallen asleep. He heard Althea shifting about, trying to find a comfortable way to sit on the slanted deck. ". . . by the time I came back to Bingtown, I was a seasoned hand. Oh, was I seasoned. But still the same old damn thing. Trell's boy this, and Trell's son that . . . I'd thought I'd made something of myself. I actually tried to go to my father and patch things up. But he was not much impressed with what I'd made of myself. No, sir, he was not. What a horse's ass . . . so I went to every ship in the harbor. Every ship. No one was hiring Kelf Trell's son. When I got to the *Vivacia*, I kept my scarf down low on my brow and kept my eyes on the deck. Asked for honest work for an honest sailor. And your father said he'd try me. Said he could use an honest man. Something about the way he said it . . . I was sure he hadn't recognized me, and I was sure he'd turn me off if I told him my name. But I did anyway. I looked at him and I said, 'I'm Brashen Trell. I used to be Kelf Trell's son.' And he said, 'That won't make your watch one minute shorter or longer, sailor.' And you know. It never did."

"Chalcedeans don't hire women," Althea said dully. Paragon wondered how much of Brashen's tale she had truly heard.

"Not as sailors," Brashen agreed. "They believe a woman aboard ship will draw serpents after you. Because women bleed, you know. Lots of sailors say that."

"That's stupid," she exclaimed in disgust.

"Yeah. Lots of sailors are stupid. Look at us." He laughed at his own jest, but she did not join him.

"There are other women sailors in Bingtown. Someone will hire me."

"Maybe, but not to do what you expect," Brashen said harshly. "Yes, there are women sailors, but most of the ones you see on the docks are working on their family boats, with fathers and brothers to protect them. Ship out alone on anything else, and you'd better choose early which shipmates you want to roll. If you're lucky, they'll be possessive enough to keep the others off you. If you're not lucky, they'll turn a nice profit from your services before you reach the next port. And most mates and captains will turn a blind eye to what goes on, to keep order on the ship. That's if they don't claim your services for themselves." He paused, then added grumpily, "And you already knew all that. You couldn't grow up around sailors and not know it. So why are you even considering this?"

Anger engulfed her. She wanted to shout that she didn't believe it or demand to know why men had to be such pigs. But she did believe it, and she knew that Brashen could not answer that question any more than she could. Silence bled into the darkness between them, and even her anger deserted her.

"So what am I to do?" she asked miserably. It did not seem to Paragon she was speaking to Brashen, but he answered anyway.

"Find a way to be reborn as a boy. Preferably one that isn't named Vestrit." Brashen rearranged himself in the hammock and drew in a long breath that emerged as a buzzing snore.

In her cramped corner, Althea sighed. She leaned her head back against the hard wood of the bulkhead and was still and silent.

The slaver was a darker silhouette against the night sky. If he felt he was in any danger of pursuit, he showed no signs of it. He had a respectable amount of canvas on but Kennit's keen eyes saw no flurry of activity aloft to indicate he felt a need for extreme speed. The night was perfect, a sweet even wind breathing over the sea, the waves willing beasts bearing the ship along. "We'll overhaul him before dawn," he observed quietly to Sorcor.

"Aye," Sorcor breathed. His voice betrayed far more excitement at the prospect than his captain felt. Over his shoulder, he said quietly to the helmsman, "Keep her in close to the shore. Hug it like your granny. If their lookout chances to glance this way, I don't want us visible against the open water." To the ship's boy he hissed, "Below. Pass the word yet again. Still and silent, no movement that isn't in response to a command. And not a light to show, not so much as a spark. Go and softly, now."

"He's got a couple of serpents off his stern," Kennit observed.

"They follow for the dead slaves thrown overboard," Sorcor said bitterly. "And for those too sick to be worth feeding. They go over the side, too."

"And if the serpents choose to turn and attack us during battle?" Kennit inquired. "What then?"

"They won't," Sorcor assured him. "Serpents learn quickly. They'll let us kill each other, well knowing they'll get the dead with not a scale lost."

"And after?"

Sorcor grinned savagely. "If we win, they'll be so fat with the crew of the slaver, they won't be able to wiggle after us. If we lose . . ." he shrugged. "It won't much matter to us."

Kennit leaned on the railing, sour and silent. Earlier in the day, they had spotted the *Ringsgold*, a fine old fat waddling cog of a liveship, near as deep as he was tall. They had had the advantage of surprise; Kennit had had the crew hang out every bit of canvas the rigging would hold, and yet the liveship had lifted and dashed off as if driven by his own private wind. Sorcor had stood silent by his side as Kennit had first been silently incredulous and then savagely angry at the turn of events. When the *Ringsgold* rounded Pointless Island to catch the favorable current there and be whisked from sight, Sorcor had dared to observe, "Dead wood has no chance against wizardwood. The very waves of the sea part for it."

"Be damned," Kennit had told him fiercely.

"Quite likely, sir," Sorcor had replied un-perturbed. He had probably already been sniffing the air for the spoor of a slaveship.

Or maybe it was just the man's infernal luck that they had raised this one so quickly. It was a typical Chalcedean slaver, deep hulled and wide waisted, all the better to pack her full of flesh. Never had Kennit seen Sorcor so lustful in pursuit, so painstaking in his stalking. The very winds seemed to bless him, and it was actually well before dawn when Sorcor ordered the sweeps out. The ballista were already wound and set, loaded with ball and chain to foul their prey's rigging and grappling hooks were ready to snare their crippled conquest. These last were a new idea of Sorcor's, one that Kennit regarded with skepticism.

"Will you lead the crew to the prize, sir?" Sorcor asked him even as the lookouts on the slaver sounded the first alarms.

"Oh, I think I shall leave that honor to you," Kennit demurred dryly. He leaned idly on the railing, putting the pursuit and battle entirely into Sorcor's hands. If the mate was dismayed by his captain's lack of enthusiasm, he covered it well. He sprang aloft, to cry his commands down to the men on deck. The men shared his battle pitch, for they leaped to obey with a will, so that the extra canvas seemed to flow over the mast and blossom with the night wind. Kennit was

selfishly grateful for the favorable wind, for it bore most of the stench
of the slaver away from them.

He felt almost detached as they closed the distance on the slaver.
In a desperate bid to outpace them, the slaver was putting on sail, the
rigging swarming with men scuttling like disturbed ants. Sorcor
cursed his delight with this and ordered the ballista fired. Kennit
thought he had acted too quickly, yet the two heavy balls linked with a
stout length of barbed and bladed chain flew well and high, crashing
into the other ship's canvas and lines, ripping and tangling as they fell
heavily to the deck below. Half a dozen men fell with the balls,
screaming until they found the deck or vanished beneath the waves.
The sound of their screams had scarcely died before Sorcor had
launched a second set of balls and chain. This one did not do quite as
much damage, but the harried crew of the slaver were now too busy
watching for other missiles to work the sails effectively, while the
canvas and lines that had fallen draped the deck and fouled the workings of the other sails. The slaver's decks were in a state of total
disarray when Sorcor ordered grappling lines swung.

Kennit felt distant and detached as he watched their hapless victim
roped in and secured. As dawn ventured over the water, Sorcor and
his raiders leaped or swung across the small distance between the two
vessels, whooping and screeching their bloodlust. Kennit himself
lifted his cuff to his nose and breathed through his sleeve to keep from
inhaling the stench of the slaver. He remained aboard the *Marietta*
with a skeleton crew. Those who remained with him were plainly
frustrated to be cheated of the slaughter, yet someone had to man the
Marietta and be ready either to repel boarders or cast loose the grappling lines if things went against them.

Kennit was a spectator to the slaughter of the slaver's crew. They
had little expected to be attacked by pirates. Their cargo was not
usually to a pirate's taste. Most pirates, like Kennit, preferred valuable, non-perishable goods, preferably easily transportable. The
chained slaves below decks were the only cargo this ship carried. Even
if the pirates had had the will to make the tedious voyage to Chalced
to sell them, the transport of such cargo demanded a watchful eye and
a strong stomach. Such livestock needed to be guarded as well as fed,
watered and provided with rudimentary sanitation. The ship itself
would have some value, Kennit supposed, though the current stench it
gave off was enough to turn his stomach.

The crew of the slaver had such weapons as they carried to keep
their cargo in order and little more than that. They did not, Kennit
reflected, seem to have much idea of how to fight an armed and

healthy man; he supposed that one became accustomed to beating or kicking men in chains and forgot what it was like to deal with any other type of opponent.

He had earlier tried to persuade Sorcor that the crew and vessel might have some ransom value, even if divested of their cargo. Sorcor had been adamantly opposed. "We kill the crew, free the cargo and sell the ship. But not back to other slavers," he had loftily stipulated.

Kennit was beginning to regret letting the man think he regarded him as an equal. He was becoming entirely too demanding, and seemed unaware of how odious Kennit found such behavior. Kennit narrowed his eyes as he considered that the crew seemed overly pleased with Sorcor's idealistic ranting. He doubted it was that they shared his lofty goals of suppressing slavery. More like that they relished the thought of unreined carnage. As he watched two of his worthy seamen together loft a still-living man over the side and into the waiting maw of a serpent, Kennit nodded his head slowly to himself. This bestial bloodshed was what they craved. Perhaps he had been keeping too tight a rein on the men for the sake of the ransom that live captives bought. He tucked that thought away for later consideration. He could learn from anyone, even Sorcor. All dogs needed to be let off their leashes now and then. He mustn't let the crew believe that only Sorcor could provide such treats.

He quickly wearied of watching the final slaughter. The slaver's crew was no match for his. There was no organization to their ship's defense, merely a band of men trying not to die. They failed at that. The mass of men that had met the pirate's boarding party rapidly diminished to knots of defenders surrounded by implacable foe. The ending was predictable; there was no suspense at all to this conquest. Kennit turned away from it. There was a sameness to men dying that bored more than disgusted him. The shrieks, the blood that gushed or leaked, the final frantic struggles, the useless pleas; he had seen it all before. It was far more enlightening to watch the two serpents.

He wondered if they had not escorted this ship for some time; perhaps they even regarded it companionably, as a sort of provider of easy feeding. They had withdrawn when the *Marietta* initially attacked, seemingly spooked by the flurry of activity. But when the sounds of battle and the shrieks of the dying began, they came swiftly back. They circled the locked ships like dogs begging at a table, vying with one another for the choicest positions. Never before had Kennit had the opportunity to observe a serpent for so long and at such close quarters. These two seemed fearless. The larger one was a scintillating crimson mottled with orange. When he reared his head and neck from the water and opened his maw, a ruff of barbs stood out around his throat and head like a lion's mane. They were fleshy, waving appendages, reminding Kennit of the stinging arms on an anemone or jellyfish. He would have been much surprised to discover they were not tipped with some sort of paralyzing poison. Certainly when the smaller turquoise worm vied with the larger one, he avoided the touch of the other's ruff.

What the smaller serpent lacked in size it made up for in aggression. It dared to come much closer to the ship's side, and when it lifted its head to the height of the slaveship's rail, it opened its maw as well, baring row upon row of pointed teeth. It hissed when it did so, sending forth a fine cloud of venomous spittle. The cloud engulfed two struggling men. Both of them immediately left off their own fight and fell gasping to the deck, writhing in a useless struggle to pull air into their lungs. They soon grew still while the frustrated serpent lashed the sea beside the ship into foam, furious that its prey remained safe aboard the ship. Kennit guessed that it was young and inexperienced.

The larger serpent seemed more philosophical. He was content to hover alongside the slaver, watching expectantly for men bearing bodies to approach the railing. He then opened his maw to catch whatever was thrown, regardless of whether it was dead or wriggling. He would seize a body in his jaws, but made no effort at chewing it. His teeth seemed devoted to the purpose of tearing. These small tidbits needed no dismembering. Instead the serpent would fling his head back and open his jaws far wider than Kennit would have believed possible. Then the body would vanish, boots and all, and Kennit could mark its progress down the creature's gullet by the distention of his sinuous throat. It was a spectacle at once chilling and fascinating.

His crew seemed to share his awe, for as the battle subsided and there were but bodies and subdued captives to dispose of, they gathered their serpent victuals on the high afterdeck of the slaver and took turns feeding the serpents from there. Some of the bound captives wept and screamed, but their cries were drowned out by the approving roars of the pirate crew as each human morsel was flung over the side. It soon became a game to toss each victim or corpse not to a serpent, but between them, to watch the great beasts vie for the meat. Those men who had remained aboard the *Marietta* felt greatly slighted to be excluded from this pastime, for though they kept to their duties on the ship, it was with many a glance in the direction of their comrades. As the serpents became sated, their aggression diminished and they were content to take turns with their feeding.

As the final captives went over the side, the first of the slaves began to emerge onto the deck. They came up from the hatches, coughing and blinking in the morning light. They clutched their tattered rags about their bony bodies against the briskness of the sea wind. As hatch cover after hatch cover was removed, the fetid stink in the air increased, as if the stench were an evil genie confined too long below decks. Kennit's gorge rose as he saw how scabrous these men were. Disease had always held a great horror for him, and he hastily sent a man to tell Sorcor it was time the vessels parted. He wanted good clean seawater between him and that pestilence-ridden hulk. He saw his messenger leap to his command, more than willing to get a closer look for himself. Kennit himself quit the afterdeck and went below to his cabin. There he set scented candles alight to ward off the trailing odor from outside.

Some moments later, Sorcor rapped smartly on his door.

"Enter," Kennit invited him brusquely.

The burly mate came in, red of hand and bright of eye. "A complete victory," he told Kennit breathlessly. "A complete victory. The ship is ours, sir. And over 350 men, women and children released from below her scurvy decks."

"Any other cargo worth speaking of?" Kennit asked dryly when Sorcor paused for breath.

Sorcor grinned. "The captain seemed to have an eye for fine clothes, sir. But he was a portly man, and his taste in colors rather wild."

"Then perhaps you will find the dead man's garments to your taste." The chill in Kennit's tone stood Sorcor up straight. "If you have finished with your adventure, I suggest we put a small crew aboard her and sail our 'prize' to port somewhere, seeing as how that wooden hulk is all we have to show for the night's work. How many men lost or wounded?"

"Two dead, sir, three cut up a bit." Sorcor sounded resentful of the question. Plainly he had been foolish enough to expect Kennit to share his exuberance.

"I wonder how many more we shall lose to disease. The stench alone is enough to give a man the flux, let alone whatever other contagion they have bred in that tub."

"It's scarcely the fault of the folk we have rescued if we do, sir," Sorcor pointed out stiffly.

"I did not say it would be. I will put it down to our own foolishness. Now. We have the ship to show for our troubles, and perhaps it will sell for a bit, but only after we have rid it of its cargo and seen to its scrubbing out." He looked at Sorcor and smiled carefully as he phrased the question he had been looking forward to. "What do you propose to do with these wretches you have rescued? Where shall we put them off?"

"We can't simply put them off on the closest land, sir. It'd be murder. Half are sick, the others weak, and there are no tools or provisions of any kind we could leave them, save ship's biscuit."

"Murder," Kennit cut in affably. "Ah, now there's a foreign concept for you and me. Not that I've been tossing folk to sea serpents of late."

"They got what they deserved!" Sorcor was beginning to look badgered. "And better than what they deserved, for what they got was quick!" He smacked a meaty fist into his other palm and nearly glared.

Kennit heaved a tiny sigh. "Ah, Sorcor, I do not dispute that. I am merely trying to remind you that we are, you and I, pirates. Murderous villains who scour the Inside Passage for vessels to overcome, loot and plunder and ransom. We do this to make a profit for ourselves. We are not nursery maids for sickly slaves, half of whom are probably as deserving of their fates as were the crew that you fed to the serpents. Nor are we heroic saviors of the downtrodden. Pirates, Sorcor. We are pirates."

"It was our deal," Sorcor pointed out doggedly. "For every liveship we chase, we go after one slaver. You agreed."

"So I did. I had hoped that after you had dealt with the reality of one 'triumph' you would see the futility of it. Look you, Sorcor. Say we strain our crew and resources to take that squalid vessel to Divvytown. Do you think the inhabitants are going to welcome us and rejoice that we put ashore 350 half-starved, ragged, sickly wretches to infest their town as beggars, whores and thieves? Do you think these slaves we have 'rescued' are going to thank you for abandoning them to their fates as paupers?"

"They're thankful now, the whole damn lot of them," Sorcor declared stubbornly. "And I know in my time, sir, I'd have been damn grateful to be set ashore anywhere, with or without a mouthful of bread or a stitch of clothes, so long as I was a free man and able to breathe clean air."

"Very well, very well." Kennit made a great show of capitulating with a resigned sigh. "Let us ride this ass to the end, if we must. Choose a port, Sorcor, and we shall take them there. I shall but ask this. On our way there, those who are able shall begin the task of cleaning out that vessel. And I should like to get underway as soon as we are decently able, while the serpents are still satiated." Kennit glanced casually away from Sorcor. It would not do to let him wallow in the gratitude of the freed captives. "I shall require you aboard the *Marietta*, Sorcor. Put Rafo in charge of the other vessel, and assign him some men."

Sorcor straightened himself. "Aye, sir," he replied heavily. He trudged from the room, a very different man from the one who had burst in the door exuberant with victory. He shut the door quietly behind himself. For a time, Kennit remained looking at it. He was straining the man's loyalty; the link that bound them together was forged mostly from Sorcor's fidelity. He shook his head to himself. It was, perhaps, his own fault. He had taken a simple uneducated sailor with a knack for numbers and navigation and elevated him to the status of mate, taught him how it felt to control men. Thinking, perforce, went with that command. But Sorcor was beginning to think too much. Kennit would soon have to decide which was worth more to him: the mate's value as second in command, or his own total control of his ship and men. Kennit sighed heavily. Tools blunted so quickly in this trade.

CHAPTER THIRTEEN

TRANSITIONS

RASHEN AWOKE WITH GRITTY EYES AND A CRICK IN HIS NECK. MORNING SUNLIGHT HAD PENETRATED THE thick panes of the bay windows that glassed one end of the chamber. It was a thick, murky light, greenish with the dried algae that coated the outside of the windows, but light nonetheless. Enough to alert him that it was daylight and time he was up and about.

He swung out of the hammock to his feet. Guilty. He was guilty of something. Spending all his pay when he had sworn that this time he would be wiser. Yes, but that was a familiar guilt. This was something else, something that bit with sharper teeth. Oh. Althea. The girl had been here last night, begging his advice, or he had dreamed her. And he had given her his bitterest counsels with not a word of hope or an offer of help from him.

He tried to shrug the concern away. After all, what did he owe the girl? Nothing. Not a thing. They hadn't even really been friends. Too big of a gap in status for that. He had just been the mate on her father's ship, and she had been the daughter of the captain. No room for a friendship there. And as for the old man, well, yes, Ephron Vestrit had done him a good turn when no one else would, had let him prove himself when no one else would. But the old man was dead now, so that was that.

Besides. Bitter as the advice had been, it was solid. If Brashen could have gone back in time, he would never have quarreled with his father. He'd have gone to the endless schooling, behaved correctly at the social functions, eschewed drunkenness and cindin, married whoever was chosen for him. And he'd be the heir now to the Trell fortune, instead of his little brother.

The thought reminded him that as he was not heir to the Trell fortune and as he had spent the rest of his money last night save for a few odd coins, he had best be worrying more about himself and less about Althea. The girl would have to take care of herself. She'd have to go home. That's all there was to it. What was the worst that would happen to her, really? They'd marry her off to a suitable man. She'd live in a comfortable home with servants and well-prepared food, wear clothing tailored especially for her and go to the endless round of balls and teas and social functions that seemed so essential to Bingtown society and the Traders especially. He snorted softly to himself. He should hope for such a cruel fate to befall him. He scratched at his chest and then his beard. He ran both hands through his hair to smooth it back from his face. Time to find work. He'd best clean himself up and head down to the docks.

"Good morning," he greeted Paragon as he rounded the bow of the ship.

The figurehead looked permanently uncomfortable, fastened to the front of the heavily leaning ship. Brashen suddenly wondered if it made his back ache, but didn't have the courage to ask. Paragon had his thickly muscled arms crossed over his bare chest as he faced out over the glinting water to where other ships came and went from the harbor. He didn't even turn toward Brashen. "Afternoon," Paragon corrected him.

"So it is," Brashen agreed. "And more than time I got myself down to the docks. Have to look for a new job, you know."

"I don't think she went home," Paragon replied. "I think that if she went home, she would have gone her old way, up the cliffs and through the woods. Instead, after she said good-bye, I heard her walking away over the beach toward town."

"Althea, you mean?" Brashen asked. He tried to sound unconcerned.

Blind Paragon nodded. "She was up at first light." The words almost sounded like a reproach. "I had just heard the morning birds begin to call when she stirred and came out. Not that she slept much last night."

"Well. She had a lot to think about. She may have gone into town this morning, but I'll wager she goes home before the week is out. After all, where else does she have to go?"

"Only here, I suppose," the ship replied. "So. You will seek work today?"

"If I want to eat, I have to work," Brashen agreed. "So I'm down to the docks. I think I'll try the fishing fleet or the slaughter boats instead of the merchants. I've heard a man can rise rapidly aboard one of the whale or dolphin boats. And they hire easy, too. Or so I've heard."

"Mostly because so many of them die," Paragon relentlessly observed. "That's what I heard, back when I was in a position to hear such gossip. That they're too long at sea and load their ships too heavy, and hire more crew than they need to work the ship because they don't expect all of them to survive the voyage."

"I've heard such things, too," Brashen reluctantly admitted. He squatted down on his haunches, then sat in the sand beside the beached ship. "But what other choice do I have? I should have listened to Captain Vestrit all those years. I'd have had some money saved up by now if I had." He gave a sound that was not a laugh. "I wish someone had told me, all those years ago, that I should just swallow my stupid pride and go home."

Paragon searched deep in his memory. "If wishes were horses, beggars would ride," he declared, and then smiled, almost pleased with himself. "There's a thought I haven't recalled for a long time."

"And true as ever it was," Brashen said disgruntledly. "So I'd best take myself down to the harbor and get myself a job on one of those stinking kill boats. More butchery than sailor's work is what I've heard of them as well."

"And dirty work it is, too," Paragon agreed. "On an honest merchant vessel, a man gets dirty with tar on his hands, or soaked with cold sea water, it's true. But on a slaughter ship, it's blood and offal and oil. Cut your finger and lose a hand to infection. If you don't die. And on those that take the meat as well, you'll spend half your sleeping time packing the flesh in tubs of salt. On the greedy ships the sailors end up sleeping right alongside the stinking cargo."

"You're so encouraging," Brashen said bleakly. "But what choice do I have? None at all."

Paragon laughed oddly. "How can you say that? You have the choice that eludes me, the choice that all men take for granted so that they cannot even see they have it."

"What choice is that?" Brashen asked uneasily. A wild note had come into the ship's voice, a reckless tone like that of a boy who fantasizes wildly.

"Stop." Paragon spoke the word with breathless desire. "Just stop."

"Stop what?"

"Stop being. You are such a fragile thing. Skin thinner than canvas, bones finer than any yard. Inside you are wet as the sea, and as salt, and it all waits to spill from you anytime your skin is opened. It is so easy for you to stop being. Open your skin and let your salt blood flow out, let the sea creatures take away your flesh bite by bite, until you are a handful of green slimed bones held together with lines of nibbled sinew. And you won't know or feel or think anything anymore. You will have stopped. Stopped."

"I don't want to stop," Brashen said in a low voice. "Not like that. No man wants to stop like that."

"No man?" Paragon laughed again, the sound breaking and going high. "Oh, I have known a few that did want to stop. And I have known a few that did stop. And it ended the same, whether they wanted to or not."

"One appears to have a small flaw."

"I am sure you are mistaken," Althea replied icily. "They are well-matched and deep-hued and of the finest quality. The setting is gold." She met the jeweler's gaze squarely. "My father never gave me a gift that was less than the finest quality."

The jeweler moved his palm and the two small earrings rolled aimlessly in his hand. In her ear lobes, they had looked subtle and sophisticated. In his palm, they merely looked small and simple. "Seventeen," he offered.

"I need twenty-three." She tried to conceal her relief. She had decided she would not take less than fifteen before she came into the shop. Still, she would wring every coin she could out of the man. Parting with them was not easy, and she had few other resources.

He shook his head. "Nineteen. I could go as high as nineteen, but no more than that."

"I could take nineteen," Althea began, watching his face carefully. When she saw his eyes brighten she added, "if you would include two simple gold hoops to replace these."

A half hour of bargaining later, she left his shop. Two simple silver hoops had replaced the earrings her father had given her on her thirteenth birthday. She tried not to think of them as anything other than a possession she had sold. She still had the memory of her father giving them to her. She did not need the actual jewelry. They would only have been two more things to worry about.

It was odd, the things one took for granted. Easy enough to buy heavy cotton fabric. But then she had to get needle, thread and palm as well. And shears for cutting the fabric. She resolved to make herself a small canvas bag as well to keep these implements in. If she followed her plan to its end, they would be the first possessions she had bought for her new life.

As she walked through the busy market, she saw it with new eyes. It was no longer merely a matter of what she had the coin to pay for and what she would have marked to her family's account. Suddenly some goods were far beyond her means. Not just lavish fabrics or rich jewelry, but things as simple as a lovely set of combs. She allowed herself to look at them for a few moments longer, holding them against her hair, as she looked into the cheap street-booth mirror and imagined how they would have looked in her hair at the Summer Ball. The flowing green silk, trimmed with the cream lace—for an instant she could almost see it, could almost step back into the life that had been hers a few scant days ago.

Then the moment passed. Abruptly Althea Vestrit and the Summer Ball seemed like a story she had made up. She wondered how much time would go by before her family opened her sea chest, and if they would guess which gifts had been intended for whom. She even indulged herself in wondering if her sister and mother would shed a tear or two over the gifts from the daughter and sister they had allowed to be driven away. She smiled a hard smile and set the combs back on the merchant's tray. No time for such mawkish daydreams. It didn't matter, she told herself sternly, if they never opened that trunk at all. What did matter was that she needed to find a way to survive. For, contrary to Brashen Trell's stupid advice, she was not going to go crawling home again like some helpless spoiled girl. No. That would only prove that everything Kyle had said about her was true.

She straightened her spine and moved with renewed purpose through the market. She bought herself a few simple foodstuffs: plums, a wedge of cheese and some rolls, no more than what she would need for the day. Two cheap candles and a tinderbox with flint and steel completed her purchases.

There was little else she could do in town that day, but she was reluctant to leave. Instead she wandered the market for a time, greeting those who recognized her and accepting their condolences on the loss of her father. It no longer stung when they mentioned him; instead it was a part of the conversation to get past, an awkwardness. She did not want to think of him, nor to discuss with relative strangers the grief she felt at her loss. Least of all did she want to be drawn into any conversation that might mention her rift with her family. She wondered how many folk knew of it. Kyle would not want it trumpeted about, but servants would talk, as they always did. Word would get around. She wanted to be gone before the gossip became widespread.

There were not many in Bingtown who recognized her anyway. For that matter, there were few other than the ship's brokers and merchants her father had done ship's business with that she recognized. She had withdrawn from Bingtown society gradually over the years without ever realizing it. Any other woman her age would have attended at least six gatherings in the last six months, balls and galas and other festivities. She had not been to even one since, oh, the Harvest Ball. Her sailing schedule had not allowed it. And the balls and dinners had seemed unimportant then, something she could return to whenever she wished. Gone now. Done and gone, dresses sewn for her with slippers to match, painting her lips and scenting her throat. Swallowed up in the sea with her father's body.

The grief she had thought numbed suddenly clutched at her throat. She turned and hurried off, up one street and down another. She blinked her eyes furiously, refusing to let the tears flow. When she had herself under control, she slowed her step and looked around her.

She looked directly into the window of Amber's shop.

As before, an odd chill of foreboding raced up her back. She could not think why she should feel threatened by a jeweler, but she did. The woman was not even a Trader, not even a proper jeweler. She carved wood, in Sa's name. Wood, and sold it as jewelry. In that instant, Althea suddenly decided she would see this woman's goods for herself. With the same resolution as if grasping a nettle, she pushed open the door and swept into the shop.

It was cooler inside, and almost dark after the brightness of the summer street. As her eyes adjusted, Althea saw the place as polished simplicity. The floor was smoothed pine planking. The shelves, too, were simple wood. Amber's goods were arranged on plain squares of deep-hued fabric on the shelves. Some of the more elaborate necklaces were displayed on the walls behind her counter. There were also pottery bowls full of loose wooden beads in every color that wood could be.

Her goods were not just jewelry either. There were simple bowls and platters, carved with rare grace and attention to grain; wooden goblets that could have honored a king's table; hair combs carved of scented wood. Nothing had been made of pieces fastened together. In each case, shapes had been discovered in the wood and called forth whole, brought to brilliance by carving and polishing. In one case a chair had been created from a huge wood bole; it was unlike any seat Althea had ever seen before, lacking legs but possessing a smoothed hollow that a slight person could curl into. Ensconced on it, knees folded beside her, sandaled feet peeping from the beneath the hem of her robe, was Amber.

It jolted Althea that for an instant she had looked right at Amber and not seen her. It was her skin and hair and eyes, she decided. The woman was all the same color, even to her clothing, and that color was identical to the honey-toned wood of the chair. She raised one eyebrow quizzically at Althea.

"You wished to see me?" she asked quietly.

"No," Althea exclaimed both truthfully and reflexively. Then she made an effort to recover, saying haughtily, "I was but curious to see this wooden jewelry that I had heard so much about."

"You being such a connoisseur of fine wood," Amber nodded.

There was almost no inflection to Amber's words. A threat? A sarcasm? A simple observation? Althea could not decide. And suddenly it was too much that this woodworker, this artisan, would dare to speak to her so. She was, by Sa, the daughter of a Bingtown Trader, a Bingtown Trader herself by right, and this woman, this upstart, was no more than a newcomer to their settlement who had dared to claim a spot for herself on Rain Wild Street. All Althea's frustration and anger of the past week suddenly had a target. "You refer to my liveship," Althea rejoined. It was all in the tone, the challenge as to what right this woman had to speak of her ship at all.

"Have they legalized slavery here in Bingtown?" Again there was no real expression to read in that fine-featured face. Amber asked the question as if it flowed naturally from Althea's last words.

"Of course not! Let the Chalcedeans keep their base customs. Bingtown will never acknowledge them as right."

"Ah. But then . . ." the briefest of pauses, "you did refer to the liveship as yours? Can you own another living intelligent creature?"

"Vivacia is mine, as I speak of my sister as mine. Family." Althea threw down the words. She could not have said why she suddenly felt so angry.

"Family. I see." Amber flowed upright. She was taller than Althea had expected. Not pretty, much less beautiful, there was still something arresting about her. Her clothing was demure, her carriage graceful. The finely pleated fabric of her robe echoed the fine plaits of her hair. Her appearance shared her carvings' simplicity and elegance. Her eyes met Althea's and held them. "You claim sisterhood with wood." A smile touched the corners of her lips, making Amber's mouth suddenly mobile, generous. "Perhaps we have more in common than I had dared to hope."

Even that tiny show of friendliness increased Althea's wariness. "You hoped?" she said coolly. "Why should you hope that we had anything in common at all?"

The smile widened fractionally. "Because it would make things easier for both of us."

Althea refused to be baited into another question.

After a time, Amber sighed a small sigh. "Such a stubborn girl. Yet I find myself admiring even that about you."

"Did you follow me the other day . . . the day I saw you down at the docks, near the *Vivacia*?" Althea's words came out almost as an accusation, but Amber seemed to take no offense.

"I could scarcely have followed you," she pointed out, "seeing as how I was there before you. I confess, it crossed my mind when I first saw you that perhaps you were following me. . . ."

"But the way you were looking at me . . ." Althea objected unwillingly. "I do not say that you lie. But you seemed to be looking for me. Watching me."

Amber nodded slowly, more to herself than to the girl. "So it seemed to me, also. And yet it was not you at all that I went seeking." She toyed with her earrings, setting first the dragon and then the serpent to swinging. "I went to the docks looking for a nine-fingered slave boy, if you can credit that." She smiled oddly. "You were what found me instead. There is coincidence, and there is fate. I am more than willing to argue with coincidence. But the few times I have argued with fate, I have lost. Badly." She shook her head, setting all four of her mismatched earrings to swaying. Her eyes seemed to look inward, recalling other times. Then she looked up and met Althea's curious gaze, and once more her smile softened her face. "But that is not true for all folk. Some folk are meant to argue with fate. And win."

Althea could think of no reply to that, so held her silence. After a moment, the woman moved to one of her shelves, and took down a basket. At least, at first glance it had appeared to be a basket. As she approached, Althea could see that it had been wrought from a single piece of wood, all excess carved away to leave a lattice of woven strands. Amber shook it as she came nearer, and the contents clicked and rattled pleasantly against one another.

"Choose one," she invited Althea, extending the basket to her. "I'd like to make you a gift."

Within the basket were beads. One glimpse of them, and Althea's impulse to haughtily refuse the largesse died. Something in the variety of color and shape caught the eyes and demanded to be touched. Once touched, they pleased the hand. Such a variety of color and grain and texture. They were all large beads, as big around as Althea's thumb. Each appeared to be unique. Some were simple abstract designs, others were animals, or flowers. Leaves, birds, a loaf of bread, fish, a tortoise . . . Althea found she had accepted the basket and was sifting through the contents while Amber watched her with strangely avid eyes. A spider, a twining worm, a ship, a wolf, a berry, an eye, a pudgy baby. Every bead in the basket was desirable, and Althea suddenly understood the charm of the woman's wares. They were gems of wood and creativity. Another artisan could surely carve as well, wood as fine could be bought, but never before had Althea seen such craft applied to such wood with such precision. The leaping dolphin bead could only have been a dolphin: there was no berry, no cat, no apple hiding in that bit of wood. Only the dolphin had been there, and only Amber could have found it and brought it out of concealment.

Althea could not choose, and yet she kept looking through the beads. Searching for the one that was most perfect. "Why do you want to give me a gift?" she asked suddenly. Her quick glance caught Amber's pride in her handiwork. She gloried in Althea's absorption in her beads. The woman's sallow cheeks were almost warm, her golden eyes glowing like a cat's before a fire.

When she spoke the warmth rode her words as well. "I would like to make you my friend."

"Why?"

"Because I can see that you go through life athwart it. You see the flow of events, you are able to tell how you could most easily fit yourself into it. But you dare to oppose it. And why? Simply because you look at it and say, 'this fate does not suit me. I will not allow it to befall me.'" Amber shook her head, but her small smile made it an affirmation. "I have always admired people who can do that. So few do. Many, of course, will rant and rave against the garment fate has woven for them, but they pick it up and don it all the same, and most wear it to the end of their days. You . . . you would rather go naked into the storm." Again the smile, fading as quickly as it blossomed. "I cannot abide that you should do that. So I offer you a bead to wear."

"You sound like a fortune teller," Althea complained, and then her finger touched something in the bottom of the basket. She knew the bead was hers before she gripped it between thumb and forefinger and brought it to the top of the hoard. Yet when she lifted it, she could not say why she had chosen it. An egg. A simple wooden egg, pierced to be worn on a string on her wrist or neck. It was a warm brown, a wood Althea did not know, and the grain of the wood ran around it rather than from end to end. It was plain compared to the other treasures in the basket, and yet it fit perfectly in the hollow of her hand when she closed her fingers about it. It was pleasant to hold, as a kitten is pleasant to stroke. "Might I have this one?" she asked softly and held her breath.

"The egg." Amber's smile came and stayed. "The serpent's egg. Yes, you might have that. You might indeed."

"Are you sure you wish nothing in return?" Althea asked baldly. She knew it was an awkward question, but something about Amber cautioned her that it was wiser to ask her a rude question than to blunder about with the wrong assumption.

"In return," Amber answered smoothly, "I only ask that you allow me to help you."

"Allow you to help me what?"

Amber smiled. "Thwart fate," she replied.

Wintrow scooped a double handful of lukewarm water from the bucket and splashed and rubbed it over his face. With a sigh, he lowered his hands back into the bucket and allowed the water to soothe them for a moment. Broken blisters, his father had assured him, were the beginning of callus. "We'll have those priest's hands toughened up in a week. You'll see," his father had jovially promised him the last time he had seen fit to notice his son's existence. Wintrow had been unable to reply.

He could not remember when he had ever been so tired before. His training told him that the deepest rhythms of his body were being broken. Instead of rising at dawn and seeking his bed when darkness closed over the land, his father and the first and second mates were forcing him into a new regimen, based on watches and bells. There was no need for their cruelty. The ship was still tied firmly to the dock, but nevertheless they persisted. What they were insisting he learn was not that difficult, if only they would let his body and mind completely rest between lessons. Instead they woke him at hours that made no sense to him, and had him clambering up and down masts and tying knots and sewing canvas and scrubbing and scouring. And always, always, with a scant smile at the corners of their lips, with an edge of mockery to every command. He was convinced he could have dealt well with anything they threw at him, if only he had not had to face that ever-present scorn. He pulled his aching hands from the bucket and gently dried them on a bit of rag.

He looked around the chain locker that had become his home. A hammock of coarse twine was draped across one corner. His clothing shared pegs with coils of line. Every bit of rope was now precisely and neatly stowed. The broken blisters on Wintrow's hands were testament to his repeated lessons.

He took down his cleanest shirt and eased into it. He thought about changing his trousers and decided it wasn't worth the effort. He'd washed out his other pair last night, but in the close confines of the storage room, they were still damp and were beginning to acquire a mildewy smell. He sank down onto his haunches; there was no comfortable place to sit. He put his aching head in his hands and waited for the bang on the door that would summon him to the captain's table. Since he had tried simply to walk off the ship yesterday, Torg had taken to locking him in his quarters during the time allotted for him to sleep.

Incredibly, he dozed off as he crouched there, jerking back to wakefulness when the door was snatched open. "Cap'n wants you." Torg greeted him. As he strode off, the apish man added, "though why anyone would want you is a puzzle to me."

Wintrow ignored the gibe and the screaming of his joints to rise and follow the man. As he walked, he tried to work his shoulders loose. It felt good to be able to stand completely upright again. Torg glanced back at him. "Hurry up, you! No one has time to put up with your dawdling."

It was more his body than his mind that responded, making an effort to put spring in his step. Although Torg had threatened him several times with a knotted rope, he'd never used it. And the fact that he only threatened him when neither his father nor the first mate were on board made Wintrow suspect it was something Torg would have liked to do but dared not. Still, just the sensing of that capacity in the man was enough to make Wintrow's flesh crawl whenever he was about.

Torg saw him right to the captain's door, as if he could not trust the boy to report himself. And Wintrow supposed he could not. Even though his father had reminded him repeatedly that Sa's precepts included obedience and honor due to one's parents, Wintrow had decided that if any opportunity presented itself at all, he would leave the ship and return however he could to his monastery. Sometimes he felt that resolve was all he had left to cling to. Torg watched him as he knocked sharply on the door, and then entered to his father's curt "Come ahead."

His father was already seated at a small table. A white cloth overlay it, and a goodly array of serving vessels graced it. It was set for two, and for an uncomfortable moment Wintrow stood in the door, wondering if he were intruding on a private meeting.

"Come in," his father said, a shade of annoyance in his voice. "And shut the door," he added in a gentler tone.

Wintrow obeyed him but remained standing by the door, wondering what was required of him now. Had he been summoned to wait table for his father and a guest? His father was dressed well, almost formally. He wore tight-fitting breeches of blue and a blue jacket over a shirt of soft cream. His hair had been plaited with oil and it gleamed like old gold in the lamplight.

"Wintrow, son, come and sit down and join me. Forget for a moment that I am the captain, and have a good meal and let us talk plainly." His father gestured at the plate and chair opposite him and smiled warmly. It only made Wintrow feel warier as he approached the table and gingerly seated himself. He smelled roast lamb and mashed turnips with butter and applesauce and peas cooked with mint. Amazing, how keen one's nose could become after a few days of hard bread and greasy stew as rations. Still, he kept his aplomb, forcing himself to unfold his napkin onto his lap and await his father's signal to begin serving himself. He said, "please," to his father's offer of wine, and "thank you" as each dish was offered him. He sensed his father watching him, but made no effort to meet his eyes as he filled and then emptied his plate.

If his father had intended this civilized meal and quiet moment as a bribe or a peace offering, it was ill-considered. For as the food filled his belly and the surroundings restored to him a sense of normality, Wintrow found a chill sense of outrage growing in him. From not knowing what to say to this man who smiled fondly as his son ate like a famished dog, Wintrow went to forcing his tongue to keep still. He tried to recall all he had been taught about dealing with adverse situations, that he should reserve judgment and action until he had grasped his opponent's motivation. So he ate and drank silently, watching his father covertly from beneath his lashes. His father actually rose himself to set their plates on a sideboard and then offered Wintrow a serving of custard with fruit. "Thank you," Wintrow forced himself to say quietly as it was set before him. There was something in the way his father re-settled himself in his chair that let him know the point of this whole meeting was about to be announced.

"You've developed a good appetite," Kyle observed genially. "Hard work and sea air will do that for a man."

"So it would seem," Wintrow replied evenly.

His father gave a gruff laugh. "So. Still smarting, are we? Come, son, I know this must seem hard to you, and perhaps just now you are still angry at me. But you must be coming to see this is what you were meant to do. Honest hard work and the company of men and the beauty of a ship under full sail . . . but I suppose you haven't known the full measure of it yet. I just want you to know, I'm not doing this to you to be harsh or cruel. A time will come when you will thank me. I promise you that. When we are done with you, you will know this ship as a true captain should, for you will have worked every measure of her, and there won't be a task on her that you haven't performed yourself." His father paused and smiled bitterly. "Unlike Althea, who just claims such knowledge. You will actually have done it, and not just when it pleased you, but as a sailor should, keeping busy every minute of your watch, and doing tasks as they need doing, not only when you are ordered to do so."

His father paused, obviously expecting some response. Wintrow kept still. After a heavy pause, his father cleared his throat. "I know what I am asking you is hard. So I will tell you plainly what awaits you at the end of this steep road. In two years, I expect to make Gantry Amsforge captain of this vessel. In two years, I expect you to be ready to serve as mate. You'll be very young for it; don't deceive yourself as to that. And it's not going to be handed to you. You'll have to show both Amsforge and I that you are ready for it. And even if and when we accept you, you'll still have to prove yourself to the crew, every day and every hour. It won't be easy. Still, it's an opportunity that damn few men have offered to them. So."

With a slow smile he reached into his jacket. He drew out a small box. He opened it himself and then turned to proffer the contents to Wintrow. It was a small gold earring, wrought in the likeness of the *Vivacia*'s figurehead. He had seen such earrings on the other sailors. Most crew-members wore some device that signaled their allegiance to their ship. An earring, a scarf, a pin, a tattoo if one were really sure of continuing employment. All were ways of declaring one's highest loyalty was given to a ship. Such an act was not fitting for a priest of Sa. Surely his father must already know his answer. But the smile on his father's face was warm as he invited him with, "This is for you, son. You should wear it proudly."

Truth. Simple truth, Wintrow counseled himself, spoken without anger or bitterness. So. Politely. Gently. "I don't want this opportunity. Thank you. You must know I would never deface my body by piercing an ear to wear that. I would rather be a priest of Sa. I believe it is my true calling. I know you believe you are offering me a—"

"Shut up!" There was deep hurt beneath the anger in his father's voice. "Just shut up." As the boy clenched his jaws and forced himself to look only at the table, his father spoke on to himself. "I'd rather hear anything from you than your mealy-mouthed prattle about being a priest of Sa. Say you hate me, tell me you can't take the work, and I'll know I can change your mind. But when you hide behind this priest nonsense . . . Are you afraid? Afraid of having your ear pierced, afraid of an unknown life?" His father's question was almost desperate. The man grasped after ways he could persuade Wintrow to his side.

"I am not afraid. I simply don't want this. Why don't you offer it to the person who truly hungers for it? Why don't you make this offer to Althea?" Wintrow asked quietly. The very softness of his words cut through his father's diatribe.

His father's eyes glinted like blue stone. He pointed his finger at Wintrow as if it were a weapon. "It's simple. She's a woman. And you, damn you, are going to be a man. For years it stuck in my craw to see Ephron Vestrit dragging his daughter after him, treating her like a son. And when you came back and stood before me in those brown skirts with your soft voice and softer body, with your mild manners and rabbitty ways, I had to ask myself, am I any better? For here before me stands my son, acting more like a woman than Althea ever has. It came to me like that. That it was time for this family—"

"You speak like a Chalcedean," Wintrow observed. "There, I am told, to be a woman is but little better than to be a slave. I think it is born of their long acceptance of slavery there. If you can believe that another human can be your possession, it is but a step to saying your wife and your daughter are also possessions, and relegate them to lives convenient to one's own. But in Jamaillia and in Bingtown, we used to take pride in what our women could do. I have studied the histories. Consider the Satrap Malowda, who reigned consortless for a score of years, and was responsible for the setting down of the Rights of Self and Property, the foundation of all our laws. For that matter, consider our religion. Sa, who we men worship as father of all, is still Sa when women call on her as mother of all. Only in Union is there Continuity. The very first precept of Sa says it all. It is only in the last few generations that we have begun to separate the halves of our whole, and divide the—"

"I didn't bring you hear to listen to your priestly clap-trap," Kyle Haven declared abruptly. He pushed himself away from the table so violently that it would have overturned if it had not been so securely fastened down. He paced a turn around the room. "You may not recall her, but your grandmother, my mother, was from Chalced. And yes, my mother behaved as was proper for a woman to behave, and my father kept to a man's ways. And I took no harm from such an upbringing. Look at your grandmother and mother! Do they seem happy and content to you? Burdened with decisions and duties that take them out into the harshness of the world, subjected to dealing with all sorts of low characters, forced to worry constantly about accounts and credits and debts? That isn't the life I swore I'd provide for your mother, Wintrow, or your sister. I won't see your mother grow old and burdened as your Grandmother Vestrit has. Not while I'm a man. And not while I can make you a man to follow after me and uphold the duties of a man in this family." Kyle Haven returned and slapped his hand firmly against the table and gave a sharp nod of his head, as if his words had determined the future of his entire family.

Words deserted Wintrow. He stared at his father and floundered through his thoughts, trying to find some common ground where he could begin reasoning with him. He could not. Despite the blood bond between them, this man was a stranger, and his beliefs were so utterly different from all Wintrow had embraced that he felt no hope of reaching him. Finally he said quietly, "Sa teaches us that no one may determine the life path of another. Even if you cage his flesh and forbid him to utter his thoughts, even to cutting out his tongue, you cannot still a man's soul."

For a moment, his father just looked at him. *He, too, sees a stranger,* Wintrow thought to himself. When he spoke, his voice was thick. "You're a coward. A craven coward." Then his father strode past him. It took all of Wintrow's nerve to keep from cowering as his sire passed him. But Kyle only threw open the door of his cabin and bellowed for Torg. The man appeared so promptly that Wintrow knew he must have been loitering nearby, perhaps eavesdropping. Kyle Haven either did not notice this or did not care.

"Take the ship's boy back to his quarters," his father ordered Torg abruptly. "Keep a good watch on him and see he learns all his duties before we sail. And keep him out of my sight." This last he uttered with great feeling, as if wronged by the world.

Torg gave a jerk of his head and Wintrow rose silently to follow him. With a sinking heart, he recognized the smirk on Torg's face. His father had given him over completely into this wretch's hands, and the man knew it.

For now the man seemed content to shepherd him forward to his miserable dungeon. Wintrow just managed to duck his head before the man pushed him across the threshold. He stumbled, but caught himself before he fell. He was too deep in despair to even pay attention to whatever mocking comment it was that Torg threw after him before slamming the door shut. He heard the man work the crude latch and knew he was shut in for the next six hours at least.

Torg hadn't even left him a candle. Wintrow groped through the darkness until his hands encountered the webbing of the hammock. Awkwardly he hauled his stiff body up into it and tried to arrange himself comfortably. Then he lay still. About him the ship moved gently on the waters of the harbor. The only sounds that reached him were muffled. He yawned hugely, the effects of his large meal and long day's work overwhelming both his anger and his despair. Out of long habit, he prepared both body and mind for rest. As much as the hammock would permit, he did the stretches of the large and small muscles of his body, striving to bring all back into alignment before rest.

The mental exercises were more difficult. Back when he had first come to the monastery, they had given him a very simple ritual called Forgiving the Day. Even the youngest child could do this; all it required was looking back over the day and dismissing the day's pains as a thing that were past while choosing to remember as gains lessons learned or moments of insight. As initiates grew in the ways of Sa, it was expected they would grow more sophisticated in this exercise, learning to balance the day, taking responsibility for their own actions and learning from them without indulging in either guilt or regrets. Wintrow did not think he was up to that tonight.

Odd. How easy it had been to love Sa's way and master the meditations in the quietly structured days of the monastery. Within the massive stone walls, it had been easy to discern the underlying order in the world, easy to look at the lives of the farmers and shepherds and merchants and see how much of their misery was self-generated. Now that he was out in the midst of it, he could still see some of that pattern, but he felt too weary to examine it and see how he could change it. He was tangled in the threads of his own tapestry. "I don't know how to make it stop," he said softly to the darkness. Doleful as an abandoned child, he wondered if any of his teachers missed him.

He recalled his final morning at the monastery, and the tree that had come to him out of the shards of stained glass. He had always taken a secret pride in his ability to summon beauty and hold it. But had it been his skill at all? Or had it been something created instead by the teachers who insulated him from the world and provided both a place and a time in which he might work? Perhaps, given the right atmosphere, anyone could do it. Perhaps the only thing about him that had been remarkable was that he had been given a chance. For an instant, he was overwhelmed by his own ordinariness. Nothing remarkable about Wintrow. An indifferent ship's boy, a clumsy sailor. Not even worth mentioning. He would disappear into time as if he had never been born. He could almost feel himself unraveling into darkness.

No. No! He would not let go. He would hang on to himself, and fight and something would happen. Something. Would the monastery send anyone to inquire after him when he did not return? "I think I'm hoping to be rescued," he observed wearily to himself. There. That was a high ambition. To stay alive and remain himself until someone else could save him. He was not sure if . . . if . . . if . . . There had been the beginning of a thought there, but the upsurging blackness of sleep drowned it.

In the dark of the harbor, Vivacia sighed. She crossed her slender arms over her breasts and stared up at the bright lights of the night market. So engrossed was she in her own thoughts that she startled to the soft touch of a hand against her planking. She looked down. "Ronica!" she exclaimed in gentle surprise.

"Yes. Hush. I would speak quietly with you."

"If you wish," Vivacia replied softly, intrigued.

"I need to know . . . that is, Althea sent me a message. She feared all was not well with you." The woman's voice faltered. "The message actually came some days ago. A servant, thinking it unimportant, had set it in Ephron's study. I only found it today."

Her hand was still set to the hull. Vivacia could read some of what she felt, though not all. "It is hard for you to go into that room, isn't it? As hard as it is to come down here and see me."

"Ephron," Ronica whispered brokenly. "Is he . . . is he within you? Can he speak through you to me?"

Vivacia shook her head sorrowfully. She was used to seeing this woman through Ephron's eyes or Althea's. They had seen her as determined and authoritative. Tonight, in her dark cloak with her head bowed, she looked so small. Vivacia longed to comfort her, but would not lie. "No. I'm afraid it isn't like that. I'm aware of what he knew, but it is commingled with so much else. Still. When I look at you, I feel as my own the love he felt for you. Does that help?"

"No," Ronica answered truthfully. "There is some comfort in it, but it can never be like Ephron's strong arms around me, or his advice guiding me. Oh, ship, what am I to do? What am I to do?"

"I don't know," Vivacia answered. Ronica's distress was awakening an answering anxiety in her. She put it in words. "It frightens me that you ask me that question. Surely you know what to do. Ephron certainly always believed you did." Reflectively, Vivacia added, "He thought of himself as a simple sailor, you know. A man who had the knack of running a ship well. You were the wisdom of the family, the one with the greater vision. He counted on that."

"He did?"

"Of course he did. How else could he have sailed off and left you to manage everything?"

Ronica was silent. Then she heaved a great sigh.

Quietly Vivacia added, "I think he would tell you to follow your own counsels."

Ronica shook her head wearily. "I fear you are right. Vivacia, do you know where Althea is?"

"Right now? No. Don't you?"

Ronica answered reluctantly. "I have not seen her since the morning after Ephron died."

"I have, several times. The last time she came to see me, Torg came down onto the docks and tried to lay hands on her. She pushed him off the dock, and walked away while everyone else was laughing."

"But she was all right?"

Vivacia shook her head. "Only as 'all right' as you or I am. Which is to say she is troubled and hurt and confused. But she told me to be patient, that all would eventually be put right. She told me not to take matters into my own hands."

Ronica nodded gravely. "Those are the very things I came down here to say tonight, also. Do you think you can keep such counsels?"

"I?" The ship almost laughed. "Ronica, I am three times a Vestrit. I fear I shall have only as much patience as my forebears did."

"An honest answer," Ronica conceded. "I will only ask that you try. No. I will ask one more thing. If Althea returns here, before you sail, will you give her a message from me? For I have no other way to contact her, save through you."

"Of course. And I will see that no one save her hears the message."

"Good, that is good. All I ask is that she come to see me. We are not at odds as much as she believes we are. But I will not go into details now. Just ask her to come to me, quietly."

"I shall tell her. But I do not know if she will."

"Neither do I, ship. Neither do I."

FAMILY MATTERS

ENNIT DID NOT TAKE THE CAPTURED SHIP TO DIV-
VYTOWN. HE DID NOT TRUST THE WALLOWING THING
not to become mired in negotiating the narrow channels
and numerous sandbars a ship must pass to get there. Instead, after a tense conference, he and Sorcor determined
that Askew would be a better port for her. Kennit had
thought it fitting; had not Askew been founded when a
storm-driven slaver took shelter up a channel and the cargo
managed a successful uprising against the crew, he had
asked Sorcor in amusement. Yes, that was true, but Sorcor
had still been opposed, for there was little more to Askew
than sand and rocks and clams. What future could these
folk have there? Better than what the slaver had offered
them, Kennit pointed out. Sorcor became surly but Kennit
insisted. The journey there had taken six slow days, far less
than it would have taken them to reach Divvytown, and
from Kennit's point of view, the time had been well spent.

Sorcor had seen a number of his rescued slaves die;
disease and starvation did not vanish simply because a man
could claim to be free. To Rafo's credit and that of his
charges, they had turned to and given the vessel a good

scrubbing. She no longer gave off the full stench of a slaver, but Kennit still insisted that the *Marietta* sail upwind of her. He would risk no wind bringing disease to his ship. He had permitted none of the freed slaves to board the *Marietta*, saying that crowding his own vessel to relieve the tight quarters on the *Fortune* would do no one any good. Instead the slaves had had to be content with spreading out on the decks and taking the living area of the devoured crew. Some of the healthier ones were pressed into service as deckhands to fill out the ranks of the skeleton crew that manned her. The unfamiliar work was hard for them, especially in their weakened state.

Despite this, and the continued deaths, the morale on the captured ship seemed high. The former slaves were pathetically grateful for fresh air, for shares of the salt pork that had once gone to the slaver's crew, and for whatever fish they could catch to supplement their diets. Sorcor had even been able to drive off the serpents with several showers of ballast shot from the ballista on the decks of the *Marietta*. Those who died now were still heaved from the decks of the ship, but the bodies splashed into the water rather than being snatched up by an avid serpent. This seemed to afford them great satisfaction, though for the life of him, Kennit could not see what difference it could make to the dead men.

They brought the ships into Askew on an incoming tide, when the push of the waters helped them up the sluggish tide channel that led into the brackish bay. The remains of a foundered ship thrust up skeletally at the shallow end of the anchorage. The village itself had sprung up as a row of huts and houses along the beach. These shelters were made from old ship's timbers, driftwood and stone. Thin smoke rose from a few chimneys. Two makeshift fishing boats were tied to a battered wharf and a half-dozen skiffs and coracles were pulled up on the sandy shore. It was not a prosperous town.

The *Marietta* led the way, and Kennit had to admit to a grudging pride that the slaves-cum-sailors that were the main crew of the *Fortune* now did not shame him. They worked lively if not as skillfully as seasoned salts, bringing the big ship in and setting her anchors well. The *Fortune* was now flying the Raven flag that was known throughout all the pirate isles as Kennit's emblem. By the time both ships had their boats away, a curious crowd had gathered on the rickety wharves to gawk at the newcomers. The rag-tag community of former slaves and refugees boasted no ship of their own larger than a fishing boat. To see two merchant ships anchor in their harbor must make them wonder what tidings or goods they brought.

Kennit was content to send Sorcor ashore with the news that they would be taking bids on the *Fortune*. He doubted that anyone in the ratty little town would have enough coin to have made the conquest worth his while, but he was determined simply to take the best offer and be rid of both the smelly ship and the slaves who had filled its hold. He did not permit himself to dwell on how much the cargo of men would have brought had he forced Sorcor to accept his wisdom and sail on to Chalced to sell them. That opportunity was lost; there was no point in dwelling on it.

From the docks, a small flotilla of rowboats was suddenly set in motion, hastening towards the *Fortune*. The slaves already crowded the railings, awaiting their chance to disembark from their floating prison. Kennit had not expected the townsfolk to be so eager to welcome his riff-raff. Well, all to the better. The sooner the *Fortune* was unloaded and sold, the sooner he could be back to more profitable pursuits. He turned aside, to give the ship's boy a curt order that he was not to be disturbed by anyone. He had no immediate desire to visit Askew. Let the slaves go first, and Sorcor, to see what sort of welcome they might receive.

Instead he spent several hours after they docked in perusing the fine charts that had been aboard the *Fortune*. Sorcor had completely overlooked the charts and papers that had been in a concealed cupboard in the captain's quarters. It was only when Kennit had finally decided to indulge his curiosity and pay a personal visit to the captured ship that they had been discovered. The papers were only of minimal interest to him, as they related only to the dead man's personal interests and properties. In passing he noticed that the slaver's wife and child had been well provided for. But the charts were another matter. In going over them, Kennit had noticed that his expectations were well founded. Charts were wealth. The information on them was often gained only at great cost, and was not casually shared with rival merchants or sailors. The slaver's charts showed only the obvious passage past the Pirate Isles. There were a few notes on rumors of other channels, but very little of the inland waterways of the islands had been charted. Seven pirate settlements were marked on the chart, two incorrectly and a third was a settlement long abandoned as too exposed to passing slaveships. Slavers saw no reason not to raid pirate settlements for extra cargo as they were passing through; it was one of Sorcor's grievances against them. Despite these obvious lacks, it was a painstaking chart of the main channel.

For some time Kennit leaned back in his chair and gazed out at the high passing clouds and considered. He decided he could accept this chart as the current level of the slavers' knowledge of the Pirate

Isles and the passages through it. So. If a man could gain control of the main channel, he could strangle all trade. Slaveships had not the leisure to explore, looking for alternate routes. Perhaps the same was true of the liveships. He tempted himself with that belief, then reluctantly shook his head. The liveships and their families had plied these waters for many years longer than the slavers had. The Chalcedean slave trade had largely created the pirates and their settlements. So he would have to assume that most Trader families who plied these waters would have better knowledge of them than the slavers. Why had not that knowledge been shared? The answer was obvious. No Trader would willingly extend his own advantage to his competitors. He leaned back in his chair. So. What had he learned, really? Nothing he had not already known. Slavers would be easier to capture than liveships. But that did not mean that capturing a liveship would be impossible, only that he might have to give more thought to it.

His mind strayed to the slaveship. It had been a ship of freed men for three days before he visited, and that had wrought some change in the level of stench, though not enough to placate Kennit's nose. He had given no real thought to it when he had put Rafo in charge of the ship, but he was acquitting himself well in his new position. Hundreds of buckets of seawater had been hauled aboard and the upper decks at least showed the benefit of it. But from the open hatch covers, a fetid stench welled up. There were simply too many live beings crowded aboard the vessel. They huddled in knots on the deck, bony limbs thrusting out of tattered rags. Some were endeavoring to help work the ship, others simply trying to stay out of the way. Some were engaged in the absorbing business of dying, interested in nothing else. As Kennit walked the length of the ship, a handkerchief held to his nose and mouth, the eyes of the slaves followed him. Every one of them spoke softly as he passed them. Eyes flooded with tears at his approach and heads were bowed before him. At first he had thought they groveled in terror of him. When he finally realized their murmurs were expressions of thanks and blessings upon him, he did not know whether to be amused or annoyed. Unsure of how to react to such a display, he resorted to his accustomed small smile, and made his way to what had been the quarters of the ship's officers.

They had lived very well indeed, compared to the plight of the poor wretches who'd made up their cargo. He found he agreed with Sorcor's assessment of the captain's taste in clothing. In a whimsical moment, he had ordered it distributed to those of the slaves who could make best use of it. The man had smoking herbs in plenty also. Kennit wondered if he had not resorted to those to spare his own nose

the stench of his cargo. It was an addiction Kennit had never succumbed to, so those, also, he ordered passed out among the slaves. He
had next discovered the charts and papers in the dead man's quarters.
These he appropriated to himself. There was little else in the cabin of
interest to him. The very ordinariness of the man's possessions would
have been a revelation to Sorcor, he thought to himself. This man had
been no monster such as Sorcor had presumed, but simply an ordinary
sea-captain and trader.

Kennit had originally intended to inspect below decks as well, to
see how sound the ship was, as well as to explore for any other valu-
ables Sorcor might have missed. He descended the ladder into the
hold and looked about him with watering eyes. Men, women, even
some children, their eyes huge in their bony faces, were a haphazard
clutter of limbs and bodies, stretching off into darkness. All faces
turned towards him, and the lantern Rafo carried sent its light to
dance in all those eyes. They reminded him of rats seen near midden
heaps by night.

"Why are they so thin?" he demanded suddenly of Rafo. "The
journey from Jamaillia is not so long as to leave folk like bones, unless
they were fed nothing at all."

Kennit was shocked to see Rafo's eyes narrow in sympathy. "Most
of them had been in debtors' prison. Many are from the same village.
Somehow they displeased the Satrap and he raised the taxes for their
valley. When none of them could pay, all of them were rounded up to
be sold as slaves. Almost the whole village, and not the first time such
a thing had happened, from what they say. They were bought and
held in pens and fed cheap until the folk trading in them had enough
to make a full load. Simple folk like these are don't bring a high price,
they say, so they try to haul a lot at once. The ship had to be packed
full in order to ensure a decent profit."

The sailor lifted his lantern higher. Empty fetters dangled like
strange cobwebs and curled on the floor like crushed snakes. Kennit
realized he had only been aware of the first row of people staring at
him. Behind him, others sprawled, crouched or sat in the darkness as
far as his eyes could reach. Other than the slaves, the hold was empty.
Bare planking. A few wisps of soiled straw caught in corners suggested
discarded bedding. The inside of the ship, too, had been sloshed and
scrubbed with seawater, but the urine-soaked wood and the noisome
bilge in the depths would not give up its evil odor. The ammoniac
stench made the tears roll freely down his cheeks. He ignored them
and hoped they were not noticeable in the dimness. By gritting his

teeth and breathing shallowly, he was able to keep from gagging. He wanted nothing so much as to be out of there, but he forced himself to pace the length of the hold.

The wretches drew closer as he passed, murmuring among themselves. It set the hair up on the back of his neck, but he refused to look behind to see how closely they followed him. One woman, braver or stupider than the rest, stepped in front of him. She suddenly offered him the bundle of rags she clutched. Against his will, he peered at it, to see the babe within. "Born on this ship," she said hoarsely. "Born into slavery, but freed by you." Her finger touched the bluish *X* that some diligent slaver had already marked beside the child's nose. She looked up at him again, a sort of fierceness in her eyes. "What could I ever offer you in thanks?"

Kennit could feel his control over his rising gorge slipping. The thought of the only thing she might offer him made his flesh crawl. The breath of her mouth smelled of rotting teeth loose in her gums. He bared his own teeth for a moment, a parody of a smile. "Name the child Sorcor. For me," he suggested in a choked voice. She seemed to miss the sarcasm in his voice, for she blessed him as she stepped back, beaming and clutching the skinny infant. The rest of the crowd jostled stiflingly closer, and several voices were lifted. "Captain Kennit, Captain Kennit!" He forced himself to stand his ground and not retreat. Instead he motioned to the sailor preceding him with the lantern, and then commanded in a wheeze, "Enough. I have seen enough." He was not able to keep the distress from his voice. He clutched his scented handkerchief to his face and ascended the closest ladder rapidly.

On deck it took him a moment to regain control of his heaving gut. He set his face and stared off at the horizon until he was sure he would not disgrace himself with any show of weakness. He forced himself to consider this prize Sorcor had won for him. The ship had appeared sound enough, but he'd never get a decent price for her, not if the buyer had a nose at all. "A waste," he growled, furious. "Such a waste!" He summarily ordered the gig to return him to the *Marietta*. It was then he had decided to head for Askew. If the ship was not going to bring a good price, then at least he would be rid of it soon, and able to go on with other things.

It was late afternoon before he decided to visit Askew himself. It would be amusing, he thought, to see both how his freed slaves were reacting to the town, and how the town was welcoming this sudden influx of population. Perhaps by now Sorcor would have seen the folly of his beneficence.

He made his will known to the ship's boy, who speedily passed the word. By the time he had smoothed his hair, settled his hat and emerged from his cabin, the ship's gig was readied to be lowered. The sailors who were to man her were as eager as dogs invited for a walk. Any town, any shoreside trip was a welcome diversion to them. Despite the brevity of the notice he had given, every man jack of them had found time to don a cleaner shirt. From their anchorage to the docks of Askew was but a few minutes of their diligent rowing. Kennit silently ignored the grins the men exchanged. They tied up at the base of the dock, and he ascended the rickety ladder to the top and then awaited his men while he wiped the slime from his fingers with his handkerchief. As if he were passing out sweetmeats to children, he drew a handful of small coins from his coat pocket. It was enough for a round of small beer for all of them. He entrusted it to the man in charge, with the nebulous warning, "Be here and ready when I come back. Don't make me wait."

The men clustered in a circle about them. Gankis spoke for them. "Cap'n. You don't need to do that. After what you done, we'd be waiting here for you if every demon of the deep was after us."

The sudden outpouring of devotion from the old pirate took Kennit aback. He could think of nothing he had done for them lately that should merit this sudden affection. In an odd way it touched him as much as it amused him. "Well. No sense waiting thirsty, boys. Do be here, though."

"No, sir, Cap'n, that we won't. Promise to be here, every one of us." The man who spoke grinned so that his old tattoo crawled and danced across his face. Turning his back on them, Kennit proceeded up the docks and towards the heart of town. Behind him, he could hear the men arguing as to how they could best enjoy their beer and still be back awaiting him on time. It pleased him to set them these little dilemmas. Perhaps it even sharpened their wits. In the meantime, he set his own wits as to puzzling out what he had done to please them. Had there been booty on the other boat that Sorcor had not informed him about? Promises of favors from the women that had been among the slaves? Suspicions, never long absent from Kennit's thoughts, suddenly took over. It might be very revealing to find out where Sorcor was right now and what he was doing. That he had let the men believe such largesse had come from the captain did not excuse him for passing it out without making Kennit aware of it.

He made his way down the main street of the small town. There were but two taverns in the town; if Sorcor was not in one, it was likely he was in the other. As it turned out, he was in neither. In what looked like a jubilant celebration, the entire population of the town seemed to be gathered in the street between the two taverns. Tables and benches had been dragged out into the light of day, and kegs rolled out and broached in the street. Kennit's suspicions became even darker. This sort of jubilation usually bespoke coins by the handful, lavishly doled. He put a knowing look upon his face, accompanied by a small, tight smile. Whatever was going on here, he must appear to be informed of it, or be a fool before all.

"Say nothing. Trust your luck," chided a tiny voice. The charm at his wrist had a tiny melodic laugh, unnerving in its sweetness. "Above all, show no fear. Luck such as yours has no patience with fear." Again, the laugh.

He dared not lift his wrist nor gaze at his token. Not in public. Nor was there time to seek a quieter spot to confer with it, for at that moment the crowd became aware of him. "Kennit!" cried a voice aloud. "Captain Kennit! Kennit!" Others took up the cry until the summer air rang with his name. Like a beast stirred from licking itself, the mob turned faces towards him and then surged at him like an oncoming wave.

"Courage. And smile!" taunted the wizardwood face.

He himself felt his sardonic grin was set in ice upon his features. His heart pounded and the sweat started down his back at the sight of the mob coming towards him, fists and mugs raised to the sky. But they could not see that. No. All they would see as they closed on him was that small smile and how straight and fearless he stood as they engulfed him. A bluff, perhaps, but a bluff only worked so long as the user believed it would. In vain he tried to pick out Sorcor's face in that oncoming wave of humanity. He wanted to find him, and, if necessity dictated it, make sure he at least died before Kennit did.

Instead the folk ringed him, their faces flushed red with both drink and apparent triumph. None, as yet, dared to touch him. They stood a respectful distance from his fists and every eye was on him. He let his gaze rove over them, looking for a weakness or for the aggressor who would strike the first blow. Instead a burly woman pushed her way to the front of the crowd ringing him, to stand before him, her meaty fists on her generous hips. "I'm Tayella," she announced in a clear and powerful voice. "I run Askew." Her eyes met his as if he might challenge that declaration. Then, to his astonishment, her eyes flooded suddenly with tears. They spilled unabashedly down her cheeks as she added in a voice that suddenly broke, "And I tell you that anything here is yours, yours for the asking. Anything, anytime. For you have brought us our own, whom we never thought to see again!"

Trust the luck. He returned her smile, and with his most gallant bow and silent heartfelt regrets for the wasted lace, offered her his handkerchief. She took it from him as if it were embroidered with gold. "How did you know?" she asked brokenly. "How could you have guessed? One and all, we were astonished."

"I have my ways," he assured her. He wondered what it was he was supposed to have known. But he did not ask, did not even flinch when her hand fell on his shoulder with a whack surely meant to be welcoming.

"Set out a fresh table and all our best. Make way for Captain Kennit! Bless the man who delivered our kin and our neighbors from slavers, and brought them here to join us in freedom and a new life. Bless the man!"

They swept him forward in a triumphant wave, to seat him at a sticky table and then heap it high with baked fish and some kind of starchy cakes made from a pounded root. A bucket of clam soup thickened with sea weed completed the festive meal. Tayella joined him there, to pour him a wooden bowl of a wine they had contrived from a sour berry. He supposed that as it was the only wine in the town, it was also the best. He tried a sip of it and managed not to wince. Tayella seemed to have had a quantity of it already. He judged it most politic to sip at his wine and let her regale him with the town's history. He scarcely glanced at the man when Sorcor came to join them. The swarthy old dog looked chastened, somehow. Humbled with amazement. To Kennit's appalled amusement, he carried the swaddled child marked with the X. The mother hovered not far away.

Tayella rose, to clamber up on top of the table and address the company at large.

"Twelve long years ago," she intoned, "we were brought here. In chains and sick and half dead, some of us. The ocean blessed us with a storm like to a hurricane. Shoved the ship right up this channel, where no slaver had ever come before or since, and run her aground. The pounding the ship took loosened a lot of things. Including a staple that secured a whole string of slave fetters. Even with our hands and feet still bound, we killed those Chalcedean bastards. And we freed our companions and we made this place our own. Not such a great place, no, but once anyone's been in the hold of a slaver, anywhere else is Sa's own paradise. We learned to live here, we learned to use the ship's boats to fish, in time we even ventured out to let others know we were here. But we knew we could never go home. Our families, our village were lost to us forever." She turned suddenly to point down at Kennit. "Until you brought it back to us today."

In consternation, he waited while she wiped more tears on his handkerchief. "Twelve years ago," she managed at last. "When they came to take us because we could not pay the Satrap's taxes, I fought them. They killed my husband and took me, but my little girl ran away. And I never thought to see her again, let alone my grandson." She gestured fondly at Sorcor and little Sorcor. More tears welled up and choked her.

It took her a bit, and soon other folk chimed in to help her and tell their own stories. By the most powerful of coincidences, most of the slaves on board the *Fortune* had come from the same village as had the original founders of Askew. But no one there believed it a coincidence. All, even dour Sorcor, credited him with deducing it and deciding to bring them here to be re-united with their kin. He had not. But Kennit knew it was not mere coincidence, but something far more powerful.

Sheerest luck. His luck. Luck to be trusted and never questioned. Casually he smoothed a finger over the wizardwood charm at his wrist. Would he scorn such luck by disdaining this chance? Of course not. Such luck demanded he dare to be worthy of it. He decided he dared. Shyly, so humbly, he asked Tayella, "Have my men told you of the prophecy I received from the Others?"

Tayella's eyes widened. She sensed something immense to come. Like a widening ring of ripples, her silence spread. All eyes turned toward him. "I have heard something of what was said," she said cautiously.

As if overcome, Kennit cast his eyes down. He let his voice drop deep, and said softly, "Here it begins." Then he drew a deeper breath and brought the words up from the depths of himself, powering them with his lungs. "Here it begins!" he announced, and contrived to make it sound as if it were an honor he was bestowing on them.

It worked. All about him, eyes shone with tears. Tayella shook her head in slow disbelief. "But what have we to offer you?" she asked, almost brokenly. "We are a village with next to nothing. No fields to till, no grand houses. How does a king begin here?"

Kennit put gentleness into his voice. "I begin as you begin. With a ship, which I have taken for you. With a crew, which I have trained for you. Work the ship. I shall leave Rafo here to teach you the ways of the Raven flag. Take whatever you will from whoever passes, and make it your own. Remember how the Satrap took all from you, and do not be ashamed to reclaim your wealth from the merchants of Jamaillia that he cossets with your blood." He glanced at the shining gaze of his first mate and was inspired. "But I warn you. Suffer no slaver to pass unchallenged. Send the crews to the serpents who will welcome them, and gather their ships here. Of all cargo that is aboard these ships, I give Askew a full half. A full half!" He repeated it loudly, to be sure they all knew of his generosity. "Keep the rest here, in safety. Sorcor and I will return, before the year is out, to take a tally, and to teach you how such things are best sold." With a wry and confiding smile, he lifted the wooden bowl of wine. "I offer you a sour toast! To sweeter and better things to come!"

As one, they roared out their adulation. Tayella did not seem to realize he had just stolen her village's control from her. Her eyes shone as brightly as the rest, she lifted her bowl as high. Even dour Sorcor joined in when they shouted his name. Triumph sharper than any he had known cut deep and sweet into his soul. His gaze met the worshipful eyes of his first mate and he knew he once more had his leash securely. He smiled at the man and even at the baby he was doting on. A laugh almost burst from Kennit's chest as this final piece tumbled into place. Sorcor believed Kennit had honored him. That Kennit had hung his name on the baby as a sort of reward to him. He did not fight the widening of his own grin. Instead, he lifted his bowl high once more. With a pounding heart, he waited for the noise to subside around him. When it did, he spoke in a deceptively soft voice. "Do as I teach you," he bade them gently. "Follow my ways, and I shall lead you to peace and prosperity!"

The roar that greeted this near deafened him. He lowered his eyes modestly, to share a secret grin with the small face on his wrist. The revelry lasted long, not just the night but over into the morning. Before it was over, most of Askew was reeling with the sour wine and Kennit's gut was curdled from trying to drink it. Not only had Sorcor found a quiet moment in which he had begged Kennit to forgive him for doubting him, but he admitted to his captain that he had believed him a heartless sort of man, cold as a serpent. Kennit did not need to ask him what had changed his mind. He had already heard, from several sources, how moved they had all been when he himself—by all accounts one of the most hardened captains of the Pirate Isles—had been reduced to tears at the sight of their misery in the hold. He had rescued them, he had wept for them, and then he had restored to them not only their freedom but their lost families. He realized too late that he could have claimed this place without giving them a ship as well, but what was done was done. And half of whatever booty they managed to seize would come to him, without effort. It was not a bad beginning. Not a bad beginning at all.

"I'd just like to see him again before he sails. So would Mother." Keffria said this and then hastily took up her teacup and sipped at it. She tried to look casual, as if this were a minor favor she asked of her husband rather than something of the greatest importance to her.

Kyle Haven wiped his mouth on his napkin and set the cloth aside on the breakfast table. "I know, my dear. I know it must be hard for you, not to see him for so long, and then to have him snatched away from you. What you have to remember is that at the end of this voyage, I'll bring him back to you a healthy and hearty young man, a son to be proud of. Right now, he scarce knows his own mind about anything. The work he is learning is hard, he's discouraged, I don't doubt his body is sore every night." He lifted his own cup, frowned into it, and set it down. "More tea. If I brought him home here to his mama and granny, he'd but take it as a sign he could whine to you. He'd whimper and beg, you would both be upset, he'd be back to where he started No, Keffria. Trust me in this. It would not be good for either of your. Or your mother. She's had a hard enough time lately, losing Ephron. Let's not make it worse for her."

Keffria quickly leaned forward to replenish her husband's cup. She had been so pleased when he had joined her for breakfast, so sure she could beg this favor of him. It seemed forever since he had set aside any time for the two of them. He came home exhausted each night and rose before each dawn to hasten back to his ship. This morning when he had lingered in her bed, she had hoped it foretold an easing in his temperament. When he had told her he had time to breakfast with her, her hopes had bubbled swiftly But she recognized that tone in his voice when he spoke of Wintrow. There was no arguing with it. Best for the sake of peace to set her hopes aside.

Over two weeks had passed since the day Kyle had sent her son from the house to the ship. In those two weeks, Kyle had volunteered no mention of her son, and replied but briefly to her queries. It was almost as it had been in the days when he had been newly gone to the monastery. Not knowing what his life had become, she could find no solid premises to anchor her worries. Still, they loomed, nebulous and threatening, whenever her mind was not otherwise occupied with worrying about her mother's grieving silence or Althea's absolute disappearance. At least, she comforted herself, she knew where he was. And Kyle was his father. Surely he would let no harm come to him, and would tell her if there was any real reason for concern. No doubt Kyle was right about the boy. Perhaps his firmness was what was called for. After all, what did she know of boys that age? She took a steadying breath and moved resolutely to her next topic of concern.

"Have you . . ." she hesitated. "Has Althea been down to the ship?"

Kyle frowned. "Not since the day that fool Torg ran her off. I had given orders she was not to come aboard, but I never meant for him to chase her off. I truly wish he had had the wit to summon me. I can tell you right now, I would have hauled that young woman home here where she belongs." His tone left no doubt that Althea's opinion in the matter would not have counted.

There was no one in the room with them save a serving maid, but Keffria lowered her voice nonetheless. "She has not been to see Mama. I know, for I asked her. And she has not come home at all. Kyle, where can she be? I've had nightmares. I fear she may be murdered, or something worse. I did have one other idea the other night . . . could she have sneaked aboard the *Vivacia*? She always had such a strong bond with the ship. She is just stubborn enough, perhaps, to creep aboard and hide herself until you were out to sea and turning back would be difficult, and then . . ."

"She's not on the ship," Kyle said shortly. His whole tone dismissed Keffria's conjectures as female silliness. "She's probably staying somewhere in town. She'll be home as soon as her ready cash runs out. And when she does come home, I want you to be strict with her. Don't fuss over her and tell her you were worried. And don't scold like an angry hen. She'll ignore that. You need to be hard with her. Leave her without a coin to her name until she starts behaving herself. Then keep the leash short." He reached across the table and took her hand gently, his touch belying the firmness of his tone. "Can I trust you in this? To do what is wisest and best for her?"

"It will not be easy. . . ." Keffria faltered. "Althea is used to getting her own way. And Mother—"

"I know. Your mother is having second thoughts about all of this. Her judgment is not the best at this time. She has lost her husband, and fears to lose her daughter as well. But she will only truly lose Althea if she gives into her and lets her go her own wild way. If she want to keep her, she must force her to come home and live her life properly. But I know that is not how your mother sees it just now. Still. Give her time, Keffria. Give them both time, for that matter, and they will see how right we are and come to thank us. What is it?"

They both turned to the tap at the door. Malta peeked around the corner. "May I come in?" she asked timorously.

"Your mother and I are having a conversation," Kyle announced. He considered that an answer to the question. Without another glance at his daughter, he turned back to his wife. "I've had time to look over the accountings for the north properties. The tenants on the Ingleby farm have not paid a full rent for the last three years. They should be moved out. Or the whole farm should be sold. One of the two."

Keffria took up her teacup and held it firmly in both hands. Sometimes when she had to correct her husband, it made her nervous and her hands trembled. Kyle disliked that. "The Ingleby farm is Mother's, Kyle. It was part of her bridal portion. And the tenants are her old nanny and her husband. They are getting up in years, and Mother had always promised Tetna that she would be provided for, so—"

Kyle set his own cup down so firmly the tea sloshed out onto the white cloth. He gave an exasperated sigh. "And that is just the type of reasoning that will bring us all down. I have nothing against charity, Keffria, or loyalty. But if she must take care of some doddering old couple, have her bring them here and put them up in the servant's wing and give them whatever tasks they can still manage. No doubt they'd be more useful here, as well as more comfortable. There is no reason to waste a whole farm on them."

"Tetna grew up there—" Keffria began again, then jumped and gasped as Kyle's callused palm struck the table in front of him.

"And I grew up in Frommers, but no one will give me a house there when I am old and we are destitute because we managed our wealth poorly. Keffria. Be silent a moment and let me finish what I am trying to say to you. I know it is your mother's. I know you have no direct say in what she does with it. I merely desire that you pass on to her my advice. And with it, the warning that no more monies will be forthcoming to support it from your father's estate. If she cannot force it to yield enough money to keep up the repairs to it, then she will have to let it decay. But no more good money thrown after bad. That's all." He turned suddenly in his chair and pointed an accusing finger at the door. "You. Malta. Are you eavesdropping on your elders? If you want to act like a spying serving girl, I can see that you have the chores of one as well."

Malta peered around the corner of the door into the room. She looked appropriately daunted. "I beg your pardon, Papa. I wanted to wait until you and Mama had finished speaking, so that I could talk to you."

Kyle gave a long-suffering sigh, and rolled his eyes at his wife.

"The children must be taught not to interrupt, Keffria. Come in, Malta, as you cannot seem to wait in a patient and seemly way. What do you want?"

Malta edged into the room, then, at a scowl from her father, hastened forward to stand before him. She bounced a curtsey at him and avoided her mother's eyes as she announced, "The Summer Ball is past, now. We had to miss it, I understand that. But Harvest Offering is seventy-two days from now."

"And?"

"I wish to go."

Her father shook his head in exasperation. "You will go. You've gone since you were six. Everyone goes who is of a Trader family. Save those like me, who must sail. I doubt I shall return in time to attend. But you know you'll go. Why do you bother me like this?"

Malta stole a glance at her mother's disapproving face and then looked up earnestly at her father. "Mother said we might not go this year. Because of mourning Grandfather, you know." She took a deep breath. "And she said that even if we did go, I was still not old enough for a proper ball gown. Oh, Papa, I do not want to go to the Harvest Offering in a little girl's frock. Delo Trell, who is the same age as I, is wearing a ball gown this year."

"Delo Trell is eleven months older than you." Keffria cut in. She could feel the heat in her cheeks, that her daughter dared bring this to her father as if it were a grievance. "And if she attends the Harvest Offering in a gown, I shall be very surprised. I myself was not presented at the Offering as a woman until I was fifteen, nearly sixteen. And we are in mourning. Nothing is expected of us this year. It is not fitting. . . ."

"It could be a dark gown. Carissa Krev was at the Ball only two months after her own mother died."

Keffria spoke firmly. "We will go only if your grandmother sees fit to go. I doubt that she will. And if we go, you will dress as is appropriate for a girl of your age."

"You dress me like a child!" Malta cried out. Her voice was tragic with pain. "I'm not a little girl anymore. Oh, Papa, she makes me wear my skirts half up my shin, with ruffles on the bottom, as if she fears I shall run and play through puddles. And she makes me plait my hair as if I were seven, and puts bows on my collars and lets me wear only flowers, no jewelry and—"

"Enough," Keffria warned her daughter, but to her surprise her husband laughed aloud.

"Come here, Malta. No, wipe your tears and come here. So," he went on when his daughter had come close enough to be pulled onto his lap. He looked down into her face. "You think you are old enough to dress as a woman, now. Next you'll be wanting young men to come calling."

"Papa, I'll be thirteen by then," Malta began but he shushed her.

He looked over his daughter's head at his wife. "If you all go," he began carefully, "would there be so much harm in letting her have a proper gown?"

"She's but a girl!" Keffria protested in dismay.

"Is she?" Kyle asked. His voice was warm with pride. "Look at your daughter, Keffria. If she is a little girl, she's a well-fleshed one. My mother always said, 'A boy is a man when he proves himself to be one, but a girl is a woman when she desires to be one.'" He stroked Malta's plaited hair and the girl beamed up at him. She gave her mother a pleading look.

Keffria tried to conceal her shock that her husband would side with her daughter against her. "Kyle. Malta. It is simply not seemly."

"What is unseemly about it? What will it hurt? This year, next year, what difference does it make when she graduates to long skirts, so long as she wears them well and they look becoming on her?"

"She is only twelve," Keffria said faintly.

"Nearly thirteen." Malta sensed her advantage and pressed it. "Oh, please, Mama, say yes! Say I may go to the Offering and have a proper gown this year!"

"No." Keffria was determined to stand her ground. "We shall only go if your grandmother does. Otherwise, it would be scandalous. On that I am firm."

"But if we do go?" Malta wheedled. She turned to her father again. "Oh, Papa, say I may have a proper dress if Mama allows me to go to the Offering."

Kyle gave his daughter a hug. "It seems a fair compromise," he suggested to Keffria. To Malta he added, "You shall go to the ball only if your grandmother does. And no teasing or nagging about it. But if she goes, then so you shall, and you shall have a proper gown."

"Oh, thank you, Papa," Malta breathed as if he had granted her a lifelong wish.

Something so like anger that it dizzied her coursed through Keffria's blood. "And now, Malta, you may go. I wish to speak to your father. And as you believe you are old enough to dress like a woman, you shall show me you have the skills of one. Finish the embroidery that has been on your loom for three weeks now."

"But that will take me all day!" Malta protested in anguish. "I wanted to call on Carissa, and see if she could go with me to Weaver Street, to look at cloth. . . ." Her voice dwindled off as she saw the look on her mother's face. Without another word, she turned and scampered from the room.

As soon as she was out of sight, her father let out a burst of laughter. There was nothing, Keffria thought, that he could have done that would have affronted her more. But when he caught sight of her face, instead of realizing his error, he but laughed the louder. "If you could see your face," he managed at last. "So angry to have your daughter get around you! But what can I do about it? You know she has always been my pet. Besides. What harm, truly, can it do?"

"It can attract to her an attention that she has not been taught to deal with as of yet. Kyle, when a woman goes to the Harvest Offering in her first ball gown, it is more than an extra length of cloth to her skirts. It is an announcement that she is presented to Bingtown as a woman of her family. And that says she is of a courtable age, that her family will consider offers for her hand."

"So?" Kyle demanded uncomfortably. "We do not have to say yes."

"She will be invited to dance," Keffria went on inexorably. "Not by the boys her age, with whom she has danced before. For they will still be seen as boys. She will be seen as a young woman. She will be dancing with men, both young and old. Not only is she still an indifferent dancer, but she has not been taught the skills of conversing with men, nor how to deal with attentions that are . . . unwanted. She may invite improper advances without being aware she is allowing them. Worse, a nervous smile or a silly giggle may make it seem she is encouraging them. I wish you had spoken to me before you had allowed her this."

In the blink of an eye, Kyle went from discomfort to irritation. He stood abruptly, flinging his napkin to the table. "I see. Perhaps I should simply live aboard the ship, to avoid inconveniencing you while you determine the fate of our family! You seem to forget that Malta is my daughter as well as yours. If she is twelve and had not yet been taught dancing and manners, perhaps you should rebuke yourself for that! First you sent my son off to be a priest, now you behave as if I shall have no say in how my daughter is raised either."

Keffria was already on her feet, grasping at his sleeve. "Kyle! Please! Come back, sit down. That is not what I meant. Of course I want you to help raise our children. It is simply that we must be careful with Malta's reputation, if we want her to be seen as a properly raised young woman."

But Kyle was not to be appeased. "Then I suggest you see to her manners and her dancing lessons, instead of sending her off to work embroidery. As for me, I have a ship to attend to. And a young man to straighten out. And *that* through a decision I had no say in at all." He shook her off as if shooing away a fly and stormed from the room. Keffria was left standing with her hand clutched over her mouth.

After a time, she sank slowly back into her chair. She took a deep breath, and then lifted her hands to her throbbing temples. Her eyes were scratchy with unshed tears. So much tension, so many quarrels lately. It seemed as if there was never a moment of peace in the house. She longed suddenly to return to the days when her father was a healthy man, and he and Althea sailed while she and her mother stayed home and cared for the house and children.

Then when Kyle had come into port, it had been like a holiday. He had been the captain of the *Daring* in those days. All had spoken well of him, how handsome, how dashing he looked. His days at home they had spent either dallying late in their bedchamber or strolling arm in arm about Bingtown. His sea chest had always brimmed with prizes for her and the children, and he had made her always feel like a newly wed bride. Ever since he had taken over the *Vivacia*, he had become so serious. And so, so . . . she tried to think of a word. "Grasping" came to mind, but she rejected it. He was simply a man in charge, she decided to herself. And with her father's death, he had extended that to everything: not just the family ship, but the household, the holdings, the children, and even, she thought woefully, her sister and her mother.

They used to talk late at night, long conversations about nothing. Kyle had liked to open the draperies and let the moonlight stream in across their curtained bed. He had spoken of the fury of the storms he had seen, and the beauty of the full sails when the wind was right, as he had touched her with hands and eyes that said he found her as fascinating as the sea. Now he spoke of little, save what cargo he had sold and what goods he'd taken on. Over and over, he reminded her that the foundering or the thriving of the Vestrit family fortunes rested on his shoulders now. Over and over he vowed to her that he would show the Bingtown Traders a thing or two about sagacious management and shrewd trading. The nights they spent together brought her neither release nor rest. The days in port he spent with his ship. And now, she admitted bitterly, what she was looking forward to was his sailing. When he left, she could at least reclaim some of the peace of regular days and routines.

She looked up at the sound of footsteps, both hoping and dreading that they heralded her husband's return. Instead her mother drifted into the room. She looked at Keffria and the remnants of food on the breakfast table as if they were less than shadows. Then her eyes roamed the room as if looking for something else. Or someone else. "Good morning, Mother," Keffria said.

"Good morning," her mother replied listlessly. "I heard Kyle leave."

"So you came down," Keffria supplied bitterly. "Mother, it pains me that you avoid him. There are things that must be discussed, that must be decided. . . ."

Her mother's smile was tight. "And while Kyle is present, that is impossible. Keffria, I am too tired and too grieved to speak tactfully. Your husband leaves no room for discussion. There is no point to my trading words with him, for we do not agree, and he will admit to no reason save his own." She shook her head. "It seems I have but two thoughts these days. I can grieve for your father, or rebuke myself for the muddle I have made of what he entrusted to me."

Despite her own recent anger with Kyle, the words stung Keffria. When she replied, it was in a low voice, freighted in hurt. "He is a good man, Mother. He only does what he believes is best for all of us."

"That may be true, but it's little comfort, Keffria." Ronica shook her head to herself. "Your father and I certainly believed he was a good man, or we would never have consented to your wedding him. But at that time, we could not have foreseen even half of what has come to pass. You might have been better off wedded to a man of Trader stock. We all might have been better off, had you married someone more familiar with our ways." Her mother came and seated herself at the table, moving like an old woman, slowly and stiffly. She turned her face away from the bright summer morning flooding the room with light as if her eyes hurt her. "Look at what we have come to, through Kyle's doing what he believes is good for us all. Althea is still missing. And young Wintrow is carried off against his will to the ship. That's not good. Not for the boy nor for the ship. If Kyle truly understood all that a liveship is, I don't think he'd have the boy aboard a new ship while he's so agitated and unhappy. From all I've heard, the first few months that a ship is quickened are crucial. Calm is what she needs, and confidence in her master, not coercion and quarreling. As for his idea of using her as a slaver . . . it makes me ill. Simply ill." She lifted her head and her gaze pinned Keffria in her place. "It shames me that you can allow your son to endure all he must see if he travels aboard a slaveship. How can you allow him to see that, let alone be a part of it? What do you think he must become to survive it?"

Her words wakened nameless dread in Keffria, but she clenched her hands under the table and sought to still them. "Kyle says he will not be harsh with Wintrow. As for the slaves, as he has pointed out to me, to make them suffer needlessly would only be to damage a valuable cargo. I did speak to him, I did, of all I have heard of slave ships. And he promised me that the *Vivacia* would not become some stinking death-hole."

"Even should Kyle treat Wintrow as gently as a girl child, he will suffer from what he sees on a slaveship. The necessary crowding, the deaths, the savage discipline to keep such a cargo under control . . . it's wrong. It's wrong, and we both know it." Her mother's voice brooked no opposition.

"But we have a slave right here in the house. Rache, that Davad lent you while Papa was so ill."

"It's wrong," Ronica Vestrit repeated in a low voice. "I realized that, and I wanted to send her back to Davad. But when I tried to send her home, she fell to her knees and begged me not to. She'll bring a good price in Chalced, she knows that, for she has a bit of learning. Her husband was already sent that way, for being a debtor. They came from Jamaillia, you know. And when they fell into debt and could not find a way out of it, both she and her husband and son were sent to the slave block. Her husband was a well-educated man, and he brought a goodly price. But she and her small son were sold cheaply, to one of Davad's agents." Ronica Vestrit's voice thickened. "She told me about her journey here. Her little boy did not survive it. Yet I do not think Davad Restart is a cruel man, at least not intentionally. Nor is he so poor a trader as to intentionally damage a valuable cargo." Her mother's voice had remained curiously flat through this telling. When she mimicked Kyle's words back to her in that same tone, it made Keffria's skin prickle.

"I think I had grown immune to death. In the years since your brothers died of the plague, I had pushed it aside as something I had endured and had done with. Now your father has gone, and it has reminded me of how sudden and how permanent is that moment of ending. Hard enough to deal with it when it is delivered by disease. But Rache's boy died because his little belly could not tolerate the tossing motion in the crowded, airless hold. He could not keep down the coarse bread and stagnant water the crew fed them. She had to watch her little boy die."

Her mother lifted her eyes to meet Keffria's and there was torment there. "I asked Rache, why did not you cry out to the crew when they came to feed you? Surely they could have given you a bit of time on the deck in the fresh wind, a little food that your boy could tolerate. She told me she did. That she begged and pleaded each time they came near to pass out the food or haul the buckets away. But the sailors behaved as if they could not hear her. She was not the only one aboard begging for mercy. Chained beside her, grown men and young women died as uselessly as her boy had. When they came and took the man next to her and her child away, they lugged him off like a meal sack. She knew they would throw his body to the serpents that followed the ship. And it made her mad.

"Oddly enough, her insanity was what saved her. For when she began to cry out, begging the serpents to break in the hull of the ship and devour her as well, when she began to call on Sa to send winds and tides to smash the ship on the rocks, her ranting moved the sailors as her pleas had not. They did not want this woman who cared so little for life as to call down death upon them all. She was beaten, but she would not be silenced. And when the ship docked briefly in Bingtown, she was put off, for the sailors vowed that the last storm they had endured was of her calling, and they'd sail no further with her aboard. Davad had to take receipt of her; she was cargo he owned. But as he could not call her a slave in Bingtown, he took her as indentured servant. And when he grew apprehensive of her stares, for she blames him for her boy's death, he sent her here to wait upon us. So you see, his gift to us in our time of need had more of fear in it than charity. And I mistrust that that is what Davad himself has become; a man governed more by fear than charity."

She paused as if reflecting. "And with a good measure of greed thrown in. I did not think Davad the type of man who could listen to a tale such as Rache's and then continue the trade that had bred it. But he has. And he pushes, quite persistently, at those he knows well to ask them to vote to legalize his trade for Bingtown as well." Again her eyes speared Keffria. "Now that you have inherited your father's holdings, you inherit his Council vote as well. No doubt Davad will begin to court you to use that vote to his bidding. And if your own economic interests align with that of slavery . . . what do you think Kyle will bid you do?"

Keffria felt paralyzed. She dared not answer. She wished to say her husband would not countenance slavery in Bingtown, but already her mind was unwillingly marking up the ledger. Were slaves legal, certain properties could suddenly become profitable once again. Grain fields. The tin mine. But apart from that, Kyle would not have to take his cargo as far as Chalced to dispose of it profitably, but could sell the slaves right here in Bingtown. Less time in transit meant more of his cargo would arrive alive and in good condition to be sold. . . .

With a shudder, Keffria suddenly considered the full import of her thought. *More of his cargo would arrive alive.* From the beginning, she had accepted that if Kyle chose to transport slaves, it was inevitable that some would die in the process. Of what? Of old age or ill health? No. Kyle was too sage to buy slaves likely to die. She had been expecting them to die from the trip. Accepting that it must happen. But why? In her journeys by ship, she had never feared for her own life or health. So only the treatment of the unwilling passengers could be the reason for the deaths. The treatment of the slaves that might well be part of Wintrow's duties as a sailor. Would her son learn to ignore the pleading cries of a young woman begging mercy for her child? Would he help fling the lifeless bodies to the serpents?

Her mother must have read something of her thoughts, for she said quietly, "Remember, it is your vote. You can cede it to your husband if you wish. Many Bingtown Trader wives in your position would do so, though Bingtown law does not require it. But remember that the Vestrit family gets one vote on the Traders' Council, and one vote only. And once you have ceded it to your husband, you cannot reclaim it. He can appoint whoever he wishes to vote his will in his absence."

Keffria suddenly felt very cold and alone. No matter how she decided this, she would suffer for it. She could not doubt that Kyle would advocate for slavery. She could almost hear his logical, rational arguments, even when he argued that slavery in Bingtown was bound to be a kinder fate for the slaves than slavery in Chalced. He would persuade her. And when he did, her mother would lose respect for her. "It is but one vote on the Traders' Council," she heard herself say faintly. "One vote of fifty-six."

"Fifty-six remaining Trader families," her mother conceded. In the next breath she went on, "and do you know how many newcomers have amassed enough leffers of land to claim a vote on the Bingtown Council now? Twenty-seven. You look shocked. Well, so was I. Evidently there are folk settling to the south of Bingtown, quietly taking up land with grants signed by the new Satrap, and then coming into Bingtown to assert their right to a place on the Bingtown Council. That second Council that we created—in a sense of fairness, that the Three-Ships Immigrants could have a place to resolve their own grievances among themselves, and a voice in governing Bingtown—is now being used against us.

"And the pressure is not just from within Bingtown. Chalced itself casts greedy eyes on our wealth. They have challenged our northern border, more than once, and that fool boy of a Satrap has all but conceded to them without a murmur. All for the sake of the gifts they send him, women and jewelry and pleasure herbs. He will not stand for Bingtown against Chalced. He will not even keep Esclepius' promises to us. Rumor has it that this new Satrap has depleted Jamaillia's treasury with his wastrel ways, and seeks to find more coin for his amusement by issuing grants of land to whoever will court his favor with gifts and promises of gifts. Not just to Jamaillian nobles does he give our land, but to his Chalcedean sycophants as well. So you may be correct in what you were about to say, Keffria. Perhaps one vote will do no good at all to stop the changes that are overtaking Bingtown."

Her mother rose slowly from her place at the table. She had taken no food, not even a sip of tea. As she drifted toward the door, she sighed. "In time, not even all fifty-six Trader votes will be enough to stem the will of this wave of newcomers. And if this new Satrap Cosgo will so violate one promise given to us by Esclepius, will he hold the others sacred? How long before the monopolies granted to us are sold to others as well? I do not like to think of what may happen here. It will be far more than the end of our way of life. What such greedy and incautious folk as these may awaken if they venture up the Rain Wild River, I do not like to think."

For one horrific instant, Keffria's mind was carried back to the birth of her third child. Or rather, her third time to be brought to childbed, for no child was born of that long pregnancy and painful labor. Only a creature her mother had neither allowed her to see nor to hold, something that had growled and snarled and thrashed wildly as her mother carried it from the room. Kyle had been at sea. Her father had been at home, and it had been left to him to do what was the burden of the Bingtown Trader families. No one had spoken of it afterwards. Even when Kyle came home from sea, he had not asked about the cradle still empty, but only accepted it and treated her with great tenderness. Once, since then, he had referred to her "stillbirth." She wondered if that was what he truly believed. He was not Trader-born; perhaps he did not believe in the price that must be paid.

Perhaps he did not grasp all that it meant to have married into a Trader family. Perhaps he did not grasp that they protected as well as profited from the Rain Wild River and all it brought down with its waters.

For a brief instant she saw her husband as a stranger, as, perhaps, a threat. Not an evil, malevolent threat, but part of a storm or immense tide that, soulless, still crushes and destroys all in its path.

"Kyle is a good man," she said to her mother. But her mother had left the room soundlessly, and her own words fell lifeless in the uncaring air.

CHAPTER FIFTEEN

NEGOTIATIONS

WE SAIL TOMORROW MORNING." TORG DIDN'T EVEN TRY TO MASK THE ENJOYMENT HE TOOK FROM IMPARTING these tidings.

Wintrow refused to look up from his work. The man's words were neither a question nor an order. He was not required to reply.

"Yep. We sail from here. Last you'll see of Bingtown for a time. We've got seven ports between here and Jamaillia. First three are in Chalced. Going to get rid of those comfer nuts. I could have told him they wouldn't sell in Bingtown, but then, no one asked me." Torg rolled his shoulders and grinned in self-satisfaction. He seemed to think that his captain's poor decision proved that Torg was a wiser man. Wintrow saw no such connection.

"Captain's going to build up a bit of a cash pot, is what I hear, and have all the more to spend on slaves in Jamaillia. We'll take on a nice haul of them, boy." He licked his lips. "Now, that's what I look forward to, especially as he'll be listening to my advice once we reach Jamaillia. That's a market I know. Yea. I know prime slave-flesh when I see it, and I'll be holding out for the best. Maybe I'll even get some skinny little girls for you to fancy. What do you think of that, laddie?"

Questions had to be answered, if one didn't want a boot in the small of one's back. "I think that slavery is immoral and illegal. And that it isn't appropriate for us to be discussing the captain's plans." He kept his eyes on his work. It was a pile of old line. His task was to untangle it, salvage what was good, and render the rest down into fibers that could either be re-twisted into line or used as chinking as needed. His hands had become as rough as the hemp he handled. When he looked at them, it was hard to recall they had once been the hands of an artist with a fine touch for glass. Across from him on the foredeck, Mild was working on his side of the pile. He envied the young sailor the agility of his callused hands. When Mild took up a piece of rope and gave it a shake, it seemed to magically untangle itself. No matter how Wintrow tried to coil a piece of line, it still always wanted to twist in the other direction.

"Oh, ho. Getting a bit snippy, are we?" Torg's heavy boot nudged him painfully. He was still bruised from an earlier kick.

"No, sir," Wintrow answered reflexively. It was getting easier, sometimes, to simply be subservient. When his father had first given him over to this brute, he had tried to speak to the man as if he had a mind. He had rapidly learned that any words Torg didn't understand he interpreted as mockery, and that explanations were only seen as feeble excuses. The less said, the fewer bruises. Even if it meant agreeing with statements he normally disagreed with. He tried not to see it as an eroding of his dignity and ethics. Survival, he told himself. It was simple survival until he could get away.

He dared to venture a question. "What ports shall we be stopping in?"

If there were one anywhere on the peninsula of Marrow, he'd be off the ship there, somehow. He didn't care how far he had to walk, or if he had to beg his way across the entire peninsula, he'd get back to his monastery. When he told his tale there, they'd listen to him. They'd change his name and place him elsewhere, where his father could never find him again.

"Nowhere near Marrow," Torg told him with vicious delight. "If you want to get back to your priesting, boy, you're going to have to swim." The second mate laughed aloud, and Wintrow saw how he had been set up to ask that question. It disturbed him that even Torg's slow wit could know so clearly where his heart was. Did he dream on it too much, did it show in his every action? He had begun to think it was the only way for him to stay sane. He constantly planned ways to slip away from the ship. Every time they latched him into the chain locker for the night, he would wait until the footsteps had died away and then try the door. He wished he had not been so impatient when he first was dragged aboard the ship. His clumsy attempts to leave had alerted both captain and crew to his intent, and Kyle had made it well known both to him and the crew that any man who let him leave the ship would pay heavily for it. He was never left alone, and those who worked alongside him resented that they could not trust him, but must guard him as well as work.

Now Torg made a great show of stretching his muscles. He lifted a booted foot to tap Wintrow's spine again. "Got to go, boys. Work to do. Mild, you're the nanny. See pretty boy here keeps busy." With a final painful nudge, Torg lumbered away down the deck. Neither boy looked up to watch him go. But when he was out of earshot, Mild observed calmly, "Someone will kill him someday and tip him over the side and no one will be the wiser." The young sailor's hands never paused in their work as he imparted this information to Wintrow. "Maybe it will be me," he added pleasantly.

The youth's calm advocation of murder chilled Wintrow. Much as he disliked Torg, as difficult as it was for him not to hate the man, he had never considered killing him. That Mild had was disconcerting. "Don't let someone like Torg distort your life and focus," he suggested quietly. "Even to think of killing for the sake of vengeance bends the spirit. We cannot know why Sa permits such men as Torg to have power over others, but we can deny him the power to distort our spirits. Yield him obedience where we must, but do not . . ."

"I didn't ask for a sermon," Mild protested irritably. He flung down the piece of line he'd been working on in disgust. "Who do you think you are? Why should you be telling me how to think or live? Don't you ever just talk? Try it sometime. Just say out loud, 'I'd really love to kill that dog-pronging bastard.' You'd be surprised what a relief it is." He turned his face away from Wintrow and spoke aloud in an apparent aside to a mast. "Dung. You try to talk to him like he's a person and he acts like you're on your knees begging his advice."

Wintrow felt a moment of outrage, followed by a rush of embarrassment. "I didn't mean it like that. . . ." He started to say he didn't think he was any better than Mild, but the lie died on his lips. He forced himself to speak truth. "No. I never talk without thinking first. I've been schooled to avoid careless words. And in the monastery, if we see or hear someone putting himself on a destructive path, then we speak out to each other. But to help each other, not to . . ."

"Well, you're not in a monastery anymore. You're here. When are you going to get that through your thick head and start acting like a sailor? You know, it's painful to watch how you let them all push you around. Get some gumption and stand up to them instead of preaching Sa all the time. Take a swing at Torg. Sure, you'll get a beating for it. But Torg is a bigger coward than you are. If he thinks there's even a chance you're going to lay for him with a marline spike, he'll back off of you. Don't you see that?"

Wintrow tried for dignity. "If he makes me behave like he does, then he's truly won. Don't you see that?"

"No. All I see is that you're so afraid of a beating you won't even admit you're afraid of it. It's just like your shirt the other day, when Torg put it up the mast to taunt you. You should have known you'd have to go get it yourself, so you should have just done it, instead of waiting until you were forced to do it. That made you lose to him twice, don't you see?"

"I don't see how I lost at all. It was a cruel joke, not worthy of men," Wintrow replied quietly.

Mild lost his temper for an instant. "There. That's what you do that I hate. You know what I mean, but you try to talk about it a whole different way. It isn't about what is 'worthy of men.' Here and now, it's about you and Torg. The only way you could have won that round was pretending that you didn't give a damn, that climbing the mast to get your shirt back wasn't anything. Instead, you got sunburned sitting around acting too holy to go get your shirt. . . ." Mild sputtered off into silence, obviously frustrated by Wintrow's lack of response. He took a breath, tried again. "Don't you get it at all? The worst was him forcing you to climb the mast ahead of him. That was when you really lost. The whole crew thinks you've got no spine now. That you're a coward." Mild shook his head in disgust. "It's bad enough you look like a little kid. Do you have to act like one all the time?"

The sailor rose in disgust and stalked away. Wintrow sat staring down at the heap of rope. The other boy's words had rattled him more than he liked to admit. He had pointed out, too clearly, that Wintrow now lived and moved in a different world. He and Mild were probably of an age, but Mild had taken up this trade of his own inclination, three years ago. He was a sailor to the bone now, and no longer the ship's boy since Wintrow had come aboard. No longer a boy at all in appearance. He was hard-muscled and agile. He was a full head taller than Wintrow as well, and the hair on his cheeks was starting to darken into proper whiskers. Wintrow knew that his slight build and boyish appearance were not faults, were not something he could change even if he saw them as faults. But somehow it had been

easier in the monastery, where one and all agreed that each would
grow in his own time and way.

Sa'Greb would never be taller than a lad, and his short stocky
limbs would have made him the butt of all jokes had he remained in
his home village. But in the monastery he was respected for the verses
he wrote. No one thought of him as "too short", he was simply
Sa'Greb. And the kind of cruel pranks that were the ordinary day to
day of this ship would never have been expected nor tolerated there.
The younger boys teased and shoved one another when they first
arrived, but those with a penchant for bullying or cruelty were swiftly
returned to their parents. Those attributes had no place among the
servants of Sa.

He suddenly missed the monastery with a sharp ache. He forced
the pain away before it could bring tears smarting to his eyes. No tears
aboard this ship; no sense in letting anyone see what they could only
view as a weakness. In his own way, Mild was right. He was trapped
aboard the *Vivacia*, either until he could make his escape or until his
fifteenth birthday. What would Berandol have counseled him? Why,
to make the best of his time here. If sailor he must be, then he were
wiser to learn it swiftly. And if he were forced to be a part of this crew
for . . . however long it would be . . . then he must begin to form
alliances, at least.

It would help, he reflected, if he had had the vaguest idea of how
one made friends with someone one's own age, but with whom one
had next to nothing in common. He took up a worn piece of line and
began to pick it apart as he pondered this very thing. From behind
him, Vivacia spoke quietly. "I thought your words had merit."

Wonderful. A soulless wooden ship, animated by a force that
might or might not be of Sa, found his words inspiring. Almost as
soon as he had the unworthy thought, Wintrow squelched it. But not
before he sensed a vibration of pain from the ship. Had not he just
been telling himself he needed allies? And here he was viciously turning on the only true ally he had. "I am sorry," he said quietly, knowing he scarcely needed to speak the words aloud. "It is the nature of
humans that we tend to pass our pain along. As if we could get rid of it
by inflicting an equal hurt on someone else."

"I've seen it before," Vivacia agreed listlessly. "And you are not
alone in your bitterness. The whole crew is in turmoil. Scarcely a soul
aboard feels content with his lot."

He nodded to her observation. "There has been too much change,
too fast. Too many men dismissed, others put on lesser wage because
of their age. Too many new hands aboard, trying to discover where

they fit into the order of things. It will take time before they feel they
are all part of the same crew."

"If ever," Vivacia said with small hope. "There is Vestrit's Old
Crew, and Kyle's Men and the New Hands. So they seem to think of
themselves, and so they behave. I feel . . . divided against myself. It
is hard to trust, hard to relax and give control to . . . the captain."
She hesitated on the title, as if she herself did not yet fully recognize
Kyle in that position.

Wintrow nodded again, silently. He had felt the tensions himself.
Some of the men Kyle had let go had been acrimonious, and at least
two others had quit in protest. The latest disturbance had been when
Kyle had demanded that one older man who was quitting return to
him the gold earring that Captain Vestrit had given him for his long
service aboard the *Vivacia*. The earring was shaped like Vivacia's figurehead and marked him as a valued member of her crew. The old
man had thrown it over the side rather than surrender it to Kyle.
Then he had stalked off down the dock, his sea-bag over his bony
shoulder. Wintrow had sensed that the old man had little to go to; it
would be hard to prove himself on board a new ship, competing with
younger, more agile hands.

"He didn't really throw it into the sea." Vivacia's voice was little
more than a whisper.

Wintrow was instantly curious. "He didn't? How do you know?"
He stood and went to the railing to look down at the figurehead. She
smiled up at him.

"Because he came back later that night and gave it to me. He said
we had been so long together, if he could not die aboard my decks, he
wished me to have at least a token of his years."

Wintrow felt himself suddenly deeply moved. The old sailor had
given back to the ship what was surely a valuable piece of jewelry, as
gold alone. Given it freely.

"What did you do with it?"

She looked uncomfortable for a moment. "I did not know what to
do with it. But he told me to swallow it. He said that many of the
liveships do that. Not commonly, but with tokens that are of great
significance. The ships swallow them and thus carry the memory of
the man who gave it for as many years as they live." She smiled at
Wintrow's astonished look. "So I did. It was not hard, although it felt
strange. And I am . . . aware of it, in an odd way. But you know, it
felt like the right thing to do."

"I am sure it was," Wintrow replied. And wondered why he was so
sure.

.   .   .

The evening wind was welcome after the heat of the day. Even the ordinary ships seemed to speak softly to one another as they creaked gently beside the docks. The skies were clear, promising a fine day tomorrow. Althea stood silently in Vivacia's shadow and waited. She wondered if she were out of her mind, to fix her heart on an impossible goal and then depend on a man's angry words as a path to it. But what else did she have? Only Kyle's impulsive oath, and her nephew's sense of fair play. Only an idiot would believe those things might be enough. Her mother had tried to seek her out through Vivacia; perhaps that might mean she had an ally at home. Perhaps, but she would not count on it.

She set a hand silently to Vivacia's silvery hull. "Please, Sa," she prayed, but had no words to follow those. She had seldom prayed. It was not in her nature to depend on anyone else to give her what she wanted. She wondered if the great Mother of All would even hear the words of one who usually ignored her. Then she felt the warm response from Vivacia through the palm of her hand, and wondered if she had truly prayed to Sa at all. Maybe, like most sailors she knew, she believed more in her ship than in any divine providence.

"He's coming," Vivacia breathed softly to her.

Althea moved a step deeper into her ship's shadow and waited.

She hated sneaking about like this, she hated having brief, clandestine meetings with her ship. But it was her only hope of success. She was sure that if Kyle had any notion of her plans, he'd do anything in his power to thwart her. Yet here she was, about to divulge those plans to Wintrow, and all on the basis of a single look exchanged with him. For a brief moment, she had seen her father's sense of honor in the boy's eyes. Now she was going to stake everything on her belief in him.

"Remember, boy, I'm watching you," Torg's voice boomed nastily in the stillness. When only silence greeted this announcement, he barked, "Answer me, boy!"

"You didn't ask me a question," Wintrow pointed out quietly. On the docks below, Althea gave the boy marks for guts, if not wisdom.

"You even try to jump ship tonight, and I'll kick your ass until your backbone splits," Torg threatened him. "You understand me?"

"I understand you," Wintrow's slight voice replied wearily. He sounded very young and very tired. Althea heard the slight scuff of bare feet, and then the sound of someone settling wearily to the deck. "I am too tired to think, let alone talk," the boy said.

"Are you too tired to listen?" the ship asked him gently.

Althea heard the indistinct sounds of a yawn. "Only if you don't mind if I fall asleep in the middle of whatever you want to tell me."

"I'm not the one who wishes you to listen," Vivacia said quietly. "Althea Vestrit waits on the docks below. She is the one with something to say to you."

"My Aunt Althea?" the boy asked in surprise. Althea saw his head appear over the railing above her. She stepped silently from the shadows to look up at him. She could see nothing of his face; he was merely a darker silhouette against the evening sky. "Everyone says you just disappeared," he observed to her quietly.

"Yes. I did," she admitted to him. She took a deep breath and her first risk. "Wintrow. If I speak frankly with you of what I plan to do, can you keep those plans a secret?"

He asked her a priest's question in reply. "Are you planning on doing something . . . wrong?"

She almost laughed at his tone. "No. I'm not going to kill your father or anything so rash as that." She hesitated, trying to measure what little she knew of the boy. Vivacia had assured her that he was trustworthy. She hoped the young ship was right. "I am going to try to out-maneuver him, though. But it won't work if he knows of my plans. So I'm going to ask you to keep my secret."

"Why are you telling anyone at all what you plan? A secret is kept best by one," he pointed out to her.

That, of course, was the crux of it. She took a breath. "Because you are crucial to my plans. Without your promise to aid me, there is no sense in my even acting at all."

The boy was silent for a time. "What you saw, that day, when he hit me. It might make you think I hate him, or wish his downfall. I don't. I just want him to keep his promise."

"That's exactly what I want, also," Althea replied quickly. "I'm not going to ask you to do anything wrong, Wintrow. I promise you that. But before I can say any more, I have to ask you to promise to keep my secret."

It seemed to her that the boy took a very long time considering this. Were all priests so cautious about everything? "I will keep your secret," he finally said. And she liked that about him. No vows or oaths, just the simple offering of his word. Through the palm of her hand, she felt the *Vivacia* respond with pleasure to her approval of him. Strange, that that should matter to the ship.

"Thank you," she said quietly. She took her courage in both

hands, and hoped he would not think she was a fool. "Do you remember that day clearly? The day he knocked you down in the dining room?"

"Most of it," the boy said softly. "The parts when I was conscious, anyway."

"Do you remember what your father said? He swore by Sa, and said that if but one reputable captain would vouch for my seamanship, he'd give my ship back to me. Do you remember that?" She held her breath.

"I do," Wintrow said quietly.

She put both hands to the ship's hull. "And would you swear by Sa that you heard him say those words?"

"No."

Althea's dreams crashed down through their straw foundations. She should have known it. How could she ever have thought the boy would stand up to his father in a great matter as this? How could she have been so stupid?

"I would vouch that I heard him say it," Wintrow went on quietly. "But I would not swear. A priest of Sa does not swear by Sa."

Althea's heart soared. It would be enough, it would have to be enough. "You'd give your word, as a man, as to what he said," she pressed.

"Of course. It's only the truth. But," he shook his head down at her, "I don't think it would do you any good. If my father will not keep his word to Sa to give me up to the priesthood, why should he keep his word on an angrily sworn oath? After all, this ship is worth much more to him than I am. I am sorry to say this to you, Althea, but I think your hopes of regaining your ship that way are groundless."

"You let me worry about that," she said in a shaky voice. Relief was flowing through her. She had one witness, and she felt she could rely on him. She would say nothing to the boy of the Traders' Council and the power it held. She had entrusted him with enough of her secret. She would burden him with no more of it. "As long as I know you will vouch for the truth, that your father spoke those words, I have hope."

He received these words in silence. For a time Althea just stood there, her hands on her silent ship. She could almost feel the boy through the ship. His desolation and loneliness.

"We sail tomorrow," he said finally. There was no joy in his voice.

"I envy you," Althea told him.

"I know you do. I wish we could change places."

"I wish it were that simple." Althea tried to set aside her jealousy.

"Wintrow. Trust the ship. She'll take care of you, and you take good care of her. I'm counting on both of you to watch out for each other." She heard in her own voice the "doting relative" tone that she had always hated when she was young. She pushed it away, and spoke as if he were any young boy setting out on his maiden voyage. "I believe you'll grow to love this life and this ship. It's in your blood, you know. And if you do," these words came harder, "if you do, and you are true to our ship, when I take her over, I'll make sure there's always a place for you aboard her. That is my promise to you."

"Somehow I doubt I'll ever ask you to keep it. It's not that I don't like the ship, it's just that I can't imagine—"

"Who are you talking to, boy?" Torg demanded. His heavy feet thudded across the deck as Althea melted back into the ship's shadow. She held her breath. Wintrow wouldn't lie to Torg. She already knew that about him. And she couldn't stand by and let the boy take a beating for her, but she also couldn't risk Torg holding her for Kyle.

"I believe this is my hour with Wintrow," Vivacia cut in sharply. "Who do you imagine he would be speaking to?"

"Is there someone on the docks down there?" Torg demanded. His bushy head was thrust out over the railing, but both the curve of Vivacia's hull and the deep shadow protected Althea. She held her breath.

"Why don't you haul your fat ass down there and see?" Vivacia asked nastily. Althea clearly heard Wintrow's gasp of astonishment. It was all she could do to keep from laughing. She sounded just like their cocky ship's boy, Mild, in one of his bolder moods.

"Yea? Well, maybe I'll just do that."

"Don't trip in the dark," the *Vivacia* warned him sweetly. "It would be a shame if you went overboard and drowned right here by the dock." The liveship's peaceful rocking suddenly increased by the tiniest of increments. And in that moment her adolescent taunting of the man took on a darker edge that stood the hair up on the back of Althea's neck.

"You devil ship!" Torg hissed at her. "You don't scare me. I'm seeing who's down there." Althea heard the thudding of his feet on the deck, but she couldn't decide if he hurried toward the gang-plank or away from the figurehead.

"Go now!" Vivacia hissed to her.

"I'm going. Good luck. My heart sails with you." Althea no more than breathed the words, but she knew the ship did not need to hear her speak so long as she touched her. She slipped away from the *Vivacia*, staying to the deepest shadows as she fled. "Sa keep them both safe, especially from themselves," she said under her breath, and this time she knew that she uttered a true prayer.

Ronica Vestrit waited alone in the kitchen. Outside the night was full, the summer insects chirring, the stars glinting through the trees. Soon the gong at the edge of the field would sound. The thought filled her stomach with butterflies. No. Moths. Moths were more fitting to the night and the rendezvous she awaited.

She had given the servants the night off, and finally told Rache pointedly that she wished to be alone. The slave woman had been so grateful to her lately that it was difficult to be rid of her sad-eyed company. Keffria had her teaching Malta to dance now, and how to hold a fan and even how to discourse with men. Ronica found it appalling that she would entrust her daughter's instruction in such things to a relative stranger, but understood also that lately Keffria and Malta had not been on the best of terms. She was not informed as to the full extent of their quarreling, and fervently hoped she would not be. She had problems enough of her own, real and serious problems, without listening to her daughter's squabbles with her granddaughter. At least Malta was keeping Rache busy and out from under foot. Most of the time.

Twice now Davad had hinted he'd like the slave to be returned to him. Each time Keffria had thanked him so profusely for all Rache's help, all the while exclaiming that she didn't know how she'd get along without her, that there had been no gracious way for Davad to simply ask for her back. Ronica wondered how long that tactic would suffice, and what she would do when it did not. Buy the girl? Become a slave-owner herself? The thought made her squeamish. But it was also endlessly aggravating that the poor woman had so attached herself to her. At any time when she was not busy with something else, Rache would be lurking outside whatever chamber Ronica was in, looking for an opportunity to leap forth and be of some service to her. She devoutly wished the woman would find some sort of life for herself. One to replace the one that her slavery had stolen from her, she asked herself wryly.

In the distance, a gong rang, soft as a chime.

She arose nervously and paced around the kitchen, only to come back to the table. She had set it and arranged it herself. There were two tall white candles of finest beeswax to honor her guest. The best china and her finest silver decked the table upon a cloth of heavy cream lacework. Trays of dainty tarts vied with platters of subtly smoked oysters and fresh herbs in bitter sauce. A fine old bottle of wine awaited as well. The grandness of the food was to indicate how she respected her guest, while secrecy and the kitchen setting reminded them both of the old agreements to both protect and defend one another. Nervously Ronica pushed the silver spoons into a minutely improved alignment. Silliness. This was not the first time that she had received a delegate from the Rain Wild Traders. Twice a year since she had been married to Ephron they had come. It was only the first time she had received one since his death. And the first time she had not been able to amass the full payment due.

The small but weighty casket of gold was two measures light. Two measures. Ronica intended to admit it, to bring it up herself before embarrassing questions could be asked. To admit it, and offer an increase in interest on the next payment. What else, after all, could she do? Or the delegate? A partial payment was better than none, and the Rain Wild folk needed her gold far more than anything else she could offer them. Or so she hoped.

Despite her anticipation, she still startled when the light tap came on the door. "Welcome!" she called without moving to open the door. Quickly she blew out the branch of candles that had illuminated the room. She saved but one, to light the two tall beeswax tapers before she extinguished it. Ornamental hoods of beaten brass with decorative shapes cut of out them were then carefully lowered over the tapers. Now the room was lit only by a scattering of leaf-shaped bits of light. Ronica nodded approval to herself at the effect, and then stepped quickly to open the door herself.

"I bid you welcome to my home. Enter, and be at home also." The words were the old formality, but Ronica's voice was warm with genuine feeling.

"Thank you," the Rain Wild woman replied. She came in, glanced about to nod her approval at the privacy and the lowered lights. She ungloved her hands, passing the soft leather garments to Ronica and then pushed back the cowl that had sheltered her face and hair. Ronica held herself steady, and met the woman's eyes with her own. She did not permit her expression to change at all.

"I have prepared refreshment for you, after your long journey. Will you be seated at my table?"

"Most gratefully," her companion replied.

The two women curtseyed to one another. "I, Ronica Vestrit, of the Vestrit Family of the Bingtown Traders, make you welcome to my table and my home. I recall all our most ancient pledges to one another, Bingtown to Rain Wilds, and also our private agreement regarding the liveship *Vivacia*, the product of both our families."

"I, Caolwn Festrew, of the Festrew Family of the Rain Wild Traders, accept your hospitality of home and table. I recall all our most ancient pledges to one another, Rain Wilds to Bingtown, and also our private agreement regarding the liveship *Vivacia*, the product of both our families."

Both women straightened and Caolwn gave a mock sigh of relief that the formalities were over. Ronica was privately relieved that the ceremony was a tradition. Without it, she would never have recognized Caolwn. "It's a lovely table you've set, Ronica. But then, in all the years we have met, it has never been anything else."

"Thank you, Caolwn." Ronica hesitated, but not to have asked would have been the false reticence of pity. "I had expected Nelyn this year."

"My daughter is no more." Caolwn spoke the words quietly.

"I am sorry to hear that." Ronica's sympathy was genuine.

"The Rain Wilds are hard on women. Not that they are easy on men."

"To outlive your child . . . that is bitter."

"It is. And yet Nelyn gifted us with three children before she went. She will be long remembered for that, and long honored."

Ronica nodded slowly. Nelyn had been an only child. Most Rain Wild women considered themselves lucky if they bore one child that lived. For Nelyn to have borne three would indeed make her memory shine. "I had taken out the wine for Nelyn," Ronica said quietly. "You, as I recall, prefer tea. Let me put the kettle on to boil and set aside the wine for you to take back with you."

"That is too kind of you."

"No. Not at all. When it is drunk, please have all who share it remember Nelyn and how she enjoyed wine."

Caolwn suddenly bowed her head. The sagging growths on her face bobbed as she did so, but they did not distract Ronica from the tears that shone suddenly in the other woman's violet eyes. Caolwn shook her head and then heaved a heavy sigh. "For so many, Ronica, the formalities are only that. The welcome is forced, the hospitality uncomfortable. But ever since you became a Vestrit and took on the duties of the visit, you have made us feel truly welcome. How can I thank you for that?"

Another woman might have been tempted to tell Caolwn then that the measure of the gold was short. Another woman might not have believed in the sacredness of the old promises and pacts. Ronica did. "No thanks are needed. I give you no more than is due you," she said, and added, because the words sounded cold, "But ceremony or no, pact or no, I believe we would have been friends, we two."

"As do I."

"So. Let me put on the kettle for tea, then." Ronica rose and instantly felt more comfortable in the homey task. As she poured the water into the kettle and blew on the embers in the hearth, she added, "Do not wait for me. Tell me, what do you think of the smoked oysters? I got them from Slek, as we always have done, but he has turned the smoking over to his son this year. He was quite critical of the boy, but I believe I like them better."

Caolwn tasted and agreed with Ronica. Ronica made the tea and brought the kettle to the table and set out two teacups. They sat together and ate and drank and spoke in generalities. Of simple things like their gardens and the weather, of things hard and personal like Ephron's and Nelyn's death, and of things that boded ill for them all, such as the current Satrap's debaucheries and the burgeoning slave trade that might or might not be related to his head tax on the sale of slaves. There was long and fond reminiscence of their families, and deep discussion of the *Vivacia* and her quickening, as if the ship were a shared grandchild. There was quiet discussion, too, of the influx of new folk to Bingtown, and the lands they were claiming and their efforts to gain seats on the Bingtown Council. This last threatened not only the Bingtown Traders, but the old compact between Bingtown and the Rain Wild Traders that kept them both safe.

The compact was a thing seldom spoken of. It was not discussed, in the same way that neither breathing nor death are topics for conversation. Such things are ever-present and inevitable. In a similar way, Caolwn did not speak to Ronica of the way grief had lined her face and silvered her hair, nor how the years had drawn down the flesh from her high cheekbones and tissued the soft flesh of her throat. Ronica forbore to stare at the scaly growths that threatened Caolwn's eyesight, nor at the lumpy flesh that was visible even in the parting of her thick bronze hair. The kindness of the dimmed candles could soften but not obscure these scars. Like the pact, these were the visible wounds they bore simply by virtue of who they were.

They shared the steaming cups of tea and the savory foods. The heavy silver implements ticked against the fine china whilst outside the summer's night breeze stirred Ronica's wind chimes to a silvery counterpoint to their conversation. For the space of the meal, they were neighbors sharing a genteel evening of fine food and intelligent conversation. For this, too, was a part of the pact. Despite the miles and differences that separated the two groups of settlers, both Bingtown Traders and Rain Wild Traders would remember that they had come to the Cursed Shore together, partners and friends and kin. And so they would remain.

So it was not until the food was finished and the women were sharing the last cup of cooled tea in the pot, not until the social conversation had died to a natural silence that the time came to discuss the final purpose of Caolwn's visit. Caolwn took a deep breath and began the formality of the discussion. Long ago the Bingtown Traders had discovered that this was one way to separate business from pleasure. The change in language did not negate the friendship the women shared, but it recognized that in manners of business, different rules applied and must be observed by all. It was a safeguard for a small society in which friends and relatives were also one's business contacts. "The liveship *Vivacia* has quickened. Is she all that was promised?"

Despite her recent grief, Ronica felt a genuine smile rise onto her face. "She is all that was promised, and freely do we acknowledge that."

"Then we are pleased to accept that which was promised for her."

"As we are pleased to tender it." Ronica took a breath and abruptly wished she had brought up the short measure earlier. But it would not have been correct nor fair to make that a part of their friendship. Hard as it was for her to speak it, this was the correct time. She groped for words for this unusual situation. "We acknowledge also that we owe you more at this time than we have been able to gather." Ronica forced herself to sit straight and meet the surprise in Caolwn's lavender eyes. "We are a full two measures short. We would ask that this additional amount be carried until our next meeting, at which time I assure you we shall pay all that we owe then, and the two additional measures, plus one-quarter measure of additional interest."

A long silence followed as Caolwn pondered. They both knew the full weight of Bingtown law gave her much leeway in what she could demand as interest for Ronica's failed payment. Ronica was prepared to hear her demand as much as a full additional two measures. She hoped they would settle at one-half to one measure. Even to come up with that much was going to tax her ingenuity to its limits. But when Caolwn did speak, the soft words chilled Ronica's blood. "Blood or gold, the debt is owed," Caolwn invoked.

Ronica's heart skipped in her chest. Who could she mean? None of the answers that came to her pleased her. She tried to keep the quaver out of her voice, she sternly reminded herself that a bargain was a bargain, but one could always try to better the terms. She took the least likely stance. "I am but newly widowed," she pointed out. "And even if I had had the time to complete my mourning, I am scarcely suitable to the pledge. I am too old to bear healthy children to anyone, Caolwn. It has been years since I even hoped I would bear another son to Ephron."

"You have daughters," Caolwn pointed out carefully.

"One wed, one missing," Ronica quickly agreed. "How can I promise you that which I do not have the possession of?"

"Althea is missing?"

Ronica nodded, feeling again that stab of pain. Not knowing. The greatest dread that any sea-going family had for its members. That someday one would simply disappear, and those at home would never know what became of him . . .

"I must ask this," Caolwn almost apologized. "It is required of me, in duty to my family. Althea would not . . . hide herself, or flee, to avoid the terms of our bargain?"

"You have to ask that, and so I take no offense." Nonetheless, Ronica was hard put to keep the chill from her voice. "Althea is Bingtown to the bone. She would die rather than betray her family's word on this. Wherever she is, if she still lives, she is bound, and knows she is bound. If you choose to call in our debt, and she knows of it, she will come to answer for it."

"I thought as much," Caolwn acknowledged warmly. But she still went on implacably. "But you have a granddaughter and grandsons as well, and they are as firmly bound as she. I have two grandsons and a granddaughter. All approach marriageable age."

Ronica shook her head, managed a snort of forced laughter. "My grandchildren are children still, not ready for marriage for years yet. The only one who is close to that age has sailed off with his father. And he is pledged to Sa's priesthood," she added. "It is as I have told you. I cannot pledge you that which I do not possess."

"A moment ago, you were willing to pledge gold you did not yet possess," Caolwn countered. "Gold or blood, it is all a matter of time for the debt to be paid, Ronica. And if we are willing to wait and let you set the time to pay it, perhaps you should be more willing to let us determine the coin of payment."

Ronica picked up her teacup and found it empty. She stood hastily. "Shall I put on the kettle for more tea?" she inquired politely.

"Only if it will boil swiftly," Caolwn replied. "Night will not linger for us to barter, Ronica. The bargain must be set and soon. I am reluctant to be found walking about Bingtown by day. There are far too many ignorant folk, unmindful of the ancient bargains that bind us all."

"Of course." Ronica sat down hastily. She was rattled. She abruptly and vindictively wished that Keffria were here. By all rights, Keffria should be here; the family fortunes were hers to control now, not Ronica's. Let her face something like this and see how well she would deal with it. A new chill went up Ronica's spine; she feared she knew how Keffria would deal with it. She'd turn it over to Kyle, who had no inkling of all that was at stake here. He had no concept of what the old covenants were; she doubted that even if he were told, he'd adhere to them. No. He'd see this as a cold business deal. He'd be like those ones who had come to despise the Rain Wild folk, who only dealt with them for the profit involved, with no idea of all Bingtown owed to them. Keffria would surrender the fate of her whole family to Kyle, and he would treat it as if he were buying merchandise.

In the moment of realizing that, Ronica crossed a line. It was not easily done, for it involved sacrificing her honor. But what was honor compared to protecting one's family and one's word? If deceptions must be made and lies must be told, then so be it. She could not recall that she had ever in her life decided so coldly to do what she had always perceived as wrong. But then again, she could not recall that she had ever faced so desperate a set of choices before. For one black moment, her soul wailed out to Ephron, to the man who had always stood behind her and supported her in her decisions, and by his trust in her decisions given her faith in herself. She sorely missed that backing just now.

She lifted her eyes and met Caolwn's hooded gaze. "Will you give me some leeway?" she asked simply. She hesitated a moment, then set the stakes high in order to tempt the other woman. "The next payment is due in mid-winter, correct?"

Caolwn nodded.

"I will owe you twelve measures of gold, for the regular payment."

Again the woman nodded. This was one of Ephron's tricks in striking a bargain. Get them agreeing with you, set up a pattern of agreement, and sometimes the competitor could be led into agreeing to a term before he had given it thought.

"And I will also owe you the two measures of gold I am short this time, plus an additional two measures of gold to make up for the lateness of the payment." Ronica tried to keep her voice steady and casual as she named the princely sum. She smiled at Caolwn.

Caolwn smiled in return. "And if you do not have it, we shall adhere to our family's original pledge. In blood or gold, the debt is owed. You shall forfeit a daughter or a grandchild to my family."

There was no negotiating that. It had been pledged years ago, by Ephron's grandmother. No Trader family would dream of going back on the given pledge of an ancestor. The nod she gave was a very stiff one, and the words she spoke she said carefully, binding the other woman with them. "But if I have for you a full sixteen measures of gold, then you will accept it as payment."

Caolwn held out a bare hand in token of agreement. The lumps and wattles of flesh that depended from the fingers and knobbed the back of it were rubbery in Ronica's grip as their handshake sealed them both to this new term. Caolwn stood.

"Once more, Ronica of the Trader family Vestrit, I thank you for your trade. And for your hospitality."

"And once more, Caolwn of the Rain Wild family Festrew, I am pleased to have welcomed you and dealt with you. Family to family, blood to blood. Until we meet again, farewell."

"Family to family, blood to blood. May you fare well also."

The formality of the words closed both their negotiations and the visit. Caolwn donned once more the summer cloak she had set aside. She pulled the hood up and well forward until all that remained of her features were the pale lavender lights of her eyes. A veil of lace was drawn down to cover them as well. As she drew on her loose gloves over her mis-shapen hands, she broke tradition. She looked down as she spoke. "It would not be so ill a fate as many think it, Ronica. Any Vestrit who joined our household I would treasure, as I have treasured our friendship. I was born in Bingtown, you know. And if I am no longer a woman that a man of your folk could look upon without shuddering, know that I have not been unhappy. I have had a husband who treasured me, and borne a child, and seen her bear three healthy grandchildren to me. This flesh, the deformities . . . other women who stay in Bingtown perhaps pay a higher price for smooth skin and eyes and hair of normal hues. If all does not go as you pray it will, if next winter I take from you one of your blood . . . know that he or she will be cherished and loved. As much because that one comes of honorable stock and is a true Vestrit as because of the fresh blood he or she would bring to our folk."

"Thank you, Caolwn." The words almost choked Ronica. Sincere as the woman's words might be, could she ever guess how they turned her bowels to ice inside her? Perhaps she did, for the lambent stare from within the hood blinked twice before Caolwn turned to the door. She took up the heavy wooden box of gold that awaited her by the threshold. Ronica unlatched the door for her. She knew better than to offer lantern or candle. The Rain Wild folk had no need of light on a summer's night.

Ronica stood in her open doorway and watched Caolwn walk off into the darkness. A Rain Wild man shambled out from the shadows to join her. He took the wooden casket of gold and tucked it effortlessly under his arm. They both lifted a hand in farewell to her. She waved in return. She knew that on the beach there would be a small boat awaiting them, and farther out in the harbor a ship that bore but a single light. She wished them well, and hoped they would have a good journey. And she prayed fervently to Sa that she would never stand thus and watch one of her own walk off into darkness with them.

In the darkness, Keffria tried once again. "Kyle?"

"Um?" His voice was warm and deep, sweet with satiation.

She fitted her body closely to his. Her flesh was warm where they touched, chilled to delicious goosebumps where the summer breeze from the open window flowed over them. He smelled good, of sex and maleness, and the solid reality of his muscle and strength were a bulwark against all night fears. Why, she demanded silently of Sa, why couldn't it all be this simple and good? He had come home this evening to say farewell to her, they had dined well and enjoyed wine together and then come together in both passion and love here. Tomorrow he would sail and be gone for however long it took him to make a trade circuit. Why did she have to spoil it with yet another discussion of Malta? Because, she told herself firmly, it had to be settled. She had to make him agree with her before he left. She would not go behind his back while he was gone. To do so would chip away the trust that had always bonded them.

So she took a deep breath and spoke the words they were both tired of hearing. "About Malta . . ." she began.

He groaned. "No. Please, Keffria, no. In but a few hours I will have to rise and go. Let us have these last few hours together in peace."

"We haven't that luxury. Malta knows we are at odds about this. She will use that as a lever on me the whole time you are gone. Whatever she wants that I forbid, she will reply, 'But Papa said I am a woman now. . . .' It will be torture for me."

With a long-suffering sigh, he rolled away from her. The bed was suddenly a cooler place than it had been, uncomfortably cool. "So. I should take back my promise to her simply so you won't be squab-

bling with her? Keffria. What will she think of me? Is this really so
great a difficulty as you are making it out to be? Let her go to the one
gathering in a pretty dress. That's all it is."

"No." It took all her courage to contradict him directly. But he
didn't know what he was talking about, she told herself frantically. He
didn't understand, and she'd left it too late to explain it all to him
tonight. She had to make him give in to her, just this once. "It's far
more than dancing with a man, in a pretty dress. She's having dance
lessons from Rache. I want to tell her that she must be content with
that for now, that she must spend at least a year preparing to be seen
as a woman in Bingtown society before she can go out as one. And I
want to tell her that you and I are united in this. That you thought it
over and changed your mind about letting her go."

"But I didn't," Kyle pointed out stubbornly. He was on his back
now, staring up at the ceiling. He had lifted his hands and laced the
fingers behind his head. Were he standing up, she thought, he'd have
his arms crossed on his chest. "I think you are making much of a small
thing. And . . . I don't say this to hurt you, but because I see it more
and more in you . . . I think you simply do not wish to give up any
control of Malta, that you wish to keep her a little girl at your side. I
sense it almost as a jealousy in you, dear. That she vies for my attention, as well as the attentions of young men. I've seen it before; no
mother wishes to be eclipsed by her daughter. A grown daughter must
always be a reminder to a woman that she is not young anymore. But I
think it is unworthy of you, Keffria. Let your daughter grow up and be
both an ornament and a credit to you. You cannot keep her in short
skirts and plaited hair forever."

Perhaps he took her furious and affronted silence for something
else, for he turned slightly toward her as he said, "We should be
grateful she is so unlike Wintrow. Look at him. He not only looks and
sounds like a boy, but longs to continue being one. Just the other day,
aboard the ship, I came upon him working shirtless in the sun. His
back was red as a lobster and he was sulking as furiously as a five-year-
old. Some of the men, as a bit of a jest, had taken his shirts and pegged
them up at the top of the rigging. And he feared to go up to get them
back. I called him to my chamber and tried to explain to him, privately, that if he did not go up after them, the rest of the crew would
think him a coward. He claimed it was not fear that kept him from
going after his shirt but dignity. Standing there like a righteous little
prig of a preacher! And he tried to make some moral point of it, that it
was neither courage nor cowardice, but that he would not risk himself
for their amusement. I told him there was very little risk to it, did he

but heed what he'd been taught, and again he came back at me with some cant about no man should put another man even to a small risk simply for his own amusement. Finally, I lost patience with him and called Torg and told him to see the boy up the mast and back to get his shirt. I fear he lost a great deal of the crew's respect over that. . . ."

"Why do you allow your crew to play boys' pranks when they ought to be about their work?" Keffria demanded. Her heart bled for Wintrow even as she fervently wished her son had simply gone after his own shirt. If he'd but risen to their challenge, they would have seen him as one of their own. Now they would see him as an outsider to torment. She knew it instinctively, and wondered that he had not.

"You've fair ruined the lad by sending him off to the priests." Kyle sounded almost satisfied as he said this, and she suddenly realized how completely he had changed the topic.

"We were discussing not Wintrow but Malta." A new tack suddenly occurred to her. "As you have insisted that only you know the correct way to raise our son in the ways of men, perhaps you should concede that only a woman can know the best way to guide Malta into womanhood."

Even in the darkness, she could see the surprise that crossed his face at the tartness of her tone. It was, she suddenly knew, the wrong way to approach him if she wanted to win him to her side. But the words had been said and she was suddenly too angry to take them back. Too angry to try to cajole and coax him to her way of thinking.

"If you were a different type of woman, I might concede the right of that," he said coldly. "But I recall you as you were when you were a girl. And your own mother kept you tethered to her skirts much as you seek to restrain Malta. Consider how long it took me to awaken you to a woman's feelings. Not all men have that patience. I would not see Malta grow up as backward and shy as you were."

The cruelty of his words took her breath away. Their slow courtship, her deliciously gradual hope and then certainty of Kyle's interest in her were some of her sweetest memories. He had snatched that away in a moment, turned her months of shy anticipation into some exercise of bored patience on his part, made his awakening of her feelings an educational service he had performed for her. She turned her head and stared at this sudden stranger in her bed. She wanted to deny that he had ever spoken such words, wanted to pretend that they did not truly reflect his feelings but had been said out of some kind of spite. Coldness welled up from within her now. Spite words or true, did not it come to the same thing? He was not the man she had always believed him to be. All these years, she had been married to a fantasy, not a real person. She had imagined a husband to herself, a tender, loving, laughing man who only stayed away so many months because he must, and she had put Kyle's face on her creation. Easy enough to ignore or excuse a few flaws or even a dozen when he made one of his brief stops at home. She had always been able to pretend he was tired, that the voyage had been both long and hard, that they were simply getting re-adjusted to one another. Despite all the things he had said and done in the weeks since her father's death, she had continued to treat him and react to him as if he were the man she had created in her mind. The truth was that he had never been the romantic figure her fancies had made him. He was just a man, like any other man. No. He was stupider than most.

He was stupid enough to think she had to obey him. Even when she knew better, even when he was not around to oppose her. Realizing this was like opening her eyes to the sun's rising. How had it never occurred to her before?

Perhaps Kyle sensed that he had pushed her a bit too far. He rolled towards her, reached out across the glacial sheets to touch her shoulder. "Come here," he bade her in a comforting voice. "Don't be sulky. Not on my last night at home. Trust me. If all goes as it should on this voyage, I'll be able to stay home for a while next time we dock. I'll be here, to take all this off your shoulders. Malta, Selden, the ship, the holdings . . . I'll put all in order and run them as they should always have been run. You have always been shy and backward. . . . I should not say that to you as if it were a thing you could change in yourself. I just want to let you know that I know how hard you have tried to manage things in spite of that. If anyone is at fault, it is I, to have let these concerns have been your task all these years."

Numbed, she let him draw her near to him, let him settle against her to sleep. What had been his warmth was suddenly a burdensome weight against her. The promises he had just made to reassure her instead echoed in her mind like a threat.

Ronica Vestrit opened her eyes to the shadowy bedroom. Her window was open, the gauzy drapes moving softly with the night wind. *I sleep like an old woman now*, she thought to herself. *In fits and starts. It isn't sleeping and it isn't waking and it isn't rest.* She let her eyes close again. Maybe it was from all those months spent by Ephron's bedside, when she didn't dare sleep too deeply, when if he stirred at all she was instantly alert. Maybe, as the empty lonely months passed, she'd be able to unlearn it and sleep deep and sound again. Somehow she doubted it.

"Mother."

A whisper light as a wraith's sigh. "Yes, dear. Mother's here." Ronica replied to it as quietly. She did not open her eyes. She knew these voices, had known them for years. Her little sons still sometimes came, to call to her in the darkness. Painful as such fancies were, she would not open her eyes and disperse them. One held on to what comforts one had, even if they had sharp edges.

"Mother, I've come to ask your help."

Ronica opened her eyes slowly. "Althea?" she whispered to the darkness. Was there a figure just outside the window, behind the blowing curtains. Or was this just another of her night fancies?

A hand reached to pull the curtain out of the way. Althea leaned in on the sill.

"Oh, thank Sa you're safe!"

Ronica rolled hastily from her bed, but as she stood up, Althea retreated from the window. "If you call Kyle, I'll never come back again," she warned her mother in a low, rough voice.

Ronica came to the window. "I wasn't even thinking of calling Kyle," she said softly. "Come back. We have to talk. Everything's gone wrong. Nothing's turned out the way it was supposed to."

"That's hardly news," Althea muttered darkly. She ventured closer to the window. Ronica met her gaze, and for an instant she looked down into naked hurt. Then Althea looked away from her. "Mother . . . maybe I'm a fool to ask this. But I have to, I have to know before I begin. Do you recall what Kyle said, when . . . the last time we were all together?" Her daughter's voice was strangely urgent.

Ronica sighed heavily. "Kyle said a great many things. Most of which I wish I could forget, but they seem graven in my memory. Which one are you talking about?"

"He swore by Sa that if even one reputable captain would vouch for my competency, he'd give my ship back to me. Do you remember that he said that?"

"I do," Ronica admitted. "But I doubt that he meant it. It's just his way, to throw such things about when he is angry."

"But you do remember him saying it?" Althea pressed.

"Yes. Yes, I remember he said that. Althea, we have much more important things to discuss than this. Please. Come in. Come back home, we need to . . ."

"No. Nothing is more important than what I just asked you. Mother, I've never known you to lie. Not when it was important. The time will come when I'll be counting on you to tell the truth." Incredibly, her daughter was walking away, speaking over her shoulder as she went. For one frightening instant, she looked so like her father as a young man. She wore the striped shirt and black trousers of a sailor on shore. She even walked as he had, that roll to her gait, and the long dark queue of hair down her back.

"Wait!" Ronica called to her. She sat down on the windowsill and swung her legs over it. "Althea, wait!" she cried out, and jumped down into the garden. She landed badly, her bare feet protesting the rocky walk under her window. She nearly fell, but managed to catch herself. She hastened across a sward of green to the thick laurel hedge that bounded it. But when she reached it, Althea was already gone. Ronica set her hands to that dense, leafy barrier and tried to push through it. It yielded, but only a little and scratchily. The leaves were wet with dew.

She stepped back from it and looked around the night garden. All was silence and stillness. Her daughter was gone again. If she had ever really been here at all.

Sessurea was the one the tangle chose to confront Maulkin. It both angered and wounded Shreever that they had so obviously been conferring amongst themselves. If one had a doubt, why had not that one come to speak of it to Maulkin himself, rather than sharing the poisonous idea with the others? Now they were all crazed with it, as if they had partaken tainted meat. The foolishness was most strong in Sessurea, for as he whipped himself into position to challenge Maulkin, his orange mane was already erect and toxic.

"You lead us awry!" he trumpeted. "Daily the Plenty grows shallower and warmer, and the salts of it more strange. You lead us where prey is scarce and then give us scant time to feed. I scent no other tangles, for no others have come this way. You lead us not to rebirth but to death."

Shreever shook out her ruff, arching her neck to release her poisons. If Maulkin were attacked by the others, she vowed he would not fight alone. But Maulkin did not even erect his ruff. As lazily as weed in the tides, he wove a slow pattern in the Plenty. It carried him over and then under Sessurea, who twined his own head about in an effort to keep his gaze upon Maulkin. Before the whole tangle, he changed Sessurea's challenge into a graceful dance in which Maulkin led.

His wisdom was as entwining as his movement when he addressed Sessurea. "If you scent no other tangle, it is because I follow the scent of those who passed here an age ago. But if you opened wide your gills, you would scent others, and not so far ahead of us. You fear the

warmth of this Plenty, and yet you were among those who first protested when I led you from warmth to coolness. You taste the strangeness of the salts and think we have gone awry. Foolish serpent! If all
were familiar, then we would be swimming back into yesterday. Follow me, and do not doubt any longer. For I lead you, not into your
own familiar yesterday, but into tomorrow, and the yesterday of your
ancestors. Doubt no longer, but swallow my truth!"

So close had Maulkin come to Sessurea as he wove his dance and
wisdom that when he lifted his mane and released his toxins, Sessurea
breathed them in. His great green eyes spun as he tasted the echo of
death and the truth that hides in it. He faltered in his defense, going
limp, and would have sunk to the bottom had not Maulkin wrapped
his length with his own. Yet even as he bore up the one who would
have denied him, the tangle cried out in unease. For above the Plenty
and yet in it, and below the Lack and yet in it, a great darkness moved.
Its shadow passed over them soundlessly save for the rush of its finless
body.

Yet when the rest of the tangle would have fled back into the
depths, Maulkin upheld Sessurea and pursued the shape. "Come!" he
trumpeted back to them all. "Follow! Follow without fear, and I
promise you both food and rebirth when the time for the gathering is
upon us!"

Shreever mastered her fear only with her loyalty to Maulkin. Of
all the tangle, she first uncoiled herself to flow through the Plenty and
follow their leader. She watched the first shivering of awareness come
back to Sessurea, and marked how gently he parted himself from
Maulkin. "I saw this," he called back to the others who still lagged and
hesitated. "This is right, Maulkin is right! I have seen this in his
memories, and now we live it again. Come. Come."

At that acknowledgment, there came forth from the shape food,
prey that neither struggled nor swam, but drifted down to be seized
and consumed by all.

"We shall not starve," Maulkin assured his followers quietly.
"Nor shall we need to delay our journey for fishing. Set aside your
doubts and reach for your deepest memories. Follow."

AUTUMN

CHAPTER SIXTEEN

NEW ROLES

THE SHIP CRESTED THE WAVE, HER BOW RISING AS IF SHE WOULD ASCEND INTO THE TORTURED SKY ITSELF. SA knew, the rain was near heavy enough to float a ship. For a long hanging instant, Althea could see nothing but sky. In the next instant, they were rushing headlong down a long slope of water into a deep trough. It seemed as if they must plunge into the rising wall of water, and plunge they did, green water covering the deck. The impact jarred the mast, and with it the yard that Althea clung to. Her numbed fingers slipped on the wet cold canvas. She curled her feet about the footrope she had braced them on and made her grip more firm. Then with a shudder, the ship was shaking it off, rising through the water and rushing up the next mountain.

"Ath! Move it!" The voice came from below her. On the ratlines, Reller was glaring at her, eyes squinted against the wind and rain. "You in trouble, boy?"

"No. I'm coming," she called back. She was cold and wet and incredibly tired. The other hands had finished their tasks and fled down the rigging. Althea had paused a moment to cling where she was and gather some strength for the climb down. At the beginning of her watch, at first sight of storm, the captain had ordered the sails hauled down and clewed up. The rain hit them first, followed by wind that seemed bent on picking them out of the rigging. They had no sooner finished and regained the deck than the cry came to double-reef the topsails and furl everything else. In seeming response to their efforts, the storm grew worse. Her watch had clambered about the rigging like ants on floating debris, clewing down, close reefing and furling in response to order after order, until she had stopped thinking at all, only moving to obey the bellowed commands. She had not forgotten why she was there; of their own accord, her hands had packed the wet canvas and secured it. Amazing, what the body could do even when the mind was numbed by weariness and fear. Her hands and feet were like cleverly trained animals now that contrived to keep her alive despite her own ambivalence.

She made her slow way down, the last to be clear of the rigging as always. The others had passed her on the way down and were most likely already below. That Reller had even bothered to ask her if she was in trouble marked him as far more considerate than the rest. She had no idea why the man seemed to keep an eye on her, but she felt at once grateful and humiliated by it.

When she had first joined the ship's crew, she had been burning to distinguish herself. She had driven herself to do more, faster and better. It had seemed wonderful to be back on a deck again. Repetitious food, badly stored; crowded and smelly living conditions; even the crudity of those she was forced to call ship-mates had all seemed tolerable in her first days aboard. She was back at sea, she was doing something and at the end of the voyage she'd have a ship's ticket to rub in Kyle's face. She'd show him. She'd regain her ship, she promised herself, and resolutely set out to learn this new ship as swiftly as she could.

But despite her best efforts, her inexperience on such a vessel was multiplied by the lesser size of her body. This was a slaughter ship, not a merchant trader. The captain's objective was not to get swiftly from one place to another to deliver goods, but to cruise a zig-zag path looking for prey. The ship carried a far larger crew than would a merchant ship of the same size, for in addition to sailing, there must be enough hands to hunt, slaughter, render and stow the harvested meat and oil below. Hence the ship was more crowded and less clean. She had held fast to her resolution to learn fast and well, but determination alone could not make her the best sailor on this stinking carrion ship. She knew, in some dim back part of her mind, that she had vastly improved her skills and stamina since signing on to the *Reaper*. She also knew that what she had achieved was still not enough to make her what her father would have called "a smart lad." Her purposefulness had wallowed down into despair. Then she had lost even that. Now she survived from day to day, and thought of little more than that.

She was one of three "boys" aboard the slaughter ship. The other two, young relatives of the captain, drew the gentler chores. They waited table for both the captain and mate, with a fair chance at getting the leavings from decent meals. They often helped the cook, too, with the lesser chores of preparing food for the main crew. She envied them that the most, she thought to herself, for it often meant they were inside, not only out of the storm's reach but close to the heat of the cook stove. To Althea, the odd boy, fell the cruder tasks of a ship's boy. The messy clean-ups, the hauling of buckets of slush and tar, and the make-up work of any task that merited an extra man. She had never worked so hard in her life.

She held tight to the mast for a moment longer, just out of reach of yet another wave that swamped the deck. From there to the shelter of the forepeak, she moved in a series of dashes and gasping moments of clinging tight to lines and rails to stay with the vessel as she plowed through wave after wave. They'd had three solid days of bad weather now. Before the current storm began, Althea had naïvely believed it would not get much worse. The experienced hands seemed to accept it as part of a normal season on the Outside. They cursed it and demanded of Sa that he end it, but always wound up telling one another tales of worse storms they had endured upon less sea-worthy vessels.

"Ath! Boy! Best get a move on if you want your share of the mess tonight, let alone to eat it while it's got a breath of warmth in it!"

Reller's words had more than a bit of threat to them, but despite that tone the old hand stayed on deck, watching her until she gained his side. Together they went below, sliding the hatch tight shut behind them. Althea paused on the step behind Reller to dash the water from her face and arms and then wring out the thick queue of her hair. Then she followed him down into the belly of the ship.

A few months ago, she would have said it was a cold, wet, smelly place. Now it was if not home, a place where the wind could not drive the rain into you so fiercely. The yellow light of a lantern was almost welcoming. She could hear food being served out, a wooden ladle clacking against the inside of a kettle and hastened to be sure of getting her rightful share.

On board the *Reaper*, there were no crew quarters. Each man found himself a sleeping spot and claimed it. The more desirable ones had to be periodically defended with fists and oaths. There was a small area in the midst of the cargo hold that the men had claimed as a sort of den. Here the kettle of food was brought by one of the ship's boys and rationed out in dollops as soon as they came off watch. There was no table, no benches to sit on, save your sea chest if you had one. For the rest, there was only the deck and the odd keg of oil to lean against. The plates were wooden trenchers, cleaned only with a wiping of fingers or bread, when they had bread. Ship's biscuit was the rule, and in a storm like this, there was small chance that Cook had tried to bake anything. Althea made her way through a jungle of dangling garments. Wet clothing hung everywhere from pegs and hooks in a pretense of drying. Althea shrugged out of her oilskin, won last week gambling with Oyo, and hung it on the peg she had claimed as her own.

Reller's threat had not been idle. He was serving himself as Althea approached, and like every man on the ship, he took what he wanted with no regard for who came after. Althea snatched up an empty trencher and waited eagerly for him to be out of the way. She sensed he was taking his time about it, trying to bait her into complaint, but she had learned the hard way to be wiser than that. Anyone could cuff a ship's boy, and they did not need the excuse of his whining to do it. Better to keep silent and get half a ladle of soup than to complain and get only a cuff for her supper. Reller crouched over the kettle and ladled up scoop after scoop from the shallow puddle of what was left. Althea swallowed and waited her turn.

When Reller saw she would not be baited, he almost smiled. Instead he told her, "There, lad. I've left you a few lumps in the bottom. Clean up the kettle, and then run it back to Cook."

Althea knew this was a kindness, in a way. He could have taken all and left her naught but scrapings and no one would have even considered speaking against him. She was happy to take the kettle and all and retire to her claimed spot to devour it.

She had a good place, all things considered. She had wedged her meager belongings up in a place where the curve of the hull met the deck above. It made it near impossible to stand upright. Here she had slung her hammock. No one else could have curled himself small enough to sleep comfortably there. She had found she could retreat there and be relatively undisturbed while she slept; no one was brushing past her in wet rain gear. So she took the kettle to her corner and settled down with it.

She scooped up what broth was left with her mug and drank it down. It was not hot—in fact, the grease had congealed in small floating blobs—but it was warmer than the rain outside and the fat tasted good to her. True to his word, Reller had left some lumps. Potato, or turnip or perhaps just a doughy blob of something meant to be a dumpling but not cooked enough. Althea didn't care. Her fingers scooped it up and she ate it. With a hard round of ship's biscuit she scraped the kettle clean of every last remnant of food.

She had no sooner swallowed the last bite than a great weariness rose up in her. She was cold and wet and ached in every bone. More than anything, she longed simply to drag down her blanket, roll up in it and close her eyes. But Reller had told her she had to take the kettle back to the cook. She knew better than to wait until after she had slept. That would be seen as shirking. She thought Reller himself might turn a blind eye to it, but if he did not, or if the cook complained, she could catch the end of a rope for it. She couldn't afford that. With a sound that could have been a whimper, she crept from her sleeping space with the kettle cradled in her arms.

She had to brave the storm-washed deck again to reach the galley. She made it in two dashes, holding on to the kettle as tightly as she held on to the ship. If she let something like that wash overboard, she knew they'd make her wish she'd gone with it. When she got to the galley, she had to kick and beat on the door; the fool cook had secured it from inside. When he did let her in, it was with a scowl. Wordlessly, she offered him the kettle, and tried not to look longingly at the fire in its box behind him. If you were favored by the cook, you could stay long enough to warm yourself. The truly privileged could hang a shirt or a pair of trousers in the galley, where they actually dried completely. Althea was not even marginally favored. The cook gestured her out the door as soon as she set the kettle down.

On the trip back, she misjudged her timing. Later, she would blame it on the cook for turning her so swiftly out of the galley. She thought she could make it in one dash. Instead the ship seemed to dive straight into a mountain of water. She felt her desperate fingers brush the line she lunged for, but she did not make good her hold. The water simply swept her feet out from under her and rushed her on her belly across the deck. She kicked and struggled wildly, trying to claw some kind of a hold on the deck with fingers and toes. The water was in her eyes and up her nose; she could not see nor find breath to shout for help. An eternal instant later, she was slammed into the ship's railing. She took a glancing blow to the side of her head that rang darkness before her eyes and near tore her ear off. For a brief moment, she knew nothing but to hold tight to the railing with both hands as she lay belly down on the swamped deck. Water rushed past her in its hurry to be overboard. She clung to the ship, feeling the seawater cascade past her, but unable to lift her head high enough to get a clear breath. She knew, too, that if she waited until the water was completely gone before she got to her feet, the next wave would catch her as well. If she didn't manage to get up now, she wasn't ever going to get up. She tried to move but her legs were jelly.

A hand grabbed the back of her shirt, hauled her choking to her knees. "You're plugging the scuppers!" someone exclaimed in disgust. She hung from his grip like a drowned kitten. There was air against her face, mixed with driving rain, but before she could take it in, she had to gag out the water in her mouth and nose. "Hang on!" she heard him shout and she wrapped her legs and arms about his legs. She managed one gargly breath of air before the water hit them both.

She felt his body swing with the impact of the water and thought surely they would both be torn loose from the ship. But an instant later, as the water retreated, he struck her a cuff to the side of the head that loosened her grip on him. Suddenly he was moving across the deck, dragging her behind him, her pigtail and shirt caught together in his grip. He hauled her up a mast; as soon as her feet and hands felt the familiar rope, they clung to them and propelled her up of their own accord. The next wave that rushed over the deck went by beneath her. She gagged and then spat a quantity of seawater into it. She blew her nose into her hand and shook it clean. With her first lungful of air, she said, "Thank you."

"You stupid little deck rat! You damn near got us both killed." Anger and fear vied in the man's voice.

"I know. I'm sorry." She spoke no louder than she had to in order to be heard through the storm.

"Sorry? I'll make you a sight more than just sorry. I'll kick your ass till your nose bleeds."

He lifted his fist and Althea braced herself to take the blow. She knew that by ship's custom she had it coming. When after a moment it did not land, she opened her eyes.

Brashen peered at her through the darkness. He looked more shaken than he had when he'd first dragged her up from the water. "Damn you. I didn't even recognize you."

She made a small gesture that could have been a shrug. Her eyes did not meet his.

Another wave made its passage across the ship. Again the ship began its wallowing climb.

"So. How have you been doing?" Brashen's voice was pitched low, as if he feared to be overheard talking to her. A mate was not expected to have chummy little chats with the ship's boy. Since discovering her, he had avoided all contact with her.

"As you see," Althea said quietly. She hated this. She abruptly hated Brashen, not for anything he had done, but because he was seeing her this way. Ground down to someone less than dirt under his feet. "I get by. I'm surviving."

"I'd help you if I could." He sounded angry with her. "But you know I can't. If I take any interest in you at all, someone will suspect. I've already made it plain to several of the crew that I've no interest in . . . other men." He suddenly sounded awkward. A part of Althea found the irony in this. Clinging to rigging on this scummy ship in the middle of a storm after he'd just offered to kick her ass, and he could not bring himself to speak of sex with her. For fear of offending her dignity. "On a ship like this, any kindness I showed you would be construed only one way. Then someone else would decide he fancied you, too. Once they found out you were a woman . . ."

"You needn't explain. I'm not stupid," Althea interrupted to stop his litany. Didn't he know she lived aboard the scum-infested tub?

"You're not? Then what are you doing aboard?" He threw the last bitter words over his shoulder before he dropped from the rigging to the deck. Agile as a cat, quick as a monkey, he made his way swiftly to the bow of the ship, leaving her clinging in the rigging and staring after him.

"The same thing you are," she replied snidely to his last words. It didn't matter that he could not hear them. The next time the water cleared the deck, she followed Brashen's example, but with considerably less grace and skill. Moments later, she was belowdecks, listening to the rush of water all around her. The *Reaper* moved through the water like a barrel. She sighed heavily, and once more dashed the water from her face and bare arms. She wrung out her queue and shook her wet feet like a cat before padding back to her corner. Her clothing was sodden against her skin, chilling her. She changed hastily into clothing that was merely damp, then wrung out what she had had on. She shook it out, hung her shirt and trousers on a peg to drip and tugged her blanket out from its hiding place. It was damp and smelled musty, but it was wool. Damp or not, it would hold the heat of her body. And that was the only warmth she had. She rolled herself into it and then curled up small in the darkness. So much for Reller's kindness. It had got her half-drowned and cost her half an hour of her sleep. She closed her eyes and let go of consciousness.

But sleep betrayed her. As weary as she was, oblivion would not come to her. She tried to relax, but could not remember how to loosen the muscles in her lined brow. It was the words with Brashen, she decided. Somehow they brought the situation back to her as a whole. Often she went for days without catching so much as a glimpse of him. She wasn't on his watch; their lives and duties seldom intersected. And when she had no reminders of what her life once had been, she could simply go from hour to hour, doing what she had to do to survive. She could give all her attention to being the ship's boy and think no farther than the next watch.

Brashen's face, Brashen's eyes, were crueler than any mirror. He pitied her. He could not look at her without betraying to her all that she had become, and worse, all that she had never been. Bitterest of all, perhaps, was seeing him recognize as surely as Althea herself had, that Kyle had been right. She *had* been her Papa's spoiled little darling, doing no more than playing at being a sailor. She recalled with shame the pride she had taken in how swiftly she could run the rigging of the *Vivacia*. But her time aloft had mostly been during warm summer days, and whenever she was wearied or bored with the tasks of it, she could simply come down and find something else to amuse herself. Spending an hour or two splicing and sewing was not the same as six hours of frantically hasty sailwork after a piece of canvas had split and needed to be immediately replaced. Her mother had fretted over her calluses and rough hands; now her palms were as hardened and thick-skinned as the soles of her feet had been, and the soles of her feet were cracked and black.

That, she decided, was the worst aspect of her life. Finding out that she was no more than adequate as a sailor. No matter how tough she got, she was simply not as strong as the larger men on the ship. She had passed herself off as a fourteen-year-old boy to get this position aboard the *Reaper*. Even if she had wished to stay with this slaughter tub, in a year or so they were bound to notice she wasn't growing any larger or stronger. They wouldn't keep her on. She'd wind up in some foreign port with no prospects at all.

She stared up into the darkness. At the end of this voyage, she had planned to ask for a ship's ticket. She still would, and she'd probably get it. But she wondered now if it would be enough. Oh, it would be the endorsement of a captain, and perhaps she could use it to make Kyle live up to his thoughtless oath. But she feared it would be a hollow triumph. Having a stamped bit of leather to show she had survived this voyage was not what she had wanted. She had wanted to vindicate herself, to prove to all, not just Kyle, that she was good at her chosen life, a worthy captain, to say nothing of being a competent sailor. Now, in the brief times when she did think about it, it seemed to her that she had only proved the opposite to herself. What had seemed daring and bold when she'd begun it back in Bingtown now seemed merely childish and stupid. She'd run away to sea, dressed as a boy, taking the first position that was offered to her.

Why, she asked herself now. Why? Why hadn't she gone to one of the other liveships and asked to be taken on as a hand? Would they have refused as Brashen had said they would? Or could she, even now, be sleeping aboard a merchant vessel cruising down the Inside Passage, sure of both wages and recommendation at the end of the voyage? Why had it seemed so important to her that she be hired anonymously, that she prove herself worthy without either her name or her father's reputation to fall back on? It had seemed such a spirited thing to do, on those summer evenings in Bingtown when she had sat cross-legged in the back room of Amber's store and sewed her ship's trousers. Now it merely seemed childish.

Amber had helped her. But for her help, with both needlework and readily shared meals, Althea would never have been able to do it. Amber's sudden befriendment of her had always puzzled Althea. Now it seemed to her that perhaps Amber had actually been intent on propelling her into danger. Her fingers crept up to touch the Serpent's Egg bead that she wore on a single strand of leather about her neck. The touch of it almost warmed her fingers and she shook her head at the darkness. No. Amber had been her friend, one of the few rare women friends she'd ever had. She'd taken her in for the days of high summer, helped her cut and sew her boy's clothing. More, Amber had donned man's clothing herself, and schooled Althea in how to move and walk and sit as if she were male. She had, she told Althea, once been an actress in a small company. Hence she'd played many roles, as both sexes.

"Bring your voice from here," she'd instructed her, prodding Althea below her ribs. "If you have to talk. But speak as little as you can. You'll be less likely to betray yourself, and you'll be better accepted. A good listener of any sex is rare. Be one, and it will make up for anything else perceived as a fault." Amber had also shown her how to wrap her breasts flat to her chest in such a way that the binding cloth appeared to be no more than another shirt worn under her outer shirt. Amber had shown her to fold dark-colored stockings to use as blood rags. "Dirty socks you can always explain," Amber had told her. "Cultivate a fastidious personality. Wash your clothing twice as much as anyone else does, and no one will question it after a time. And learn to need less sleep. For you will either have to rise before any others or stay up later in order to keep the privacy of your body. And this I caution you most of all. Trust no one with your secret. It is not a secret a man can keep. If one man aboard the ship knows you are a woman, then they all will."

This was the only area in which Amber had, perhaps, been mistaken. For Brashen knew she was a woman, and he had not betrayed her. At least, he hadn't so far. A sudden irony came to Althea. She grinned bitterly to herself. *In my own way I took your advice, Brashen. I arranged to be reborn as a boy, and not one called Vestrit.*

Brashen lay on his bunk and studied the wall opposite him. It was not far from his face. Was a time, he thought ruefully, when I would have scorned this cabin as a clothes closet. Now he knew what a luxury even a tiny space to himself could be. True, there was scarce room to turn around once a man was inside, but he did have his own berth, and no one slept in it but him. There were pegs for his clothing, and a corner just large enough to hold his sea chest. In the bunk, he could brace himself against the ledge that confined his body and almost sleep secure when he was off watch. The captain's and the mate's cabins were substantially larger and better appointed, even on a tub like this. But then on many ships the second mate had no better quarters than the crew. He was grateful for this tiny corner of quiet, even if it had come to him by the deaths of three men.

He had shipped as an ordinary seaman, and spent the first part of his trip growling and elbowing in the forecastle with the rest of his watch. Early on, he had realized he had not only more experience but a stronger drive to do his job well than the rest of his fellows. The *Reaper* was a slaughter ship out of Candletown far to the south, on the northern border of Jamaillia. When the ship had left the town many months ago in spring, it had left with a mostly conscripted crew. A handful of professional sailors were the backbone of the crew, charged with battering the newcomers into shape as sailors. Some were debtors, their work sold by their creditors as a means of forcing them to pay back what they owed. Others were simple criminals purchased from the Satrap's jails. Those who had been pickpockets and thieves had soon learned better or perished; the close quarters aboard a slaughter ship did not encourage a man to be tolerant of such vice in his fellows. It was not a crew that worked with a will, nor one whose members were likely to survive the rigors of the trip.

By the time the *Reaper* reached Bingtown, she'd lost a third of her crew to sickness, accidents and violence aboard. The two-thirds that remained were survivors; they'd learned to sail, they'd learned to pursue the slow-moving turtles and the so-called brack-whales of the southern coast inlets and lagoons. Their services were not, of course, to be confused with the skills of the professional hunters and skinners who rode the ship in the comparative comfort of a dry chamber and idleness. The dozen or so men of that ilk never set a hand to a line or stood a watch; they idled until their time of slaughter and blood. Then they worked with a fury, sometimes going without sleep for days at a time while the reaping was good. But they were not sailors and they were not crew. They would not lose their lives save that the whole ship went down or one of their prey turned on them successfully.

The ship had beat her way north on the outside of the pirate islands, hunting, slaughtering and rendering all the way. At Bingtown, the *Reaper* had put in to take on clean water and supplies and to make such repairs as they had the coin to pay for. The mate had also actively recruited more crew, for the journey out to the Barren Islands. It had been nearly the only ship in the harbor that was hiring.

The storms between Bingtown and the Barrens were as notorious as the multitude of sea mammals that swarmed there just prior to the winter migration. They'd be fat with the summer feedings, the sleek coats of the young ones large enough to be worth the skinning and unscarred from battles for mates or food. It was worth braving the storms of autumn to take such prizes—soft furs, the thick layer of fat, and beneath it all the lean, dark-red flesh that tasted both of sea and land. The casks of salt that had filled the hold when they left Candletown would soon be packed instead with salted slabs of the prized meat, with hogsheads of the fine rendered oil, while the scraped hides would be packed with salt and rolled thick to await tanning.

It would be a cargo rich enough to make the *Reaper*'s owners dance with glee, while those debtors who survived to reach Candletown again would emerge from their ordeal as free men. The hunters and skinners would claim a percentage of the total take and begin to take bids on their services for the next season based on how well they had done this time. As for the true sailors who had taken the ship all that way and brought her back safely, they would have a pocketful of coins to jingle, enough to keep them in drink and women until it was time to sail again for the Barrens.

A good life, Brashen thought wryly. Such a fine berth as he had won for himself. It had not taken much. All he had had to do was scramble swiftly enough to catch the mate's eye and then the captain's. That, and the vicious storm that had carried off two men and crippled the third who was a likely candidate for this berth.

Yet it was not any peculiar guilt at having stepped over dead men to claim this place and the responsibilities that went with it that bothered him tonight. No. It was the thought of Althea Vestrit, his benefactor's daughter, curled in wet misery in the hold in the close company of such men as festered there. "There's nothing I can do about it." He spoke the words aloud, as if by giving them to air he could make them ease his conscience. He hadn't seen her come aboard in Bingtown; even if he had, he wouldn't have recognized her easily. She was a convincing mimic as a sailor lad; he had to give her that.

His first hint that she was aboard had not been the sight of her. He'd glimpsed her any number of times as "a ship's boy" and given no thought to it. Her flat cap pulled low on her brow and her boy's clothes had been more than sufficient disguise. The first time he'd seen a rope secured to the hook on a block with a double blackwall hitch rather than a bowline, he'd raised an eyebrow. It was not that rare of a knot, but the bowline was the common preference. Captain Vestrit, however, had always preferred the blackwall. Brashen hadn't given much thought to it at the time. A day or so later, coming out on deck before his watch, he'd heard a familiar whistle from up in the rigging. He'd looked up to where she was waving at the look-out, trying to catch his attention for some message, and instantly recognized her. "Oh, Althea," he'd thought to himself calmly, and then started an instant later as his mind registered the information. In disbelief, he'd stared up at her, mouth half-agape. It was her: no mistaking her style of running along the footropes. She'd glanced down, and at sight of him had so swiftly averted her face that he knew she'd been expecting and dreading this moment.

He'd found an excuse to linger at the base of the mast until she came down. She'd passed him less than an arm's length away, with only one pleading glance. He'd clenched his teeth and said nothing to her, nor had he spoken to her since then until tonight. Once he had recognized her, he'd known the dread of certainty. She wouldn't survive the voyage. Day by day, he'd waited for her to somehow betray herself as a woman, or make the one small error that would let the sea take her life. It had seemed to him simply a matter of time. The best he had been able to hope for her was that her death would be swift.

Now it appeared that would not be the case. He allowed himself a small, rueful smile. The girl could scramble. Oh, she hadn't the muscle to do the work she was given. Well, at least not as fast as the ship's first mate expected such work to be done. It wasn't, he reflected, so much a matter of muscle and weight that she lacked; she could do the work well enough, actually, save that the men she worked alongside overmatched her. Even a few inches of extra reach, a half stone of extra weight to fling against a block-and-tackle's task could make all the difference. She was like a horse teamed with oxen; it wasn't that she was incapable of the work, only that she was mismatched.

Additionally, she had come from a liveship to one of mere wood; her family liveship, at that. Had Althea even guessed that pitting one's strength against dead wood could be so much harder than working a willing ship? Even if the *Vivacia* hadn't been quickened in his years aboard her, Brashen had known from the very first time he touched a line of her that there was some underlying awareness there. The *Vivacia* was far from sailing herself, but it had always seemed to him that the stupid incidents that always occurred aboard other ships didn't happen on her. On a tub like the *Reaper*, work stair-stepped. What looked like a simple job, replacing a hinge, for instance, turned into a major effort once one had revealed that the faulty hinge had been set in wood that was half rotten and out of alignment as well. Nothing, he sighed to himself, was ever simple on board the *Reaper*.

As if in answer to the thought, he heard the sharp rap of knuckles against his door. It wasn't his watch, so that could only mean trouble. "I'm up," he assured his caller. In an instant he was on his feet and had the door opened. But this was not the mate come to call him to extra duties on this stormy night. Instead Reller stepped in hesitantly. Water still streamed down his face and dripped from his hair.

"Well?" Brashen demanded.

A frown divided the man's wide brow. "Shoulder's paining me some," he offered.

Brashen's duties included minding the ship's medical supplies. They'd started the voyage with a ship's doctor, he'd been told, but had lost him overboard one wild night. Once it had been discovered that Brashen could read the spidery letters that labeled the various bottles and boxes of medicines, he'd been put in charge of what remained of the medical stores. He personally doubted the efficacy of many of them, but passed them out according to the labels' instructions.

So now he turned to the locked chest that occupied almost as much space as his own sea chest did and groped inside his shirt for the key that hung about his neck. He unlocked the chest, frowned into it for a moment, and then took out a brown bottle with a fanciful green label on it. He squinted at the writing in the lantern's unsteady light. "I think this is what I gave you last time," he guessed aloud, and held the bottle up for Reller's inspection.

The sailor peered at it as if a long stare would make the letters intelligible to him. At last he shrugged. "Label was green like that," he allowed. "That's probably it."

Brashen worked the fat cork loose from the thick neck and shook out onto his palm half a dozen greenish pellets. They looked, he thought to himself, rather like a deer's droppings. He'd have only been mildly surprised to discover that's what they actually were. He returned three to the bottle and offered the other three to Reller. "Take them all. Tell Cook I said to give you a half measure of rum to wash those down, and to let you sit in the galley and stay warm until they start working."

The man's face brightened immediately. Captain Sichel was not free with the spirits aboard ship. It would probably be the first taste Reller had had since they'd left Bingtown. The prospect of a drink, and a warm place to sit for a time made the man's face glow with gratitude. Brashen knew a moment's doubt but then reflected that he had no idea how well the pellets would work; at least he could be sure that the rough rum they bought for the crew would help the man to sleep past his pain.

As Reller was turning to leave, Brashen forced himself to ask his question. "My cousin's boy . . . the one I asked you to keep an eye on. How's he working out?"

Reller shrugged. He jiggled the three pellets loosely in his left hand. "Oh, he's doing fine, sir, just fine. He's a willing lad." He set his hand to the latch, clearly eager to be gone. The promised rum was beckoning him.

"So," Brashen went on in spite of himself. "He knows his job and does it smartly?"

"Oh, that he does, that he does, sir. A good lad, as I said. I'll keep an eye on Athel and see he comes to no harm."

"Good. Good, then. My cousin will be proud of him." He hesitated. "Mind, now, don't let the boy know any of this. Don't want him to think he'll get any special treatment."

"Yes sir. No sir. Good night, sir." And Reller was gone, shutting the door firmly behind him.

Brashen shut his eyes and took a deep breath. It was as much as he could do for Althea, asking a reliable man like Reller to keep an eye on her. He checked to make sure the catch on his door was secure, and then re-locked the cabinet that held the medical supplies. He crawled back into the narrow confines of his bunk and heaved a heavy sigh. It was as much as he could do for Althea. Truly, it was. It was.

Eventually, he was able to fall asleep.

· · ·

Wintrow didn't like the rigging. He had done his best to conceal that from Torg, but the man had a bully's unerring instinct. As a result, a dozen times a day he would fabricate a reason why Wintrow had to climb the mast. When he had sensed the repetition was dulling Wintrow's trepidation, he had added to the task, giving him things to carry aloft and place in the crow's nest, only to send him to fetch them back down almost as soon as he'd regained the deck. Torg's latest commands had him not only climbing the rigging, but going out to the ends of the spars and clinging there, heart in his mouth, waiting for Torg's shouted command to return. It was simple hazing, of the stupidest, most predictable sort. Wintrow expected such from Torg. It had been harder to comprehend that the rest of the crew accepted his torment as normal. When they paid any attention at all to what Torg was subjecting him to, it was usually with amusement. No one intervened.

And yet, Wintrow reflected as he clung to a spar and looked down at the deck so far below him, the man had actually done him a favor. The wind rushed past him, the canvas was full bellied with it, and the line he perched on sang with the tension. The height of the mast exaggerated the ship's motion through the water, amplifying every roll into an arc. He still did not like being up there, but he could not deny there was an exhilaration to being there that had nothing to do with enjoyment. He had met a challenge and bested it. Left to himself, he would never have sought to take his own measure in this way. He squinted his eyes to the wind that rushed past his ears deafeningly. For a moment he toyed with the idea that perhaps he did belong here, that maybe deep within the priest there could be the heart of a sailor.

A small, odd noise came to his ears. A vibration of metal. He wondered if it was some fitting about to give way, and his heart began to beat a bit faster. Slowly he worked his way along the ratline, looking for the source of the sound. The wind mocked him, bringing the sound and then blasting it away. He had heard it a few times before he recognized that there were variations in tone and a rhythm to the sound that defied the steady rush of the wind. He got to the crow's nest and clung to the side.

Within the lookout's post was Mild. The sailor had folded himself up into a comfortable braced squat. His eyes were closed to slits, a tiny jaw harp braced against his cheek. He played it one-handed, the sailor's way, using his own mouth as a sounding box as his fingers danced on the metal prongs that were the keys. His ears were turned to his private music as his eyes scanned the horizon.

Wintrow thought he was unaware of him until the other boy's

eyes darted briefly to his. His fingers stilled. "What?" he demanded, not taking the instrument from the side of his face.

"Nothing. You on watch?"

"Sort of. Not much to watch for."

"Pirates?" Wintrow ventured.

Mild snorted. "They don't bother a liveship, usually. Oh, I've heard rumors from when we were in Chalced, that one or two got chased, but for the most part they leave us alone. Most liveships can outrun any wooden ship under identical conditions, unless the liveship has a really carp crew. And the pirates know that even if you catch up with a liveship, you're in for the fight of your life. And even if they win, what do they have? A ship that won't sail for them. I mean, do you think Vivacia would welcome strangers aboard her and accept them running her? Not much!"

"Not much," Wintrow agreed. He was pleasantly surprised—both by Mild's obvious affection and pride for the ship, and by the boy's conversation with him. Mild seemed flattered by the boy's rapt attention, for he narrowed his eyes knowingly and went on, "The way I see it, right now the pirates are doing us a big favor."

Wintrow bit. "How?"

"Well. How to explain it . . . you didn't get ashore in Chalced, did you? Well, what we heard there was that pirates were suddenly attacking some of the slavers. At least one taken, and rumors of others being threatened. Well. It's end of autumn now, but by spring, Chalced needs a powerful lot of slaves to do the spring plowing and planting. If pirates are picking off the regular slavers, well, by the time we run into Chalced with a prime load, it will be a seller's market. We'll get so much for our haul, we can probably go straight home to Bingtown."

Mild grinned and nodded in satisfaction, as if somehow Kyle getting a good price for slaves would reflect well on him. He was likely only repeating what he'd heard the elders of the crew say. Wintrow said nothing. He looked far out over the heaving water. There was a heavy, sick place under his heart that had nothing to do with seasickness. Whenever he thought forward to Jamaillia and the actual act of his father buying slaves to sell, a terrible sorrow welled up in him. It was like having the guilt and pain of a shameful memory in advance of the event. After a moment, Mild picked up the conversation again.

"So. Torg's got you up here again?"

"Yeah." Wintrow surprised himself, stretching his shoulders and then leaning back casually against his grip. "Doesn't bother me so much anymore."

"I can tell. That's why they do it." When Wintrow lifted his brows, Mild grinned at him. "Oh, you thought it was a special torture just for you? No. Torg likes picking on you. Sa's balls, Torg likes picking on anyone. Anyone he can get away with, anyway. But running the ship's boy up and down the mast is a tradition. When I first come aboard, I hated it. Brashen was mate then, and I thought he was the son of a sow. Once he realized I was nervous about coming up here, he saw to it that every one of my meals ended up here. 'You want to eat, go get it,' he'd tell me. And I'd have to climb the mast and crawl around up here until I found a bucket with my mess in it. Damn, I hated him. I was so scared and slow, my food was almost always cold when I found it, and half the time there'd be rain sloshing around with it. But I learned, same as you, not to mind it after a while."

Wintrow was silent, thinking. Mild's fingers danced again over the keys, picking out a lively little tune. "Then Torg doesn't hate me? This is some kind of training?"

Mild stopped with a snort of amusement. "Oh, no. Depend on it. Torg hates you. Torg hates everyone that he thinks is smarter than he is, and that's most of us aboard. But he knows his job, too. And he knows that if he wants to keep it, he's got to make you into a sailor. So, he'll teach you. He'll make it as painful and unpleasant as he can, but he'll teach you."

"If he's such a hateful person, why does my . . . the captain keep him on as second mate?"

Mild shrugged. "Ask your Da," he said cruelly. Then he grinned, almost making that a joke. He went on, "I hear that Torg had been with him quite a while, and stuck with him on a real bad trip on the ship they used to be on. So when he came to the *Vivacia*, he brought Torg with him. Maybe no one else would hire him and he felt an obligation. Or maybe Torg's got a nice tight ass."

Wintrow's jaw went slack at the implication. But Mild was grinning again. "Hey, don't take it so serious. No wonder everyone loves to tease you, you're such a mark."

"But he's my father," Wintrow protested.

"Naw. Not when you're serving aboard his ship. Then he's just your captain. And he's an okay captain, not as good as Ephron was, and some of us still think Brashen should have took over when Cap'n Vestrit stepped off. But he's okay."

"Then why did you say . . . that about him?" Wintrow was genuinely mystified.

"Because he's the captain," Mild laboriously explained. "Sailors always say and do like that, even if you like the man. Because you know he can shit on you any time he wants. Hey. You want to know something? When we first found out that Cap'n Vestrit was getting off and putting a new man on, you know what Comfrey done?"

"What?"

"He went to the galley and took the cap'n's coffee mug and wiped the inside with his dick!" Delight shone in Mild's gray eyes. He waited in anticipation for Wintrow's reaction.

"You're teasing me again!" A horrified smile dawned on his face despite himself. It was disgusting, and degrading. It was too outrageous to be true, for a man to do that to another man he hadn't even met yet, just because that man would have power over him. It was unbelievable. And yet . . . and yet . . . it was funny. Suddenly Wintrow grasped something. To do that to a man you knew would be cruel and vicious. But to do that to an unknown captain, to be able to look up at man who had life-and-death power over you and imagine him drinking the taste of your dick with his coffee . . . He looked aside from Mild, feeling with disbelief the broad grin on his face. Comfrey had done that to his father.

"Crew's gotta do a few things to the cap'n, and the mate. Can't let them get away with always thinking they're gods and we're dung."

"Then . . . you think they know about stuff like that?"

Mild grinned. "Can't be around the fleet too long and not know it goes on." He twanged a few more notes, then shrugged elaborately. "They probably just think it never happens to them."

"Then no one ever tells them," Wintrow clarified for himself.

"Of course not. Who'd tell?" A few notes later, Mild stopped abruptly. "You wouldn't, would you? I mean, even if he is your Da and all . . ." His voice trailed off as he realized that he might have been very indiscreet.

"No, I wouldn't tell," Wintrow heard himself say. He found a foolish grin on his face as he added wickedly, "But mostly because he *is* my father."

"Boy? Boy, get your butt down here!" It was Torg's voice, bellowing up from the deck.

Wintrow sighed. "I swear, the man can sense when I'm not miserable, and always takes steps to correct it."

Wintrow began the long climb down. Mild leaned over slightly to watch his descent and called after him, "You use too many words. Just say he's on your ass like a coat of paint."

"That, too," Wintrow agreed.

"Move it, boy!" Torg bellowed again, and Wintrow gave all his attention to scrambling down.

Much later that night, as he meditated in forgiveness of the day, he wondered at himself. Had not he laughed at cruelty, had not his smile condoned the degradation of another human being? Where was Sa in that? Guilt washed over him. He forced it aside; a true priest of Sa had little use for guilt. It but obscured; if something made a man feel bad then he must determine what about it troubled him, and eliminate that. Simply to suffer the discomforts of guilt did not indicate a man had improved himself, only that he suspected he harbored a fault. He lay still in the darkness and pondered what had made him smile and why. And for the first time in many years, he wondered if his conscience was not too tender, if it had not become a barrier between him and his fellows. "That which separates is not of Sa," he said softly to himself. But he fell asleep before he could remember the source for the quote, or even if it were from scripture at all.

Their first sighting of the Barrens came on a clear cold morning. The voyage northeast had carried them from autumn to winter, from mild blue weather to perpetual drizzle and fog. The Barrens crouched low on the horizon. They were visible not as proper islands, but only as a place where the waves suddenly became white foam and spume. The islands were low and flat, little more than a series of rocky beaches and sand plains that chanced to be above the high tide line. Inland, Althea had heard there was sand and scrubby vegetation and little more than that. Why the sea bears chose to haul out there, to fight and mate and raise their young, she had no idea. Especially as each year at this time, the slaughter boats came to drive and kill hundreds of their kind. She squinted her eyes against the flying salt spray and wondered what kind of deadly instinct brought them back here every year despite their memories of blood and death.

The *Reaper* came into the lee of the cluster of islands at about noon, only to find that one of their rivals had already claimed the best anchorage. Captain Sichel cursed at that, cursed as if it were somehow the fault of his men and his ship that the *Karlay* had beaten them here. Anchors were set and the hunters roused from their stupor of inactivity. Althea had heard that they'd quarreled over their gambling a few days ago and all but killed one of their number who they'd suspected of cheating. It was nothing to her; they were foul-mouthed and ill-tempered on the occasions when she'd had to fetch for them in her duties as ship's boy. She was not at all surprised they were turning on one another in their close quarters and idleness. And what they did to one another was no concern to her at all.

Or so she had thought. It was when they were safely anchored and she was looking forward to the first day of comparative quiet that they'd had in weeks that she suddenly discovered that it would affect her. Officially, she was off duty. Most of her watch were sleeping, but she had decided to take advantage of the light and the relatively quiet weather to mend some of her clothes. Doing close work by lantern light had begun to bother her eyes of late, to say nothing of the close air belowdecks. She'd found a quiet corner, in the lee of the house. She was out of the wind and the sun had miraculously found them despite the edge of winter in the air. She had just begun to cut squares of canvas from her worst worn pair of trousers to patch the others when she heard the mate bellow her name.

"Athel!" he roared, and she leapt to her feet.

"Here, sir!" she cried, heedless of the work that had spilled from her lap.

"Get ready to go ashore. You'll be helping the skinners; they're short a man. Lively, now."

"Yessir," she replied, as it was the only possible reply, but her heart sank. That did not slow her feet, however. She snatched up her work and carried it down the hatch with her, and set it aside to finish on some unforeseeable tomorrow. She jammed her callused feet into felted stockings and heavy boots. The barnacled rocks would not be kind to bare feet. She snugged her knit cap more closely about her ears and dashed back up the steps to the deck. She was not a moment too soon, for the boats were already being raised by the davits. She lunged into one and took a place at an oar.

The sailors manned the oars while the hunters hunched their shoulders to the spray and icy wind and grinned at one another in anticipation. Favorite bows were gripped and held well out of the water's reach, while oiled bags of arrows rolled sluggishly in the shallow bilge water of the skiff. Althea leaned hard on her oar, trying to match her companion. The boats of the *Reaper* moved together toward the rocky shores of the islands, each with a complement of hunters, skinners and sailors. She noticed, almost in passing, that Brashen pulled at the oars in one of the other boats. He'd be in charge of the sailors ashore then, she decided. She resolved to give him no reason to notice her. She'd be working with the hunters and skinners anyway; there was no need for their paths to cross. For an instant she wondered just what her task would be, then shrugged it off as useless curiosity. They'd tell her, soon enough.

Just as the rival ship had taken the best anchorage, so, too, her hunters had taken the prime island. By tradition the ships would not encroach on one another's hunting territories. Past experience had taught them all that it led only to dead men and less profit for all. So the island where they put ashore was bare of all other human life. The rocky beaches were deserted, save for some very old sows resting in the shallows. The adult males had already left, beginning the migration back to wherever these creatures wintered. On the sandy inland plains, Althea knew they would find the younger females and this year's crop of offspring. They would have lingered there, feeding off the late runs of fish and gathering fat and strength before they began their long journey.

The hunters and skinners remained in the boats when the rowers jumped overboard into the shallows and seized the gunwales of the skiffs to run the boats ashore. They timed this action to coincide with a wave to help them lift the boat clear of the sharp rocks. Althea waded out on the beach with the others, her soaked legs and wet boots seeming to draw in the cold.

Once ashore, she quickly found her duties, which seemed to be to do whatever the hunters and skinners didn't care to do for themselves. She was soon burdened with all the extra bows, arrows, knives and sharpening stones. She followed the hunters inland with her arms heavily laden. It surprised her that the hunters and skinners walked so swiftly and talked so freely amongst themselves. She would have supposed this hunt to require some kind of stalking and stealth.

Instead, at the top of the first rise, the gently rolling interior of the island was revealed to her. The sea bears sprawled and slept in clusters on the sand and amongst the scrub brush. As the men crested the hill, the fat creatures scarcely deigned to notice them. Those that did open their eyes regarded their approach with as little interest as they took in the dung-picker birds that shared their territory.

The hunters chose their positions. She was speedily relieved of the bags of arrows she had carried for them. She stood well back of them as they strung their bows and selected their targets. Then the deadly rain of arrows began. The animals they struck bellowed and some galloped awkwardly in circles before they died, but the creatures did not appear to associate their pain and deaths with the men upon the rise above them. It was almost a leisurely slaughter, as the hunters chose target after target and sent arrows winging. The throats were the chosen targets, where the broad-headed arrows opened the veins. Blood spilled thick. That was the death they meted out, that animals might bleed to death. This left the supple furs of their hides intact, as well as yielding meat that was not too heavy with blood. Death was not swift, nor painless. Althea had never seen much of meat slaughter, let alone killing on such a scale. It repulsed her, and yet she stood and watched, as she was sure a true youth would have done, and tried not to let her revulsion show on her face.

The hunters were businesslike about their killing. As soon as the final arrows were expended, they moved down to reclaim them from the dead beasts, while the skinners came behind them like gorecrows to a battle scene. The bulk of the live animals had moved off in annoyance from the struggles and bellows of those struck and dying. They still seemed to feel no panic, only a distaste for the odd antics that had disturbed their rest. The leader of the hunters glanced at Althea in some annoyance. "See what's keeping them with the salt," he barked at her, as if she had known she would have this duty and had neglected it. She scrambled to this command, just as glad to leave the scene of slaughter. The skinners were already at work, stripping the hide from each beast, salvaging tongues, hearts, and livers before rolling the entrails out of the way and leaving the naked fat-and-meat creatures on their own hides. The knowledgeable gulls were already coming to the feast.

She had scarcely crested the rise before she saw a sailor coming toward her, rolling a cask of salt ahead of him. Behind him came a line of others, and she suddenly realized the scope of their task. Cask after cask of salt was making its way up the rise, while a raft of empty barrels was being brought ashore by yet another crew of sailors. All over the island, this was happening. The *Reaper* herself was securely anchored with no more than a skeleton crew aboard to maintain her. All the others had been pushed into the vast task of off-loading and ferrying kegs of salt and empty barrels ashore. And all, she realized, must then be transported back, the barrels heavy with salted meat or hides. Here they would stay to continue this harvest for as long as animals and empty barrels remained.

"They want the salt now," she told the sailor pushing the first keg. He didn't even bother to reply. She turned and ran back to her party of hunters. The hunters were already raining death down on another wing of the vast herd, while the skinners seemed to have finished fully half of what the hunters had already brought down.

It was the beginning of one of the seemingly endless bloody days that followed. To Althea fell the tasks that everyone else judged them-selves too busy to do. She ferried hearts and tongues to a central cask, salting each organ as she added it to the barrel. Her clothes grew sticky and stiff with blood, dyed brown with repeated staining, but that was no different for anyone else. The erstwhile sailors who had been the debtors of Jamaillia were swiftly taught to be butchers. The slabs of yellowish fat were sliced clean of the meat and packed into clean barrels to be ferried back to the ship. Then the carcasses were boned out to conserve space in the barrels, the slabs of dark red meat were well salted before they were laid down, and then over all a clean layer of salt before the casks were sealed. Hides were scraped clean of any clinging fat or red strips of flesh the skinners might have left, and then spread out with a thick layer of salt on the skin side. After a day of drying thus, they were shaken clean of salt, rolled and tied, and taken to the ship in bundles. As the teams of butchers moved slowly forward, they left red-streaked bones and piles of gut-sacks in their wake. The sea birds descended to this feast, adding their voices to those of the killers and the cries of the those being killed.

Althea had hoped that she might gain some immunity to their bloody work, but with each passing day, it seemed to grow both more monstrous and more commonplace. She tried to grasp that this wide-spread slaughter of animals went on year after year, but could not. Not even the tangles of white bones on the killing fields could convince her that last year had seen slaughter on the same scale. She gave over thinking about it, and simply did her tasks.

They built a rough camp on the island, on the same site as last year's camp, in the lee of a rock formation know as The Dragon. Their tent was little more than canvas stretched to break the wind, and fires for warmth and cooking, but at least it was shelter. The sweet heavy smells of blood and butchery still rode the wind that assailed them, but it was a change from the close quarters of the ship. The men built smoky fires with the resinous branches of the scrub brush that grew on the island and the scarce bits of driftwood that had washed up. They cooked the sea-bears' livers over them, and she joined in the feasting, as glad as anyone over the change in their diet and the chance to eat fresh meat again.

In some ways, she was glad of her change in status. She worked for the hunters and skinners now, and her tasks were separate from those of the rest of the crew. She envied no one the heavy work of rolling the filled kegs back up the rise, over the rocky beach and then ferrying them back to the ship and hoisting them aboard and stowing them. It was mindless, back-breaking work. Drudgery such as that had little to do with sailing, yet no one of the *Reaper*'s crew was excused from it. Her own tasks continued to evolve as the hunters and skinners thought of them. She honed knives. She retrieved arrows. She salted and packed hearts and tongues. She spread hides and salted hides and shook hides and rolled hides and tied hides. She coated slabs of meat with salt and layered it into casks. The frequent exchange of blood and salt on her hands would have cracked them had not they been constantly coated with thick animal fat as well.

The weather had held fine for them, blustery and cold but with no sign of the drenching rains that could ruin both hides and meat. Then came an afternoon when the clouds suddenly seemed to boil into the sky, beginning at the horizon and rapidly encroaching on the blue. The wind honed itself sharper. Yet the hunters still killed, scarcely sparing a glance at the clouds building up on the horizon, tall and black as mountains. It was only when the first sleet began to arrow down that they gave over their own deadly rain and began shouting angrily for the skinners and packers to make haste, make haste before meat and fat and hides were lost. Althea scarcely saw what anyone could do to defy the storm, but she learned swiftly. The stripped hides were rolled up with a thick layer of salt inside them. All were suddenly pressed into work as skinners, butchers and packers. She abruptly found herself with a skinning knife in her hands, bent over a carcass still warm, drawing the blade from the sea bear's gullet to its vent.

She had seen it done often enough now that she had lost most of her squeamishness. Still, a moment's disgust uncoiled inside her as she peeled the soft hide back from the thick layer of fat. The animal was warm and flaccid beneath her hands, and that first opening of its body released a waft of death and offal. She steeled herself. The wide, flat blade of her skinning knife slipped easily between fat and skin, slicing it free of the body while her free hand kept a steady tug of tension upon the soft fur. She holed the hide twice on her first effort, trying to go too fast. But when she relaxed and did not think about what she was doing so much as how to do it well, the next hide came free as simply as if she were peeling a Jamaillian orange. It was, she realized, simply a matter of thinking how an animal was made, where hide would be thick or thin, fat present or absent.

By her fourth animal, she realized it was not only easy for her, but that she was good at it. She moved swiftly from carcass to carcass, suddenly uncaring of the blood and smell. The long slice to open the beast, the swift skinning, followed by a quick disemboweling. Heart and liver were freed with two slashes and the rest of the gut-sack rolled free of the body and hide. The tongue, she found, was the most bothersome, prying open the animal's mouth and reaching within to grasp the still-warm wet tongue and then hew it off at the base. Had it not been such a valuable delicacy she might have been tempted to skip it entirely.

At some point she lifted her head, to peer around her through the driving sleet. The cold rain pounded her back and dripped into her eyes, but until that moment of respite, she had been almost unaware of it. Behind her, she realized, were no less than three teams of butchers trying to keep up with her. She had left behind her a wide trail of stripped carcasses. In the distance, one of the hunters appeared to be speaking to the mate about something. He made an off-hand gesture towards her and she suddenly knew with certainty that she was the topic of their conversation. She once more bent her head to her work, her hands flying as she blinked away the cold rain that ran into her eyes and dripped from her nose. A small fire of pride began to burn within her. It was dirty, disgusting work, carried out on a scale that was beyond greed. But she was good at it. And it had been so long since she had been able to claim that for herself, her hunger for it shocked her.

There came a time when she looked around her and found no more animals to skin. She stood slowly, rolling the ache from her shoulders. She cleaned her knife on her bloody trousers, and then held her hands out to the rain, letting the icy water flush the blood and gobbets of fat and flesh from them. She wiped them a bit cleaner on her shirt and then pushed the wet hair back from her eyes. Behind her, men bent to work over the flayed carcasses in her wake. A man rolled a cask of salt toward her, while another followed with an empty hogshead. When a man stopped beside her and righted the cask, he lifted his eyes to meet hers. It was Brashen. She grinned at him. "Pretty good, eh?"

He wiped rain from his own face and then observed quietly, "Were I you, I'd do as little as possible to call attention to myself. Your disguise won't withstand a close scrutiny."

His rebuke irritated her. "Maybe if I get good enough at this, I won't need to be disguised any more."

The look that passed over his face was both incredulous and horrified. He stove in the end of the salt cask, and then gestured at her as if he were bidding her get to work salting hides. But what he said was, "Did these two-legged animals you crew with suspect for one moment that you were a woman, they'd use you, one and all, with less concern than they give to this slaughter. Valuable as you might be to them as a skinner, they'd see no reason why they couldn't use you as a whore as well. And they would see it that by your being here you had expected and consented to such use."

Something in his low earnest voice chilled her beyond the rain's touch. There was such certainty in his tone she could not imagine arguing with it. Instead she hurried off to meet the man with the hogshead, bearing with her the tongue and heart from her final beast. She continued with this task, keeping her head low as if to keep rain from her eyes and trying to think of nothing, nothing. If she had stopped to think of how easy that had become lately, it might have frightened her.

That evening when she returned to camp, she understood for the first time the naming of the rock. A trick of the last light slanting through the overcast illuminated The Dragon in awful detail. She had not seen it before because she had not expected it to be sprawled on its back, forelegs clutching at its black chest, outflung wings submerged in earth. The contortions of its immense body adumbrated an agonized death. Althea halted on the slight rise that offered her this view and stared in horror. Who would carve such a thing, and why on earth did they camp in its lee? The light changed, only slightly, but suddenly the eroded rock upthrust through the thin soil was no more than an oddly shaped boulder, its lines vaguely suggestive of a sprawled animal. Althea let out her pent breath.

"Bit unnerving the first time you catch it, eh?" Reller asked at her elbow.

She started at his voice. "Bit," she admitted, then shrugged her shoulders in boyish bravado. "But for all that, it's just a rock."

Reller lowered his voice. "You so sure of that? You ought to climb up on its chest some time, and take a look. That part there, that looks like forelegs . . . they clutch at the stump of an arrow shaft, or what's left of one. No, boy, that's the for-real carcass of a live dragon, brought down when the world was younger'n an egg, and rotting slow ever since."

"No such things as dragons," Althea scoffed at his hazing.

"No? Don't be telling me that, nor any other sailor was off the Six Duchies coast a few years back. I saw dragons, and not just one or two. Whole phalanx of 'em, flying like geese, in every bright color and shape you can name. And not just once, but twice. There's some as say they brought the serpents, but that ain't true. I'd seen serpents years before that, way down south. Course, nowadays, we see a lot more of 'em, so folk believe in 'em. But when you've sailed as long as I, and been as far as I, you'll learn that there's a lot of things that are real but only a few folk have seen 'em."

Althea gave him a skeptical grin. "Yea, Reller, pull my other leg, it's got bells on," she retorted.

"Damn pup!" the man replied in apparently genuine affront.

"Thinks 'cause he can slide a skinning knife he can talk back to his betters." He stalked off down the rise.

Althea followed him more slowly. She told herself she should have acted more gullible; after all, she was supposed to be a fourteen-year-old out on his first lengthy voyage. She shouldn't spoil Reller's fun, if she wanted to keep on his good side. Well, the next time he trotted out a sea tale, she'd be more receptive and make it up to him. After all, he was as close as she had to a friend aboard the *Reaper*.

The *Vivacia* made her fourth port on a late autumn evening. The light was slanting across the sky, breaking through a bank of clouds to fall on the town below. Wintrow was on the foredeck, spending his mandatory evening hour with Vivacia. He leaned on the railing beside her and stared at the white-spired town snugged in the crook of the tiny harbor. He had been silent, as he often was, but lately the silence had been more companionable than miserable. She blessed Mild with all her heart. Since he had extended his friendship to Wintrow the boy had begun to thrive.

Wintrow, if not cheerful, was at least gaining a bit of the cockiness that was expected of a ship's boy. When that post had been Mild's, he had been daring and lively, into mischief when he was not being the ship's jester for anyone who had a spare moment to share with him. When Mild had acquired the status of hand, he had settled into a more sober attitude toward his work, as was right. But Wintrow had suffered badly in comparison. It had showed all too plainly that his heart was not in his work. He had ignored or misunderstood the sailor's attempts to jest with him, and his doldrums spirits had not been conducive to anyone wishing to spend time to him. Now that he was beginning to smile, if only occasionally, and to good-naturedly rebut some of the sailor's jests, he was beginning to be accepted. They were more prone now to give the word of advice or warning that prevented him from making mistakes that multiplied his work load. He built on each small success, mastering his tasks with the rapidity of a mind trained to learn well. An occasional word of praise or camaraderie was beginning to waken in him a sense of being part of the crew. Some now perceived that his gentle nature and thoughtful ways were not a weakness. Vivacia was beginning to have hopes for him.

She glanced back at him. His black hair was pulling free of his queue and falling into his eyes. With a pang, she saw a ghost there, an echo of Ephron Vestrit when he had been that age. She twisted and reached a hand to him. "Put your hand in mine," she told him quietly, and for a wonder he obeyed her. She knew he still had a basic distrust of her, that he was not sure if she was of Sa or not. But when he put his own newly callused hand into hers, she closed her immense fingers around his, and they were suddenly one.

He looked through his grandfather's eyes. Ephron had loved this harbor and this island's folk. The shining white spires and domes of their city were all the more surprising given the smallness of their settlement. Back beneath the green eaves of the forest were where most of the Caymara folk lived. Their homes were small and green and humble. They tilled no fields, broke no ground, but were hunters and gatherers one and all. No cobbled roads led out of the town, only winding paths suitable for foot traffic and hand carts. They might have seemed a primitive folk, save for their tiny city on Claw Island. Here every engineering instinct was given vent and expression. There were no more than thirty buildings there, not including the profusion of stalls that lined their market street and the rough wooden buildings that fronted the waterfront for commercial trade. But every one of the buildings that comprised the white heart of the city was a marvel of architecture and sculpting. His grandfather had always allowed himself time to stroll through the city's marble heart and look up at the carved faces of heroes, the friezes of legends, and the arches on which plants both live and carved climbed and coiled.

"And you brought it here, much of the marble facing. Without you and him . . . oh, I see. It is almost like my windows. Light shines through them to illuminate the labor of my hands. Through your work, Sa's light shines in this beauty . . ."

He was breathing the words, a sub-vocal whisper she could barely hear. Yet more mystifying than his words was the feeling he shared with her. A moving toward unity that he seemed to value above all else was what he appreciated here. He did not see the elaborately carved facades of the buildings as works of art to enjoy. Instead, they were an expression of something she could not grasp, a coming together of ship and merchant and trading folk that had resulted not just in physical beauty but . . . *arcforia-Sa*. She did not know the word, she could only reach after the concept. Joy embodied . . . the best of men and nature coming together in a permanent expression . . . justification of all Sa had bequeathed so lavishly upon the world. She felt a soaring euphoria in him she had never experienced in any of his other kin, and suddenly recognized that this was what he missed so hungrily. The priests had taught him to see the world with these eyes, had gently awakened in him a hunger for unadulterated beauty and goodness. He believed his destiny was to pursue goodness, to find and exult it in all its forms. To believe in goodness.

She had sought to share and teach. Instead, she had been given and taught. She surprised herself by drawing back from him, breaking the fullness of the contact she had sought. This was a thing she needed to consider, and perhaps she needed to be alone to consider it fully. And in that thought she recognized yet again the full impact Wintrow was having on her.

He was given shore time. He knew it did not come from his father, nor from Torg. His father had gone ashore hours ago, to begin the negotiations for trade. He had taken Torg with him. So the decision to grant him shore time with the others seemed to come from Gantry, the first mate. It puzzled Wintrow. He knew the mate had full charge of all the men on board the ship, and that only the captain's word was higher. Yet he did not think Gantry had even been fully cognizant of his existence. The man had scarcely spoken to him directly in all the time he had been aboard. Yet his name was called out for the first group of men allowed time ashore, and he found his heart soaring with anticipation. It was too good a piece of luck to question. Each time they had anchored or docked in Chalced, he had stared longingly at the shore, but had never been allowed to leave the ship. The thought of solid ground underfoot, of looking at something he had not seen before, was ecstatically dizzying. Like the others fortunate enough to be in the first party he dashed below, to don his shore clothes and run a brush through his hair and re-plait his queue. Clothes gave him one moment of indecision.

Torg had been given charge of purchasing Wintrow's kit before they left Bingtown. His father had not trusted Wintrow with money and time in which to buy the clothes and supplies he would need for the voyage. Wintrow had found himself with two suits of canvas shirts and trousers for his crew work, both cheaply made. He suspected that Torg had made more than a bit of profit between what coin his father had given him and what he had actually spent. He had also supplied Wintrow with a typical sailor's shore clothes: a loudly striped woven shirt and a pair of coarse black trousers, as cheaply made as his deck clothes. They did not even fit him well, as Torg had not been too particular about size. The shirt especially hung long and full on him. His alternative was his brown priest's robe. It was stained and worn now, darned in many places, and hemmed shorter to solve the fraying and provide material for patches. If he put it on, he would once more be proclaiming to all that this was what he was, a priest, not a sailor. He would lose what ground he had gained with his fellows.

As he donned the striped shirt and black trousers, he told himself that it was not a denial of his priesthood, but instead a practical choice. If he had gone among the folk of this strange town dressed as a priest of Sa, he would likely have been offered the largesse due a wandering priest. It would have been dishonest to seek or accept such gifts of hospitality, when he was not truly come among them as a priest but only as a visiting sailor. Resolutely he set aside the niggling discomfort that perhaps he was making too many compromises lately, that perhaps his morality was becoming too flexible. He hurried to join those going ashore.

There were five of them going ashore, including Wintrow and Mild. One of them was Comfrey, and Wintrow found that he could neither keep his eyes off the man nor meet his gaze squarely. There he sat, the man who had perpetrated the coffee-cup obscenity on his father, and Wintrow could not decide whether to be horrified by him or amused. He seemed a fellow of great good cheer, making one jest after another to the rest of the crew as they leaned on the oars. He wore a ragged red cap adorned with cheap brass charms, and his grin was missing a tooth. When he caught Wintrow stealing glances at him, he tipped the boy a wink and asked him loudly if he'd like to tag along to the brothel. "Likely the girls'll do you for half price. Little men like you sort of tickle their fancy is what I hear." And despite his embarrassment, Wintrow found himself grinning as the other men laughed. He suddenly grasped the good nature behind a great deal of the teasing.

They hauled the small boat up on the beach and pulled her well above the tide line. Their liberty would only last until sundown, and two of the men were already complaining that the best of the wine and women would not be found on the streets until after that. "Don't you believe them, Wintrow," Comfrey said comfortingly. "There's plenty to be had at any hour in Cress; those two just prefer the darkness for their pleasures. With faces like those, they need a bit of shadow even to persuade a whore to take them on. You come with me, and I'll see you have a good time before we have to be back to the ship."

"I've a few errands of my own before sundown," Wintrow excused himself. "I want to see the carvings on the Idishi Hall, and the friezes on the Heroes' Wall."

All the men looked at him curiously, but only Mild asked, "How do you know about that stuff? You been to Cress before?"

He shook his head, feeling both shy and proud. "No. But the ship has. Vivacia told me about them, and that my grandfather had found them beautiful. I thought I'd go see for myself."

A total silence fell, and one of the deckhands made a tiny gesture with his left little finger that might have been an invocation of Sa's protection against evil magic. Again Mild was the one to speak. "Does the ship really know everything that Cap'n Vestrit knew?"

Wintrow gave a small shrug. "I don't know. I only know that what she chooses to share with me is very . . . vivid. Almost as if it became my memory." He halted, suddenly uncomfortable. He found that he did not want to speak about it at all. It was private, he discovered, that link between himself and the *Vivacia*. No, more than private. An intimacy. The silence became uncomfortable again. This time Comfrey rescued them. "Well, fellows, I don't know about you but I don't get beach time all that often. I'm for town and a certain street where both the flowers and the women bloom sweet." He glanced at Mild. "See that both you and Wintrow are back to the boat on time. I don't want to have to come looking for you."

"I wasn't going with Wintrow!" Mild protested. "I've got a lot more in mind than looking at walls."

"I don't need a guardian," Wintrow added. He spoke aloud what he thought might be troubling them. "I won't try to run away. I give you my word I'll come back to the boat well before sundown."

The surprised looks on their faces told him they had never even considered this. "Well, course not," Comfrey observed drily. "No place on Claw Island to run to, and the Caymarans ain't exactly friendly to strangers. We weren't worrying about you running off, Wintrow. Cress can be dangerous for a sailor out and about on his lonesome. Not just a ship's boy, but any sailor. You ought to go with him, Mild. How long can it take for him to look at a wall anyway?"

Mild looked extremely unhappy. Comfrey's words were not an order; he did not have the power to give him an order. But if he ignored his suggestion and Wintrow got into some kind of trouble . . .

"I'll be fine," Wintrow said insistently. "It won't be the first time I've been in a strange city. I know how to take care of myself. And our time is wasted just standing here arguing. I'll meet you all back here at the boat, well before sundown. I promise."

"You'd better," Comfrey said ominously, but there was an immediate lightening of spirit. "You come find us at the Sailors' Walk as soon as you've seen this wall of yours. Be there ahead of time. Now that you're starting to act like a sailor on board, it's time we marked you as one of our own." Comfrey tapped the elaborate tattoo on his arm while Wintrow grinned and shook his head emphatically. The older sailor thumbed his nose at him. "Well. Be on time, anyway."

Wintrow knew that if anything did happen to him now, they could all agree that he'd insisted on going off by himself, that there had been nothing they could do about it. It was a bit disconcerting to see how quickly they abandoned him. He was still part of the group as they walked down the beach, but when they reached the commerce docks, the men veered like a flock of birds, heading for the waterfront bars and brothels. Wintrow hesitated a moment, watching them go with an odd sort of longing. They laughed loudly, a bunch of sailors out on the town, exchanging friendly shoves and gestures suggestive of their afternoon plans. Mild bounced along at their heels almost like a friendly dog, and Wintrow was suddenly certain that he was newly accepted to that brotherhood, that he had only been promoted to it because Wintrow had come to take his place on the bottom rung of the ship's hierarchy.

Well, it didn't bother him. Not really, he told himself. He knew enough of men's ways to realize that it was natural for him to want to be a part of the group, to do whatever he must do to belong. And, he told himself sternly, he knew enough of Sa's ways to know that there were times when a man had to set himself apart from the group, for his own good. Bad enough, really, that he had not so much as muttered a single word against their afternoon's plans for whoring and drunkeness. He tried to find reasons for that but knew they were only excuses, and set the whole question aside in his mind. He had done what he had done, and tonight he would meditate on it and try to find perspective on it. For now, he had a whole city to see in the space of a few hours.

He had his grandfather's memory of the city's layout to guide him. In an odd way, it was almost as if the old captain walked with him, for he could see the changes that had occurred since the last time Ephron had visited this port. Once, when a shopkeeper came out to adjust the awning over his heaped baskets of fruit, Wintrow recognized him and nearly greeted him by name. Instead he just found himself grinning at the man, thinking that his belly had done a bit of rounding out in the last few years. The man glared at him in turn, looking the boy up and down as if he were affronted. Wintrow decided his smile had been too familiar and hastened on past him, heading into the heart of the city.

He came to Well Square and stopped to stare in awe. Cress had an artesian spring for its water supply. It surged up in the center of a great stone basin, with enough force to mound the water in the center as if a great bubble were trying to rise from the depths. From the main basin it had been channeled into others, some for the washing of clothes, some for potable water and still others for watering of animals. Each basin had been fancifully decorated with images of its purpose so that there could be no mistake in its utility. The overflow too was gathered and funneled off out of sight into a drainage system that no doubt ended in the bay. Interspersed among the various basins were plantings of flowers and shrubs.

A number of young women, some with small children playing beside them, were taking advantage of the clear and warm afternoon to wash clothing. Wintrow halted and stood looking at the scene they made. Some of the younger women stood in the washing basin, skirts looped up and tied about their thighs as they pounded and rubbed the laundry clean and then wrung it out against their legs. They laughed and called to one another as they worked. Young mothers sat on the basin's edge, washing clothes and keeping a watchful eye on babes and toddlers that played at the fountain's edge. Baskets were scattered about, holding laundry both wet and dry. There was something so simple and yet so profound about the scene that it nearly brought tears to Wintrow's eyes. Not since he had left the monastery had he seen folk so harmoniously engaged in work and life. The sun shone on the water and the Caymaran women's smooth hair gleamed on the wet skin of their arms and legs. He gazed avidly, taking it all in as balm that soothed his roughened spirit.

"Are you lost?"

He turned quickly to the words. They could have been spoken kindly, but had not been. One look at the eyes of the two city guardsmen left him no doubt of their hostility. The one who had spoken was a bearded veteran, with a white stripe tracing an old scar through his dark hair and down his cheek. The other was a younger man, brawny in a professional way. Before Wintrow could reply to the query, the second guard spoke. "The waterfront's down that way. That's where you'll find what you're looking for." He pointed with a truncheon back the way Wintrow had come.

"What I'm looking for . . . ?" Wintrow repeated blankly. He looked from one tall man to the other, trying to fathom their hard faces and cold eyes. What had he done to cause offense? "I wanted to see the Heroes' Frieze and the carvings on the Idishi Hall."

"And on the way," the first guard observed with ponderous humor, "you thought you might stop off to watch some young women getting wet in a fountain."

There seemed nothing he could say. "The fountains themselves are objects of beauty," he attempted.

"And we all know how interested sailors are in objects of beauty." The guard put the emphasis on the last three words with heavy sarcasm. "Why don't you go buy some 'objects of beauty' down at the Blowing Scarf? Tell them Kentel sent you. Maybe I'll get a commission."

Wintrow looked down, flustered. "That isn't what I meant. I do, seriously, wish to take time to see the friezes and carvings." When neither man replied, he added defensively, "I promise, I'll be no trouble to anyone. I have to be back to my ship by sundown anyway. I just wanted to look about the town a bit."

The older man sucked his teeth briefly. For a moment, Wintrow thought he was reconsidering. "Well, we 'seriously' think you ought to get back down where you belong. Down by the docks is where sailors 'look about our town.' The street for your kind is easy to find; we call it the Sailors' Walk. Plenty there to amuse you. And if you don't head back that way now, young fellow, I promise you that you will have trouble. With us."

He could hear his heart beating, a muffled thunder in his ears. He couldn't decide which emotion was stronger, but when he spoke, it was the anger he heard, not the fear. "I'm leaving," he said brusquely. But even if the anger was stronger, it was still hard to turn his back on the men as he walked past them. The skin on his back crawled, half expecting to feel the blow of a truncheon. He listened for footsteps behind him. What he did hear was worse. A derisive snort of laughter, and a quietly mocking comment from the younger man. He neither turned to it nor walked faster, but he could feel the muscles in his neck and shoulders knotting with his fury. My clothing, he told himself. It isn't me they've judged, but my clothing. I should not take their insults to heart. Let it go by, let it go by, let it go by, he breathed to himself, and after a time, he found that he could. He turned at the next corner and chose a different path up the hill. He would let their words go by, but he would not be defeated by their attitude. He intended to see the Idishi Hall.

He wandered for a time, bereft of his grandfather's guidance, for he had never taken this route through the city. He was stopped twice, once by a young boy who offered to sell him some smoking herbs and, more distressingly, by a woman who wished to sell herself to him. Wintrow had never been so approached before, and it was worse that the tell-tale sores of a flesh disease were plain around her mouth. He forced himself to refuse her courteously twice. When she refused to be put off, only lowering her price and offering him "any way you like, anything you fancy at all," he finally spoke plainly. "I have no wish to share your body or your disease," he told her, and heard with a pang how cruel his honesty sounded. He would have apologized but she did not give him time, spitting at him before she turned and flounced away. He continued walking, but found that she had frightened him more than the city guards had.

Finally he gained the heart of the city proper. Here the streets were paved and every building that fronted on the street had some decoration or design to recommend it. These were obviously the public structures of Cress, where laws were made and judgments passed and the higher business of the city conducted. He walked slowly, letting his eyes linger, and often stopping to step back into the street to try to see a structure as a whole. The stone arches were some of the most amazing work he had ever seen.

He came to a small temple of Odava, the serpent-god, with the traditional rounded doors and windows of the sect. He had never especially cared for this particular manifestation of Sa, and had never met a follower of Odava who would admit that the serpent-deity was but another facet of Sa's jewel face. Nonetheless, the graceful structure still spoke to him of the divine and the many paths folk trod in seeking it out. So finely was the stone of this building worked that when he set his hand to it, he could scarcely feel the seam of the builders' joining. He stood thus for a time, reaching out as he had been trained to do to sense structure and stresses in the building. What he discovered was a powerful unity, almost organic in its harmony. He shook his head in amazement, scarcely noticing the group of men in white robes banded with green and gray who had emerged from a door behind him and now walked past and around him with annoyed glances.

After a time he came to himself, and realized, too, that the afternoon was fleeing more swiftly than he had expected it to. He had no more time to waste. He stopped a matron to courteously ask her the way to the Idishi Hall. She took several steps back from him before she answered, and then it was only with a toss of her hand that indicated a general direction. Nonetheless, he thanked her and hurried on his way.

The streets in this part of the city had more pedestrian traffic. More than once he caught folk looking at him oddly. He suspected that his clothes proclaimed him a stranger to their town. He smiled and nodded, but hastened along, too pressed for time to be more social.

The Idishi Hall was framed by its site. A hollow in the side of a hill cupped the building lovingly in its palm. From Wintrow's vantage, he could look down on it. The verdant forest behind it set off the gleaming white of its pillars and dome. The contrast of the lush and random growth and the precise lines of the hall took Wintrow's breath away. He stood transfixed; it was an image he wished to carry with him forever. People were coming and going from the hall, most dressed in gracefully draped robes in cool tones of blues and greens. It could not have been more lovely if it had been a contrived spectacle. He softened the focus of his eyes, and took several deep breaths, preparing to absorb the scene before him with complete concentration.

A heavy hand fell on his shoulder. "Sailor boy is lost again," the younger city guard observed. Even as Wintrow's head swiveled to the man's words, he received a shove that sent him sprawling on the paving stones. The older guard looked down at him and shook his head, almost regretfully.

"I guess we'll have to see him back to where he belongs this time," he observed as the brawny guard advanced on Wintrow. There was a deadly softness to his words that chilled Wintrow's heart. Even more chilling were the three people who had halted to watch. None of them spoke nor made any effort to interfere. When he looked appealingly at them, seeking help, their eyes were guiltless, showing only their interest in what would happen next.

The boy struggled to his feet hastily and began backing away. "I've done no one any harm," he protested. "I simply wanted to see the Idishi Hall. My grandfather saw it and . . ."

"We don't welcome waterfront rats coming up our streets and dawdling about staring at folk. Here in Cress, we don't let trouble start." The older man was speaking but Wintrow scarcely heard him. He spun about to flee, but in one lunge the brawny guard had him by the back of his collar. He gripped it hard, half strangling Wintrow and then shaking him. Dazed, Wintrow felt himself lifted from the ground and then propelled suddenly forward. He tucked into the fall, rolling with the momentum this time. One uneven paving stone caught him in the short ribs as he did so, but at least no bones broke. He came to his feet almost smoothly but not quite swiftly enough to avoid the younger guardsman. Again he seized Wintrow, shook him and then threw him in the general direction of the waterfront.

This time he collided with the corner of a building. The shock took the skin from his shoulder but he kept to his feet. He ran a few staggering steps, with the grinning inexorable guard in pursuit. Behind him the older soldier followed them almost leisurely, lecturing as he came. It seemed to Wintrow that his words were not for him, but to remind the folk who were halting to watch that they were only doing their jobs. "We've nothing against sailors, so long as they keep themselves and their vermin to the waterfront where they belong. We tried to be nice to you, boy, just because you are such a pup. If you'd gone to the Sailors' Walk, you'd have found it suited you well, I'm sure. Now you're bound for the waterfront anyway. You could have saved all of us a lot of effort and yourself a lot of bruises if you'd only listened."

The calm reasonableness of the older man's voice was almost more horrifying than the other guard's efficient enjoyment of his task. The man was quick as a snake. Somehow he once more had hold of Wintrow's collar. This time he snapped the boy out as a dog flings a rat, sending him slamming into a stone wall. Wintrow felt his head strike the stone and saw a brief flash of darkness. He tasted blood. "Not a sailor," he blurted out. "I'm a priest. A priest of Sa."

The young guard laughed. The older man shook his head in mock regret for the boy. "Oho. That makes you a heretic as well as waterfront scum. Haven't you heard that the followers of Odava have no use for those who would submerge him as but a part of their own god? I was about to tell Flav you'd had enough, but another knock or two might hasten your enlightenment."

The guard's hand was closing on his collar, dragging him to his feet. In a panic, Wintrow let his head slip through the overlarge collar and whipped his arms in as well. He literally fell out the bottom of his shirt as the guard hauled up on the collar of it. Fear spurred him and he scrabbled away, already running as he came to his feet. There was a burst of laughter from the onlookers. He had one brief glimpse of the younger guard's surprised face and the older man's beard split in a grin of amusement. The old man's laughter and the younger man's angry shout followed him but Wintrow was running now, running full tilt. The lovely stonework that had earlier transfixed him was now but something to pass on his way back to his ship and safety. The wide straight streets that had been so open and welcoming now seemed designed only to expose him to pursuit. He dodged past people on the street, and they shrank back from him and then stared after him curiously. He ran shirtless, turning corners as he came to them, afraid of looking back lest they still be pursuing him.

When the streets narrowed and began winding through rows of wooden warehouses and ramshackle inns and brothels, he slowed from his now-staggering run. He looked around himself. A tattoo shop. A cheap chandlery. A tavern. Another tavern. He came to an alley and stepped into it, heedless of the scattered garbage he waded through. Halfway down it, he leaned against a door-jamb and caught his breath. His back and shoulder burned where stone had abraded the skin from them. He touched his mouth cautiously; it was already beginning to puff up. The lump on his head was no more than that, just a bad bump. For a sickening second he wondered how badly the guard had intended to hurt him. Had he wanted to crack his skull, would he have continued beating him until he was dead if he hadn't run away? He had heard of sailors and strangers being "roughed up" by the city guard, even in Bingtown. Was this what was meant by that? He had always assumed that it happened only to those who were drunk or ill-mannered or in some other way offensive.

Yet today it had happened to him. Why? "Because I was dressed as a sailor," he said quietly to himself. For one ghastly instant he considered that this might be a punishment from Sa for not having worn his priest's robe. He had denied Sa and as retribution Sa had denied him His protection. He pushed the unworthy thought away. So children and the superstitious spoke of Sa, as if he were nothing but a much larger and more vengeful human rather than the god of all. No. That was not what was to be learned from this. What was the lesson then? Now that the danger was past, his mind sought refuge in the familiar exercise. There was always something to be learned from any experience, no matter how horrendous. As long as a man kept sight of that, his spirit could prevail against anything. It was only when one gave in and believed the universe to be nothing more than a chaotic collection of unfortunate or cruel events that one's spirit could be crushed.

The breath came more easily to his lungs. His mouth and throat were parched dry but he was not ready yet to go and look for water. He pushed the need to the back of his awareness and reached instead for the calm center of himself. He took the deep steadying breaths and opened himself to perceive the lesson. He willed that his own mind would not shape it, nor his emotions. What was to be learned from this? What should he carry away?

The thought that came floating to the top of his mind shocked him. With great clarity, he saw his own gullibility. He had seen the beauty of the city, and interpreted it to mean that folk of beautiful spirit lived here. He had come here expecting to be greeted and welcomed in the light of Sa. So strong had been his pre-judgment that he had failed to heed any of the warnings that now glared so plainly. His crew-mates had warned him, the city guard's hostility had been a warning, the baleful glances from the townspeople . . . he had been like an overly friendly child approaching a growling dog. It was his own fault he'd been bitten.

A wave of desolation deeper than anything he'd ever felt swept over him. He was unprepared for it and sank with it, letting it sweep away his balance from him. Hopeless, it was all hopeless. He'd never regain his monastery, never return to the life of meditation he so missed. He would become like so many others he'd met, convinced that all men were born his enemy and that only crass gain created friendship or love. So often he'd heard folk mock Sa's ideal that all folk had been created to become creatures of goodness and beauty. Where, he asked himself bitterly, was the goodness in the young guard who'd taken such pleasure in roughing him up today? Where was the beauty in the ulcer-lipped woman who had wanted to lie with him for the sake of money? He suddenly felt young and stupid, gullible in the worst way. A fool. A stupid fool. The pain of this hurt was as real as his bruises, his heart actually felt heavy in his chest. He squeezed his eyes shut to it, wishing he could be somewhere else, be someone else who didn't feel this way.

After a moment he opened his eyes and stood up. The worst of it was that he still had to go back to the ship. This experience would have been hard enough even if he had had the safety and peace of the monastery to return to. To go from this to the stupid squabbling aboard the *Vivacia*, to return to Torg's gleeful brutality and his father's disparagement of him was almost more than his heart could bear. Yet what was the alternative? To hide himself and remain in Cress as a penniless and despised vagabond? He sighed heavily but his heart only sank deeper in his chest. He waded through softening garbage to the mouth of the alley and then glanced up at the westering sun. The time that had seemed so brief for sight-seeing was now a long empty stretch until sundown. He decided to find the rest of the *Vivacia*'s crew. He could think of nothing else he wanted to see or do in Cress.

He trudged shirtless down the street, ignoring the grins of those who remarked his fresh bruises and scrapes. He came upon a group of men, obviously part of the crew of another ship enjoying some free time. They all wore head scarves that once had been white with a black bird marked on the front. They were laughing and shouting congenial insults to one another as they moved as a group from a brothel to a tavern. Their eyes fell upon Wintrow. "Oh, poor lad!" One exclaimed in mock sympathy. "Turned you down, did she? And kept your shirt to boot?" This witticism brought a general chorus of guffaws. He walked on.

He turned a corner and was suddenly sure he'd found the Sailors' Walk. Not only the Blowing Scarf was on this street, with a signboard depicting a woman clad only in a scarf that the wind was blowing away from her, but the signboards on the other erstwhile taverns were equally suggestive. The crudity of the signboards signaled the specialties of those who worked within the brothels. Obviously the makers had had small faith in any sailor's ability to read.

There were other, cheaper amusements fronting the street. One stall offered lucky charms, potions and amulets: dried cauls to protect a man from drowning, bits of horn to ensure virility, magic oils that could soothe a storm to stillness. Wintrow passed the stall by with a look of pity for those gullible enough to be seeking its wares. Further down the street, in a marked-off square, a beast-tamer was offering passers-by the chance to wrestle his bear for a purse of gold. Even muzzled as he was with his claws blunted to stubs, the bear looked formidable. A short chain hobbled his hind legs, while a heavier chain led from his collar to his owner's fist. The bear shifted constantly, an anxious, restless mountain. His small eyes prowled the crowd. Wintrow wondered what sort of an idiot would be talked into accepting such a challenge. Then with a sinking heart he recognized a grinning Comfrey leaning on a companion and talking to the beast-tamer. A small crowd of on-lookers, most of them sailors, were excitedly placing side bets.

He was tempted to walk on by and look for Mild. Then he recognized Mild amongst those placing bets. With a sigh, he went to join him. Mild recognized him with a grin of delight as he approached. "Hey, come on, Wintrow, you're in luck. Comfrey's going to wrestle the bear. Put your money down, and you can double it." He leaned closer to Wintrow. "It's a sure thing. We just saw a man win. All he had to do was get up on the bear's back and the bear gave up right away. The beastmaster didn't want to let anyone else wrestle him after that, but Comfrey insisted." Mild suddenly goggled at Wintrow. "Hey. What happened to your shirt?"

"I lost it wrestling with the City Guards." Wintrow was almost able to make a joke of it. He was a bit hurt at how easily Mild accepted his words, until he noticed the tang to the other boy's breath. A moment later he saw him shift something about in his lower lip. Cindin. The focus of his eyes quivered with the stimulant. Wintrow felt uneasy for him. The drug was forbidden aboard ship; if he even came aboard still intoxicated, he'd be in trouble. The rash optimism it gave a man did not make him a prudent sailor. Wintrow thought he should say something, suggest caution to him somehow, but could find no words. "I just wanted to let you all know I'd be waiting for you back at the boat. I've finished my sight-seeing, and I'm headed there now."

"No. No, don't go!" The other boy grabbed his arm. "Stay and watch this. You'll be sorry if you don't. You sure you don't want to bet a coin or two? The odds don't get better than this. And the bear's tired. He's got to be tired. He's already wrestled half a dozen times."

"And the last man won?" Curiosity was getting the better of Wintrow.

"Yea. That's right. Once he got up on the bear's back, the bear just folded up like a sleeping cat. Made the beast-tamer scowl, I'll tell you, to have to give him the purse." Mild linked arms with him. "I got my last five coppers riding on this. 'Course, Comfrey has more than that. He did well at the gaming table earlier today." Again Mild peered at him. "You sure you don't have any money you want to put down? The whole crew's betting on Comfrey."

"I haven't a coin of my own. Not even a shirt." Wintrow pointed out again.

"That's right. That's right. Never mind, it's . . . here he goes!"

With a grin and a wave to his gathered shipmates, Comfrey stepped into the marked-off square. No sooner had he crossed the line than the bear reared up onto his hind legs. His fettered legs kept his steps small as he lumbered slowly toward Comfrey. The sailor wove one way and then abruptly dodged the other to slip past the bear and get behind him.

But he never had a chance. As if it were a move he had practiced a hundred times, the bear turned and swatted the sailor down. His powerful front legs had a much greater reach than Wintrow would have credited. The impact of the blow slammed Comfrey face first to the ground.

"Get up, get up!" his ship-mates were yelling, and Wintrow found himself shouting with the rest. The bear continued his restless, shifting dance. He had dropped to all fours again. Comfrey lifted his face from the dusty street. Blood was streaming from his nose, but he seemed to take encouragement from his ship-mates' cheers. He sprang abruptly to his feet and dashed past the bear.

But the bear rose, tall and solid as a wall, and one outstretched paw greeted Comfrey's head in passing. This time the sailor was flung to his back, his head rebounding from the dirt. Wintrow flinched and looked away with a groan. "He's done," he told Mild. "We'd better get him back to the ship."

"No, no. He'll get up, he can do this. Come on, Comfrey, it's just a big old stupid bear. Get up, man, get up!" The other sailors from the *Vivacia* were shouting as well, and for the first time Wintrow picked out Torg's hoarse voice among the crowd. Evidently he had been dismissed by his captain to take some entertainment of his own.

Wintrow was suddenly sure he'd have something witty to say about his missing shirt. Abruptly, he wished that he had never left the ship. This day had been one long string of disasters.

"I'm going back to the boat," he said again to Mild, but Mild paid no attention. He only gripped his arm the harder.

"No, look, he's getting up, I told you he would. That's the way, Comfrey, come on man, you can do it."

Wintrow doubted that Comfrey heard anything Mild shouted. The man looked dazed still, as if instinct alone were compelling him to get to his feet and get away from the bear. But the instant he moved, the animal was on him again, this time clutching him in a hug. It looked laughable, but Comfrey cried out in a way that suggested cracking ribs.

"Do you give, then?" the beast-tamer shouted to the sailor, and Comfrey nodded his head violently, unable to get enough wind to speak.

"Let him go, Sunshine. Let him go!" the tamer commanded, and the bear dropped Comfrey and waddled away. He sat down obediently in the corner of the square and nodded his muzzled head all about as if accepting the cheers of the crowd.

Save that no one was cheering. "I had my every coin on that!" one sailor shouted. He added a muttered comment about Comfrey's virility that seemed to have little relation to bear wrestling. "It wasn't fair!" another added. That seemed to be the general consensus of those who had bet, but Wintrow noticed that not one of them followed it up with a reason why it was not fair. He himself had his own suspicions, but saw no reason to voice them. Instead he moved forward to offer Comfrey some help in getting to his feet. Mild and the others were too busy commiserating on what they had lost. "Comfrey, you dumb ass!" Torg called across the ring. "Can't even get past a hobbled bear." A few other sour remarks confirmed that general opinion. The crew of the *Vivacia* were not the only sailors to have lost their bets.

Comfrey got to his feet, coughing, then bent over to spit out a mouthful of blood. For the first time, he recognized Wintrow. "I nearly had him," he panted. "Damn near had him. Lost everything I'd won earlier. Well, I'm broke now. Damn. If I had just been a bit faster." He coughed again, then belched beerily. "I nearly won."

"I don't think so," Wintrow said quietly, more to himself than to Comfrey. But the man heard him.

"No, really, I almost had him, lad. If I'd a been a bit smaller, a bit quicker, we'd all have gone back to the ship with fat pockets." He wiped blood from his face with the back of his hand.

"I don't think so," Wintrow rejoined. To comfort him, he added, "I think it was rigged. I think the man that won was in league with the bear man. They show you something that seems to make the bear give up, only it's something he's been taught to do. And then when you try it, the bear has been taught to expect you to try it. So you get stopped. Don't feel bad, Comfrey, it wasn't your fault. It was a trick. Let's get you back to the ship now." He put a helping arm around the man.

But Comfrey abruptly wheeled away from him. "Hey! Hey, you. Bear man! You cheated. You cheated me and my friends." In the shocked silence that followed, Comfrey proclaimed, "I want my money back!"

The beast-tamer had been in the act of gathering his winnings preparatory to leaving. He made no reply but took up his animal's chain. Despite Comfrey's shout, he would have just walked off, if several sailors from another ship hadn't stepped in front of him. "That true?" one demanded. "Did you cheat? Is this rigged?"

The beast-tamer glanced about at the angry onlookers. "Of course not!" he scoffed. "How could it be rigged? You saw the man, you saw the bear! They were the only two in the square. He paid for a chance to wrestle the bear and he lost. It doesn't get any simpler than that!"

In a sense, what the man said was true, and Wintrow expected the sailors to grudgingly agree with it. He had not taken into account how much they had drunk, nor how much money they had lost. Once the accusation of cheating had been raised, a simple denial was not going to calm them. One, more quick witted than the others, suddenly said, "Hey. Where did that fellow go, the one who won earlier? Is he your friend? Does the bear know him?"

"How should I know?" the bear owner demanded. "He's probably off spending the money he won from me." A brief shadow of unease had flickered across the beast-tamer's face, and he glanced about the crowd as if looking for someone.

"Well, I think the bear's been trained for this," someone declared angrily. It seemed to Wintrow the most obvious and, in this context, the stupidest statement that he'd heard yet.

"It wasn't a fair contest. I want my money back," another declared, and almost immediately this statement was taken up by the rest of the crowd. The bear's owner again seemed to seek someone in the crowd, but found no allies there.

"Hey. We said we want our money back!" Torg pointed out to him. He swaggered up to put his face close to the beast-tamer's. "Comfrey's my shipmate. You think we're going to stand by and see him beat up and us cheated out of our hard-earned money? You made our man look bad, and by Sa's balls, we don't stand still for that!" Like many a bully, he knew how to best rally men to their own self-interest. He glanced around at the men watching him and then turned back to the beast-tamer. He nodded significantly. "Think we can't just take it if you choose not to give it?" There was a rumbling of agreement from the others.

The beast-tamer was outnumbered and knew it. Wintrow could almost seem him cast about for compromises. "Tell you what," he declared abruptly. "I didn't cheat and my bear didn't cheat, and I think most of you know that. But I can be fair and more than fair. Any one of you wants, I'll let him wrestle the bear for free. If he wins, I pay off all the bets same as if that man had won. He loses, I keep the money. Fair enough? I'm giving you a chance to win back your money for free." After a brief pause, a muttering of agreement ran through the crowd. Wintrow wondered what fool would be the next to feel the bear's strength.

"Here, Win, you go against him," Comfrey suggested. He gave the boy a shove forward. "You're little and quick. All you got to do is get past him and onto his back."

"No. No, thank you." As quickly as Comfrey had pushed him forward, Wintrow stepped back. But the sailor's words had been overheard, and another man from another ship took it up.

"Yea. Let their ship's boy give it a try. He's little and quick. I bet he can get past the bear and get our money back for us."

"No!" Wintrow repeated louder, but his voice was lost in the general chorus of assent. It was not just his own shipmates urging him on, but the crowd in general.

Torg swaggered up to him and looked him up and down. He smelled of beer. "So," he sneered. "You think you can win our money back for us? Somehow I doubt it. But give it a try, boy." He gripped Wintrow's arm and dragged him toward the bear's square. "Our ship's boy wants to give it a try."

"No," Wintrow hissed at him. "I don't."

Torg frowned at him. "Just get past him and onto his back," he explained in an elaborately patient voice. "That should be easy for a skinny little weasel like you."

"No. I won't do it!" Wintrow declared loudly. A chorus of guffaws greeted this, and Torg's face darkened with embarrassed fury.

"Yes, you will," he declared.

"Boy doesn't want to do it. Got no guts," Wintrow clearly heard a man say.

The beast-tamer had his animal back in the square. "So. Your boy going to try or not?"

"Not!" Wintrow declared loudly, as Torg firmly announced, "He will. He just needs a minute." He rounded on Wintrow. "Look here," he hissed at him. "You're shaming us all. You're shaming your ship! Get in there and get our money back for us."

Wintrow shook his head. "You want it done, you do it. I'm not stupid enough to take on a bear. Even if I got past him and got on his back, there's no guarantee he'll give in. Just because he did it before . . ."

"I'll do it!" Mild volunteered. His eyes were bright with the challenge.

"No," Wintrow objected. "Don't do it, Mild. It's stupid. If you weren't humming on cindin, you'd know that. If Torg wants it done, let Torg do it."

"I'm too drunk," Torg admitted freely. "You do it, Wintrow. Show us you got some guts. Prove you're a man."

Wintrow glanced at the bear. It was a stupid thing to do. He knew it was a stupid thing to do. Did he need to prove anything to Torg, of all people? "No." He spoke the word loudly and flatly. "I'm not going to do it."

"The boy doesn't want to try, and I'm not going to stand around here all day. Money's mine, boys." The beast-tamer gave an elaborate shrug and grinned around.

Someone in the crowd made an unflattering remark about the *Vivacia*'s crew in general.

"Hey. Hey, I'll do it." It was Mild again, grinning as he volunteered.

"Don't do it, Mild!" Wintrow entreated him.

"Hey, I'm not afraid. And someone's got to win our money back." He shifted restlessly on his feet. "Can't go off leaving this town believing the crew of the *Vivacia*'s got no nerve."

"Don't do it, Mild! You'll get hurt."

Torg gave him a savage shake. "Shup up!" He belched. "Shut up!" he repeated more clearly. "Mild ain't afraid! He can do it if he wants. Or do you want to do it? Hurry up, decide! One of you has got to win our money back. We're nearly out of time."

Wintrow shook his head. How had it suddenly come down to this, to him or Mild getting into a square with a bear to win back someone else's money in a rigged game? It was preposterous. He looked around at the crowd, trying to find one rational face to side with him. A man caught his gaze. "Well, who is it?" he demanded. Wintrow shook his head wordlessly.

"Me!" Mild declared with a grin and danced a step or two. He stepped into the square and the beast-tamer released the bear's chain.

Later Wintrow would wonder if the tamer had not been irritating the animal somehow the whole time they were waiting. The bear did not lumber toward Mild, nor mince forward on his hobbled legs. Instead he lunged on all fours for the boy, slamming his huge head against him and then gripping him with his huge paws. The bear reared up with Mild yelling and struggling in his grasp. Blunted or not, his claws shredded the young sailor's shirt until a shout from his owner made him throw the boy aside. Mild landed hard outside the bear's square. "Get up!" someone yelled, but Mild did not. Even the bear's owner looked rattled at the violence of it. He grabbed the bear's chain and tugged hard on it to convince the animal he had control of it.

"It's over!" he declared. "You all saw it, it was fair. The bear won. The boy's out of bounds. And the money is mine!"

There were some grumbles but no one challenged him this time as he trudged off. The bear minced along at his heels. One sailor glanced over at Mild still lying in the dust and then spat. "Gutless, the whole lot of them," he declared and glared at Wintrow meaningfully. Wintrow returned his glare and then went to kneel in the dust beside Mild. He was still breathing. His mouth was half open and he was drawing in dust with every breath. He had landed so hard, chest first, it would be a miracle if his ribs were not at least cracked.

"We've got to get him back to the ship," he said and glanced up at Comfrey.

Comfrey looked down at him with disgust. Then he looked away as if he were not there. "Come on, boys, time to get back to the ship." Heedless of any injuries Mild might have, he seized the lad by his arm and dragged him upright. When Mild sagged like a rag doll, he scooped up the boy and flung him over his shoulder. The other two sailors from the *Vivacia*'s crew trailed off after him. None of them deigned to notice Wintrow's existence.

"It wasn't my fault!" Wintrow declared aloud. But somehow he wondered if it was.

"Was so," Torg pointed out. "You knew he was full of cindin. He shouldn't have been in there, but he had to go because you were too much the coward. Well." Torg grinned with satisfaction. "Now they all know you for what you are, boy. Before it was just me that knew what a water-assed coward you were." Torg spat into the dusty street and walked away from him.

For a time Wintrow stood alone staring at the kicked over corners of the square. He knew he had done the right thing and made the right choices. But a terrible sense of a lost chance was welling up in him. He suspected he had just lost his opportunity to be accepted as part of the *Vivacia*'s crew. To be considered a man among men. He glanced up at the westering sun, and then hastened to catch up with the men who now despised him.

CHAPTER SEVENTEEN

KENNIT'S WHORE

THE RAINS OF AUTUMN HAD WASHED DIVVYTOWN AL-
MOST CLEAN. THE LAGOON WAS HIGHER, THE CHAN-
nels deeper, and as the *Marietta* approached home port, the
hearts of those aboard her were lighter than they had ever
been before. It had nothing to do with the hold full of
pirated cargo. While it was a respectable haul, they'd done
better any number of times.

"It's that we're someones now, when we come into a
port. Folk know us, and turn out to welcome us. Did I tell
you that, in Littleport, Mistress Ramp turned her whole
house over to us, for a whole watch, for free? And it wasn't
just the Mistress telling her girls to do for us; they were
willing, by Sa. Anything we wanted . . ." Sorcor's voice
trailed off in amazement at their good fortune.

Kennit repressed a sigh. He'd only heard the tale a
score of times before. "All that disease, for free," he said
quietly, but Sorcor took his words for a jest and grinned at
his captain fondly. Kennit turned his head and spat over the
side. When he turned back to Sorcor, he managed to smile
back at him. "Caution the men to remember that few
prophets are treated well in their home towns."

Sorcor's brows knitted in puzzlement.

Kennit did not sigh. "I mean that although others, elsewhere, may regard our freeing of slaves and fitting them out as pirates with a share in our territory as an act of philanthropy, some here will see us as creators of competition. And they will judge it their duty to curb our ambitions."

"You mean they're going to be jealous, and they'll rub our faces in the dirt if they get the chance."

Kennit considered a moment. "Exactly."

A slow smile crawled across Sorcor's scarred visage. "But, Cap'n, that's exactly what the men are looking forward to. Them trying to put us in our places."

"Ah."

"And, Cap'n?"

"Yes, Sorcor."

"The men sort of took a vote, sir. And them what didn't agree was persuaded to change their minds. Every man will be taking a draw this time, sir, and letting you sell off the cargo whole." Sorcor vigorously scratched the side of his face. "I suggested they might want to let Divvytown know they all believe in their captain. Now, mind, they weren't all willing to say they'd do it this way every time. But this time, well, it's your toss."

"Sorcor!" exclaimed Kennit, and his smile widened fractionally. "That was well done."

"Thankee, sir. I thought it might please you."

The two men stood for a few moments longer, watching the shore draw nearer. The rattling rain of the day before had forced the last browning leaves from the deciduous trees, not that there were many of them. Dark large-leaved evergreens were the dominant trees on the hills above and around Divvytown. Closer to the water, medusa-vine and creeper-root had taken over the edge lands, with a towering cedar defying its own sodden roots to flourish here and there. In the freshness after the rain, Divvytown looked almost inviting. Wood smoke rose from chimneys, adding its scent to that of the iodine of the seaweed and the briny water. Home. Kennit tried the word out in his mind. No. It didn't fit. Port. Yes.

Sorcor hastened away, shouting at some deckhand who wasn't moving quite swiftly enough to please him. Sorcor was notoriously hard to please when they were bringing the ship into port. It was never enough for him that the ship was docked well; she must be sailed in smartly, as if putting on a display for every lounger who might be watching from the beach. As, this time, they were.

Kennit made a mental tally of their captures since they had last tied up here. Seven ships under their belts, four of them slavers. They'd made five pursuits of liveships, with nothing even approaching success in that area. He was almost resigned to giving up that part of his plan. Perhaps he could achieve the same ends simply by capturing enough slaveships. He and Sorcor had worked a bit of math the other night over a mug or two of rum. All of it was speculative, but the results were always pleasant. No matter how well or how poorly the four ships succeeded in piracy, half of the take would come back to the *Marietta*. In each capture, Kennit had awarded the captaincy of the taken vessel to one of his seasoned men. That, too, had been inspired, for now those that remained on board the *Marietta* actively vied for his attention, hoping to distinguish themselves sufficiently to earn ships of their own. The only drawback was that it might eventually deplete their own crew of proven men. He put that worry out of his mind. By then he would have a flotilla, no, a fleet of pirate ships under his command. And they would be bound to him, not just by debt but by gratitude.

He and Sorcor had carefully spaced their sub-vessels throughout the Inside, spending much time in discussing where these new citizens would be most welcome, not to mention where the pickings were thickest for an inexperienced ship. He was satisfied they had done well. Even those freed slaves who had not chosen to follow him into a life of piracy must think of him with gratitude and speak well of him. He trusted that when the time came for them to speak their loyalties, they would recall how he had rescued them. He nodded sagely to himself. King of the Pirate Isles. It could be done.

The three plunder ships they had taken had not been noteworthy. One had not even been especially sea-worthy, so when the fires got out of control, they had let it sink. They had salvaged most of the easily negotiable cargo by then anyway. The other two ships and the crews had been ransomed through Kennit's usual brokers. He shook his head to himself at that. Was he getting too confident of himself? He should move around more, use other people. Otherwise it would only be a matter of time before several merchants banded together to have an attempt at revenge on him. The last ship's captain had been a surly bastard, kicking and attempting to strike out long after he had been securely bound. He'd cursed Kennit and warned him that there were rewards for his capture now, not only in Jamaillia but even in Bingtown. Kennit had thanked him and let him make the rest of his trip to Chalced sitting in his own bilge water, chained like a slave. He'd been courteous enough when Kennit finally had him hauled onto deck. Kennit decided he had always underrated the effects that dark and wet and chains could have on a man's spirit. Well, one was never too old to learn.

They came into Divvytown in good order, and his men disembarked like visiting royalty, purses already a-jingle with coins. Kennit and Sorcor followed them shortly, leaving a handful of chosen men aboard who would be well rewarded for postponing their own pleasures. As he and Sorcor strolled up the docks, ignoring the blatant offerings of the pimps, whores and drug mongers, he reflected that no matter who inspected them, at least one of them would be seen as having good taste. Sorcor, as always, was dressed in a wide array of fine clothes in colors that bedazzled the eye. The silk scarf that belted his waist had come from the plump pale shoulders of a noblewoman they had ransomed. The jeweled dagger stuck in it had come from her son, a brave boy who had not known when to surrender. He'd had the yellow silk shirt tailored in Chalced. Given the bulkiness of the man's muscled shoulders and thick chest, the wide pale expanse of fluttering fabric reminded Kennit of a ship under sail. In contrast, he had chosen sober colors for himself, trusting the fabric and tailoring to draw the eye. Few in Divvytown would appreciate the rarity of the lace that spilled so extravagantly from cuff and collar, but even in their ignorance they would have to admire it. His high black boots shone while the blue breeches, waistcoat and jacket accentuated both his muscle and his leanness. That the man who had tailored these clothes had been a freed slave who charged him nothing at all for the privilege of serving him only enhanced Kennit's satisfaction with his appearance.

Sincure Faldin had bought cargoes from Kennit before, but never before had he so obviously fawned on him as he did now. As he had suspected, the rumors of the freed slaves and the newly flagged Raven ships that now sailed for Kennit had reached Divvytown weeks ago. The man who welcomed them at Faldin's door showed them, not to his office but to his parlor. This small, stuffily warm room saw little use, Kennit surmised from the stiffness of the fabric on the cushioned chairs. They sat for a few moments, Sorcor uneasily drumming his fingers on his thighs, before a smiling woman entered with a tray of wine and tiny sweet biscuits. If Kennit was not mistaken, the woman who brought the wine was Faldin's own wife. She curtseyed to them silently and then quickly retired from the room. When Faldin himself appeared but moments later, the strength of his scent and the smoothness of his hair attested to recent personal grooming. Like many native to Durja, he favored brilliant colors and extravagant embroidery. The vested expanse of his girth put Kennit in mind of a wall tapestry. The earrings he wore were an elaborate twining of gold and silver. Kennit mentally added five per cent to what he had hoped to get for their cargo.

"You honor my establishment, Captain Kennit, by seeking us first," Faldin greeted them. "And is this not your first mate, Sincure Sorcor, of whom I have heard so many tales?"

"It is," Kennit replied before Sorcor could stammer a reply. He smiled to Faldin's courtesy. "You speak of us honoring you with our trade. And how is that, Sincure Faldin?" Kennit asked drily. "Have not we sought out your business before?"

The Sincure smiled and made a deprecating gesture. "Ah, but then, if you will excuse my saying so, you were but one more pirate. Now, if all we hear is true, you are Captain Kennit the Liberator. Not to mention, Captain Kennit, the co-owner of four more ships than the last time I saw you."

Kennit inclined his head gracefully. He was glad to see that Sorcor had the wit to keep still and but watch how this was done. He waited silently for the offer he was almost certain would come. It did. Sincure Faldin allowed himself a moment to settle deeply into a chair opposite them. He picked up the wine bottle and poured a generous measure for himself, and then added more to their glasses as well. He took a deep breath before he spoke.

"And so, before we negotiate for but one more ship-load of cargo, I suggest we might consider the benefits to both of us if I were always your first choice, for many ship-loads of cargo."

"I see the benefit to you, if you were assured of always having the pick of our plunder. But I confess I see small good for ourselves out of such an arrangement."

Sincure Faldin laced his fingers over his extravagant vest. He smiled benevolently. "You see no good in having a partner always ready and willing to dispose of whatever you bring in? You see no good in consistently getting the best price for your cargo, large or small? For with a partner ashore, you'd not have to sell all you have in a day or two. A partner ashore would warehouse it for you, disposing of it only when the market for it was strongest. You see, Captain Kennit, when you come into a town and sell off a hundred kegs of fine rum, all at once, why, the very quantity of the cargo makes the fineness suddenly common. With a partner ashore with a warehouse, those same kegs could be held and sold off a few at a time, increasing their rarity and thus their price. Moreover, a partner ashore would not sell all those kegs in Divvytown. No. Why, with a small ship at his disposal, he could ply the surrounding islands and settlements as well, cultivating a market for you. And once or twice a year, that ship could make a trip to, say, Bingtown or Jamaillia itself, there to sell off the very finest pickings of your year's taking to merchants more than able to pay the best prices."

Sorcor was looking a bit too impressed. Kennit resisted the urge to nudge him with his boot; he would only have looked startled and puzzled as well. Instead Kennit leaned back in his uncomfortable chair as if relaxing. "Simple economics," he announced casually. "Your suggestions are far from unique, Sincure Faldin."

Faldin nodded, not at all flustered by this. "Many great ideas are not unique. They only become unique when the men who have the wherewithal actually to implement them come together." He paused, weighing the wisdom of his next words. "It is gossiped about Divvytown that you have ambitions. Ambitions, I might add, that are far from unique. You would rise to power amongst us. Some say the word 'king' and smile in their beards. I do not. I have not proffered the word 'king' to you at all in my business offer. And yet, if we applied ourselves, one might rise to that much power and wealth and authority. With or without the word 'king' attached to one. Words such as that tend to unsettle folks. But I trust it is not the word you aspire to, but the state of being."

Sincure Faldin leaned back, his words spoken. Sorcor's eyes leaped from Faldin to Kennit. His glance was wide, full of wonder. It is one thing to hear one's captain speak of a desire for power. It was entirely another to find that a respected merchant might take such words seriously.

Kennit moistened his lips. He glanced down to find his amulet grinning at him. The wicked little face winked up at him, then folded its lips tightly as if enjoining him to silence. It was all Kennit could do to keep from staring at it. He found he had sat up straight. Resolutely he stilled his own features and looked away from the wizardwood charm. He glanced up at Faldin. "What you propose goes far beyond merely doing business together. 'Partner,' you have said, more than once. 'Partner,' dear Sincure Faldin, is a word that my first mate and I hold in especial regard. So far, we have extended it only to each other. We two know the full depth of that word. 'Partner.' Money alone does not buy it." He hoped that Sorcor would not miss that reminder of mutual loyalty. Faldin was looking a bit alarmed now. Kennit smiled at him. "However. We are still listening," he pointed out to Faldin. Once more he leaned back in his chair.

The merchant took a deep breath. He glanced from one man to another, as if assessing them. "I see what you do, sirs. You gather not only wealth, but influence. The loyalty of men and the power of ships are behind that loyalty. But what I have to offer you is something not as easily gathered. Something that only time can establish." He paused for emphasis. "Respectability."

Sorcor shot Kennit a puzzled glance. Kennit made a tiny motion of his hand. *Hold*, the hand motion told him. *Stand as you are.* "Respectability?" Kennit put an edge of mockery on the word.

Faldin swallowed, then plunged on. "To gain what you want, sir, you must offer folk assurances. Nothing steadies a community's regard for a man like respectability. If I might be so bold as to point out, you have no real ties here. No houses, no lands, no wives and families, no blood ties to those who make up this town. At one time, those things were not important. What were we, what were any of us, except pariahs and outcasts, runaway slaves, petty criminals fleeing justice, debtors and rebels and vagabonds?" He waited for their grudging nods. "But that, Captain Kennit and Sincure Sorcor, was a generation or two ago." Excitement was building in his voice. "I am sure, sirs, that this is what you have seen as clearly as I have seen myself. Times are changing us. I myself have been here a score of years. My wife was born in this town, as were my children. If a proper society is to rise from the mud and shanties here, well, we will be its cornerstones. We and others like us, and those who have joined our families."

If there had been some sort of a signal, it had escaped Kennit. But the timing was too exquisite to be coincidental. Sincura Faldin and two young women entered the room bearing trays of fruit and bread and smoked meats and cheese. Faldin's features in feminine were plainly marked on the two girls. His daughters. His bargaining chips on the board, the passcards to respectability. They were not Divvytown sluts. Neither dared to look at Kennit, but one sent Sorcor a shy smile and a glance from beneath lowered lashes. They were, Kennit surmised, probably even virgins, never allowed to walk on the streets of Divvytown unless Mama's watchful eyes were upon them. Nor were they bad-looking. Durja still spoke in their pale skin and honey hair, but their eyes were almond-shaped and hazel. Both were plump as ripe fruit, their bared arms round and white. They set out food and drink for each man and for their Mama.

Sorcor had lowered his eyes to his plate, but was sucking speculatively on his lower lip. He suddenly lifted his glance and boldly stared at one of the sisters. A blush raced up her cheeks at his glance. She did not meet his eyes, but she did not turn aside from his stare either. The younger girl could have been no more than fifteen, her sister at most seventeen. Smooth and unscarred they were, a man's transport into a gentle world where women were soft and quiet and saw willingly to their husbands' needs. A world many men probably dreamed about, Kennit thought, and Sorcor was most likely one of them. What other prize could be farther from the grasp of the scarred and tattooed pirate than the willing embrace of a pale virgin? That which was most unattainable was always most desirable.

Faldin pretended not to notice the pirate's ogling of his daughter. Instead he exclaimed, "Ah, refreshment. Let us take a moment from our business. Gentlemen, I welcome you to the hospitality of my home. I believe you've met Sincura Faldin. These two are my daughters, Alyssum and Lily." Each girl nodded her head in turn, then took her place between their mother and father.

And these two, Kennit reflected, were but the first offer from Divvytown. Not necessarily the best. Nor did this "respectability" have to come from Divvytown. There were other pirate towns on other islands, and merchants more wealthy than Faldin. There was no need to be hasty in choosing. No need at all.

The sun had tracked much of the sky before Kennit and Sorcor emerged from Sincure Faldin's premises. Kennit had disposed of his cargo profitably; more, he had done so without fully committing himself to a permanent alliance with Faldin. After his daughters and lady had left the room, Kennit had taken the tack that while the value of a business association with Faldin could not be doubted, no one could be so heartless as to hasten into any other aspects of such an "alliance." He had left Faldin with the dubious security of knowing that he would be allowed to show his goodwill by offering the first bid on any goods the *Marietta* brought into Divvytown. The man was merchant enough to know it was a poor offer, and wise enough to know it was the best he would get at this time. So he smiled stiffly and accepted it.

"I could almost see him ciphering the numbers on the back of his tongue. How much would he have to overpay us for our next three cargoes to assure us of his goodwill?" Kennit offered the jest wryly to Sorcor.

"The younger one . . . was she Alyssum, or Lily?" Sorcor asked cautiously.

"Don't worry about it," Kennit suggested callously. "I am sure that if you don't fancy her name, Faldin will allow you to change it. Here." He handed Sorcor the tally sticks they had negotiated so easily. "I'll trust these to you. Don't let them deliver less coin than was promised before you allow him to unload. You'll take the ship's watch tonight?"

"Of course," the burly pirate replied distractedly.

Kennit did not know whether to frown or smile. So easily could the man be bought with the offer of unsullied flesh. Kennit scratched his chin. He watched Sorcor turn towards the docks and swagger off into the gathering autumn twilight. He gave his head a minute shake. "Whores," he congratulated himself quietly. "Whores make it all so much simpler." A wind had come up. Winter was no farther away than a new moon, or a few day's sail to the north. "I've never cared for the cold," he said softly to himself.

"No one does," a small voice commiserated. "Not even whores."

Slowly, as if the token were an insect that might take flight if startled, Kennit raised his wrist. He glanced about the street, then feigned refastening a cuff-link. "And why do you speak to me this time?" he demanded softly.

"Your pardon." The tiny smile was mocking as his own. "I thought you had spoken to me first. I was just agreeing."

"There is no strange weight, then, to be put on your words?"

The tiny wizardwood charm pursed its lips as if considering. "No more than I might put to yours," the face suggested. He gave his master a pitying look. "I know no more than you know, sirrah. The only difference between us is that I admit more easily what I know. Try it yourself. Say this aloud: But in the long run, a whore can cost one more than the most wastrel wife."

"What?"

"Eh?" An old man passing in the street turned back to him. "You spoke to me?"

"No. Nothing."

The old man peered at him closer. "You're Captain Kennit, h'ain't you? From the *Marietta*? Goes around freeing slaves and telling them to be pirates?" His coat was fraying at the cuffs, and one boot was split along the seam. But he carried himself as if he were a man of consequence.

Kennit had nodded twice. To the last he replied, "Well, so some say of me."

The old man coughed wheezily, and then spat to one side. "Well, some also say they don't like the idea. They say you're getting too full of yourself. Too many pirates means the pickings get slimmer. And too many pirates preying on slaveships can irritate the Satrap to where he sends his galleys up our way. Knocking off fat merchant ships, well, that's one thing, laddie. But the Satrap gets a cut of those slave sales. We don't want to be digging in the pockets of the man what funds the warships, if you get my drift."

"I do," Kennit said stiffly. He considered killing the old man.

The geezer wheezed and then spat again. "But what I say," he continued in a creakier voice. "Is more power to you. You put it to him, laddie, and give him a couple thrusts for me as well. Time someone showed him that blue ink on a man's face don't mean he's not a man any more. Not that I'd say that to just anyone around here. There's some as would think I needed shutting up, if they heard me speak so. But, seeing as how it was you, I thought I'd tell you this: not everyone that keeps silent is against you. That's all. That's all." He went off into his wheezing cough again. It sounded painful.

Kennit was amused to find himself rummaging in his pocket. He came up with a silver coin and passed it to the man. "Try a bit of brandy for that cough, sir. And good evening to you."

The old man looked at the coin in amazement. Then he held it up and shook it after Kennit as he strode away. "I'll drink your health, sir, that I will!"

"To my health," Kennit muttered to himself. Having begun talking to himself, it now seemed he could not stop. Perhaps it was a side effect of random philanthropy. Did not most madnesses occur in pairs? He pushed the thought aside. Too much thinking only led to bleakness and despair. Better not to think, better to be a man like Sorcor, who was probably even now imagining a blushing virgin in his bed. He'd be better off simply buying a woman who could blush and squeak convincingly, if that was what appealed to him.

He was still distracted when he strode up to Bettel's bagnio. For such a chill evening, there were more idlers outside her door than he would have expected. Two of them were her regular toughs, cocky and grinning as usual. Someday, he promised himself, he'd do something permanent to their smirks. "Evening, Captain Kennit," one dared to address him lazily.

"Good evening." He enunciated the reply, freighting it with a different meaning entirely. One of the idlers abruptly brayed aloud, a whiskey laugh that sent his fellows off into sniggering laughter. Brainless. He took the steps briskly, thinking that the music sounded louder tonight, the notes more brittle. Within, he endured the services of the serving boy, nodding perfunctorily that he was satisfied before passing into the inner chamber.

There, finally, there were enough things out of routine that he was moved to lightly touch the hilt of the sword at his belt. Too many folk were in this room. Customers did not linger here. Bettel did not permit it. If a man came to pay for a whore, then he could take his purchase to a private room to enjoy as he pleased. This was not some cheap sailors' whorehouse, where the wares could be fondled and sampled before one bought. Bettel ran a proper house, discreet and dignified.

But tonight the reek of cindin was heavy in the air, and men slouched insolently in the chairs where the whores usually displayed themselves. The prostitutes who remained in the room were standing or perched on laps. Their smiles seemed more brittle, their laughter more forced, and Kennit noticed how swiftly their eyes strayed to Bettel herself. This time her black locks had been trained into ringlets. They swung stiff and shining. Despite her layers of powder, a mist of perspiration shone on her forehead and upper lip, and the reek of cindin was stronger on her breath.

"Captain Kennit, you dear man!" she greeted him with her usual contrived affection. She came at him, arms wide as if to embrace him. At the last moment she dropped them to clasp her hands joyously before her. Her fingernails were gilded. "Just wait until you see what I have for you!"

"I'd rather not wait," Kennit replied irritably. His eyes wandered the room.

"For I knew you were coming, you see!" she burbled on. "Oh, we hear of it right away, when the *Marietta* comes to dock. And here in Divvytown, we've heard all the tales of your adventures. Not that we wouldn't be so delighted if you ever chose to favor us with the telling yourself." She batted her lash-laden eyes up at him, and rolled her breasts forward against the confines of her dress.

"You know my usual arrangements," he pointed out to her, but she had seized hold of his hand and was threatening to engulf it in her bosom as she clasped it fondly to her.

"Oh, your usual arrangements!" she cried gaily. "Fie on the usual, Captain Kennit, dear. That is not why a man comes to Bettel's house, for the 'usual.' Now come with me and see. Just see what I've saved for you."

There were at least three men in the room who were following their conversation with more attention than seemed polite. None of them, Kennit noted, looked particularly pleased as Bettel tugged him over to a candle-lit alcove off the main room. Curious and cautious, he glanced within.

Either she was a new arrival, or had been working on his previous visits. She was striking if one fancied small, pale women. She had large blue eyes in a heart-shaped face with painted pink cheeks. Her plump little mouth was painted red. Short golden hair was dressed in tight curls all over her head. Bettel had dressed her in pale blue, and decked her in gilt jewelry. The girl stood up from the tasseled cushions where she had been seated and smiled sweetly up at him. Nervously, but sweetly. Her nipples had been tipped with pink to make them stand out more noticeably beneath the pale gauze of her dress.

"For you, Captain Kennit," Bettel purred. "As sweet as honey, and pretty as a little doll. And our largest room. Now. Will you want your meal set out first, as usual?"

He smiled at Bettel. "Yes, I will. And in my usual room, with my usual woman to follow. I do not play with dolls. They don't amuse me."

He turned and walked away from her, headed toward the stair. Over his shoulder, he reminded her. "Have Etta bathe first. And remember, Bettel, a decent wine."

"But Captain Kennit!" she protested. The nervousness in her voice was suddenly a shrilling of fear. "Please. At least try Avoretta. If you do not fancy her, there will be no charge."

Kennit was ascending the stairs. "I do not fancy her, so there is no charge." The small of his back ached with tension. He had seen avidity kindle in the men's eyes as he started up the main staircase. He reached the top of the landing and opened the door to the narrow stair beyond it. He entered it, shutting the door behind him. Several long, light strides took him to the second small landing where the sole lantern burned. Here the stairway bent back on itself. He waited soundlessly around the corner. He drew his sword silently and un-sheathed his belt knife as well. He heard the door below softly open and then close again. By their cautious tread, at least three men were behind him on the stairs. He smiled grimly. Better here, in tight quarters with them below him than out on the dark of the streets. With a bit of luck he'd take at least one by surprise.

He did not have to wait long. They were too eager. As the first one stepped around the corner, the tip of Kennit's blade flicked across the man's throat. That simple. Kennit gave him a good shove. He tumbled back into his fellows, gargling incoherently, and as they stumbled backwards down the stairs, Kennit followed, dashing out the lamp as he passed it and then flinging the hot glass and spilling oil down on them. They cursed in the dark now, with a dying man's weight pressing them back down the stairs. Kennit made several random downward thrusts with his sword to encourage their retreat. He hoped the dying man would be low, collapsing against their legs. Stabbing him again would be a waste of effort, so he placed his thrusts higher and had the satisfaction of two cries of pain. Perhaps the stairway and closed door would muffle them. He was sure that further surprises awaited him upstairs. No sense in spoiling their anticipation.

He heard these three hit the downstairs door and sprang forward then, thrusting with both sword and dagger into any flesh he could find. Here he had the advantage, for anything that was not himself was the enemy, whereas they had as good a chance of striking an ally as him in the dark, close confines of the stairwell. One man at least was fumbling wildly for the doorknob, cursing when he could not find it. Eventually he did, but only in time to open it and allow himself and his dying companions to spill out onto the landing. At the base of the staircase, Bettel looked up in horror from her parlor.

"Rats," Kennit informed her. Another tidy flick of his sword, to be sure the last man stayed down and died. "Vermin on your staircase. You really should not allow this, Bettel."

"They forced me! They forced me. I tried to keep you from going up there, you know I did!" The woman's wail followed him as he turned back to the staircase. He shut the door firmly on it, hoping it had not carried all the way to the chamber at the top of the house. Soft-footed as a cat he padded up the darkened stairs. He let his sword's tip lead the way. When he reached the second door, he paused. If they were alarmed at all—no, if they were sly at all—they'd have a man waiting outside this door. He eased the latch open, took a fresh grip on both weapons, and then shouldered his way through the door, coming in as low and silently as he could. No one was there.

The door to his usual chamber was shut. Voices came through it, pitched softly. Men's voices. At least two, then. They sounded impatient. No doubt they'd seen him through the window as he approached Bettel's house. Why hadn't they ambushed him at the top of the stairs? Perhaps because they'd expected their fellows to overpower him and drag him into this chamber for them?

He considered, then pounded roughly on the door. "Got him!" he cried hoarsely, and was rewarded by a fool who jerked the door open for him. Kennit put his knife low in the man's belly and then dragged it up with all his strength. It did not do as much damage as he had hoped it would; worse, it tangled in the man's loose shirt. Kennit was forced to abandon it in him. He gave the man a backwards shove and then sprang forward to meet the next man's blade. His blade engaged Kennit's neatly, turned aside his thrust, then thrust in turn. A gentlemanly approach to fencing, Kennit realized, as he set the man's blade tip out of alignment with his throat. A mistaken sense of gallantry and showmanship.

Kennit whipped a glance about the room. There was one more man sitting with studied composure in his chair before the fire. He held a glass of claret in one hand, but was prudent enough to have his hand on the drawn sword across his knees. Etta was flung naked across the bed. They had bloodied both the woman and the linens. "Ah. King Kennit has come calling on his lady," the seated man observed lazily. He gestured with his glass at the whore. "I don't think she'll be up to receiving you just now. Our day's amusement has left her . . . indisposed."

It was meant to distract him and it almost worked. It was distressing. No. It angered him. This clean and pleasant chamber, the comparative safety of Bettel's house had been taken away. He'd never be able to relax in this room again. The bastards!

A part of him was aware of shouts in the street outside. More of them. He'd have to finish this one quickly, and then get the one in the chair. But even as he pressed his reach advantage, the mocking man rose and advanced on Kennit with his sword. That one, at least, was not stupid enough to think that fair play had anything to do with killing. Kennit was not stupid enough to think he had much of a chance against two blades. He wished he hadn't had to leave his knife in the other man.

A stupid time to die, he told himself, as he parried one blade with his sword and knocked the other aside with his arm. He was thankful for the thick fabric of his sleeve that absorbed most of the impact. Seeing how he must defend himself, his attacker instantly switched to slashing attacks rather than thrusts. Kennit began a constant harried retreat from both blades, with no time to do anything except defend and evade. The other two men laughed and shouted to one another as they fought, mocking words about kings and slaves and whores. He did not listen, he could not listen, one moment's distraction would be his death. All his attention went to the two blades and the two men who powered them. Time to decide, he recognized grimly. Do I make them kill me now, quickly, or fight until I can no longer defend myself well, and they can play cats to my mouse?

He was as startled as they were when the quilted comforter was snapped open and flung over one of them. As he was fighting clear of it, the rest of the bedding quickly followed, fat down-stuffed pillows, billowing sheets that draped his enemies' blades and tangled their feet. A sheet settled over one man, draping him like a walking corpse. Apt, Kennit smiled to himself. Kennit's blade popped through the linen drapery and as he drew it back, a great scarlet blossom opened on it. Etta, cursing and shrieking, gathered up an immense double-armful of feather bed and flung it and herself upon the last attacker. Kennit quickly made sure of the man he had stabbed. By the time he turned, Etta had found the other man's head beneath the blanket and was pounding it up and down on the floor. The bedding muffled his cries as he struggled to get clear of the shrouding stuff. Kennit casually stabbed him several times, and then, out of breath, put the sword where he judged the man's heart to be. The thrashing lump under the blankets stilled. Etta kept on pounding his head against the floor.

"I think you can stop that now," Kennit pointed out. She did, abruptly, but the sound continued.

They both turned to the pounding footsteps coming up the stairs. Etta, crouched naked over her kill, looked savage as a feral cat as she unconsciously bared her teeth to the sound. Kennit waded through the welter of bodies and bedding to secure the door. He tried to slam it but the first man's body was in the way. He bent to drag the body free, and before he could close the door, it flew wide open so hard it bounced off the wall. Kennit caught it before it could rebound into Sorcor's face. Sorcor was red-faced from running as were the men who burst into the room behind him. "An old man," he gasped. "Came to the ship. Said you might have trouble here."

"Now that was a bit of silver well spent," a small voice observed. Sorcor glanced at Etta, thinking she had spoken, then self-consciously turned his head from the naked, battered woman. She staggered upright. She glanced at the other men staring at her and then stooped awkwardly, to drag up a corner of one blanket to cover herself. It revealed a man's hand and arm flung lifelessly on the floor.

"Trouble." Kennit observed drily. "A bit." He sheathed his sword. He gestured at the body in the door. "Pass me my knife, please."

Sorcor crouched to pull it out of the man. "You were right," he observed needlessly. "There's been talk against us in the town, and some are angered by what we do. Is this Rey? Of the *Sea-Vixen*?"

"I don't know," Kennit admitted. "He never introduced himself." He stooped and dragged some of the bedding off the other dead men.

"It was Rey," Etta said in a low voice through bruised lips. "I knew him well enough." She took a breath. "All of these were *Sea-Vixen* men." She gestured at the man whose head she had pounded against the floor. "That was their captain. Skelt." In a lower voice she added, "They kept saying they'd show you that every pirate is his own king. That they didn't need you, and you couldn't rule them."

"That makes six," one of Kennit's crew observed in awe. "Cap'n took down six men by himself."

"How many were outside?" Kennit asked curiously as he resheathed the knife Sorcor gave him.

"Four. They were ten to one against you. Brave sods, weren't they?" Sorcor asked heavily.

Kennit shrugged. "Did I wish to make sure a man was killed, I'd do the same." He gave Sorcor a small smile. "They still lost. Ten men. They feared me very badly, to wish to be so sure I'd be dead." His smile widened. "Power, Sorcor. Other men see us gathering it to ourselves. This attempt is but proof that we are moving towards our goal." He became aware of the eyes of his men. "And taking our crew with us," he said reassuringly, and nodded his smile all round. The five pirates with Sorcor grinned back at him.

Sorcor put his own blade away. "Well. Now what?" he asked heavily.

Kennit considered briefly. He pointed to his men. "You and you. Together. Make the rounds of the taverns and whorehouses. Find our ship-mates and warn them. Quietly. I suggest it is wisest for all to sleep aboard tonight, with a stout watch posted. Sorcor and I will be doing so. But only after we've made ourselves seen about town, alive and whole. And all of you, I warn you: No bragging about this. This was nothing, do you understand? Not even a story worth the telling. Let other men do the telling for us; the tale will grow faster that way." The men nodded, grinning appreciatively to one another. "You and you. You will follow Sorcor and I as we show ourselves about, but you won't be with us. Understand? You watch our backs, and you listen for what others say about us at their own tables. Listen, and remember, for I will want a full accounting."

They nodded their understanding. He glanced about the room. There was something else he should do here, something he'd been intending to do. Etta stood silent, looking at him. A tiny ruby sparkled in her earlobe. "Oh, and you." He pointed to the last man. "See to my woman."

The sailor flushed red, and then white. "Yes, sir. Uh. How, sir?"

Kennit shook his head angrily. He had things to do, and they bothered him with details. "Oh, take her down to the ship. Put her in my cabin for later." If the town considered Etta his woman, then he must put her out of casual reach. He must appear to have no vulnerabilities. He knit his brow. Was that all? Yes.

Etta dragged the sheet free of the last body. Standing straight as a queen, she wrapped the blood-stained linen around her shoulders. Kennit glanced about the room one last time, then took in his men's proud and incredulous grins. Even Sorcor was smiling. Why? Ah. The woman. They would have expected carnage like this to kill his appetite for her. That they believed it hadn't made him more of a man in their eyes. Lust had not motivated him; he did not find bruises on a woman arousing. But his supposed lust for her was what they were admiring. Well, let them think it, then. He glanced back to the blushing man. "See she is provided with warm water for a bath. Feed her. And find appropriate garments for her as well." He supposed this meant he'd have to keep her in his cabin. At least let her be clean, then.

His eyes returned to Sorcor's. "Well, you've got your orders," his first mate pointed out gruffly to the smirking men. "Move!"

A round of ayes and his two runners rattled off down the stairs. The man assigned to Etta crossed the room, hesitated awkwardly, then scooped her up in his arms as if she were a large child. To Kennit's surprise, Etta wilted against him gratefully. Kennit, Sorcor, and their guards started down the stairs with the man carrying Etta coming behind them. They met Bettel on the landing. Her hands fluttered before her as she exclaimed, "Oh! You're alive!"

"Yes," Kennit agreed.

In her next breath, she exclaimed angrily, "Do you think you're taking Etta out of here?"

"Yes," Kennit called over his shoulder up the stairs.

"What about all these dead men?" she shrieked after him as they strode out of her house.

"Those you may keep," Kennit replied.

Etta caught at the front door with her hand as she and her bearer passed through it. She slammed it shut behind them.

CHAPTER EIGHTEEN

MALTA

IT ALL WOULD HAVE GONE PERFECTLY IF NOT FOR THAT FAT FOOL DAVAD RESTART.

Malta had found the money under her pillow on the morning that her father left to go to sea. She recognized his cramped handwriting from the missives her mother occasionally received while her father was off trading. *"For my not-so-little daughter,"* Papa had written. *"Green silk would suit you best."* Inside the soft little bag had been four gold coins. She had not been sure what they were worth; they were foreign coins, from one of the lands he visited when he was trading. What Malta had been instantly certain of was that they would be enough for the most sumptuous gown that Bingtown had ever seen.

In the days that followed, whenever she had doubts, she had held the note and re-read it and assured herself that she had her father's permission to do this. Not only his permission, but his assistance: the money was proof of that. His connivance, her mother would say later, darkly.

Her mother was so predictable. As was her grandmother. Her grandmother had declined to attend the Harvest Offering Ball, citing mourning Grandfather as a reason. And that was all the excuse her mother needed to tell her that no one in the Vestrit family was going to the Ball. And thus, she said, there was to be no argument over dresses or frocks or gowns. She had Rache giving her dancing lessons now, and they were seeking a good etiquette teacher as well. In the meantime, Rache would help her with those lessons, also. And that was more than enough for now for a young girl of her age.

The severity of her mother's tone had surprised her. When Malta had been brave enough to say, "But my father said . . ." her own mother had turned on her with something close to fury in her eyes.

"Your father is not here," she had pointed out coldly. "I am. And I know what is proper for a young Bingtown girl. As should you. Malta, there is time and more than enough time for you to be a woman. It is natural for you to be curious about such things, and natural, too, for you to wish for lovely gowns and wonderful evenings dancing with handsome young men. But too much curiosity and eagerness . . . well. It could lead you down the same path as your Aunt Althea took. So trust me. I will be the one to tell you when the time is right for such things. I also know there is much more to the Harvest Ball than pretty dresses and bright-eyed young men. I am a woman of Bingtown, and a Bingtown Trader and I know such things. Not your father. So keep your peace about this, or you will lose what you have gained."

Then her mother had stalked out of the breakfast room, not even giving Malta time to argue. Not that she would have. She had decided that she did not need to argue. Arguing would only have made her mother suspicious and watchful. There was no sense in making her own tasks harder.

Her father had suggested green silk, and fortunately there had been a good supply of it in Aunt Althea's sea chest. She had been aching to know what was in there since it had been delivered to the house, but her mother had wearily told her it was none of her concern. But it hadn't been locked—Aunt Althea never remembered to lock anything—and as Althea certainly was never going to use it, Malta saw no sense in letting the lovely fabric stay there and fade. Besides, by using this fabric, she'd have more coin to spend on a really good dressmaker. She was only being thrifty. Had not her father told her that was a good trait in a woman?

From Delo Trell, Malta obtained the name of a good dressmaker. It shamed her to have to ask her friend, but even in that important area, her mother and grandmother were so old-fashioned. Almost all their dresses were still made at home, with Nana measuring and fitting and sewing, and sometimes even Mama and Grandmother helping with the sewing and trimming themselves. And so they never had anything that was the latest style from Jamaillia. No. Oh, they would see something they liked at the Ball or the Presentation, and then they would copy it onto the next gown they made. But that was always what it was: a copy. No one was ever astonished by what one of the Vestrit women wore to a social gathering. No one ever gossiped about them or put heads together behind their fans to whisper enviously. They were too respectable. And too boring.

Well, Malta had no intention of being either as staid as her matronly mother, nor as mannish as her wild Aunt Althea. Instead she intended to be mysterious and magical, shyly demure and unknowable, and yet daring and extravagant. It had been hard to express all that to the dressmaker, a disappointingly old woman who clicked her tongue over the green silk Malta brought her. "Sallow," she had said, shaking her gray head. "It will make you look sallow. Pinks and reds and oranges. Those are your colors." Her thick Durja accent made it seem like a pronouncement. Malta folded her lips and said nothing. Her father was a trader who had seen the whole wide world. Surely he knew what colors looked best on women.

Then Fayla went on to measure her endlessly, muttering all the time through a mouthful of pins. She cut and hung paper shapes all over Malta, and paid no attention at all when Malta protested that the neck seemed too high and the skirts too short. The third time Malta objected, Fayla Cart had spat the mouthful of pins out into her own hand and glared at her. "You want to look like a trollop? A sallow trollop?" she demanded.

Malta shook her head wordlessly as she tried to recall what a trollop flower looked like.

"Then you listen to me. I sew you a nice dress, a pretty frock. A dress your mama and papa happy to pay me for. Okay?"

"But . . . I've brought the money to pay. My own money. And I want a woman's gown, not a little girl's frock." With every word she spoke, Malta became bolder.

Fayla Cart stood slowly, rubbing at her back. "A woman's gown? Well, who's going to wear this dress, you or some woman?"

"I am." Malta forced her voice to stay firm.

Fayla scratched at her chin. A hair was growing out of a warty-looking mole there. She shook her head slowly. "No. You are too young. You will only look silly. You listen to me, I make you a pretty frock. No other girl will have one like it, they will all stare and tug their mamas' skirts and whisper about you."

Without warning, Malta tore the paper shape loose from herself and stepped out of it. "I am not eager to have *girls* staring at me," she said haughtily. "Good day to you."

And she left the shop, her green silk under her arm, and went down the street to find a dressmaker of her own, one that would listen to her. She tried not to wonder if Delo Trell had purposely sent her to that horrible old woman, if Delo did not think that Malta still belonged in a little girl's starched skirts. Lately Delo had begun to give herself airs, to imply loftily that there were many things that Malta, young little Malta, simply could not understand about Delo's life now. As if they had not been playmates since they could walk!

The young seamstress Malta chose wore her own skirts as if they were silk scarves, at once clinging and revealing her legs. She did not quibble about the color of the fabric, nor try to hide Malta in paper. Instead she measured her swiftly and spoke of things like butterfly sleeves and how a spill of lace could flatter a young woman's developing bosom into an illusion of fullness. Malta knew then she had chosen well, and had all but skipped home with a tale of being unable to find a free shimshay to excuse her lateness.

From that one decision of finding her own dressmaker had flowed all her good fortune. The woman had a cousin who made slippers; she sent Malta to him when she came in for the second fitting of the dress. And she would need jewelry, Territel reminded her. She pointed out to Malta that the reality of jewelry was not nearly as important as the effect it created with sparkle and shine. Cut glass would do as well as real gems, and then her budget would allow her larger and more glittering pieces. She had yet another cousin, and she came to show Malta her wares during the third fitting. When Malta returned for her final fitting, the slippers and jewelry were ready to be picked up as well. And Territel so kindly showed her how to paint her lips and eyes in the newest way, and even sold Malta some of her own powders and skin paints. The woman could not have been kinder. "To have it exactly as I dreamed of it is well worth every coin," Malta told her, and gladly gave over to her the pouch of gold that her father had provided. That had been but two days before the Harvest Ball.

It had been a feat both of nerve and creativity to smuggle the paper-wrapped gown home and successfully conceal it not only from Mama but from Nana, too. That old woman didn't have enough to do anymore. Now that Selden was old enough for tutors and didn't need watching every minute, Nana seemed to be constantly spying on Malta. All of the "tidying" she did in Malta's chambers was no more than an excuse for going through her things. Nana was constantly asking her questions that were none of the old servant's business. "Where did you get that scent? Does your mother know that you wore those earrings into town?"

In the end the solution had been simple. She directed Rache to store the wrapped gown, jewelry and slippers in her own quarters. Her grandmother had recently granted Rache a whole cottage to herself, one that gave onto the pond garden. Malta did not know what Rache had done to deserve this private space, but she found it useful that Rache had it. No one thought anything of her spending time with Rache. After all, was not the slave woman teaching her dance steps and body carriage and etiquette? It was only too funny, of course, that a slave should know such things. Delo and Malta giggled about it often in the brief times they had together. Delo, of course, now thought that she was too old and womanly to be spending time with a mere girl like Malta. Well, that would change as soon as Malta presented herself at the Harvest Offering Ball.

Rache was also the one to assist her with her dressing on the night of the Ball. Malta had not informed her ahead of time. That would have given the slave woman too much time to ponder things and then run and tattle to her grandmother or mother. Instead she had simply gone down to Rache's cottage and asked her for the package. She had told Rache to help her dress, and the woman had complied, an odd smile on her face. Malta could see now the complete usefulness of an obedient slave. When she was fastened into the gown, she sat down before Rache's own small mirror to don her jewelry a piece at a time, and then to carefully paint her lips and eyes. As the seamstress had shown her, she traced the outer edges of her ears and earlobes in the same color as her eyelids. The effect was both exotic and alluring. The slave woman seemed completely amazed at what she was doing. She was probably astonished that Malta had such womanly skills as these.

When the shimshay that Malta had arranged earlier arrived at her door, Rache seemed only mildly alarmed. And where was her young lady off to? An evening at Kitten Shuyev's house, Malta told her. Kitten's mother and father had arranged a puppeteer to come and amuse her and her younger brother while the parents went to the Harvest Ball. It was well known that Kitten's ankle was still quite painful since her pony had thrown her. Malta was going to go over and cheer her up. As they both had to miss the Harvest Ball, they might as well do it together.

Malta had had complete confidence in her own casual lies. Rache had been taken in completely, nodding and smiling and saying that she did not doubt at all that Kitten would be well-amused. The only discomfort was the dark winter cloak that Malta had to wear over her gown on the way to the Ball. It did not go with such a fine dress. But it would not do to have dust from the street soil her dress, nor did she wish to have anyone see her before she made her entrance into the gathering. A shimshay was not exactly the traditional way to arrive at the Ball. Everyone else would be taking their carriages there, or riding their flashiest mounts. Well, there was nothing she could do about that. Her flashiest mount was the fat pony that she and Selden shared. She had begged in vain for a horse of her own. As usual, her mother had said no, that if she wanted to take the time to learn to ride properly, she could learn on her mother's own mare. Her mother's mare was older than Malta. Even if she had wanted to use the nag, there would be no getting a riding horse out of the stables at this hour without her mother hearing of it. Besides. Given the fluttering nature of her skirts, she did not think horseback would be seemly.

But despite it all, despite the heavy winter cloak that misted her face with perspiration on this mild night, despite the rude little song the shimshay driver seemed to think was humorous, despite the fact that she knew her mother was going to be furious afterwards, it was all terribly exciting. "I'm doing it. I'm really doing it," she breathed to herself over and over. It gave her a heady sense of power to have finally stepped forward and taken control of her own life. She did not realize how tired she had grown of staying home and being her mother's child. Her mother was so staid and matronly and settled. She never did anything that people did not expect of her.

For the last year, while Grandfather was dying, the house had been the most boring place on earth. Not that it had ever been exciting. Not like other people's homes. Other Trader families held gatherings at their homes, and not just of Trader folk. Some welcomed the newcomers and their families. The Beckerts once had a whole evening of fun with a troupe of jugglers that some newcomer family had hired. Polia Beckert had told her all about it the next day, how the young boys in the troupe had worn little more than a wrap of cloth about their loins, and how they had juggled fire and knives and glass balls. There was never anything like that in the Vestrit home. Grandmother used to have some of the old lady Traders over, but all they did was sit in a room and embroider together and sip wine and talk of how much better everything used to be. But even they had not come for a long time. When Grandfather's illness became severe, Grandmother stopped inviting anyone over to the house. All had been quiet and dullness and dimmed rooms for almost a year. Mother even stopped playing her harp in the evenings—not that Malta had missed it. Whenever Mama played, she tried to teach Malta the notes as well. Sitting about plucking harp strings was not Malta's idea of an interesting evening.

"Stop here!" she hissed at the shimshay driver, and then louder, "No. Here. Stop here! I'll walk up to the door. I said, I'll walk, you idiot!"

He was nearly in the circle of light that the torches threw off before he stopped. And he had the effrontery to laugh at her anger. She gave him exactly what she owed him for the trip and not a penny more. Let him laugh about that. He avenged himself by not presenting her his hand to dismount. Well, she didn't need his hand, she was young and lively, not some crippled-up old woman. She stepped a little bit on the hem of her gown as she clambered down, but she did not stumble or tear it. "Come back for me at midnight," she commanded him imperiously. That was an early end to Harvest Ball, but, little as she cared to admit it, she did not wish to push her mother too far. Too far, and Grandmother's authority might be angered as well. Besides, the presentation was always done shortly after midnight, and Malta had never cared for that part of the Harvest Ball. It was simply too creepy. One year, when Malta was only seven, the representative from the Rain Wilds had unmasked for the presentation. Malta had been dumbfounded at his body. It was as if a child had begun as a human, but in growing had somehow outgrown the human body, putting out odd bones, unusual height, flesh that might have pouched organs unknown to a human's body. She had been in awe when her grandfather touched hands with him and called him "brother." Her grandfather had put their family's presentation into the Rain Wild man's hands himself. For many nights afterwards, when the image of the Rain Wilder had given her nightmares, she had taken comfort in knowing how brave her grandfather was. She need fear no such monsters. Still, "Midnight sharp," she repeated.

The driver looked down meaningfully at the few coins in his hand. "Oh, without doubt, young mistress," he said sarcastically. He started his horse and as the nag's hoofbeats faded into the night, Malta had a moment's uneasiness. What if he did not return? She could not imagine walking all the way home in the dark, least of all in a long gown and soft slippers. Resolutely she pushed the thought away. Nothing, she would let nothing stand between her and her enjoyment of this night.

Carriages were pulling up to the Traders' Concourse. Malta had been here before, many times, but tonight the hall seemed larger and more imposing. The glows of the torches made the marble shine with an almost amber tone. From each carriage Traders were alighting, in couples or family groups, all dressed in their best. The rich gowns of the women swept the paving stones. The girls wore the last of the year's flowers in their hair, and the little boys were scrubbed and groomed to implausible orderliness. And the men . . . For a time, Malta stood in the shadows and watched almost greedily as they stepped down from carriages or dismounted from horses. The fathers and grandfathers she quickly dismissed. With her eyes she followed the young husbands and the men so obviously and flamboyantly still single.

She watched them as they arrived, and she wondered. How did one choose, how did a woman know? There were so many kinds, and yet in her whole lifetime, a woman could possess but one. Or two, perhaps, if her husband died young and left her a widow while she could yet bear children. Still, she supposed, if one truly loved her husband, she wouldn't hope for that to happen, no matter how curious she might be. Still. It did not seem fair. There, on the black horse, pulling him in so abruptly that the horse's hooves clattered on the paving stones, that was Roed Caern. His hair flowed down his back in a black stream, as glistening as his horse's mane and as unbound. His shoulders strained the seams of his tailored coat. He had a sharp nose and narrow lips, and Delo had shivered when she spoke of him. "Oh, but he's a cruel one," she had said so knowingly, and then only rolled her eyes when Malta had demanded to know what she had meant.

Jealousy gnawed at Malta's heart that Delo knew such things and she did not. Delo's brother frequently invited his friends to dine at his home. Roed was one such. Oh, why couldn't she have a brother like Cerwin, who rode and hunted and had handsome friends, instead of doltish Wintrow with his saggy brown robes and beardless chin? She followed Roed's striding steps with her eyes, and marked how he gave way suddenly with a deep and courtly bow to allow a young wife to precede him into the hall. Her husband looked none too pleased at his gallantry.

Yet another carriage pulled up. The Trentor family's, the crest on the door proclaimed it. The white horses that pulled it had ostrich plumes on their headstalls. Malta watched the family alight, the parents dressed so sedately in dove gray, followed by three unwed daughters, all in shades of goldenrod and holding hands as if they feared some man would try to separate such devout sisters. Malta snorted softly at their fearfulness. Krion came last. He was dressed in gray, like his father, but the scarf at his throat was a deeper gold than that his sisters wore. His hands were gloved in white tonight. Krion always wore gloves, to cover the terrible scars where he had stumbled into a fire as a child. He was ashamed of his hands, and modest, too, of the poetry he wrote. He never read it aloud himself, leaving that task to his devoted sisters. His hair was auburn and as a boy he had been as freckled as an egg. His eyes were green. Delo had confided to Malta that she thought she was in love with him. Someday, she said, she hoped to be the one to stand before chosen friends and read his latest verses aloud. Such a gentle spirit, Delo had breathed, and then sighed.

Malta watched him ascend the steps, and sighed herself. She longed to be in love. She longed to know more of men, to speak knowingly of this one or that, to blush at the mention of a name or frown sternly at the glance of dark eyes. Her mother was wrong, wrong when she said there was plenty of time, to wait to be a woman. The years of being a woman with a choice were far too few. All too soon women married and grew fat with babies. Malta did not dream of a solid husband and a well-filled crib. She hungered for this, these nights in the shadows, these hungers of the soul, and the attention of men who could not claim to possess her.

Well, it would not happen to her hiding in the shadows. Resolutely she took her cloak from her shoulders. She bundled it up and tossed it under a bush to retrieve later. She almost wished that her mother and grandmother were here, that she were arriving in a carriage, certain that her hair had not been mussed, that the paint on her lips was straight and fresh still. For an instant she imagined them all arriving here together, her handsome father presenting her his arm to escort her into the Ball. But with that thought came an image of awkward little Wintrow trotting along behind them in his brown priest's robe, and Mother in some stiflingly modest dress. Malta winced. She was not ashamed of her family. She would have enjoyed having them here, if only they knew how to behave properly and could dress well. Had she not asked, over and over, for her mother to come to the Ball this year? Well, they had refused her that. If she was to enter life as a woman, Malta would have to do it on her own. And she would be brave, allowing only a hint of her tragedy and loneliness to show on her face. Oh, she would be merry tonight, laughing and charming, but in an unguarded moment, perhaps one knowing eye would look at her and know the neglect she suffered at home, ignored and passed over by her family. She took a deep breath and walked forward towards the torchlight and the wide beckoning doors.

The horses pulling the Trentor family carriage clopped away. Another took its place. The Trells, Malta realized with both delight and dread. Delo would be in that carriage. Her parents and older brother Cerwin would, unfortunately, be with her. If Malta greeted them as they alighted, Delo's parents would be bound to ask where Mama and Grandmother were. Malta was not ready to face awkward questions just yet. Still, it would be so fun to go in arm and arm with Delo, two dazzling young women of the Bingtown Traders entering society together. She ventured a step closer. If Delo's parents and brother preceded her, there was a chance she could hiss to Delo and have her wait for her.

As Malta had hoped, Delo's parents got out first. Her mama was dazzling. Her gown was simple and deep blue. The neckline left her throat and shoulders bare save for a single silver chain with a row of pendant perfume gems. How Malta wished her own mother would appear, just once, so elegantly dressed. Even from where she lurked, she could smell the heady scent of the gems. Delo's mama took her papa's arm. He was tall and thin. His linen jacket and trousers were also blue, flattering his wife's gown. They ascended the steps to the hall like folk from a legend. Behind them, Cerwin waited impatiently for Delo to clamber out of the carriage. Like his father, his coat and trousers were blue, his boots a softly gleaming black. He wore a single gold earring in one ear, and his black hair was daringly curled into long locks. Malta, who had known him all her life, suddenly felt an odd little shiver in her belly. Never before had he looked so handsome to her. She longed to astonish him with her presence.

Instead, she herself was astonished when Delo finally appeared in the carriage door. Her dress echoed the color of her mother's, but there the resemblance stopped. Her hair was plaited into a crown decked with fresh flowers, and a flounce of lace graced her short skirts to make them almost mid-calf. Matching lace trimmed the high collar and cuffs. She wore no jewelry at all.

Malta could not contain herself. She swept up to Delo like an avenging spirit. "But you said you were going to wear a gown this year! You said your mama had promised you would," she greeted her friend. "What happened?"

Delo looked up at Malta miserably. Then her eyes widened in astonishment and her mouth opened. No sound came out of it.

Cerwin stepped protectively in front of her. "I don't believe you could know my sister," he said in a haughty voice.

"Cerwin!" Malta exclaimed in annoyance. She peered past him at Delo. "What happened?"

Delo's eyes widened another fraction. "Malta? Is that you?"

"Of course it's me. Did your mama change her mind?" A nasty suspicion began to unfold in Malta's mind. "You must have had dress fittings. You must have known you weren't going to be allowed to wear a gown!"

"I didn't think you'd be here!" Delo wailed miserably, while Cerwin Trell asked incredulously, "Malta? Malta Vestrit?" His eyes moved over her in a way that she knew was rude. Rude or not, it made another shiver run over her.

"Trell?" Shukor Kev was dismounting from his horse. "Trell, is that you? Good to see you. And who is this?" His incredulous glance went from Malta to Cerwin. "You can't bring her to the Harvest Ball, friend. You know it's only for Traders." Something in his tone made Malta uncomfortable.

Another carriage had pulled up. The footman was having trouble opening the door, the catch appeared to be stuck. Malta tried not to stare. It was not ladylike. But the footman caught sight of her and appeared to be so struck by her appearance that he completely forgot his task. Within the carriage, a portly man thudded his shoulder against the door, which flew open, narrowly missing her. And Davad Restart, in all his portly clumsy glory, nearly tumbled out into the street.

The footman had caught at her arm to steady her as she stepped hastily back from the wide-flung door. Had he not had hold of her arm, she could have easily stepped away and avoided disaster. Instead she was there as Davad caught his balance by snatching at the door and then trod squarely on the hem of her dress. "Oh, I beg pardon, I do," he declared fervently, and then the words died on his lips at he looked her up and down. So transformed was she that for a time she was sure he did not recognize her. She could not resist. She smiled at him.

"Good evening, Trader Restart," she greeted him. She curtseyed, a trickier task in the longer skirts than she had thought it would be. "I trust you are well."

Still, he goggled at her. After a moment, he opened his mouth and squeaked out, "Malta? Malta Vestrit?"

Another carriage came to take the place of the Trells'. This one was resplendent in green and gilt, Rain Wild colors. That would be the representatives from the Rain Wild families. The ball would begin as soon as they were seated.

Behind her, like an echo, came Shukor's incredulous, "Malta Vestrit? I don't believe it!"

"Of course." She smiled up at Davad again, enjoying the astonished way his eyes leapt from the necklace at her throat to the lace that frothed at her bosom. He suddenly glanced behind her. She turned, but there was no one there. Damn. Delo had gone into the Ball without her! She turned back to Davad, but he was staring wildly about. As the door of the Rain Wild carriage opened, he suddenly seized her by the shoulders and thrust her behind him, almost inside the still open door of his carriage. "Be still!" he hissed. "Say nothing at all!"

He turned back and bowed low as the Rain Wild representatives exited their carriage. Malta peeped past him. There were three of them this year. Two tall and one short was all she could tell of them, hooded and cloaked as they were. The dark fabric of their cloaks was something she had never seen before. It was black when they were still, but any motion set it to dancing in scintillant colors. Green, blue and red shone briefly in the darkness at the tiniest movement.

"Trader Restart," one greeted him. A woman's reedy voice.

"Trader Vintagli," he replied, bowing even deeper. "I welcome you to Bingtown and the Harvest Ball."

"Why, thank you, Davad. Shall I see you within, then?"

"Most certainly," he replied. "As soon as I find my gloves. I seemed to have dropped them on the floor of my carriage."

"How careless of you!" she rebuked him. Her voice caressed the words oddly. She then moved on after her companions.

The still autumn air reeked of Restart's sudden sweat. The moment the doors of the hall closed behind the Rain Wild family, he spun about to confront Malta. He seized her by one arm and shook her.

"Where is your grandmother?" he demanded. Then before she could reply, he asked as urgently, "Where is your mother?"

She should have lied. She could have said they had already gone in, or that she had just now stepped out for a breath of cooler air. Instead, she said simply, "I've come alone." She glanced aside from him, and spoke more softly, adult to adult. "Since Grandfather died, I'm afraid they've become more house-bound than ever. It's so sad. But I knew that if I did not get out and about, I should simply go mad. You can't imagine how gloomy it has been for me—"

She gasped as he clutched her arm more tightly and urged her towards the coach. "Quickly! Before anyone else sees you . . . you haven't spoken to anyone else, have you?"

"I . . . no. Well, only Delo and her brother. I just arrived you see, and . . . let go of me! You're mussing my dress."

It both frightened and shocked her, the way he shoved her into his carriage and climbed determinedly in after her. What did he have in mind? She had heard tales of men driven by passion and lust to do impulsive things, but Davad Restart? He was old! The idea was too disgusting! He slammed the door, but this time it refused to catch. He held it shut as he called up, "Driver! To the Vestrit town house. Quickly." To Malta he said, "Sit down. I'm taking you home."

"No! Let me out, I want to go to the Harvest Ball. You can't do this to me. You're not my father!"

Trader Restart was panting as he clutched the door handle and held it shut. The carriage started forward with a lurch and Malta sat down hard.

"No, I'm not your father," Restart agreed harshly. "And tonight I thank Sa I am not, for I am sure I'd have no idea what to do with you. Poor Ronica! After everything else she's been through this year. Wasn't it bad enough that your aunt vanished completely without you presenting yourself at the Harvest Ball dressed like a Jamaillian strumpet? What will your father say about this?" He pulled a large kerchief from his sleeve and mopped his sweating face with it. He was wearing, she noted, the same blue trousers and jacket that he'd worn the two previous years. They strained at his girth; from the smell of cedar in the carriage, she doubted he'd taken them out of his clothing chest before tonight. And he dared to speak to her of clothing and fashion!

"I had this dress specially made for me, and for this night. With money my Papa gave me, I might add. So I scarcely think he would be angry that I had used it as he suggested. What he might want to know, however, is what you mean by snatching his young daughter off the street and dragging her off against her will. I do not think he will be pleased."

She had known Davad Restart for years, and knew how easily cowed he was when her grandmother snapped at him. She had expected at least a bit of that same deference for herself. Instead he surprised her by snorting. "Let him come to me and ask me, when he gets back to port, and I will tell him that I was trying to save your reputation. Malta Vestrit, you ought to be ashamed of yourself. A little girl like you, dressed up like a common . . . and then daring to show yourself so at the Harvest Ball. I pray to Sa that no one else recognized you. And nothing you can say will convince me that your mother or grandmother knew anything of that dress or your coming to the Ball when any proper girl would still be mourning her grandfather."

She could have said a dozen things in reply to that. A week later, she had thought of them all, and knew exactly how she should have said them. But at the time no words would come to her and she sat silent and helplessly furious as the swaying carriage bore her resolutely homeward.

When they arrived, she did not wait for Davad Restart, but pushed past him to climb out of the carriage and hurry up to the door before him. Unfortunately a tassel of her skirt caught on the edge of the carriage door. She heard it tear and turned back with an exclamation of despair but it was too late. The tassel and a hand's-length of pale green silk dangled from the doorframe. Davad glanced at it, then slammed the door on it. He stalked past her to the house door and loudly rang for the servants.

Nana answered it. Why had it to be Nana? She stared at Davad crossly, and then looked past him at Malta, who returned her glare haughtily. For an instant Nana merely looked affronted. Then she gave a gasp of horror and shrieked, "Malta! No, it cannot be you. What have you done, what have you done?"

That brought the whole household down on her. First her mother appeared, and fired a dozen angry questions at Davad Restart, none of which he could answer. Then her grandmother, in her nightgown and wrapper, her hair bundled up in a night scarf, appeared to scold her mother for making such a hue and cry in the night. At the sight of her, Grandmother had suddenly gone pale. She had dismissed all the servants save Nana, who she sent off for tea. She gripped Malta firmly by the wrist as she led her down the hall to what had been Grandfather's study. Only when Davad, Keffria and Malta were inside and the door shut firmly had she turned to her.

"Explain yourself," she commanded.

Malta drew herself up. "I wished to go to the Harvest Ball. Papa had said I might, and that I might go in a gown, as befitted a young woman. I have done nothing I am ashamed of." Her dignity was impeccable.

Her grandmother pursed her pale lips. When she spoke, there was ice in her voice. "Then you are truly as empty-headed as you appear to be." She turned aside from Malta, dismissing her completely. "Oh, Davad, how can I ever thank you for whisking her home? I hope you have not put your own reputation at risk while saving ours. Did many people see her like this?"

Trader Restart looked distinctly uncomfortable. "Not many. I hope. Cerwin Trell and his little sister. Some friend of his. I pray they were all." He paused as if considering whether or not to lie. "The Vintagli family arrived, to represent the Rain Wilds, while she was there. But I do not think they saw her. For once, perhaps, my girth served some useful purpose." He rubbed his belly ruefully. "I hid her behind me, and snatched her into my carriage the moment they had passed. My footman was there, too, of course." He added reluctantly, "And there were other Trader families, coming and going, but I trust that I did not make too much of a scene." His face was troubled as he added hesitantly, "Of course, you knew nothing of any of this?"

"I am both relieved and ashamed to admit I knew nothing," her grandmother said sternly. Her eyes were full of accusations as she turned to Malta's mother. "Keffria? Did you know what your daughter was up to?" Before her mother could reply, Grandmother went on, "And if you did not, how could you not?"

Malta had expected her mother to burst into tears. Her mother always burst into tears. Instead she turned on her daughter. "How could you do this to me?" she demanded. "And why? Oh, Malta, why?" There was terrible grief in her words. "Didn't I tell you that you only had to wait? That when the time was right, you would be properly presented? What could have persuaded you to . . . do this?" Her mother looked devastated.

Malta knew a moment's uncertainty. "I wanted to go to the Harvest Ball. I told you that. Over and over, I begged to be allowed to go. But you would not listen, even after Papa said I could go, even after he promised me I could have a proper gown." She paused, waiting for her mother to admit that promise. When she only stared at her aghast, Malta shouted, "Well, it's your own fault if you're surprised! I was only doing what Papa had promised me I could do."

Something in her mother's face hardened. "If you had any idea of how badly I want to slap you just now, you'd keep a more civil tongue, girl."

Never had her mother spoken to her like that before. Girl, she called her, as if she were a servant! "Why don't you, then?" Malta demanded furiously. "This evening has been ruined for me in every other way! Why don't you just beat me here, in front of everyone, and have done with it?" The tragedy of her ruined plans rose up and choked her.

Davad Restart looked aghast. "I really must be going," he said hastily, and rose.

"Oh, Davad, sit down," Grandmother said wearily. "There is tea coming. We owe you at least that for this rescue tonight. Don't be put off by my granddaughter's sense of drama. Although beating Malta might make us all feel better at this point, we've never resorted to that—yet." She gave Trader Restart a wan smile and actually took his hand. She led the fat little man back to his chair and he sat down as she bade him. It made Malta queasy. Couldn't they see what a disgusting little man he was, with his face and balding pate shining with sweat and his ill-fitting out-of-style clothes? Why were they thanking him for humiliating her?

Nana entered the room with a tray of tea things. She also had a bottle of port tucked under one arm, and a towel draped over the same arm. She set the bottle and the tray down on the table and then turned to present Malta with a towel. It was damp. "Clean your face," the old serving woman told her brusquely. The adults all glanced at her, then looked away. They would grant her the privacy in which to obey. For an instant she was grateful. Then it dawned on her what they were doing to her, telling her to wash her face like a dirty child.

"I will not!" she cried, and flung the wet towel to the floor.

A long moment of silence followed. Then her grandmother asked her conversationally, "Do you realize you look like a whore?"

"I do not!" Malta declared. She had another moment of doubt, but thrust it aside. "Cerwin Trell did not seem to find me unattractive this night. This dress and this way of painting my eyes are what is currently fashionable in Jamaillia."

"For the whores, perhaps," Grandmother continued implacably. "And I did not say you were 'unattractive.' You are simply not attractive in a way any proper woman would be comfortable with."

"Actually," Davad Restart began uncomfortably, but Grandmother continued, "We are not in Jamaillia, nor are you a whore. You are the daughter of a proud Trader family. And we do not so flaunt our bodies or our faces in public. I wonder that somehow this has escaped your notice before this."

"Then I wish I were a whore in Jamaillia!" Malta declared hotly. "Because anything else would be better than being suffocated here. Forced to dress and act like a little child when I am near a woman grown, forced to always be quiet, be polite, be . . . unnoticed. I don't want to grow up like that, I don't want to be like you and Mother. I want to . . . to be beautiful, and noticed, and have fun, and have men want to be near me and send me flowers and presents. And I don't want to dress in last year's fashions and behave as if nothing ever excited me or angered me. I want . . . ."

"Actually," Davad broke in awkwardly, "there has been a, uh, similar fashion in Jamaillia. Since last year. One of the Satrap's, uh, Companions appeared thus. Uh, in the guise of a, uh, street woman. Not at a public function, but at a very large private gathering. To proclaim her, shall we say, complete devotion to the Satrap and his needs. That she was willing to, well, to be seen and treated as his, well . . ." Davad took a deep breath. "This is not something I usually would discuss with any of you," he pointed out awkwardly. "But it did happen, and there were, uh, shall we say echoes of it seen in fashionable dress in the months that followed. The ear paint, the uh, accessible panels of the skirts . . ." He suddenly flushed very red and subsided.

Grandmother only shook her head angrily. "This is what our Satrap has come to. He breaks the promises of his grandfather and father, and reduces the Companions of his Heart to whores for his bodily pleasures. Time was when a family was proud to have one of their daughters named as a Companion, for it was a post that demanded wisdom and diplomacy. What are they now? His seraglio? It disgusts me. And I will not see my granddaughter dressed as such, no matter how popular the garb becomes."

"You want me to be old and dowdy, like you and mother," Malta declared. "You want me to go from being an infant to being an old woman. Well, I won't. Because that's not what I want."

"Never in my life," Keffria declared suddenly, "have I spoken so to my mother. And I won't tolerate you speaking so to your grandmother. If—"

"If you had, maybe you would have had a life!" Malta pointed out suddenly. "But no! I bet you've always been mousy and silent and obedient. Like a cow. Shown one year and wed the next, like a fine fat cow taken to auction! One season of dancing and fun, and then married off to have babies with whatever man offered the best bargain to your parents." She had shocked the whole room. She looked around at them all. "That's not what I want, Mother. I want a life of my own. I want to wear pretty clothes, and go to wonderful places. I don't want to marry some nice Trader boy you pick out for me. I want to visit Jamaillia some day, I want to go to the Satrap's Court, and not as a married woman with a string of babies following me. I want to be free of all that. I want—"

"You want to ruin us," grandmother said quietly, and poured tea. Cup after tidy cup, calmly and efficiently as she spoke her damning words. "You want, you say, and give no thought at all to what we all need." She glanced up from her tea duties, to inquire, "Tea or port, Davad?"

"Tea," he said gratefully. "Not that I can stay long. I must hasten back, to at least be in time for the Presentation of the Offerings. I have no one else to give my presentation in my place, you know. And Trader Vintagli seemed to wish to speak to me. They will not expect you this year, of course, because of your mourning. . . ." His voice trailed off awkwardly.

"Tea? Very well, then." Her grandmother filled in smoothly. Her eyes moved from Davad to Nana. "Nana, dear. I hate to ask this of you, but would you see Malta off to bed? And see she washes well first. I am so sorry to put this on you."

"Not at all, Mistress. I see it as my duty."

And Nana did. Large and implacable as she had been when Malta was a child, she took her wrist and dragged her from the room. Malta went quietly, for the sake of her own dignity, not out of any acquiescence. She did not fight as Nana disrobed her, and she climbed herself into the steaming bath that Nana poured for her. She did not, in fact, speak a word to her large and imperious nanny, not even to interrupt Nana's boring monologue about how ashamed of herself she should be.

Because she was not ashamed, Malta told herself. Nor cowed at all. When her father came home, they would all have to answer for their mistreatment of her. For now, she would be satisfied with that.

That, and the shivery sensation that Cerwin Trell's glance had awakened in her. She thought of his eyes and felt it again. Cerwin, at least, knew that she was no longer a little girl.

CHAPTER NINETEEN

TESTIMONY

DOES IT HURT MUCH?"

"CAN YOU FEEL PAIN?"

"Not as men do, no, but I understand the distress you must—"

"Then why do you ask? Any answer I give will have no real meaning to you."

A long silence followed. Vivacia lifted her smooth arms and crossed them over her breasts. She stared straight ahead of herself. She fought the rising tide of grief and despair inside her. It was not getting any better between Wintrow and her. Since Cress, with every passing day his resentment of her increased. It made what might have been pleasant days into torture.

The wind was blowing from the north, pushing them southwards to warmer climes. The weather had been fair, but all else had been ill. The crew was at odds with Wintrow and hence with her. She had picked up from the men's talk the gist of what had happened on the beach. In her limited way, she understood it. She knew that Wintrow still believed his decision had been correct. And she knew, with the wisdom of her stored memories, that his grandfather would have agreed with him. But all it took to make him miserable was for him to know that the rest of the crew considered him a coward, and that his father seemed to concur with their opinion. And that was all it took for her to feel a misery as deep.

Despite his misery, he had not given up. In her eyes, that spoke greatly for the spirit inside him. Shunned by his ship-mates, consigned to a life he could not relish, he still continued to work hard and learn. He jumped as quickly to orders as any of them did, and endeavored each day to shoulder a man's share of the work. He was now as capable as any ship's boy and was moving rapidly to master the tasks of an able deckhand. He applied his mind as well as his body, comparing how his father managed the sails to the commands that Gantry issued. Some of his eagerness was simply the starvation of a mind accustomed to learning opportunities. Bereft of books and scrolls, he now absorbed the lessons of wind and wave instead. He accepted the physical labor of his ship-board life just as he had once accepted the menial work of the monastery's orchard. They were the tasks a man must do when he was part of such a life, and it behooved a man to do them well. But Vivacia also knew that there was a second motivation for his mastering of seamanship. He strove to show the crew by his deeds that he was neither fearful of necessary risks nor disdainful of a sailor's work. It was the Vestrit in him that kept his neck stiff and his head up despite the scorn of Torg and his fellows. Wintrow would not apologize for his decision in Cress. He did not feel he had done wrong. That did not keep him from smarting under the crew's contempt for him.

But that had been before the accident.

He sat cross-legged on the deck, his injured hand cradled into his lap. She did not need to look at him to know that he, too, stared towards a distant horizon. The small islands they were passing held no interest to him. On a day like this, Althea would have leaned on the railing, eyes avid. It had rained heavily yesterday, and the many small streams of the islands were full and rushing. Some meandered out into the salt water; others fell in sheets of silver as waterfalls from the steeper, rockier islands. All contributed fresh water that floated for a time atop the salt, changing the colors of the waters the ship moved through so serenely. These islands teemed with bird life; sea birds, shore birds and those who inhabited the towering cliffs, all contributed their notes to the chorus. Winter might be here, but in these islands it was a winter of rain and lush plant growth. To the west of them, the Cursed Shore was cloaked in one of its familiar winter fogs. The steaming waters of the many rivers that flowed from that coast mellowed the climate here even as they shrouded the Pirate Islands in mist. These islands would never know a snowfall, for the warm waters of the Inside Passage kept true winter forever at bay. Yet green and inviting as the islands might be, Wintrow had thoughts only for a more distant harbor, far to the south, and the monastery a day's journey inland from it. Perhaps he could have endured better if there was even the faintest hope that their journey would pause there. But it would not. His father was not so foolish as to offer him the vague hope of escape. Their trade would make them stop in many ports of call, but Marrow was not one of them.

As if the boy could sense her thoughts as clearly as Althea had, he suddenly dropped his head over his bent knees. He did not weep. He was past weeping, and rightfully wary of the harsh mockery that any show of weakness called forth from Torg. So they were both denied even that vent from the wretchedness that coiled inside him and threatened to tear him apart. After a time he took a deep breath and opened his eyes. He stared down at his hand loosely fisted in his lap.

It had been three days since the accident. A stupid mishap, as almost all such are in hindsight, of the commoner sort aboard a ship. Someone had released a line before Wintrow expected it. Vivacia did not believe it had been deliberate. Surely the crew's feeling against him did not run that high. Only an accident. The twisting of the hemp line had drawn Wintrow's gripping hand with it, ramming his fingers into a pulley block. Anger bubbled deep within Vivacia as she recalled Torg's words to the boy as he lay curled on the deck, his bleeding hand clasped to his chest. "Serves you right for not paying attention, you gutless little plugger. You're just stupid lucky that it was only a finger and not your whole hand smashed. Pick yourself up and get back to your work. No one here is going to wipe your nose and dry your little eyes for you." And then he had walked away, leaving Mild to come wordless with guilt with his almost clean kerchief to bind Wintrow's finger to the rest of his hand. Mild, whose hands had slipped on the line that Wintrow had been gripping. Mild, whose cracked ribs were still wrapped and healing.

"I'm sorry," Wintrow said in a low voice. More than a few moments had passed in silence. "I shouldn't speak so to you. You offer me more understanding than anyone else aboard . . . at least you endeavor to understand what I feel. It's not your fault, truly, that I am so unhappy. It's just being here when I wish I were somewhere else. Knowing that if you were any other ship save a liveship, my father would not force me to be here. It makes me blame you, even though you have no control over what you are."

"I know," Vivacia replied listlessly. She did not know which was worse, when he spoke to her or when he was silent. The hour each morning and each afternoon that he spent with her were ordered by his father. She could not say why Kyle forced him into proximity with her. Did he hope some bond would miraculously develop? Surely he could not be so stupid. At least, he could not be so stupid as to suppose he could force the boy to love her. Being what she was, and he being who he was, she had no choice but to feel a bond with him. She thought back to the high summer evening that now seemed so long ago, that first night he had spent aboard with her, and how well they had begun together. If only that had been allowed to grow naturally . . . but there was no sense in pining for that, no more sense than when she let her thoughts drift back to Althea. How she wished she were here now. Hard enough to be without her, let alone to constantly wonder what had become of her. Vivacia sighed.

"Don't be sad," Wintrow told her, and then, hearing the stupidity of his words, sighed himself. "I suppose this is as bad for you as it is for me," he added.

She could think of too much to reply to that, and so said nothing. The water purled past her bow, the even breeze sped them on. The man on the wheel had a competent touch; he should have, he was one of Captain Vestrit's choosing and had been aboard her for almost a score of years. It was an evening to be satisfied, sailing south from winter cold back into warmth, and so her unhappiness pierced her all the more keenly.

There were things the boy had said to her, over the past few days, words he had spoken in anger and frustration and misery. A part of her recognized such words for what they were: Wintrow railed against his fate, not her. Yet she could not seem to let go of them, and they cut her like hooks whenever she allowed herself to think of them. He had reviled her yesterday morning after a particularly bad night's watch, telling her that Sa had no part in her being and she partook nothing of his divine force, but was only a simulacrum of life and spirit, created by men for the serving of their own greed. The words had shocked and horrified her, but even worse was when Kyle had strode up from behind the boy and knocked him flat to the deck in fury that he would so goad her. Even the kinder men among the crew had spoken ill of Wintrow after that, saying the boy was sure to curse their luck with his evil words. Kyle had seemed ignorant that she would feel the blow he had struck Wintrow as keenly as the boy himself had. Nor had he paused to think that perhaps that was not the way to help Wintrow develop kindly feelings toward her. Instead Kyle ordered the lad below to the extra chores he hated most. She was left alone to mull over the boy's poisonous words and wonder if they were not, after all, absolutely true.

The boy made her think. He made her think of things no other Vestrit had ever considered while on her decks. Half his life, she reflected, seemed to be considering how he saw that life in respect to the existence of others. She had known of Sa, for all the other Vestrits had revered him in a cursory way. But none of them had pondered the existence of the divine, nor thought to see the reflection of divinity in life around them. None of them had believed so firmly that there was goodness and honor inherent in every man's breast, nor cherished the idea that every being had some special destiny to fulfill, that there was some need in the world that only that life lived correctly could satisfy. Hence none of them had been so bitterly disappointed as Wintrow had been in his everyday dealings with his fellows.

"I think they're going to have to cut my finger off." He spoke hesitantly and softly, as if his voicing of the fear might make it a reality.

Vivacia held her tongue. It was the first time since the accident that he had initiated a conversation. She suddenly recognized the deep fear he had been hiding behind his harsh words to her. She would listen and let him share with her whatever he could.

"I think it's more than broken. I think the joint is crushed." Simple words, but she felt the cold dread coiled beneath them. He took a breath and faced the actuality he'd been denying. "I think I've known it since it happened. Still I kept hoping. . . . But my whole hand has been swelling since this morning. And it feels wet inside the bandaging." His voice went smaller. "So stupid. I've cared for other's injuries before, not as a healer, but I know to how to clean a wound and change a dressing. But this, my own hand . . . I haven't been able to muster the courage to look at it since last night." He paused. She heard him swallow.

"Isn't it odd?" he went on in a higher, strained voice. "I was there once when Sa'Garit cut a man's leg off. It had to be done. It was so obvious to all of us. But the man kept saying, 'no, no, let's wait a bit longer, perhaps it will get better,' when hour by hour we could see it getting worse. Finally his wife persuaded him to let us do what had to be done. I wondered, then, why he had kept putting it off, instead of simply getting it over with. Why cling to a rotting hunk of flesh and bone, simply because it used to be a useful part of your body?"

His voice suddenly closed itself off. He curled forward over his hand again. And now she could sense the throbbing of his pain, the beat, beat, beat in his hand that echoed every pulse of his body's heart.

"Did I ever really look at my hands before, really think about them? A priest's hands . . . one always hears about a priest's hands. All my life, I had perfect hands. Ten fingers, all working and nimble . . . I used to create stained-glass windows. Did you know that, Vivacia? I used to sit and plunge myself so deeply into my work . . . my hands would move of their own accord, it almost seemed. And now . . ."

He fell silent again. Vivacia dared to speak. "A lot of sailors lose fingers. Or whole limbs. Yet those sailors still . . ."

"I'm not a sailor. I'm a priest. I was to be a priest! Until my father condemned me to this. He's destroying me. He deliberately seeks to destroy me. He and his men make mock of my belief, when I try to hold to my ideals they use them against me. I cannot withstand what he is doing to me, what they are all doing to me. They are destroying . . ."

"Yet those sailors still remain who they are, lost limbs or not." Vivacia continued implacably. "You are not a finger, Wintrow. You're a man. You cut your hair, your nails, and you are still Wintrow and a man. And if you are a priest, then you will remain one, nine fingers or ten. If you must lose a finger, then you must lose a finger. But do not use it as an excuse to stop being yourself." She paused, almost savoring the boy's astonished silence. "I know little of your Sa, Wintrow. But I know much of the Vestrits. What you are born to be, you will be, whether it be priest or sailor. So step up and be it. Let them do nothing to you. Be the one who shapes yourself. Be who you are, and eventually all will have to recognize who you are, whether they are willing to admit it or not. And if your will is that you will shape yourself in Sa's image, then do so. Without whimpering."

"Ship." He spoke the word softly, but it was almost like a benediction. He placed his good hand flat on her planking. After a moment's hesitation, he placed his injured hand, palm down, beside it. For the first time since Althea had left the ship, she felt one of her own deliberately reach towards her for strength. She doubted that he knew that was what he did; perhaps as he bowed his head and spoke soft words, he thought he prayed to Sa. But no matter who he addressed his plea for strength to, she was the one who answered it.

"Wintrow," she said quietly, when his soft words were done. "Go to your father now and tell him it must be done. And demand that it be done here, beside me. In my name, if they will not heed your wish."

She had feared he would hesitate. Instead he rose gracefully. Without a word to anyone else he made his way to the captain's gallery, where he rapped smartly on the door with his good hand.

"Enter," Kyle replied.

She could not see all that went on within herself, but she was aware of it in a way humans had never given her a word for. So she knew the thundering of Wintrow's heart, and sensed too the small leap of triumph he felt when his father looked up from his bills of lading to startle at the sight of his son standing so boldly before him.

"What do you do here?" Kyle demanded harshly. "You're the ship's boy, no more than that. Don't bring your whining to me."

Wintrow stood quietly until his father was finished. Then in an even voice he spoke. "I need this finger cut off. It was crushed, and now it's infected. I can tell already it won't get better." He took a small, swift breath. "I'd like it done while it's only the finger and not the whole hand."

When Kyle finally replied, his voice was thick and uncertain. "You are sure of this? Did the mate tell you so? He does the doctoring aboard the ship."

"It scarcely needs a doctor's eye. See for yourself." With a casualness Vivacia was sure Wintrow did not feel, he began to unwind the crusted bandaging. His father made a small sound. "The smell is bad, also," Wintrow confirmed, still in that easy voice. "The sooner you cut it off for me, the better."

His father rose, scraping his chair back over the deck. "I'll get the mate for you. Sit down, son."

"I'd rather you did it, sir, if it's all the same to you. And up on deck, by the figurehead." She could almost feel Wintrow's calculated glance about the room. "No sense in bleeding in your stateroom," he added, almost as an afterthought.

"I can't . . . I've never . . ."

"I can show you where to cut, sir. It's not that different from boning out a fowl for the pot. It's just a matter of cutting out the joint. That's another thing they taught me in the monastery. Sometimes it surprised me, how much cooking had in common with medicine. The herbs, the knowledge of . . . meat. The knives."

It was some kind of a challenge, Vivacia realized. She didn't understand it in full. She wondered if even Wintrow did. She tried to work it through in her head. If Kyle refused to cut the infected finger from his son's hand, he somehow lost. Lost what? She was not sure, but she suspected it had something to do with who truly controlled Wintrow's life. Perhaps it was a challenge from the boy for his father to admit fully to himself the life he had forced his son into, to make him confront completely the harshness of it. There was in it also the foolish challenge to risk his body that he had refused in town. They had called him a coward for that, and deemed him fearful of pain. He would prove to them all now that it had not been pain he feared. A shiver of pride in him traveled over her. Truly, he was unlike any Vestrit she had ever carried before.

"I'll call the mate," Kyle Vestrit replied firmly.

"The mate won't do," Wintrow asserted softly.

Kyle ignored him. He stepped to the door, opened it and leaned out to bellow, "GANTRY!" for the mate. "I'm captain of this ship," he told Wintrow in the intervening space of quiet. "And on this ship, I say what will or will not do. And I say who does what. The mate does this sort of doctoring, not I."

"I had thought my father might prefer to do it himself," Wintrow essayed quietly. "But I see you have no stomach for it. I'll wait for the mate on the foredeck, then."

"It's not a matter of stomach," Kyle railed at him, and in that moment Vivacia glimpsed what Wintrow had done. He had shifted this, somehow, from a matter between the ship's boy and the captain to something between a father and a son.

"Then come and watch, father. To give me courage." Wintrow made his request. No plea, but a simple request. He stepped out of the cabin without waiting to be dismissed, not even pausing for an answer. As he walked away, Gantry approached the door, to be harshly ordered to fetch his surgeon's kit and come to the foredeck. Wintrow did not pause but paced calmly back to the foredeck.

"They're coming," he told Vivacia quietly. "My father and the mate, to cut off my finger. I pray I don't scream."

"You've the will," Vivacia promised him. "Put your hand flat to my deck for the cut. I'll be with you."

The boy made no reply to that. A light breeze filled her sails and blew to her the scent of his sweat and fear. He only sat patiently picking the last of the bandaging from his injured hand. "No." He spoke the word with finality. "There's no saving this. Better to be parted from it before it poisons my whole body." She felt him let go of the finger, felt him remove it from his perception of his body. In his mind, he had already done the deed.

"They come," Vivacia said softly.

"I know." He gave a nervous giggle, chilling to hear. "I feel them. Through you."

It was his first acknowledgment of such a thing. Vivacia wished it could have come at a different time, when they could have spoken about it privately, or simply been alone together to explore the joining. But the two men were on the foredeck, and Wintrow reflexively surged to his feet and turned to face them. His injured hand rested upon the palm of his good one like an offering.

Kyle jerked his chin toward his son. "Boy thinks you need to take his finger off. What do you think?"

Wintrow's heart seemed to pause in his chest, then begin again. Wordlessly he presented his hand to the mate. Gantry glanced at it and bared his teeth in his distaste. "The boy is right." He spoke to his captain, not Wintrow. He gripped Wintrow's right wrist firmly and turned his hand to see the finger from all sides. He gave a short grunt of disgust. "I'll be having a word with Torg. I should have seen this hand before now. Even if we take the finger off now, the lad will need a day or so of rest, for it looks to me like the poison from the finger has worked into the hand."

"Torg knows his business," Kyle replied. "No man can predict everything."

Gantry looked levelly at his captain. There was no argument in his voice as he observed, "But Torg has a mean streak to him, and it comes out worst when he thinks he has one who should be his better at his mercy. It's what drove Brashen awry; the man was a good hand, save when Torg was prodding him. Torg, he picks a man, and doesn't know when to leave off riding him." Gantry went on carefully, "It's not a matter of favoritism. Don't fear that. I don't care what this lad's name is, sir. He's a working hand aboard the ship, and a ship runs best when all hands can work." He paused. "I'll be having a word with Torg," he repeated, and this time Kyle made no reply. Gantry's next words were to Wintrow.

"You're ready to do this." It wasn't really a question, mostly an affirmation that the boy had seen the right of it.

"I am." Wintrow's voice had gone low and deep. He went down on one knee, almost as if he were pledging his loyalty to someone, and set his injured hand flat on Vivacia's deck. She closed her eyes. She concentrated on that touch, on the splayed fingers pressing against the wizardwood planking of the foredeck. She was wordlessly grateful that the foredeck was planked with wizardwood. It was almost an unheard-of use for the expensive wood, but today she would see that it would be worth every coin the Vestrits had pledged for it. She gripped his hand, adding her will to his that it would not move from the place where he had set it.

The mate had crouched beside him and was unrolling a canvas kit of tools. Knives and probes rested in canvas pockets, while needles were pierced through the canvas. Some were ready threaded with fine fish-gut twine. As the last of the kit bounced open, it revealed the saws, toothed both fine and coarse. Wintrow swallowed. Beside them Gantry set out bandages of lint and linen.

"You'll want brandy," Gantry told him harshly. The man's heart was a deep trembling inside him. Vivacia was glad he was not unfeeling about this.

"No." The boy's word was soft.

"He may want it. Afterwards." She dared to speak up. Wintrow did not contradict her.

"I'll fetch it," Kyle said harshly.

"No." Both she and Wintrow spoke the word together.

"I wish you to stay," Vivacia said more softly. It was her right. But in case Kyle did not understand it, she spoke it aloud. "When you cut Wintrow, I bleed. In a manner of speaking," she added. She forced her own nervousness down. "I have a right to demand that you be here, with me, when something as unsettling as this is happening on my deck."

"We could take the boy below," Kyle offered gruffly.

"No," she forbade him again. "If this mutilation must be done, I wish it done here, where I may witness it." She saw no need to tell him that no matter where on the ship it was done, she would be aware of it. If he was that ignorant of her full nature, let him remain so. "Send one of the others."

Kyle turned to follow her gaze, and almost startled. The rumor had spread quickly. Every hand that was not occupied had somehow found an excuse to draw closer to the foredeck. Mild, white-faced, almost jumped out of his skin when Kyle pointed at him. "You. Fetch the brandy and a glass. Quickly."

The boy jumped to the command, his bare feet slapping the deck as he hastened away. No one else moved. Kyle chose to ignore them.

Wintrow took a deep breath. If he had noticed those who had gathered to watch, he gave no sign of it. His words were spoken to Gantry. He lifted his left hand and pointed carefully to his injured right. "There is a place, right here . . . in the knuckle. That's where I want you to cut. You'll have to go in . . . with the point of the knife . . . and sort of feel as you cut. If you feel the knuckle of your own hand, you can find the spot I mean. That way there will be no jag

of bone left. . . . And afterwards, I want you to draw the skin together over the . . . space. And stitch it." He cleard his throat and
spoke plainly. "Careful is better than fast. A clean slice, not a chop."

Between each phrase, Wintrow drew a steadying breath. His voice
did not quite shake, nor did his hand as he pointed carefully to what
had been the index finger of his right hand. The finger that might
have worn a priest's pledge ring someday, had he been allowed to keep
it. *Sa, in your mercy, do not let me scream. Do not let me faint, nor look
away. If I must do this, let me do it well.*

The undercurrent of the boy's thoughts was so strong, Vivacia
found herself joined with him. He took a final breath, deep and
steadying, as Gantry chose a knife and held it up. It was a good one,
shining and clean and sharp. Wintrow nodded slowly. Behind him
came the patter of Mild's feet and his whisper of "I've brought the
brandy, sir," but it seemed to come from far away, as faint and meaningless as the cries of the sea-birds. Wintrow was doing something,
Vivacia realized. With each breath, the muscles of his body slackened.
He dwindled inside himself, going smaller and stiller, almost as if he
were dying. He's going to faint, she thought, and pity for him filled
her.

Then in the next instant he did something she did not understand.
He left himself. He was not gone from his body, but in some strange
way he was apart from it. It was almost as if he had joined her and
looked through her eyes at the slender boy kneeling so still upon the
foredeck. His hair had pulled free from his sailor's queue. A few
strands danced on his forehead, others stuck to it with sweat. But his
black eyes were calm, his mouth relaxed as he watched the shining
blade come down to his hand.

Somewhere there was great pain, but Wintrow and Vivacia
watched the mate lean on the blade to force it into the boy's flesh.
Bright red blood welled. *Clean blood,* Wintrow observed somewhere.
The color is good, a thick deep red. But he spoke no word and the sound
of the mate swallowing as he worked was almost as loud as the shuddering breath Kyle drew in as the blade sank deep into the boy's
knuckle. Gantry was good at this; the fine point of the blade slipped
into the splice of the joint. As it severed it, Wintrow could feel the
sound it made. It was a white pain, shooting up his finger bone,
traveling swift and hot through his arm and into his spine. *Ignore it,* he
commanded himself savagely. In a willing of strength unlike anything
Vivacia had ever witnessed before, he kept the muscles of his arm
slack. He did not allow himself to flinch or pull away. His only concession was to grip hard the wrist of his right hand with his left, as if

he could strangle the coursing of the pain up his arm. Blood flowed freely now, puddling between his thumb and middle finger. It felt hot on Vivacia's deck planking. It soaked into the wizardwood and she drew it in, cherishing this closeness, the salt of it, the copper of it.

The mate was true to Wintrow's wishes. There was a tiny crunch as the last gristle parted under the pressure of the blade, and then he drew the knife carefully across to sever the last bit of skin. The finger rested on her deck now, a separate thing, a piece of meat. Wintrow reached down carefully with his left hand to pick up his own severed finger and set it aside. With the thumb and forefinger of his left hand, he pinched the skin together over the place where his right forefinger had been.

"Stitch it shut," he told the mate calmly as his own blood welled and dripped. "Not too tight; just enough to hold the skin together without the thread cutting into it. Your smallest needle and the finest gut you have."

Wintrow's father coughed and turned away. He walked stiffly to the railing, to stand and stare out at the passing islands as if they held some deep and sudden fascination for him. Wintrow appeared not to notice, but Gantry darted a single glance at his captain. Then he folded his lips, swallowed hard himself, and took up the needle. The boy held his own flesh together as the mate stitched it and knotted the gut thread. Wintrow set his bloodied left hand flat to the deck, bracing himself as the mate bandaged the place where the finger had been. And the whole time he gave no sign, by word or movement, that he felt any pain at all. He might have been patching canvas, Vivacia thought. No. He was aware, somewhere, of the pain. His body was aware, for the sweat had flowed down the channel of his spine and his shirt was mired in it, clinging to him. He felt the pain, somewhere, but he had disconnected his mind from it. It had become only his body's insistent signal to him that something was wrong, just as hunger or thirst was a signal. A signal that one could ignore when one must.

Oh, I see. She did not, quite, but was moved at what he was sharing with her. When the bandaging was done, he rocked back on his heels but was wise enough not to try to stand. No sense in tempting fate right now. He had come too far to spoil it with a faint. Instead he took the cup of brandy that Mild poured for him with shaking hands. He drank it down in three slow swallows, not tossing it back but drinking as one drank water when very thirsty. The glass was bloodied with his fingerprints when he handed it back to Mild.

He looked around himself. Slowly he called his awareness back into his body. He clenched his teeth against the white wave of pain from his hand. Black dots swam for an instant before his eyes. He blinked them away, focusing for a time on the two bloody handprints he had left on the *Vivacia*'s deck. The blood had soaked deep into the wizardwood. They both knew that no amount of sanding would ever erase those twin marks. Slowly he lifted his gaze and looked around. Gantry was cleaning the knife on a rag. He returned the boy's gaze, his brow furrowed but a small smile on his face. He gave him the smallest of nods. Mild's face was still pale, his eyes huge. Kyle gazed out over the rail.

"I'm not a coward." He didn't speak loud, but his voice carried. His father turned slowly to the challenging words. "I'm not a coward," Wintrow repeated more loudly. "I'm not big. I don't claim to be strong. But I'm neither a weakling nor a coward. I can accept pain. When it's necessary."

A strange odd light had come into Kyle's eyes. The beginnings of a smile hovered at the corners of his mouth. "You *are* a Haven," he pointed out with quiet pride.

Wintrow met his gaze. There was neither defiance nor the will to injure, but the words were clear. "I'm a Vestrit." He looked down to the bloody handprints on *Vivacia*'s deck, to the severed forefinger that still rested there. "You've made me a Vestrit." He smiled without joy or mirth. "What did my grandmother say to me? 'Blood will tell.' Yes." He stooped to the deck and picked up his own severed finger. He considered it carefully for a moment, then held it out to his father. "This finger will never wear a priest's signet," he said. To some he might have sounded drunken, but to Vivacia his voice was broken with sorrow. "Will you take it, sir? As a token of your victory?"

Captain Kyle's fair face darkened with the blood of anger. Vivacia suspected he was close to hating his own flesh and blood at that moment. Wintrow stepped lightly toward him, a very strange light in his eyes. Vivacia tried to understand what was happening to the boy. Something was changing inside him, an uncoiling of strength was filling him. He met his father's gaze squarely, yet in his own voice was nothing of anger, nor even pain as he stepped forward boldly, to a place close enough to invite his father to strike him. Or embrace him.

But Kyle Haven moved not at all. His stillness was a denial, of all the boy was, of all he did. Wintrow knew in that instant that he would never please his father, that his father had never even desired to be pleased by him. He had only wanted to master him. And now he knew he would not.

"No, sir? Ah, well." With a casualness that could not have been faked, Wintrow walked to the bow of the ship. For a moment he made

a show of studying the finger he held in his hand. The nail, torn and
dirtied in his work, the mangled flesh and crushed bone of it. Then he
flipped the small piece of flesh overboard as if it were nothing at all,
had never been connected to him in any way. There he remained, not
leaning on the railing but standing straight beside her. He looked far
ahead to a distant horizon. To a future he had been promised that now
seemed far further than days or distance could make it. He swayed
very slightly on his feet. No one else moved or spoke. Even the
captain was still, his eyes fastened to his son as if their gaze could
pierce him. Cords of muscle stood out on his neck.

Gantry spoke. "Mild. Take him below. See him to his berth.
Check on him at each bell. Come to me if he runs a high fever or is
delirious." He rolled up his tools and tied the canvas round them. He
opened a wooden case and sorted through some bottles and packets in
it. He did not even look up as he added quietly, "You others should
find your duties before I find them for you."

It was enough of a threat. The men dispersed. His words had been
simple, the commands well within the range of his duties as mate. But
no one could miss that in a very evasive way, Gantry had come between the captain and his son. He had done it as smoothly as he might
for any other man aboard who had brought himself too sharply to the
captain's attention. It was not an unheard of thing for the mate to do;
he'd done it often enough before when Kyle had first taken over the
Vivacia. But never before had he interfered between the captain and
his son. That he had done so now marked his acceptance of Wintrow
as a genuine member of the crew, rather than as the captain's spoiled
son, brought along for the sake of his discipline.

Mild made himself small and unnoticed as he waited. After a time,
Captain Haven turned without a word and stalked aft. Mild watched
him go for a time, then jerked his eyes away, as if it were somehow
shameful to watch his captain retreat to his own quarters.

"And Mild," Gantry suddenly went on, as if there had been no
pause. "Assist Wintrow in moving his gear and bedding to the forecastle. He'll bunk with the rest of the men. Once he's settled, give him
this. No more than a spoonful and bring the rest back to me right
away. It's laudanum," he added, raising his voice for Wintrow's benefit. "I want him to sleep. It'll speed the healing." He handed the boy
the fat brown bottle, then rose and tucked the rest of his supplies
under his arm. With no more than that, Gantry turned and walked
away.

"Yessir," Mild agreed. He moved up shyly to Wintrow's side.
When the other boy did not deign to notice him, he nerved himself to

tug at Wintrow's sleeve. "You heard what the mate said," he reminded him awkwardly.

"I'd rather stay here." Wintrow's voice had gone drifting and dreamy. The pain, Vivacia realized, must be paid for sooner or later. He had kept his body from reacting to it at the time, but the price now was complete exhaustion.

"I know," Mild said, almost kindly. "But it was an order."

Wintrow sighed heavily and turned. "I know." With the docility of weariness, he followed the other boy below.

A short time later Vivacia was aware that Gantry had gone back to take the wheel himself. It was something he did when he was disturbed and wanted time to think. He was not, she thought to herself, a bad mate. Brashen had been better, but Brashen had been with her longer. Gantry's touch on the wheel was sure and steady, reassuring but not distrustful of her.

She looked down furtively and opened her hand. The finger lay in her palm. She did not think anyone had seen her catch it. She could not have explained why she had done so, save that it had been a part of Wintrow, and she was unwilling to lose even so small a fragment of him. It was so tiny compared to her own larger-than-life digits. A thin, jointed rod of bone, coated with flesh and skin, and in the end of it, the finely ridged nail. Even crushed and bloody, it fascinated her with its delicacy and detail. She compared it to her own hand. Her carver had done a competent job, with her joints and nails and even the tendons on the back of her hand. But there was no fine pattern of follicles on the back of her fingers, no tiny hairs, no whorling prints on the pads of her fingers. She bore, she decided regretfully, only a passing resemblance to a true creature of flesh and blood.

For a time longer she examined her treasure. Then she glanced furtively aft before she lifted it to her lips. She could not throw it away and she had no place to keep it, save one. She placed it in her mouth and swallowed. It tasted like his blood had smelled; of salts and copper and in an odd way, like the sea itself. She swallowed it down, to become part of herself. She wondered what would become of it, deep inside her wizardwood gullet. Then she felt it being absorbed, in much the same way the deck planks had soaked up his blood.

She had never eaten anything meat before. She had never known hunger or thirst. Yet in the taking of Wintrow's severed flesh into herself, she satisfied some longing that had gone nameless before. "We are one, now," she whispered to herself.

In a bunk in the forecastle, Wintrow turned over restlessly. The laudanum could soften but not still the throbbing in his hand. His flesh felt hot and dry, tight over the bones of his face and arm. "To be one with Sa," he said in a small cracked voice. The priest's ultimate goal. "I shall be one with Sa," he repeated more firmly. "It is my destiny."

Vivacia had not the heart to contradict him.

It was raining, the relentless pelting rain that was the hallmark of winter in Bingtown. It ran down his carved locks and dripped from his beard onto his bare chest. Paragon crossed his arms on his chest, and then shook his head, sending heavy drops flying. Cold. Cold was mostly something he remembered from sensations humans had stored for him. *Wood cannot get cold*, he told himself. *I'm not cold.* No. It was not a matter of temperature, it was just the annoying sensation of water trickling over him. He wiped a hand over his brow and shook the water from it.

"I thought you said it was dead." A husky contralto voice spoke unnervingly near him. That was another problem with rain; the sound of it filled his ears, numbing them to important sounds like footsteps on wet sand.

"Who's there?" he demanded. His voice sounded angry. Anger was a better thing to show humans than fear. Fear only made them bolder.

No one replied. He hadn't expected anyone to answer, really. They could see that he was blind. They'd probably creep about and he'd never know where they were until the rock hit. He put all his concentration into listening for stealthy footsteps. But when the second voice spoke, it was not far from where the first had originated. He recognized it right away by the Jamaillian accent. Mingsley.

"I thought it was. It never moved nor spoke at all the last time I was here. Dav—my intermediary assured me that it was alive still, but I doubted him. Well. This puts a whole new slant on this." He cleared his throat. "The Ludlucks have been reluctant to deal, and now I see why. I thought I was bidding on dead wood. My offer was far too low. I shall have to approach them again."

"I think I've changed my mind." The woman's voice was low. Paragon couldn't decide what emotion she was repressing. Disgust? Fear? He could not be sure. "I don't think I want anything to do with this."

"But you seemed so intrigued earlier," Mingsley objected. "Don't be squeamish now. So the figurehead is alive. That only increases our possibilities."

"I am intrigued by wizardwood," she admitted reluctantly. "Someone brought me a tiny piece to work on once. The customer wanted me to carve it into a shape of a bird. I told him, as I tell you, that the work I do is determined by the wood I am given, not by any whim of my own or the customer's. The man urged me to try. But when I took the wood from him, it felt . . . evil. If you could steep wood with an emotion, I'd say that one was pure malice. I couldn't bear to even touch it, let alone carve it. I told him to take it away."

Mingsley chuckled as if the woman had told an amusing story. "I've found," he said loftily, as if speaking in generalities, "that the finely tuned sensibilities of an artist are best soothed with the lovely sound of coins being stacked. I am sure we can get past your reservations. And I can promise you that the money from this would be incredible. Look at what your work brings in now, using ordinary wood. If you fashioned beads from wizardwood, we could ask . . . whatever we wanted. Literally. What we would be offering buyers has never been available to them before. We're two of a kind in this. Outsiders, seeing what all the insiders have missed."

"Two of a kind? I am not at all sure we can even talk." There was no compromise to the woman's tone, but Mingsley seemed deaf to it.

"Look at it," he gloated. "Fine straight grain. Silvery color. Plank after plank and I haven't spotted a single knot. Not one! Wood like that, you can do anything with it. Even if we remove the figurehead, have you restore it, and sell it separately, there is still enough wizardwood in this hulk to found an industry. Not just your beads and charms; we have to think bigger than that. Chairs, and bedsteads, and tables, all elaborately carved. Ah! Cradles. Imagine the status of that, rocking your firstborn to sleep in a cradle all carved from wizardwood. Or," the man's voice suddenly grew even more enthused, "perhaps you might carve the headboard of the cradle with women's faces. We could find out how to quicken them, teach them to sing lullabies, and we'd have a cradle that could sing a child to sleep!"

"The thought makes my blood cold," the woman said.

"You fear this wood, then?" Mingsley gave a short bark of laughter. "Don't succumb to Bingtown superstition."

"I don't fear wood," the woman snapped back. "I fear people like you. You charge into things blindly. Stop and think. The Bingtown Traders are the most astute merchants and traders this part of the world has ever seen. There must be a reason why they do not traffic in this wood. You've seen for yourself that the figurehead lives. But you don't ask how or why! You simply want to make tables and chairs of the same substance. And finally, you stand before a living being and blithely speak of chopping up his body to make furniture."

Mingsley made an odd sound. "We have no real assurances that this is a live being," he said tolerantly. "So it moved and it spoke. Once. Jumping jacks on sticks move, as do puppets on strings. Parrots talk. Shall we give them all the status of a human?" His tone was amused.

"And now you are willing to spout whatever nonsense you must to get me to do your will. I've been down to the north wall where the liveships tie up. As have you, I'll wager. The ships I saw there are clearly alive, clearly individuals. Mingsley. You can lie to yourself and convince yourself of anything you wish. But don't expect me to accept your excuses and half-truths as reasons I should work for you. No. I was intrigued when you told me there was a dead liveship here, one whose wood could be salvaged. But even that was a lie. There is no point to me standing out here in the rain with you any longer. I've decided this is wrong. I won't do it."

Paragon heard her striding away, heard Mingsley call after her, "You're stupid. You're walking away from more money than you can even imagine."

Her footsteps halted. Paragon strained his ears. Would she come back? Her voice alone came, pitched in a normal tone but carrying clearly. "Somehow," she said coldly, "you have confused profitable and not profitable with right and wrong. I, however, have not."

Then he could hear her walking away again. She strode like an angry man. The rain began to pelt even harder; the drops would have stung human flesh. He heard Mingsley grunt with distaste at the new downpour.

"Artistic temperament," he scoffed to himself. "She'll be back." A pause. Then, "Ship. You, ship. Are you truly alive?"

Paragon chose not to reply.

"It's not smart to ignore me. It's only a matter of time before I own you. It's in your own best interests to tell me what I need to know. Are you separate from the ship, or truly a part of it?"

Paragon faced the pounding rain and did not reply.

"Would it kill you if I cut you free of your ship?" Mingsley asked in a low voice. "For that is what I intend to do."

Paragon did not know the answer to that. Instead, he invited Mingsley, "Why don't you come close enough to try?"

After a short time, he heard the man leave.

He waited there, in the stinging rain. When he heard her speak again, he did not start. He did turn his head slowly, to hear her better.

"Ship? Ship, may I come closer?"

"My name is Paragon."

"Paragon, may I come closer?"

He considered it. "Aren't you going to tell me your name?" he finally countered.

A short hesitation. "I am called Amber."

"But that is not your name."

"I've had a number of names," she said after a time. "This is the one that suits me best, here and now."

She could, he reflected, simply have lied to him and said it was her name. But she had not. He extended an open hand toward the sound of her voice. "Amber," he accepted her. It was a challenge, too. He knew how huge his hand was in comparison to a human's. Once his fingers closed around her hand, he'd be able to jerk her arm out of its socket. If he chose to.

He listened to her breath, to the sound of the rain pocking the packed sand of the beach. Abruptly she took two quick steps towards him and set her gloved left hand in his. He closed his immense fingers over her small ones. "Paragon," she said breathlessly.

"Why did you come back?"

She laughed nervously. "As Mingsley put it, I am intrigued by you." When he made no reply to that, she went on, "I have always been more curious than wise. Yet any wisdom I have ever gained has come to me from my curiosity. So I have never learned to turn away from it."

"I see. Will you tell me about yourself? As you see, I am blind."

"I see that only too well." There was pity and regret in her voice. "Mingsley called you ugly. But whoever shaped your brow and jaw, your lips and nose, was a master carver. I wish I could have seen your eyes. What kind of a person could destroy such art?"

Her words moved him, but they also nudged him toward a thing he could not, would not recall. Gruffly he replied, "Such compliments! Are they meant to distract my mind from the fact that you have not answered my request?" He released her hand.

"No. Not at all. I am . . . Amber. I carve wood. I make jewelry from it, beads and ornaments, combs and rings. Sometimes larger pieces, such as bowls and goblets . . . even chairs and cradles. But not many of those. My talent seems strongest on smaller work. May I touch your face?"

The question came so swiftly that he found himself nodding before he had considered. "Why?" he asked belatedly.

He felt her come closer to him. The scant warmth of her body interceded with the chill of the rain. He felt her fingers brush the edge of his beard. It was a very slight touch and yet he shivered to it. The reaction was too human. Had he been able to draw back, he would have.

"I cannot reach you. Could you . . . would you lift me up?"

The vast trust she offered made him forget she had not answered his first question. "I could crush you in my hands," he reminded her.

"But you will not," she told him confidently. "Please."

The urgency in her plea frightened him. "Why do you think I would not? I've killed before, you know! Whole crews of men! All of Bingtown knows that. Who are you not to fear me?"

For answer, she set her bare wet hand to the skin of his arm. She flowed through his grain; the warmth of her shot through him the way the heat of a woman's hand on a man's thigh can inflame his whole body. Both ways, he suddenly knew, the flow was both ways, he was within her flesh as much as she was within his timbers. Her humanity sang in him. He wallowed in her senses. Rain had soaked her hair and clothes to her body. Her skin was cold, but her body warmed itself from within. He felt the sigh of air in her lungs like wind against his sails had been, the rush of blood through her flesh almost like the sea water thrilling past his hull.

"You are more than wood!" she cried aloud. Discovery was in her voice and he knew the sudden terror of betrayal. She was inside him, seeing too much, knowing too much. All the things he had set aside from himself, she was awakening. He did not mean to push her so hard, but she cried out as she fell on the wet sand and rocky beach. He heard her gasping for breath as the rain fell all around them.

"Are you hurt?" he asked gruffly after a time. Things were calming inside him.

"No," she spoke quietly. Then, before he could apologize, "I'm sorry," she said. "Despite everything, I expected you to be . . . wood. I've a gift for wood. When I touch it, I know it, I know how its grain bends, where it runs fine or coarse. . . . I thought I could touch you and guess how your eyes had been. I touched you, thinking to find only wood. I should not have been so . . . forgive me. Please."

"It's all right," he replied gravely. "I did not mean to push you away so abruptly. I did not intend you should fall."

"No, it was my own fault. And you were right to push me away. I . . ." She halted again and for a time the only sounds were the rain. The shush of the waves came louder now. The tide had turned and the water was venturing closer. "Please, may we begin again?" she suddenly asked.

"If you wish," he said awkwardly. This woman . . . he did not understand this woman at all. So quickly she had trusted him, and now so swiftly she moved towards friendship. He was not accustomed to things like this happening, let alone happening so quickly. It frightened him. But more frightening was the thought that she might go away and not come back. He searched himself for some trust of his own to offer her. "Would you like to come in, out of the rain?" he invited her. "I'm at a terrible list, and it's no warmer within than without, but at least you'd be out of the rain."

"Thank you," she said quietly. "I'd like that. I'd like that a great deal."

WINTER

CHAPTER TWENTY

C R I M P E R S

THERE WERE FEW SAFE HARBORS ON THE OUTSIDE PAS-
SAGE WORTHY OF THE NAME, BUT NOOK WAS ONE OF
them. It was a tricky place to get into on an outgoing tide,
but once within, it was one of the few places where both
ships and sailors could rest easy for a night or two. Most
ports on the Outside were regularly scoured by the winter
storms that blew in off the Wild Sea and pounded the
beaches mercilessly, sometimes for weeks on end. A wise
captain kept his ship well away from land on her way south,
for the closer she came to the outer banks, the greater the
chance she would be driven ashore and pounded to pieces
on the rocks. If their water supplies had not gone too foul
even for sailors to drink, chances were that the *Reaper*
would not have taken the risk of coming into Nook.

But she had, and so the crew was having one blessed
evening of shore liberty, of women, of food that was not salt
and water that was not green with scum. The holds of the
Reaper were full, cask after cask of salted meat, stacks of
rolled hides, tubs of oil and fat. It was a rich cargo, hard
won, and the crew were justifiably proud of having filled
her so swiftly. It had been but fifteen months since the

Reaper had left her home port of Candletown. Their return journey had been far swifter than their outbound one. The professional sailors knew they had well earned the bonuses they expected at the end of the trip, while the hunters and skinners had kept their own tallies as to what their shares would be. Those forced into sailing knew that all they had to do now was survive as far as home, and they would disembark as free men.

Athel, the ship's boy, had distinguished himself by earning a skinner's bonus on top of his regular wages. This had made him somewhat popular with those on the ship who enjoyed playing dice, but the shy boy had turned down all offers to accept his scrip against his forthcoming bonus. To the surprise of all, he had also refused the offer to move in with the skinners and hunters and become one of them, preferring to remain as a common crew member. When pushed to answer why, the boy would only grin and say, "D'ruther be a sailor. Sailor can ship out on any kind of vessel. But hunters and skinners, they have to come north at least once a year. This is my first time north; didn't like it much."

It was actually the best answer he could have given. Hunters and skinners were left admiring themselves for how tough they were, while the sailors nodded approvingly to themselves at the wisdom of his choice. Brashen had to wonder if Althea had taken all that into account or simply made a lucky decision. He watched her across the tavern. She sat at the end of a bench, nursing the same mug of dark beer that she'd first ordered. She nodded to the talk at the table, she laughed in all the right places, and she looked convincingly bashful when the whores approached her. She was, he thought, finally a member of the ship's crew.

That afternoon on the slaughter beach had changed her. She had proven to herself that she could excel, when the task did not demand brute strength or bulk to accomplish it. For as long as they'd been ashore there, her first task had become to skin, and with the passing days, she had only become swifter at it. She had brought that confidence back on board with her, taking to herself the tasks where nimbleness and swiftness counted more than size. She still struggled when she had to work alongside the men, but that was expected of a boy. That she had excelled in one area had given them faith that in time she would grow into her other tasks as well.

Brashen swallowed the last two mouthfuls of beer in his mug and held it up for more. And, he thought to himself, she had the sense not to get drunk with her shipmates. He nodded to himself. He'd underestimated her. She'd survive this voyage, so long as she kept on as she had begun. Not that she could spend many years sailing as a boy, but she'd get by for this one.

A barmaid came to refill his mug. He nodded to her and pushed a coin across the table. She took it gravely and bobbed a curtsey before she darted off to the next table. A pretty little thing she was; he wondered that her father allowed her to work in the common room. Her demeanor made it plain she was not one of the women working the room as whores, but he wondered if every sailor would respect that. As his eyes followed her about the room at her tasks, he noted that most of them did. One man tried to catch at her sleeve after she had served him, but she evaded him nimbly. When she reached Athel, however, she paused. She smiled as she questioned the ship's boy. Althea made a show of glancing into her mug, and then allowing the girl to refill it for her. The smile the tavern girl gave the supposed lad was a great deal friendlier than she had offered the other customers. Brashen grinned to himself; Althea did make a likely looking boy, and the bashfulness the ship's boy professed probably made her more alluring than most. Brashen wondered if the discomfort Althea exhibited was entirely feigned.

He set his mug back on the counter in front of him, and then opened his coat. Too warm. He actually felt too warm in here. He smiled to himself, replete with well-being. The room was warm and dry, the deck was still under his feet. The anxiety that was a sailor's constant companion eased for a moment. By the time they reached Candletown with their cargo, he would have earned enough to give him breathing space. Not that he'd be so foolish as to spend it all. No. This time, at least, he'd hearken back to Captain Vestrit's advice and set a bit by for himself. He even had a choice now. He knew the *Reaper* would be more than willing to keep him on. He could probably stay with the ship for as long as he wanted. Or he could take his ship's ticket in Candletown, and look about a bit there. Maybe he'd find another ship there, something a bit better than the *Reaper*. Something cleaner, something faster. Back to merchant sailing, piling on the canvas and skipping from port to port. Yes.

He felt a once-familiar burn in his lower lip and hastily shifted the quid of cindin. It was as potent as the seller had promised, to eat through his skin that fast. He had another mouthful of beer to cool it. It had been years since he'd indulged in cindin. Captain Vestrit had been an absolute tyrant on that point. If he even suspected a man of using it, on shore or on ship, he'd check his lower lip. Any sign of a burn put him off the ship at the next port, with no pay. He'd won the small plug earlier at a gaming table, another amusement he hadn't indulged much of late. But, damn it all, there came a time when a man had to unwind, and this was as good a time as any. He hadn't been irresponsible. He never bet anything he couldn't lose. He'd started out with some sea-bear teeth he'd carved into fish and such in his bunk time. Almost from the start of the game, he'd won steadily. Oh, he'd come near to losing his deck knife, and that would have been a sore blow, but then his luck had turned sweet and he'd won not only the cindin plug but enough coins for the evening's beer.

He almost felt bad about it. The fellows he had fleeced of the coin and cindin were the mate and steward of the *Jolly Gal*, another oil ship in the harbor. Only the *Jolly Gal* had an empty hold and full kegs of salt. She and her crew were just on their way out to the killing grounds. This late in the season, they'd have a hard time filling her up. Wouldn't surprise Brash if she stayed on the grounds the season through, going from sea bear to small whale. Now there was ugly, dangerous work. Damn glad he wouldn't be doing it. His winning tonight was a sign, he was sure of it. His luck was getting better and his life was going to straighten itself out. Oh, he still missed the *Vivacia*, and old Captain Vestrit, Sa cradle him, but he'd make a new life for himself.

He drank the last of the beer in his mug, then rubbed at his eyes. He must have been wearier than he thought he was, to feel so suddenly sleepy. Cindin usually enlivened him. It was the hallmark of the drug, the benign sense of well-being coupled with the energy to have fun. Instead he felt as if the most wonderful thing that could happen to him now would be a warm, soft bed. A dry one, that didn't smell of sweat and mildew and oil and oakum. With no bugs.

He had been so busy building this image of paradise in his mind that he startled to find the tavern maid before him. She smiled up at him mischievously when he jumped and then gestured at his mug. She was right, it was empty again. He covered it with his hand and shook his head regretfully. "I'm out of coin, I'm afraid. It's all to the good. I'll want a clear head when we leave port tomorrow anyway."

"Tomorrow? In this blow?" she asked sympathetically.

He shook his head, confirming his own reluctance. "Storm or no storm, we have to face it. Time and tide wait on no man, or so they tell us. And the sooner we leave, the sooner we're home."

"Home," she said, and smiled again. "Then this one is on me. To a swift trip home, for you and all your crew."

Slowly he removed his hand from the top of his mug and watched her pour. Truly, his luck was changing. "You're from the same ship as those men, aren't you? The *Reaper*?"

"That's us," he confirmed. He shifted the cindin in his mouth again.

"And you're the mate of the *Reaper*, then."

"Just barely. I'm the third."

"Ah. You're Brashen, then?"

He nodded and could not keep from grinning. There was something flattering about a woman knowing his name before he knew hers.

"They're saying the *Reaper* has filled her hold and is headed back. Must have been a good crew?" She raised one eyebrow whenever she asked a question.

"Good enough." He was starting to enjoy this conversation. Then, in her next breath, she betrayed the true reason for her generosity.

"That's your ship's boy on the end, there? He's not much of a drinker."

"No, he's not. Doesn't talk much either."

"I noticed," she said ruefully. She took a breath, then suddenly asked, "Is it true what they say about him? That he can skin sea bears near as fast as they shoot them?"

She did think Althea, or Athel was comely, then. Brashen grinned to himself. "No, it's not true at all," he said solemnly. "Athel is much faster than the hunters. That's the problem we've had with the lad, he was down there skinning them out before they were shot. Our hunters had to spend all their time chasing down the naked bears he'd already skinned."

He took a swallow of the beer. For an instant she just stared at him, eyes wide. Then, "Oh, you," she rebuked him with a giggle and gave him a playful push. Relaxed as he was, he had to catch at the bar to keep from falling. "Oh, sorry!" she cried and caught at his sleeve to help him right himself.

"It's all right. I'm just more tired than I thought I was."

"Are you?" she asked more softly. She waited until his eyes met hers. Her eyes were blue and deeper than the sea. "There's a room in back with a bed. My room. You could rest there for a while. If you wanted to lie down."

Just before he was certain of her meaning, she cast her eyes aside and down. She turned and walked away from him. He picked up his mug again and just as he sipped from it, she said over her shoulder, "Just let me know. If you want to." She paused as she was, looking back at him, one eyebrow raised quizzically. Or was it invitingly?

A man's luck turning is like a favorable tide. One has to make the most of it while it's there. Brashen drained off the last of his mug and stood up. "I'd like that," he said quietly. It was true. Whether the offer of a bed included the girl or not, it sounded very good. What was there to lose? He shifted the cindin in his mouth again. It was very, very good.

"One more round," Reller announced. "Then we'd better get back to the ship."

"Don't wait on us," one of the hands giggled. "Head back, Reller. We'll be along soon enough." He started to sag his head down onto his arms.

Reller reached across the table and gave him a shake. "None of that, Jord. No passing out here. Once we get to the ship you can drop to the deck and snore like a pig for all I care. But not here."

Something in his tone got Jord's attention. He lifted his head blearily. "Why's that?"

Reller leaned across the table. "Deckhand from the *Tern* gave me a warning earlier. You know that *Jolly Gal*, tied up just to the lee of us? Crew had the red-heaves before they got here. They lost seven men. The skipper has been about town for three days, trying to hire on more crew but with no luck. Word is that he's getting desperate; they got to get out to the grounds. Every day they stay here is likely another week they'll have to spend hunting. Fingers from the *Tern* told me our crew would be wise to stick together and sleep on board tonight. One of their hunters has gone missing for two days now, and you know what they think. So when we go back to the ship we all go back together. Less you want to wake up northward bound on the *Jolly Gal*."

"Crimpers?" Jord asked in a sort of horror. "Working here in Nook?"

"Where better?" Reller asked in a low voice. "Man don't come back to his ship on time, no one's going to stay tied up here to look for him. Easy to lay in an alley, pick off a few tars from a home-bound vessel, the poor sots wake up back on the hunting waters. I tell you, this isn't a town where a sailor should walk about alone."

Jord abruptly hauled himself to his feet. "I've had a gut full of these northern waters. No way I'll even take a chance on that. Come on, fellows. Let's to the ship."

Reller glanced about. "Hey, where'd Brash go? Wasn't he sitting over there?"

"He went with a girl, I think." Althea spoke up for the first time. She heard the disapproval in her voice and saw the faces turn toward her in surprise. "One I thought was looking at me," she added sourly. She picked up her mug, took a sip, and set it down. "Let's go. The beer here tastes like piss, anyway."

"Oh, you know what piss tastes like, do you?" Jord mocked her.

"Don't need to. All I need to know is that this stuff smells just like your bunk, Jord."

"Aw, a bunk sniffer, eh?" Jord guffawed drunkenly. The others joined in the laughter and Althea just shook her head. Afloat or ashore, the humor and witticisms were the same. She actually found herself eager to return to the ship. The sooner they sailed from this armpit, the sooner they'd get to Candletown. She pushed back from the table. Jord leaned over to look in her mug. "You going to drink that?" he demanded.

"Be my guest," she told him and turned to follow the others out of the tavern into the storm. From the corner of her eye she saw Jord toss it off and then make a face.

"Ew. Guess you got the bottom of the cask or something." He wiped his mouth on his sleeve and followed.

Outside the storm was still blowing. Althea wondered wearily if it ever did not storm in the forsaken hole. She squinted her eyes into the rain-laden wind that tore at her clothes and hair. In two steps she forgot that she had ever been warm and dry. Back to life as the ship's boy.

She almost didn't hear the inn-keeper calling from behind her. Reller turned, and when she glanced back to see what he was staring at, she saw the man leaning out the door of his tavern. "You Athel?" he yelled into the storm.

Reller pointed silently at her.

"Brashen wants you. He's had a bit much to drink. Come and haul him out of here!"

"Wonderful," she snarled to herself, wondering why he had picked on her. Reller motioned her to go back.

"Meet us back at the ship!" he roared into the wind and she nodded. She turned back to the inn wearily. She didn't look forward to staggering through the storm with Brash leaning on her. Well, this was the sort of task that fell to ship's boys. If he puked, she'd get to clean that up, too.

Muttering to herself, she climbed the steps and then stepped into the tavern. The keeper motioned towards a door in the back. "He's in there," he said disgustedly. "Nearly passed out on one of the girls."

"I'll get him out of here," Althea promised and dripped her way past the tables and benches of drinkers to the door. She opened it on a dimly lit chamber. There was a bed, and the tavern maid with her blouse unlaced. The girl was bent over Brashen as Althea came in. She looked up at Althea and smiled helplessly. "I don't know what to do," she said, still smiling. "Won't you help me?"

Perhaps if Althea had truly been a ship's boy, she would have been distracted by the girl's bared breasts and would simply have stepped into the room. She probably would not have stared at Brashen as she did, thinking that he did not look like a man passed out in a bed but rather like a man who had been struck down and then arranged on a bed. In that momentary pause, she caught a flicker of motion to her left. She dodged back, catching the blow on the side rather than on the top of her head. The club crashed into the top of her shoulder as well, numbing her right arm down to her fingertips. She staggered forward with a cry as the man who had clubbed her slammed the door shut behind her.

The girl was in on it. Althea grasped that instantly, and spurred by her pain, she struck the tavern maid in the face as hard as she could with her left hand. It was not her best punch, but the girl seemed shocked as much as hurt. Clutching at her face, she staggered back with a scream as Althea spun to face the man beside the door. "You heartless little bastard!" the man spat, and swung at her. Althea ducked it and sprang for the door behind him. She managed to pull it part way open. "Crimpers!" she shouted with every bit of breath in her body. A white flash of light knocked her to the floor.

Voices came back first. "One from the *Tern*, the one they've been looking for. He was tied up in the beer cellar. One from the *Carlyle*, and these two from the *Reaper*. Plus it looks like there's a couple more out back with some earth scraped over them. Probably hit them too hard. Tough way for a sailor to go."

There was a shrug in the second voice that replied, "Well, tough is true, but we never seem to run out of them."

She opened her eyes to overturned tables and benches. Her cheek was in a puddle of something; she hoped it was beer. Men's legs and boots were in front of her face, close enough to step on her. She tipped her head to look up at them. Townsmen wearing heavy leathers against the storm's chill. She pushed against the floor. On her second try she managed to sit up. The movement set the room to rocking before her.

"Hey, the boy's coming round," a voice observed. "What did you hit Pag's girl for, you sot?"

"She was the bait. She's in on it," Althea said slowly. Men. Couldn't they even see what was right in front of their faces?

"Maybe, maybe not," the man replied judiciously. "Can you stand?"

"I think so." She clutched at an overturned chair and managed to get to her feet. She was dizzy and felt like throwing up. She touched the back of her head cautiously, then looked at her red fingers. "I'm bleeding," she said aloud. No one seemed greatly interested.

"Your mate's still in there," the man in boots told her. "Better get him out of there and back to your ship. Pag's plenty mad at you for punching his daughter. Didn't no one ever teach you any manners about women?"

"Pag's in on it, too, if it's going on in his back room and beer cellar," Althea pointed out dully.

"Pag? Pag's run this tavern for ten years I know about. I wouldn't be saying such wild things if I were you. It's your fault all his chairs and tables are busted up, too. You aren't exactly welcome here any more."

Althea squeezed her eyes shut and then opened them. The floor seemed to have steadied. "I see," she told the man. "I'll get Brashen out of here." Obviously Nook was their town, and they'd run it as they saw fit. She was lucky the tavern had been full of other sailors who weren't fond of crimpers. These two townsmen didn't seem overly upset about how Pag made his extra money. She wondered. If there wasn't a knot of angry sailors still hovering near the fire, would they be letting her and Brashen go even now? She'd better get while the going was good.

She staggered to the door of the back room and looked in. Brashen was sitting up on the bed, his head bowed into his hands. "Brash?" she croaked.

"Althea?" he replied dazedly. He turned toward her voice.

"It's Athel!" she asserted grumpily. "And I'm getting damn tired of being teased about my name." She reached his side and tugged uselessly at his arm. "Come on. We got to get back to the ship."

"I'm sick. Something in the beer," he groaned. He lifted a hand to the back of his head. "And I think I was sapped, too."

"Me, too." Althea leaned closer to him and lowered her voice.

"But we've got to get out of here while we can. The men outside the door don't seem too upset about Pag's crimping. The sooner we're out of here, the better."

He caught the idea quickly, for one as bleary as he looked. "Give me your shoulder," he ordered her, and staggered upright. She took his arm across her shoulders. Either he was too tall or she was too short for it to work properly. It almost felt as if he was deliberately trying to push her down as they staggered out of the back room and then through the tavern to the door. One of the men at the fireside nodded to them gravely, but the two townsmen merely watched them go. Brashen missed a step as they went down the stairs and they both nearly fell into the frozen muck of the street.

Brashen lifted his head to stare into the wind and rain. "It's getting colder."

"The rain will turn to sleet tonight," Althea predicted sourly.

"Damn. And the night started out so well."

She trudged down the street with him leaning heavily on her shoulder. At the corner of a shuttered mercantile store she stopped to get her bearings. The whole town was black as pitch and the cold rain running down her face didn't help any.

"Stop a minute, Althea. I've got to piss."

"Athel," she reminded him wearily. His modesty consisted of stumbling two steps away as he fumbled at his pants.

"Sorry," he said gruffly a few moments later.

"It's all right," she told him tolerantly. "You're still drunk."

"Not drunk," he insisted. He put a hand on her shoulder again. "There was something in the beer, I think. No, I'm sure of it. I'd have probably tasted it, but for the cindin."

"You chew cindin?" Althea asked incredulously. "You?"

"Sometimes," Brashen said defensively. "Not often. And I haven't in a long time."

"My father always said it's killed more sailors than bad weather," Althea told him sourly. Her head was pounding.

"Probably," Brashen agreed. As they passed beyond the buildings and came to the docks he offered, "You should try it sometime, though. Nothing like it for setting a man's problems aside."

"Right." He seemed to be getting wobblier. She put her arm around his waist. "Not far to go now."

"I know. Hey. What happened back there? In the tavern?"

She wanted so badly to be angry then but found she didn't have the energy. It was almost funny. "You nearly got crimped. I'll tell you about it tomorrow."

"Oh." A long silence followed. The wind died down for a few breaths. "Hey. I was thinking about you earlier. About what you should do. You should go north."

She shook her head in the darkness. "No more slaughter boats for me after this. Not unless I have to."

"No, no. That's not what I mean. Way north, and west. Up past Chalced, to the Duchies. Up there, the ships are smaller. And they don't care if you're a man or a woman, so long as you work hard. That's what I've heard anyway. Up there, women captain ships, and sometimes the whole damn crew are women."

"Barbarian women," Althea pointed out. "They're more related to the Out Islanders than they are to us, and from what I've heard, they spend most of their time trying to kill each other off. Brashen, most of them can't even read. They get married in front of rocks, Sa help us all."

"Witness stones," he corrected her.

"My father used to trade up there, before they had their war," she went on doggedly. They were out on the docks now, and the wind suddenly gusted up with an energy that nearly pushed her down. "He said," she grunted as she kept Brashen to his feet, "that they were more barbaric than the Chalcedeans. That half their buildings didn't even have glass windows."

"That's on the coast," he corrected her doggedly. "I've heard that inland, some of the cities are truly magnificent."

"I'd be on the coast," she reminded him crankily. "Here's the *Reaper*. Mind your step."

The *Reaper* was tied to the dock, shifting restlessly against her hemp camels as both wind and waves nudged at her. Althea had expected to have a difficult time getting him up the gangplank, but Brashen went up it surprisingly well. Once aboard, he stood clear of her. "Well. Get some sleep, boy. We sail early."

"Yessir," she replied gratefully. She still felt sick and woozy. Now that she was back aboard and so close to her bed, she was even more tired. She turned and trudged away to the hatch. Once below she found some few of the crew still awake and sitting around a dim lantern.

"What happened to you?" Reller greeted her.

"Crimpers," she said succinctly. "They made a try for Brashen and me. But we got clear of them. They found the hunter off the *Tern*, too. And a couple of others, I guess."

"Sa's balls!" the man swore. "Was the skipper from the *Jolly Gal* in on it?"

"Don't know," she said wearily. "But Pag was for sure, and his girl. The beer was drugged. I'll never go in his tavern again."

"Damn. No wonder Jord's sleeping sound, he got the dose that was meant for you. Well, I'm heading over to the *Tern*, hear what that hunter has to say," Reller declared.

"Me, too."

Like magic, the men who were even partially awake rose and flocked off to hear the gossip. Althea hoped the tale would be well-embroidered for them. For herself, she wanted only her hammock and to be under sail again.

It took him four tries to light the lantern. When the wick finally burned, he lowered the glass carefully and sat down on his bunk. After a moment he rose, to go to the small looking glass fastened to the wall. He pulled down his lower lip and looked at it. Damn. He'd be lucky if the burns didn't ulcerate. He'd all but forgotten that aspect of cindin. He sat down heavily on his bunk again and began to peel his coat off. It was then he realized the left cuff of his coat was soaked with blood as well as rain. He stared at it for a time, then gingerly felt the back of his head. No. A lump, but no blood. The blood wasn't his. He patted his fingers against the patch of it. Still wet, still red. Althea? he wondered groggily. Whatever they had put in the beer was still fogging his brain. Althea, yes. Hadn't she told him she'd been hit on the head? Damn her, why hadn't she said she was bleeding? With the sigh of a deeply wronged man, he pulled his coat on again and went back out into the storm.

The forecastle was as dark and smelly as he remembered it. He shook two men awake before he found one coherent enough to point out her bunking spot. It was up in a corner a rat wouldn't have room to turn around in. He groped his way there by the stub of a candle and then shook her awake despite curses and protests. "Come to my cabin, boy, and get your head stitched and stop your sniveling," he ordered her. "I won't have you laying abed and useless for a week with a fever. Lively, now. I haven't all night."

He tried to look irritable and not anxious as she followed him out of the hold and up onto the deck and then into his cabin. Even in the candle's dimness, he could see how pale she was, and how her hair was crusted with blood. As she followed him into his tiny chamber, he barked at her, "Shut the door! I don't care to have the whole night's storm blow through here." She complied with a sort of leaden obedience. The moment it was closed he sprang past her to latch it. He turned, seized her by the shoulders, and resisted the urge to shake her. Instead he sat her firmly on his bunk. "What is the matter with you?" he hissed as he hung his coat on the peg. "Why didn't you tell me you were hurt?"

She had, he knew, and half-expected that to be her reply. Instead she just raised a hand to her head and said vaguely, "I was just so tired. . . ."

He cursed the small confines of his room as he stepped over her feet to reach the medicine chest. He opened it and picked through it, and then tossed his selections on the bunk beside her. He moved the lantern a bit closer; it was still too dim to see clearly. She winced as his fingers walked over her scalp, trying to part her thick dark hair and find the source of all the blood. His fingers were wet with it; it was still bleeding sluggishly. Well, scalp wounds always bled a lot. He knew that, it should not worry him. But it did, as did the unfocused look to her eyes.

"I'm going to have to cut some of your hair away," he warned her, expecting a protest.

"If you must."

He looked at her more closely. "How many times did you get hit?"

"Twice. I think."

"Tell me about it. Tell me everything you can remember about what happened tonight."

And so she spoke, in drifting sentences, while he used scissors to cut her hair close to the scalp near the wound. Her story did not make him proud of his quick wits. Put together with what he knew of the evening, it was clear that both he and Althea had been targeted to fill out the *Jolly Gal*'s crew. It was only the sheerest luck that he was not chained up in her hold even now.

The split he bared in her scalp was as long as his little finger and gaping open from the pull of her queue. Even after he cut the hair around it to short stubble and cleared the clotted strands away, it still oozed blood. He blotted it away with a rag. "I'll need to sew this shut," he told her. He tried to push away both the wooziness from whatever had been in his beer and his queasiness at the thought of pushing a needle through her scalp. Luckily Althea seemed even more beclouded than he was. Whatever the crimpers had put in the beer worked well.

By the lantern's shifting yellow light, he threaded a fine strand of gut through a curved needle. It felt tiny in his calloused fingers, and slippery. Well, it couldn't be that much different from patching clothes and sewing canvas, could it? He'd done that for years. "Sit still," he told her needlessly. Gingerly he set the point of the needle to her scalp. He'd have to push it in shallowly to make it come up again. He put gentle pressure on the needle. Instead of piercing her skin, her scalp slid on her skull. He couldn't get the needle to slide through.

A bit more pressure and Althea yelled, "Wah!" and suddenly batted his hand away. "What are you doing?" she demanded angrily, turning to glare up at him.

"I told you. I've got to stitch this shut."

"Oh." A pause. "I wasn't listening." She rubbed at her eyes, then reached back to touch her own scalp cautiously. "I suppose you do have to close it," she said ruefully. She squeezed her eyes shut, then opened them again. "I wish I could either pass out or wake up," she said woefully. "I just feel foggy. I hate it."

"Let me see what I have in here," he suggested. He knelt on one knee to rummage through the ship's stores of medicines. "This stuff hasn't been replenished in years," he grumbled to himself as Althea peered past his shoulder. "Half the containers are empty, the herbs that should be green or brown are gray, and some of the other stuff smells like mold."

"Maybe it's supposed to smell like mold?" Althea suggested.

"I don't know," he muttered.

"Let me look. I used to restock the *Vivacia*'s medicines when we got to town." She leaned against him to reach the chest in the small space between the bunk and the wall. She inspected a few bottles, holding them up to the lamp light and then setting them aside. She opened one small pot, wrinkled her nose in distaste at the strong odor, and capped it again. "There's nothing useful in there," she decided, and sat back on the bunk. "I'll hold it closed and you just stitch it. I'll try to sit still."

"Just a minute," Brashen said grudgingly. He had saved part of the plug of cindin. Not a very large part, just a bit to give him something to look forward to on a bad day. He took it out of his coat pocket and brushed lint off it. He showed it to Althea and then carefully broke it in two pieces. "Cindin. It should wake you up a bit, and make you feel better. You do it like this." He tucked it into his lower lip, packed it down with his tongue. The familiar bitterness spread through his mouth. If it hadn't been for the taste of the cindin, he thought ruefully, he might have tasted the drug in his beer. He pushed that aside as a useless thought and nudged the cindin away from the earlier sore.

"It'll taste very bitter at first," he warned her. "That's the worm-wood in it. Gets your juices going."

She looked very dubious as she tucked it into her lip. She made a wry face and then sat meeting his eyes, waiting. After a moment she asked, "Is it supposed to burn?"

"This is pretty strong stuff," he admitted. "Shift it around in your lip. Don't leave it in one place too long." He watched the expression on her face slowly change, and felt an answering grin spread over his own. "Pretty good, huh?"

She gave a low laugh. "Fast, too."

"Starts fast, ends fast. I never really saw any harm to it, as long as a man was finished before he came on watch."

He watched her awkwardly move the plug in her lip. "My father said that men used it when they should have been sleeping instead. Then they came on watch all used up. And if they were still on it when they were working, they'd be too confident, and take unneeded risks." Her voice trailed off. " 'Risk-takers endanger everyone,' he always said."

"Yes. I remember," Brashen agreed gravely. "I never used cindin aboard the *Vivacia*, Althea. I respected your father too much."

For a moment silence held, then she sighed. "Let's do this," she suggested.

"Right," he agreed. He took up the needle and thread again. She followed it with her eyes. Maybe he'd made her too alert. "There's no room in here to work," he complained. "Here. Lie down on the bunk and turn your head. Good." He crouched down on the floor beside the bunk. This was better, he could almost see what he was doing. He dabbed away the sluggishly welling blood and picked out a few stray hairs. "Now hold the gash shut. No, your fingers are in the way. Here. Like this." He arranged her hands, and it was no accident that one of her wrists was mostly over her eyes. "I'll try to be quick."

"Be careful instead," she warned him. "And don't stitch it too tight. Just pull the edges together as evenly as you can, but not so they hump up."

"I'll try. I've never done this before, you know. But I've watched it done more than once."

She moved the plug of cindin in her lip, and he remembered to shift his own. He winced as it touched a sore from earlier in the evening. He saw her jaws clench and he began. He tried not to think of the pain he inflicted, only of doing a good job. He finally got the needle to pierce her scalp. He had to hold the skin firmly to her skull as he brought the tip of the curved needle up on the other side of the cut. Drawing the thread through was the worst. It made a tiny ripping noise as it slipped through, very unnerving to him. She set her teeth and shuddered to each stitch, but did not cry out.

When it was finally done, he tied the last knot and then snipped away the extra thread.

"There," he told her, and tossed the needle aside. "Let go, now. Let me see how I did."

She dropped her hands to the bed. Sweat misted her face. He studied the gash critically. His work was not wonderful, but it was holding the flesh closed. He nodded his satisfaction to her.

"Thanks." She spoke softly.

"Thank you." He finally said the words. "I owe you. But for you, I'd be in the hold of the *Jolly Gal* by now." He bent his head and kissed her cheek. Then her arm came up around his neck and she turned her mouth to the kiss. He lost his balance and caught himself awkwardly with one hand on the edge of the bunk, but did not break the kiss. She tasted of the cindin they were sharing. Her hand grasped the back of his neck gently and that touch was as stimulating as the kiss. It had been so long since anyone had touched him with gentleness.

She finally broke the kiss, moving her mouth aside from his. He leaned back from her. "Well," he said awkwardly. He took a breath. "Let's get a bandage on your head."

She nodded at him slowly.

He took up a strip of cloth and leaned over her again. "It's the cindin, you know," he said abruptly.

She moved it in her lip. "Probably. And I don't care if it is." Narrow as the bunk was, she still managed to edge over in it. Invitingly. She set her hand to his side and heat seemed to radiate out from it. A shiver stood his hair up in gooseflesh. The hand urged him forward.

He made a low sound in his throat and tried one last time. "This isn't a good idea. It's not safe."

"Nothing is," she told him, almost sadly.

His fingers were awkward on the laces of her shirt, and even after she shrugged out of it, there was a wrapping about her chest. He unwound it to free her small breasts and kiss them. Thin, she was so thin, and she tasted of the salt water, oakum and even the oil that was their cargo. But she was warm and willing and female, and he crammed himself into the too-narrow, too-short bunk to be with her. It was likely the cindin that made her dark eyes bottomless, he tried to tell himself. Startling it was that such a sharp-tongued girl would have a mouth so soft and pliant. Even when she set her teeth to the flesh of his shoulder to still her wordless cries, the pain was sweet. "Althea," he said softly into her hair, between the second and third times. "Althea Vestrit." He named not just the girl but the whole realm of sensation she had wakened in him.

Brash. Brashen Trell. Some small part of her could not believe she was doing this with Brashen Trell. Not this. Some small, sarcastic observer watched incredulously as she indulged her every impulse with his body. He was the worst possible choice for this. Then, *too late to worry about it,* she told herself, and pulled him even deeper inside her. She strained against him. It made no sense, but she could not find the part of her that cared about such things. Always, other than that first time, she'd had the sense to keep this sort of thing impersonal. Now not only was she giving in to herself and him with an abandonment that shocked her, but she was doing this with someone she had known for years. And not just once, no. He had scarcely collapsed upon her the first time before she was urging him to begin again. She was like a starving woman suddenly confronted with a banquet. The heat in her was strong, and she wondered if that were the cindin. But just as great was the sudden need she was admitting for this close human contact, the touching and sharing and holding. At one point she felt tears sting her eyes and a sob shake her. She stifled it against his shoulder, almost afraid of the strength of the loneliness and fears that this coupling seemed to be erasing. For so long she had been strong; she could not bear to display her weakness like this to anyone, let alone to someone who actually knew who she was. So she clutched him fiercely and let him believe it was part of her passion.

She did not want to think. Not now. Now she just wanted to take what she could get, for herself. She ran her hands over the hard muscles of his arms and back. In the center of his chest was a thick patch of curly hair. Elsewhere on his chest and belly there was black stubble, the hair chafed away by the coarse fabric of his clothes and the ship's constant motion. Over and over he kissed her, as if he could not get enough of it. His mouth tasted of cindin, and when he kissed her breasts, she felt the hot sting of the drug on her nipples. She slipped her hand down between their bodies, felt the hard slickness of him as he slid in and out of her. A moment later she clapped her hand over his mouth to muffle his cry as he thrust into her and then held them both teetering on the edge of forever.

For a time she thought of nothing. Then from somewhere else, she abruptly came back to the narrow sweaty bunk and his crushing weight upon her and her hair caught under his splayed hand. Her feet were cold, she realized. And she had a cramp in the small of her back. She heaved under him. "Let me up," she said quietly, and when he did not move at first, "Brashen, you're squashing me. Get off!"

He shifted and she managed to sit up. He edged over on the bunk so that she was sitting in the curl of his prone body. He looked up at her, not quite smiling. He lifted a hand, and with a finger traced a circle around one of her breasts. She shivered. With a tenderness that horrified her, he drew the sole blanket up to drape her shoulders. "Althea," he began.

"Don't talk," she begged him suddenly. "Don't say anything." Somehow if he spoke of what they had just done, it would make it more real, make it a part of her life that she'd have to admit to later. Now that she was satiated, her caution was coming back. "This can't happen again," she told him suddenly.

"I know. I know." Nonetheless, his eyes followed his hand as he traced his fingers down her throat to her belly. He tapped at the ring and charm in her navel. "That's . . . unusual."

In the gently shifting lantern light, the tiny skull winked up at them. "It was a gift from my dear sister," Althea said bitterly.

"I . . ." he hesitated. "I thought only whores wore them," he finished lamely.

"That's my sister's opinion as well," Althea replied stonily. Without warning, the old hurt lashed her.

She suddenly curled herself smaller and managed to lie down in the bunk beside him. He snugged her into the curve of his body. The warmth felt good, as did the gentle tickling as he toyed with one of her breasts. She should push his hand away, she knew. She should let this go no further than it had. Getting up and getting dressed and going back to the forecastle would be the wisest thing she could do. Getting up in the chill cabin and putting her cold wet clothes back on . . . She shivered and pressed against his warmth. He shifted to put both arms around her and hold her close. Safe.

"Why did she give you a wizardwood charm?" She could hear the reluctant curiosity in his voice.

"So I wouldn't get pregnant and shame my family. Or catch some disfiguring disease that would let all Bingtown know what a slut I was." She deliberately chose the hard word, spat it out at herself.

He froze for an instant, then soothed his hand down her back. Stroking her, then gently kneading at her shoulders and neck until she sighed and relaxed into him again. "It was my own fault," she heard herself say. "I should never have told her about it. But I was only fourteen and I felt like I had to tell someone. And I couldn't tell my father, not after he discharged Devon."

"Devon." He spoke the name, making it not quite a question.

She sighed. "It was before you came on board. Devon. He was a deckhand. So handsome, and always with a jest and a smile for anything, even misfortune. Nothing daunted him. He'd dare anything." Her voice trailed off. For a time she thought only of Brash's hand gently moving over her back, unknotting the muscles there as if he were untangling a line.

"That was where he and my father differed, of course. 'He'd be the best deckhand on this ship if he had common sense,' Papa once told me. 'And he'd make a good first, if he only knew when to get scared.' But Devon didn't sail like that. He was always complaining that we could carry more sail than we did, and when he worked aloft, he was always the fastest. I knew what my father meant. When the other men tried to keep up with him, for pride's sake, then work was done faster but not as thoroughly. Mistakes were made. And sailors got hurt. None seriously, but you know how my father was. He always said it was because the *Vivacia* was a liveship. He said accidents and deaths on board a liveship are bad for the ship; the emotions are too strong."

"I think he was right," Brashen said quietly. He kissed the back of her neck.

"I know he was," Althea said in mild annoyance. She sighed suddenly. "But I was fourteen. And Devon was so handsome. He had gray eyes. He'd sit about on deck after his watch was over, and whittle things for me and tell me stories of his wandering. It seemed like he'd been everywhere and done everything. He never exactly spoke against Papa, to me or to the rest of the crew, but you could always tell when he thought we were sailing too cautious. He'd get this disdainful little smile at the corner of his mouth. Sometimes just that look could make my father furious with him, but I'm afraid I thought it was adorable. Daring. Mocking danger." She sighed. "I believed he could do no wrong. Oh, I was in love."

"And he acted on that, when you were fourteen?" Brashen's voice was condemning. "On your father's ship? That's far past the line of daring, into stupidity."

"No. It wasn't like that." Althea spoke reluctantly. She didn't want to tell him any of this, yet somehow she could not stop. "I think he knew how I adored him, and he sometimes flirted with me, but in a joking way. So I could treasure his words, even as I knew he didn't mean them." She shook her head at herself. "But one night I got my chance. We were tied up at a dock in Lees. Quiet night. My father had gone into Lees on business, and most of the crew had liberty. I had the watch. I had had liberty earlier that day, and I'd gone into town and bought myself, oh, earrings, and some scent and a silk blouse and a long silk skirt. And I was wearing it all, all rigged out for him to see whenever he came back from the taverns. And when I saw him coming back to the ship early, by himself, my heart started hammering so hard I could barely breathe. I knew it was my chance.

"He came aboard with a bound, like he always did, landing on the deck like a cat and stood before me." She gave a snort of laughter. "You know, we must have talked, I must have said something, he must have said something. But I can't recall a word of it, only how happy I was to finally be able to tell him how much I loved him, with no need to be careful, for no one would overhear us. And he stood and grinned to hear me say it, as if he could not believe how fortune had favored him. And . . . he took my arm and walked me across the deck. He bent me over a hatch cover, and lifted my skirts and pulled down my knickers . . . and he took me right there. Bent over a hatch cover, like a boy."

"He raped you?" Brashen was aghast.

Althea choked back an odd laughter. "No. No, it wasn't rape. He didn't force me. I didn't know a thing about it, but I was sure I was in love. I went willingly, and I stood still for it. He wasn't rough, but he was thorough. Very thorough. And I didn't know what to expect, so I suppose I wasn't disappointed. And afterwards, he looked at me with that adorable grin and said, 'I hope you remember this the rest of your life, Althea. I promise I will.' " She took a deep breath. "Then he went below and came back up with his sea-bag all packed and left the ship. And I never saw him again." A silence stretched out. "I kept watching and waiting for him to come back. When we left port two days later, I found out Papa had fired him as soon as we had docked."

Brashen let out a low groan. "Oh, no." He shook his head. "Taking you was his revenge against your father."

She spoke slowly. "I never thought of it quite that way. I always thought that it was just something he dared to do, reckoning he wouldn't get caught." She forced herself to ask him, "You really think it was revenge?"

"Sounds like it to me," Brashen said quietly. "I think that's the worst thing I've ever heard," he added softly. "Devon. If I ever meet him, I'll kill him for you." The sincerity in his voice startled her.

"The worst was afterwards," she admitted to him. "We got to Bingtown a couple of weeks later. And I was sure I must be pregnant.

Just positive of it. Well, I dared not go to my father, and Mother wasn't much better. So I went to my married sister Keffria, sure that she could advise me. I swore her to silence and then I told her." Althea shook her head. She moved the cindin in her lip again. It had left a sore. The flavor was almost gone now.

"Keffria?" Brashen pushed her. He sounded as if he genuinely wanted to know the rest of the story.

"Was horrified. She started crying, and told me I was ruined forever. A slut and a whore and a shame to my family name. She stopped speaking to me. Four or five days later, my blood days came, right on time. I found her alone and told her, and told her if she ever told Papa or Mama, I'd say she was lying. Because I was so scared. From all she had said, I was sure that they'd throw me out and never love me again if they knew."

"Hadn't she promised not to tell?"

"I didn't trust her to keep her word. I was already pretty sure she'd told Kyle, from the way he started treating me. But she didn't yell at me or anything. She hardly spoke at all when she gave me the navel ring. Just told me that if I wore it, I wouldn't get pregnant or diseased, and that it was the least that I owed my family." Althea scratched the back of her neck, then winced. "It was never the same after that between us. We learned to be civil to one another, mostly to stop our parents from asking questions. But I think that was the worst summer of my life. Betrayal on top of betrayal."

"And after that, I suppose, you sort of did what you pleased with men?"

She should have known he'd want to know. Men always seemed to want to know. She shrugged, resigned to the whole truth. "Here and there. Not often. Well, only twice. I had a feeling that it hadn't been . . . done right. The way the men on the *Vivacia* talked, I suspected it should at least have been fun. It had just been . . . pressure, and a bit of pain, and wetness. That was all. So I finally got up my nerve and tried a couple more times, with different men. And it was . . . all right."

Brashen lifted his head to look into her eyes. "You call this 'all right'?"

Another truth she didn't want to part with. She felt like she was giving away a weapon. "This was not 'all right.' This has been what it was always supposed to be. It was never like this before for me." Then, because she could not bear the softness that had come into his eyes, she had to add. "Maybe it was the cindin." She fished the tiny fragment that was left out of her lip. "It made little sores inside my mouth," she complained and looked away from the small hurt on his face.

"Like as not, it was the cindin," he admitted. "I've heard it affects women that way, sometimes. Most women don't use it much you know, because it can, um, make you bleed. Even when it's not your time." He looked suddenly embarrassed.

"Now he tells me," she muttered aloud. His grip on her had loosened. The cindin was wearing off and she was suddenly sleepy. And her head had begun a nasty throbbing. She should get up. Cold room. Wet clothes. In a minute. In a minute, she'd have to get up and go back to being alone. "I have to go. If we get caught like this . . ."

"I know," he said, but he didn't move. Except to slide his hand in a long caress down her body. A shiver seemed to follow his touch.

"Brashen. You know this can't happen again."

"I know, I know." He breathed the words against her skin as he kissed the back of her neck slowly. "This can't happen again. No more. No more after this last time."

CHAPTER TWENTY-ONE

RONICA LOOKED UP FROM HER ACCOUNT LEDGERS WITH A SIGH. "YES? WHAT IS IT?"

Rache looked uneasy. "Delo Trell is in the sitting room."

Ronica raised her eyebrows. "Why?" Delo usually ran in and out as she wished. She and Malta had been best friends for at least two years now, and the formalities between the girls had eroded long ago.

Rache looked at the floor. "Her older brother is with her. Cerwin Trell." Rache hesitated.

Ronica frowned to herself. "Well, I can see him now, I suppose. Not here, put him in the morning room. Did he say what he wanted?"

Rache bit her lip for a moment. "I'm sorry, ma'am. He said he was here to call upon Malta. With his sister."

"What?" Ronica shot to her feet as if jabbed.

"I do not know your ways all that well, in this regard. But to me, it did not seem . . . correct. So I asked them to wait in the sitting room." Rache looked very uncomfortable. "I hope I have not caused an awkwardness."

"Don't worry about it," Ronica said crisply. "Malta invited this 'awkwardness.' But young Trell should have better manners as well. They are in the sitting room, you said?"

"Yes. Should I . . . bring refreshments?" The two women looked at one another. In the face of this social dilemma, the lines between mistress and servant were near invisible.

"I . . . yes. Thank you, Rache. You are correct. This is best handled with formality rather than scolding him like a rude boy. Even if that is how he has behaved." Ronica bit her lower lip for a moment. "Advise Keffria of this as well, and ask her to join us. Bring refreshments and serve them. Then, wait a bit before you tell Malta she has guests waiting. She has created this, she should witness how it is dealt with."

Rache took a breath, a soldier preparing for battle. "Very well."

After she had left the room, Ronica lifted her hands to her face and rubbed her eyes. She glanced back at the accounting ledgers she had set aside, and shook her head. Her eyes and head ached from poring over them anyway, and she had yet to find any way to make the debts on the pages any smaller or the credits any larger. This, at least would be a distraction. An unpleasant distraction from an impossible problem. Ah, well. She patted at her hair, then straightened her spine and headed towards the sitting room. If she hesitated, she'd lose her nerve. Cerwin Trell might be young, but he was also the heir to a powerful Trader family. She needed to put him in his place, but without direct insult. It would be a fine line to tread.

At the sitting room door she paused to take a breath and set her hand to the latch.

"Mother."

Ronica turned to see Keffria bearing down on her like a runaway horse. Small glints of anger shone in her usually docile eyes. Her lips were set in a firm line. Ronica could not recall having seen her daughter like this. She lifted a cautioning hand to her. "The Trell family is not to be offended," she reminded her very quietly. She saw Keffria hear her words, evaluate them, and set them aside.

"Neither are the Vestrits," she hissed in a low voice. The inflection was so like her father that it paralyzed Ronica. Keffria pushed open the door and preceded her into the room.

Cerwin looked up with a guilty start from where he perched on the edge of a divan. Even Delo looked startled. She cocked her head to peer past Keffria and Ronica.

Ronica spoke before Keffria could. "Malta will join us in a moment, Delo. I am sure your friend will be very happy to see you. And what a pleasure to have you call on us, Cerwin. It has been, oh, let's see. Why, do you know, I can't recall the last time you came to visit us."

Cerwin surged to his feet and bowed. He straightened and smiled, but not easily. "I believe my parents brought me to Keffria's wedding. Of course, that was some years back."

"About fifteen," Keffria observed. "You were an inquisitive little boy, as I recall. Didn't I catch you trying to grab the goldfish in the garden fountains?"

The boy was still standing. Ronica tried to recall his age. Eighteen? Nineteen? "I suppose you did. Yes, I do recall something of that. Of course, as you say, I was just a little boy then."

"That you were," Keffria replied before Ronica could speak. "And I would never blame a little child for seeing something bright and pretty and desiring to possess it." She smiled at Cerwin as she added, "And here is Rache with some refreshments for us. Do sit down and be comfortable."

Rache had brought coffee and small cakes and cream and spices on a tray. She set it up on a small table, and left the room. Keffria served them. For a time the only talk was whether or not cream and spices were preferred in the coffee. When all were served, Keffria seated herself and smiled round at their guests. Delo was sitting nervously on the edge of her seat, and she kept glancing towards the door. Ronica guessed she was hoping Malta would appear and take her out of the grown-up setting. At least, so she hoped.

Keffria immediately returned to her attack. "So. What does bring you calling here today, Cerwin?"

He met her eyes boldly, but his voice was soft as he said, "Malta invited me . . . us. I had taken Delo into the market for an afternoon of shopping. We chanced to meet Malta and we all took some refreshment together. And Malta extended to us an invitation to call on her at home."

"She did." Keffria's tone did not question his story. Ronica hoped her dismay did not show as plainly as her daughter's. "Well. The silly child never told us to expect you. But that is how girls are, I suppose, and Malta worse so than most. Her head is full of foolish fancies, I am afraid, and they crowd out all common sense and courtesy."

Ronica heard Keffria's words with half an ear. She was already wondering how often Malta had slipped away to market on her own, and if the meeting had truly been as chance as Trell made it sound. She looked at Delo speculatively; could the two girls have planned the "accidental" encounter?

As if on cue, Malta entered the room. She glanced around in consternation at them all taking refreshments together so socially. A sly wariness came over her face, very ugly to Ronica's eye. When had the girl become capable of such deliberate waywardness? It was plain she had hoped to greet Delo and Cerwin on her own. At least she did not appear to have expected them today. Although her hair was freshly brushed and there was a touch of paint on her lips, her dress at least was appropriate to a girl of her age. She wore a simple woolen shift, embroidered at the throat and hem. Yet there was something in the way she wore it, sashed tight to show her waist and pull the fabric firm against her rounding bosom that suggested there was a woman in the child's clothes. And Cerwin Trell had risen to his feet as if it were a young woman entering rather than a little girl.

This was worse than Ronica had feared.

"Malta," her mother greeted her. She smiled at her daughter. "Delo has come over to visit with you. But won't you have some cakes and coffee with us first?"

Delo's and Malta's eyes met. Delo swallowed and licked her lips. "And afterwards, perhaps you can show us the trumpet vine that you said was on bud." She cleared her throat and spoke louder than was needed as she added to Keffria, "Malta was telling us about your hothouse room when last we met. My brother is very interested in flowers."

Keffria smiled, a stretching of her lips. "Is he? Then he shall have a tour. Malta spends so little time in the flower rooms, I am surprised that she even recalled we had a trumpet vine. I shall show it to Cerwin myself. After all," and she turned the smile on Cerwin, "I can scarcely trust him alone with my goldfish, after what he tried the last time!"

Ronica almost felt sorry for the boy, as he forced a smile to his face and tried not to show his full understanding of her words.

"I am sure I would enjoy that very much, Keffria."

Ronica had expected to have to take control of this situation. But in this area, at least, Keffria seemed to have finally assumed her full role. Ronica said little other than courtesy talk as they finished the coffee and cakes. Instead, she watched. She was soon convinced that Malta and Delo were conspirators in this, with Delo far more uneasy and guilt stricken over it than Malta. Malta looked, if not at ease, at least determined. She focused herself and her conversation at Cerwin in a way he could not help but respond to. Cerwin himself seemed well aware of the impropriety of the situation, but like a mouse fascinated by a snake, he could not seem to recover himself from it. Instead he strove to remain focused on Keffria's stream of polite conversation, while Malta smiled at him over the rim of her coffee cup. Mentally, Ronica shook her head. Keffria had worried that Malta was too naïve to be brought into Bingtown society as a young woman, fearing that men might take advantage of her. The opposite was more likely true. Malta watched Cerwin with the avidity of a stalking cat. Deep in her heart, Ronica wondered which was more important to her; the man or the hunting of him. Cerwin was young, and from what little Ronica had seen of him, inexperienced in games such as these. If Malta won him too easily . . . and he showed little sign of resisting her attentions . . . then Malta might discard him for more challenging conquests.

Ronica was looking at her granddaughter with new eyes. What she saw there she found no more admirable in a woman than in a man. A little predator, she was. Ronica wondered if it were already too late to do anything about it. When had the pretty little girl metamorphosed into not a woman but a grasping, conquering female? She found herself thinking that perhaps it was just as well Kyle had drawn Wintrow back from the priesthood. If one of them must inherit the Vestrit Trader legacy, she would rather it went to him than to Malta as she was now.

Her thoughts turned to Wintrow. She hoped the boy was doing well. It would be more realistic, she knew, to hope he was surviving. There had been one message from the monastery. A certain Berandol had written to inquire after the boy, and ask when they might expect him to return. Ronica had turned the missive over to Keffria. Let her answer it as she saw fit.

There were times when Ronica wanted to punish Keffria savagely for not having the spine to stand up to Kyle. She wanted to force her to confront every bit of the pain that man had managed to cause in the few short months since Ephron had died. Wintrow had been virtually kidnapped and forced into slavery on his own family ship. Sa only knew what had become of Althea; sometimes that was the hardest for Ronica, to lie awake at night and wonder endlessly what had become of her wayward daughter. Did her body rot in a hasty grave somewhere? Did she live somewhere in Bingtown in dreadful circumstances, doing whatever she must to support herself? This last Ronica doubted. She had made too many inquiries and received not even a tidbit of gossip about her daughter. If Althea lived, she had left Bingtown. Under what circumstances, though?

Bingtown was no longer the civilized place it had been but five years ago. These newcomers had brought all sorts of vices with them, and very contagious attitudes toward both servants and women. The newcomers were mostly men. She did not know how they treated their women at home, but the women in their households now were servants only nominally different from slaves. And slaves were often treated as less than animals. The first time Ronica had seen a new-comer man strike one of his servants in the face right there in the market, she had been shocked. Not that the man had done it; there were ill-tempered tyrants among the Bingtown Traders as there were anywhere else, folk who lost their tempers with servants or kin and lashed out at them. Usually they ended up with what they deserved: servants who stole and lied and did as little as possible. But the servant in the market only cowered away from his master; he did not speak out at all, did not threaten to leave his employer or even complain it was an injustice. And somehow by not speaking out on his own behalf, he made it impossible for anyone else to object. One hesitated, won-dering, did he perhaps truly deserve the blow? Was he acknowledging his own fault in the matter by accepting it? And so no one else spoke out for the man.

Now it had evolved that there were two classes of servants in Bingtown. True servants, like Nana, paid a living wage and entitled to their own dignity and lives—for waiting on the Vestrits was only her job, not her life. And the newcomers' servants, who were no more than slaves, whose very existence was to please any whim of their owners. It was not legal, but how did one go about proving a man was a slave and not merely a servant? When asked, such servants immedi-ately and fearfully asserted they were, indeed, servants whose wages were sent home to their families. Many insisted they were content as they were, and had chosen their lives. It always made Ronica a bit queasy to wonder what threats held them in such abject fearfulness. Obviously the threats had been carried out more than once, for the slaves to so fear them.

"Good day, Ronica Vestrit."

She did not startle. She had that much poise. Cerwin was before her, nodding his head in a gentleman's bow to her. She nodded gravely in return. "Good day, Cerwin Trell. I hope you enjoy our garden room. And if you enjoy the trumpet vine, perhaps Keffria can give you a cutting from it. As harsh as it may seem, we cut ours back quite severely to encourage it to bloom and to have a graceful shape."

"I see," he said, and she was sure that he did. He thanked her and then followed Keffria from the room. Malta and Delo, heads together, followed them. Malta's pent frustration showed in her flared nostrils and flat lips. Clearly she had expected to get Cerwin alone, or at least in no more than the company of his sister. To what end? Probably the girl herself did not know.

Possibly that was the most frightening thing about all this; that Malta had flung herself into it so aggressively with so little knowledge of the consequences.

And whose fault was that, Ronica was forced to ask herself as she watched them go. The children had been growing up in her household. She had seen them often, at table, underfoot, in the gardens. And yet they had been, always, the children. Not tomorrow's adults, not small people growing towards what they must someday be, but the children. Selden. Where was Selden, at this moment, what was he doing? Probably with Nana, probably with his tutor, supervised and secure. But that was all she knew of him. A moment of panic washed over her. There was so little time, it might even now be too late to shape them. Look at her own daughters. Keffria, who only wanted someone to tell her what to do, and Althea, who only desired that she do her own will always.

She thought of the numbers on her ledgers, that no act of mere will could change. She thought of the debt she owed the Festrews of the Rain Wilds. Blood or gold, that debt was owed. In a sudden wrenching of her perceptions, it was not her problem. It was Selden's and it was Malta's, for were not they the blood that might pay the debt? And she had taught them nothing. Nothing.

"Mistress? Are you all right?"

She lifted her eyes to Rache. The woman had entered, gathered up the coffee things on a tray, then come to stand next to where her mistress stared black-eyed off into the distance. This woman, a servant-slave in her own house, entrusted with the teaching of her granddaughter. A woman she hardly knew at all. What did her mere presence in the household teach Malta? That slavery was to be accepted—was that the shape of things to come? What did that say to Malta about what it meant to be a woman in the Bingtown society to come?

"Sit down," she heard herself saying to Rache. "We need to talk. About my granddaughter. And about yourself."

"Jamaillia," said Vivacia softly.

The word woke him and he lifted his head from the deck where he'd been sleeping in the winter sunlight. The day was clear, neither cool nor warm, and the wind was leisurely. It was that hour of the afternoon designated for him to "pay attention to the ship," as his father so ignorantly put it. He had been sitting on the foredeck mending his trousers and quietly conversing with the figurehead. He did not recall lying down to sleep.

"I'm sorry," he said, rubbing his eyes.

"Don't be," the ship said simply. "Would that I could truly sleep as humans do, turning away from the day and all its cares. That one of us can is a blessing to us both. I only woke you because I thought you would enjoy seeing this. Your grandfather always said that this was the prettiest view of the city, out here where you cannot see any of its faults. There they are. The white spires of Jamaillia."

He stood, stretched and then stared out across the blue waters. The twin headlands reached out to surround the ship like welcoming arms. The city lined the coast between the steaming mouth of the Warm River and the towering peak of the Satrap's Mountain. Lovely mansions and estate gardens were separated from one another by belts of trees. On a ridge behind the city rose the towers and spires of the Satrap's Court. Commonly referred to as the "upper city," it was the heart of Jamaillia City. The capital city that gave its name to the whole satrapy, center of civilization, the cradle of all learning and art, glistened in the afternoon sunlight. Green and gold and white she shone, like a jewel in a setting. Her white spires soared higher than any tree, and so intensely white were they that Wintrow could not look at them without squinting. The spires were banded with gold, and the foundations of the buildings were rich green marble from Saden. For a time Wintrow gazed out on it hungrily, seeing for the first time what he had heard of so often.

Some five hundred years ago, most of Jamaillia had burned to the ground. The Satrap of that time had then decreed that his royal city would be rebuilt more magnificently than ever, and that all of the buildings should be of stone so that such a disaster could never befall Jamaillia again. He called together his finest architects and artists and stonemasons, and with their aid and three decades of work, the Court of the Satrap was raised. The next-to-highest white spire that pointed to the sky denoted the residence of the Satrap. The only spire that soared higher was that of the Satrap's Temple to Sa, where the Satrap and his Companions worshipped. For a time Wintrow gazed at it, filled with awe and wonder. To be sent to dwell in the monastery that served that temple was the highest honor to which a priest could aspire. The library alone filled seventeen chambers, and there were three scribing chambers where twenty priests were constantly employed in renewing or copying the scrolls and books. Wintrow thought of the amassed learning there, and awe filled him.

Then bitterness came to darken his soul. So, too, had Cress seemed fair and bright, but it had still been a city of greedy, grasping men. He turned his back on it and slid down to sit flat on the deck. "It's all a trick," he observed. "All a rotten trick men play on themselves. They get together and they create this beautiful thing and then they stand back and say, 'See, we have souls and insight and holiness and joy. We put it all in this building so we don't have to bother with it in our everyday lives. We can live as stupidly and brutally as we wish, and stamp down any inclination to spirituality or mysticism that we see in our neighbors or ourselves. Having set it in stone, we don't have to bother with it anymore.' It's a trick men play on themselves. Just one more way we cheat ourselves."

Vivacia spoke softly. If he had been standing, he might not have heard the words. But he was sitting, his palms flat to her deck, and so they rang through his soul. "Perhaps men are a trick Sa played on this world. 'All other things I shall make vast and beautiful and true to themselves,' perhaps he said. 'Men alone shall be capable of being petty and vicious and self-destructive. And for my cruelest trick of all, I shall put among them men capable of seeing these things in themselves.' Do you suppose that is what Sa did?"

"That is blasphemy," Wintrow said fervently.

"Is it? Then how do you explain it? All the ugliness and viciousness that is the province of humanity, whence comes it?"

"Not from Sa. From ignorance of Sa. From separation from Sa. Time and again I have seen children brought to the monastery, boys and girls with no hint as to why they are there. Angry and afraid, many of them, at being sent forth from their homes at such a tender age. Within weeks, they blossom, they open to Sa's light and glory. In every single child, there is at least a spark of it. Not all stay; some are sent home, not all are suited to a life of service. But all of them are suited to being creations of light and thought and love. All of them."

"Mm," the ship mused. "Wintrow, it is good to hear you speak as yourself again."

He permitted himself a small, bitter smile and rubbed at the knot of white flesh where his finger had been. It had become a habit, a small one that annoyed him whenever he became aware of it. As now. He folded his hands abruptly and asked, "Do I pity myself that much? And is it so obvious to all?"

"I am probably more sensitized to it than anyone else could be. Still. It is nice to jolt you out of it now and then." Vivacia paused. "Will you be going ashore, do you think?"

"I doubt it." Wintrow tried to keep the sulkiness from his voice. "I haven't touched shore since I 'shamed' my father in Cress."

"I know," the ship replied needlessly. "But, Wintrow, if you do go ashore, be careful of yourself."

"Why?"

"I don't know, exactly. I think it is what your great-great-grandmother would have called a premonition."

Vivacia sounded so unlike herself that Wintrow stood up and peered over the bow railing at her. She was looking up at him. Every time he thought he had become accustomed to her, there would be a moment like this. The light was unusually clear today, what Wintrow always thought of as an artist's light. Perhaps that accounted for how luminous she appeared to him. The green of her eyes, the rich gloss of her ebony hair, even her fine-grained skin shone with the best aspects of both polished wood and healthy flesh. She flushed pink to have him stare at her so, and in response to that he felt again the sudden collision of his love for her and his total benightedness as to what she truly was. It rocked him, as it always did. How could he feel this . . . passion, if he dared to use that word, for a creation of wood and magic? His love had no logical roots he could find . . . there was no prospect of marriage and children to share, no hunger for physical satiation in one another, there was no long history of shared experiences to account for the warmth and intimacy he felt with her. It made no sense.

"Is it so abhorrent to you?" she asked him in a whisper.

"It isn't you," he tried to explain. "It is that this feeling is so unnatural. It is like something imposed on me rather than something I truly feel. Like a magic spell," he added reluctantly. The followers of Sa did not deny the reality of magic. Wintrow had even seen it done, on rare occasions, small spells to cleanse a wound or spark a fire. But those were acts of a trained will coupled with a gift to have a physical effect. This sudden rush of emotion, triggered, as much as he could determine, solely by prolonged association, seemed to him something else entirely. He liked the *Vivacia*. He knew that, it made sense to him. He had many reasons to like the ship: she was beautiful and kind and sympathetic to him. She had intelligence, and watching her use that intelligence as she built chains of thought was a pleasure. She was like an untrained acolyte, open and willing to any teaching. Who would not like such a being? Logic told him he should like the ship, and he did. But that was separate from the wave of almost painful emotion that would sweep through him at odd moments like this. He would perceive her as more important than home and family, more important than his life at the monastery. At such moments, he could imagine no better end to his life than to fling himself flat upon her decks and be absorbed into her.

But no. The goal of a life lived well was to become one with Sa.

"You fear that I subvert the place of your god in your heart."

"I think that is almost what I fear," he agreed with her reluctantly. "At the same time, I do not think it is something that you, as Vivacia, impose upon me. I think it has to do with what a liveship is." He sighed. "If anyone consigned me to this, it was my own family, my great-great-grandmother when she saw fit to commission the building of a liveship. You and I, we are like buds grafted onto a tree. We can grow true to ourselves, but only so much as our roots will allow us."

The wind gusted up suddenly, as if welcoming the ship into the harbor. Wintrow stood and stretched. He was more aware of the differences in his body these days. He did not think he was getting any taller, but his muscles were definitely harder than they had been. A glimpse in a looking-glass the other day had shown him the roundness gone from his face. Changes. A leaner, fitter body and nine fingers to his hands. But they were still not enough changes to suit his father. When his fever had finally gone down and his hand was healing well, his father had summoned him. Not to tell him he'd been pleased by Wintrow's show of bravery or even to ask how his hand was. Not even to say he'd noticed his improved skills as a seaman. No. Only to tell him how stupid he had been, that he had had the chance in Cress to win the crew's approval and be seen as truly a part of them. And he had let it go by.

"It was a sham," he'd told his father. "The whole setup with the bear and the man who won were just a lure. I knew that right away."

"I know that!" his father had declared impatiently. "That's not the point. You didn't have to win, you idiot. Only to show them you have spunk. You thought to prove your courage by standing silent while Gantry cut off your finger. I know you did, don't deny it. Instead you only showed yourself as some sort of . . . religious freak. When they expected guts, you showed yourself a coward. And when any normal man would have cried out and cursed, you behaved like a fanatic. At the rate you're going, you'll never win this crew. You'll never be part of them, let alone a leader they respect. Oh, they may pretend to accept you, but it won't be real. They'll just be waiting for you to let your guard down, so they can really put it to you. And you know something? That's what you've earned from them. And damn me if I don't hope you get it!"

His father's words still echoed through him. In the long days that had passed since then, he had thought he sensed a grudging acceptance by the crew. Mild, as swift to forgive as he was to take offense, had been most quick to resume a tolerant attitude towards him. But Wintrow could no longer relax and accept it. Sometimes, at night, when he tried to reach for his old meditative states, he could convince himself that the situation was contrived. His father had poisoned his attitude towards the other crew members. His father did not wish to see them accept him; therefore he would see to it, however he could, that Wintrow remained an outcast. And that, he told himself as he painstakingly traced the convoluted logic of such insanity, was why he must never trust completely to the crew's acceptance and friendship. Because if he did, his father would find some way to turn them against him.

"Every day," he said quietly, "it becomes harder for me to know who I am. My father plants doubts and suspicions in me, the coarseness of life aboard this ship accustoms me to casual cruelty amongst my fellows and even you, even the hours I spend with you are shaping me, carrying me away from my priesthood. Towards something else. Something I don't think I want to be."

These words were hard for him to speak. They hurt him as much as they hurt her. That was the only thing that let her keep silent.

"I don't think I can stand it much longer," he warned her. "Something will have to give way. And I fear it will be me." He met her eyes unflinchingly. "I've just been living from day to day. Waiting for something or someone else to change the situation." His eyes studied her face, looking for a reaction to his next words. "I think I need to make a real decision. I believe I need to take action on my own."

He waited for her to say something, but she could think of no words. What was he hinting he might do? What could the boy do against his father's dominance?

"Hey, Wintrow! Lend a hand!" someone shouted down to the deck.

The call back to drudgery. "I have to go," he told Vivacia. He took a deep breath. "Right or wrong, I've come to love you. But—" He shook his head, suddenly wordless.

"Wintrow! Now!"

Like a well-trained dog, he sprang to obey. She watched him scamper up the rigging with familiar ease. That facility told as much as his words did of his love for her. He still complained, and often. He still suffered the torments of a divided heart. But when he gave words to his unhappiness they could discuss it and both learn more of one another in the process. He thought now that he could not bear it, but she knew the truth. Inside him was strength, and he would bear up despite unhappiness. Eventually they would be whole, the both of them. All that they needed was time. She had known ever since that first night together that he was truly destined to be aboard her. It was not easy for him to accept. He had struggled long against the idea. But even in his defiant words today, she sensed a pending resolution to that struggle. Her patience would be rewarded.

She looked about the harbor with new eyes. In many ways, Wintrow was absolutely correct about the city's underlying corruption. Not that she would want to reinforce that with the boy. He needed no help from her to be gloomy. Better for Wintrow that he focus his thoughts on what was clean and good about Jamaillia. The harbor was lovely in the winter sunlight.

She did and yet did not recall it all. Ephron's memory of it was a man's view, not a ship's. He had focused on the docks and merchants awaiting his trade goods, and the architectural wonder of the city above them. Ephron had never noticed the curling tendrils of filthy water bleeding into the harbor from the city's sewers. Nor could he have smelt with every pore of his hull the underlying stench of serpent. Her eyes skimmed the placid waters but there was no sight of the cunning, evil creatures. They were below, worming about in the soft bottom muck of the harbor. Some foreboding made her swing her gaze to the section of the harbor where the slavers anchored. Their foul stench came to her in hints on the wind. The smell of serpent was mixed with that of death and feces. That was where the creatures coiled thickest, over there beneath those miserable ships. Once she was unloaded and refitted for her new trade, she would be anchored alongside them, taking on her own load of misery and despair. Vivacia crossed her arms and held herself. Despite the sunny day, she shivered. Serpents.

Ronica sat in the study that had once been Ephron's and was now slowly becoming hers. It was in this room that she felt closest to him still, and in this room that she missed him most. In the months since his death, she had gradually cleared away the litter of his life, replacing it with the untidy scattering of her own bits of papers and trifles. Yet Ephron was still there in the bones of the room. The massive desk was far too large for her, and sitting in his chair made her feel like a small child. Oddities and ornaments of his far-ranging voyages characterized this room. A massive sea-washed vertebra from some immense sea creature served as a footstool, while one wall shelf was devoted to carved figurines, sea shells and strange body ornaments from distant folk. It was an odd intimacy to have her ledgers scattered across the polished slab of his desk top, to have her teacup and discarded knitting draped on the arm of his chair by his fireplace.

As she often did when perplexed, she had come here to think and try to decide what Ephron would have counseled her. She was curled on the divan on the opposite side of the fireplace, her slippers discarded on the floor. She wore a soft woolen robe, well worn from two years' use. It was as comfortable as her seat. She had built the fire herself, and kindled it and watched it burn through its climax. Now the wood was settling, glowing against itself, and she was relaxed and warm but seemed no closer to an answer of any kind.

She had just decided that Ephron would have shrugged his shoulders and delegated the problem back to her, when she heard a tap at the heavy wood-paneled door.

"Yes?"

She had expected Rache, but it was Keffria who entered. She wore a night-robe and her heavy hair was braided and coiled as for sleep, but she carried a tray with a steaming pot and heavy mugs on it. Ronica smelled coffee and cinnamon.

"I had given up on your coming."

Keffria didn't directly answer that. "I decided that as long as I couldn't sleep, I might as well be really awake. Coffee?"

"Actually, that would be good."

This was the sort of peace they had found, mother and daughter. They talked past one another, asking no questions save regarding food or some other trifle. Keffria and Ronica both avoided anything that might lead to a confrontation. Earlier, when Keffria had not come as invited, Ronica had assumed that was why. Bitterly she had reflected that Kyle had taken both her daughters from her: driven the one away and walled the other up. But now she was here, and Ronica found herself suddenly determined to regain at least something of her daughter. As she took the heavy steaming mug from Keffria, she said, "I was impressed by you today. Proud."

A bitter smile twisted Keffria's face. "Oh, I was, too. I single-handedly triumphed in defeating the conniving plot of a sly thirteen-year-old girl." She sat down in her father's chair, kicked off her slippers and curled her feet up under her. "Rather a hollow victory, Mother."

"I raised two daughters," Ronica pointed out gently. "I know how painful victory can be sometimes."

"Not over me," Keffria said dully. There was self-loathing in her tone as she added, "I don't think I ever gave you and Father a sleepless night. I was a model child, never challenging anything you told me, keeping all the rules, and earning the rewards of such virtue. Or so I thought."

"You were my easy daughter," Ronica conceded. "Perhaps because of that, I under-valued you. Over-looked you." She shook her head to herself. "But in those days, Althea worried me so that I seldom had a moment to think of what was going right . . ."

Keffria exhaled sharply. "And *you* didn't know the half of what she was doing! As her sister, I . . . but in all the years, it hasn't changed. She still worries us, both of us. When she was a little girl, her willfulness and naughtiness always made her Papa's favorite. And now that he has gone, she has disappeared, and so managed to capture your heart as well, simply by being absent."

"Keffria!" Ronica rebuked her for the heartless words. Her sister was missing, and all she could be was jealous of Ronica worrying about her? But after a moment, Ronica asked hesitantly, "You truly feel that I give no thoughts to you, simply because Althea is gone?"

"You scarcely speak to me," Keffria pointed out. "When I muddled the ledger books for what I had inherited, you simply took them back from me and did them yourself. You run the household as if I were not here. When Cerwin showed up on the doorstep today, you charged directly into battle, only sending Rache to tell me about it as an afterthought. Mother, were I to disappear as Althea has, I think the household would only run more smoothly. You are so capable of managing it all." She paused and her voice was almost choked as she added, "You leave no room for me to matter." She hastily lifted her mug and took a long sip of the steaming coffee. She stared deep into the fireplace.

Ronica found herself wordless. She drank from her own mug. She knew she was making excuses when she said, "But I was always just waiting for you to take things over from me."

"And always so busy holding the reins that you had no time to teach me how. 'Here, give me that, it's easier if I just do it myself.' How many times have you said that to me? Do you know how stupid and helpless it always made me feel?" The anger in her voice was very old.

"No," Ronica said quietly. "I didn't know that. But I should have. I really should have. And I am sorry, Keffria. Truly sorry."

Keffria snorted out a sigh. "It doesn't really matter, now. Forget it." She shook her head, as if sorting through things she could say to find the words she must. "I'm taking charge of Malta," she said quietly. She glanced up at her mother as if expecting opposition. Ronica only looked at her. She took a deeper breath. "Maybe you doubt that I can do it. I know I doubt it. But I know I'm going to try. And I wanted to ask you . . . No. I'm sorry, but I have to tell you this. Don't interfere. No matter how rocky or messy it gets. Don't try to take it away from me because it's easier to do it yourself."

Ronica was aghast. "Keffria, I wouldn't."

Keffria stared into the fire. "Mother, you would. Without even knowing you were, just as you did today. I took what you had set up, and handled it from there. But left to myself, I would not have called Malta down at all. I would have told Cerwin and Delo that she was out or busy or sick, and sent them politely on their way, without giving Malta the chance to simper and flirt."

"That might have been better," Ronica conceded in a low voice. Her daughter's words hurt. She had only been trying to think swiftly and handle things quickly to prevent a disaster. But although her daughter's words stung, she could also hear the truth of them. So she closed her lips tightly and took a sip of her coffee. "May I know what you plan?" she asked after a few moments.

"I scarcely know myself," Keffria admitted. "She is so far gone, and she has so little respect for me . . . I may not be able to do anything with her. But I have a few ideas of ways to begin. I'm going to take Rache away from her. No more dance or etiquette lessons unless she earns them. If and when they resume, she will have to extend to Rache the same courtesy and respect that Selden gives his tutor. The lessons will be at a set time every day, not whenever Malta is bored and wishes a diversion. If she misses one, she will have to earn the time back with chores." Keffria took a breath. "I intend that she will only earn the privileges of a woman by doing the work of a woman. So." She took a breath and then met her mother's eyes. "I am taking back my ledger books from you. I will not let Malta grow up as ignorant as I am. Malta is going to have to spend some time reconciling the ledgers every week. I know she will blot them and spoil pages and make mistakes and copy pages over. We will both have to endure that, as will she. She will have to enter the numbers and tot them up. And she . . . we, that is . . . will have to accompany you when you meet with the brokers and the tradesmen and the overseers. She needs to learn how the estates and trading accounts are handled."

Again Keffria paused, as if waiting to deal with an objection. Ronica said nothing.

"She will, of course, have to behave well at those times. And dress as befits a girl who is becoming a woman. Not cheaply and suggestively, but not childishly, either. She will need some new clothing. I intend that she shall share in the making of it. And that she will learn to prepare food, and supervise the servants."

Ronica nodded gravely each time Keffria added another task to those Malta must learn. When she finally paused, her mother spoke. "I think you have made wise plans, and Malta can benefit greatly from what you propose to teach her. But I do not think she will come willingly to this. It is not fashionable at all for a woman to know how to do such things, let alone to actually do them. In fact, Bingtown now sees such behavior as plebeian. It will hurt her pride to do it. I doubt she will be a willing student."

"No. She will not," Keffria concurred. "And that is why I have yet another task. Mother, I know you will not agree with this, but I think it is the only way to rein her to my will. Not a coin must she be given to spend on her own, save that it comes from me. I will have to instruct the shopkeepers and tradesmen that they are no longer to extend her the family's credit. It will be humiliating to do, but . . ." she paused as if considering. "Yes. I will widen that to include Selden as well. I suppose it is not too early to begin with him. Perhaps I should never have allowed Malta to have so easily whatever she desired."

To this Ronica nodded, suppressing a heartfelt sigh of relief. There were already on the desk a handful of chits with Malta's imprint on them, for sweets and baubles and outrageously priced perfumes. Malta's casual spending had not been easy to allow for, but it was yet another thing that Ronica had been unwilling to bring up to Keffria. Now she honestly wondered why. "She is your daughter," Ronica added. "But I fear this will not be easy, on any of us. And," she added unwillingly, "there is yet another thing she must be taught about. Our contract with the Festrew family."

Keffria raised one eyebrow. "But I am married," she pointed out.

Ronica felt a sudden pang of sympathy for her daughter. She recalled how she had felt, the first time she realized that her growing daughters were now vulnerable to a bargain struck generations ago. "That you are," she agreed quietly. "And Althea is missing. And our debts grow faster far than our credits. Keffria, you must recall the terms of the Vestrit bargain. Blood or gold. Once Malta is presented to Bingtown society as a woman, then she is forfeit to the Festrews, if we do not have the gold to make the payment. And," she added unwillingly, "at the midsummer, I was short. I have promised to pay it in full by midwinter, plus a penalty." She could not find the courage to admit to her daughter what a large penalty she had accepted. "If not," she went on with difficulty, "Caolwn Festrew may invoke her right to claim blood from us. Althea, if she is found by then. Malta, if she is not."

Ronica could find no more words. She watched understanding and horror grow in Keffria's eyes. Followed, inevitably, by anger. "It is not fair. I never agreed to such a bargain! How can Malta be forfeit to a contract signed generations before she was born? It makes no sense, it isn't fair!"

Ronica gave her a moment or two. Then she said the words familiar to any Trader's daughter or son. "It's Trader. Not fair, always; not right, always. Sometimes not even understandable. But it's Trader. What did we have when we came to the Cursed Shores? Only ourselves, and the value of a man's word. Or a woman's. We pledged our loyalty to each other, not just for the day or the year, but to all generations. And that is why we have survived here where no others had before. We pledged ourselves to the land, also, and to what it demands. That, I imagine, is another topic you have not yet discussed with Malta. You should, and soon, for you know that she must have heard rumors."

"But . . . she is only a child," Keffria pleaded. As if by agreeing with her, her mother could somehow change the facts that time had imposed on them.

"She is," Ronica agreed carefully. "But only for a short time longer. And she must be prepared."

PLOTS AND PERILS

S O. IT DIDN'T WORK OUT QUITE AS CAPTAIN KENNIT THE PIRATE KING HAD PLANNED, DID IT?"

"Shut up." Kennit spoke more in weariness than rancor. It had been a distressing and taxing day. They had sighted a liveship, a wide-bellied merchant-trader of the old style, a wallowing sow of a ship. She had been quite a way ahead of them, picking her way through the shallows of Wrong Again channel. She sat deep in the water, heavy with some rich cargo. At the very least, they should have been able to force her to run aground. The *Marietta* had put on sail and swept up on her, close enough to hear the figurehead calling out the soundings and headings to the steersman. They came close enough to see the faces of the men that manned her, close enough to hear their cries as they recognized his Raven flag and shouted encouragement to one another. Sorcor launched his balls-and-chains at their rigging, only to have the ship sidle aside from it at the last moment. In fury, Kennit called for fire-balls, and Sorcor reluctantly complied. One of them struck well, splattering on a sail that obligingly burst into flames. But almost as swiftly as the flames ran up the canvas, the sail collapsed on itself, billowing down to where a frantic crew could trample it and douse it with water. And with every passing moment, somehow, impossibly, the liveship pulled steadily away from them.

Kennit had shrieked at his crew like a madman, demanding canvas, oars, anything they might muster to push a bit more speed out of the ship. But as if the very gods opposed him, a winter squall blew in, one of the horrible island squalls that sent the winds racketing in every possible direction. Gray rain sheeted down, blinding them. He cursed, and climbed the mast himself, to try to keep sight of her. His every sense strained after her, and time after time, he caught glimpses of her. Each time she had been farther ahead of him. She swept around a headland, and when the *Marietta* rounded it, the liveship was gone. Simply gone.

Now it was evening, the night wind filled the *Marietta*'s sails and the monotonous rains had ceased. His crew was tip-toeing around him, unaware that his seething displeasure with them had boiled itself dry. He stood on the afterdeck, watching witch-fire dance in their wake, and sought some inner peace.

"I suppose this means you owe Sorcor another slaver, doesn't it?" the charm observed affably.

"I wonder, if I cut you from my wrist and threw you overboard, would you float?"

"Let's find out," the small face suggested agreeably.

Kennit sighed. "The only reason I continue to tolerate you is because you cost me so much in the first place."

The twin countenance pursed his lips at him. "I wonder if you shall say that of the whore, also, in days to come."

Kennit clenched his eyes shut. "Cannot you be silent and leave me alone for even a moment?"

A soft step and the whisper of brushing fabric on the deck behind him. "Did you speak to me?" Etta asked.

"No."

"I thought you said something . . . you wished to be alone? I can return to the cabin, if you like." She paused, and added more softly, "But I would much prefer to join you, if it would please you."

Her perfume had reached him now. Lavender. Irresolution assailed him and he turned his head to regard her. She curtsied low to him, a lady greeting her lord.

"Oh, please," he growled in disbelief.

"Thank you," she replied warmly. Her slippered feet pattered softly across the deck and Etta was suddenly beside him. She did not touch him. Even now, she knew better than to be that familiar. Nor did she lean casually on the rail beside him. Instead, she stood, her back straight, a single hand resting upon the rail. And she looked at him. After a time, he could not stand it. He turned his head to meet her stare.

And she smiled at him. Radiantly. Luminously.

"Lovely," breathed the small voice at his wrist. And Kennit had to concur. Etta lowered her eyes and looked aside from him, as if momentarily shy or confused. She wore yet another new costume. The sailor who had brought her aboard had followed his original directive, supplying her with a tub of warm water for bathing, but had been at a loss as to what to provide her to wear. Clearly rough sailor's clothing would not do for his captain's lady. With a great deal of trepidation, he had laid out the captain's own night-robe for her, and then hesitantly offered her several bolts of rich cloth from their latest trove. Kennit had at first been disgruntled at this largesse, but then resigned to it. Needles and thread were always plentiful aboard a sailing ship, and Etta had kept herself well occupied with her sewing tasks. Kennit eventually concluded that the man had actually been brilliant. While the woman was occupied with needlework, she could not bother him. The clothing Etta styled for herself was unlike anything Kennit had ever before seen on a woman, and actually quite sensible for shipboard life.

Not that he was resigned to her living aboard the ship. He had simply not yet found a good place to stash her. It was convenient to him that she was an adaptable sort. Not once had she complained since he had brought her aboard. Unless one counted the second day, when she stormed the galley and upbraided the cook for over-salting the stew he had sent to Kennit's table. As often as not she now oversaw the preparation of their cabin-served meals. And perhaps the food had improved as a result of that.

But she was still a whore, he reminded himself. Despite her crown of sleek short hair that caught the ship's lights and returned it as sheen, despite the emerald-green silk of her loose-sleeved blouse, or the brocaded trousers she tucked it into, despite the cloth-of-gold sash that narrowed her lean waist, she was still just his whore. Even if a tiny ruby twinkled in her ear-lobe, and a lush fur-lined cloak sheltered her body from the night wind.

"I have been thinking about the liveship that eluded you today," she dared to say. She lifted her eyes to his, dark eyes too bold for his taste. She seemed to sense that, for she cast them down again, even before he barked, "Don't speak to me of that."

"I won't," she promised him gently. But after a moment, she broke her word, as women always did. "The swiftness of a willing liveship is legendary," she said quietly. She stared out at their wake and spoke to the night. "I know next to nothing of piracy," she next admitted. As if that might surprise him. "But I wonder if the very willingness of the ship to flee swiftly might not be somehow turned against it."

"I fail to see how," Kennit sneered.

She licked her lips before she spoke, and for just an instant, his whole attention was caught by that tiny movement of wet pink tongue-tip. An irrational surge of desire flamed up in him. Damn her. This constant exposure to a woman was not good for a man. He breathed out, a low sound.

She gave him a quick sideways glance. If he had been certain it was amusement at him that curved the corners of her lips, he would have slapped her. But she spoke only of piracy. "A rabbit kills itself when it runs headlong into the snare," she observed. "If one knew the planned course of a liveship, and if one had more than one pirate vessel at one's disposal . . . why, then, a single ship could give chase, and urge the liveship to run headlong into an ambush." She paused and cast her eyes down to the water again. "I am told that it can be quite difficult to stop a ship, even if the danger ahead is seen. And it seems to me there are many narrow channels in these waters, where a sailing ship would have no alternative but to run aground to avoid a collision."

"I suppose it might be done, though it seems to me that there are a great many 'ifs' involved. It would require precisely the right circumstances."

"Yes, I suppose it would," she murmured. She gave her head a small shake to toss the hair back from her eyes. Her short sleek hair was perfectly black, as the night sky is black between the stars. He need not fear to kiss her; she had no man save him these days. She saw him watching her. Her eyes widened and suddenly she breathed more quickly and deeply. He abruptly matched his body to hers, pinning her against the rail, mastering her. He forced her mouth open to his, felt the small, hard nipples of her slight breasts through the thin, body-warmed silk of her blouse. He lifted his mouth from hers.

"Never," he said roughly, "presume to tell me my business. I well know how to get what I want. I need no woman to advise me."

Her eyes were full of the night. "You know very well," she agreed with him huskily.

.   .   .

He heard them long before they reached him. He knew it was full dark night, for the evening birds had ceased their calls hours ago. From the damp that beaded him, he suspected there was a dense fog tonight. So Paragon waited with trepidation, wondering why two humans would be picking their way down the beach toward him in the dark and fog. He could not doubt that he was their destination; there was nothing else on this beach. As they drew closer, he could smell the hot oil of a burning lantern. It did not seem to be doing them much good, for there had been frequent small curses as they worked their stumbling way towards him. He already knew one was Mingsley. He was coming to know that man's voice entirely too well.

Perhaps they were coming to set fire to him. He had taunted Mingsley the last time he was here. Perhaps the man would fling the lantern at him. The glass would break and flaming oil would splash over him. He'd die here, screaming and helpless, a slow death by fire.

"Not much farther," Paragon heard Mingsley promise his companion.

"That's the third time you've said that," complained another voice. His accent spoke of Chalced even more strongly than Mingsley's did of Jamaillia. "I've fallen twice, and I think my knee is bleeding. This had damn well better be worth it, Mingsley."

"It is, it is. Wait until you see it."

"In this fog, we won't be able to see a thing. Why couldn't we come by day?"

Did Mingsley hesitate in his reply? "There has been some bad feeling about town; the Old Traders don't like the idea of anyone not an Old Trader buying a liveship. If they knew you were interested . . . well. I've had a few not-so-subtle warnings to stay away from here. When I ask why, I get lies and excuses. They tell me no one but a Bingtown Trader can own a liveship. You ask why, you'll get more lies. Goes against all their traditions, is what they'd like you to believe. But actually, there's a great deal more to it than that. More than I ever suspected when I first started negotiating for this. Ah! Here we are! Even damaged, you can see how magnificent he once was."

The voices had grown closer as Mingsley was speaking. A sense of foreboding had been growing within Paragon, too, but his voice was steady as he boomed out, "Magnificent? I thought 'ugly' was the word you applied to me last time."

He had the satisfaction of hearing both men gasp.

Mingsley's voice was none too steady as he attempted to brag, "Well, we should have expected that. A liveship is, after all, alive." There was a sound of metal against metal. Paragon guessed that a lantern had been unhooded to shed more light. The smell of hot oil came more strongly. Paragon shifted uneasily, crossing his arms on his chest. "There, Firth. What do you think of him?" Mingsley announced.

"I'm . . . overwhelmed," the other man muttered. There was genuine awe in his voice. Then he coughed and added, "But I still don't know why we're out here and at night. Oh, I know a part of it. You want my financial backing. But just why should I help you raise three times what a ship this size would cost us for a beached derelict with a chopped-up figurehead? Even if it can talk."

"Because it's made of wizardwood." Mingsley uttered the words as if revealing a well-kept secret.

"So? All liveships are," Firth retorted.

"And why is that?" Mingsley added in a voice freighted with mystery. "Why build a ship of wizardwood, a substance so horrendously expensive it takes generations to pay one off? Why?"

"Everyone knows why," Firth grumbled. "They come to life and then they're easier to sail."

"Tell me. Knowing that about wizardwood, would you rush to commit your family's fortunes for three or four generations, just to possess a ship like this?"

"No. But Bingtown Traders are crazy. Everyone knows that."

"So crazy that every damn family of them is rich," Mingsley pointed out. "And what makes them rich?"

"Their damn monopolies on the most fascinating trade goods in the world. Mingsley, we could have discussed economics back at the inn, over hot spiced cider. I'm cold, the fog has soaked me through, and my knee is throbbing like I'm poisoned. Get to the point."

"If you fell on barnacles, likely you are poisoned," Paragon observed in a booming voice. "Likely it will swell and fester. He's lined you up for at least a week of pain."

"Be quiet!" Mingsley hissed.

"Why should I?" Paragon mocked him. "Are you that nervous about being caught out here, tinkering with what doesn't concern you? Talking about what you can never possess?"

"I know why you won't!" Mingsley suddenly declared. "You don't want him to know, do you? The precious secret of wizardwood, you don't want that shared, do you? Because then the whole stack of blocks comes tumbling down for the Bingtown Traders. Think about it, Firth. What is the whole of Bingtown founded on, really? Not some ancient grant from the Satrap. But the goods that come down the Rain Wild River, the really strange and wondrous stuff from the Rain Wild themselves."

"He's getting you in deeper than you can imagine," Paragon warned Firth loudly. "Some secrets aren't worth sharing. Some secrets have prices higher than you'll want to pay."

"The Rain Wild River, whose waters run cold and then hot, brown and then white. Where does it really come from, that water? You've heard the same legends I have, of a vast smoking lake of hot water, the nesting grounds of the firebirds. They say the ground there trembles constantly and that mist veils the land and water. That is the source of the Rain Wild River . . . and when the ground shakes savagely, then the river runs hot and white. That white water can eat through the hull of any ship almost as swiftly as it eats through the flesh and bones of a man. So no one can go up the Rain Wild River to trade. You can't trek up the banks either. The shores of the river are treacherous bogs, the hanging vines drip scalding acid, the sap of the plants that grow there can raise welts on a man's flesh that burn and ooze for days."

"Get to the point," Firth urged Mingsley angrily, even as Paragon shouted, "Shut up! Close your foul mouth! And get away from my beach. Get away from me. Or come close enough to be killed by me. Yes. Come here, little man. Come to me!" He reached out blindly, swinging his arms wide, his hands open to grasp.

"Unless you have a liveship." Mingsley revealed. "Unless you have a liveship, hulled with wizardwood, impervious to the hot white water of the river. Unless you have a liveship, who knows from the moment it is quickened the one channel up the river. That is the true source of the Bingtown monopoly on the trade. You have to have a liveship to get in the game." He paused dramatically. "And I'm offering you the chance to get one."

"He's lying," Paragon shouted desperately. "Lying! There's more to it, so much more to it. And even if you owned me, I wouldn't sail for you. I'd roll and kill you all! I've done it before, you've heard the tales. And if you haven't, ask in any tavern. Ask about the *Paragon*, the *Pariah*, the death ship! Go ahead, ask, they'll tell you. They'll tell you I'll kill you!"

"He can be forced," Mingsley said with quiet confidence. "Or removed. The hull is what is most important, a good riverman could sound us out a channel. Think what we could do with a wizardwood ship. There's some tribe up there that the Bingtown Traders traffic with. One trip would be all it would take. Firth, we could pay them double what the Old Traders pay them, and still make a profit. This is our chance to get in on a trade that's been closed to outsiders since Bingtown was founded. I've got the contacts, the owners are listening for the right cash offer. All I need is the backing. And you've got that."

"He's lying to you," Paragon bellowed out into the night. "He's going to get you killed. And worse! Much worse. There are worse things than dying, you Chalcedean scum. But only a Bingtown Trader would know that. Only a Bingtown Trader could tell you that."

"I think I'm interested," Firth said quietly. "But there are better places to discuss this."

"No!" howled Paragon. "You don't know what he's selling you, you don't know what grief you'd be buying. You've no idea, no idea at all!" His voice broke suddenly. "I won't go with you, I won't, I won't. I don't want to, and you can't make me, you can't, I'll kill you, I'll kill you all!"

Again he flailed out wildly. If he had been able to reach the beach, he would have thrown sand, rocks, seaweed, anything. But his hands found nothing. He halted suddenly, listening. The footsteps were receding.

". . . tell anyone?"

"Not a concern, really," he heard Mingsley reply confidently. "You heard him. He's mad, completely insane. No one listens to him. No one even comes out here. Even if he had someone to tell, they'd never believe him. That's the beauty of this, my friend. It's so far outside of any one else's imagining. That ship has rested there for years. Years! And no one ever thought of this before . . ."

His voice dwindled, and was damped away by the muffling fog and the shush of the waves.

"NO!" Paragon shrieked out into the night. He reached back with his fists to drum and batter on his own planking. "No!" he cried again. Denial and defiance. And hopelessness. They weren't listening to him. No one ever listened to him. That had always been the problem. They'd ignore everything he told them. They'd take him out and he'd have to kill them all. Again.

"Serpent!"

Althea's voice rang out clear and cold as the night that surrounded them. She clung with near-numbed fingers, her feet braced against the look-out's platform. Her eyes strained through the darkness to track the creature even as she heard the thundering of the crew's feet on the deck below, heard her cry passed on. Hatches were flung open as all hands hit the decks to do whatever they could do to withstand this latest attack.

"Where?"

"Three points off the starboard bow, sir! A big one."

They were all big, she reflected bitterly as she strove to tighten her weary grip. She was cold and wet and tired, and the healing injury on her scalp still throbbed all the time. In the cold of a night like this, the throbbing became a dull agony as the chill tightened her skin. The fever had passed days ago, and Reller had snipped and tugged the stitches out when the itching had become unbearable. Reller's clumsiness and coarse jokes about her pain were infinitely preferable to the guarded tenderness she saw in Brashen's eyes whenever she chanced to be near him. Damn him. And damn him again, for here she was thinking of him when her very life depended on her focusing her mind on her task. Where had the serpent gone? One moment she had seen it, and now it was gone.

In answer to her question, the ship gave a sudden starboard lurch. Her feet slid on her ice-rimed perch, and she found her life depending on the clutch of her numbed fingers. Without even thinking, she wrapped her arm about a line and held on. On the deck below she could hear Captain Sichel cursing and demanding that the hunters do something, shoot the damned thing before it took them all to the bottom! But even as the hunters with bows drawn ran to one side of the ship, the serpent had doubled back and nudged them from the other side. It was not a sharp impact like being rammed. It was a strong upward push, like a shark nosing a dead carcass floating on the water. The ship heeled over and men scrabbled across the decks.

"Where is it?" the captain demanded furiously as Althea and the other look-outs strained their eyes into the darkness. The cold wind streamed past her, the waves heaved and she saw serpents in the curve of every swell. They dissolved into fear and imagination when she tried to focus on them.

"He's gone!" one of the other look-outs cried, and Althea prayed he was right. This had gone on too long, too many days and nights of sudden random attacks followed by anxious hours of ominous cessation. Sometimes the serpents crested and writhed alongside the ship, always just out of reach of a bowshot. Sometimes there were half a dozen, hides scintillating in the winter sun, reflecting blue and scarlet and gold and green. And sometimes, like tonight, there would be but one monstrous creature, coming to mock them by effortlessly toying with their lives. Sighting serpents was nothing new to Althea. Once, they had been so rare as to be legendary; now they infested certain areas on the Outside, and followed slave ships through the Inside Passage. She'd seen a few in her time aboard the *Vivacia*, but always at a distance and never threatening. This proximity to their savagery made them seem new creatures.

Between one breath and the next, the ship heeled over. Hard. The horizon swung and suddenly Althea's feet were flung from under her. For an instant she flapped from the spar like a flag. On the canted deck below sailors roared and flailed wildly as they slid and tumbled. She hitched her belly tight and kicked up a foot to catch a ratline. In a moment she was secure again even as the ship tilted further. The serpent had come up under the ship, and lifted it high to roll her hard to starboard. "Hang on!" someone roared, and then she heard a shrill cry cut short. "He took him!" someone shrieked, and the cry was followed by a confusion of voices, demanding of one another, "Did you see that? Who did he get? Picked him off like a ripe plum! That's what this thing is after!" The ship righted itself and through the chaos of voices, she clearly heard Brashen cursing. Then, "Sir!" His voice rang desperate in the night. "Can we not put some hunters on the stern, to keep him off our rudder? If he takes that out . . ."

"Do it!" the captain barked.

There was the clatter of running feet. Althea clung to her perch dizzily, feeling sick not with the sudden lurching of the ship but from the abruptness of death that had visited them. The serpent would be back, she was certain. He would rock the ship like a boy shaking cherries from a tree. She didn't think the beast was powerful enough to overturn the ship completely, but she was not certain. Land had never seemed so far away. Land, solid land, that could not shift beneath her, that did not conceal ravenous monsters who could erupt at any time.

She remained at her post, hating that she could not see what was happening on the deck right below her. She did not need to know, she reminded herself. What she did need to do was keep good watch and cry a warning that might save a man's life. Her eyes were weary from peering into the darkness, her hands no more than icy claws. The wind snatched the warmth from her body. But, she reminded herself, it also filled the sails and pushed the ship on. Soon, they would be out of these serpent-infested waters. Soon.

The night deepened around the ship. Clouds obscured both moon and stars. The only light in the world was that of the ship herself. Down on the deck, men worked at fabricating something. Althea moved swiftly and often, a small spider in a web of wet rigging, trying to keep some warmth in her body as she maintained her futile watch. All she could hope to see was some disturbance in the faint luminescence of the ocean's moving face.

Eventually the ship's bell rang and her replacement came to relieve her. She scampered down the now-familiar rigging, moving swiftly and gracefully despite the cold and her weariness. She hit the deck cat-lightly and stood a moment kneading her stiff hands.

On the deck, she was given a crewman's measure of rum thinned with hot water. She held it between her near-numb hands and tried to let it warm her. Her watch was over. Any other time, she would have gone to her hammock, but not tonight. Throughout the ship, cargo was being lashed down more tightly to prevent it shifting if the serpent attacked again. On the deck, the hunters were constructing something that involved a lot of salt meat and about fifty fathom of line. They were both laughing and cursing as they put it together, swearing that the serpent would be sorry it had ever seen this ship. The man who had been devoured had been one of the hunters. Althea had known him, had even worked alongside him on the Barrens, but it was hard to grasp the completeness of his death. It had happened too swiftly.

To her, the curses and threats of the hunters sounded thin and impotent, the tantrum of a child pitted against the inevitability of fate. In the darkness and the cold their anger seemed pathetic. She did not believe they could prevail. She wondered what would be worse, to drown or be eaten. Then she pushed all such thought aside, to fling herself into the work of the moment. On the deck was a hodge-podge of items jarred loose by the serpent's attack. All must be carefully restowed. Below decks, men worked the pumps. The ship had not sprung, but they had taken in water. There was work and plenty to spare.

The night passed as slow as the flow of black tar. From alert vigilance, all decayed to a state of frayed anxiety. When everything was made as tight as it could be, when the bait was readied and the trap set, all waited. Yet Althea doubted that anyone save the hunters hoped the serpent would return to receive their vengeance. The hunters were men whose lives centered around successful killing. For another creature to stalk and successfully devour one of their own was a sudden reversal of roles they could not accept. To the hunters, it was manifest that the serpent must return to be killed. Such was the right-ful nature of the world. The sailors, however, were men who lived constantly with the knowledge that, sooner or later, the ocean would take them. The closest to winning they could come was to tell death, "Tomorrow." The sailors working the ship strove only to put as much ocean behind them as they could. Those who had no tasks napped where they could on deck, well-tucked into nooks and crannies where a man could brace himself. Those who could not sleep haunted the rails, not trusting to the look-outs who stared from the masts above into blackness.

Althea was leaning thus, eyes straining to pierce the night, when she felt Brashen take a place beside her. Without even turning, she knew it was him. Perhaps she was that familiar with how he moved, or perhaps without realizing it, she had caught some trace of his scent on the air. "We're going to be all right," he said reassuringly to the night.

"Of course we are," she replied without conviction. Despite the greater danger they all faced, she was still acutely aware of her per-sonal discomfort around Brashen. She would have given a great deal to be able to recall dispassionately all they had said and done that night. She did not know what to blame it on—the drugged beer, the blow to the head or the cindin—but she was not entirely sure she recalled things as they had happened. She could not, for the life of her, recall what had possessed her to kiss him. Maybe, she reflected bleakly, it was because she did not want to recall that those things had happened at all.

"Are you all right?" he asked in a quiet voice that freighted the words with more meaning.

"Quite well, thank you. And yourself?" she asked with impeccable courtesy.

He grinned. She could not see it, but she could hear it in his voice. "I'm fine. When we get to Candletown, all of this is going to seem like a bad dream. We'll have a drink and laugh about it."

"Maybe," she said neutrally.

"Althea," he began, just as the ship gave a lurch beneath them and then began to rise. She caught frantically at the railing and clung tight. As the ship listed over, the sea seemed to rise towards her. "Get back from the rail," Brashen snapped at her, and then flung himself aft shouting, "Feed it to him! Get it over the side, feed it to him!"

The deck under her feet kept inclining towards the vertical. Everywhere sailors shouted out their anger and terror. The ship

screamed, too, a terrible creaking of wood accustomed to being supported by water and now pushed up out of it. The flexibility of the
ship that made it possible for the *Reaper* to withstand the pounding of
the sea told against her now. Althea could almost feel the pain of
planks as fore to aft the whole structure twisted and racked. The
rigging groaned and the canvas swung. She found herself crouched on
the railing rather than clinging to it, gripping it with both hands. She
looked up the slanting deck. Sanded smooth and clean, it offered no
handholds to retreat from the edge of the ship. Below her the black
sea boiled suddenly as the serpent's tail lashed the water for more
purchase.

A man above her roared in sudden, helpless fury. He had lost his
grip, and now he slid down the sloping deck towards her. He wouldn't
strike her. If she just stayed where she was, she'd be safe. He'd hit the
railing and probably go over, but she'd be safe. If she just stayed as she
was.

Instead she found herself letting go with one hand, and reaching
for him. He struck the railing, she seized his coat and suddenly they
were both swinging, attached to the ship only by her hand's grip and
one of his legs crooked over the railing. "No," she heard herself gasp
as she felt her muscles cracking with the strain. They clutched at each
other and the ship, the man's hands clutching her so tightly she
thought he'd break her bones as he instinctively tried to scrabble up
her body to the ship. Below her, the water seethed.

Aft of her, there was a concerted yell of effort and a huge net-
wrapped wad of gobbets of oily sea-bear meat was flung over the side.
Althea caught a glimpse of a section of chain following it and then line
began to pay out. The meat had no more than touched the surface of
the water before an immense open maw rose from beneath the waves
to engulf it. She could have touched the scaled curve of its neck as it
dived after the bait. She caught a glimpse of layered teeth and huge
eyes, then it was gone, a hump of serpent body arching beneath her
feet.

There was a triumphant shout and then Brashen was shouting to
snub it off, snub it off! As abruptly as the deck had tilted up, it was
falling away, while rope was snaking out across the deck as if they had
dropped an anchor. Althea and her companion were abruptly on the
ship's railing instead of dangling over the side of it. They both scrabbled frantically to get their whole bodies onto the deck. The bait line
snapped suddenly taut, and the whole ship shuddered to that tug as
the hook was set. Then there was a shriek of torn wood and the huge

cleat that had anchored the line was jerked free. The cleat vanished over the side. The lashed-together line of barrels that followed took out a section of the ship's rail in their passage into the sea. The empty barrels popped under the water as if made of stone rather than wood. As the ship righted itself, there was a general rush of men towards the railing. All scanned the dark sea for some sign of the vanished serpent. Men were poised, silent and motionless, looking and listening. A soft-voiced hunter spoke into the silence. "He can't stay under forever. Not with all those barrels tied to that hook-and-chain."

Privately, Althea wondered. What could they really know of what a serpent could or could not do? Might those scissoring teeth be capable of severing the chain leader that bound the meat to the roped-together kegs? Perhaps the serpent was so powerful, it could take the kegs to the bottom with it and not even feel the strain.

As if in answer to her thought, there was a sudden shout from the other side of the ship. "There! See them, they just bobbed up! Look at them go! And she's down again!"

"So now it's a she," Althea muttered to herself.

She started to cross the deck but was stopped by the mate's yell. "All of you, quit your gawking. While the damn thing is busy, let's get out of here."

"You're not going to run it down and kill it?" One of the hunters demanded in astonishment. "You don't want to be the first ship to bring a serpent's head and hide back to port? A man could drink for a year on even the telling of such a story!"

"I want to live to get to port," the mate replied sourly. "Let's get some canvas on!"

"Cap'n?" the hunter protested.

Captain Sichel stared out to where they had last seen the serpent. His whole body was tense with hatred, and Althea guessed that he longed to pursue it with the same mindless tenacity as a hound on a scent. She stood still and silent, scarcely breathing, as she thought to herself, *no, no, no, no, no.*

Just as the hunters started to talk cheerfully amongst themselves about harpoons and boats and partners, the captain shook himself as if awakening from a dream. "No," he said quietly, regretfully. And then, "No," more firmly and loudly. "It would be a stupid risk. We've got a full hold of cargo to deliver. We won't risk it. Besides. I've heard some say a mere touch of a serpent's skin will numb a man's muscles and drag him down to death. Let the hell-spawn go. That wad of sea-bear meat hooked in its gorge will kill it, most like. If it comes back, why, then we'll fight it with everything we've got. But for now, let's get out of here. Let it drag those kegs down to the bottom with it, for all I care."

Althea would have expected the men to spring to such a command, but they went reluctantly, with many a glance at the black patch of sea where the serpent had last sounded. The hunters manifested their anger and frustration openly. Some threw down their bows with a clatter, while others meaningfully kept their arrows drawn as they scanned the night sea with narrowed eyes. If the serpent showed again, they'd feather it. As Althea hauled herself up into the rigging, she prayed it would stay away. At the farthest edge of the world, the sun was clambering up out of the ocean's depths. She could see a shimmer of gray where it would soon burst free. As illogical as it was, she almost believed that if the sun managed to rise before the serpent returned, they would all survive. Something in her instinctively longed for light and day to put an end to this long nightmare.

Beside the ship, the serpent suddenly rose like a log turned on end by a whirlpool. The creature shot up, shaking its head wildly, its jaws gaping wide as it sought to dislodge the hook. As it whipped its maned head frantically, small gobs of bloody mucus flew wildly from its maw. Tiny flecks of stinging slime pattered against the canvas. One struck Althea's cheek and burned. She cried out wordlessly and wiped it away with a sleeve. A terrifying numbness spread out from the burn. Other cries from other sailors let her know she was not the only one hit. She clung where she was and tried to be calm. Would the stuff kill her?

On the deck below, the hunters whooped triumphantly and rushed to the side of the ship where the serpent stood on its tail and tried to free itself from the barbed bait it had swallowed. The chain rattled against its teeth and the kegs bobbed on the water nearby. Arrows sang and harpoons were flung. Some fell short or went wide of their target, but a handful found their mark. The serpent trumpeted its agony as it fell back into the water. It was a shrill sound, more akin to the scream of a woman than the roar of a bull. It dived again, for the kegs vanished like popping bubbles.

Above Althea, a man cried out more loudly, a loose, wordless sound. He fell, his body striking a spar near her. He teetered a moment, and Althea caught the sleeve of his shirt. But his body overbalanced and the sleeve tattered free in her grip. She heard him strike the deck far below. She was left gazing stupidly at the rotted cloth that she clutched. The serpent's slime had eaten through the heavy cotton fabric like moths through woven wool.

She wondered what it was doing to her face. A graver thought than that came to her, and she cried out, "The serpent's slime is eating our canvas!"

Other cries confirmed her. Another man, hands burned and numbed, was clutched by his comrades as they awkwardly worked him down to the deck. His head lolled on his shoulders, and his mouth and nose both leaked fluid. Althea did not think he was completely aware any more. It was a terrible sight, but more terrible were the small rips that were appearing in the canvas. As the wind pressed on the sail, the fabric first holed and then began to split. The captain watched with a wary eye, measuring the speed the ship was managing to hold against how long it would take to drag up the spare sails and set them. His plan seemed to be to get as far as he could from the serpent grounds before he paused to replace canvas. Althea agreed with it.

A cry aft turned her head. She did not have a clear view, but the shouts from below told her that the serpent had been sighted again. "The bastard's coming right after us!" someone yelled, and the captain bellowed for the hunters to go aft, and be ready to drive it off with arrows and harpoons. Althea, clinging to her perch, caught one clear glimpse of the creature bearing down on them. Its mouth still gaped wide, the chain dangling from the corner. Somehow it had severed the heavy hemp line that had attached the barrels to it. The arrows and harpoons stood out from its throat. Its immense eyes caught a bit of the first feeble light of dawn and reflected it as red anger. Never before had Althea seen an emotion shine so fiercely in an animal's countenance. Taller and taller it reared up from the water, impossibly tall, much too long to be something alive.

It struck the ship with every bit of force it could muster. The immense head landed on the afterdeck with a solid smack, like a giant hand upon a table. The bow of the ship leaped up in response and Althea was nearly thrown clear of the rigging. She clung there, voicing her terror in a yell that more than one echoed. She heard the frantic twanging of arrows loosed. Later, she would hear how the hunters sprung fearlessly forward, to thrust their spears into the creature over and over. But their actions were unneeded. It had been dying even as it charged up on them. It lay lifeless on the deck, wide eyes staring, maw dribbling a milky fluid that smoked where it fell on the wooden deck. Gradually the weight of its immense body drew its head back and down, to vanish back into the dark waters from whence it had sprung. Half the after-rail went with it. It left a trough of scarred wood smoking in its wake. Hoarsely, the captain ordered the decks doused with sea water.

"That wasn't just an animal," a voice she recognized as Brashen's said. There was both awe and fear in his voice. "It wanted revenge before it died. And it damn near got it."

"Let's get ourselves out of here," the mate suggested.

All over the ship, men sprang to with a will as the grudging sun slowly reached toward them over the sea.

He came to the foredeck in the dead of night on the fourth day of their stay in Jamaillia. Vivacia was aware of him there, but she was aware of him anywhere on board her. "What is it?" she whispered. The rest of the ship was still. The single sailor on anchor watch was at the stern, humming an old love song as he gazed at the city's scattered lights. A stone's throw away, a slaver rocked at anchor. The peace of the scene was spoiled only by the stench of the slaveship and the low mutter of misery from the chained cargo within it.

"I'm going," he said quietly. "I wanted to say good-bye."

She heard and felt his words, but they made no sense to her. He could not mean what the words seemed to say. Panicky, she reached for him, to grope inside him for understanding, but somehow he held that back from her. Separate.

"You know I love you," he said. "More important, perhaps, you know I like you, too. I think we would have been friends even if we had not been who we are, even if you had been a real person, or I just another deckhand—"

"You are wrong!" she cried out in a low voice. Even now, when she sensed his decision to abandon her hovering in the air, she could not bring herself to betray him. It was not, could not be real. There was no sense in crying an alarm and involving Kyle in this. She would keep it private, between the two of them. She kept her words soft. "Wintrow. Yes, in any form we would be friends, though it cuts me to the quick when you seem to say I am not a real person. But what is between us, ship and man, oh, that could never be with any other! Do not deceive yourself that it could. Don't salve your conscience that if you leave me I can simply start chatting with Mild or share my opinions with Gantry. They are good men, but they are not you. I need you, Wintrow. Wintrow? Wintrow?"

She had twisted about to watch him, but he stood just out of her eye-shot. When he stepped up to her, he was stripped to his underwear. He had a very small bundle, something wadded up inside an oilskin and tied tight. Probably his priest's robe, she thought angrily to herself.

"You're right," he said quietly. "That's what I'm taking, and nothing else. The only thing of mine I ever brought aboard with me. Vivacia. I don't know what else I can say to you. I have to go, I must, before I cannot leave you. Before my father has changed me so greatly I won't know myself at all."

She struggled to be rational, to sway him with logic. "But where will you go? What will you do? Your monastery is far from here. You have no money, no friends. Wintrow, this is insanity. If you must do this, plan it. Wait until we are closer to Marrow, lull them into thinking you've given up and then . . ."

"I think if I don't do this now, I will never do it at all." His voice was quietly determined.

"I can stop you right now," she warned him in a hoarse whisper. "All I have to do is sound the alarm. One shout from me and I can have every man aboard this vessel after you. Don't you know that?"

"I know that." He shut his eyes for a moment and then reached out to touch her. His fingertips brushed a lock of her hair. "But I don't think you will. I don't think you would do that to me."

That brief touch and then he straightened up. He tied his bundle to his waist with a long string. Then he clambered awkwardly over the side and down the anchor chain.

"Wintrow. You must not. There are serpents in the harbor, they may . . ."

"You've never lied to me," he rebuked her quietly. "Don't do it now to keep me by you."

Shocked, she opened her mouth, but no words came. He reached the cold, cold water and plunged one bare foot and leg into it. "Sa preserve me," he gasped, and then resolutely lowered himself into the water. She heard him catch his breath hoarsely in its chill embrace. Then he let go of the chain and paddled awkwardly away. His tied bundle bobbed in his wake. He swam like a dog.

Wintrow, she screamed. Wintrow, Wintrow, Wintrow. Soundless screams, waterless tears. But she kept still, and not just because she feared her cries would rouse the serpents. A terrible loyalty to him and to herself silenced her. He could not mean it. He could not do it. He was a Vestrit, she was his family ship. He could not leave her, not for long. He'd get ashore and go up into the dark town. He'd stay there, an hour, a day, a week, men did such things, they went ashore, but they always came back. Of his own will, he'd come back to her and acknowledge that she was his destiny. She hugged herself tightly and clenched her teeth shut. She would not cry out. She could wait, until he saw for himself and came back on his own. She'd trust that she truly knew his heart.

"It's nearly dawn."

Kennit's voice was so soft, Etta was scarcely sure she had heard it. "Yes," she confirmed very quietly. She lay alongside his back, her body not quite touching his. If he was talking in his sleep, she did not wish to wake him. It was seldom that he fell asleep while she was still in the bed, seldom that she was allowed to share his bedding and pillows and the warmth of his lean body for more than an hour or two.

He spoke again, less than a whisper. "Do you know this piece? 'When I am parted from you, The dawn light touches my face with your hands.'"

"I don't know," Etta breathed hesitantly. "It sounds like a bit of a poem, perhaps. . . . I never had much time for the learning of poetry."

"You have no need to learn what you already are," he said quietly. He did not try to disguise the fondness in his voice. Etta's heart near stood still. She dared not breathe. "The poem is called *From Kytris, To His Mistress*. It is older than Jamaillia, from the days of the Old Empire." Again there was a pause. "Ever since I met you, it has made me think of you. Especially the part that says, 'Words are not cupped deeply enough to hold my fondness. I bite my tongue and scowl my love, lest passion make me slave.'" A pause. "Another man's words, from another man's lips. I wish they were my own."

Etta let the silence follow his words, savored them as she committed them to memory. In the absence of his breathless whisper, she heard the deep rhythm of his breathing in harmony with the splash and gurgle of the waves against the ship's bow. It was a music that moved through her with the beating of her blood. She drew a breath and summoned all her courage.

"Sweet as your words are, I do not need them. I have never needed them."

"Then in silence, let us bide. Lie still beside me, until morning turns us out."

"I shall," she breathed. As gentle as a drifting feather alighting, she lay her hand on his hip. He did not stir, nor turn to her. She did not mind. She did not need him to. Having lived for so long with so little, the words he had spoken to her now would be enough to last her a life. When she closed her eyes, a single tear slid forth from beneath her lashes.

In the dimness of the captain's cabin, a tiny smile curved his wooden features.

CHAPTER TWENTY-THREE

JAMAILLIA SLAVERS

HERE WAS A SONG HE HAD LEARNED AS A CHILD, ABOUT THE WHITE STREETS OF JAMAILLIA SHINING IN THE SUN. Wintrow found himself humming it as he hurried down a debris-strewn alley. To either side of him, tall wooden buildings blocked the sun and channeled the sea wind. Despite his efforts, the salt water had reached his priest's robe. The damp bure slapped and chafed against him as he walked. The winter day was unusually mild, even for Jamaillia. He was not, he told himself, very cold at all. As soon as his skin and robe dried completely, he'd be fine. His feet had become so callused from his days on shipboard that even the broken crockery and splintered bits of wood that littered the alley did not bother him much. These were things he should remember, he counseled himself. Forget the growling of his empty belly, and be grateful that he was not overly cold.

And that he was free.

He had not realized how his confinement on the ship had oppressed him until he waded ashore. Even before he had dashed the water from his skin and donned his robe, his heart had soared. Free. He was many days from his monastery, and he had no idea how he would make his way there, but he was determined he would. His life was his own again. To know he had accepted the challenge made his heart sing. He might fail, he might be recaptured or fall to some other evil along the way, but he had accepted Sa's strength and acted. No matter what happened to him after this, he had that to hold to. He was not a coward.

He had finally proved that to himself.

Jamaillia was bigger by far than any city he had ever visited. The size of it daunted him. From the ship, he had focused on the gleaming white towers and domes and spires of the Satrap's Court in the higher reaches of the city. The steaming of the Warm River was an eternal backdrop of billowing silk to these marvels. But he was in the lower part of the city now. The waterfront was as dingy and miserable as Cress had been, and more extensive. It was dirtier and more wretched than anything he had ever seen in Bingtown. Dockside were the warehouses and ship outfitters, but above them was a section of town that seemed to consist exclusively of brothels, taverns, druggeries and rundown boarding houses. The only permanent residents were the curled beggars who slept on doorsteps and within scavenged hovels propped up between buildings. The streets were near as filthy as the alleys. Perhaps the gutters and drains had once channeled dirty water away; now they overflowed in stagnant pools, green and brown and treacherous underfoot. It was only too obvious that nightsoil from chamberpots was dumped there as well. A warmer day would probably have produced an even stronger smell and swarms of flies. So there, he reminded himself as he skirted a wider puddle, was yet another thing to be grateful for.

It was early dawn, and this part of the city slept on. Perhaps there was little that folk in this quarter of town deemed worth rising for. Wintrow supposed that night would tell a different story on these streets. But for now, they were deserted and dead, windows shuttered and doors barred. He glanced up at the lightening sky and hastened his steps. It would not be too much longer before his absence from the ship would be noticed. He wanted to be well away from the waterfront before then. He wondered how energetic his father would be in the search for him. Probably very little on his own account; he only valued Wintrow as a way to keep the ship content.

Vivacia.

Even to think the name was like a fist to his heart. How could he have left her? He'd had to, he couldn't go on like that. But how could he have left her? He felt torn, divided against himself. Even as he savored his liberty, he tasted loneliness, extreme loneliness. He could not say if it was his, or hers. If there had been some way for him to take the ship and run away, he would have. Foolish as that sounded, he would have. He had to be free. She knew that. She must understand that he had to go.

But he had left her in the trap.

He walked on, torn within. She was not his wife or his child or his beloved. She was not even human. The bond they shared had been imposed upon them both, by circumstance and his father's will. No more than that. She would understand, and she would forgive him.

In the moment of that thought, he realized that he meant to go back to her. Not today, nor tomorrow, but someday. There would come a time, in some undecided future, perhaps when his father had given up and restored Althea to the ship, when it would be safe for him to return. He would be a priest and she would be content with another Vestrit, Althea or perhaps even Selden or Malta. They would each have a full and separate life, and when they came together of their own independent wills, how sweet their reunion would be. She would admit, then, that his choice had been wise. They would both be wiser by then.

His conscience suddenly niggled at him. Did he hold the intent to return as the only way to assuage his conscience? Did that mean, perhaps, that he suspected what he did today was wrong? How could it be? He was going back to his priesthood, to keep the promises made years ago. How could that be wrong? He shook his head, mystified at himself, and trudged on.

He decided he would not venture into the upper reaches of the city. His father would expect him to go there, to seek sanctuary and aid from Sa's priests in the Satrap's temple. It would be the first place his father would look for him. He longed to go there, for he was certain the priests would not turn him away. They might even be able to aid him to return to his own monastery, though that was a great deal to ask. But he would not ask them, he would not bring his father banging on their doors demanding his return. At one time, the sanctuary of Sa's temple would have protected even a murderer. But if the outer circles of Jamaillia had degraded to this degree, he somehow doubted that the sanctity of Sa's temple would be respected as it once was. Better to avoid causing them trouble at all. There was really no sense to pausing in the city at all. He would begin his long trek across the Satrapy of Jamaillia to reach his monastery and home.

He should have felt daunted at the thought of that long journey. Instead he felt elated that, at long last, it was finally begun.

He had never thought that Jamaillia City might have slums, let alone that they would comprise such a large part of the capital city. He passed through one area that a fire had devastated. He estimated that fifteen buildings had burned to the ground, and many others nearby showed scorching and smoke. None of the rubble had been cleared away; the damp ashes gave off a terrible smell. The street became a footpath beaten through debris and ash. It was disheartening, and he reluctantly gave more credence to all the stories he had heard about the current Satrap. If his idle luxury and sybaritic ways were as decadent as Wintrow had heard, that might explain the overflowing drains and rubbish-strewn streets. Money could only be spent once. Perhaps taxes that should have repaired the drains and hired street watchmen had been spent instead on the Satrap's pleasures. That would account for the sprawling wasteland of tottering buildings, and the general neglect he had seen down in the harbor. The galleys and galleasses of Jamaillia's patrol fleet were tied there. Seaweed and mussels clung to their hulls, and the bright white paint that had once proclaimed they protected the interests of the Satrap was peeling and flaking away from their planks. No wonder pirates now plied the inner waterways freely.

Jamaillia City, the greatest city in the world, the heart and light of all civilization, was rotting at the edges. All his life he had heard legends of this city, of its wondrous architecture and gardens, its grand promenades and temples and baths. Not just the Satrap's palace, but many of the public buildings had been plumbed for water and drains. He shook his head as he reluctantly waded past yet another overflowing gutter. If the water was standing and clogged here below, how much better could things be in the upper parts of the city? Well, perhaps things were much better along the main thoroughfares, but he'd never know. Not if he wanted to elude his father and whatever searchers he sent after him.

Gradually the circumstances of the city improved. He began to see early vendors offering buns and smoked fish and cheese, the scents of which made his mouth water. Doors began to be opened, people came out to take the shutters down from the windows and once more display their wares to the passing foot traffic. As carts and foot traffic began to crowd the streets, Wintrow's heart soared. Surely, in a city of this size, with all these people milling about, his father would never find him.

Vivacia stared across the bright water to the white walls and towers of Jamaillia. In hours, it had not been that long since Wintrow left. Yet it seemed lifetimes had passed since he had clambered down the anchor

chain and swum away. The other ships had obscured her view of him.
She could not even be absolutely certain he had reached the beach
safely. A day ago, she would have insisted that if something had happened to him, she would have felt it. But a day ago, she would have
sworn that she knew him better than he did himself, and that he could
never simply leave her. What a fool she had been.

"You must have known when he left! Why didn't you give an
alarm? Where did he go?"

Wood, she told herself. *I am only wood. Wood need not hear, wood need
not answer.*

Wood should not have to feel. She stared up at the city. Somewhere up there, Wintrow walked. Free of his father, free of her. How
could he so easily sever that bond? A bitter smile curved her lips.
Perhaps it was a Vestrit thing. Had not Althea walked away from her
in much the same way?

"Answer me!" Kyle demanded of her.

Torg spoke quietly to his captain. "I'm so sorry, sir. I should have
kept a closer watch on the boy. But who could have predicted this?
Why would he run, after all you've done for him, all you wanted to
give him? Makes no sense to a man like me. Ingratitude like that's
enough to break a father's heart." The words were spoken as if to
comfort, but Vivacia knew that every sentence of Torg's commisera-
tion only deepened Kyle's fury with Wintrow. And with her.

"Where did he go and when? Damn you, answer me!" Kyle raged.
He leaned over the railing. He dared to seize a heavy lock of her hair
and pull it.

Swift as a snake, she pivoted. Her open hand slapped him away
like a man swipes at an annoying cat. He went sprawling on the
deck. His eyes went wide in sudden fear and shock. Torg fled, trip-
ping in his fear and then scrabbling away on all fours. "Gantry!" he
called out wildly. "Gantry, get up here!" He scurried off to find the
first mate.

"Damn you, Kyle Haven," she said in a quiet vicious voice. She
did not know where the tone or the words came from. "Damn you to
the bottom of the briny deep. One by one, you've driven them away.
You took my captain's place. You drove his daughter, the companion
of my sleeping days, from my decks. And now your own son has fled
your tyranny and left me friendless. Damn you."

He stood slowly. Every muscle in his body was knotted. "You'll be
sorry—" Kyle began in a voice that shook with both fear and fury, but
she cut him off with a wild laugh.

"Sorry? How can you make me sorrier than I already am? What

deeper misery can you visit upon me than to drive from me those of my own blood? You are false, Kyle Haven. And I owe you nothing, nothing, and nothing is what you shall have from me."

"Sir." Gantry's voice came in a low respectful tone. He stood on the main deck, a safe distance from both man and figurehead as he spoke. Torg hovered behind him, both savoring and fearing the conflict. Gantry himself stood straight, but his tanned face had gone sallow. "I respectfully suggest you come away from there. You can do no good, and, I fear, much harm. Our best efforts should be made to search for the lad now, before he goes too far and hides too deep. He has no money, nor friends here that we know of. We should be in Jamaillia City right now, putting out word that we are seeking him. And offer a reward. Times are hard for many folk in Jamaillia. Like as not, a few coins will have him back on board before sunset."

Kyle made a show of considering Gantry's words. Vivacia knew that he stood where he was, almost within her reach, as a show of boldness. She was aware, too, of Torg watching them, an almost avid look on his face. It disgusted her that he relished this quarrel between them. Abruptly she didn't care. Kyle wasn't Wintrow, he wasn't kin to her. He was nothing.

Kyle nodded to Gantry, but his eyes never left her. "Your suggestion has merit. Direct all crew members who have shore time to put out the word that we'll give a gold piece for the boy returned safe and sound. Half a gold piece in any other condition. A silver for word of where he is, if such word helps us take him ourselves." Kyle paused. "I'll be taking Torg and heading down to the slave marts. The damn boy's desertion has cost me an early start this day. No doubt the best stock will be taken already. I might have had a whole company of singers and musicians, if I had been down there early on the morning we arrived. Have you any idea what Jamaillian singers and musicians would have been worth in Chalced?" He spoke as bitterly as if it were Gantry's failure. He shook his head in disgust. "You stay here and see to the modifications in the hold. That needs to be completed as swiftly as possible, for I intend to sail as soon as we have both boy and cargo on board."

Gantry was nodding to his captain's words, but several times Vivacia felt his eyes on her. She twisted as much as she could to stare coldly at the three men. Kyle would not look at her, but Gantry's uneasy glance met her eyes once. He made a tiny motion with his hand, intended for her, she was sure, but she could not decide what it meant. They left the foredeck and both went down into the hold. Some time later she was aware of both Torg and Kyle leaving. And good riddance to them both, she told herself. Again her eyes wandered the white city cloaked in the faint steaming of the Warm River. A city veiled in cloud. Did she hope they would find Wintrow and drag him back to her, or did she hope he would escape his father and be happy? She did not know. She remembered a hope that he would come back to her of his own will. It seemed childish and foolish now.

"Ship? Vivacia?" Gantry had not ventured onto the foredeck. Instead he stood on the short ladder and called to her in a quiet voice.

"You needn't be afraid to approach me," she told him sulkily. Despite being one of Kyle's men, he was a good sailor. She felt oddly ashamed to have him fear her.

"I but wanted to ask, is there anything I can do for you? To . . . ease you?"

He meant to calm her down. "No," she replied shortly. "No, there is nothing. Unless you wish to lead a mutiny." She stretched her lips in a semblance of a smile, to show him she was not serious in her request. At least, not quite yet.

"Can't do that," he replied, quite solemnly. "But if there's anything you need, let me know."

"Need. Wood has no needs."

He went away as softly as he had come, but in a short time, Findow appeared, to sit on the edge of the foredeck and play his fiddle. He played none of the lively tunes he used to set the pace for the crew when they were working the capstan. Instead he played soothingly, tunes with more than a tinge of sadness to them. They were in keeping with her mood, but somehow the simple sound of the fiddle strings echoing her melancholy lifted her spirits and lessened her pain. Salt tears rolled down her cheeks as she stared at Jamaillia. She had never wept before. She had supposed that tears themselves would be painful, but instead they seemed to ease the terrible tightness inside her.

Deep inside her, she felt the men working. Drills twisted into her timbers, followed by heavy eye-bolts. Lengths of chain were measured across her and then secured to stanchions or heavy staples. Oncoming supplies were mostly water and hard-tack and chains. For the slaves. Slaves. She tried the word on her tongue. Wintrow had believed slavery to be one of the greatest evils that existed in the world, but when he had tried to explain it to her, she could not see much difference between the life of a slave and the life of a sailor. All, it seemed to her, were owned by a master and made to work for as long and hard as that master saw fit. Sailors had very little say about their lives. How could it be much worse to be a slave? She had not been able to grasp it. Perhaps that was why Wintrow had been able to leave her so easily. Because she was stupid. Because she was not, after all, a human being. Tears welled afresh into her eyes, and the slaver *Vivacia* wept.

Even before they could see the ship itself, Sorcor declared he knew she was a slaver by the tallness of her masts. They were visible through the trees as she came around the island.

"More sail to run faster, to deliver 'fresh' cargo," he observed sarcastically. Then he shot Kennit a pleased grin. "Or perhaps the slavers are learning they have something to fear. Well, run as they may, they won't outdistance us. If we put on some sail now, we'll be on her as soon as she rounds the point."

Kennit shook his head. "The shoals are rocky there." He considered a moment. "Run up a Trader flag and drag some rope to make us appear heavy laden. We'll just be a fat little merchant vessel ourselves, shall we? Hang off and don't approach too close until she's going into Rickert's Channel. There's a nice sandy shoal just past there. If we have to run her aground to take her, I don't want to hole her."

"Aye, sir." Sorcor cleared his throat. It was not clear whom he next addressed. "When we take a slaver, it's usually pretty bloody. Serpents snapping up bodies is not a fit sight for a woman's eyes, and slavers always have a snake or two in their wakes. Perhaps the lady should retire to her cabin until this is over."

Kennit glanced over his shoulder at Etta. It now seemed to him that any time he came on deck, he could find her just behind his left shoulder. It was a bit disconcerting, but he'd decided the best way to deal with it was to ignore it. He found it rather amusing that Sorcor would refer to a whore so deferentially, and pretend that she needed some sort of sheltering from the harsher realities of life. Etta, however, looked neither amused nor flattered. Instead there were deep sparks in her dark eyes, and a pinch of color at the top of each cheek. She wore sturdier stuff this day, a shirt of azure cotton, dark woolen trousers and a short woolen jacket to match. Her black knee boots were oiled to a shine. He had no idea where those had come from, though she had prattled something about gaming with the crew a few nights ago. A gaudy scarf confined her black hair, leaving only the glossy tips free to brush across her wind-reddened cheeks. Had he not known Etta, he might have mistaken her for a young street tough. She certainly bristled enough at Sorcor to be one.

"I think the lady can discern what is too bloody or cruel for her taste, and retire at that time," Kennit observed dryly.

A small cat smile curved Etta's lips as she brazenly pointed out, "If I enjoy Captain Kennit by night, surely there is little I need to fear by day."

Sorcor flushed red, scars standing white against his blush. But Etta only shot Kennit a tiny sideways glance to see if he would preen to her flattery. He tried not to, but it was pleasing to see Sorcor discomfited by his woman's bragging of him. He permitted himself a tiny quirk of his lip acknowledging her. It was enough. She saw it. She flared her nostrils and turned her head, his tigress on a leash.

Sorcor turned away from them both. "Well, boys, let's run the masquerade," he shouted to the crew and they tumbled to his command. Kennit's Raven came down and the Trader flag, taken long ago with a merchant ship, was run up and the rope drags put over the side. All but a fraction of their crew went below. Now the *Marietta* moved sedately as a laden cargo ship, and the sailors who manned her deck carried no weapons. Even as the slaver rounded the point and became completely visible to them, Kennit could tell they would overtake her easily.

He observed her idly. As Sorcor had observed, her three masts were taller than usual, to permit her more sail. A canvas tent for the crew's temporary shelter billowed on the deck; no doubt the sailors working the ship could no longer abide the stench of their densely packed cargo, and so had forsaken the forecastle for airier quarters. The *Sicerna*, as the name across her stern proclaimed her, had been a slaver for some years. The gilt had flaked from her carvings, and stains down her sides told of human waste sloshed carelessly overboard.

As predicted, a fat yellow-green serpent trolled along in the ship's wake like a contented mascot. If the girth of the serpent was any indication, this slaver had already put a good part of its cargo overboard. Kennit squinted at the slaver's deck. There were a great deal more people standing about on the deck than he would have expected. Had the slavers taken to carrying a fighting force to protect themselves? He frowned to himself at the idea, but as the *Marietta* slowly overtook the *Sicerna*, Kennit realized that the folk huddled together on the deck were slaves. Their worn rags flapped in the brisk winter rings, and while individuals shifted, no one appeared to move freely. The captain had probably brought a batch up on deck to give them a breath of fresh air. Kennit wondered if that meant they had sickness down below. He had never known a slaver to worry solely about his wares' comfort.

Sorcor was closing up the distance between them now, and the reek of the slave ship carried plainly on the wind. Kennit took a lavender-scented kerchief from his pocket and held it lightly to his face to mask the effluvium. "Sorcor! A word with you," he called.

Almost instantaneously, the mate was at his side. "Cap'n?"

"I believe I shall lead the men this time. Pass the word firmly amongst them. I want at least three of the crew left alive. Officers, preferably. I've a question or two I'd like answered before we feed the serpents."

"I'll pass the word, sir. But it won't be easy to hold them back."

"I have great confidence they can manage it," Kennit observed in a voice that left little doubt as to the hazards of disobedience.

"Sir," Sorcor replied, and went to pass the word to those on deck and to the armed boarders who waited below.

She waited until Sorcor was out of earshot before Etta asked in a low voice, "Why do you choose to risk yourself?"

"Risk?" He considered it a moment, then asked her, "Why do you ask? Do you fear what would happen to yourself if I were killed?"

The lines of her mouth went flat. She turned aside from him. "Yes," she said softly. "But not in the way you think I do."

They had crept up to hailing distance, when the captain of the *Sicerna* called to them across the water.

"Stand off!" he roared. "We know who you be, no matter what flag you show."

Kennit and Sorcor exchanged a look. Kennit shrugged. "The masquerade ends early."

"Hands on deck!" Sorcor bellowed cheerfully. "And heave the ropes up."

The decks of the *Marietta* resounded to the pounding of eager feet. Pirates crowded the railing, grappling lines and bows at the ready. Kennit cupped his hands to his mouth. "You may surrender," he offered the man as the lightened *Marietta* closed with her prey.

For an answer, the man barked some command of his own. Six stalwart sailors abruptly seized up an anchor lying on the deck. Screams sounded as they hove it over the side. And in its wake, as swiftly as if they had eagerly leaped, went a handful of men who had been manacled to it. They vanished instantly, their screams bubbled into silence. Sorcor stared in shock. Even Kennit had to admit a sort of awe at the other captain's ruthlessness.

"That was five slaves!" bellowed the captain of the *Sicerna*. "Stand off! The next measure of chain has twenty fastened to it."

"Probably the sickly ones he didn't expect to last the journey anyway," Kennit opined. From the deck of the other vessel, he could hear voices, some raised in pleas, others in terror or anger.

"In Sa's name, what do we do?" Sorcor breathed. "Those poor devils!"

"We do not stand off," Kennit said quietly. Loudly, he called back, "*Sicerna*. If those slaves go over the side, you pay with your own lives."

The other captain threw back his head and laughed so ringingly that the sound came clear across the water to them. "As if you would let any of us live! Stand off, pirate, or these twenty die."

Kennit looked at the agony in Sorcor's face. He shrugged. "Close the distance! Grapples away!" he shouted. His men obeyed. They could not see the indecision in the mate's eyes, but all heard the screams of twenty men as a second anchor dragged them down. They took part of the ship's railing with them.

"Kennit," Sorcor groaned in disbelief. His face paled with horror and shock.

"How many spare anchors can he have?" Kennit asked as he sprang to lead the boarding party. Over his shoulder he flung back, "You were the one who told me you would have preferred death to slavery. Let us hope it was their preference as well!"

His men were already hauling on the grappling lines, drawing the two ships closer, while his archers kept up a steady rain of arrows against the defenders who sought to pluck the grapples out and throw them overboard. The crew of the *Marietta* outnumbered that of the *Sicerna* at least three times over. The embattled defenders were well-armed, but obviously unfamiliar with their weapons. Kennit drew his blade and jumped the small gap between the boats. He landed, then gut-kicked a sailor with one arrow standing out of his shoulder as he wrestled with his own bow. The man went down and one of Kennit's knifed him in passing. Kennit spun on him. "Leave three alive!" he spat angrily. No one else challenged his boarding, and with drawn sword he went seeking the vessel's captain.

He found him on the opposite side of the vessel. He, the mate and two sailors were hastily trying to launch the ship's boat. It hung swinging over the water from its davits, but one of the release lines was jammed. Kennit shook his head to himself. The entire ship was filthy; they should not be surprised at a seized-up block if they could not even keep the deck clear.

"Avast!" he shouted with a grin.

"Stand clear," the *Sicerna*'s captain warned him, leveling a hand-held cross bow at his chest.

Kennit lost respect for him. He had been far more impressive when he acted instead of threatening first. And then, arcing up from the water came the sinuous neck of the serpent. Perhaps the man did not wish to expend his bolt until he knew which target was more threatening. As the serpent's head lifted from the water, Kennit saw the body of a slave gripped in the serpent's jaws. Twin chains hung from the man's body. To one side, a manacle still gripped a hand and arm. The other chain dangled slack and empty. The serpent gave a sudden worrying shake to the body, then a slight toss. The great jaws closed more firmly on its catch, shearing away the still-manacled hands at the elbows. The chain splashed back into the water. The serpent threw back its head and gulped the rest of the man down. As the bare feet vanished down its throat, it gave its head another shake. Then it eyed the men in the boat with interest. One of the sailors cried out in horror. The captain aimed his weapon at the monster's wide eyes.

The moment the crossbow was not pointed at his chest, Kennit sprang forward. He poised his blade to chop one of the davit lines that supported the boat. "Throw down the weapon and come back on board," Kennit ordered him. "Or I'll feed you to the serpent now!"

The man spat at Kennit, then fired the bolt unerringly into the serpent's swirling green eye. The bolt vanished from sight into the creature's brain. Kennit guessed it was not the first serpent the man had shot. As the creature went into a frenzy of lashing and screaming, the man drew his own knife and began sawing at the line just above the hook that secured it to the boat. "We'll take our chances with the serpents, you bastard!" he screamed at Kennit as the undulating serpent sank beneath the waves. "Rodel, cut your line loose!"

Rodel, however, did not share his skipper's optimism regarding the serpent. The terrified sailor gave a cry of despair and flung himself from the dangling boat back to the ship's deck. Kennit disabled him with a cut to his leg and then put his attention back on the boat. He ignored the cries of the squirming sailor who tried vainly to stem the flow of his blood.

With a single stride Kennit sprang into the swinging boat. He set the tip of his blade to the captain's throat. "Back," he suggested with a smile. "Or die here."

The seized-up block-and-tackle suddenly broke free. One end of the suspended boat dropped abruptly, spilling men into the sea even as the serpent once more erupted to the surface. Kennit, lithe and lucky as a cat, sprang clear of the falling boat. One hand caught the railing of the *Sicerna*, and then the other. He was hauling up his dangling legs when the serpent lifted its head from the water to regard him. Its ruined eye ran ichor and blood. It opened its maw wide and screamed, a sound of fury and despair. Its blinded eye faced towards the men who struggled in the water, while Kennit dangled before the good eye like a fishing lure. Frantically, he swung one leg up over the railing and hooked it there. As softly as a well-trained pet takes a tidbit from its master's fingers, the serpent closed its jaws on his other leg.

It hurt, it burned like a red-hot leg-iron, and he screamed. Then the pain suddenly flowed away from him. A chill, delightfully numbing, chased the pain away as hot water purges cold from the skin. He felt it flowing up his body. Relief, such relief from the pain. He felt his leg relax with it, and then the numbness was flowing higher. His scream died away to a groan.

"NO!" The whore shrieked the word as she flew across the deck. Etta must have been watching from the deck of the *Marietta*. No one blocked her way. The deck was mostly cleared of live men; they had probably fallen back at sight of the serpent rising again. Some impromptu weapon, a boarding ax or a kitchen cleaver, flashed in the sunlight as Etta brandished it. She was screaming, a stream of gutter invective and threats directed toward the serpent that even now was lifting him up. Some reflex made him cling to the ship's railing with all his might. That was not much anymore. Strength had fled him. Whatever venom the serpent had put into his wound was already rendering him helpless. When Etta seized him in a wild embrace that also included the ship's railing, he scarcely felt her grip. "Let him go!" she commanded the serpent. "Let him go, you bitch thing, you slimy sea-worm, you whore's ass! Let him go!"

The enfeebled serpent tugged on his booted leg, stretching him out over the water. Etta hauled determinedly back. The woman was stronger than he had thought. He saw more than felt the serpent set its teeth more firmly. Like a hot knife through butter, those teeth sheared through flesh and muscle. He had a glimpse of exposed bone, looking oddly honeycombed where the serpent's saliva ate into it. The creature turned its great head like a hooked fish, preparing to give a shake that would either tear him loose from the railing or snatch his leg from his body. Sobbing, Etta raised her weapon. "Damn you!" she screamed, "damn you, damn you, damn you!" Her puny blade fell, but not as Kennit had expected. She did not waste the blow on the serpent's heavily scaled snout. Instead the blade cracked loudly against his weakened bone. She severed his leg just below the serpent's teeth, cutting it off a nice bite as it were. He saw blood gout from the ragged worried stump of his leg as she hauled him hastily backward, crabbing across the deck with him in her grip. He dimly heard the awe-stricken cries of his men as the serpent raised its head still higher, and then suddenly collapsed back into the sea, boneless as a piece of string. It would not rise again. It was dead. And Etta had fed it his leg.

"Why did you do that?" he demanded of her faintly. "What have I ever done to you that you would chop my leg off?"

"Oh, my darling, oh, my love!" she was caterwauling, even as the darkness swirled around him and took him down.

The slavemart stank. It was the worst smell that Wintrow had ever encountered. He wondered if the smell of one's own kind in death and disease was naturally more offensive than any other odor. Instinctively, he wished to be away from here. It was a bone-deep revulsion. Despite the misery he saw, his sympathy and outrage were overwhelmed by his disgust. Hurry as he might, he could not seem to find an escape from this section of the city.

He had seen animals confined in large numbers before, even animals gathered together for slaughter, but their misery had been dumb and uncomprehending. They had chewed their cuds and lashed their tails at flies as they awaited their fates. Animals could be held in pens or yards. They did not need to be secured in both manacles and leg-irons. Nor did animals shout or sob their misery and frustration in words.

"I can't help you, I can't help you." Wintrow heard himself muttering the words aloud and bit down on his tongue. It was true, he assured himself. He could not help them. He could no more break their chains than they could. Even if he had been able to undo their fetters, what then? He could not erase the tattoos from their faces, could not help them flee and escape. Evil as their fates were, it was best if he left each one to face it and make the best he could of it. Some, surely, would find freedom and happiness later in their lives. This extreme of misery could not last forever.

As if in agreement with that thought, a man passed him trundling a barrow. Three bodies had been dumped in it and, despite their emaciation, the man pushed it with difficulty. A woman trailed after him, weeping disconsolately. "Please, please," she burst out as they passed Wintrow. "At least let me have his body. What good is it to you? Let me take my son home and bury him. Please, please." But the man pushing the barrow paid her no notice. Nor did anyone else in the hurrying, crowded street. Wintrow stared after them, wondering if perhaps the woman was crazy, perhaps it was not her son at all and the man with the barrow knew it. Or perhaps, he reflected, everyone else in the street was crazy, and had just seen a heart-sick mother begging for the dead body of her son, and had done nothing about it. Including himself. Had he so swiftly become inured to human pain? He lifted his eyes and tried to see the street scene afresh.

It overwhelmed him. In the main part of the street, folk strolled arm in arm, dawdling to look at booths just as they might in any marketplace. They spoke of color and size, of age and sex. But the livestock and goods they perused were human. There were simple coffles standing in courtyards, a string of people chained together, offered in lots or singles, for general work on farms or in town. At the corner of the courtyard, a tattooist plied his trade. He lounged in a chair beside a leather-lined head vise and an immense block of stone with an eye-bolt worked into it. For a reasonable price, the chant rose, a reasonable price, he would mark any newly purchased slave with the buyer's emblem. The boy calling this out was tethered to the stone. He wore only a loincloth, despite the winter day, and his entire body had been lavishly embellished with tattoos as a means of advertising his master's skill. For a reasonable price, a reasonable price.

There were buildings that housed slaves, their specialties advertised on their swinging signs. Wintrow saw an emblem for carpenters and masons, another for seamstresses, and one that specialized in musicians and dancers. Just as any type of folk might fall into debt, so one might acquire any type of slave. Tinker, tailor, soldier, sailor, Wintrow thought to himself. Tutors and wet nurses and scribes and clerks. Why hire what you could buy outright? That seemed to be the philosophy here in the slavemart, yet Wintrow wondered how those shopping for slaves could not see themselves in their faces, or recognize one's neighbors. No one else seemed disturbed by it. Some might hold a lace kerchief fastidiously to the nose, distressed by the odor. They did not hesitate to demand a slave stand, or walk, or trot in a circle the better to inspect him. Latticed-off areas were provided for the more private inspection of the females for sale. It seemed that, in the eyes of the buyers, a failure of finances instantly changed a man from a friend or neighbor into merchandise.

Some, it appeared, were not too badly housed and kept. They were the more valuable slaves, the well-educated and talented and skilled. Some few of those even appeared to take a quiet pride in their own worth, holding themselves with pride and assurance despite being marked with a tattoo across the face. Others were what Wintrow heard referred to as "map-faces," meaning that the history of their owners could be traced by the progression of different tattoos. Usually such slaves were surly and difficult; tractable slaves often found permanent homes. More than five tattoos usually marked a slave as less than desirable. They were sold more cheaply and treated with casual brutality.

The face tattooing of slaves, once regarded as a barbaric Chalcedean custom, was now the norm in Jamaillia City. It pained Wintrow to see how Jamaillia had not only adopted it, but adapted it. Those marketed as dancers and entertainers often bore only small and pale tattoos, easily masked with make-up so that their status would not disturb the pleasure of those being entertained. While it was illegal still to purchase slaves solely to prostitute them, the more exotic tattoos that marked some of them left no doubt in Wintrow's mind as to what profession they'd been trained to. It was easier, often, to see their tattoos instead of meet their eyes.

It was while he was passing a street-corner coffle that a slave hailed him. "Please, priest! The comfort of Sa for the dying."

Wintrow halted where he stood, unsure if he were the one addressed. The slave had stepped as far from his coffle as his fetters would allow. He did not look the sort of man who would seek Sa's comfort; tattoos sprawled over his face and down his neck. Nor did he look as if he were dying. He was shirtless and his ribs showed and the fetter on his ankle had chafed the flesh there to running sores, but other than that, he looked tough and vital. He was substantially taller than Wintrow, a man of middle years, his body scarred by heavy use. His stance was that of a survivor. Wintrow glanced past him, to where his owner stood a short way off, haggling with a prospective buyer. The owner, a short man who spun a small club as he talked, caught Wintrow's gaze briefly and scowled in displeasure, but did not leave off his bargaining.

"You. Aren't you a priest?" The slave asked insistently.

"I was training to be a priest," Wintrow admitted, "though I cannot fully claim that title as yet." More decisively he added, "But I am willing to give what comfort I can." He eyed the chained slaves and tried to keep suspicion from his voice as he asked, "Who needs such comfort?"

"She does." The man stepped aside. A woman crouched miserably behind him. Wintrow saw then that the other slaves clustered around her, offering her the warmth and scant shelter of their gathered bodies. She was young, surely not more than twenty, and bore no visible injuries. She was the only woman in the group. Her arms were crossed over her belly, her head bowed down on her chest. When she lifted

her face to regard him, her blue eyes were dull as river stones. Her
skin was very pale and her yellow hair had been chopped into a short
brush on her head. The shift she wore was patched and stained. The
shirt that shawled her shoulders probably belonged to the man who
had summoned Wintrow. Like the man and the other slaves in the
coffle, her face was over-written with tattoos. She bore no traces of
injury that Wintrow could easily see, nor did she appear frail. On the
contrary, she was a well-muscled woman with wide shoulders. Only
the lines of pain on her face marked her illness.

"What ails you?" Wintrow asked, coming closer. In some corner
of his soul, he suspected the coffle of slaves were trying to lure him
close enough to seize him. As a hostage, perhaps? But no one made
any threatening moves. In fact, the slaves closest to the woman turned
their backs to her as much as they could, as if to offer this token of
privacy.

"I bleed," she said quietly. "I bleed and it does not stop, not since
I lost the child."

Wintrow crouched down in front of her. He reached out to touch
the back of her arm. There was no fever, in fact her skin was chill in
the winter sunlight. He gently pinched a fold of her skin, marked how
slowly the flesh recovered. She needed water or broth. Fluids. He
sensed in her only misery and resignation. It did feel like the acceptance of death. "Bleeding after childbirth is normal, you know." He
offered her. "And after child loss as well. It should stop soon."

She shook her head. "No. He dosed me too strong, to shake the
child loose from me. A pregnant woman can not work as hard, you
know. Her belly gets in the way. So they forced the dose down me and
I lost the child. A week ago. But still I bleed, and the blood is bright
red."

"Even a flow of bright red blood does not mean death. You can
recover. Given the proper care, a woman can—"

Her bitter laugh cut off his words. He had never heard a laugh
with so much of a scream in it.

"You speak of women. I am a slave. No, a woman need not die of
this, but I shall." She took a breath. "The comfort of Sa. That is all I
am asking of you. Please." She bowed her head to receive it.

Perhaps in that moment Wintrow finally grasped what slavery
was. He had known it for an evil, been schooled to the wickedness of it
since his first days in the monastery. But now he saw it and heard the
quiet resignation of despair in this young woman's voice. She did not
rail against the master who had stolen her child's life. She spoke of his
action as if it were the work of some primal force, a wind storm or

river flood. His cruelty and evil did not seem to concern her. Only the end product she spoke of, the bleeding that would not cease, that she expected to succumb to. Wintrow stared at her. She did not have to die. He suspected she knew that as well as he did. If she were given a warm broth, bed and shelter, food and rest, and the herbs that were known to strengthen a woman's parts, she would no doubt recover, to live many years and bear other children. But she would not. She knew it, the other slaves in her coffle knew it and he almost knew it. Almost knowing it was like pressing his hand to the deck to await the knife. Once the reality fell, he could never be the same again. To accept it would be to lose some part of himself.

He stood abruptly, his resolve strong, but when he spoke his words were soft.

"Wait here and do not lose hope. I will go to Sa's temple and get help. Surely your master can be made to see reason, that you will die without care." He offered a bitter smile. "If all else fails, perhaps we can persuade him a live slave is worth more than a dead one."

The man who had first summoned him looked incredulous. "The temple? Small help we shall get there. A dog is a dog, and a slave is a slave. Neither is offered Sa's comfort there. The priests there sing Sa's songs, but dance to the Satrap's piping. As to the man who sells our labor, he does not even own us. All he knows is that he gets a percentage of whatever we earn each day. From that, he feeds and shelters and doses us. The rest goes to our owner. Our broker will not make his piece smaller by trying to save Cala's life. Why should he? It costs him nothing if she dies." The man looked down at Wintrow's incomprehension and disbelief. "I was a fool to call to you." Bitterness crept into his voice. "The youth in your eyes deceived me. I should have known by your priest's robe that I would find no willing help in you." He gripped Wintrow suddenly by the shoulder, a savagely hard pinch. "Give her the comfort of Sa. Or I swear I will break the bones in your collar."

The strength of his clutch left Wintrow assured he could do it. "You do not need to threaten me," Wintrow gasped. He knew that the words sounded craven. "I am Sa's servant in this."

The man flung him contemptuously on the ground before the woman. "Do it then. And be quick." The man lifted a flinty gaze to stare beyond him. The broker and the customer haggled on. The customer's back was turned to the coffle, but the broker faced them. He smiled with his mouth at some jest of his patron and laughed, ha, ha, ha, a mechanical sound, but all the while his clenched fist and the hard look he shot at his coffle promised severe punishment if his bargaining were interrupted. His other hand tapped a small bat against his leg impatiently.

"I . . . it cannot be rushed," Wintrow protested, even as he knelt before the woman and tried to compose his mind.

For answer, she tottered to her feet. He saw then that her legs were streaked with blood, that the ground beneath her was sodden with it. It had clotted thick on the fetters on her ankles. "Lem?" she said piteously.

The other slave stepped to her quickly. She leaned on him heavily. Her breath came out a moan.

"It will have to be rushed," the man pointed out brusquely.

Wintrow skipped the prayers. He skipped the preparations, he skipped the soothing words designed to ready her mind and spirit. He simply stood and put his hands on her. He positioned his fingers on the sides of her neck, spreading them until each one found its proper point. "This is not death," he assured her. "I but free you from the distractions of this world so that your soul may prepare itself for the next. Do you assent to this?"

She nodded, a slow movement of her head.

He accepted her consent. He drew a slow, deep, breath, aligning himself with her. He reached inside himself, to the neglected budding of his priesthood. He had never done this by himself. He had never been fully initiated into the mysteries of it. But the mechanics he knew, and those at least he could give her. He noticed in passing that the man stood with his body blocking the broker's view and kept watch over his shoulder. The other slaves clustered close around them, to hide what they did from passing traffic. "Hurry," Lem urged Wintrow again.

He pressed lightly on the points his fingers had unerringly chosen. The pressure would banish fear, would block pain while he spoke to her. As long as he pressed, she must listen and believe his words. He gave her body to her first. "To you, now, the beating of your heart, the pumping of air into your lungs. To you the seeing with your eyes, the hearing with your ears, the tasting of your mouth, the feeling of all your flesh. All these things do I trust to your own control now, that you may command them to be or not to be. All these things, I give back to you, that you may prepare yourself for death with a clear mind. The comfort of Sa I offer you, that you may offer it to others." He saw a shade of doubt in her eyes still. He helped her realize her own power. "Say to me, 'I feel no cold.' "

"I feel no cold," she faintly echoed.

"Say to me, 'The pain is no more.' "

"The pain is no more." The words were soft as a sigh, but as she spoke them, lines eased from her face. She was younger than he had thought. She looked up at Lem and smiled at him. "The pain is gone," she said without prompting.

Wintrow took his hands away, but stood close still. She rested her head on Lem's chest. "I love you," she said simply. "You are all that has made this life bearable. Thank you." She took a breath that came out as a sigh. "Thank the others for me. For the warmth of their bodies, for doing more that my less might not be noticed. Thank them. . . ."

Her words trailed off and Wintrow saw Sa blossoming in her face. The travails of this world were already fading from her mind. She smiled, a smile as simple as a babe's. "See how beautiful the clouds are today, my love. The white against the gray. Do you see them?"

As simply as that. Unchained from her pain, her spirit turned to contemplation of beauty. Wintrow had witnessed it before but it never ceased to amaze him. Once a person had realized death, if they could turn aside from pain they immediately turned toward wonder and Sa. It took both steps, Wintrow knew that. If a person had not accepted death as a reality, the touch could be refused. Some accepted death and the touch, but could not let go of their pain. They clung to it as a final vestige of life. But Cala had let go easily, so easily that Wintrow knew she had been longing to let go for a long time.

He stood quietly by and did not speak. Nor did he listen to the exact words she spoke to Lem. Tears coursed down Lem's cheeks, over the scars of a hard life and the embedded dyes of his slave tattoo. They dripped from his roughly shaven chin. He said nothing, and Wintrow purposely did not hear the content of Cala's words. He listened to the tone instead and knew that she spoke of love and life and light. Blood still moved in a slow red trickle down her bare leg. He saw her head loll on her shoulder as she weakened, but the smile did not leave her face. She had been closer to death than he had guessed; her stoic demeanor had deceived him. She would be gone soon. He was glad he had been able to offer her and Lem this peaceful parting.

"Hey!" A bat jabbed him in the small of his back. "What are you doing?"

The slave broker gave Wintrow no time to answer. Instead he pushed the boy aside, dealing him a bruising jab to the short ribs as he did so. It knocked the wind out of his lungs and for a moment, all he could do was curl over his offended mid-section, gasping. The broker stepped boldly into the midst of his coffle, to snarl at Lem and Cala. "Get away from her," he spat at Lem. "What are you trying to do, get her pregnant again, right here in the middle of the street? I just got rid of the last one." Foolishly, he reached to grab Cala's unresisting shoulder. He jerked at the woman but Lem held her fast even as he uttered a roar of outrage. Wintrow would have recoiled from the look in his eyes alone, but the slave broker snapped Lem in the face with the small bat, a practiced, effortless movement. The skin high on Lem's cheek split and blood flowed down his face. "Let go!" the broker commanded him at the same time. Big as the slave was, the sudden blow and pain half-stunned him. The broker snatched Cala from his embrace, and let her fall sprawling into the bloody dirt. She fell bonelessly, wordlessly, and lay where she had bled, staring beatifically up at the sky. Wintrow's experienced eye told him that in reality she saw nothing at all. She had chosen to stop. As he watched, her breath grew shallower and shallower. "Sa's peace to you," he managed to whisper in a strained voice.

The broker turned on him. "You've killed her, you idiot! She had at least another day's work in her!" He snapped the bat at Wintrow, a sharply stinging blow to the shoulder that broke the skin and bruised the flesh without breaking bones. From the point of his shoulder down, pain flashed through his arm, followed by numbness. Indeed, a well-practiced gesture, some part of him decided as he yelped and sprang back. He stumbled into one of the other hobbled slaves, who pushed him casually aside. They were all closing on the broker and suddenly his nasty little bat looked like a puny and foolish weapon. Wintrow felt his gorge rise; they would beat him to death, they'd jelly his bones.

But the slave broker was an agile little man who loved his work and excelled at it. Lively as a frisking puppy, he spun about and snapped out with his bat, flick, flick, flick. At each blow, his bat found slave flesh, and a man fell back. He was adept at dealing out pain that disabled without damaging. He was not so cautious with Lem, however. The moment the big man moved, he struck him again, a sharp snap of the bat across his belly. Lem folded up over it, his eyes bulging from their sockets.

And meanwhile, in the slavemart, the passing traffic continued. A raised eyebrow or two at this unruly coffle, but what did one expect of map-faces and those who mongered them? Folk stepped well wide of them and continued on their way. No use to call to them for help, to protest he was not a slave. Wintrow doubted that any of them would care.

While Lem gagged up bile, the broker casually unlocked the blood-caked fetters from Cala's ankles. He shook them clear of her dead feet, then glared at Wintrow. "By all rights, I should clap these onto you!" he snarled. "You've cost me a slave, and a day's wages, if I'm not mistaken. And I am not, see, there goes my customer. He'll want nothing to do with this coffle, after they've shown such bad temperament." He pointed the bat after his fleeing prospect. "Well. No work, no food, my charmers."

The little man's manner was so acridly pleasant, Wintrow could not believe his ears. "A woman is dead, and it is your fault!" he pointed out to the man. "You poisoned her to shake loose a child, but it killed her as well. Murder twice is upon you!" He tried to rise, but his whole arm was still numb from the earlier blow, as was his belly. He shifted to his knees to try to get up. The little man casually kicked him down again.

"Such words, such words, from such a cream-faced boy! I am shocked, I am. Now I'll take every penny you have, laddie, to pay my damages. Every coin, now, be prompt, don't make me shake it out of you."

"I have none," Wintrow told him angrily. "Nor would I give you any I had!"

The man stood over him and poked him with his bat. "Who's your father, then? Someone's going to have to pay."

"I'm alone," Wintrow snapped. "No one's going to pay you or your master anything for what I did. I did Sa's work. I did what was right." He glanced past the man at the coffle of slaves. Those who could stand were getting to their feet. Lem had crawled over by Cala's body. He stared intently into her upturned eyes, as if he could also see what she now beheld.

"Well, well. Right for her may be wrong for you," the little man pointed out snidely. He spoke briskly, like rattling stones. "You see, in Jamaillia, slaves are not entitled to Sa's comfort. So the Satrap has ruled. If a slave truly had the soul of a man, well, that man would never end up a slave. Sa, in his wisdom, would not allow it. At least, that's how it was explained to me. So. Here I am with one dead slave and no day's work. The Satrap isn't going to like that. Not only are you a killer of his slaves, but a vagrant, too. If you looked like you could do a decent day's work, I'd clap some chains and a tattoo on you right now. Save us all some time. But. A man must work within the law. Ho, guard!" The little man lifted his bat and waved it cheerily at a passing city guard. "Here's one for you. A boy, no family, no coin, and in debt to me for damage to the satrap's slaves. Take him in custody, would you? Here, now! Stop, come back!"

The last exclamation came as Wintrow scrabbled to his feet and darted away from them both. Only Lem's cry of warning made him glance back. He should have ducked instead. The deftly flung spinning club caught him alongside the head and dropped him in the filthy street of the slavemart.

CHAPTER TWENTY-FOUR

RAIN WILD TRADERS

BECAUSE ANYTHING OUT OF THE ORDINARY RATTLES ME, THAT'S WHY," GRANDMA SNAPPED.

"I'm sorry," Malta's mother said in a neutral voice. "I was only asking." She stood behind Grandmother at her vanity table, pinning up her hair for her. She didn't sound sorry, she sounded weary of Grandma's eternal irritability. Malta didn't blame her. Malta was sick of them both being so crabby. It seemed to her that all they focused on was the sad side of life, the worrying parts. Tonight there was a big gathering of Old Traders and they were taking Malta with them. Malta had spent most of the afternoon arranging her hair and trying on her new robe. But here were her mother and grandmother, just dressing at the last minute, and acting as if the whole thing were some worrisome chore instead of a chance to get out and see people and talk. She just couldn't understand them.

"Are you ready yet?" she nudged them. She didn't want to be the last one to get there. There would be a lot of talking tonight, a Rain Wild and Trader business discussion her mother had said. She couldn't see why her mother and grandmother found that so distressing. No doubt that

would be sit-still-and-try-not-to-be-bored time. Malta wanted to arrive while there was still talking and greeting and refreshments being
offered. Then maybe she could find Delo and sit with her. It was
stupid that it was taking them so long to get ready. They should have
each had a servant to assist with dressing hair and laying out garments
and all the rest of it. Every other Trader family had such servants. But
no, Grandma insisted that they could no longer afford them and
Mama had agreed. And when Malta had argued they had made her sit
down with a big stack of tally sticks and receipts and try to make sense
of them in one of the ledger books. She had muddled the page, and
Grandma made her copy it over. And then they had wanted to sit
around and talk about what the numbers meant and why the numbers
said they couldn't have servants anymore, only Nana and Rache.
Malta would be very glad when Papa got back. She was sure there was
something they were missing. It made no sense to her. How could
they suddenly be poor? Nothing else had changed. Yet there they
were, in robes at least two years old, dressing one another's hair and
snipping at each other as they did it. "Can we go soon?" she asked
again. She didn't know why they wouldn't answer.

"Does it look like we can go soon?" her mother demanded.
"Malta, please try to be useful instead of driving me mad. Go and see
if Trader Restart's carriage has arrived."

"Oh, not him!" Malta protested. "Please, please tell me we are not
riding with him in that smelly old carriage of his. Mother, the doors
don't even stay shut or open properly. I am going to be so humiliated
if we have to go with—"

"Malta, go and see if the carriage is here," her grandmother
tersely commanded her. As if her mother had not already said it.

Malta sighed and stalked off. By the time they got there, the food
and drink would be gone and everyone would be seated on the council
benches. If she had to go and sit through a whole council meeting, she
at least wanted to be there for the fun part. As she walked down the
hall, she wondered if Delo would even be there. Cerwin would. His
family had been treating him like an adult for years. Maybe Delo
would be there, and if she was, Malta could find a way to get permission to sit with her. It would be easy to get Delo to sit next to her
brother. She hadn't seen Cerwin since the day Mother had insisted on
showing him around the garden room. But that didn't mean that
Cerwin was no longer interested.

At that thought, she made a quick side trip to the water closet.
There was a small looking-glass there. The light was not good, but
Malta still smiled at what she saw. She had swept her dark hair up

from her face, braiding it and then securing it to the crown of her head. Artless tendrils danced on her forehead and brushed the tops of her cheeks. They still would allow her only flowers as adornments, but she had chosen the last tiny roses that still bloomed in the garden room. They were a deep red, with a heady sweet fragrance. Her robe for this evening was very simple, but at least it was not a little girl's frock. It was a Trader's robe, such as all the Traders wore to such meetings. Hers was a deep magenta, almost the same shade as the roses in her hair. It was traditionally the Vestrit color. Malta would have preferred a blue, but the magenta did look good on her. And at least it was new.

She'd never had a Trader's robe before. In a way, they were stuffy garments, round necklines, ankle length, belted at the waist like a monk's robe. She admired the shining black leather of her wide belt, the stylized initial that formed the buckle. She had cinched it tight, to better emphasize the swell of her hips and to pull the fabric tauter over her breasts. Papa was right. She did have a woman's shape already; why should she not have a woman's clothes and privileges? Well, it was only a matter of time before he was back, and then things would change around here. His trading would go well, he'd come home with pockets full of money, and then he would hear of how she had been mistreated and cheated of her promised gown and . . .

"Malta!" Her mother jerked the door open. "What are you doing in here? Everyone is waiting for you. Get your cloak and hurry up!"

"Is the carriage here?" she asked her mother's back as she hurried after her.

"Yes," Mama replied with asperity. "And Trader Restart has been standing beside it waiting for us."

"Well, why didn't he knock or ring the bell or . . ."

"He did," her mother snapped. "But as usual, you were off in some daydream of your own."

"Do I have to wear my cloak? We'll be in the carriage and then the hall, and my old cloak looks stupid with my new robe."

"It's cold out. Wear your cloak. And, please, try to remember your manners tonight. Pay attention to what is said. The Rain Wild families don't ask for an audience of all the Old Traders without good cause. I have no doubt that whatever is said tonight will affect the fates of us all. And remember that the Rain Wild folk are kin to us. Don't stare, have your best manners and . . ."

"Yes, Mother." The same lecture she had already delivered six times at least today. Did she think Malta was deaf, or stupid? Hadn't

she been told ever since she was born that they were kin to the Rain
Wild families? That reminded her. As they went out the door past a
stern-faced Nana, Malta began, "I've heard that the Rain Wild folk
have a new ware. Flame jewels. I heard that the beads are clear as
raindrops, but there are small tongues of flames that dance in each
one."

Her mother did not even answer. "Thank you so much for waiting, Davad. And this is so far out of your way as well," she was saying
to the dumpy little man.

He beamed at her mother, his face shining with pleasure and
grease as he helped her up into the carriage. Malta didn't say a word to
him and managed to hop in before he could touch her arm. She hadn't
forgotten nor forgiven him for her last carriage ride. Her mother had
settled in next to her grandmother. Oh, they couldn't expect her to sit
next to Trader Restart. It was just too disgusting. "May I sit in the
middle?" she said, and managed to squeeze herself in between them.
"Mother, about the flame jewels . . ." she began hopefully, but
Trader Restart started speaking as if she weren't even there.

"All settled? Well, here we go, then. Now, I shall have to sit by the
door here to hold it shut, I'm afraid. I told my man to see to having
the catch repaired, but when I ordered the carriage out tonight, I
found it had not been done yet. It's enough to drive one mad. What is
the good of having servants if they pay no attention when you tell
them to do something? It's almost enough to make a man wish for
slavery here in Bingtown. A slave knows that his master's goodwill is
his only hope of comfort and well-being, and it makes him pay attention to his orders."

And on and on and on, all the way to Trader Concourse. Trader
Restart talked and her mother and grandmother listened. At most
they only politely differed with him even though she had heard her
grandmother say a hundred times that she thought slavery would ruin
Bingtown. Not that Malta agreed with her. She was sure Papa would
not have become involved with it if it were not profitable. Still, she
thought it was rather spineless, the way her grandmother said one
thing at home, and then didn't stand up for her views with Restart.
The strongest thing she said was, "Davad, I have only to imagine
myself a slave to know that it is wrong." As if that were some final
argument. Malta was thoroughly bored with the whole discussion
long before the carriage stopped. And she still hadn't managed to
finish telling her mother about the flame jewels.

But at least they weren't the last ones to arrive. Not quite. It took
every bit of self-control Malta could muster to sit still while Restart

fumbled with the faulty door-catch, and then maneuvered himself out the opening. She followed right away, stepping nimbly down before he could take her hand in his moist, meaty palm. The man made her want to go and wash.

"Malta!" her mother called to her sharply as she started up the walk. She didn't even lower her voice as she said, "Wait there. We shall all go in together."

Malta folded her lips and breathed out once through her nose. She did it on purpose: her mother enjoyed publicly speaking to her as if she were still a child. She waited for them, but when they caught up with her, she purposely lagged behind, not so far that her mother would call her, but far enough that she wasn't quite with them and Trader Restart.

The Trader Concourse was dark. Well, not entirely, but certainly not lit as it had been for the Harvest Ball. A mere two torches burned to illuminate the pathway, and the windows of the hall showed dimly through shutter cracks. That was probably because this meeting had been called by the Rain Wild families. They did not enjoy light, or so it was said. Delo said it was something about their eyes, but Malta suspected that if they all were as ugly as the one she had seen, they just didn't want everyone looking at them. Warty. That was how she had heard them described. Warty and deformed. A little shiver ran up her spine. She wondered how many of them would be here tonight.

Another carriage rattled up behind Davad's just as his coachman clucked to his horses. It was an old style of carriage, with heavy lace panels obscuring the windows. Malta lagged to see who would get out of it. In the dim light, she had to peer to see the crest on the door. It was unfamiliar, not an Old Trader crest. That meant they had to be Rain Wild. No one else would dare to be here tonight. She walked on, but could not resist glancing over her shoulder to see who would get out. A family disembarked, six figures, all cloaked and hooded in dark colors. But as each stepped out, the touch of gloved hand to collar or cuff set tiny amber, red and orange lights to flickering at each location. The hair stood up on the back of her neck and then she realized what they were. Flame jewels. Malta halted where she stood. Oh, the rumors of them could not do them justice. She caught her breath and stared. The closer they came, the more magnificent they were.

"Malta?" She heard the warning in her mother's voice.

"Good evening." It was a husky woman's voice that came from within the shadowed depths of the hood. And now Malta could see that the hood was veiled with a curtain of lace as well. What could be so hideous, as to need hiding even in darkness? The flame jewels she wore were scarlet, weighing down the edges of her veil. She was dimly aware of hurried footsteps behind her, the soft susurrus of fabric. She startled when her mother spoke right at her elbow. "Good evening. I am Keffria, of the Vestrit Trader family."

"Jani of the Rain Wild's Khuprus gives you greeting," the hooded woman replied.

"May I present my daughter, Malta Haven of the Vestrit family?"

"You may indeed." The woman's voice was a cultured purr. Malta belatedly remembered to bow. The woman chuckled approvingly. When she spoke, it was to Malta's mother. "I do not believe I have seen her at a Gathering before. Has she just entered society?"

"In truth, this is her first Gathering. She has not been presented yet. Her grandmother and I believe she must learn the duties and responsibilities of a Trader woman before she is presented as one." In contrast to Jani, her mother's voice was courteous and hasty, as if correcting a wrong impression.

"Ah. That does sound like Ronica Vestrit. And I do approve of such philosophy. I fear it is becoming rarer in Bingtown these days." Her tone smooth and rich as cream now.

"Your flame jewels are beautiful," Malta blurted out. "Are they very expensive?" Even as she said it, she heard how childish she sounded.

"Malta!" her mother rebuked her.

But the Rain Wild woman chuckled throatily. "Actually, the scarlets are the most common and the easiest to awaken. But I still love them best. Red is such a rich color. The greens and blues are rarer far, and much harder to stir. And so, of course, they are the ones we charge most dearly for. The flame jewels are the exclusive province of the Khuprus, of course."

"Of course," her mother replied. "It is quite thrilling to see this new addition to the Khuprus merchandise. The rumors of them have not done them justice." Her mother glanced over her shoulder. "Oh, dear! We have delayed you, I fear. We should probably all go in lest they begin without us."

"Oh, they will wait on me, I am certain," Jani Khuprus observed heavily. "It is at my behest we are all gathered here. But you are right, there is no courtesy in keeping others waiting. Keffria, young Malta. A pleasure to speak with you both."

"Our pleasure," her mother demurred, and stepped aside deferentially to allow the hooded woman to precede her. As her mother took her arm, she gripped it just a fraction tighter than was comfortable. "Oh, Malta," she sighed in rebuke, and then firmly escorted her in. Just within the doors of the Trader Concourse, Grandmother awaited them. Her lips were folded tightly. She curtsied deeply to Jani Khuprus as she passed, then turned wide eyes on Malta and her mother.

Her mother waited a few moments to be sure Jani Khuprus was out of earshot, then hissed, "She presented herself to her!"

"Oh, Malta," her grandmother groaned. Sometimes Malta felt her name was a sort of club. Almost any time either of them said it, they expressed anger or disgust or impatience with the world. She hung her cloak on a peg, then turned with a shrug.

"I just wanted to see her flame jewels," she tried to explain, but as usual, neither of them was listening to her. Instead they hurried her inside the hall. It was dimly lit with tall standing branches of tapers. A third of the space had been given over to an elevated stage. The floor that she had always seen cleared for dancing was now lined with rows of chairs. And it was as she had feared. They were late. The tables of food were picked over and folk were either seated already or seeking their seats. "Can I go and sit with Delo?" she asked hastily.

"Delo Trell is not here," Grandmother pointed out acidly. "Her parents had the good sense to leave her at home. Which is where I wish you were, also."

"I didn't ask to come," Malta replied, even as her mother said, "Mother!" in rebuke. A few moments later, Malta found herself seated between them at the end of a long row of cushioned chairs. Davad Restart sat at the very end. There was an elderly couple in front of them, a pox-scarred man and his pregnant wife behind them, and on the other side of Mama were two heavy-jowled brothers. They weren't even interesting to look at. By sitting up tall and craning her head, she finally found Cerwin Trell. He was six rows in front of them, and almost at the opposite end of the row. There were empty seats behind the Trells. She was sure her mother had deliberately chosen to seat her so far away.

"Sit still and pay attention," her grandmother hissed.

Malta sighed and slumped back in her seat. Up front, Trader Trentor was midway through a long invocation to Sa. It seemed to be a long list of everything that had ever gone wrong for any of the Trader families. Instead of being angry that Sa had let such things befall them, he groveled along about how Sa always came to their aid.

If it had been Krion instead of his uncle, perhaps it would have been interesting. In the seats reserved for the Rain Wild Traders, several cowled heads were bent forward. She wondered if they were already dozing.

After the invocation, there was the speech of welcome by Trader Drur. It repeated the same tired litany. All were kin, all were Traders, ancient oaths and bonds, loyalty and unity, blood and kin. Malta found a flaw in the weave of her new robe. It was right at the edge of her knee. When she tried to point it out to her mother, she looked annoyed and made a shushing motion with her hand. When Drur finally resumed his seat and Jani Khuprus came forward, Malta sat up and leaned forward.

The Rain Wild Trader had taken off her heavy outer cloak and hood but her features were still obscured. She wore a lighter mantle of ivory, also hooded, and the lace veil that covered her face was actually a part of that garment. The flame jewels still shone as brilliantly and had lost none of their effect in the dimly lit room. As she spoke, her veiled face often turned to different corners of the room. Whenever she turned her head, the veil moved, and the flame gems flared up more brightly. There were fifteen of them, all as glistening red as pomegranate kernels, but about the size of shelled almonds. She couldn't wait to tell Delo that she had seen them up close and even spoken to Jani Khuprus about them.

The matriarchal woman suddenly lifted both hands and voice, and Malta focused on what she was saying. "We can no longer wait and hope. None of us can afford to do so. For if we do, our secrets shall be secrets no longer. Had not the river protected us, eating their ship to splinters as they fled, we would have been forced to kill them all ourselves. Bingtown Traders! How could this have happened to us? What has become of your vows? Tonight you listen to Jani Khuprus, but be assured I speak for all the Rain Wild Traders. This was more than a threat we faced."

She paused. A long silence filled the Concourse. Then a mutter of voices rose. Malta assumed she was finished. She leaned over to her mother, and whispered, "I'm going to go get something to drink."

"Sit still and be silent!" her grandmother hissed at both of them. There were deep lines of tension in her brow and around her mouth. Her mother didn't say a word. Malta sat back with a sigh.

One of the jowly brothers to their left rose abruptly. "Trader Khuprus!" he called out. When all heads turned to him, he asked simply, "What do you expect us to do?"

"Keep your promises!" Jani Khuprus snapped. Then, in a slightly milder tone, as if her own reply had surprised her, she added, "We must remain united. We must send representatives to the Satrap. For obvious reasons, they cannot come from Rain Wild families. But we would stand united with you in the message."

"And that message would be?" someone queried from another part of the hall.

"I'm really thirsty," Malta whispered. Her mother frowned at her.

"We must demand the Satrap honor our original covenant. We must demand he call back these so called New Traders, and cede back to us any lands he has deeded them."

"And if he refuses?" This from a Trader woman in the back of the hall.

Jani Khuprus shifted uneasily. She did not want to answer the question. "Let us first ask him to honor the word of his forebears. We have never even asked him. We have complained and grumbled amongst ourselves, we have disputed individual claims. But not once have we stood up as a people and said, 'Honor your word if you expect us to honor ours.'"

"And if he refuses?" the woman repeated steadily.

Jani Khuprus lifted her gloved hands and then let them fall back to her sides. "Then he is without honor," she said in a quiet voice that still carried to every part of the hall. "What have the Traders to do with those who are without honor? If he fails in his word, then we should withdraw ours. Stop sending him tribute. Market our goods wherever we please, rather than funneling the best of them through Jamaillia." In an even quieter voice, she said, "Drive out the New Traders. Rule ourselves."

A cacophony of voices broke out, some raised in outrage, others shrill with fear, and still others roaring their approval. At the end of the row, Davad Restart stood suddenly. "Hear me!" he shouted, and when no one paid attention, he climbed up on top of his chair, where he balanced ponderously. "HEAR ME!" he roared out, a surprising sound from such an ineffectual man. All eyes turned to him and the babble died down.

"This is madness," he announced. "Think what will happen next. He won't let Bingtown go that easily. The Satrap will send ship-loads of soldiers. He will confiscate our holdings. He will deed them over to the New Traders, and make slaves of our families. No. We must work with the New Traders. Give them, not all, but enough to make them content. Make them a part of us, as we did with the Three-Ships Immigrants. I'm not saying we should teach them all we know, or that they should be allowed to trade with Rain Wild Traders, but . . ."

"Then what are you saying, Restart?" someone demanded angrily from the back of the hall. "As long as you're speaking for your New Trader friends, just how much do they want of us?"

Someone else chimed in, "If the Satrap were interested in sending ships up the Inside Passage, he'd have cleaned out the pirates long ago. They say the old patrol galleys are rotting at their quays, for lack of taxes to man them or repair them. All the money goes for the Satrap to entertain himself. He cares nothing about the serpents and pirates that devour our trade. All he cares is that he be amused. The Satrap is no threat to us. Why should we bother with demands. Let's just run these New Traders off ourselves. We don't need Jamaillia!"

"Then where would we sell our goods? All the richest trade is to the south, unless you want to deal with the northern barbarians."

"That's another thing. The pirates. The old covenant said the Satrap would protect us from sea marauders. If we're making demands, we should tell him that—"

"We do need Jamaillia! What are we without Jamaillia? Jamaillia is poetry and art and music, Jamaillia is our mother culture. You can't cut off trade there and still—"

"And the serpents! The damn slavers draw the serpents, we should demand that slavers be outlawed from the Inside Passage—"

"We are an honorable folk. Even if the Satrap cannot recall how to keep his word, we are still bound by—"

"—will take our homes and lands and make slaves of us all. We'll be right back where our forebears were, exiles and criminals, with no hope of reprieve."

"We should set up our own patrol ships, to start with. Not just to keep New Traders away from the mouth of the Rain Wild, but to hunt serpents and pirates as well. Yes, and to make clear to Chalced once and for all that the Rain Wild River is not their border, but that their control stops at Hover Inlet. They've been pushing—"

"You'd have us in two wars at once then, battling both Chalced and Jamaillia! That's stupid. Remember, were it not for Jamaillia and the Satrap, Chalced would have tried to overrun us years ago. That's what we risk if we cut ourselves free of Jamaillia. War with Chalced!"

"War? Who speaks of war? All we need to ask is that the Satrap Cosgo keep the promises that Satrap Esclepius made to us!"

Once more the hall erupted with a chorus of angry voices. Traders stood on their chairs, or shouted from where they stood. Malta couldn't make sense of any of it. She doubted anyone could. "Mother," she whispered pleadingly. "I am dying of thirst! And it's so stuffy in here. Can I just go outside for a breath of air?"

"Not now!" her mother snapped.

"Malta, shut up," her grandmother added. She didn't even look at her, she seemed to be trying to follow a conversation between two men three rows ahead of them.

"Please," Jani Khuprus was calling from the stage. "Hear me, please! Please!" As the babble died down, she spoke more quietly, forcing folk to be silent to hear her. "This is our biggest danger. We quarrel among ourselves. We speak with many voices, and so the Satrap heeds none of them. We need a strong group of people to take our words to the Satrap, and we must be united and sincere in what we say. One strong voice he must heed, but as long as we tear at one another like . . ."

"I have to use the back house," Malta whispered. There. That was something they never argued with. Her grandmother gave a disapproving shake of her head, but they let her go. Davad Restart was so intent on what Jani Khuprus was saying he scarcely noticed her slip past him.

She stopped at the refreshment table to pour herself a glass of wine. She was not the only one to have left her seat. In different parts of the hall, knots of folk were forming and talking, all but ignoring the Rain Wild Trader. Some folk were arguing amongst themselves, others nodding in mutual agreement with her words. Almost everyone there was substantially older than she was. She looked for Cerwin Trell, but he was still seated with his family and appeared to be avidly interested in what was going on. Politics. Privately Malta believed that if everyone just ignored them, life would go on as it always had. The arguments would probably last the rest of the evening and spoil the party. She sighed and took her wine with her as she stepped outside into the crisp winter night.

It was full dark now. The footpath torches had burned down. Above the icy winter stars sparkled. She glanced up at them now and thought of flame jewels. The blues and the greens were the rarest. She couldn't wait to tell Delo that. She knew how she would say it, as if it were something she just assumed that everyone knew. Delo was the best for sharing such things with, because Delo was a hopeless gossip. She'd repeat it to everyone. Hadn't she spread word among all the girls about Malta's green gown? Of course, she had also told them about Davad Restart making Malta go home. She'd been an idiot to tell Delo the whole truth, but she'd been so mad, she just had to talk to someone. And tonight would make up for that embarrassment. She wouldn't tell Delo how bored she had been, only that she had stood outside and chatted with Jani Khuprus herself about flame jewels. She strolled down past the coaches, sipping at her wine. Some of the coachmen sat within the carriages, out of the cold, while others hunched on the boxes. Some few had gathered at the corner of the drive to gossip amongst themselves, and probably share a sip or two from a flask.

She walked almost to the end of the drive, past Davad's coach and then the Rain Wild's one. She'd left her ratty old cloak inside and was starting to feel the chill of the evening. She held her arms close to her chest, resolving not to spill wine down her front, and strolled on. She stopped to examine the crest on a coach door. It was a silly one, a rooster wearing a crown. "Khuprus," she said to herself, and lightly traced it with a finger, committing it to memory. The metal glowed briefly in her finger's wake, and she realized the crest was made of jidzin. It was not as popular now as it once was. Some of the older street performers still made their cymbals and finger-chimes from jidzin. The metal shimmered whenever it was struck. It was a wonderful treat to the eyes, but in reality brass sounded better. Still, it was one more thing to tell Delo. She strolled idly on, and imagined how she would phrase it. "Odd, to think how a human touch sets off both jidzin and flame jewels," she ventured aloud. No, that wasn't quite it. She needed a more dramatic statement than that.

Almost beside her, a blue eye winked into existence. She stepped back hastily, then peered again. Someone was standing there, leaning against the Khuprus coach. The blue glow was a jewel fastened at his throat. He was a slight figure, heavily cloaked in the Rain Wild style. His neck was swathed in a scarf, his face veiled like a woman's. He was probably their coachman. "Good evening," she said boldly, to cover up her momentary surprise, and started to walk by him.

"Actually," he said in a quiet voice, "it needn't be a human touch. Any motion can set them flaring, once they've been wakened. See?" He extended a gloved hand towards her, then gave his wrist a shake. Two small blue gems popped into evidence on his cuff. Malta had to stop and stare. It was not a pale blue, but a deep sapphire blue that danced alone in the darkness.

"I thought the blues and greens were the rarest and most valuable," she observed. She took a sip of the wine she still carried. That seemed more polite than asking how a coachman came to have such things.

"They are," he admitted easily. "But these are very small ones. And slightly flawed, I am afraid. They were chipped in the recovery process." He shrugged. She saw the movement in the rise and fall of the gem at his throat. "They probably won't burn long. No more than a year or two. But I couldn't bear to see them thrown away."

"Of course not!" Malta exclaimed, almost scandalized. Flame jewels thrown away? Shocking. "You say they burn? Are they hot, then?"

He laughed, a soft chuckle. "Oh, not in the ordinary way. Here. Touch one." Again he extended his arm towards her.

She unwrapped her arms from around herself to extend a timid finger. She tapped one cautiously. No. It did not burn. Emboldened, she touched it again. It was smooth and cool like glass, although she could feel a tiny nick in one place. She touched the other one, then wrapped her arms around herself again. "They're beautiful," she said, and shivered. "It's freezing out here. I'd better go back inside."

"No, don't . . . I mean . . . Are you cold?"

"A little. I left my cloak inside." She turned to go.

"Here. Take mine." He had stood up straight and was unfastening his cloak.

"Oh, thank you, but I'm fine. I couldn't take your cloak from you. I just need to get back inside." The very thought of his cloak from his warty back touching her flesh made her chill deepen. She hurried away, but he followed her.

"Here. Try just my scarf, then. It doesn't look like much, but it's amazingly warm. Here. Do try it." He had it off, flame gem and all, and when she turned, he draped it over her arm. It was amazingly warm, but what stopped her from flinging it back at him was the blue flame jewel winking up at her.

"Oh," she said. To wear one, even for just a few moments . . . that was too great an opportunity to pass by. She could always take a bath when she got home. "Would you hold this, please?" she asked him, and held out the wineglass. He took it from her and she wasted no time in draping the scarf around her neck and shoulders. He had been wearing it like a muffler, but its airy knit could be shaken out until it was nearly a shawl. And it was warm, very warm. She arranged it so that the blue jewel rested between her breasts. She looked down at it. "It's so beautiful. It's like . . . I don't know what it's like."

"Some things are only like themselves. Some beauty is incomparable," he said quietly.

"Yes," she agreed, staring into the stone's depth.

After a moment, he reminded her, "Your wine?"

"Oh." She frowned to herself. "I don't want it anymore. You may have it, if you wish."

"I may?" There was a tone of both amusement and surprise in his voice. As if some delicate balance between them had just shifted in his favor.

She was momentarily flustered by it. "I mean, if you want it . . ."

"Oh, I do," he assured her. The veil that covered his face was split. He was deft at slipping the glass through, and he drained the wine off with a practiced toss. He held the emptied glass up to the starlight and gazed at it for a moment. She felt that he glanced at her before he slipped the glass up his sleeve. "A keepsake," he suggested. For the first time, Malta realized that he was older than she and perhaps their conversation was not quite proper, that all of these casual exchanges might be taken to mean something deeper. Nice girls did not stand about in the dark chatting with strange coachmen.

"I had best go inside. My mother will be wondering where I am," she excused herself.

"No doubt," he murmured his assent, and again that amusement was there. She began to feel just a tiny bit afraid of him. No. Not afraid. Wary. He seemed to sense it, for when she tried to walk away, he followed her. He actually walked beside her, as if he were escorting her. She was halfway afraid he would follow her right into the Concourse, but he stopped at the door.

"I need something from you, before you go," he suddenly requested.

"Of course." She lifted her hands to the scarf.

"Your name."

She stood very still. Had he forgotten she was wearing his scarf with the flame jewel on it? If he had, she wasn't going to remind him. Oh, she wouldn't keep it. Not forever, just long enough to show Delo.

"Malta," she told him. Enough of a name that he could find out who had his scarf when he recalled it. Not so much that he could recover it too quickly.

"Malta . . ." he let it hang, prompting her. She pretended not to understand. "I see," he said after a moment. "Malta. Good evening, then, Malta."

"Good evening." She turned and hurried through the great doors of the hall. Once within, she hastily removed the scarf and jewel. Whatever the scarf was woven of, it was fine as gossamer. When she bunched it in her hands, it was small enough to fit completely inside the pocket sewn into her cloak. She stowed it there. Then, with a small smile of satisfaction, she returned to the hall. Folk in there were still taking turns at speeches. Covenants, compromises, rebellions, slavery, war, embargoes. She was sick of it all. She just wished they would give up and be quiet so her mother would take her home, where she could admire the flame jewel in the privacy of her own room.

The rest of the tangle did not seem to sense that anything was amiss. Sessurea, perhaps, was a bit uneasy, but the others were content. Food was plentiful and easily obtained, the atmosphere of this Plenty was warm, and the new salts woke exciting colors in the fresh skins that their shedding revealed. They shed frequently, for the feeding was rich and growth was easy. Perhaps, Shreever thought discontentedly, that was all the others had ever sought. Perhaps they thought this indolent life of feeding and shedding was rebirth. She did not.

She knew Maulkin sought far more than this. The rest of the tangle was short-sighted not to perceive Maulkin's anxiety and distress. North he had led them, following the shadow of the provider. Several times he had halted at warm flows of un-briny water, tasting and tasting yet again the strange atmospheres. The others had always wanted to hasten after the provider. Once Sessurea had shocked them by extending his ruff and challenging their passage to halt them in their foolish following. But moments later, Maulkin had closed his jaws in bafflement, and left the warm flow, to once more take his place in the provider's shadow.

Shreever had not been overly distressed when the provider had halted and Maulkin had been content to stay near it. Who was she to question one who had the memories of the ancients? But when the provider had reversed its path to go south, and Maulkin had bid them follow it yet again, she had become anxious. Something, she felt, was not right. Sessurea seemed to share her unease.

They glimpsed other tangles, following other providers. All seemed content and well fed. At such times, Shreever wondered if the fault were in her. Perhaps she had dreamed of too much, perhaps she had taken the holy lore too literally. But then she would mark how distracted Maulkin was, even in the midst of feeding. While the others snapped and gorged, he would abruptly cease feeding and hang motionless, jaws wide, gills pumping as he quested for some elusive scent. And often, when the provider had halted for a time and the others of the tangle were resting, Maulkin would rise, nearly to the Lack, to begin a twining dance with lidded eyes. At such times, Sessurea watched him almost as closely as she did. Over and over again their leader knotted his body and then flowed through the knot, sensitizing the entire length of his skin to all the atmosphere could tell him. He would trumpet lightly and fitfully to himself, snatches of nonsense interspersed with holy lore. Sometimes he would lift his head above the Plenty and into the Lack, and then let himself sink again, muttering of the lights, the lights.

Shreever could endure it no longer. She let him dance until exhaustion began to dim his false-eyes. In a slow wavering of weariness, he began to drift toward the bottom. Ruff slack and unchallenging, she approached his descent and matched it. "Maulkin," she bugled quietly. "Has your vision failed? Are we lost?"

He unlidded his eyes to stare at her. Almost lazily he looped a loose coil around her, drawing her down to tangle with him in the soft muck. "Not merely a place," he told her almost dreamily. "It is a time as well. And not just a time and a place, but a tangle. A tangle such as has not been gathered since ancient times. I can almost scent a One Who Remembers."

Shreever shivered her coils, trying to read his memory. "Maulkin. Are not you One Who Remembers?"

"I?" His eyes were lidding again. "No. Not completely. I can almost remember. I know there is a place, and a time, and a tangle. When I experience them, I will know them without question. We are close, very close, Shreever. We must persevere and not doubt. So often the time has come and gone, and we have missed it. I fear that if we miss it yet again, all our memories of the ancient times will fade, and we will never be as we were."

"And what were we?" she asked, simply to hear him confirm it.

"We were the masters, moving freely through both the Lack and the Plenty. All that one knew, everyone knew, and all shared the memories of all time, from the beginning. We were powerful and wise, respected and revered by all the lesser creatures of mind."

"And then what happened?" Shreever asked the rote question.

"The time came to be re-shaped. To mingle the essences of our very bodies, and thus to create new beings, partaking of new vitality and new strengths. It was time to perform the ancient cycling of joining and sundering, and growing yet again. It was time to renew our bodies."

"And what will happen next?" she completed her part of the ritual.

"All will come together at the time and the place of the gathering.

All memory shall be shared again, all that was held safe by one shall be given back to all. The journey to rebirth shall be completed, and we shall rise in triumph once more."

"So it shall be," Sessurea confirmed from nearby in the tangle. "So it shall be."

CHAPTER TWENTY-FIVE

CANDLETOWN

C ANDLETOWN WAS A LIVELY LITTLE TRADE PORT ON THE
MARROW PENINSULA. ALTHEA HAD BEEN HERE BEFORE,
with her father. As she stood on the deck of the *Reaper* and
looked around at the busy harbor, it suddenly seemed that if
she jumped from the ship and ran down the docks, she must
find the *Vivacia* tied up and her father on board her just as it
used to be. He'd be in the captain's salon, receiving merchants from the city. There would be fine brandy and
smoked fish and aged cheese set out, and the atmosphere
would be one of comradely negotiation as he offered his
cargo in exchange for their wares or coin. The room would
be both clean and cozy, and Althea's stateroom would be as
it once had been, her personal haven.

The sudden ache of longing she felt for the past was a
physical pain in her chest. She wondered where her ship
was, and how she was faring under Kyle's usage. She hoped
Wintrow had become a good companion to her, despite the
jealousy that assured her that no one could ever know the
Vivacia as well as she did. Soon, she promised both herself
and her distant ship. Soon.

"Boy!"

The sharp word came from close behind her, and she jumped before she recognized both Brashen's voice and the teasing snap in the word. Still, "Sir?" she asked, turning hastily.

"Captain wants to see you."

"Yes, sir," she replied and jumped up to go.

"Wait. A moment."

She hated the way he glanced about to see if anyone was near, or even watching them. Didn't he realize that to anyone else that was an obvious signal of something clandestine between them? Worse still, he stepped close to her, to be able to speak more softly.

"Dinner ashore tonight?" He tapped his pouch, so the coins inside gave a jingle. A newly stamped ship's tag hung from his belt beside it.

She shrugged. "If I get liberty, perhaps I will." She chose deliberately to miss the invitation in his question.

His eyes traveled over her face lingeringly. "That serpent burn is nearly gone. For a time, I feared you'd carry a scar."

Althea shrugged, refusing to meet the tenderness in his eyes. "What's one more scar on a sailor? I doubt anyone else aboard has noticed it or will."

"Then you've decided to stay on with the ship?"

"I'll work it as long as we're in port. But I think I've a better chance of getting a ship back to Bingtown from here than from the other little ports the *Reaper* will visit after this." She knew she should let it lie at that, but sudden curiosity made her ask, "And you?"

"I don't know yet." He grinned suddenly at her and confided, "They've offered me second. Almost twice the pay I started out at and it looks much better on a ticket than a third. I might stay aboard her, just for that. I've told them yes, but I haven't signed ship's articles yet." He was watching her face very carefully as he said, "On the other hand, if we found a sound ship heading back to Bingtown, it might be good to see home again, too."

Her heart dropped into her belly. No. This mustn't continue. She forced a casual smile to her lips and a laugh. "Now, what are the chances that we'd both end up on the same ship again? Pretty slim, I'd say."

Still, he watched her so closely. "Depends on how hard we tried," he offered. He took a breath. "I did put in a word for you here. Said I thought you did more the work of a real sailor than a ship's boy. The first agreed with me. Like as not, that's what the captain wants to see you about, to make you a better offer if you stay on."

"Thank you," she said awkwardly. Not because she felt grateful, but because she felt the first sparks of anger kindling. Did he think she needed his "good word" to be seen as an able-bodied seaman? She was well worth the wages they paid a regular hand, especially as she could skin, too. She felt as if he'd cheated her of her dignity and her own worth, by putting in his good word. She should have stopped at that, but heard herself add, "I think they've seen that about me already."

He knew her too damn well. "I didn't mean it that way," he hastily apologized. "Anyone can see you're worth your pay. You were always a good sailor, Althea. And your time on the *Reaper* has made you an even better one. If I had to work rigging in a storm, I'd choose you to be up there with me. A man can count on you, aloft or on deck."

"Thank you," she said again, and this time it came out even more awkwardly, for she meant it. Brashen did not give out compliments casually. "I'd best report to the captain if I want to keep his good opinion of me," she added, as a way to be quickly away from him.

She turned away from him, but he called after her, "I've got liberty. I'm off to the Red Eaves. Good food, and better ale and cheap. See you ashore."

She hurried away from him, and hoped that by ignoring the odd look Reller sent her way she could dismiss it. Damn him. She'd hoped to live aboard and work the off-loading and re-supplying of this ship until she had a berth on another one. But if Brashen made it too awkward, she'd have to go ashore and pay for a room. Her lips were folded tight as she knocked at Captain Sichel's door. She tried to smooth her face into a more presentable expression when she heard his terse, "Come ahead."

She had only glimpsed the officer's mess once or twice on the trip. Now as she entered it, she found it even less impressive than she had before. True, this was a hard-working ship and oil and meat were messy cargoes, but her father would never have tolerated the clutter she saw here. Captain Sichel sat at the table, while the first stood at his shoulder. There was a strongbox on the table, and a ledger as well as a stack of leather tickets and the ship's seal. She knew that a number of the men had been paid off earlier that day. Those who had come aboard as debtors or prisoners had walked off as free men. True, they'd received no pay to show for the long year aboard the ship, only the stamped leather tag to show they'd put in their time, and a receipt to show their debt worked off. She caught herself wondering what sort of homes most of the men were returning to, or if their homes still existed. Then she felt the captain's expectant stare and called her mind back to herself.

"Reporting, sir," she told him smartly.

He glanced down at the open ledger before him. "Athel. Ship's boy. And I've a note here that you earned a bonus skinning for us as well. That right, boy?"

"Yessir." He knew it, she knew it. She waited for whatever else he wanted to say.

He flipped back through another book on the table, and ran his finger down the entries. "I've a note here in the ship's log that it was your quick action that kept our third from being crimped, and yourself as well. Not to mention several men from other ships. And," he flipped the pages forward to another marker in the logbook, "the mate has noted that on the day we hooked the serpent, your quick action kept another man from going overboard. That so, boy?"

She struggled to keep the grin off her face but could do nothing about the pleased flush that rose to her cheeks. "Yessir," she managed, and added, "I didn't think anyone had made note of those things."

The captain's chair creaked as he leaned back in it. "We take more notice of most things than the men aboard suspect. With this large of a crew, and half of them jail scrapings, I depend on my ship's officers to watch closely, to see who is worth his salt and who isn't." He cocked his head at her. "You came on at Bingtown as a ship's boy. We'd like to keep you on, Athel."

"Thank you, sir." And no offer of a raise in either pay or status? So much for Brashen's good word.

"That suits you, then?"

She took a breath. Her father had always preferred honesty in his men. She'd try it here. "I'm not sure, sir. The *Reaper*'s a fine ship, and I've no complaint against her. But I've been thinking I'd like to make my way back to Bingtown, and get there sooner than the *Reaper* would take me. What I'd like to do, sir, is take my pay and my ticket now, but stay aboard her and work as long as she's in port. And if I didn't find another berth before the *Reaper* sailed, perhaps I could stay aboard her after all."

So much for honesty. The captain's look had darkened. Plainly he believed he'd made her a fair bid in offering to keep her on. He wasn't pleased that she'd consider looking about for a better one. "Well. You've a right to your pay and your ticket, of course. But as to your maybe, perhaps attitude, well, we set a great store on loyalty to the ship. Plainly you think you could do better elsewhere."

"Not better, no sir. The *Reaper*'s a fine vessel, sir, a fine vessel. I was just hoping to find one that would take me home a bit sooner."

"A sailor's home is his vessel," Captain Sichel observed heavily.

"Home port is what I meant, sir," Althea amended weakly. Plainly she was not handling this well.

"Well. Let's tally you out and pay you off. And I'll give you your ticket as well, for I've no quarrel with the job you did. But I won't have you idling about my deck and hoping for a better position. The *Reaper* is scheduled to sail within the month. If you come back before we up anchor and want your position back, well, we'll see. It may be filled easily, you know."

"Yessir." She bit her lip to keep from saying more. As the captain totted up her pay and bonus and counted it out to her, she gave him marks for his own honesty. Blunt and merciless as he had been, he still counted out her correct pay, down to the last copper shard. He passed it to her, and while she pocketed it, he took up a ship's tag and with mallet and stamp drove the *Reaper*'s mark into it. He wiped ink over it to make it stand out better, and then took up a leather scribing tool. "Full name?" he asked casually.

Odd, the places where the world caught up with one. Somehow she had never foreseen this moment. She took a breath. It had to be in her name, or it would be worth nothing at all. "Althea Vestrit," she said quietly.

"That's a girl's name," the captain complained as he began to carve the letters into the ticket.

"Yessir," she agreed quietly.

"What in Sa's name made your parents hang a girl's name on you?" he asked idly as he started on the "Vestrit."

"I suppose they liked it, sir," she answered. Her eyes didn't leave his hands as he carefully scored the letters into the leather. A ship's ticket, and all the proof she needed to make Kyle keep his oath and give her back her ship. The scribing hand slowed, then halted. The captain looked up and met her eyes. A frown deepened on his face. "Vestrit. That's a Trader name, isn't it?"

Her mouth was suddenly dry. "Yes—" she began, but he cut her off with a wave of his hand.

He swung his attention to his first mate. "Vestrits had that ship, what was her name? A liveship?"

The mate shrugged, and Captain Sichel turned back to her sharply. "What was the ship's name?"

"The *Vivacia*," Althea said quietly. Pride crept into her voice whether she willed it or no.

"And the captain's daughter worked the deck alongside the crew," Captain Sichel said slowly. He stared at her hard. "You're that girl, aren't you?" His voice was hard now, the words an accusation.

She held herself very straight. "Yessir."

He flung the carving implement down in disgust. "Get her off my ship!" he snapped at the first.

"I'll go, sir. But I need that ticket," Althea said as the mate advanced on her. She stood her ground. She wasn't going to shame herself by fleeing from him now.

The captain gave a snort of disgust. "You'll get no ticket from me, not with my ship's stamp on it! Do you think I'll let you make me the mock of the slaughter fleet? Shipped a woman aboard all season and never even knew it? That would be a fine laugh on me! I ought to shake your pay out of your pockets for such a lie. No wonder we had such troubles with serpents, worse than we ever had before. Everyone knows a woman aboard a ship draws serpents. We're damn lucky we got here alive, no thanks to you. Get her out of here!" This last he bellowed at his mate, whose expression showed he shared his captain's opinion.

"My ticket," Althea said desperately. She lunged for it, but the captain snatched it up. She'd have to assault him to get it. "Please," she begged him as the mate grabbed her arm.

"Get out of here and off my ship!" he growled in return. "Be damn glad I'm giving you time to pack your gear. If you don't get out of here now, I'll have you put off on the docks without it. Lying whore-bitch. How many of the crew did you sleep with to keep your secret?" he asked as the mate forced her toward the door.

None, she wanted to say angrily. None at all. But she had slept with Brashen, and though that was no one's business but hers, it would have made a lie of her denial. So, "This is not fair," was all she could manage to choke out.

"It's fairer than your lying to me was!" Captain Sichel roared.

The mate thrust her out of the room. "Get your gear!" he growled in a savage whisper. "And if I hear so much as a rumor of this in Candletown, I'll hunt you down myself and show you how we deal with lying whores." The push he gave her sent her stumbling across the deck. She caught her balance as he slammed the door behind him. She swayed with the strength of her anger and disappointment as she stared at the slab of wood that had closed between her and her ticket. None of it seemed real. The months of hard work, and all for what? The handful of coins that was all a ship's boy was worth. She would have gladly given them all back, and everything else she owned for the scrap of leather that he was, no doubt, cutting up even now. As she turned slowly away, she caught Reller staring at her. He raised an eyebrow quizzically.

"They've turned me off the ship," she said briefly. It was true and the simplest explanation.

"What for?" the sailor demanded, following her as she headed towards the forecastle to gather her meager belongings.

She just shrugged and shook her head. "Don't want to talk," she said gruffly, and hoped she sounded like an angry adolescent boy instead of a woman on the verge of hysterical tears. Control, control, control, she whispered to herself as she clambered one last time into the cramped and stuffy place she had called home all winter. It was the work of a few moments to snatch up her possessions and shove them down into her sea-bag. She swung it to her shoulder and left the ship. As her foot touched the dock, she looked around her with new eyes. Candletown. A hell of a place to be with nothing but a handful of coins and a sea-bag.

A man turned his head and stared at him oddly. Brashen glanced at him and then looked away. He realized he was striding down the street with a foolish grin on his face. He shrugged his shoulders to himself. He had a right to grin. He was proud of her. She had looked just like any tough ship's lad, standing there on the *Reaper*'s deck. Her casual acceptance of his invitation, the cocky angle of her cap had all been perfect. In retrospect, this voyage that he had expected to kill her had actually been good for her. She'd recovered something, something he'd believed Kyle had hammered out of her once he took over as captain of the *Vivacia*. The lack of it was what had made her unbearable those last two voyages. It had changed her cheekiness to bitchiness, her sense of fair play to vindictiveness. On the day her father had died, he had thought that spark of the old Althea had been extinguished. He had seen no sign of it until that day on the Barrens when she was skinning out sea bears. Something had changed in her that day. The change had begun there and grown stronger, just as she herself had grown stronger and tougher. The night she had come to him in Nook, he had suddenly and completely realized that she had returned to being the old Althea. He had realized, too, how much he had missed her.

He took a deep breath of land air and liberty. His pay was in his pockets, he was free as a bird, and had the prospect of some very good company for the evening. What could be better? He began watching for the signboard of the Red Eaves. The first mate had grinned and recommended the inn to him as a clean place for a thrifty sailor when Brashen had mentioned he might spend the night ashore. The mate's smile had plainly indicated he did not expect Brashen to spend the night alone. For that matter, neither did Brashen. He caught sight of the inn's red eaves long before he saw its modest signboard.

Within, he found it clean but almost austere. There were only two tables and four benches, all sanded clean as a good ship's deck. The floors were covered with raked white sand. The fire in the hearth was built of driftwood; the flames danced in many colors. The place was empty of customers. He stood some time in the open room before a man gimped out to greet him. He was wiping his hands on his apron as he came. He looked Brashen up and down almost suspiciously before he gave him, "Good day."

"Your house was recommended to me. How much for a room and a bath?"

Again there was that scrutiny, as if the man were deciding what Brashen could afford. He was a man of middle years, a sea-scarred fellow who now walked on a badly twisted leg. That was probably what had put an end to his sailing. "Three," he said decisively. Then he added, "You're not the kind to come in drunk and break things up, are you? For if you are, then the Red Eaves has no room for you."

"I'll come in drunk, yes, but I don't break things up. I sleep."

"Emph. Well, you're honest, that's in your favor." He held his hand out for the coin, and as soon as he had it in hand, he pocketed it. "Take the room to the left at the top of the stairs. If you want a bath, there's a pump-house and a fireplace and tub in the shed out back. Fire's banked, but it doesn't take much time to stir it up. See to yourself and take as long as you want, but mind you leave all as tidy as you found it. I keep a tidy place here. Some don't like that, they want to come in and drink and eat and shout and fight until all hours. That's what you want, you'll have to go somewhere else. Here an honest man can pay for a clean bed and get it. Pay for a well-cooked meal and get it: not fancy, but good clean food, cooked today, and an honest mug of good beer with it. But this isn't a tavern or a whore-house nor a place to make bets and game for money. No, sir. It's a clean place. A clean place."

He found himself nodding woodenly to the garrulous old man. Brashen was beginning to suspect that the mate who had sent him here had been having a bit of fun with him. Still, here he was, and it was quiet and clean and quite likely a better place to entertain Althea than a crowded, noisy tavern. "I'll be heading out back to take a bath, then," he announced when the landlord paused for breath. "Oh, and a

shipmate of mine may be coming here to meet me. He'll be asking for
Brashen. That's me. The lad is named Athel. Would you bid him wait
for me?"

"Aye, I'll let him know you're here." The landlord paused. "Not a
carouser, is he? Not the type to come in here drunk and spew on my
floor and knock over my benches, is he?"

"Athel? No indeed, not him. No indeed." Brashen beat a hasty
retreat out the back door. In a small shed set in a cobbled yard, he
found the water pump, a bath trough and a fireplace as the landlord
had promised. Like the rooming house, the pump-house was almost
excessively tidy. And the several rough towels that hung on pegs
looked clean, if well used, and the trough did not show a ring of some
other man's grease. Just as well, Brashen told himself, to stay at a clean
place. He pumped several buckets of water and put them to heat. His
shore clothes were in the bottom of his duffel. They were clean,
though smelling a bit musty. He hung out his striped shirt and stockings and good woolen trousers to air near the fireplace. There was a
pot of soft-soap and he helped himself to it. He took off several layers
of grease and salt and possibly a layer of skin as well before he was
finished. For the first time in weeks he took his hair out of its braid,
washed it well and then bound it back again. He would have liked to
lie and soak in the tub, but he didn't want to keep Althea waiting. So
he rose and dried himself and trimmed his beard back to its former
shape and donned his clean shore clothes. Such a treat to put on clean,
warm, dry clothes over clean, warm, dry skin. The bath had left him
almost lethargic, but that was nothing that a good meal and a cold
mug of beer wouldn't cure. He stuffed his dirty clothes back in his sea-
bag and did a quick tidy of the room. Tomorrow, he'd find a laundry
to have all his clothes washed out, save for those so tarry as to be
hopeless. Feeling a new man, he went back to the main house to have
a meal and wait for Althea.

She had never been in a foreign port alone before. Always before, she
had had shipmates and a ship to return to when the night grew dark. It
was not late afternoon yet, but the day suddenly seemed both more
chill and more gray. She looked around herself yet again. The world
was suddenly an edgeless, formless place. No ship, no duties, no family ties. Only the coin in her pocket and the duffel on her back to
concern her. A strange mixture of feelings suddenly assailed her; she
felt at once forlorn and alone, devastated at their refusal to give her a
ticket, and yet oddly powerful and independent. Reckless. That was
the word. It seemed there was nothing she could do that would make

things worse than they already were. She could do anything she wanted just now, and answer to no one, for no one else would care. She could get shamelessly drunk or spend every coin she had on a sybaritic night of food, wine, music and exotic surroundings. Of course there was tomorrow to worry about, but one always had to reckon with tomorrow. And if she chose to slam into one head first, there was no one to forbid it, or to say shame to her the next day.

It wasn't as if careful planning had paid off well for her lately.

She gave a final heist to her bag and then deliberately set her cap at a jauntier angle. She strode down the street, taking in every detail of the town. This close to the waterfront, it was ship's brokers and chandlers and cheap seaman's boarding houses, interspersed with taverns, whorehouses, gaming rooms and druggeries. It was a rough section of town for a rough pack of folk. And she was part of them now.

She chose a tavern at random and went inside. It looked no different from the taverns in Bingtown. The floor was strewn with reeds, not very fresh. Trestle tables bore ancient ring stains from many mugs. The benches looked much-mended. The ceilings and walls were dark with oily smoke from cooking and lamps. There was a large fireplace at one end, and there the sailors had gathered thickest, close to the warmth and the smell of stew. There was a tavern-keeper, a lean, mournful-looking man, and a gaggle of serving maids, some sullen, some giggly. A staircase at the back led up to rooms above. The conversational roar pushed at her as solidly as a wind.

She found a spot at a table, not as close to the fire as she wished, but still much warmer than it had been outside, or in the forecastle of the ship. She set her back to the wall at the mostly empty table. She got a mug of beer that was surprisingly good, and a bowl of stew that was badly seasoned, but still a vast improvement over ship's food. The chunk of bread that went with it more than made up for it. It had not been out of the oven for more than a few hours. It was dark and thick with grain and chewy. She ate slowly, savoring the warmth, the food, and the beer, refusing to think of anything else. She considered getting a room upstairs, but the thumps, thuds, shrieks and laughter that drifted down the staircase made her aware that the rooms were not intended for sleeping. One tavern maid approached her halfheartedly, but Althea simply pretended not to understand. The girl seemed as glad to go on her way.

She wondered how long one had to be a whore before one got tired of it. Or used to it. She found her hand had gone to her belly and was touching the ring through her shirt. Whore, the captain had called her, and said she'd brought the serpents down on the ship. Ridiculous. But that was how they had seen her. She took a bite of her bread and looked around the room and tried to imagine what it would be like to randomly offer herself to the men there in hopes of money. They were a rancid lot, she decided. The sea might make a man tough, but for the most part, it also made him ugly. Missing teeth, missing limbs, hands and faces weathered dark as much by tar and oil as by wind and sun; there were few men there that appealed to her. Those that were young and comely and well-muscled were neither clean nor mannered. Perhaps, she reflected, it was the oil trade. Hunting and killing and rendering, blood and salt and oil made up their days. The sailors on the merchant vessels had been cleaner, she thought. Or perhaps only the ones on the *Vivacia*. Her father had pushed the men to be clean to keep the vessel free of vermin as well.

Thinking of the *Vivacia* and her father did not hurt as much as it once had. Hopelessness had replaced the pain. She brought her mind about and sailed straight into the thought she'd been refusing. It was going to be damn close to impossible to ever get a ship's ticket in her name. All because she was a woman. The defeat that washed abruptly over her almost sickened her. The food in her belly was suddenly a sour weight. She found she was trembling as if she were cold. She pressed her feet against the floor, and set her hands to the edge of the table to still them. *I want to go home*, she thought miserably. *Somewhere that I am safe and warm and people know me.* But no, home was none of those things, not anymore. The only place those things existed for her was in the past, back when her father had been alive and the *Vivacia* had been her home. She reached for those memories, but found them hard to summon. They were too distant, she was too disconnected from them. To long for them only made her more alone and hopeless. Brashen, she thought suddenly. He was as close to home as she could get in this dirty town. Not that she intended to seek him out, but it suddenly occurred to her that she could. That was something she could do, if she wanted to, if she wanted to be reckless and truly care nothing about tomorrow. She could find Brashen, and for a few hours, she could feel warm and safe. The thought was like the smell of a well-laden table to a starving man.

But she wouldn't do it. No. Brashen would not be a good idea. If she went to meet him, he would think that meant she was going to bed him again. She deliberately considered that idea. She felt a slow stirring of interest. She gave a snort of disgust and forced herself to truly consider it. The sounds from upstairs seemed suddenly both degrading and silly. No. She wasn't really interested in doing that with anyone, let alone Brashen. Because if they did, that would be the worst idea of all, because sooner or later one or the other of them, or both of them, would be back in Bingtown. Bedding Brashen on the ship had not been a good idea. They had both been tired and half-drunk, to say nothing of the cindin. That was the only reason it had happened. But if she went to meet him tonight and it happened again, then he might think it meant something. And if they encountered one another in Bingtown . . . well, what happened on the ship was one thing, but in Bingtown it would be quite another. Bingtown was home. So. She would not go to meet him and she would not bed him. That was all quite decided with her.

So the only question that remained was what she was going to do with the rest of the evening, and the night to follow. She held up her mug to get a tavern maid's attention. As the girl filled it, Althea pasted a sickly grin on her face. "I'm more tired than I thought," she said artlessly. "Can you recommend a quiet rooming house or inn? One where I can get a bath as well?"

The girl scratched the back of her neck vigorously. "You can get a room here, but it's not quiet. Still, there's a bath house down the street."

Watching the girl scratch, Althea decided that even if the tavern were silent, she wouldn't want to sleep in one of their beds. She hoped to get rid of any vermin she'd acquired on the ship, not invite more. "A quiet place?" she asked the girl again.

The girl shrugged. "The Gilded Horse, if you don't mind paying well for what you get. They've got musicians there, too, and a woman who sings. And little fireplaces in the best rooms, I've heard. Windows in some of the rooms, too."

Ah. The Gilded Horse. Dinner with her father there, roast pork and peas. She'd given him a funny little wax monkey she'd bought in a shop, and he'd told her about buying twenty casks of fine oil. A different lifetime. Althea's life, not Athel's.

"No. Sounds too expensive. Someplace cheap and quiet."

She frowned. "Don't know. Not many places in this part of town are quiet. Most sailors, they don't want quiet, you know." She looked at Althea as if she were a bit strange. "There's the Red Eaves. Don't know if they have baths there, but it's quiet. Quiet as a tomb, I heard."

"I heard of that place earlier," Althea said quickly. "Anywhere else?"

"That's it. Like I said, quiet isn't what most sailors come to town to find." The girl looked at her oddly. "How many places do you need to hear about?" she asked, and then took the coin for the beer she had poured and sauntered off.

"Good question," Althea conceded. She took a slow drink of her beer. A man who smelled badly of vomit sat down heavily next to her. Evening was coming on and the tavern was starting to fill up. The man belched powerfully and the smell that wafted toward her made her wince. He grinned at her discomfiture and leaned confidentially closer. "See her?" he demanded of Althea as he pointed to a sallow-faced woman wiping a table. "I did her three times. Three times, and she only charged me for the once." He leaned back companionably against the wall and grinned at her. Two of his top teeth were broken off crookedly. "You ought to give her a go, boy. She'd teach you a few things, I'd wager." He winked broadly.

"I'm sure you'd win that wager," Althea agreed amiably. She drank off the last of her beer and rose. She took up her sea-bag again. Outside it had begun to rain. A wind was sweeping in with it, and it promised heavier rainfall soon. She decided to do the simplest thing. She'd find a room that suited her, pay for it, and get a good night's sleep. Tomorrow was soon enough to think of something significant to do. Such as find a shipboard job that would take her back to Bingtown as swiftly as possible.

Bingtown. It was home. It would also mark the end of her dream of recovering the *Vivacia*. She pushed that thought aside.

By the time it was fully dark, she had sampled six different rooming houses. Almost all the rooms were over taverns or tap rooms. Every one of them had been noisy and smoky, some with whores on the premises for the convenience of those staying there. The one she settled on was no different from the others, save that there had just been a brawl there. The city guard had come, temporarily driving out the more lively customers. Those who remained after the brawl seemed either worn out or sodden. There were three musicians in a corner and now that the paying customers were mostly dispersed, they were playing for themselves. They talked and laughed softly, and occasionally stopped in mid-piece to go back and try something a different way. Althea sat close enough to listen in on their intimacy and far enough away not to intrude. She envied them. Would she ever have friends like that? She had enjoyed her sailing years aboard ship with her father, but there had been a price. Her father had been her only real friend. The captain and owner's daughter could never fully share the deep friendships of the forecastle crew. When she was at home, it was much the same. She had long ago lost touch with the little girls she had played with as a child. Married by now, most of them, she thought. Probably to the little boys they had spied on and giggled about. And here she was, in ragged sailor-boy togs in a foreign port in a run-down tavern. And alone. With no prospects save crawling home with her tail between her legs.

And getting more maudlin every minute. Time to go to bed. Right after this last mug, it would be time to go up to the room she had secured for the night.

Brashen walked in the door. His gaze swept the room and settled on her immediately. For a frozen instant he just stood where he was. She knew by his stance that he was angry. He'd been in a fight, too. The redness under his left eye would be a black eye before morning. But she doubted that was what he was still angry about. There was a tightness to his wide shoulders under his clean striped shirt, and small sparks deep in his dark eyes. There was no reason for her to feel guilty or ashamed. She hadn't promised to meet him, she'd only said she might. So the sudden shrinking she felt surprised her. He strode across the tavern and glanced about to find an unbroken chair. There wasn't one, and he had to sit on the end of her bench. He leaned forward to speak to her and his words were clipped.

"You could have simply said no. You didn't have to leave me sitting and worrying about you."

She drummed her fingers lightly on the table. For a few seconds she watched them and then looked up to meet his eyes. "Sorry, sir," she reminded him. "Didn't think as you'd worry about the likes of me."

She saw his eyes dart to the musicians, who were paying no attention to them at all. "I see," he said levelly. His eyes said much more. She'd hurt him. She hadn't meant to, hadn't really thought about that aspect of it at all. He got up and walked away. She expected he would leave, but instead he interrupted the tavern-keeper, who was sweeping up broken crockery. Brashen brought his own mug of beer back to the table and resumed his seat. He didn't give her a chance to speak at all. "I got worried. So I went back to the ship. I asked the mate if he knew where you'd gone."

"Oh."

"Yes. Oh. What he said about you was not . . ." His words trailed off and he touched the darkening bruise on his face. "I won't be sailing aboard the *Reaper* again," he said abruptly. He glared at her as if it were her fault. "Why were you so stupid as to tell them your real name?"

"The mate told you about it?" she asked in reply. Unbelievably, her mood dropped yet another notch. If he was talking about it, it was going to lessen her chances of getting aboard another ship as a boy. Despair hit her like green water.

"No. The captain. After the mate escorted me in there and they demanded to know if I had known you were a woman."

"And you told them you had?" Worse and worse. Now they would be convinced she had whored herself out to buy Brashen's silence.

"There seemed little point in lying."

She didn't want to know the rest, about who had hit whom first and when. None of it seemed to matter anymore. She just shook her head.

But Brashen wasn't going to let it be. He took a gulp of his beer, then demanded, "Why did you give them your real name? How could you expect to sail again on a ticket that had your real name on it?" He was incredulous at her stupidity.

"On the *Vivacia*," she said faintly. "I expected to use it to sail on the *Vivacia*. As her captain and owner."

"How?" he asked suspiciously.

And she told him. The whole story, and even as she spoke of Kyle's careless oath and her hopes of using it against him, even as Brashen shook his head at her foolish plan, she wondered why she was telling him. What was it about him that had her spilling her guts to him, about things that were none of his business?

He left a small space of silence at the end of her story. Then he shook his head yet again. "Kyle would never keep his word on a chance oath like that. You'd have to take it to Traders' Council. And even with your mother and your nephew speaking in your behalf, I doubt they'd take you seriously. People say things, in the heat of anger. . . . If the Traders' Council started forcing every man who swore an oath in anger to live up to them, half of Bingtown would be murdered." He shrugged. "On the other hand, it doesn't surprise me that you'd try. I always thought that, sooner or later, you'd try to take the *Vivacia* back from Kyle. But not like that."

"How, then?" she asked him testily. "Sneak aboard and cut his throat while he's asleep?"

"Ah. So that occurred to you, too," he observed dryly.

She found herself grinning in spite of herself. "Almost immediately," she admitted. Then her smile faded. "I have to take the *Vivacia* back. Even though I now know I'm not really ready to captain her. No, don't laugh at me. I may be thick, but I do learn. She's mine, in a way no other ship ever could be. But the law is against me and my family is against me. One or the other, I might fight. But to-gether . . ." Her voice died away and she sat still and silent for a time. "I spend a lot of time not thinking about her, Brashen."

"Me, too," he commiserated. He probably meant the remark in sympathy, but she bristled to it. How could he say that? Vivacia wasn't his family ship. How could he possibly feel about her as Althea did? The silence stretched between them. A group of sailors came in the door and claimed an adjacent table. She looked at Brashen and could think of nothing to say. The door opened again and three longshore-men came in. They began calling for beer before they were even seated. The musicians glanced about as if awakening, and then launched into a full rendition of the bawdy little tune they'd been tinkering with. Soon it would be a noisy, crowded room again.

Brashen drew circles on the table with the dampness from his mug. "So. What will you do now?"

There. The very question that had been stabbing her all day. "I guess I'll go home," she said quietly. "Just like you told me to do months ago."

"Why?"

"Because maybe you were right. Maybe I'd better go and mend things there as best I can, and get on with my life."

"Your life doesn't have to be there," he said quietly. "There are a lot of other ships in the harbor, going to a lot of other places." He was too offhandedly casual as he offered, "We could go north. Like I told you. Up in the Six Duchies, they don't care if you're a man or a woman, so long as you can do the work. So they're not that civilized. Couldn't be much worse than life on board the *Reaper*."

She shook her head at him wordlessly. Talking about it made her feel worse, not better. She said the words anyway. "The *Vivacia* docks in Bingtown. If nothing else, I could see her sometimes." She smiled in an awful way. "And Kyle is older than I am. I'll probably outlive him, and if I'm on good terms with my nephew, maybe he'll let his crazy old aunt sail with him sometimes."

Brashen looked horrified. "You can't mean that!" he declared. "Spend your life waiting for someone else to die!"

"Of course not. It was a joke." But it hadn't been. "This has been a horrible day," she announced abruptly. "I'm ending it. Good night. I'm going up to bed."

"Why?" he asked quietly.

"Because I'm tired, stupid." It was suddenly more true than it had ever been in her life. She was tired to her bones, and deeper. Tired of everything.

The patience in his voice was stretched thin as he said, "No. Not that. Why didn't you come to meet me?"

"Because I didn't want to bed you," she said flatly. Even too tired to be polite anymore.

He managed to look affronted. "I only invited you to share a meal with me."

"But bed was what you had in mind."

He teetered on the edge of a lie, but his honesty won out. "I thought about it, yes. You didn't seem to think it went so badly last time. . . ."

She didn't want to be reminded. It was embarrassing that she had enjoyed what they had done, and all the more so because he knew she had enjoyed it. At the time. "And last time, I also told you it couldn't happen again."

"I thought you meant on the ship."

"I meant anywhere. Brashen . . . we were cold and tired, we'd been drinking, there was the cindin." She halted, but could find no graceful words. "That's all it was."

His hand moved on the table top. She knew then just how badly he wanted to touch her, to take her hand. She put her hands under the table and gripped them tightly together.

"You're certain of that?" His words probed his pain.

"Aren't you?" She met his eyes squarely, defying the tenderness there.

He looked aside before she did. "Well." He took a deep breath, and then a long drink from his mug. He leaned towards her on one elbow and tried for a convincing grin as he suggested, "I could buy the cindin if you wanted to supply the beer."

She smiled back at him. "I don't think so," she replied quietly.

He shrugged one shoulder. "If I buy the beer as well?" The smile was fading from his face.

"Brashen." She shook her head. "When you get right down to it," she pointed out reasonably, "we hardly even know one another. We have nothing in common, we aren't—"

"All right," he cut her off gruffly. "All right, you've convinced me. It was all a bad idea. But you can't blame a man for trying." He drank the last of his beer and stood up. "I'll be going, then. Can I offer you a last piece of advice?"

"Certainly." She braced herself for some tender admonition to take care of herself, or be wary.

Instead he said, "Take a bath. You smell pretty bad." Then he left, sauntering across the room and not even looking back from the door.

If he had stopped at the door to grin and wave, it would have dispersed the insult. Instead, she was left feeling affronted. Just because she had refused him, he had insulted her. As if to pretend he had never wanted her, because she was not perfumed and prettied up. It certainly hadn't bothered him the last time, and as she recalled, he had smelled none too fresh himself. The gall of the man. She lifted her mug. "Beer!" she called to the sour innkeeper.

Brashen hunched his shoulders to the dirty rain that was driving down. As he walked back to the Red Eaves he carefully thought about nothing. He stopped once to buy a stick of coarse cindin from a street corner vendor miserable in the rain, and then walked on. When he reached the doors of the Red Eaves, he found them barred for the night. He pounded on them, unreasonably angry at being shut out in the rain.

Above his head, a window opened. The landlord stuck his head out. "Who's there?" he demanded.

"Me. Brashen. Let me in."

"You left the washing room a mess. You didn't scrub out the trough. And you left the towels in a heap."

He stared up at the window in consternation. "Let me in," he repeated. "It's raining!"

"You are not a tidy person!" the innkeeper shouted down at him.

"But I paid for a room!"

For an answer, his duffel bag came flying out the window. It landed in the muddy streets with a splat that spattered Brashen as well. "Hey!" he shouted, but the window above him shut firmly. For a time he knocked and then kicked at the barred door. Then he shouted curses up at the closed window. He was throwing great handfuls of greasy mud up at it when the city guards came by and laughingly told him to move along. Evidently it was a situation they had seen before, and more than once.

He slung his filthy sea-bag over his shoulder and strode off into the night to find a tavern.

CHAPTER TWENTY-SIX

GIFTS

THE WINTER MOONLIGHT IS CRISP. IT MAKES THE SHAD-
OWS VERY SHARP AND BLACK. THE SHORE ROCKS ARE
sitting in pools of ink, and your hull rests in absolute blackness. Then, because of my fire, there's an overlay of another
kind of shadows. Ones that jump and shift. So, when I look
at you, parts of you are stark and sharp in the moonlight,
and other parts are made soft and mellow by the firelight."

Amber's voice was almost hypnotic. The warmth of her
driftwood fire, kindled with great difficulty earlier in the
evening, touched him distantly. Warm and cold were things
he had learned from men, the one pleasant, the other unpleasant. But even the concept that warm was better than
cold was a learned thing. To wood, it was all the same. Yet
on a night like tonight, warm seemed very pleasant indeed.

She was seated—cross-legged, she had told him—on a
folded blanket on the damp sand. She leaned back against
his hull. The texture of her loose hair was finer than the
softest seaweed. It clung to the grain of his wizardwood
hull. When she moved, it dragged across his planks in
strands before it pulled free.

"You almost make me remember what it was like to see.

Not just colors and shapes, but the times when sight was a pleasure to indulge in."

She didn't reply but lifted her hand and put the palm flat against his planking. It was a gesture she used, and in some ways it reminded him of making eye-contact. A significant glance exchanged without eyes. He smiled.

"I brought you something," she said into the comfortable silence.

"You brought me something?" he wondered aloud. "Really?" He tried to keep the excitement out of his voice. "I don't think anyone has ever brought me anything before."

She sat up straight. "What, never? No one's ever given you a present?"

He shrugged. "Where would I keep a possession?"

"Well . . . I did think of that. This is something you could wear. Like this. Here, give me your hand. Now, I'm very proud of this, so I want to show it to you a piece at a time. It took me a while to do this, I had to oversize them, to get them to scale, you know. Here's the first one. Can you tell what it is?"

Her hands were so tiny against his as she opened the fingers of his hand. She set something in his palm. A piece of wood. There was a hole in it, and a heavy braided cord ran through it. The wood had been sanded and smoothed and shaped. He turned it carefully in his fingers. It curved, but here there was a projection and at the end of it, a fanning out. "It's a dolphin," he said. His fingers followed the curve of the spine again, the flare of the flukes. "This is amazing," he laughed aloud.

He heard the delight in her voice. "There's more. Move along the cord to the next one."

"There's more than one?"

"Of course. It's a necklace. Can you tell what the next one is?"

"I want to put it on," he announced. His hands trembled. A necklace, a gift to wear, for him. He didn't wait for her to reply, but took it by the cord and shook it open. He set it carefully over his head. It tangled for a moment against the chopped mess of his eyes, but he plucked it clear and set it against his chest. His fingers ran rapidly over the beads. Five of them. Five! He felt them again more slowly. "Dolphin. Gull. Seastar. This is . . . oh, a crab. And a fish. A halibut. I can feel its scales, and the track where its eye moved. The crab's eyes are out on the end of their stalks. And the starfish is rough, and there are the lines of suckers underneath. Oh, Amber, this is wonderful. Is it beautiful? Does it look lovely on me?"

"Why, you are vain! Paragon, I never would have guessed." He had never heard her so pleased. "Yes, it looks beautiful on you. As if it belongs. And I had worried about that. You are so obviously the work of a master carver that I feared my own creations might look childish against your fineness. But, well, to praise my own work is scarcely fitting, but I shall. They're made from different woods. Can you tell that? The starfish is oak, and the crab I found in a huge pine knot. The dolphin was in the curve of a willow knee. Just touch him and follow the grain with your fingers. They are all different grains and colors of wood; I don't like to paint wood, it has its own colors, you know. And I think they look best on you so, the natural wood against your weathered skin."

Her voice was quick and eager as she shared these details with him. Intimate as if no one in the world could understand such things better. There was no sweeter flattery than the quick brush of her hand against his chest. "Can I ask you a question?" she begged.

"Of course." His fingers traveled slowly from one bead to the next, finding new details of texture and shape.

"From what I've heard, the figurehead of a liveship is painted. But when the ship quickens, the figurehead takes on color of its own. As you have. But . . . how? Why? And why only the figurehead, why not all the ship's parts that are made of wizardwood?"

"I don't know," he said uneasily. Sometimes she asked him these sorts of questions. He did not like them. They reminded him too sharply of how different he was from her. And she always seemed to ask them just when he was feeling closest to her. "Why are you the colors you are? How did you grow your skin, your eyes?"

"Ah. I see." She was silent for a moment. "I thought perhaps it was something you willed. You seem such a marvel to me. You speak, you think, you move . . . can you move all of yourself? Not just your carved parts, like your hands and lips, but your planking and beams as well?"

Sometimes. A flexible ship could withstand the pounding of wind and waves better than one fastened too tightly together. Planks could shift a tiny bit, could give with the stresses of the water. And sometimes they could shift a bit more than that, could twist apart from each other to admit a sheet of silent water that spread and deepened as cold and black as night itself. But that would be unforgivable, cold-hearted treachery. Unforgivable, unredeemable. He jerked away from the burning memory and did not speak the word aloud. "Why do you ask?" he demanded, suddenly suspicious. What did she want from him? Why did she bring him gifts? No one could really like him, he knew that. He'd always known that. Perhaps this was all just a trick, perhaps she was in league with Restart and Mingsley. She was here to spy out all his secrets, to find out everything about wizardwood and then she would go back and tell them.

"I didn't mean to upset you," Amber said quietly.

"No? Then what did you mean to do?" he sneered.

"Understand you." She did not respond in kind to his tone. There was no anger in her voice, only gentleness. "In my own way, I am as different from the folk of Bingtown as I am from you. I'm a stranger here, and no matter how long I live here or how honestly I run my business, I will always be a newcomer. Bingtown does not make new folk welcome. I get lonely." Her voice was soothing. "And so I reach out to you. Because I think you are as lonely as I am."

Lonely. Pitiful. She thought he was pitiful. And stupid. Stupid enough to believe that she liked him when she was really just trying to discover all his secrets. "And because you would like to know the secrets of wizardwood," he tested her.

His gentle tone took her in. She gave a quiet laugh. "I'd be a liar if I said I wasn't curious. Whence comes the wood that can turn to life? What sort of a tree produces it, and where do such trees grow? Are they rare? No, they must be rare. Families go into debt for generations to possess one. Why?"

Her words echoed Mingsley's too closely. Paragon laughed aloud, a harsh booming that woke the cliff birds and sent them aloft, crying in the darkness. "As if you didn't know!" he scoffed. "Why does Mingsley send you here? Does he think you will win me over? That I will sail willingly for you? I know his plans. He thinks if he has me, he can sail fearlessly up the Rain Wild River, can steal trade there that belongs rightfully only to the Bingtown Traders and the Rain Wild Traders." Paragon lowered his voice thoughtfully. "He thinks because I am mad, I will betray my family. He thinks that because they hate me and curse me and abandon me that I will turn on them." He tore the bead necklace from his throat and flung it down to the sand. "But I am true! I was always true and always faithful, no matter what anyone else said or believed. I was true and I am still true." He lifted his voice in hoarse proclamation. "Hear me, Ludlucks! I am true to you! I sail only for my family! Only for you." He felt his whole hull reverberate with his shout.

Chest heaving, he panted in the winter night. He listened, but heard nothing from Amber. There was only the snapping of the driftwood fire, the querulous notes of the cliff birds as they re-settled awkwardly in the dark, and the endless lapping of the waves. No sound at all from her. Maybe she had run off while he was shouting. Maybe she had crept off into the night, ashamed and cowardly. He swallowed and rubbed at his brow. It didn't matter. She didn't matter. Nothing mattered. Nothing. He rubbed at his neck where the necklace cord had snapped. He listened to the waves creep closer as the tide rose. He heard the driftwood collapse into the fire, smelled the gust of smoke as it did so. He startled when she spoke.

"Mingsley didn't send me." He heard her abruptly stand. She walked to the fire and he heard the shifting of wood in it. Her voice was quiet and controlled when she spoke. "You are right, the first time I came here, he brought me. He proposed to cut you into bits, purely for the sake of your wizardwood. But from the first time I saw you, my heart cried out against that. Paragon, I do wish I could win you over. You are a wonder and a mystery to me. My curiosity has always been greater than my wisdom. But largest of all is my own loneliness. Because I am a long way from home and family, not just in distance but in years."

Her words were quick and hard as falling stones. She was moving about as she spoke. He heard the brush of her skirts. His quick ears caught the small sound of two pieces of wood clicking together. His beads, he suddenly thought in desolation. She was gathering them up. She would take her gift away.

"Amber?" he said pleadingly. His voice went high on her name and broke, as it sometimes did when he was afraid. "Are you taking my beads away?"

A long silence. Then, in a voice almost gruff, she said, "I didn't think you wanted them."

"I do. Very much." When she didn't say anything, he gathered his courage. "You hate me now, don't you?" he asked her. His voice was very calm, save that it was too high.

"Paragon, I . . ." her voice dwindled away. "I don't hate you," she said suddenly, and her voice was gentle. "But I don't understand you either," she said sadly. "Sometimes you speak and I hear the wisdom of generations in your words. Other times, without warning, you are a spoiled ten-year-old."

Twelve years old. Nearly a man, damn you, and if you don't learn to act like a man on this voyage, you'll never be a man, you worthless, whining titty-pup. He lifted his hands to his face, covered the place where his eyes had been, the place the betraying tears would have come from. He moved one hand, to put it firmly over his mouth so the sob would not escape. *Don't let her look at me just now,* he prayed. *Don't let her see me.*

She was still talking to herself. "I don't know how to treat you, sometimes. Ah. There's the crab. I have them all now. Shame on you, throwing these like a baby throws toys. Now be patient while I fix the string."

He took his hand away from his mouth and took a steadying breath. He voiced his worst fear. "Did I break . . . are they broken?"

"No, I'm a better workman than that." She had moved back to her blanket by the fire. He could hear the small sounds of her working, the tiny taps of the beads against each other. "When I made these, I kept in mind that they'd be exposed to wind and rain. I put a lot of oil and wax on them. And they landed on sand. But they won't withstand being thrown against rocks, so I wouldn't do that again, if I were you."

"I won't," he promised. Cautiously, he asked, "Are you angry at me?"

"I was," she admitted. "I'm not anymore."

"You didn't shout at me. You were so quiet I thought you had left."

"I almost did. I detest shouting. I hate being shouted at, and I never shout at anyone. That doesn't mean I never get angry, though." After a moment's pause, she added, "Or that I never get hurt. 'Only my pain is more silent than my anger.' That's a quote from the poet Tinni. Or a paraphrase, actually, a translation."

"Tell me the whole poem," Paragon begged, leaping swiftly to this safe topic. He wanted to get away from speaking of anger and hatred and spoiled children. Perhaps if she told him the poem, she would forget that he had not apologized. He did not want her to know that he could not apologize.

"Nana has said that she would rather stay on at half-pay, if we can still afford that." Ronica spoke the words into the quiet room. Keffria sat in the chair on the opposite side of the hearth, where her father had sat in the times when he was home. She held a small embroidery frame, and skeins of colored thread were arranged on the arm of the chair, but she no longer pretended to work. Ronica's hands were likewise idle.

"Can we afford that?" Keffria asked.

"Only just. If we are willing to eat simply and live simply. I'm almost embarrassed to say how grateful and relieved I am that she offered. I felt so guilty letting her go. Most families want a young woman to watch over their children. It would have been hard for her to find another place."

"I know. And Selden would have been devastated." She cleared her throat. "So. What about Rache?"

"The same," her mother said shortly.

Keffria began carefully, "If our finances are so strained, then perhaps paying Rache a wage is not as essential—"

"I don't see it that way," Ronica stated abruptly.

Keffria was silent, simply looking at her.

After a short time, Ronica was the one to glance aside. "Beg pardon. I know I've been too sharp with everyone lately." She forced her voice to be conversational. "I feel it is important that Rache be paid something. Important for all of us. Not so important that I would put Malta at risk for it, but far more important than new frocks and hair ribbons."

"Actually, I agree," Keffria said quietly. "I but wanted to discuss it with you. So. With those expenses agreed on . . . will we still have enough to pay the Festrews?"

Her mother nodded. "We have the gold, Keffria. I've set it aside, the full amount we owe, and the penalty. We can pay the Festrews. What we can't pay is anyone else. And there are a few who will come between now and then, demanding payment."

"What will you do?" Keffria asked. Then, remembering, she changed it to, "What do you think we should do?"

Ronica took a breath. "I suggest we wait and see who comes, and how insistent they are. The *Vivacia* is due before long. Some may be willing to be put off until she arrives, others may demand extra interest. If we are unlucky, there will be some that demand immediate payment. Then we will have to sell something from the holdings."

"But you believe that should be a final resort?"

"I do." Her mother spoke firmly. "Carriages, horses, even jewelry are all things that come and go. I don't think we've truly missed what we've sold. Oh, I know it has grated on Malta not to have new clothes this winter, but I don't think her suffering as been as acute as her temper. It is good for her to learn a little thrift; she has not had to practice it much at any other time in her life."

Keffria bit her tongue. Her daughter had become a painful topic, one she wished to discuss as little as possible. "But land?" she prompted her mother. It was a discussion they had had before. She didn't really know why she brought it up again.

"The holdings are another matter. As more and more folk come to Bingtown, the best land becomes ever more precious. If we sold what we have now, our best offers would come from new folk. That goes without saying. If we sell to them, we lose much goodwill from our Old Trader kin. We deliver more power into the hands of the new folk. And, to me the most telling point, we are selling something that can never be replaced. One can always buy a new carriage or some earrings. But there is no more bottom land near Bingtown to be had. Once ours is gone, we've given it up forever."

"I think you are right. And you believe we can hold out until the *Vivacia* returns?"

"I do. We had word that she hailed the *Vestroy* as they passed one another in Markham's Straits. That means she is right on schedule getting into Jamaillia. The southbound trip is always the trickiest this time of year." Her mother was only speaking what they both already knew. What was so reassuring about again sharing these thoughts? A belief that perhaps if one spoke them often enough, fate would listen and heed their plans? "If Kyle does as well with selling slaves as he believed he would, then when he returns, we should have enough to put ourselves current with our creditors." Ronica's voice was carefully neutral when she mentioned the slaves. She still did not approve. Well, neither did Keffria. But what else could they do?

"If he does well with the slaves, then we will have enough," she echoed her mother. "But only just enough. Mother, how long can we go on just keeping abreast of our debts? If prices for grain fall any lower, we shall be falling behind. Then what?"

"Then we shall not be alone," her mother said in a dire voice.

Keffria took a breath. The things they had hoped would come to pass, they spoke of often. Now she dared to voice their unuttered fear. "Do you truly believe there will be an uprising against the Satrap? A war?" Even to speak of war against Jamaillia was difficult. Despite her being born in Bingtown, Jamaillia was still home. It was the motherland, the source, the pride of the folk of Bingtown, the seat of all civilization and learning. Jamaillia, gleaming white city to the south.

Her mother sat silent a long time before she replied. "A great deal will depend on how the Satrap replies to our envoys. There has been another disturbing rumor; they say the Satrap will hire Chalcedean mercenaries as escorts for Jamaillian trade ships and privateers to get rid of the pirates in the Inside Passage. Already people are arguing, saying we cannot allow armed Chalcedean ships in our harbor and waters. But I do not think there will be outright war. We are not a warring people, we are traders. The Satrap must know that all we are asking is that he keep his word to us. Our envoys carry with them the original charter for our company. It will be read aloud to the Satrap and his Companions. No one can deny what was promised us. He will have to call back the New Traders."

Keffria thought her mother was doing it again—speaking aloud what they hoped would be, trying to forge a reality from words. "Some thought he might offer us money in reparation," she ventured.

"We would not take it," her mother said quickly. "I was frankly shocked by Davad Restart when he suggested we should set an amount and seek it. One does not buy back one's word." Her voice went bitter as she added, "Sometimes I fear Davad has forgotten who he is. He spends so much time with the New Traders and takes their part so often. We stand between the world and our Rain Wild kin. Shall we take money for our family?"

"It is hard for me to care about them just now. Whenever I think of them, I feel them as a threat to Malta."

"A threat?" Ronica sounded almost offended. "Keffria, we must keep in mind that they are but holding us to our original agreement. Exactly the same thing we are requiring of the Satrap."

"Then it does not feel at all to you as if we would be selling her into slavery, if a time came when we did not have the payment and they claimed blood instead?"

Ronica was silent a moment. "No, it does not," she said at last. Then she sighed. "I would not be happy to see her go. But, you know, Keffria, I have never heard of any Bingtown man or woman who was kept against their will by the Rain Wild Traders. They seek wives and husbands, not servants. Who would wish to wed someone against their inclination? Some folk go there of their own accord. And some, who go there as part of a contract, return when it suits them. You remember Scilla Appleby? She was carried off to the Rain Wilds when her family failed in a contract. Eight months later, they brought her back to Bingtown, because she was unhappy there. And two months after that, she sent them word that she had made a mistake, and they came for her again. So it cannot be all that bad."

"I heard that her family shamed her into returning. That her grandfather and mother both felt she had disgraced the Applebys and broken their pledge when she came back to Bingtown."

"I suppose that could be so," her mother conceded doubtfully.

"I don't want Malta to go there against her will," Keffria said bluntly. "Not for duty nor for pride. Not even for our good name. If it came down to it, I think I would help her run away myself."

"Sa help me, I fear I would, too." Her mother's words came some minutes later, uttered in a voice that seemed dragged from her.

Keffria was shocked. Not just by what her mother was admitting, but by the depth of emotion that her voice betrayed. Ronica spoke on. "There have been times when I hated that ship. How could anything be worth so much? Not just gold they pledged, but their own descendants!"

"If Papa had continued in the Rain Wild trade, the *Vivacia* would most likely be paid off by now," Keffria pointed out.

"Most likely. But at what cost?"

"So Papa always said," Keffria said slowly. "But I never understood it. Papa never explained it or talked about it in front of us girls. The only time I ever asked him about it, he just told me he thought it was an unlucky path to choose. Yet all the other families who have liveships trade with the Rain Wild families. As the Vestrits own a liveship, we have the right to do so, too. Yet Papa refused it." She spoke very carefully as she continued, "Perhaps it is a decision we should reconsider. Kyle would be willing. He made that clear when he asked about charts of the Rain Wild River. Before that day, we had not discussed it. I thought that perhaps Papa had already explained to him. Before that day, he had never asked me why we stopped trading up the River. It just never came up."

"And if you manage things cleverly, it never will again," Ronica said shortly. "Kyle up the Rain Wild River would be a disaster."

And here was another uncomfortable topic. Kyle. Keffria sighed. "I remember that when Grandfather was alive, he took the *Vivacia* upriver. I remember the gifts he used to bring us. A music box that twinkled as it played." She shook her head. "I don't even know what became of that." More quietly she added, "And I never truly understood why Papa wouldn't trade up the river."

Ronica stared into the fire as if she were telling an old tale. "Your father . . . resented the contract with the Festrews. Oh, he loved the ship, and would not have traded her for the world. But much as he loved the *Vivacia*, he loved you girls more. And like you, he saw the contract as a threat to his children. He disliked being bound by an agreement he'd had no say in." Ronica lowered her voice. "In some ways, he thought ill of the Festrews, that they would hold him bound by such a cruel bargain. Perhaps they saw things differently in those days. Perhaps . . ." Her words faltered for a time. Then, "I suppose I lied to you just now. I speak the way I know I should think: that a bargain is a bargain, and a contract is a contract. But that contract was made in older, harder times. Still, it binds us."

"But father resented it," Keffria said, to draw her mind back to that.

"He despised the terms. He often pointed out that no one ever completely discharged a debt to the Rain Wilds. New debts were always stacked upon the old ones, so that the chains binding the contracting families together only got stronger and stronger as the years passed. He hated that idea. He wanted there to come a time when the ship would be ours, free and clear, and if we chose to pack up and leave Bingtown, we could do so."

The very idea shook Keffria to the foundations of her life. Leave Bingtown? Her father had actually thought of taking the family away from Bingtown?

Her mother spoke on. "And though his father and grandmother had traded in Rain Wild goods, he always felt they were tainted. That was how he put it. Tainted. Too much magic. He always felt that sooner or later, such magic would have to be paid for. And he did not think it was . . . honorable, in a way, for him to bring back to our world the magic of another place and time, a magic that had, perhaps, been the downfall of another folk. Perhaps the downfall of the entire Cursed Shores. Sometimes he spoke of it, late at night, saying he feared we would destroy ourselves and our world, just as the Elder folk did."

Ronica fell silent. Both women were still, thinking. These things were so seldom spoken aloud. Just as the charts of difficult channels represented a major trading advantage, so did the hard-won knowledge shared by Bingtown and Rain Wild Traders. The secrets they shared were as great a basis for their wealth as the goods they bartered.

Ronica cleared her throat. "So he did a thing both brave and hard. He stopped trading up the river. It meant he had to work twice as hard and be gone three times as much to turn the same profit. Instead of the Rain Wilds, he sought out the odd little places in the inland channels, to the south of Jamaillia. He traded with the native folk there, for goods that were exotic and rare. But not magical. He swore that would make our fortune. And if he had lived, it probably would have."

"Did Papa think the Blood Plague was due to the magic?" Keffria asked carefully.

"Where did you hear such a thing?" Ronica demanded.

"I was very little. It was right after the boys died. Davad was here, I remember. And Papa was crying and I was hiding outside the door. You were all in this same room. I wanted to come in but I was afraid to. Because Papa never cried. And I heard Davad Restart curse the Rain Wild Traders, saying they had dug up the disease in their mining of the city. His wife and children were dead, too. And Davad said . . ."

"I remember," Ronica said suddenly. "I remember what Davad

said. But what you were too small to understand was that he was in the throes of a terrible grief. A terrible grief." Ronica shook her head and her eyes were bleak, remembering. "A man says things at such times that he doesn't truly mean. Or even believe. Davad badly needed someone or something to blame for his loss. For a time he blamed the Rain Wild Traders. But he got past that a long time ago."

Keffria took a careful breath. "Is it true, that Davad's son—"

"What was that?" Her mother's sudden exclamation cut off Keffria's words. They both sat up and were still, listening. Ronica's eyes were so wide, the white showed all round them.

"It sounded like a gong," Keffria whispered into the gathered silence. It was eerie to hear a Rain Wild gong when they had been discussing them. She thought that she heard the scuff of footsteps in the hallway. With a wild look at her mother, she leapt to her feet. When she reached the door and pulled it open, her mother was right behind her. But all she caught was a brief glimpse of Malta at the end of the hall.

"Malta!" she called out sharply.

"Yes, mother?" The girl came back from around the corner. She was in her night-robe and carrying a cup and saucer.

"What are you doing up at this hour?" Keffria demanded.

For answer, Malta held up the cup. "I couldn't sleep. I made myself some chamomile tea."

"Did you hear an odd sound, a few moments ago?"

Malta shrugged. "Not really. Perhaps the cat knocked something down."

"Perhaps not," Ronica muttered worriedly. She brushed past Keffria and headed towards the kitchen. Keffria followed her and Malta, cup in hand, trailed after them curiously.

The kitchen was dark save for the glow of the banked fires. There were the familiar, somehow safe smells of the room: the cook fire, the yeasty smell of the slow bread put out to rise for the morning's baking, the lingering aroma of the night's meat. Ronica had brought a candle from the den; she crossed the familiar room to the outside door and tugged it open. Winter cold flowed in, making mist ghosts in the room.

"Is there anyone there?" Keffria asked as the candle guttered in the breeze.

"Not anymore," her mother replied grimly. She stepped out of the door onto the icy porch. She looked all around, and then stooped down to retrieve something. She came back into the kitchen and shut the door firmly.

"What is it?" Keffria and Malta asked together.

Ronica set the candle down on the table. Beside it she placed a small wooden box. She peered at it for a moment, then turned a narrowed gaze on Malta.

"It's addressed to Malta."

"It is?" Malta cried in delight. "What is it? Who is it from?" She surged towards the table, her face alight with anticipation. She had always loved surprises.

Her grandmother put a firm hand on top of the box as Malta reached for it. Her denial was plain. "What it is," Ronica went on in an icy tone, "I believe, is a dream-box. It is a traditional Rain Wild courting gift."

Keffria felt her heart pause inside her. She couldn't get her breath, but Malta only tugged at the box under her grandmother's forbidding grip. "What's in it?" she demanded. "Give it to me."

"No." Ronica's voice was full of authority. "You will come back with us to your grandfather's study. You have some explaining to do, young woman."

Ronica scooped up the box and strode from the room.

"Mother, it's not fair, it's addressed to me! Make Grandma give it to me. Mother? Mother!"

Keffria realized she was leaning on the table. She straightened up slowly. "Malta. Didn't you hear what your grandmother just told you? It's a courting gift! How could this be?"

Malta shrugged elaborately. "I don't know! I don't even know who it's from or what's in it! How can I tell you something about it if Grandma won't even let me look at it?"

"Come to the study," Keffria instructed her with a sigh. Malta raced off ahead of her. By the time Keffria entered the room, she was already arguing with her grandmother.

"Can't I at least look at it? It's for me, isn't it?"

"No. You can't. Malta, this is serious, far more serious than you seem to understand. This is a dream-box. And it's marked with the crest of the Khuprus family. They are perhaps the most prestigious family of the Rain Wild Traders. It was not a coincidence that they came to represent all the Rain Wild families at the last gathering. They are not a family to offend, or to take lightly. Knowing that, do you still want this box?" Ronica held it out to the child.

"Yes!" Malta replied indignantly and made a grab for it. Ronica snatched it back.

"Malta!" cried Keffria. "Don't be foolish. It's a courting gift. It must be sent back, but very politely. It must be made clear to them that you are too young to consider any man's suit. But in a very courteous way."

"No, I'm not," Malta protested. "I'm too young to be promised to a man, yet, but why can't I consider his suit? Please, Grandma, at least let me see what's in it!"

"It's a dream-box," Ronica said brusquely. "So it has a dream in it. You don't open it to see what's in it, you open it to have the dream."

"How can there be a dream in a box?" Keffria asked.

"Magic," Ronica said brusquely. "Rain Wild magic."

The sudden intake of Malta's breath betrayed her excitement. "Can I have it tonight?"

"No!" Ronica exploded. "Malta, you are not listening. You cannot have it at all. It has to be returned as it is, unopened, with an extremely courteous explanation that somehow there has been a misunderstanding. If you open this box and have this dream, you have consented to his suit. You have given him permission to court you."

"Well, what's so terrible about that? It's not like I'm promising to marry him!"

"If we allow you to open it, then we are accepting his suit as well. Which is the same thing as saying that we consider you a woman, and eligible to have suitors. Which we do not," Ronica finished firmly.

Malta crossed her arms on her chest, then flung herself back into a chair. She stuck her chin out. "I shall be so glad when my father comes home," she declared sulkily.

"Will you?" asked Ronica acidly.

Watching them both, Keffria felt invisible. And useless. To watch these two strong wills clash was like watching young bulls in the spring, when they pushed and snorted and challenged one another. There was a battle going on here, a battle for dominance, to determine which of these women was going to set the rules for the household while Kyle was away. No, she suddenly realized. Kyle was but a game-piece Malta threw in. Because Malta had already discovered she could manipulate her father. He was no match for her juvenile deviousness; as she grew, he would be even less of a problem to her. Plainly, she believed that only her grandmother stood in her path. Her own mother she had dismissed as insignificant.

Well, wasn't she? For years she had washed about with the ebb and flow of the household. Her father had sailed, her mother ran the on-shore holdings. She lived in her father's house still, as she always had. When Kyle had come home, they had spent his wages mostly on amusing themselves. Now her father was dead, and Kyle and her mother were battling over the helm, while Malta and her mother struggled over who would set the rules of the household. No matter how it was decided, Keffria would remain invisible and unheeded. Malta paid no attention to her floundering attempts at authority. No one did.

Keffria crossed the room abruptly. "Mother, give me the gift," she demanded peremptorily. "As my daughter has caused this unfortunate misunderstanding, I believe it is up to me to rectify the matter."

For a moment, she thought her mother would deny her. Then, with a glance at Malta, she handed it over to her. Keffria took the small wooden box. It weighed light in her hands. She became aware that it gave off a sweet scent, spicier than sandalwood. Malta's eyes tracked the box into her possession the way a hungry dog follows a piece of raw meat. "I shall write to them first thing in the morning. I think I can ask the *Kendry* to ferry it upriver for me."

Her mother was nodding. "But take care to wrap the box well. It would not do for anyone else to know what is being returned. The refusal of a courting suit, for any reason, is a delicate thing. It would be best if this were kept a secret between the two parties." As Keffria nodded to this, her mother suddenly turned to Malta. "Do you fully understand that, Malta? This cannot be spoken of to others, not to your little friends, not to the servants. This misunderstanding must be ended swiftly and completely."

The sullen girl looked at her mutely.

"Malta!" barked Keffria, and her daughter jumped. "Do you understand? Answer."

"I understand," she mumbled. She shot a defiant glance up at her mother, then wadded herself farther into her chair.

"Good. It's all settled then." Keffria had decided to end the battle while she was still winning. "And I'm ready to go to bed."

"Wait." Ronica's voice was serious. "There is one thing more you should know about a dream-box, Keffria. They are not common items. Each one is individually made, keyed to a certain person."

"How?" Keffria asked unwillingly.

"Well, of course I don't know. But one thing I do know is that to create one, the maker must begin with a personal item from the intended recipient." Her mother sighed as she leaned back in her chair. "Such a thing did not come to our door randomly. It was addressed to Malta specifically." Ronica shook her head and looked grieved. "Malta must have given something of hers to a Rain Wild man. Something personal that he construed as a gift."

"Oh, Malta, no!" Keffria cried in dismay.

"I did not," Malta sat up defiantly. "I did not!" She raised her voice in a shout.

Keffria got up and went to the door. Once she was sure it was firmly closed, she came back to confront her daughter. "I want the truth," she said quietly and simply. "What happened and when? How did you meet this young man? Why would he think you'd accept a courting gift from him?"

Malta glanced from one to the other. "At the Trader gathering," she admitted in disgust. "I went outside for some air. I said good evening to a coachman as I passed by. I think he was leaning on the Khuprus coach. That's all."

"What did he look like?" Ronica demanded.

"I don't know," Malta said, her words slowed with sarcasm. "He was from the Rain Wilds. They wear veils and hoods, you know."

"Yes, I do know," her grandmother retorted. "But their coachman does not. You foolish girl, do you think they drove a coach down the river? The Rain Wild families store their coaches here, and use them only when they come to Bingtown. So their hired drivers are from Bingtown. If you talked to a veiled man, you talked to a Rain Wild Trader. What did you say, and what did you give him?"

"Nothing," Malta flared. "I said 'good evening' as I passed him. He said the same. That's all."

"Then how does he know your name? How does he make you a dream?" Ronica pressed.

"I don't know," Malta retorted. "Maybe he guessed my family from my robe color, and asked someone." Suddenly, to Keffria's complete amazement, Malta burst into tears. "Why do you always treat me like this? You never say anything nice to me, it's always accusations and scolding. You think I'm some kind of a whore or a liar or something. Someone sends me a present, you won't even let me look at it, and you say it's all my fault. I don't know what you want from me anymore. You want me to be a little girl, but then you expect me to know everything and be responsible for everything. It's not fair!" She lowered her face into her hands and sobbed.

"Oh, Malta," Keffria heard herself say wearily. She went swiftly to her daughter, and put her hands on her shaking shoulders. "We don't think you're a whore and a liar. We're simply very worried about you. You're trying to grow up so fast, and there are so many dangers you don't understand."

"I'm sorry," Malta sobbed. "I shouldn't have gone outside that night. But it was so stuffy in there, and so scary with everyone yelling at each other."

"I know. I know, it was scary." Keffria patted her child. She hated to see Malta weep like this, hated that she and her mother had pressed her until she had broken down. At the same time, it was almost a relief. The defiant, bitter Malta was someone Keffria didn't know. This Malta was a little girl, crying and wanting to be comforted. Perhaps they had broken through tonight. Perhaps this Malta was someone she could reason with. She bent down to hug her daughter, who returned the embrace briefly and awkwardly.

"Malta," she said softly. "Here. Look here. Here is the box. You can't keep it or open it: it has to be returned tomorrow intact. But you can look at it."

Malta gave a sniff and sat up. She glanced at the box on her mother's palm, but did not reach for it. "Oh," she said after a moment. "It's just a carved box. I thought it might have jewels on it or something." She looked away from it. "Can I go to bed now?" she asked wearily.

"Of course. You go on to bed. We'll talk more in the morning, when we've all had some rest."

A very subdued Malta sniffed once, then nodded. Keffria watched her slowly leave the room, and then turned back to her own mother with a sigh. "Sometimes it's so hard, watching her grow up."

Ronica nodded sympathetically. But then she added, "Lock up that box somewhere safe for the night. I'll get a runner in the morning to carry your letter and the box down to the docks to the *Kendry*."

It was just a few hours shy of dawn when Malta took the small box back to her room. It had been exactly where she had known it would be: in her mother's "secret" cupboard at the back of her wardrobe in her dressing chamber. It was where she always hid the naming-day presents and her most expensive body oils. She had been afraid Mother would put it under her pillow, or perhaps even open the box and claim the dream for herself. But she hadn't.

Malta shut the door behind her and sat down on her bed with the box in her lap. Such a small present for them to raise such a fuss about. She lifted the box to her nose and inhaled. Yes, she had thought it carried a sweet scent. She got out of bed again and padded quietly across to her own wardrobe. In a box up in the corner, under several old dolls, was the scarf and the flame jewel. In the dark room it seemed to burn more brightly than ever. For a time she just watched it before she recalled why she had taken it out. She sniffed the scarf, then brought it back to her bed to compare it to the box. Different scents, both exotic. Both sweet, but different.

This box might not even have come from the veiled man, then. The mark on it was like the one on the coach, yes, but perhaps it had just been bought from the Khuprus family. Maybe it was really from Cerwin. Over the years, she'd left plenty of personal things over at Delo's home. It would have been very easy, and actually, it was much more likely when she thought about it. Why would a chance-met stranger send her an expensive gift? Like as not, this was a courting gift from Cerwin. The crowning piece of her logic suddenly fell into place. If the veiled Rain Wild man had puzzled out who she was and sent her a present, wouldn't he have reminded her to return his scarf and flame jewel at the same time? Of course he would. So this wasn't from him. This was from Cerwin.

She stuffed the scarf and jewel under her pillow, and curled up with the box in the curve of her body. With one forefinger, she traced the line of her lips. Cerwin. She ran her finger down over her chin, traced a line between her breasts. What kind of a dream would he have chosen for her? Her lips curved in a smile. She suspected she knew. Her heart fluttered in her chest.

She closed her eyes and opened the box. Or tried to. She opened her eyes and peered at it. What she had taken to be the catch was not. By the time she finally worked out how to open it, she was quite annoyed with it. And when she did get it open, it was empty. Simply empty. She had imagined a sparkling dream dust, or a burst of light or music or fragrance. She stared into the empty corners of the box, then felt inside it to be sure she wasn't missing anything. No. It was empty. So, what did that mean? A joke? Or merely that the gift was the cleverly carved and sweet-scented box? Maybe it wasn't even supposed to be a dream-box, maybe that was some old-fashioned idea that her grandmother had come up with. Dream-boxes. Malta had never heard of one before tonight. In a wave of irritation, it all became clear. Her grandmother had only said that so her mother wouldn't let her have the box. Unless, perhaps, one of them had opened it and taken out whatever was in there and kept it for themselves.

"I hate them both," Malta hissed in a savage whisper. She flung the box down to the rug beside her bed and threw herself back on her pillows. She knew she should get up and go and put the box back in her mother's wardrobe, but a part of her didn't care. Let them find out she had taken it. She wanted them to know that she knew they'd stolen her present. She crossed her arms unrepentantly on her chest and closed her eyes.

Stillness. Emptiness. Only a voice. A whisper. *So, Malta Vestrit. You have received my gift. Here we mingle, you and I. Shall we make a sweet dream together? Let us see.* A tiny thread of awareness that this was a dream faded out of reach.

She was inside a burlap bag. It covered her head and draped down almost to her knees. It smelled of dust and potatoes. She was fairly sure it had been used as a harvest sack. She was being carried over someone's shoulder, carried rapidly and triumphantly, snatched and carried off against her will. The one who carried her had companions. They hooted and laughed in victory, but the man who carried her was too full of satisfaction to give vent to such boyish noises. The night was cool and foggy-moist against her legs. Her mouth was gagged, her hands bound behind her. She wanted to struggle but was afraid that if she did, he might drop her. And she had no idea where she was or what else might befall her if she did escape her captor. Frightening as it was, it was still the safest place she could be at this moment. She knew nothing of the man who carried her, except that he would fight to the death to keep her.

They reached somewhere. They all stopped, and the one carrying her slung her to her feet. He kept a grip on her. She heard a muffled conversation, quick words spoken low in a language she didn't understand. The others seemed to be laughingly urging something that the one who had carried her amiably but firmly refused. After a time, she heard footsteps receding. She sensed the others had gone. She was alone save for the man who still held her bound wrists. She trembled.

There was the cold kiss of metal against her wrists and suddenly her hands were free. She immediately clawed her way free of the sack, and pulled the wet gag from her mouth. She was still half-blinded by the dust and fibers from the rough burlap. She brushed roughly at her face and hair and then turned to confront her captor.

They were alone in a dark and foggy night. A city and a crossroads. She could tell no more than that. He stood watching her expectantly. She could see nothing of his features. His dark hood was pulled far forward; he watched her from its depths. The night smelled swampy and thick, the only lights were fog-muffled torches far down the street. If she ran, would he pounce on her? Was this a cat's game?

If she escaped, would she be plunging herself into greater danger? In time it seemed to her that he was watching her and letting her make up her mind about what she would do.

After a time, he made a sign with his head that she should follow him. He walked away swiftly down one of the streets and she went with him. He moved quickly and confidently through the labyrinthine city. After a time, he took her hand. She did not pull away. The fog was thick and wet, blinding, almost choking, and it was so dark she could make out nothing of her greater surroundings. Openings in the fog showed her tall buildings to either side of the alley they walked. But the darkness and silence seemed complete. Her companion seemed certain of his way. His large hand was warm and dry as it clasped her chilled one.

He finally turned aside, to lead her down some steps and then open a door. When the door was opened, sound boomed out. Music, laughter and talk, but all of a style and language she did not know, and so it was all just noise. Deafening noise, so that even if she had been able to understand her companion, she would not have been able to hear him. It was some kind of an inn or tavern, she surmised. There were many small round tables, each with a single short candle burning in the center. He led her to an empty one, and gestured her to a seat. He sat down across from her. He pushed back his hood.

For a long time in the dream, they just sat there. Perhaps he listened to the music, but to her it was a sound so uniformly loud that she felt deafened. By the candlelight, she could finally see her companion's face. He was handsome, in a pale way. Beardless and blond, his eyes a warm brown. He had a small soft mustache. His shoulders were wide, his arms well-muscled. He did nothing at first, save look at her. After a time, he reached across the table and she put her hand in his. He smiled. She suddenly felt they had come to so perfect an understanding that she was glad there were no words that could interfere. A long time seemed to pass. Then he reached into a pouch and brought out a ring with a simple stone on it. She looked at it, and then shook her head. She was not refusing the ring; she was only saying that she did not need an outward symbol. The agreement they had already reached was too flawless to complicate with such things. He put the ring away. Then he leaned across the table towards her. Heart thundering, she leaned forward to meet him. He kissed her. Only their mouths met. She had never before kissed a man, and it stood gooseflesh up all over her to feel the softness of his mustache beside her lips, the swift brush of his tongue that bade her lips part to his. All time stopped, hovering like a nectar bird in that one sweet moment of decision, to open or remain closed.

Somewhere, a distant male amusement, but one that approved. *You have a warm nature, Malta. Very warm. Even if your ideas of courtship hark back to that most ancient custom of abduction.* It was all fading now, whirling away from her, leaving only that tickle of sensation on her mouth. *I think we shall dance well together, you and I.*

CHAPTER TWENTY-SEVEN

PRISONERS

WINTROW WAS IN A LARGE SHED. IT WAS OPEN ON ONE SIDE AND NOTHING IMPEDED THE FLOW OF WINTER cold into it. The roof overhead was sound, but the walls were little more than rough slab wood cobbled over a beam framework. The stall he was in opened onto a walkway. It faced a long row of identical stalls. The slat sides of it gave him only nominal privacy. There was a scattering of straw on the floor for him to curl up on and a filthy bucket in one corner to contain his wastes. The only thing that prevented him from simply walking away were the leg-irons on his ankles that were chained to a heavy metal staple driven deeply into an iron-hard beam. He had worn most of the skin off his ankles determining that human strength was not going to budge the staple. It was his fourth day here.

In one more day, if no one came to redeem him, then he could be sold as a slave.

This had been carefully explained to him twice by a jovial keeper, on his first and second day of confinement. The man came once a day with a basket of rolls. He was followed by his half-wit son, who pulled a cart with a tub of water on it, and ladled out a cupful of it to every prisoner.

The first time he explained it, Wintrow had begged him to carry word of his plight to the priests in Sa's temple. Surely they would come to claim him. But the keeper had declined to waste his time. The priests, he had explained, did not meddle in civil affairs anymore. The Satrap's prisoners were a civil affair, nothing at all to do with Sa or his worship. The Satrap's prisoners, if not redeemed, became the Satrap's slaves, to be sold off to benefit the royal treasury. That would be a sad end to such a short life. Had not the boy some family the keeper might contact? The keeper's wheedling tone clearly conveyed that he would be happy to convey any message, so long as there was a good chance of a bribe or reward. Surely his mother must be worried about him by now? Had he no brothers who would pay his fine and get him released?

Each time Wintrow had bitten his tongue. He had time, he told himself, to work out his own solution to this problem. Having the man send word to his father would only land him back in his original captivity. That was no solution at all. Surely something else would occur to him if he simply thought hard enough.

And his situation was certainly conducive to thought. There was little else to do. He could sit, stand, lie or squat in the straw. Sleep held no rest. The noises of the stalls invaded his dreams, populating them with dragons and serpents that argued and pleaded with human tongues. Awake, there was no one to talk to. One side of his enclosure was the outer wall of the shed. In the stalls to either side of him, a succession of prisoners had come and gone: a disorderly drunk rescued by his weeping wife, a prostitute who had stabbed her customer and been branded in retribution, a horse-thief who had been taken away to hang. Justice, or at least punishment, was swift in the Satrap's cells.

A straw-littered aisle fronted his cage. Another row of similar stalls were on the opposite side of it. Slaves were held in those ones. Unruly and undesirable slaves, map-faces with scarred backs and legs came and went from the leg-irons. They were sold cheaply and used hard, from what Wintrow could see. They did not talk much, even to each other. Wintrow judged they had little left to talk about. Take all self-determination from a man's life, and all that is left for him to do is complain. This they did do, but in a dispirited way that indicated they expected no changes. They reminded Wintrow of chained and barking dogs. The sullen map-faces across the way would be good for heavy labor and crude work in fields and orchards, but little more than that. This he had surmised from listening in on their talk. Most of the men and women stabled across from him had been slaves for years, and fully expected to end their lives as slaves. Despite Wintrow's disgust with the concept of slavery, it was hard to feel sorry for some of them. Some had obviously become little more than beasts of labor, decrying their hard lot but no longer having the will to struggle against it. After watching them for a few days, he could understand why some worshippers of Sa could look at such slaves and believe they were so by Sa's will. It was truly hard to imagine them as free men and women with mates and children and homes and livelihoods. He did not think they had been born without souls, predestined to be slaves. But never before had he seen people so bereft of humanity's spiritual spark. Whenever he watched them, a cold slug of fear crawled slowly through his guts. How long would it take for him to become just like them?

He had one day left in which to think of something. Tomorrow, in the morning, they would come and take him to the tattooing block. They'd chain his wrists and ankles to the heavy staples there, and force his head down into the leather-wrapped vise. There they would put the small mark that designated him as the Satrap's slave. If the Satrap chose to keep him that would be the only tattoo he ever wore. But the Satrap would not choose to keep him. He had no special skills worthy of the Satrap holding onto him as a slave. He would be put up for immediate sale. And when he was sold, a new mark, the sigil of some new owner, would be needled into his face.

He had teetered back and forth for several hours. If he called for the keeper, and the man sent a runner down to the harbor, his father would come and get him. Or send someone to fetch him. Then he would go back to the ship, and become once more a prisoner there. But at least his face would be unscarred. If he did not call for his father's aid, he would be tattooed, and sold, and tattooed again. Unless he either escaped or worked free of slavery, he would forever remain someone else's property, at least legally. In either case, he would never become a priest of Sa. As he was determined to fulfill his vocation to be a priest, determined to return home to his monastery, the whole question came down to which situation offered him the better chance of escape.

And on that fine conclusion, his thoughts halted and teetered. He simply didn't know.

So he sat in the corner of his pen and idly watched the buyers who came to peruse the cheap and undesirable slaves across from him. He was hungry and cold and uncomfortable. But the worst sensation of all was his indecision. That was what kept him from curling up in a morose ball and sleeping.

He did not recognize Torg walking slowly along the fronts of the slave stalls for several minutes. Then, when he did, he was shocked when his heart gave a leap of near joy. What it was, he realized, was relief. Torg would see him and tell his father. He would not have to make what he had always suspected was a cowardly decision. Torg would do it for him. And when his father came for him, he could not mock him that he had cried out for help from him.

Much insight into himself could have been gained from a contemplation of these things, but Wintrow reined his mind away from it. Perhaps he did not want to know himself quite that well. Instead he abruptly stood up. He moved to the corner of his pen to lounge defiantly against the wall. He crossed his arms on his chest and waited for Torg to notice him.

It was surprisingly difficult to stand still and silent and wait for Torg to notice him. Torg was making his way slowly down the opposite row, examining every slave, dickering with the keeper, and then either nodding or shaking his head. The keeper had a tally block he was marking as they came. After a time, it puzzled Wintrow. Torg seemed to be buying a substantial number of slaves, but these were not the artisans and educated slaves that his father had spoken of acquiring.

He watched Torg swagger along, obviously impressed with his own importance as a buyer of human flesh. He strutted for the keeper as if he were a man worth impressing, inspecting the slaves with fine disregard for their dignity or comfort. The longer Wintrow watched him, the more he despised the man. Here, then, was the counterpoint to the slaves' loss of spirit and spark: a man whose self-importance fed on the humiliation and degradation of others.

And yet there was a horrible kernel of fear in Wintrow's waiting, too. What if Torg did not turn and notice him? What then? Would Wintrow abase himself by calling out to the man? Or let him pass by, and face a future full of dealing with other Torgs? Just as Wintrow thought he would cry out, just as he bit down on his own tongue to keep it from betraying him, Torg glanced at him. And away, and then back, as if he could not believe what his eyes had shown him. His eyes widened, and then a grin split his face. He immediately left his task to stride over to Wintrow.

"Well, well," he exclaimed in vast satisfaction. "I do believe I've earned myself quite a bonus here. Quite a bonus." His eyes roved up and down Wintrow, taking in the straw clinging to his worn robe, to the shackles around his chafed ankles and his face white with cold. "Well, well," he repeated. "Doesn't look as if your freedom lasted long, holy boy."

"Do you know this prisoner?" the keeper demanded as he came to stand beside Torg.

"Indeed I do. His father is . . . my business partner. He has been wondering where his son disappeared to."

"Ah. Then it is fortunate for you that you have found him today. Tomorrow, his freedom would have been forfeit for his fine. He would have been tattooed the Satrap's slave, and sold."

"The Satrap's slave." The grin came back to Torg's face. His pale eyebrows danced over his gray eyes. "Now, there's an amusing idea." Wintrow could almost see the slow workings of Torg's brain. "How much is the boy's fine?" he demanded suddenly of the keeper.

The old man consulted a tally cord at his waist. "Twelve bits of silver. He killed one of the Satrap's other slaves, you know."

"He what?" For a moment Torg looked incredulous. Then he burst out laughing. "Well, I doubt that, but I don't doubt there's quite a tale attached to it. So. If I come back with twelve silver bits tonight, I buy him free. What if I don't?" He narrowed both his eyes and grinned as he asked, more of Wintrow than the keeper, "What would he sell for tomorrow?"

The keeper shrugged. "Whatever he would bring. New slaves are generally auctioned. Sometimes they have friends or family who are willing to buy them free. Or enemies eager to have them as slaves. The auction bidding can be quite fierce. And sometimes amusing as well." The keeper had seen who had the power and was playing to him. "You could wait it out, and buy him back. Perhaps you'd save a coin or two. Perhaps you'd have to pay more. But he would be marked by then, marked with the Satrap's sigil. You or his father could grant him his freedom after that, of course. But he'd have to have some tattoo from you, and some sort of paper or ring to say he was free."

"Couldn't we just burn the tattoo off?" Torg asked callously. His eyes devoured Wintrow's face, looking for some kind of fear. Wintrow refused to show any. Torg would never dare to let it go so far. This was but the same kind of mockery and taunting the man always indulged in. If Wintrow gave any sign of being upset by it, Torg would only indulge in more of it. He let his eyes wander past Torg as if he were no longer interested in him or his words.

"Burning off a slave tattoo is illegal," the keeper pronounced ponderously. "A person with a burn scar to the left of his nose is assumed to be an escaped and dangerous slave. He'd be brought right back here, if he were caught. And tattooed again with the Satrap's sign."

Torg shook his head woefully, but his grin was evil. "Such a shame, to mark such a sweet little face as that, eh? Well," he turned abruptly aside from him. With a jerk of his head, he indicated the slaves he had not yet inspected. "Shall we continue?"

The keeper frowned. "Do you want me to send for a runner? To take word of this boy to his father?"

"No, no, don't trouble yourself. I'll see his father hears of his whereabouts. He's not going to be pleased with the boy. Now, what about this woman? Has she any special skill or training?" His voice caressed the last two words, making it a cruel joke on the elderly hag who crouched before them.

Wintrow stood trembling in his pen. The anger he felt inside him threatened to burst him wide open. Torg would leave him here, in cold and filth, for as long as he could. But he'd tell his father, and then come down here with him to witness their confrontation. With a sudden cold sinking of his heart, Wintrow considered how vast his father's anger would be. He'd feel humiliated as well. Kyle Haven did not like to be humiliated. He'd find ways of expressing that to his son. Wintrow leaned against the wall of his pen miserably. He should have just waited and endured. It was less than a year now to his fifteenth birthday. When it came, he would declare himself a man independent of his father's will, and just step off the ship wherever it was. This foolish attempt at running away was only going to make the months stretch longer. Why hadn't he waited? Slowly he sank down to sit in the straw in the corner of his pen. He closed his eyes to sleep. Sleeping was far better than considering his father's anger to come.

"Get out," Kennit repeated in a low growl. Etta stood where she was, her face pale, her mouth firm. One hand held a basin of water, the other was draped in bandaging.

"I thought a fresh bandage might be more comfortable," she dared to say. "That one is stiff with dry blood and—"

"Get out!" he roared. She whirled, sloshing water over the rim of the basin and fled. The door of his cabin thudded shut behind her.

He had been awake and clear-headed since early morning, but those were the first words he had spoken to anyone. He had spent most of that time staring at the wall, unable to grasp that his luck had forsaken him. How could this have happened to him? How was it possible for Captain Kennit to suffer this? Well. It was time. Time to see what the bitch had done to him, time to take command again. Time. He braced his fists deep in his bedding and hauled himself upright to a sitting position. When his injured leg dragged against the bedding, the pain was such that he felt ill. A new sweat broke out on him, plastering his stinking nightshirt to his back once more. Time. He grabbed the bedclothes and tore them aside. He looked down at the leg she had ruined.

It was gone.

His nightshirt had been carefully folded and pinned back from it. There were his legs, swarthy and hairy as ever. But the one just stopped short, snubbed off in a dirty brownish wad of bandaging right below his knee. It couldn't be. He reached toward it, but could not touch it. Instead, stupidly, he put his hand on the empty linen where the rest of his leg should have been. As if the fault might have been with his eyes.

He keened, then drew a breath and held it. He would not make another sound. Not one sound. He tried to remember how it had come to this. Why had he ever brought the crazy bitch aboard, why had they been attacking slaveships in the first place? Merchant ships, that was where the money was. And they didn't have a herd of serpents trailing after them, ready to grab a man's leg. This was their fault, Sorcor's and Etta's. But for them, he'd still be a whole man.

Calm. Calm. He had to be calm, he had to think this through. He was trapped here, in this cabin, unable to walk or fight. And Etta and Sorcor were both against him. What he had to figure out now was if they were in league with one another. And why had they done this to him? Why? Did they hope to take the ship from him? He took another breath, tried to organize his thoughts. "Why did she do this to me?" A second thought occurred to him. "Why didn't she just kill me then? Was she afraid my crew would turn on her?" If so, then perhaps she and Sorcor were not in league. . . .

"She did it to save your life." The tiny voice from his wrist was incredulous. "How can you be this way? Don't you remember it at all? A serpent had you by the leg, he was trying to pick you up and flip you into the air so he could gulp you down. Etta had to cut your leg off. It was the only way to keep him from getting all of you."

"I find that very difficult to believe," he sneered at the charm.

"Why?"

"Because I know her. That's why."

"As do I. Which is why that answer doesn't make sense either," the face observed cheerily.

"Shut up."

Kennit forced himself to look at the wrapped stump. "How bad is it?" he asked the charm in a low voice.

"Well, for starters, it's gone," the charm informed him heartlessly. "Etta's hatchet chop was the only clean part of the severing.

The part the serpent did was half chewed and half sort of melted away. The flesh reminded me of melted tallow. Most of that brown stuff isn't blood, it's oozing pus."

"Shut up," Kennit said faintly. He stared at the clotted, smeary bandaging and wondered what was beneath it. They had put a folded cloth beneath it, but there was still a smear of ochre stuff across his fine, clean linen. It was disgusting.

The little demon grinned up at him. "Well, you asked."

Kennit took a deep breath and bellowed, "Sorcor!"

The door flew open almost immediately, but it was Etta who stood there, teary and distraught. She hastened into the room. "Oh, Kennit, are you in pain?"

"I want Sorcor!" he declared, and even to himself it sounded like the demand of a petulant child. Then the brawny first mate filled the doorway. To Kennit's dismay, he looked as solicitous as Etta as he asked, "Is there aught I can do for you, Captain?" Sorcor's unruly hair stood up as if he had been pulling at it, and his face was sallow beneath its scars and weathering.

He tried to remember why he had called for Sorcor. He looked down at the disgusting mess in his bed. "I want this cleaned up." He managed to sound firmly in command, as if he were speaking of a sloppy deck. "Have a hand heat some water for a bath for me. And lay out a clean shirt." He looked up at Sorcor's incredulous stare and realized he was treating him more like a valet than his second in command. "You understand that how I appear when I interrogate the prisoners is important. They must not see me as a crippled wreck in a wad of dirty bedding."

"Prisoners?" Sorcor asked stupidly.

"Prisoners," Kennit replied firmly. "I directed that three were to be saved, did I not?"

"Yessir. But that was . . ."

"And were not three saved for me to question?"

"I have one," Sorcor admitted uneasily. "Or what's left of one. Your woman has been at him."

"What?"

"It was his fault," Etta growled low as a threatening cat. "All his fault that you were hurt." Her eyes had gone to alarming slits.

"Well. One, you say," Kennit attempted a recovery. What kind of a creature had he brought aboard his ship? *Don't think of that just now. Take command.* "See to my orders, then. When I've made myself presentable, I'll want the prisoner brought here. I don't wish to see much of the crew just now. How did the rest of the capture go?"

"Slick as a plate of guts, sir. And we got a little bonus with this one." Despite the anxiety etched in Sorcor's face, he grinned. "Seems this ship was a bit special. Carrying a bunch of regular slaves, but forward was a batch that were a gift from the Satrap of Jamaillia himself to some high muckamuck in Chalced. A troupe of dancers and musicians, with all their instruments and fancy duds and pots of face paint. And jewels, several nice little casks of sparklies . . . I stowed those under your bunk, sir. And an assortment of fine cloths, lace, some silver statues and bottled brandies. A very nice little haul. Not weighty, but all of the best quality." He gave a sideways glance at Kennit's stump. "Perhaps you'd like to sample some of the brandy now yourself."

"In a bit. These dancers and musicians . . . are they tractable? How do they feel about having their journey interrupted?" Why hadn't they thrown them overboard with the rest of the crew?

"Wonderful, sir. They'd all been taken as slaves, you see. The company was in debt, so when the owners went bust, the Satrap ordered the dancers and musicians seized as well. Which wasn't quite legal, but being the Satrap, I suppose he doesn't have to worry about that part. No, they're happy as clams at being captured by pirates. Their captain already has them at work, making up songs and dances to tell the whole story of it. You being the hero of the piece, of course."

"Of course." Songs and dances. Kennit suddenly felt unaccountably weary. "We're . . . at anchor. Where? Why?"

"Cove don't have a name that I know, but it's shallow here. The *Sicerna* was taking on water; had been for some time. Slaves in the bottom hold were just about waterlogged all the time. Seemed best to anchor her up where she couldn't sink too far while we rigged extra pumps for her. Then I thought we'd make for Bull Creek. We've got plenty of man-power to keep the pumps going all the way there."

"Why Bull Creek?" Kennit asked.

Sorcor shrugged. "There's a decent haul-out beach there." He shook his head. "She'll take some work before she'll be sea-worthy again. And Bull Creek has been raided twice in the last year by slavers, so I think we'll be welcomed there."

"There. You see," Kennit said faintly. He smiled to himself. Sorcor was right. The man had learned much from him. Put a ship there, speak persuasively there, and he could win another little town over. What could he say to them. "If the Pirate Isles had one ruler . . . that raiders feared . . . folk could live . . ." A tremble ran through him.

Etta rushed at him. "Lie back, lie back. You've gone white as a sheet. Sorcor, go for those things, the bath and all that. Oh, and bring in the basin and bandaging I left on the deck outside. I'll want them now." Kennit listened in dismay as she ordered his mate about with a fine disdain for protocol.

"Sorcor can bandage this," Kennit declared mistrustfully.

"I'm better at it," she asserted calmly.

"Sorcor—" he began again, but now the first mate dared to interrupt him with, "Actually, sir, she has quite a nice touch for it. Took care of all our boys after the last set to, and did a fine job of it. I'll see to the wash water." Then he was gone, leaving Kennit helpless and alone with the bloodthirsty wench.

"Now sit still," she told him, as if he could get up and run away. "I'm going to lift your leg up and put a pad underneath it so we don't soak all your bedding. Then when we're finished, we'll give you clean linens." He clenched his teeth and squinted his eyes and managed not to make a sound as she lifted his stump and deftly slid more folded rags under it. "Now I'm going to wet the old bandages before I try to take them off. They pull less that way."

"You seem to know a great deal about this," he gritted out.

"Whores get beaten up a lot," she pointed out pragmatically. "If the women in a house don't take care of each other, who will?"

"And I should trust the care of my injury to the woman who cut my leg off?" he asked coolly.

All her motion ceased. Like a flower wilting, she sank down on the floor beside his bed. Her face was very pale. She leaned forward until her forehead rested on the edge of his bed. "It was the only way I could save you. I'd have cut off both my hands instead of your leg, if that would have saved you."

This declaration struck Kennit as so profoundly absurd that he was speechless for a moment. The charm, however, was not. "Captain Kennit can be a heartless pig. But I assure you that I understand that you did what you had to do to preserve me. I thank you for your deed."

Shock warred with fury that the charm would so betray itself to another. He immediately clapped his hand over it, only to feel tiny teeth sink savagely into the meat of his palm. He snatched his hand away with a gasp of pain as Etta lifted her face to regard him with tear-filled eyes. "I understand," she said hoarsely. "There are many roles a man has to play. It is probably necessary that Captain Kennit be a heartless pig." She shrugged her shoulders and tried to smile. "I do not hold it against the Kennit who is mine."

Her nose had turned red and her leaky eyes were most distressing. Worse, she dared to believe him capable of thanking her for cutting off his leg. Mentally he cursed his sly, malicious charm for putting him in such a fix, even as he grasped at the straw of hope that she truly believed such words could come from his lips. "Let's say no more about it," he suggested hastily. "Make the best you can of the wretched mess of my leg."

The water she used to soak the bandaging free was warm as blood. He scarely felt it, until she began gingerly to peel the layers of linen and lint from the wound. Then he turned his head aside and focused on the wall until the edges of his vision began to waver. Sweat sheeted his body. He wasn't even aware that Sorcor had come back until the mate offered him an open bottle of brandy.

"A glass?" Kennit asked disdainfully.

Sorcor swallowed. "From the look of your leg, I thought it might be a waste of time."

If Sorcor hadn't said that, Kennit might have been able not to look at his stump. But now as the sailor fumbled clumsily in a cupboard for an appropriate glass, Kennit turned his head slowly to look down to where his sound, strong, muscular leg had once been.

The dirty bandaging had actually cushioned the shock. Seeing his leg end in a wad of stained fabric was not the same as seeing his leg stop in a mangle of chewed and seared flesh. The end of it looked partially cooked. His gorge rose, and sour bile bubbled into the back of his throat. He swallowed it back, refusing to disgrace himself in front of them. Sorcor's hand was shaking as he offered him the glass. Ridiculous. The man had dealt worse injuries than the one he was looking at now. Kennit took the glass and downed the brandy at a gulp. Then he took a shaky breath. Well, perhaps his luck had held in one odd way. At least the whore knew how to doctor him.

Snatching even that bare comfort away from him, Etta said in a quiet whisper to Sorcor, "This is a mess. We need to get him to a healer. And quickly."

He counted three breaths as he drew them. He gestured with the glass at Sorcor, but when the man tried to fill his glass, Kennit took the bottle from him instead. One drink. Three breaths. Another drink. Three breaths. No. It was time, it was time now.

He pushed himself up to a full sitting position again. He looked down at the thing on the bed that had been his leg. Then he untied the lace of his nightshirt at his throat. "Where is my wash water?" he demanded brusquely. "I have no wish to sit here in my own stink. Etta. Leave off that until I am washed. Lay out clean garments for me, and find clean linens for this bed. I will be properly washed and dressed before I interrogate my prisoner."

Sorcor cast a sideways glance at Etta before he said quietly, "Begging your pardon, sir, but a blind man isn't going to notice how you're dressed."

Kennit looked at him evenly. "Who is our prisoner?"

"Captain Reft of the *Sicerna*. Etta made us fish him out."

"He was not blinded in the battle. He was intact when he fell in the water."

"Yes sir." Sorcor glanced at Etta and swallowed. So. That was the basis of this deferential wariness the mate now had for his whore. It was almost amusing. It was evidently one thing for Sorcor to dismember a man in battle, and quite another for the whore to torment one in captivity. He had not known Sorcor was prey to such niceties.

"Perhaps a blind man might not know how I was attired, but I would," Kennit pointed out. "See to your orders. Now."

But even as he spoke, there was a tap at the door. Sorcor admitted Opal, who bore two steaming wooden buckets of water. He set them down on the floor. He didn't even dare look at Kennit, let alone speak to him. "Mister Sorcor, sir, them music people want to make music on our deck for the captain. They said I should uh, 'beg your indulgence.' And," the boy's brow furrowed with an effort to recall the foreign words, "um, they want to, uh, 'express extreme gratitudes' . . . something like that."

Kennit felt a tiny twitch of movement against his wrist. He glanced down at the charm hidden in the cradle of his folded arms. It was making frantic faces of assent and enthusiasm. The traitorous little bastard-thing actually seemed to think he would heed its advice. It was mouthing some words at him.

"Sir?" Sorcor asked deferentially.

Kennit feigned rubbing his head to bring the charm near his ear. "A king should be gracious to his grateful subjects. A gift disdained can harden any man's heart."

Kennit abruptly decided it was good advice, regardless of the source.

"Tell them it would give me great pleasure," Kennit told Opal directly. "Harsh as my life has been, I am not a man who disdains the finer pleasures of the arts."

"Sar!" the boy blasphemed in admiration. He nodded, his face flushing with pride in his captain. A serpent might bite his leg off, but he'd still have time for culture. "I'll tell them, sir. Harsh life, finer pleasures," he reminded himself as he scurried from the room.

As soon as the boy was out of the room, Kennit turned to Sorcor. "Go to the prisoner. Give him enough water and food to revive him. Etta, my bath, please."

After the mate had left, she eased him out of his night-robe. She washed him with a sponge, as Chalcedeans did. He had always thought it a nasty way to bathe, a mere smearing of sweat and dirt instead of a clean washing away, but she managed it well enough that he actually felt clean. As she attended to the more intimate parts of such a washing, he reflected that perhaps there was more than one way for a woman to be useful to a man. The bathing and wrapping of his injury was still unpleasant enough that afterwards she had to once more wash sweat from his back, chest and brow. Soft music began, a gentle composition of strings and chimes and women's voices. It was actually pleasant.

Etta matter-of-factly ripped a side seam out of one pair of his trousers to allow her to dress him almost painlessly, and then stitched it up around him again. She buttoned his shirt for him, and then groomed his hair and beard as skillfully as any valet. She took more than half his weight to help him to his chair while she stripped the bed and made it up afresh. It had never occurred to him that Etta might possess such talents. Clearly he had not appreciated how useful she might be to him.

When he was properly washed and attired, she disappeared briefly, only to return with a tray of food. He had not even been aware of his hunger until he smelled the hot soup and light bread. When the sharpest pangs of his appetite were dulled, he set down his spoon to ask quietly, "And what inspired you to make free with my prisoner?"

She gave a tiny sigh. "I was so angry," she shook her head at herself. "So angry when they hurt you. When they made me hurt you. I vowed I'd get a liveship for you if it was the last thing I ever did. Plainly that was what you wished to ask the prisoners about. So. At the times when I was worn to death of sitting by your bedside but still could not sleep, I went to see them."

"Them?"

"There were three, at first." She shrugged casually. "I believe I have the information you want. I checked and rechecked it most carefully. Nonetheless, I took care to keep one alive, as I was sure you'd wish to confirm it for yourself."

A woman of many talents. And intelligent, too. He'd probably have to kill her soon. "And you discovered?"

"They had word of only two liveships. The first is a cog, the *Ophelia*. She left Jamaillia City before they did, but she still had

Bingtown goods to trade, so she'd be making other stops as she came north." Etta shrugged. "She could be behind them still, she could be ahead of them. There is no way to be sure. The only other liveship they've seen lately was in Jamaillia City. She came into the harbor the day before they left. She didn't plan to be staying there long. She was unloading cargo, and being refitted to haul a load of slaves north to Chalced."

"That makes no sense, to use a liveship so," Kennit exclaimed in disgust. "They lied to you."

Etta gave a tiny shrug. "That's always possible, I suppose. But they lied very well, individually, at different times." She wadded his sweaty shirt up with the stained linen from his bed. "They convinced me."

"Easy enough to convince a woman. And that was the whole of what they told you?"

She gave him a look that dared to be cool. "Likely the rest was lies, too."

"I would hear it, anyway."

She sighed. "They did not know much. Most of it was rumor. The two ships were in harbor together for less than a day. The *Vivacia* is owned by a Bingtown Trader family named Haven. The ship will be making for Chalced by the Inside Passage as swiftly as she can. They hoped to buy mostly artisans and skilled workers, but might take on some others just for ballast. A man named Torg was in charge of everything, but he didn't seem to be the captain. She's newly quickened. This is her maiden voyage."

Kennit shook his head at her. "Haven isn't a Trader name."

She spread her hands at him. "You were right. They lied to me." She turned her face from him, and stared stonily at a bulkhead. "I'm sorry I bungled the questioning."

She was becoming intractable. If he'd had two good legs under him, he'd have strode up to her and pushed her onto her back on the bed and reminded her what she was. Instead, he'd have to flatter her. He tried to think of something nice to say to her, to make her pleasant again. But the interminable throbbing of his missing leg had suddenly become a pounding pain. He wanted only to lie down, to go back to sleep and avoid all of this. And he'd have to ask her to help him.

"I'm helpless. I can't even get back into my bed alone," he said bitterly. In rare honesty he declared, "I hate for you to see me this way." Outside, the music changed. One strong man's voice took up a chant, at once forceful and tender. He cocked his head to make out the oddly familiar words. "Ah," he said softly to himself. "I know it now. 'From Kytris, To His Mistress.' A lovely piece." He tried again to find a compliment to give her. He couldn't think of any. "You could go out on deck and listen to the music, if you wished," he offered her. "It's quite an old poem, you know." The edges of his vision wavered. His eyes watered with his pain. "Have you heard it before?" he asked, trying to keep his voice steady.

"Oh, Kennit." She shook her head, suddenly and inexplicitly contrite. Tears stood in her eyes as she came to him. "It sounds more sweet to me here than anywhere else. I'm sorry. I'm such a heartless wench sometimes. Look at you, white as a sheet. Let me help you lie down."

And she did, as gently as she could manage. She sponged his face with cool water. "No," he protested feebly. "I'm cold. I'm too cold."

She covered him gently, and then lay down along his good side. The warmth of her body was actually pleasant, but the lace on the front of her shirt scratched his face. "Take your clothes off," he directed her. "You're warmest when you're naked."

She gave a short laugh, at once pleased and surprised. "Such a man," she rebuked him. But she rose to obey him.

There was a knock at the door. "What?" Kennit demanded.

Sorcor's voice sounded surprised. "I've brought you the prisoner, sir."

It was all too much trouble. "Never mind," he said faintly. "Etta already questioned him. I've no need of him anymore."

Her clothing fell to the floor around her. She climbed into the bed carefully, easing her warmth up against him. He was suddenly so tired. Her skin was soft and warm, a balm.

"Captain Kennit?" Sorcor's voice was insistent, worried.

"Yes," he acknowledged.

Sorcor jerked the door open. Behind him two sailors held up what remained of the captain of the *Sicerna*. They met their captain's eyes, then both gaped at him in amazement. Kennit turned his head to follow their gaze. Beside him in the bed, Etta held the blanket firmly below her naked shoulders and just above the slight curve of her breasts. The music from the deck came more loudly into the room. He turned his head back to the prisoner. Etta had more than blinded him. She had dismantled the man a bit at a time. Disgusting. He didn't want to look at that just now. But he had to keep up appearances. He cleared his throat. Get it over with.

"Prisoner. Did you tell my woman the truth?"

The wreckage between the two sailors lifted a ruined face towards his voice. "I swear I did. Over and over again. Why would I lie?" The man began to weep noisily. He snuffled oddly with his nostrils slit. "Please, good sir, don't let her at me no more. I told her the truth. I told her everything I knew."

It suddenly seemed like too much trouble. The man had obviously lied to Etta and now he was lying to Kennit as well. The prisoner was useless. The pain from his leg was banging against the inside of Kennit's skull. "I'm . . . occupied." He did not want to admit how exhausted he was simply from taking a bath and getting dressed. "Take care of him, Sorcor. However you see fit." The meaning of his words was plain and the prisoner's voice rose in a howl of denial. "Oh. And shut the door on your way out," Kennit further instructed him.

"Sar," he heard a deckhand sigh as the door closed behind them and the wailing prisoner. "He's going at her already. Guess nothing keeps Captain Kennit down."

Kennit turned very slightly toward the warmth of Etta's body. His eyes closed and he sank into a deep sleep.

CHAPTER TWENTY-EIGHT

VICISSITUDES

I T DIDN'T QUITE SEEM REAL UNTIL THEY LAID HANDS ON HIM. THE OLD KEEPER HE COULD PROBABLY HAVE fought off rather easily, but these were heavy middle-aged men, stolid and muscled and experienced in their work. "Let go of me!" Wintrow cried angrily. "My father is coming to get me. Let go!" Stupidly, he reflected later. As if simply telling them to let go would make them do it. It was one of the things he was to learn. Words from a slave's mouth meant nothing. His angry cries were no more intelligible to them than the braying of an ass.

They did things with his arm joints, twisting them so that he stumbled angrily in the direction they wished him to go. He had not quite got over his surprise at being seized when he found himself already pressed firmly up against the tattooist's block. "Be easy," one of the men bid him gruffly as he jerked Wintrow's wrist shackles tight against a staple. Wintrow jerked back, hoping to pull free before the pin could be set, but he only took skin off his wrists. The pin was already set. As quickly as that they had him, hunched over, wrists chained close to his ankles. One of the men gave him a slight push and he nudged his own head into a leather collar set vertically on the block. The other man gave a quick tug on the leather strap that secured it a hair's-breadth short of choking him. As long as he didn't struggle, he could get enough air to breathe. Fettered as he was, it would have been hard to draw a deep breath. The collar about his neck made even his short panting breaths an effort that required attention. They had done it as efficiently as farmhands castrating calves, Wintrow thought foggily. The same expert callousness, the precise use of force. He doubted they were even sweating. "Satrap's sigil," one said to the tattooist, and the man nodded and moved a wad of cindin in his cheek.

"My flesh was not made by me. I will not puncture it to bear jewelry, nor stain my skin, nor embed decoration into my visage. For I am a creation of Sa, made as I am intended to be. My flesh is not mine to write upon." He had scarce breath enough to quote the holy writ as a whisper. But he spoke the words and prayed the man would hear them.

The tattooist spat to one side, spittle stained with blood. A hard addict, then, one who would indulge in the drug even when his mouth was raw with ulcers. "T'ain't my flesh to mark either," he exclaimed with dim humor. "It's the Satrap's. Now, his sigil I could do blindfolded. You hold still, it goes faster and smarts less."

"My father . . . is coming . . . to pay for me." He fought for air to say these essential words.

"Your father is too late. Hold still."

Wintrow had no time to wonder if holding still would be an assent to this blasphemy. The first needle was off target, striking not his cheek but the side of his nose and piercing into the side of his nostril. He yelped and jerked. The tattooist slapped him smartly on the back of the head. "Hold still!" he commanded him gruffly.

Wintrow clenched his eyes shut and set his jaw.

"Aw, I hate it when they wrinkle up like that," the tattooist muttered in disgust. Then he went swiftly to work. A dozen jabs of his needle, a quick swipe at the blood and then the sting of a dye. Green. Another dozen jabs, swipe, sting. It seemed to Wintrow as if each time he took a breath, he was getting less air. He was dizzy, afraid he would faint, and furious with himself for being ashamed. How could fainting shame him? They were the ones doing this to him. And where was his father, how could he be late? Didn't he know what would happen to his son if he was late?

"Now leave it alone. Don't touch it, don't scratch it, or you'll just make it hurt worse." A distant voice was speaking over a roaring in his ears. "He's done, take him away and bring another."

Hands tugged at his shackles and his collar, and then he was being strong-armed again, being forced off to somewhere else. He stumbled, half-dazed, taking one deep breath after another. His destination turned out to be a different stall in a different row in a different shed. This could not have happened, he told himself. It could not have happened to him, his father would not have left him to be tattooed and sold. His captors halted him by a pen set aside for new slaves. The five slaves he shared it with each bore a single oozing green tattoo.

His shackles were secured to a pin set in the floor and the men left him there. The moment they let go of his arms, Wintrow lifted his hand to his face. He touched it gingerly, feeling the puffing and seeping of his outraged flesh. A pink-tinged liquid ran slowly down his face and dripped from his chin. He had nothing to blot it.

He stared around at the other slaves. He realized he had not said a word since he had spoken to the tattooist. "What happens now?" he asked dazedly of them.

A tall, skinny youth picked his nose with a dirty finger. "We get sold," he said sarcastically. "And we're slaves the rest of our lives. Unless you kill someone and get away." He was sullenly defiant, but Wintrow heard it was only words. Words were all that were left of his resistance. The others seemed not even to have that much. They stood or sat or leaned, and waited for whatever would happen to them next. Wintrow recognized the state. Severely injured people fell into it. Left to themselves, they would simply sit and stare and sometimes shiver.

"I can't believe it," Wintrow heard his own voice whisper. "I can't believe Torg didn't tell my father." Then he wondered why he had ever expected that Torg would. What was the matter with him, why had he been so stupid? He'd trusted his fate to a sadistic brutal idiot. Why hadn't he sent word for his father, why hadn't he told the keeper the first day? Come to think of it, why had he fled the ship? Had it really been so bad there? At least there had been an end in sight, a two-year wait to his deliverance from his father. Now there was no end to it. And he would not have the *Vivacia* to sustain him. The thought of her brought a terrible pang of loneliness welling up in him. He'd betrayed her, and he'd sent himself into slavery. This was real. He was a slave now. Now and forever. He curled up in the dirty straw on his side, clasping his knees to his chest. In the distance, he seemed to hear a roaring wind.

The *Vivacia* rocked disconsolately in the placid harbor. It was a lovely day. The sunlight glittered on fabled white Jamaillia City. The winds were from the south today, ameliorating the winter day and the stench of the other slavers anchored alongside her. Not so long now to spring. Farther south, where Ephron had used to take her, fruit trees would be cascades of white or pink blossoms. Somewhere to the south, it was warm and beautiful. But she would be going north, to Chalced.

The banging and sawing from within her were stilled at last; all her modifications for being a slaver were complete. Today would be spent loading the last of the supplies, and tomorrow her human cargo would be ferried out to her. She would sail away from Jamaillia, alone. Wintrow was gone. As soon as she lifted anchor, one or more of the sluggish serpents in the harbor muck below would uncoil and follow her. Serpents would be her companions from now on. Last night, when the rest of the harbor was still, a small one had risen, to slink about among the anchored slavers. When it came to her, it had lifted its head above the water, to gaze at her warily. Something about its stare had closed her throat tight with terror. She had not even been able to call the watch. If Wintrow had been aboard, at least someone would have sensed her fear and come to her. She dragged her thoughts free of him. She'd have to take care of herself now. Loss clawed at her heart. She denied it. She refused it all. It was a lovely day. She listened to the waves slap against her hull as she rocked at anchor. So peaceful.

"Ship? Vivacia?"

She turned her head slowly and looked back and up. It was Gantry, standing on her foredeck and leaning on the rail to speak to her.

"Vivacia? Could you stop that, please? It's unnerving the whole crew. We're two hands short today; they didn't come back from liberty. And I think it's because you've frightened them off."

Frightened. What was so frightening about isolation and loneliness and serpents no one else ever saw?

"Vivacia? I'm going to have Findow come play his fiddle for you. And I've got liberty myself today for a few hours, and I promise you I'll spend every moment of it looking for Wintrow. I promise you that."

Did they think that would make her happy? If they found Wintrow and dragged him back to her, forced him to serve her, did they think she would be content and docile? Kyle would believe that. That was how Kyle had brought Wintrow aboard her in the first place. Kyle understood nothing of the willing heart.

"Vivacia," Gantry asked with despair in his voice. "Please. Please, can you just stop rocking? The water is smooth as glass today. Every other ship in the harbor is still. Please."

She felt sorry for Gantry. He was a good mate, and a very able seaman. None of this was his fault. He shouldn't have to suffer for it.

But then, neither should she.

She made an effort to find her strength. He was a good sailor; she owed him some small explanation. "I'm losing myself," she began, and then heard how peculiar that sounded. She tried again. "It's not so hard, when I know someone is coming back. But when I don't, it suddenly gets harder to hold on to who I am. I start thinking . . . no. Not thinking. Almost like a dream, but we liveships cannot sleep. But it's like a dream, and in the dream I'm someone else. Something else. And the serpents touch me and that makes it worse."

The man only looked more worried now. "Serpents," he repeated doubtfully.

"Gantry," she said in a very faint voice. "Gantry, there are serpents here in the harbor. Hiding down at the bottom in the muck."

He took a deep breath and sighed it out. "So you told me before. But, Vivacia, no one else has seen any sign of them. So, I think you might be mistaken." He paused, hoping for a response.

She looked away from him. "If Wintrow were here, he would feel them. He'd know I wasn't being foolish."

"Well," Gantry said reluctantly. "I'm afraid he's not here. And I know that makes you unhappy. And maybe it makes you fearful, just a bit." He paused. His voice took on a cajoling tone, as if she were a nervous child. "Maybe there are serpents down there. But if there are, what can we do about them? They're not hurting us. I think we should both just ignore them, don't you?"

She turned her head to stare at him, but he would not meet her gaze. What did he think of her? That she was imagining serpents? That her grief at Wintrow abandoning her was making her crazy? She spoke quietly. "I'm not mad, Gantry. It is . . . hard . . . for me to be alone like this. But I'm not going crazy. Maybe I'm even seeing things more clearly than I used to. Seeing things my own way, not a . . . Vestrit way."

Her efforts to explain only confused him. "Well. Of course. Uh." He looked away from her.

"Gantry, you're a good man. I like you." She almost didn't say the words. But then she did. "You should get onto a different ship."

She could smell the sudden fear in his sweat when he spoke to her. "Now, what other ship could compare to you?" he asked her hastily.

"After sailing aboard you, why would I want to take ship on another?" False heartiness in his voice.

"Maybe because you want to live," she said in a very low voice. "I've a very bad feeling about this voyage. A very bad feeling. Especially if I must make it alone."

"Don't talk like that!" he said roughly, as if she were an unruly hand. Then, in a calmer voice, he offered, "You won't be alone. I'll be here with you. I'll go and tell Findow to come fiddle for you, shall I?"

She shrugged. She had tried. She fixed her eyes on the distant spire of the Satrap's palace.

After a while, he went away.

She had been afraid Captain Tenira would recognize her. She had danced with his son at the Winter gathering, three years ago. But if the Bingtown Trader saw any resemblance between Athel the sailor and Althea the daughter of Ephron Vestrit, he gave no sign of it. He looked her up and down critically, then shook his head. "You've the look of a good sailor to you, boy. But I've told you. I don't need another hand. My crew is full." He spoke as if that settled the matter.

Althea kept her eyes down. Two days ago she had spotted the *Ophelia* in the harbor. The sight of the old liveship's silvery hull and smiling figurehead had moved her with a depth that shocked her. A question or two in the waterfront taverns had given her all the information she needed. The liveship was homeward bound, heading back for Bingtown in a matter of days. In the instant of hearing that, Althea had resolved that one way or another, she would be on board her. She had hung about the docks, watching and waiting for her chance to catch the captain alone. Her plan was simple. She'd first try to hire aboard as a ship's boy. If that didn't work, she'd reveal to him who she was and beg for passage home. She didn't think he'd turn her down. Still, it had taken all her courage to follow Tenira to this waterfront tavern and wait while he dined. She had stood in a corner, waiting until he had finished eating before she approached him. When he set down his fork and leaned back in his chair, she'd placed herself before him. Now she summoned all her courage. "Sir, begging your pardon, sir. I'd work for nothing, just for my passage back to Bingtown."

The captain turned in his chair to face her and crossed his arms on his chest. "Why?" he asked suspiciously.

Althea looked at the tavern floor between her bare feet and bit her lip. Then she looked up at the captain of the liveship *Ophelia*. "Got my wages from the *Reaper* . . . at least, I still got part of them. I'd like to get home, sir and give them to my mother." Althea swallowed awkwardly. "Before they're all gone. I promised her I'd come home with money, sir, Da being in a bad way. And I been trying to, but the longer I look for a ship back to Bingtown, the more I spend each day." She looked back at the floor. "Even if you don't pay me anything, I'd probably get home with more money if I ship now than if I wait around and try for a paying berth."

"I see." Captain Tenira looked at the plate on the table before him and pushed it casually away. His tongue plucked at something in his back teeth for a moment. "Well. That's admirable. But I'd still be feeding you, I think. And working aboard a liveship isn't quite the same any other kind of a vessel. They're lively in a way that has nothing to do with wind or weather. And Ophelia can be a willful lady."

Althea bit her lips to suppress a smile. The *Ophelia* was one of the oldest liveships, the first generation as it were. She was a blowzy old cog, bawdy and lewd when the mood took her, and patrician and commanding at other times. A willful lady was the kindest way she had ever heard Ophelia described.

"Her hands have got to be more than quick and smart," Captain Tenira was lecturing. "They've got to be steady. You can't be afraid of her or superstitious about her. And you can't let her bully you either. Ever been aboard a liveship, boy?"

"A bit," Althea admitted. "Before I started sailing, I'd go down to the North Wall in Bingtown and talk to them sometimes. I like 'em, sir. I'm not afraid of them."

The captain cleared his throat. In a different voice, he pointed out, "And a merchant vessel is a lot different from a slaughter ship. We move a lot faster, and we keep a lot cleaner. When the mate tells you to jump, you jump right away. Think you can do that?"

"Yes sir, I can do that. And I'm clean, and I keep my area clean." Althea was nodding like a puppet.

"Well." The captain considered. "I still don't need you, you know. Serving on a liveship is something a lot of men would jump through any hoop to do. You're stepping into a position I'd have no trouble filling with an older, experienced man."

"I know, sir. I appreciate that, sir."

"See that you do. I'm a hard master, Athel. You may regret this before we reach Bingtown."

"Begging your pardon, sir, but I'd heard that about you. That you was hard, but fair." She let her eyes meet his again. "I don't fear to work for a fair man."

It was just enough honey. The captain almost smiled. "Go and report to the mate, then. His name's Grag Tenira. Tell him I've hired you on, and that you want to chip rust on the anchor chain."

"Yes sir," Althea replied with just enough of a grimace. Chipping rust off the anchor chain was an endless task. Then she reminded herself that even chipping rust off an anchor chain on a liveship was better than any other task she'd ever done aboard the *Reaper*. "Thankee, sir."

"Go along, then," Captain Tenira told her genially. He sat forward in his chair to take up his ale mug and wave it at a passing tavern boy.

Althea let out a huge sigh of relief as soon as she was on the boardwalk outside. She scarcely felt the chill wind that flowed past her. Tenira hadn't recognized her, and she now decided it was unlikely he ever would. As lowly ship's boy, it was unlikely she would be face to face with the captain much. Now that he'd seen her as Athel, he'd probably continue to see her as Athel. She was confident she could get past Grag Tenira as well. Athel the ship's boy looked nothing like Althea the dance partner. Her heart soared suddenly as she realized she'd done it. She had passage back to Bingtown. And if all she had heard of Captain Tenira was true, she'd gain a few coins on the trip. The man was fair. If he saw her working hard, he'd reward her. She found a smile on her face. Ophelia would be leaving tomorrow. All she had to do was go and get her sea-bag and head down to the ship and find a place to hang a hammock. Tomorrow she'd be on her way home.

And aboard a liveship again. Her heart approached that with mixed feelings. The *Ophelia* was not the *Vivacia*. There would be no bond there. On the other hand, Ophelia would not be some dead piece of wood pushed around only by wind and waves. It would be good to be back on board a responsive vessel again. And she'd be glad to see the last of this greasy little town.

She turned her feet towards the run-down inn where she had been staying. She'd board Ophelia tonight and sail tomorrow. There wasn't time to find Brashen and bid him farewell. She had no idea where he was. Why, for all she knew, he might have shipped out again by now. Besides, what was the point? She'd go her way, he'd go his. That was simply how it was. She had no real connection to the man at all. None at all. She didn't even know why she was thinking about him. Certainly there was nothing left to say to him. And seeing him again would only bring up difficult words and topics.

. . .

The office of the ship's agent was small and stuffy. The fireplace held a roaring blaze for such a tiny room. It seemed smoky after the fresh windy day outside. Brashen tugged at his collar, then forced his hands to lie still in his lap.

"I hire for the ship *Springeve*. That is how much trust the captain places in me. And it is a trust I take gravely. If I send him out with a sloppy man, or a drunk, I can cost the ship time, money, and lives. So I am careful who I hire."

The agent, a small, balding man, paused to suck at a pipe. He seemed to be waiting for a reply, so Brashen tried to think of one. "It's a heavy responsibility," he hazarded.

The agent exhaled a yellowish smoke. The acridity of it bit at Brashen's eyes and throat but he tried not to show it. All he wanted was the mate's position they had posted on the bill outside the door. The *Springeve* was a small, shallow draft trading vessel that worked her way up and down the coast between Candletown and Bingtown. The cargo she picked up or let off in each town determined her next port of call. That was how the agent delicately explained it. To Brashen, it sounded suspiciously as if the *Springeve* worked with the pirates, buying and selling stolen cargoes from other ships. Brashen wasn't sure he wanted to get involved in that sort of work. Actually, he was damn sure that he didn't want to do any work at all, of any kind. But he was out of money and almost out of cindin. So he had to work, and this berth was as good as any. The man was talking again, and Brashen tried to look as if he'd been paying attention.

". . . so we lost him. It was a shame, he'd been with us for years. But, as I'm sure you know . . ." he took another long draw from his pipe and breathed it out through his nose. "Time and tide wait for no man. Nor does perishable cargo. The *Springeve* has to sail and we need a new mate. You seem familiar with the waters we've discussed. We may not be able to pay you what you think you're worth."

"What could you pay me?" Brashen asked bluntly. Then he smiled, to try and soften the roughness of the words. His headache had abruptly returned, and if the man breathed smoke in his face one more time, he thought he'd puke.

"Well." The small man bridled a bit at his question. "That depends, of course. You've your ticket from the *Reaper*, but nothing to show for the other experience you claim. I'll need to think about this."

He meant he hoped someone with more tickets would apply. "I see. When will you know if you want me?" Another question phrased too baldly. Once he had said it, he could hear it, but he seemed unable to govern his words before they came out of his mouth. He smiled at the man again, and hoped his smile was not as sickly as he felt.

"Possibly by early morning."

When the man took a draw from his pipe, Brashen bent over and pretended to adjust the cuff of his trousers. He waited until the man breathed out before he straightened up again. There was still a cloud of yellowish fumes waiting for him. He coughed, then cleared his throat. "I'll check back with you then, shall I?" A knot of anxiety was forming in Brashen's gut. He'd have to face another day without food, another night sleeping outside. With every day that passed like that, he'd have less of a chance at a decent berth. A hungry, dirty, unshaven man was not what an agent sought for in a ship's mate.

"Yes. Do that," the agent said absently. He was already shuffling papers on his desk, Brashen dismissed from his mind. "And come ready to sail, for if we want you, we shall want you right away. Good day."

Brashen stood slowly. "That is swash. You won't say if you want me or how much you'll pay me, but I should be on my toes to leave if you wink at me. I don't think so." *You're being stupid*, some rational part of himself was yelling. *Shut up, shut up, shut up!* But the words were out and he knew he'd only look stupid as well as rude if he tried to recall them now. He tried to put an arch civility into his tone as he added, "Good day to you, sir. I regret we couldn't do business together."

The ship's agent looked both insulted and worried. "Wait!" he exclaimed almost angrily. "Wait."

Brashen halted and turned to him, one eyebrow raised inquiringly.

"Let's not be hasty." The man's eyes shifted in indecision. "I'll tell you what we can do. I'm going to talk to the *Reaper*'s man sometime today. If he says all's square with you, then we'll pay you the same wages you had there. That's fair."

"No. It's not." Having adopted a hard-nosed stance, he had no choice but to stick with it. And he didn't really want the agent to chat with anyone from the *Reaper*. "On the *Reaper* I was a third. If I sign with the *Springeve*, I'll be the mate. Not the captain, nor a sailor before the mast. The mate, who is held liable for anything that goes wrong aboard. The *Springeve* may be a smaller vessel, but it's a bigger job. The crew on a trader has to be worked harder and faster than the crew on a slaughter ship. And I'll wager the *Springeve* brings in more coin than the *Reaper* ever did, if she's worth her salt at all. If I sail as mate on the *Springeve*, I'll want the same wages the last mate was paid."

"But he had years of experience on her!" the agent squeaked.

"I've years of experience as a mate on the *Vivacia*, a substantially larger vessel. Come. Pay me what you paid the last man. If you made money with him, I'll guarantee you'll make just as much with me."

The agent sank back into his chair. "You've the arrogance of a good mate," he conceded grudgingly. "All right. Come ready to sail, and at mate's wages. But I warn you, if you show badly, the captain will put you off at the next port, no matter how small it is."

"I'll do you one better, as I'm an honest man and a hard worker," Brashen offered. "I'll report to the ship now. If she's to leave day after tomorrow, I'll want at least that much time to be sure all aboard is stowed right, and to make sure the crew understands I'm the mate now. It give the captain a full day to test my mettle. He doesn't like how I do things, he tells me to walk. Is that fair?"

It was the right time to offer him such a concession. It let the agent save a bit of his pride as he narrowed his eyes thoughtfully, and then nodded. "That's fair. You know where the *Springeve* is tied up?"

Brashen grinned at him. "Do I look the sort of man who'd ask for a position aboard a vessel I hadn't seen? I know where she's tied. I and my sea-bag will be aboard her, should you change your mind about me. But I don't think you will."

"Well. All right. Good day to you, then."

"Good day."

Brashen left the man's office, shutting the door firmly behind him. Once outside, he walked briskly down the street, a man with a purpose. He was relieved to find that his sea-bag was still in a straw pile behind the livery stable where he had slept last night. Now if that had been stolen, he would have been in a real fix. He opened it and glanced through it quickly, to be sure that nothing had been filched from it. Not that he had much of value in there, but what was his was his. He poked through the bag. His cindin supply was still there. It was dwindling, but it would be enough. He wouldn't be using it while he was on duty, anyway. He never used cindin on duty. Like as not, he'd set it aside and not even use it while he was aboard. After all, for the years he had been on board the *Vivacia*, he hadn't used it at all, not even when he had liberty on shore.

Thinking of the *Vivacia* woke a dull pang in him. When he'd lost his place on her, he'd lost a lot. He tried to imagine how things could have been if Ephron Vestrit hadn't sickened. He knew he'd still be sailing aboard her. Althea, too. The thought of her jabbed him. He didn't even know where she was in this dirty town. Stupid and stubborn, that was him. There had been no reason, really, to stalk off like that on that night. So she'd said they didn't even know one another. That was just words, he knew better, she knew better.

She knew him so well she had wanted nothing further to do with him.

He stopped on the street, lowered his sea-bag and took out the remaining cindin. He broke a small piece off the stick and tucked it into his cheek. Not much, just enough to help him look lively until he had a proper meal aboard. Odd, how a couple nights of a near-empty belly could make even hard-tack and salt beef sound good. For a moment the cindin stung, then he shoved it into a better position with his tongue and it was fine. He took a deep breath past the bitterness in his mouth and felt all the world come into a sharper focus. He tossed his sea-bag to his shoulder again and headed towards the docks.

It would be good to have a definite place in the world again. And the *Springeve* promised to be an interesting ship. As often as he'd been up and down the Inside Passage on the *Vivacia*, they hadn't done much stopping. Captain Vestrit had done most of his buying to the south of Jamaillia. Brashen had been to a hundred exotic little ports in that part of the world. Now it would be interesting to re-acquaint himself with the Pirate Isles. He wondered if anyone would remember him there.

Midday had come and gone, as near as Wintrow could tell. At least, that was what his stomach told him. He touched his face again, then looked at his fingertips. The ooze from the new tattoo felt tacky. He wondered what it looked like. He could see the same green sigil on the faces of the others in the pen with him, but somehow he couldn't imagine it on his own visage. They were slaves, it was somehow not shocking to see them tattooed. But he was not a slave. It was a mistake. His father was supposed to have come and rescued him. Like a bubble popping, he saw the complete illogic of this. Yesterday, their faces had been as clean as his own. Like him, they were newly come to this status. But somehow he could not yet think of himself as a slave. It was all a great mistake.

For some time, he had been hearing sounds, the murmur of a crowd, voices raised to speak above the din. But no one had come to see them, save a solitary guard making his rounds lethargically.

He cleared his throat. No one turned to look at him. He spoke anyway. "Why aren't there any buyers? At the other pens, there were buyers walking up and down, taking slaves."

The dirty boy spoke wearily. "Then you musta been by map-face pens. They take whatever offer they can get for them, almost. Skilled slaves get bought up by companies that rent them out. They get auctioned so the companies will bid against each other. New slaves," he suddenly paused, then cleared his own throat. He was a bit husky as he went on. "New slaves like us get auctioned, too. It's called the mercy law. Sometimes your family or friends will buy you, and then give you your freedom back. I used to think it was pretty funny. Me and my friends used to come down to the auctions, and bid on new slaves. Just to run the money up, watch their brothers or fathers break a sweat." He cleared his throat again abruptly and turned back to the corner of the pen. "Never thought I'd be here."

"Maybe your friends will buy you," Wintrow suggested quietly.

"Whyn't you shut up before I bust your teeth?" the boy snarled at him, and Wintrow guessed there would be no family or friend bidding for him. Or any of the others by their looks. One was a woman past her middle years. Her face looked as if she normally smiled, but it had collapsed on itself today. She rocked slightly as she sat in the straw. There were two diffident young men, probably in their middle twenties, dressed in rough farmers' clothes. They sat beside each other, silent and empty-eyed. Wintrow wondered if they were brothers, or perhaps friends. The other woman in the pen was of an indeterminate age between disillusioned and hard. She sat huddled in a heap, her arms clasping her knees. Her lips made a flat line, her eyes were permanently narrowed. There were disease lesions on her mouth.

The short winter day was nearly over when they came for the slaves. These were men Wintrow had never seen before. They carried short clubs and a length of heavy chain. As each slave was unshackled, he was fastened to it until they had a coffle of new slaves. "That way," one of the men said. The other didn't bother with words. He just gave Wintrow a heavy prod with his stick to hasten him along.

Wintrow's reluctance to be sold on a block like a cow warred with his weariness of the uncertainty of the last few days. At least something definite was happening to him now even if he had no control over it. He held his handfuls of chain and shuffled awkwardly after the others. He looked around as he went, but there was not much to see. Most of the pens they passed were empty now. The crowd noises grew louder, and they suddenly came out into an open courtyard. Slave sheds ringed it. In the middle was a raised platform with steps going up to it, not unlike a gallows. A crowd of folk stood before it, gaping up at the wares, laughing, drinking, exchanging pleasantries and comments with one another. And buying other humans. Wintrow suddenly smelled spilled beer and the tantalizing smell of fatty, smoked

meat. There were food vendors working the crowd. Beyond the platform, Wintrow caught a glimpse of a row of tattoo stands, all quite
busy.

A lively market day, he thought to himself. No doubt some folk
had woken up early today, looking forward to this. A day in town,
seeing friends, dickering for bargains. A stroll to the auction to see
what was available in slaves today.

For a time they were kept bunched at the bottom of the steps
while the auctioneer finished with the batch on the platform. A few
serious buyers pushed through the crowd to view them more closely.
Some shouted questions to the handlers, as to age, condition of teeth,
past experience. These the handlers repeated to the slave in question,
as if they could not hear and understand the buyer themselves. One
queried Wintrow's age. "Fourteen," he replied quietly.

The buyer made a derogatory noise. "I'd have taken him for
twelve. Push up his sleeve, let's see his arm." And when the handler
complied, "Well, there's a bit of muscle there. What kind of work do
you know, boy? Kitchen? Poultry?"

Wintrow cleared his throat. What was he? A slave with good skills
was treated better, or so he had been told. He might as well make the
most of what cards he did hold. "I was in training to be a priest. I've
worked in orchards. I can do stained glass. I can read, write, and
figure. And I've been a ship's boy," he added reluctantly.

"Too full of himself," the buyer sneered. He turned away, shaking
his head at a companion. "He'll be hard to train. He already thinks he
knows too much."

While he was trying to think of an appropriate reply to that, a jerk
on his chain brought him to attention. The others were already climbing the steps and Wintrow staggered up after them. For a few moments, all he could concentrate on was the steep steps and the short
chains that linked his ankles. Then he took his place in the row of
slaves on the torch-lit wooden stage.

"New slaves, fresh slaves, no bad habits yet, you'll have to teach
them those yourself!" The auctioneer began his spiel. The crowd
responded with half-hearted chuckles. "Now here's what I've got, see
for yourself, and you decide which one will lead off the bidding. I got
a couple stout hands here, good for farm, field or stable; got a warm-
hearted granny here, perfect for keeping an eye on your little ones;
got a woman here, seen a bit of hard use but still got some good years
in her; and a couple of boys, lively, healthy boys, young enough to be
taught anything. Now, who wants to open up the bidding? Don't be

shy, you just holler it out and let me know what one's caught your eye." The auctioneer gestured invitingly to the field of faces that looked up eagerly at the merchandise on the platform.

"Mayvern! The old woman! Three silver!" Wintrow found the desperate young woman in the crowd. A daughter perhaps, or a younger friend. The old woman on the platform beside him lifted her hands to her face, covering as if she were ashamed or afraid to hope. Wintrow thought his heart would break. Then he caught a glimpse of something that made it flip over in his chest instead. His father's height and fair hair stood out in the crowd like a flag beckoning him to home and safety. He was discussing something with a man behind him.

"Father!" he cried out, and saw Kyle Haven's head turn to the platform in disbelief. He saw Torg beside him, his hand going to his mouth as if in amazement, mimicking his astonishment very well. One of the handlers thudded Wintrow in the ribs with his stick.

"Be still. Wait your turn," he commanded him.

Wintrow scarcely felt the blow or heard the words. All he had eyes for was his father's face, looking up at him. He seemed so small and far away in that sea of faces. In the gathering dark, Wintrow could not be sure of his expression. He stared down at his father and prayed to Sa. Neither his mind nor his lips shaped any words; it was a simple plea for mercy. He saw his father turn to Torg for a hasty conference of some sort. He wondered if, this late in the day, his father had money left to spend. But he must, or he would have taken what he'd bought and gone back to the ship. Wintrow tried to smile hopefully, but could not quite remember how. What was his father feeling just now? Anger, relief, shame, pity? It didn't matter, Wintrow decided. His father could not look at him and not buy him. Could he? After all, what would his mother say?

Nothing, if she wasn't told, Wintrow suddenly realized. Nothing at all, if all she knew was that her son had run away in Jamaillia City.

The auctioneer's lash slapped the table in front of him. "Sold!" he roared out. "For ten silvers, and you are welcome to her, my lady fair. Now. Who wants to open the next bid? Come on, now, there's some likely slaves up here. Look at the muscle on these field workers. Spring planting is only a few months away, farmers. Can't be ready too soon!"

"Father! Please!" Wintrow shouted, and then flinched away as the handler jabbed him again.

Slowly, Kyle Haven lifted his hand. "Five shards. For the boy."

The crowd had a general laugh at this insulting bid. One bought a

bowl of soup for five copper shards, not a slave. The auctioneer recoiled slowly, his hand to his chest. "Five shards?" he asked in mock
dismay. "Oh, laddie, what did you do to displease papa so? Five shards
I'm offered, five shards is where we start. Anyone else interested in
this five-shard slave?"

A voice came up from the crowd. "Which boy is the one who can
read, write, and figure?"

Wintrow kept silent, but a guard helpfully replied, "He's the one.
Was in training to be a priest. Says he can work stained glass, too."

This final claim in such an apparently young boy put the others in
doubt. "A full copper!" someone laughingly bid.

"Two!"

"Stand up straight," the guard bid him and followed this advice
with a nudge from his stick.

"Three," his father said sullenly.

"Four!" This was from a laughing young man at the edge of the
crowd. He and his companions nudged one another and shifted, their
gazes going from Wintrow to his father. Wintrow's heart sank. If his
father became aware of their game, there was no telling how he'd
react.

"Two silvers," someone called, apparently thinking she could
make a quick end of the bidding with a large increase. Two silvers, he
was to learn later, was still a low bid for a new and unpromising slave,
but it was within the realm of acceptability.

"Two silvers!" the auctioneer called out with enthusiasm. "Now,
my friends and neighbors, we are taking this young man seriously. He
reads, writes and figures! Claims to do stained glass, but we shan't
make much of that, shall we? A useful lad, bound to get bigger as he
can't get smaller; a tractable, trainable boy. Do I hear three?"

He did, and it was not from Wintrow's father or the hecklers. The
bids shot up to five silvers before the real buyers began shaking their
heads and turning aside to examine other waiting merchandise. The
boys at the edge of the crowd continued bidding until Torg was sent
to stand beside them. He scowled at them, but Wintrow clearly saw
him offer them a handful of coins to leave off their game. Ah. So that
was how it was done and the whole purpose of it.

A few moments later, his father bought him for seven silvers and
five whole coppers. Wintrow was unfastened from the coffle, and led
forward by his manacles exactly as a cow might be. At the bottom of
the steps, he was turned over to Torg. His father had not even come
forward to receive him. A tide of uneasiness arose in Wintrow. He
held his wrists out to Torg to have the chains removed, but the sailor

feigned not to notice them. Instead he inspected Wintrow as if he were indeed just any other slave that his master had just purchased. "Stained glass, eh?" he scoffed, and got a general laugh from the handlers and other idlers at the base of the auction stage. He gripped the chain between Wintrow's wrist and dragged him forward. Wintrow was forced to stumble after him, his ankles still hobbled.

"Take the chains off," Wintrow told him as soon as they were free of the crowd.

"And give you a chance to run again? I don't think so," Torg replied. He was grinning.

"You didn't tell my father I was held here, did you? You waited. So I'd be marked like a slave and he'd have to buy me back."

"I don't know what you're talking about," Torg replied genially. He was in fine fettle. "Were I you, I think I'd be grateful that your father happened to stay at the auctions this long, and saw you and bought you. We sail tomorrow, you know. Got our full load, he was just thinking to pick up a few last-minute bargains. Got you instead."

Wintrow shut up. He debated the wisdom of telling his father what Torg had done. Would it sound like he was whining, would his father even believe him? He searched the faces they passed, looking for his father in the gathering dusk. What expression would he wear? Anger? Relief? Wintrow himself was caught between trepidation and gratitude.

Then he did catch sight of his father's face. He was far off, and not even looking towards Wintrow and Torg. He appeared to be bidding on the two farm hands who were being sold together. He didn't even glance at his own son in chains.

"My father's over there," Wintrow pointed out to Torg. He halted stubbornly. "I want to speak to him before we go back to the ship."

"Come on," Torg grunted cheerfully. "I don't think he wants to speak to you." He grinned to himself. "In fact, I doubt he thinks you'd make a good first mate anymore when he gives the captaincy over to Gantry. I think he fancies me for that job, now." He uttered this with great satisfaction, as if he expected Wintrow to be astounded by it.

Wintrow stopped walking. "I want to speak to my father, now."

"No," Torg replied simply. His greater bulk and muscle easily overmatched Wintrow's resistance. "Walk or be dragged, it's all one to me," he assured him. Torg's eyes were roving, looking over the heads of a cluster of folk standing about. "Ah," he exclaimed suddenly, and surged forward, hauling Wintrow behind him.

They halted before a tattooist's block. He was just freeing a dazed woman from the collar while her impatient buyer tugged on her shackles for her to hurry and follow him. The tattooist looked up at Torg and nodded. "Kyle Haven's mark?" he asked, gesturing at Wintrow affably. Evidently they had been doing a lot of business.

"Not this one," Torg said, to Wintrow's instant and vast relief. He supposed there was some freedom trinket or sign to purchase here. His father would not be happy about that extra expense either. Wintrow was already wondering if there were not some way to gently abrade or bleach the new tattoo from his face. Painful as that would be, it would be far better than to wear this sign on his face the rest of his life. The sooner he put this misadventure behind him, the better. He had already decided that when his father did decide to speak to him, Wintrow would give him an honest promise to remain aboard the ship and serve him well to the end of his fifteenth year. Perhaps it was time he accepted the role Sa's will had placed him in. Perhaps this was supposed to be his opportunity to reconcile with his father. The priesthood, after all, was not a place but an attitude. He could find a way to continue his studies aboard the *Vivacia*. And Vivacia herself was something to look forward to, he found. A small smile began to dawn on his face as he thought of her. Somehow he'd have to make up to her for his desertion, he'd have to convince her that—

Torg grabbed him by the back of his hair and forced his head down into the collar. The tattooist snubbed it tight. Panicked, Wintrow fought it, but only succeeded in strangling himself. Too tight, they'd pulled it too tight. He was going to pass out, even if he tried to just stand still and breathe, he wasn't getting enough air and he couldn't even tell them that. Dimly he heard Torg say, "Mark him with a sign like this earring. He's going to be ship's property. Bet it's the first time in the history of Jamaillia City that a liveship bought a slave of her own."

CHAPTER TWENTY-NINE

DREAMS AND REALITY

"THE DREAM-BOX IS MISSING."

MALTA LOOKED FROM ONE SOLEMN FACE TO THE other. Both her mother and grandmother were watching her intently. Her eyes widened in surprise. "How could it be? Are you certain?"

Her mother spoke quietly. "I am very certain."

Malta came the rest of the way into the room and took her place at the breakfast table. She lifted the cover from the dish in front of her. "Not porridge again? We can't possibly be this poor! How could the box be missing?"

She looked up to meet their eyes again. Her grandmother's glance was narrowed as she said, "I thought perhaps you might know."

"Mother had it last. She didn't give it to me, she barely let me touch it," Malta pointed out. "Is there any fruit or preserves to go on this stuff?"

"No. There is not. If we are to pay our debts in a timely fashion, we are going to have to live simply for a while. You have been told that."

Malta heaved a sigh. "I'm sorry," she said contritely. "Sometimes I forget. I hope Papa gets home soon. I'll be so glad when things are as they are supposed to be again." She looked up at her mother and grandmother again and essayed a smile. "Until then, I suppose we should just be thankful for what we have." She sat up straight, put an agreeable look on her face, and spooned up some of the porridge.

"So. You have no thoughts on the missing dream-box?" her grandmother pressed.

Malta shook her head and swallowed. "No. Unless . . . did you ask the servants if they moved it when they tidied? Nana or Rache might know something."

"I put it away. It was not left out where it might be moved by chance. Someone had to come inside my room, search for it, and then remove it."

"Is anything else missing?" Malta asked quickly.

"Nothing."

Malta ate another spoonful of porridge thoughtfully. "Could it have just . . . disappeared?" she asked with a half-smile. "I know, maybe that is silly. But one hears such extravagant tales of the goods of the Rain Wild. After a time, one almost begins to believe anything is possible."

"No. It would not have disappeared," her grandmother said slowly. "Even if it had been opened, it would not disappear."

"How do you know so much about dream-boxes?" Malta asked curiously. She poured herself a cup of tea and sweetened it well with honey as she waited for a reply.

"A friend of mine was given one once. She opened the box and dreamed the dream. And she accepted the young man's suit. But he died before they were wed. I believe she married his brother a few years later."

"Ick," observed Malta. She took another spoonful of porridge and added, "I can't imagine marrying a Rain Wilder. Even if they are supposed to be our kin, and all. Can you imagine kissing someone who was all warty? Or having breakfast with him in the morning?"

"There is more to men than how they look," her grandmother observed coldly. "When you realize that, I may start treating you as a woman." She turned her disapproving stare on her own daughter now. "Well. What are we going to do?"

Malta's mother shook her head. "What can we do? Explain, most politely, that somehow the gift was lost before we could return it. But that we still cannot consider the suit, as Malta is far too young."

"We can't possibly tell them we lost his gift!" her grandmother exclaimed.

"Then what can we do? Lie? Say we are keeping it but refusing the suit anyway? Pretend we never got it and ignore the situation?" Keffria's voice was getting more and more sarcastic with each suggestion she made. "We'd only end up looking more foolish. As it was my fault, I shall write the letter, and I shall take the blame. I shall write that I had put it in a place I deemed safe, but it was gone in the morning. I shall offer most sincere apologies and reparation. But I shall also refuse the suit, and most tactfully point out that such a gift so early in a courting is scarcely appropriate. . . ."

"By Rain Wild standards, it is," Grandmother disagreed. "Especially for the Khuprus family. Their wealth is legendary. The boy probably considered it little more than a trinket."

"Mm. Maybe we *should* marry Malta off to him, then," her mother offered facetiously. "We could certainly use a wealthy relative these days."

"Mother!" Malta exclaimed in irritation. She hated it when her mother said things like that.

"It was a joke, Malta. Don't fly into a fit about it." Keffria stood up from the table. "Well. This is not going to be an easy letter to compose, and I have little time if I am to get it to the *Kendry* before she sails. I had best get busy."

"Assure them that if we find the box, it will be returned," her grandmother suggested.

"Of course. And I do intend to search my room again. But I'd best get this letter written if I am to have anything to send with the *Kendry* when she sails." Malta's mother hastened out of the room.

Malta scooped up the last spoonful of porridge from her bowl, but she was not quite fast enough.

"Malta," her grandmother said in a soft but firm voice. "I want to ask you, one last time, if you stole the box from your mother's room. No, think before you answer. Think what this means to our family honor, to your reputation. Answer truthfully, and I promise not to be angry with you about your first lie." Her grandmother waited, holding her breath, watching Malta like a snake.

Malta set down her spoon. "I did not steal anything," she said in a quivering voice. "I don't know how you can believe such things of me. What have I ever done to you, to deserve these accusations all the time? Oh, I wish my father were here, to see how I am treated while he is away. I am sure this is not the life he intended for his only daughter!"

"No. He'd have auctioned you off like a fat calf by now," her grandmother said shortly. "Do not flap your emotions at me. You may fool your mother but you don't fool me. I tell you this plainly. If you have taken the dream-box and opened it, well, that is bad enough a hole for us to dig out of. But if you persist in lying and keep that thing . . . oh, Malta. You cannot flaunt a courtship from one of the major Trader families of the Rain Wilds. This is not a time for your childish little games. Financially, we are teetering. What has saved us thus far is that we are known for keeping our word. We don't lie, we don't cheat, we don't steal. We pay our debts honestly. But if folk lose faith in that, if they start believing we do not keep our word, then we are lost, Malta. Lost. And young as you are, you will have to help pay the forfeit for that."

Malta stood slowly. She flung down her spoon so it rang against her plate. "My father will be home soon, with a fat purse from his hard work. And he will pay off your debts and protect us from the ruin your stubbornness has brought us to. We'd have no problems if Grandpa had traded up the Rain Wild River, like any other man with a liveship. If you'd listened to Davad and sold off the bottom land, or at least let him use his slaves to work it for shares, we wouldn't be in this hole. It's not my stubbornness that threatens this family, but yours."

Her grandmother's face had gone from stern to shock. Now her mouth was pinched white with fury. "Do you listen at doors, sweet granddaughter? To the words of a dying man to his wife? I had thought many things of you, Malta, both good and bad. But I never suspected you of being a prying little eavesdropper."

Malta wagged her head coldly. She made her voice sweet. "I was told it was how one became accepted as a woman in this family. To know the family holdings and finances, to be aware of both dangers and opportunities. But it seems to me you would rather risk any opportunity for the sake of keeping my father in ignorance. You don't really see him as a member of this family, do you? Oh, he's fine for fathering children and keeping my mother content. But you want nothing of him beyond that. Because then he might threaten your own plan. To keep power and control for yourself, even if it means ruin for the family." Malta had not known the depth of her own anger until she heard it poured out as venom.

Her grandmother's voice was shaking as she replied. "If your father is ignorant of our ways, it is because he never took the time to learn them. If he had, I would not be so fearful of the power he already wields, Malta." The woman took a breath. "You show me, here and now, that you have understanding I did not suspect in you. If you had shown us the depth of your understanding before, perhaps your mother and I would have seen you as more adult than child. For now, understand this. When Ephron . . . when your grandfather died, I could have retained far more control of the family fortune than I did. His wish was that Althea have the ship. Not Keffria and your father. It was I who persuaded him that your father would be a better choice for captain. Would I have done that, if my hope were to keep control for myself? If I opposed your father being a full member of this family? I believed in his stability and wisdom. But he was not content to inherit. He brought too much change, too fast, with no real understanding of what he was changing, or why such change would be bad. He never consulted any of us about it. Suddenly, it was all his own will and what he thought was best. I do not keep him in ignorance, Malta. His ignorance is a fortress he has built himself and defended savagely."

Malta listened, but it was almost against her will. Her grandmother was too clever for her. She knew there were lies hidden there, she knew the old woman was twisting the truth about her handsome, dashing, bold father. But she wasn't smart enough to unravel the deception. So she forced a smile to her lips. "Then you won't mind if I tell him what I know, to dispel his ignorance that offends you so. You won't mind if I tell him there never were any charts of the Rain Wild River. That the quickened ship is her own guide. Surely I should dispel that ignorance for him."

She watched her grandmother's face closely, to see how she would take Malta knowing this secret. But the old woman's face did not betray her. She shook her head. "You make a threat, child, and you don't even know that you threaten yourself. There are both costs and dangers to dealing with the Rain Wild Traders. Our kin they are, and I speak no ill against them. The bargains we have struck with them I will keep. But Ephron and I long ago decided that we would make no new bargains, no new commitments with them. Because we wanted our children and our grandchildren, yes, even you, to make their own decisions. So we lived a harder life than we needed to, and our debts were not paid off as swiftly as they might have been. We did not mind the sacrifice." Her grandmother's voice began to quaver wildly. "We sacrificed for you, you spitting little cat. And now I look at you and wonder why. Chalcedean salt water runs in your veins, not Bingtown blood."

The old woman turned and rushed from the room. There was no dignity and strength in her retreat. Malta knew that meant she had won. She had faced her down, once and for all, and now they all would have to treat Malta differently. She had won, she had proved her will was as strong as her grandmother's. And she didn't care, not really, about that last thing her grandmother had said. It was all a lie anyway, about sacrifices made for her. It was all a lie.

A lie. And that was another thing. She hadn't meant to lie to her about the box. She wouldn't have done it, if the old woman had not been so sure she had both stolen it and lied about it. If Ronica Vestrit had looked at her and wondered a little if she were innocent, Malta would have told her the truth. But what was the good of telling people the truth when they already believed you were wicked and the truth would just prove it to them? She might just as well lie twice and be the liar and thief that her grandmother not only believed she was, but hoped she was. Yes, that was true, her grandmother wanted her to be bad and wicked, because then she'd feel justified in the horrid way she treated Malta's father. It was all her grandmother's own fault. If you treated people badly, then it all just came back on you.

"Malta?" The voice was very soft, very gentle. A hand came to rest tenderly on her shoulder. "Are you all right, my dear?"

Malta whirled, seizing up her porridge bowl and dashing it at the floor at Rache's feet. "I hate porridge! Don't serve it to me again! I don't care what else you have to cook for me, don't serve me porridge. And don't touch me! You don't have the right. Now clean that up and leave me alone!"

She pushed the shocked slave out of the way and stormed out of the room. Slaves. They were so stupid. About everything.

"Paragon. There's something I have to talk to you about."

Amber had spent the afternoon with him. She'd brought a lantern with her, and explored inside him. She'd walked slowly through his hold, the captain's chamber, the chart room, every compartment inside his hull. In the course of it, she'd asked many questions, some of which he could answer, others he would not or could not. She'd found the things that Brashen had left and boldly arranged them to suit herself. "Some night I'll come out here and sleep with you, shall I?" she had proposed. "We'll stay up late and tell each other stories until dawn." She'd been intensely interested in every odd bit of junk she found. A bag with dice in it, still tucked up in a crack where some sailor had hidden it so he could game on watch and not be caught. A scratched out message on one bulkhead. "Three days, Sa help us all," it read, and she had wanted to know who had carved it and why. She had been most curious about the blood stains. She had gone from one to another, counting up to seventeen irregular blotches on his deck and in various holds. She had missed six others, but he didn't tell her that, nor would he recall for her the day that blood had been shed or the names of those who had fallen. And in the captain's quarters she had found the locked compartment that should have held his log books, but did not. The lock was long shattered, even the plank door splintered and torn awry. The logs that should have been his memory were gone, all stolen away. Amber had picked at that like a gull at a body. Was that why he would not answer her questions? Did he have to have his logs to remember? Yes? Well, then, how did he remember her visits, or Mingsley's? He had no log of those things.

He had shrugged. "A dozen years from now, when you have lost interest in me and no longer come to visit, I shall probably have forgotten you as well. You do not stop to think that you are asking me of events that most likely occurred long before you were born. Why don't you tell me about your childhood. How well do you remember your infancy?"

"Not very well." She changed the subject abruptly. "Do you know what I did yesterday? I went to Davad Restart and made an offer to buy you."

Her words jolted him into silence. Then he coldly replied, "Davad Restart cannot sell me. He does not own me. Nor can a liveship be bought and sold at all, save from kin to kin, and then only in dire circumstance."

It was Amber's turn to be silent. "Somehow, I thought you would know of these things. Well. If you do not, then you should, for they concern you. Paragon, among the New Traders, there have been rumors for months that you are for sale. Davad is acting as the intermediary. At first, your family was stipulating that you must not be used as a ship any longer because they . . . they didn't want to held responsible for any deaths. . . ." Her voice trailed off. "Paragon. How frankly can I speak to you? Sometimes you are so thoughtful and wise. Other times . . ."

"So you offered to buy me? Why? What will you make from my body? Beads? Furniture?" His edge of control was very thin, his words sharp with sarcasm. How dare she!

"No," she said with a heavy sigh. Almost to herself she muttered, "I feared this." She took a deep breath. "I would keep you as you are and where you are. Those were the terms of my offer."

"Chained here? Beached forever? For seagulls to shit on, and crabs to scuttle beneath? Beached here until all of me that is not wizardwood rots away and I fall apart into screaming pieces?"

"Paragon!" She cried out the word, in a voice between pain and anger. "Stop this. Stop it now! You must know I would never let that befall you. You have to listen to me, you have to let me talk until you've heard it all. Because I think I will need your help. If you go off now into wild accusations and suspicions, I cannot help you. And more than anything, I want to help you." Her voice went lower and softer on those words. She drew another deep breath. "So. Can you listen to me? Will you give me at least a chance to explain myself?"

"Explain," he said coldly. Lie and make excuses. Deceive and betray. He'd listen. He'd listen and gather what weapons he could to defend himself against all of them.

"Oh, Paragon," she said hoarsely. She put a palm flat to his hull. He tried to ignore this touch, to ignore the deep feeling that thrummed through her. "The Ludluck family, your family, has come on hard times. Very hard times. It is the same for many of the Old Trader families. There are many factors: slave labor, the wars in the north . . . but that doesn't matter to us. What matters is that your family needs money now, the New Traders know that, and they seek to buy you. Do not think ill of the Ludlucks. They resisted many offers. But when finally the money offered was very high, then they specified that they could not sell to anyone who wished to actually use you as a ship." He could almost feel her shake her head. "To the New Traders, that simply meant that your family wanted more money, much more money, before they would sell you as a working ship."

She took a deep breath and tried to go on more calmly. "Now, about then, I began to hear rumors that the only ship that can go up the Rain Wild River and come back intact is a liveship. Something about your wizardwood being impervious to the caustic white floods that sometimes come down the river. Which makes sense in light of how long you have rested here and not rotted, and it makes me understand why families would go into debt for generations to possess a ship like you. It is the only way to participate in the trade on the Rain Wild River. So now, as that rumor has crept about, the offers have risen. The New Traders who bid on you promise they will blame no one if you roll, and bid against each other." She paused. "Paragon, do you hear me?" she asked quietly.

"I hear you," he replied as he gazed out sightlessly over the ocean. He kept all expression out of his voice as he added, "Do go on."

"I will. Because you should know this, not because I take pleasure in it. So far, the Ludlucks have still refused all offers. I think perhaps they fear what the other Old Traders might think of them, if they sold you and opened up the Rain Wild River trade to the newcomers. Those goods are the last complete bastion of the Bingtown Traders. Or perhaps, despite their neglect of you, there still remains some family feeling. So. I made an offer. Not as great as the others have bid, for I don't have the wealth they do. But coupled with my offer was my promise that you would remain intact and unsailed. For I think the Ludlucks still care about you. That in an odd way, they keep you here to keep you safe."

"Ah, yes. Chaining up one's odder relatives and keeping them confined to a garret or cellar or other out of the way place has long been how Bingtown dealt with madness or deformity." He gave a bitter laugh. "Consider the Rain Wild Traders, for example."

"Who?"

"Exactly. Who? No one hears of them, no one knows of them, no one considers our ancient convenants with them. Least of all me or you. Pray, go on. After you buy me and leave me intact and don't sail me, what did you have in mind?"

"Oh, Paragon." She sounded completely miserable now. "If it were up to me—if I could dream as a child does and believe those dreams could come true—I would say, then, I would have artisans come here, to right you and build a cradle to support you upright. And I would come and live aboard you. On the cliffs above you, I would plant a garden of scent and color, a bird-and-butterfly garden, with trailing vines to hang all the way down to the beach and bloom sweetly. And around you I would sculpt stone and create tidepools and populate them with sea stars and sea anemones and those little scarlet crabs." As she raved on of this strange vision, her voice grew more and more impassioned. "I would live inside you and work inside you and in the evening I would dine on the deck and we would share our day. And if I dared to dream larger than that, why, then I would dream that someday I could obtain wizardwood and work it wisely enough to restore your eyes and your sight. In the mornings we would look out to the sun rising over the sea, and in the evenings we would look up to it setting over our cliff garden. I would say to the world, do what you will, for I am done with you. Destroy yourself or prosper, it is all one to me, as long as you leave us alone. And we would be happy, the two of us."

For a time he was at a loss to say anything. The childish fantasy caught him up and wrapped around him and suddenly he was not the ship but a boy who would have run in and out of such a place, pockets full of shiny stones and odd shells, gulls' feathers and . . .

"You are not my family, and you can never be my family." He dropped the words on the dream like a heavy shoe on a butterfly.

"I know that," she said quietly. "I said it was but a dream. It is what I long to do, but in truth, I do not know how long I can remain in Bingtown or with you. But Paragon, it is the only hope I have of saving you. If I go to the Ludlucks, myself, and say that you have said you could be content in such a way, perhaps they might take the lesser offer from me, for the sake of the bond. . . ." Her voice wisped away as he crossed his arms over the star scar on his broad chest.

"Save me from what?" he asked her disdainfully. "Such a nursery tale as you can spin, Amber. I confess, it is a charming image. But I am a ship. I was created to be sailed. Do you think I choose to lie here on this beach, idle, and near mad with that idleness? No. If my family chooses to sell me into slavery, let it at least be a familiar slavery. I have no desire to be your playhouse." Especially not as she had just admitted that she would eventually leave him, that her friendship with him was only because something else kept her in Bingtown. Sooner or later, she would leave him, just as all the others had. Sooner or later, all humans abandoned him.

"You had best go back to Davad Restart and withdraw your offer," he advised her when the silence had grown very long.

"No."

"If you buy me and keep me here, I will hate you forever, and I will bring you ill luck such as you cannot even imagine."

Her voice was calm. "I don't believe in luck, Paragon. I believe in fate, and I believe my fate has more terrible and heart-rending facets to it than even you can imagine. You, I know, are one of them. So, for the sake of the child who rants and threatens from within the wooden bones of a ship, I will buy you and keep you safe. Or as safe as fate will allow me." There was no fear in her voice. Only an odd tenderness as she reached up to set her palm flat to his planking.

"Just wrap it up," he told her brusquely. "It will heal."

Etta shook her head. Her voice was very soft as she told him, "Kennit, it is not healing." She set her hand gently to the flesh above his injury. "Your skin is hot and tender. I see you wince at every touch. These fluids that drain do not look to me like the liquids of healing but the—"

"Shut up," he ordered her. "I'm a strong man, not some sniveling whore in your care. I will heal, and all will be well once more. Wrap it for me, or do not, I scarcely care. I can bandage it myself, or Sorcor can. I have no time to sit here and listen to you wish bad luck on me." A sudden pain, sharp as any toothache, rushed up his leg. He gasped before he could stop himself, then gripped the edges of his bunk hard to keep from screaming.

"Kennit. You know what needs to be done." She was pleading with him.

He had to wait until he had breath to speak. "What needs to be done is feed you to a serpent so I can have a measure of peace in my life again. Go, get out of here, and send Sorcor to me. There are plans to be made, and I don't have time for your fretting."

She gathered up the sodden bandaging into a basket and left the room without another word. Good. Kennit reached for the sturdy crutch that leaned against his bunk. He had had Sorcor fashion it for him. He hated the thing, and when the deck pitched at all, it was virtually useless. But with it, on a calm day at anchor like today, he could get from his bunk to his chart table. He hopped there, in short painful hops that seared his stump with every jolt. He was sweating by the time he reached the table. He leaned forward over his charts, resting his weight on the edge of the table.

There was a tap at the door.

"Sorcor? Come in."

The mate stuck his head around the edge of the door. His eyes were anxious. But at the sight of his captain standing at his chart table, he beamed like a child offered sweets. He ventured into the room. Kennit noted he had yet another new vest, one with even more embroidery. "That healer did you some good, then," he greeted Kennit as he came in the door. "I thought he might. Those other two, I didn't think much of them. If you're going to have someone work on you, get an old man, someone who's been around a bit and . . ."

"Shut up, Sorcor," Kennit said pleasantly. "He was no more useful than the other two. The custom in Bull Creek seems to be that if you cannot cure an injury, you create a different one to distract your victim from your incompetency. Why, I asked him, did he think he could heal a new slice to my leg if he could not cure the one I had? He had no answer to that." Kennit shrugged elaborately. "I am tired of these backwater healers. Like as not, I shall heal just as fast without their leeches and potions."

The smile faded from Sorcor's face as he came slowly into the captain's room. "Like as not," he agreed dully.

"This last one as much as said so himself," Kennit asserted.

"Only because you threatened him until he agreed with you," Etta pointed out bitterly from the doorway. "Sorcor, stand up to him. Tell him he must let them cut the leg higher, above the foulness. He will listen to you, he respects you."

"Etta. Get out."

"I have nowhere to go."

"Go buy something in town. Sorcor, give her some money."

"I don't need money. All in Bull Creek know I am your woman, if

I so much as look at anything, they push it into my arms and beg me to take it. But there is nothing I truly want, anywhere, save that you should get better."

Kennit sighed heavily. "Sorcor. Please shut the door. With the woman on the other side of it."

"No, I promise, please Kennit, I'll be quiet. Let me stay. You talk to him, then, Sorcor, reason with him, he'll listen to you. . . ."

She kept it up like a whining dog and all the while Sorcor was quite gently pushing her out of the room and latching the door behind her. Kennit would not have been so gentle if he'd been able to deal with her himself. That, of course, was the whole problem. She saw him as weak, now, and would try to get her will in everything. Ever since she'd tortured his prisoners, he'd suspected she enjoyed the idea of cutting up helpless men. He wondered if there were some way he could leave her in Bull Creek.

"And how are things in town?" Kennit asked Sorcor pleasantly as if he had just entered.

Sorcor just stared at him for a moment. Then he seemed to decide to humor Kennit. "Couldn't be better. Unless you'd come ashore and talk to the merchants yourself. They've all but begged that you come and be their guest. I already told you once. They saw our Raven flag coming into the harbor and turned out the whole town for us. Little boys were shouting your name from the docks, 'Captain Kennit, Captain Kennit.' I heard one tell another that when it came to pirates, you were better than Igrot the Terrible."

Kennit startled, then made a sour face. "I knew Igrot when I was a lad. His reputation exaggerates him," he said quietly.

"Still, that's something, when folk compare you to the man that burned twenty towns and—"

"Enough of my fame," Kennit cut him off. "What of our business?"

"They've re-supplied us handsomely, and the *Sicerna* is already hove down for repair." The burly pirate shook his head. "There's a lot of rot in her hull. I'm surprised the Satrap would entrust a gift's delivery to a rotten tub like that."

"I doubt he inspected her hull," Kennit suggested drily. "And they welcomed the new population we brought them?"

"With open arms. Last slave raid carried off the best smith in town. We've brought them two new ones. And the musicians and such are all the talk of the place. Three times now they acted out *The Liberation of the* Sicerna. Got a right handsome lad being you, and a great worm made of paper and silk and barrel hoops that comes right up. . . ." Sorcor's voice died away abruptly. "It's a real fancy show, sir. I don't think there's anyone in town who hasn't seen it."

"Well. I am glad that the loss of my leg proved entertaining for so many."

"Now that's not it, sir," Sorcor began hastily, but Kennit waved him to silence.

"My liveship," he announced.

"Oh, Sar," Sorcor groaned.

"Did we not have an agreement?" Kennit asked him. "I believe we've just captured and liberated a slaveship. As I recall, it is now my turn to go after a liveship."

Sorcor scratched at his beard. "That weren't quite the agreement, sir. It was that if we saw a slaver, we went after her. And then the next liveship we saw, we'd go after. But you're talking about hunting a liveship, or laying in wait for one."

"It all amounts to the same thing," Kennit dismissed his objection.

"No, begging your pardon, sir, but it don't. I've been giving it some thought, sir. Maybe we ought to lay off both for a time. Just go back to pirating like we used to. Go after some fat merchant ships, like we used to do. Get us some money, have some good times. Stay away from slavers and serpents for a while." Sorcor's thick fingers fumbled with the gilt buttons on his vest as he offered this. "You've shown me life can be different than what I thought. For both of us. You got yourself a nice woman. She makes a real difference around here. I see now what you were trying to get me to understand. If we went back to Divvytown with a good haul, well, like Sincure Faldin was saying about being respectable and settled and all . . ."

"Once we have a liveship under us, you can have your choice of virgins, Sorcor," Kennit promised him. "A new one each week, if that is what pleases you. But first, my liveship. Now. If we can assume that anything we learned from the *Sicerna*'s crew is true, then it is likely we still have at least one liveship south of us still. Come and look at the chart with me. It seems to me that luck has placed us in a fine position. To the south of us, here, we have Hawser Channel. A nasty bit of water at any time, but especially at the change of tides. Any ship going north has to go through it. Do you see?"

"I see," Sorcor conceded grudgingly.

Kennit ignored his reluctance. "Now, in Hawser Channel we have Crooked Island. The good passage is to the east of the island. It's shallow in a few spots, but the shoals don't shift much. To the west of the island is a different story. The current runs strong, especially at the tide changes. Close to the island we have shoals that constantly form and reform. To the west we have the aptly named Damned Rocks." He paused. "Do you recall them?"

Sorcor frowned. "I'll never forget them. You took us in there that one time the Satrap's galley got after us. Current caught us and we shot through there like an arrow. Took me three days to believe I came out of it alive."

"Exactly," Kennit concurred. "A much swifter passage than if we had gone to the east of Crooked Island."

"So?" Sorcor asked warily.

"So? So we anchor here. A beautiful view of the approach to Hawser Channel. Once we see the liveship enter the channel, we take the west passage. As the liveship emerges, there we are, waiting for her, anchored in mid-channel. The east passage still has a respectable current. The liveship will have no choice but to run aground in the shoal here." He lifted his eyes from the chart to meet Sorcor's solemn look with a grin. "And she is ours. With minimum damage, if any."

"Unless she simply rams us," Sorcor pointed out sourly.

"Oh, she won't," Kennit assured him. "Even if she did, we'd still just board her and take her anyway."

"And lose the *Marietta*?" Sorcor was horrified.

"And gain a liveship!"

"This is not a good idea. A hundred things could go wrong," Sorcor objected. "We could be smashed to bits on the Damned Rocks. That's not a piece of water I'd ever willingly run again. Or if her draft is shallower than ours, we might take all those risks and she might still just slip past us quick-like while we were still anchored. Or . . ."

He meant it. He actually meant it, he wasn't going to go along with the idea. How dare he? He'd be nothing without Kennit. Nothing at all. A moment before, he'd been swearing he owed all he was to his captain, and now he would deny him his chance at a liveship.

A sudden change in tactics occurred to Kennit.

He lifted a hand to stem the mate's words. "Sorcor. Do you care for me at all?" he asked with disarming directness.

That stopped his words, as Kennit had known it would. The man almost blushed. He opened his mouth and then stammered, "Well, Captain, we've sailed together for a time now. And I can't recall a man who's treated me fairer, or been more . . ."

Kennit shook his head and turned aside from him as if moved. "No one else is going to help me with this, Sorcor. There's no one I trust as I do you. Since I was a boy, I've dreamed of a liveship. I always believed that someday I'd walk the deck of one, and she'd be mine.

And—" He shook his head and let his voice thicken. "Sometimes a man fears he may see the end sooner than he'd believed. This leg . . . if what they say is true for me . . ." He turned back to Sorcor, opened his blue eyes wide to meet Sorcor's dark ones. "This may be my last chance," he said simply.

"Oh, sir, don't talk like that!" Tears actually started to the scarred mate's eyes. Kennit bit his lip hard to keep the grin away. He leaned closer to the chart table to hide his face. It was a mistake, for his crutch slipped. He caught at the table edge, but the tip of his rotten stump still touched the floor. He cried out with the agony of it and would have fallen if Sorcor had not caught him.

"Easy. I've got you. Easy now."

"Sorcor," he said faintly. He regained his grip on the chart table, and leaned hard on his arms to keep from collapsing. "Can you do this for me?" He lifted his head. He was shaking now, he could feel it. It was the strain of standing on one leg. He wasn't accustomed to it, that was all. He didn't truly believe he'd die of this. He'd heal, he always healed, no matter how badly he was injured. He could do nothing about the grimace of pain that twisted his face or the sweat that had started fresh on his face. Use it. "Can you give me this last chance at it?"

"I can do it, sir." The dumb faith vied with heartbreak in Sorcor's eyes. "I'll get your liveship for you. You'll walk her decks. Trust me," he begged Kennit.

Despite his pain, Kennit laughed in his throat. He changed it to a cough. Trust him. "What choice do I have?" he asked himself bitterly. Somehow the words slipped out aloud. He swung his gaze to where Sorcor regarded him worriedly. He forced a sick smile to his lips, warmth to his voice. He shook his head at himself. "All these years, Sorcor, who else have I ever trusted? I have no choice but to put the burden once more upon our friendship."

He reached for his crutch. He took hold of it, but realized he did not have the strength to hold it firmly. The healing of his stump was drawing off every bit of strength he had. He blinked his heavy eyes. "I shall have to ask for your help to reach my bed as well. My strength deserts me."

"Captain," Sorcor said. The groveling affection of a dog was in the word. Kennit stored the thought away to consider when he felt better. Somehow asking Sorcor's aid had made the man more dependent on his approval than ever. He had chosen his first mate well, he decided. Were he in Sorcor's position, he would have instinctively grasped that now was his best opportunity to seize full power. Luckily for Kennit, Sorcor was slower-witted than he.

Sorcor stooped awkwardly and actually lifted Kennit bodily to carry him back to his bed. The abrupt movement stirred his pain to a new intensity. Kennit clutched at Sorcor's shoulders and his brain swam dizzily. For an instant he was overwhelmed by an ancient memory of his father: black whiskers and whiskey breath and sailor stink, whirling and laughing in a drunken dance with the boy Kennit in his arms. A time both terrifying and happy. Sorcor set him down gently on his bunk. "I'll send Etta in, shall I?"

Kennit nodded feebly. He reached after the memory of his father, but the chimera danced and mocked him from his shadowy childhood. Instead another face smiled down on him, sardonic and elegant. "A likely urchin. Perhaps something useful can be made of him." He tossed his head against his pillow, shaking the memory from his mind. The door closed behind the first mate.

"You don't deserve these people," a small voice said quietly. "Why they love you is beyond me. I would tell you that I would rejoice in your downfall the day they find you out, save that is also the day their hearts will break. By what luck do you deserve the loyalty of such folk?"

Wearily he lifted his wrist. The little face, strapped so tightly over his pulse point, glared up at him. He snorted a brief laugh at its indignant expression. "By *my* luck. By the luck in my name and the luck in my blood, I deserve them." Then he laughed again, this time at himself. "The loyalty of a whore and a brigand. Such wealth."

"Your leg is rotting," the little face said with sudden malignance. "Rotting up the bone. It will stink and drip and burn the life from your flesh. Because you lack the courage to cut your own foulness from your body." It sneered a grin at him. "Do you wit my parable, Kennit?"

"Shut up," he said heavily. He had begun to sweat again. Sweating in his nice clean shirt, in his fresh clean bed. Sweating like a stinking old drunk. "If I am evil, what shall we say of you? You are part and parcel of me."

"This piece of wood had a great heart once," the charm declared. "You have put your face upon me and your voice comes from my mouth. I am bound to you. But wood remembers. I am not you, Kennit. And I swear I shall not become you."

"No one . . . asked you . . . to." His breath was coming harder. He closed his eyes and sank away.

CHAPTER THIRTY

DEFIANCE AND ALLIANCE

ER FIRST SLAVE DEATH HAPPENED IN EARLY AFTER-
NOON. THE LOADING HAD GONE SLOWLY AND POORLY.
A wind from the east had churned up a nasty chop in the
water while the building clouds on the horizon promised
yet another winter storm by morning. The coffles of slaves
were being ferried out to where Vivacia was anchored, and
the slaves were being prodded up the rope ladder hung over
her side. Some of the slaves were in poor condition; others
were afraid of the ladder, or simply awkward getting from
the rocking boat to the ladder on the side of the rocking
ship. But the man who died, died because he wanted to. He
was halfway up the ladder, climbing awkwardly because his
legs were still fettered together. He suddenly laughed out
loud. "Guess I'll take the short road instead of the long
one," he sang out. He stepped away from the ladder and let
go. He dropped like an arrow into the sea, the weight of
chain on his ankles pulling him straight down. He could not
have saved himself even if he had changed his mind.

In the dark waters far below her hull, a knot of serpents
suddenly uncoiled. She sensed their lashing struggle for a
share of the meat. The salt of a man's blood flavored the

seawater briefly as it washed against her hull. Her horror was all the deeper that the men on her decks suspected nothing. "There are serpents below!" she called back to them, but they ignored her just as they ignored the pleas of the slaves.

After that, an angry Torg had the slaves roped together. This made it even more awkward for them to climb aboard, but he seemed to take some vengeful delight in reminding them that any man who jumped would have to answer to the rest of his coffle. No one else tried it, and Torg congratulated himself on his slyness.

Inside her holds, it was even worse. The slaves breathed out misery, until a miasma of unhappiness filled her from within. They were packed like fish in a barrel, and fastened to one another as well, so that they could not even shift without the co-operation of their chain-mates. The holds were dark with their fear; they pissed it out with their urine, wept it out with their tears until Vivacia felt saturated with human wretchedness.

In the chain locker, vibrating in harmony with her and adding his own special note to the woe, was Wintrow. Wintrow, who had abandoned her, was once again aboard her. He sprawled in the dark on the deck, ankles and wrists still weighted with chains, face pocked and stained with her image. He did not weep or moan, nor did he sleep. He simply stared into the blackness and felt. He shared her awareness of the slaves and their misery.

Like the beating of a heart she did not have, Wintrow thrummed with the slaves' despair. He knew the entire gauntlet of their despondency, from the half-wit who could not comprehend the change in his life to the aging sculptor whose early works still decorated the Satrap's personal quarters. In the lowest and darkest of her holds, scarcely above the bilge, was a layer of those least valuable. Map-faces, little more than human ballast they were, and the survivors would be sold for whatever they might bring in Chalced. In a safe dry hold that had oftimes held bales of silk or casks of wine, artisans huddled. To these were given the comfort of a layer of straw and enough chain to stand upright, if they took turns at it. Kyle had not secured as many of these as he had hoped for. The bulk of his cargo in the main hold were simple laborers and tradesmen, journeymen fallen on hard times, smiths and vineyard-dressers and lacemakers, plunged into debt by illness or addiction or poor judgment, and now paying the forfeit of their debts with their own flesh.

And in the forecastle were men with a different sort of pain. Some of the crew had had reservations about the captain's plan from the beginning. Others had given it no thought, had assisted in installing the chains and eye-bolts as if they were just another kind of netting to restrain cargo. But in the past two days, it had all become real. Slaves were coming aboard, men and women and some half-grown children. All were tattooed. Some wore their fetters with experience and others still stared and struggled against the chains that bound them. None had traveled in the cargo hold of a ship before; slaves that left Jamaillia went to Chalced. None ever came back. And each man in the crew was learning, some painfully, not to look at eyes or faces and not to heed voices that pleaded or cursed or ranted. Cargo. Stock. Bleating sheep shoved into pens until the pens would hold no more. Each man was coming to terms with it in his own way, was inventing other ways of seeing tattooed humans, other words to associate with them. Comfrey's joshing manner had vanished on the first day of loading. Mild, in his effort to find the relief of levity somewhere, made jokes that were not funny, that were sand in the wounds of an abraded conscience. Gantry held his peace and did his work, but knew that once this trip was up, he would not sail on a slaver again. Only Torg seemed to find contentment and satisfaction. In the depths of his greasy little soul, he was now living the cherished fantasy of his youth. He walked down the lines of his lashed-down cargo, savoring the confinement that finally made him feel free. He had already marked for himself those in need of his attentions, those who would benefit from his extra "discipline." Torg, Vivacia reflected, was a piece of carrion that, overturned, now showed its working maggots to the daylight.

She and Wintrow echoed one another's misery. And working inside her despair was the deep conviction that this never could have happened to her if her family had only been true to her. If one of her true blood had captained this ship, that captain would have had to share what she was feeling. She knew Ephron Vestrit would never have exposed her to this. Althea would have been incapable of it. But Kyle Haven heeded her not. If he had any misgivings, he had not shared them with anyone. The only emotion Wintrow recognized from his father was a cold burning anger that bordered on a hatred for his own flesh and blood. Vivacia suspected that Kyle saw them as a double-pronged problem: the ship that would not heed his wishes because of a boy that would not be what his father commanded him to be. She feared that Kyle was determined to break one or the other of them. And both, if he could.

She had kept her silence. Kyle had not brought Wintrow forward last night when he had hauled him on board. He had thrown Wintrow into his old confinement and then come forward himself to brag of his son's capture. In a voice pitched to carry to every man working on deck, he recounted to her how he had found his son a slave, and bought him for the ship. Once they were underway, he'd have the boy brought to her, and she might command him as she pleased—for his father, by Sa's damned eyes, was through with him.

His monologue lengthened, measured against her silent outward stare. Kyle's voice rose until his fury had him practically spitting. A shift of the breeze brought her the whisky of his breath. So. That was a new vice for Kyle Haven, coming aboard her drunk. She would not reply to him. He saw her and Wintrow as but parts of a machine, a block-and-tackle that, once joined a certain way, must then work a certain way. Had they been a fiddle and bow, she reflected, he would have smashed them together over and over again, demanding that they make music.

"I've bought you the damn worthless boy!" he finished his rant at her. "That was what you wanted, that's what you've got. He's all marked as yours, he's yours for every day left in his miserable, useless life." He spun and started to stride away, then turned back suddenly to growl at her back, "And you'd damn well better be content with him. For it's the last time I'll try to please you."

It was only in that instant that she finally heard the jealousy in his voice. Once he had coveted her, a beautiful, expensive ship, the rarest kind of a ship. A man with a ship such as she became a member of that elite brotherhood of those who captained liveships and traded in the exotic goods of the Rain Wild River and became the envy of any man who captained anything else. He had known her value, he had desired her and courted her. When he eliminated Althea, he thought he had vanquished every rival for her. But in the end, his attentions had not been enough for her. She had turned from him to a worthless twig of a boy who did not grasp her value. Like a spurned lover, Kyle saw his dream of truly possessing her crumbling. The shards of it held only the bitter dregs of hatred.

Well, it was mutual, she told herself coldly.

More difficult to name was the emotion she now felt toward Wintrow. Perhaps, she thought, it was not so different from what Kyle felt for her.

The next morning, Mild came to lean on her railing while he surreptitiously tucked a small piece of cindin in his lip. She frowned to herself. She did not like him using the drug, did not like how it blurred her perception of him. On the other hand, she could certainly understand why he felt he needed it today. She waited until he had secreted the remainder of the stick in the rolled cuff of his sleeve, and then spoke quietly.

"Mild. Tell the captain I wish Wintrow brought to me. Now."

"Oh, Sar," the boy blasphemed quietly. "Ship, why you want to put me in that spot? Can I just tell him you'd like a word with him?"

"No. Because I would not. I'd rather have no words with him at all. I simply want Wintrow brought to me. Now."

"Aw, please," the young sailor begged. "He's all in a lather already cause some of the map-faces are acting sick. Torg says they're faking it; they say if he don't put them somewhere better, they're all going to die."

"Mild." It was all in the tone of the word.

"Yes, ma'am."

She waited, but not for long. Kyle came storming across the deck, jumped to the foredeck. "What do you want now?" he demanded.

She considered ignoring him, decided against it. "Wintrow. As I believe you've been told."

"Later. When we're under way and the little cur can't jump ship again."

"Now."

He left without a word.

She was still not certain what she felt just now for Wintrow. She was glad he was aboard again. Yet she also had to confront the selfishness inherent in such gladness. And the humiliation that no matter how he had spurned her and abandoned her, she still would welcome him back. Where was her pride? she asked herself. For the moment he had come aboard, filthy, weary and sickened with despair, she had renewed her link to him. She had clutched at him and all that made him a Vestrit as a way to secure her own identity again. Almost immediately she had felt better, much more herself. It was a certainty she drew from him, an affirmation of herself. She had never been aware of that before now. She had known she was joined to him, but had thought of it as the "love" that humans so treasured. Now she was not sure. Uneasily she wondered if there were something evil in the way she clung to him and drew her perception of herself from him. Perhaps it was what he had always sensed in their bond that had made him try to escape her.

It was a terrible division, to feel such need for someone, and yet to feel angry that the need existed. She did not want to exist as a being dependent on another for her validity. She was going to confront him now, demand to know if he saw her as a parasite and if that was why he had fled her. She feared he would tell her that was the truth, that she gave nothing to him, only took. Yet as much as she feared that, she would ask him. Because she had to know. Did she truly have a life and spirit of her own, or was she but a Vestrit shadow?

She gave Haven a few more minutes. Still, no one was dispatched to Wintrow's door.

This was intolerable.

Earlier she had noted that their cargo was not evenly loaded. The crew was not used to stowing humans. It was not so much that it had to make a difference, but it could. She sighed, then subtly shifted her weight. She began to list to starboard. Just a tiny bit. But Kyle was, in some ways, a good captain, and Gantry was an even better mate.

They would notice the list. They would restow the cargo before getting under way. At which time she would develop a port list. And perhaps drag her anchor a bit. She stared stonily off at the shore. In the developing overcast, the white towers of Jamaillia City were dull, the dead white of empty shells. She swayed with the rocking of the ship, making the motion more pronounced. And she waited.

They sat together in the big darkened kitchen. Once, Keffria reflected, she had loved this room. When she was very small, she had loved to come here with her mother. Back then, Ronica Vestrit had often given intimate parties, and it was her especial pleasure to prepare the foods she herself would serve to her guests. Then the kitchen had been a lively place, for the boys would play with their blocks under the great wooden table, while she stood on a stool and watched her mother mince fine the savory herbs that would season the little meat rolls. Keffria would help her shell the hard-cooked eggs, or pop the lightly steamed almonds out of their little brown jackets.

The Blood Plague had ended those days. Sometimes Keffria thought that everything that was merry and light-hearted and simple in their household had died with her brothers. Certainly there had never been any gay little parties after that. She did not recall her mother ever again preparing dainties as she had then, or even spending much time in the kitchen. Now that they had reduced their servants, Keffria came in to help with the cooking herself on busy days. But Ronica did not.

Until tonight. They had come to the kitchen as the shadows of the day began to lengthen. In an awful parody of those old days, they had cooked together, chopping and peeling, simmering and stirring, all the while discussing the selection of wines and teas, how strong to make the coffee and which cloth to set out on the table. They spoke very little of why the Festrews had contacted them to say they would come tonight. Even though the payment was not due for some days now, it waited in a strongbox by the door. Unspoken between them was the uneasy knowledge that there had been no reply at all to Keffria's letter. The Khuprus were not the Festrews; there was likely no connection at all. Likely.

Keffria had known since she was a woman that the Rain Wild Traders came twice a year to accept payment on the liveship. She had known, too, that when the ship quickened, the size of the payments would increase. That was customary. The size of the payments reflected the belief that liveships would be used in trade on the Rain Wild River, in the very profitable and exotic Rain Wild goods. Most liveship owners became swiftly very wealthy as soon as their ships quickened. The Vestrits, of course, had not. Sometimes, Keffria allowed herself to wonder if her father's decision about magical goods had been a wise one. Sometimes, like tonight.

When the food was prepared and the table set, the two women sat down quietly by the hearth. Keffria made tea and poured cups for herself and her mother.

"I still think we should invite Malta to join us," she ventured. "She should learn. . . ."

"That one has learned far more than we suspect," her mother said wearily. "No, Keffria. Indulge me in this. Let you and I hear the Festrews out together, and together decide our course. I fear that the decisions we make tonight may chart the course of the Vestrit family." She met her daughter's eyes. "I do not say these words to hurt, but I do not know how to put it kindly. We two are the last of the Vestrit women, I fear. Malta is Haven to the bone. I do not say Kyle Haven is a bad man. I say only that what conspires here tonight is for Bingtown Traders to decide. And the Havens are not Bingtown Traders."

"Have it as you will," Keffria said tiredly. Someday, she thought to herself without rancor, you will be dead and I will no longer be caught in the middle. Perhaps then I shall simply give it all over to Kyle, and spend the time tending my gardens. Thinking of nothing else, save whether the roses need pruning or if it is time to split the iris clumps. Resting at last. She was sure Kyle would leave her alone. These days, when she thought of her husband, it was like ringing a cracked bell. She could recall the wonderful sound his name had once produced in her heart, but she could no longer hear it or make it. Love, she thought dejectedly, was after all, based on things. Family love, the love in her marriage, even her daughter's love for her. All based on things and the power to control the things. If you gave up power to people, then they loved you. Funny. Since she had discovered that, she little cared if anyone loved her or not anymore.

She sipped at her tea and watched the fire burn. From time to time she added wood to it. There were still pleasures to be found in simple things: the warmth of the fire, a good cup of tea. She would savor what was left to her.

A distant gong rang from somewhere across the field. Her mother rose hastily, to make a final check of everything. The lights in the room had long been dimmed, but now she added to the candles the leaf hoods to disperse their light even more. "Make fresh tea," she said quietly. "Caolwn likes tea." Then her mother did a rather peculiar thing. She went to the interior door of the kitchen, and opened it suddenly. She stepped out quickly, to peer up and down the hall, as if she expected to surprise someone.

When she came back into the room, Keffria asked her, "Is Selden out of bed again? He is such a little night owl."

"No, no one was there," her mother said distractedly. Then she shut the door firmly and came back to the table. "You recall the greeting ritual?" she suddenly asked Keffria.

"Of course. Don't worry, I won't shame you."

"You have never shamed me," her mother replied absently. Keffria could not say why her words made her heart leap so strangely.

Then the tap came on the door and Ronica stepped forward to open it. Keffria came to her shoulder. Outside the door stood two cloaked and hooded shapes. One wore a scattering of red flame jewels on her face veil. It was an effect both eerie and beautiful. Jani Khuprus. A feeling of dread swept up from her belly. The dream-box. For an instant dismay dizzied her. Keffria waited desperately for her mother to speak, to rescue them all somehow. Her mother stood still and silent, shocked. She offered no greeting. Keffria took a breath and prayed she would get it all right. "I bid you welcome to our home. Enter, and be at home also."

They both stepped back to allow the Rain Wild Traders to enter. Keffria braced herself as they removed their gloves, hoods and veils. The one woman's violet eyes were almost hidden by the wobbly growths on her eyelids. It was difficult for Keffria to meet her gaze and smile in a welcoming way, but she did. Yet Jani Khuprus, she of the flame jewels, was surprisingly smooth-faced for a Rain Wild Trader. She could almost have walked down a Bingtown street by daylight and not been stared at. Her markings were subtle. A pebbly outline traced the edges of her lips and eyelids. The whites of her eyes glowed bluish in the dim room, as did her hair, teeth and nails. It was not unattractive, in a shivery way. Ronica was still silent, as in a dream Keffria spoke the words. "We have prepared refreshment for you, after your long journey. Will you be seated at our table?"

"Most gratefully," they replied, almost as one.

All the women curtseyed to one another. Again, Keffria had to speak to break her mother's silence. "I, Keffria Vestrit, of the Vestrit Family of the Bingtown Traders, make you welcome to our table and our home. We recall all our most ancient pledges to one another, Bingtown to Rain Wilds, and also our private agreement regarding the liveship *Vivacia*, the product of both our families."

"I, Caolwn Festrew, of the Festrew Family of the Rain Wild Traders, accept your hospitality of home and table. I recall all our most ancient pledges to one another, Rain Wilds to Bingtown, and also our private agreement regarding the liveship *Vivacia*, the product of both our families." The one woman paused, and suddenly indicated the woman at her side. "I bring to your table and your home my guest who after this shall be your guest. Can you extend your welcome to Jani Khuprus, our kinswoman?" Her gaze was fixed on Keffria's face. It was up to her to respond.

"I do not know the formal reply to such a request," she admitted frankly. "So I shall simply say that any guest of our long-time friend Caolwn is more than welcome in our home. Allow me but a moment to set out another plate and silver." She desperately hoped that so august a personage as the head of the Khuprus clan would not be offended by her informality.

Jani smiled, and glanced at Caolwn as if seeking permission to speak. Caolwn gave her a small smile. "I, for one, am just as glad to set aside formality as well. Let me say that this unexpected visit is more my doing than Caolwn's. I begged her to arrange it and to allow me to accompany her, that she might introduce me to your home. If it has presented any difficulty for you, I wish to apologize now."

"None at all," Keffria replied quietly. "Please, let us be at ease with one another, as neighbors, friends and family ought to be." Her words included her mother as well as the other two. As if by accident, she let her hand brush her mother's in a silent plea for her to end her shocked stillness.

Caolwn had turned to regard Ronica oddly. "My old friend, you are silent tonight. Are you comfortable with the guest I bring?"

"How could I be otherwise?" Ronica said faintly. In a stronger voice, she added, "I but defer to my daughter tonight. She has come into her inheritance. It is more fitting that she welcome you now, rather than I, and that she speak for the Vestrits."

"And she has done so eloquently," Jani Khuprus said with genuine warmth in her voice. She smiled at them all. "Oh, I fear I have not done this well. I had thought that coming myself might be the most comfortable way to begin this, but perhaps a letter would have been better."

"It is quite all right, I assure you," Keffria spoke as she set an extra glass in place and then drew up another chair to the table. "Let us all be seated and enjoy food and tea and wine together. Or I have coffee, if anyone would prefer it." She had a sudden odd desire to know Jani Khuprus better before the reason for her visit was broached. Slowly. Slowly. If this riddle must be unfolded, she wanted it to be slowly, to be sure she understood it fully.

"You have set a lovely table," Jani Khuprus observed as she took her place at it. It did not escape Keffria that she seated herself first, nor that Caolwn deferred to her. She was suddenly glad that the olives were the finest, that her mother had insisted the almond paste be prepared fresh tonight, that only the very best of what they had cooked be set out upon the table. It was a lovely table of rich and dainty food such as Keffria had not seen in months. Whatever their financial limits might be, Ronica had not allowed it to affect this feast, and Keffria was glad of it.

For a time, table talk was all there was. Slowly Ronica recovered both poise and charm. She led the conversation into safe channels. Compliments on the food, the wine, the coffee and other generalities accompanied the meal. But Keffria noticed that whenever Jani took over the conversation, which was often, the little stories and anecdotes she told served to illustrate the wealth and power of her family. They were not told braggingly; there was no intent to humble the Vestrits or their table. In each case, she compared the food or the company favorably to some grander occasion or personage. She was, Keffria decided, deliberately trying to share information about her family. Her husband was still alive, she had three live sons and two live daughters, an immense family by Rain Wild standards. The new wealth from the discovery of the flame jewels was allowing them more time to travel and entertain, to bring into her home objects of beauty and the knowledge of scholarship. Was not that truly the greatest benefit of wealth, that it allowed one to treat family and friends to what they deserved? If they cared to journey up the river, they would be most welcome in her home.

It was like the courting dance of a bird, Keffria reflected. Her heart turned over in her chest again. Jani Khuprus suddenly turned to look at her, as if Keffria had made some small sound that had attracted her eyes. With no warning, she smiled dazzlingly and said, "I did receive your message the other day, my dear. But I confess, I did not understand it. That was one of the reasons I begged Caolwn to arrange this visit, you know."

"So I surmised," Keffria said faintly. She glanced at her mother. Ronica met her eyes and gave her a tiny nod. She drew strength from her restored calm. "Truly, I found myself in a most embarrassing position. I thought it best simply to write and be honest about what had happened. I assure you, if the dream-box is found, it will be swiftly returned."

That was not quite as graciously phrased as it could have been. Keffria bit her lower lip. Jani cocked her head sideways.

"That, of course, was what confused me. I called my son to me and questioned him. Such an impulsive and passionate act could only have been the doing of my youngest. Reyn stammered a bit, and blushed a great deal, for prior to this, he has shown no interest in courting. But he admitted the dream-box. And the scarf and flame jewel as well." She shook her head with maternal fondness. "I have scolded him for this, but I fear he is quite unrepentant. He is very taken with your Malta. He did not, of course, discuss the dream they shared. That would be quite, uh, indelicate of a gentleman. But he did tell me he was certain she looked with favor on his suit." She smiled round at them again. "So I shall presume the box was found and enjoyed by the young lady."

"So we should all presume, I am sure," Ronica said suddenly before Keffria could speak. The two Vestrit women exchanged a glance whose meaning could not have been concealed from anyone.

"Oh, dear," Jani sighed apologetically. "I take it you do not share your young woman's enthusiasm for my son's courtship."

Keffria's mouth had gone dry. She sipped at her wine, but it did not seem to help. Instead she coughed awkwardly, and then choked. She was just getting her breath when her mother spoke for her.

"I am afraid our Malta is a mischievous little thing. Full of pranks and tricks is our girl." Ronica's tone was light, but the look on her face was sympathetic. "No, Jani, it is not your son's courtship that we look on with disfavor. It is Malta's age and her childish behavior. When Malta is old enough to have suitors, he will most certainly be welcomed by us. And if he gains her favor, we could only feel honored by such a joining. But Malta, although she may have the appearance of a young woman, has only a child's years, and I fear, a child's love of pretense and mischief. She is barely thirteen. She has not yet been presented. He must have seen her in her Trader robe, at the gathering you called. I am sure that if he had seen her as she usually dresses, in a little girl's frocks, he would have realized his . . . error."

A silence descended. Jani looked from one woman to the other. "I see," she said finally. She seemed to feel uncomfortable now. "This, then, is why the young woman is not present tonight."

Ronica smiled at her. "She is long abed, as most children her age are." Her mother took a sip of her wine.

"I find myself in an awkward position," she said slowly.

"I fear ours is much more ungainly," Keffria cut in smoothly. "I wish to be completely honest. We were both shocked, just now, at the mention of a scarf and flame jewel. I assure you we had no knowledge of such a gift. And if the dream-box has been opened . . . no, I am sure it has been, for your son has shared the dream . . . well, Malta is the culprit there also." She sighed heavily. "I must apologize most humbly for her ill manners." Despite her efforts at control, Keffria found her throat tightening. "I am distressed." She heard her voice begin to shake. "I did not believe her capable of such deception."

"My son will certainly be discomfited," Jani Khuprus said quietly. "I fear he is too naïve. He is close to twenty, but never before has he evinced any interest in courting a bride. And now, I fear, he has been precipitate. Oh, dear." She shook her head. "This puts a different face on many things." She exchanged a glance with Caolwn and the other woman met it with an uncomfortable smile.

Caolwn explained softly. "The Festrew family has ceded to the Khuprus family the contract for the liveship *Vivacia*. All rights and debt have been transferred to them."

Keffria felt she staggered and fell out into the white silence. She scarcely needed the words that followed from Jani. "My son negotiated this with the Festrews. I came tonight to speak for him. But clearly what I was to say is inappropriate now."

No one needed to explain. The debt would have been offered back as a bridal gift. An extravagantly expensive bridal gift, a typical Rain Wild gesture, but on a scale Keffria had never before imagined. A liveship debt canceled for one woman's marriage consent? It was preposterous.

"Such a dream as it must have been," her mother murmured drily.

It was inappropriate, almost coarse in its implications. Keffria would always wonder if her mother had guessed what would happen next. As all the women burst into sudden laughter at the susceptibility of men, the awkwardness dispersed. They were all suddenly mothers caught up in the clumsiness of their offspring's fumbling courtship.

Jani Khuprus took a breath. "It seems to me," she said ruefully, "That our problem is not so great a one as time cannot solve it. So my son must wait. It will not harm him." She smiled with motherly tolerance from Ronica to Keffria. "I will speak to him most seriously. I shall tell him that his courtship cannot commence until your Malta has presented herself as a woman." She paused, mentally calculating. "If that is this spring, then the wedding can be in summer."

"Wedding? She will barely be fourteen!" Keffria cried out incredulously.

"She would be young," Caolwn agreed. "And adaptable. For a Bingtown woman marrying into a Rain Wild family, that is advantageous." She smiled and the fleshy protruberances on her face wobbled hideously at Keffria. "I was fifteen."

Keffria drew a deep breath; she was not sure if she would shriek at them, or simply order them from the house. Her mother's hand fell on her arm and squeezed it. She managed to close her mouth.

"It is far too early for us to speak of a marriage," Ronica said bluntly. "I have told you that Malta is fond of childish pranks. I fear this may be one of them, that she has not considered your son's courtship with the seriousness it deserves." Ronica looked slowly from Caolwn to Jani. "There is no need for haste."

"You speak as a Bingtown Trader," Jani replied. "You live long lives and bear many children. We do not have the luxury of time. My son is almost twenty. Finally, he has discovered a woman he desires, and you tell us he must wait? Over a year?" She leaned back in her chair. "It will not do," she said quietly.

"I will not force my child," Keffria asserted.

Jani smiled knowingly. "My son does not believe it is a question of forcing anyone. And I believe my son." She looked from one to the other. "Come, we are all women here. If she were as childish as you say, the dream-box would have revealed that to him." When no one spoke, she went on in a dangerously soft voice, "The offer is handsome. You cannot be hoping for more, from anyone."

"The offer is more than handsome, it is staggering," Ronica replied swiftly. "But we are all women here. As such, we know that a woman's heart cannot be bought. All we ask is that you wait until Malta is a bit older, to be sure she knows her own mind."

"Surely, if she has opened the dream-box and dreamed a shared dream, we can say she knows her own mind. Especially, it would seem,

if she has had to defy both her mother and grandmother to do so."
Jani Khuprus' voice was losing its velvet courtesy.

"The act of a willful child should not be seen as the decision of a
woman. I tell you, you must wait." Ronica's voice was firm.

Jani Khuprus stood. "Blood or gold, the debt is owed," she invoked. "The payment is due soon, Ronica Vestrit. And you have already been short with it once. By our contract, we can determine the
coin of its payment."

Ronica stood, to match herself against Jani. "There, in the cask by
the door. There is your gold. I give it to you freely, the just payment
on a debt owed." She shook her head, wide and slow. "I will not, I will
never, give you child or grandchild of mine, save that she goes by her
own will. That is all I am saying to you, Jani Khuprus. And it shames
us both that such a thing must be spoken aloud."

"Do you say you will not honor your contract?" Jani demanded.

"Please!" Caolwn's voice was suddenly shrill. "Please," she went
on in a softer tone when all turned to her. "Let us recall who we are.
And let us recall that we do have time. It is neither as short as some
would believe it, nor as generous as others could wish, but we do have
time. And we do have the hearts of two young people to consider."
Her slitted violet eyes flitted from one countenance to another, seeking cooperation. "I propose," she said quietly, "a compromise. One
that may spare all of us much grief. Jani Khuprus must accept your
gold. This time. For she is as surely bound by what I and Ronica
agreed, here in this same kitchen, as Ronica is ultimately bound by the
contract itself. On that we all agree, do we not?"

Keffria held her breath, did not move, but no one seemed to be
looking at her. Jani Khuprus was the first to nod, stiffly. The nod that
eventually came from Ronica was more like a bowing of the head in
defeat.

Caolwn gave a sigh of relief. "This would be my compromise. I
speak, Ronica, as a woman who has known Jani's Reyn for all his life.
He is a most honorable and trustworthy young man. You need not fear
he will take advantage of Malta, regardless of whether she be girl or
woman. And that is why I believe you could let him begin his courtship now. Chaperoned, of course. And with the stipulation that there
will be no more gifts such as could turn a girl's head more with greed
than love. Simply allow Reyn to regularly present himself to her. If
she is truly a child, he will see this promptly, and be more abashed
than any of us can imagine to have made such a mistake. But if she is
truly a woman, give him a chance, the first chance of any, to win her

heart for himself. Is this too much to ask? That he be allowed to be her first suitor?"

It went far to repair many things between them that Ronica looked to Keffria for a decision. Keffria licked her lips. "I think I can allow this. If they are well chaperoned. If there are no expensive gifts to turn her head." She sighed. "In truth, Malta has opened this door. Perhaps this should be her first lesson as a woman. That no man's affection is to be taken lightly."

The circle of women nodded agreement.

CHAPTER THIRTY-ONE

SHIPS AND SERPENTS

IT WAS A CRUDE TATTOO, DONE HASTILY AND ONLY IN BLUE INK. BUT FOR ALL THAT, IT WAS HER IMAGE marked on the boy's face. She stared at him aghast. "This falls upon me," she had said. "But for me, none of this would have befallen you."

"That is true," he agreed with her wearily. "But that does not mean it is your fault."

He turned away from her to sit down heavily on the deck. Did he even guess how his words wounded her? She tried to share his feelings, but the boy who had vibrated with pain the night before was now a great stillness. He put his head back and drew a great breath of the clean wind sweeping her decks. He sighed it out.

The man at the wheel tried to force her back out into the main channel. With almost idle malice, she leaned against it, weltering as he forced her over. That for Kyle Haven, who thought he could bend her to his will.

"I don't know what to say to you," Wintrow confessed quietly. "When I think of you, I feel shamed, as if I betrayed you by running away. Yet when I think of myself, I am disappointed, for I nearly managed to regain my life. I don't wish to abandon you, but I don't wish to be trapped here either." He shook his head, then leaned back against the railing. He was ragged and dirty, and Torg had not taken the chains from his wrists and ankles when he left him there. Wintrow now spoke over his shoulder as he looked up at her sails. "Sometimes I feel I am two people, reaching after two different lives. Or rather, joined to you, I am a different person from who I am when we are apart. When we are together, I lose . . . something. I don't know what to call it. My ability to be only myself."

A prickling of dread ran over Vivacia. His words were too close to what she had planned to say to him. She had left Jamaillia City the morning before this, but only now had Torg brought Wintrow to her. For the first time she had seen what they had done to him. Most jolting was her crude image in colored ink on the boy's cheek. Nothing marked him as a sailor now, let alone the captain's son. He looked like any slave. Yet despite all that had befallen him, he was outwardly calm.

Answering her thought, he observed, "I don't have anything left for feelings anymore. Through you, I am all the slaves at once. When I allow myself to feel that, I think I shall go mad. So I hold back from it and try to feel nothing at all."

"These emotions are too strong," Vivacia agreed in a low voice. "Their suffering is too great. It overwhelms me, until I cannot separate myself." She paused, then went on haltingly, "It was worse when they were aboard and you were not. Just your being gone made me feel as if I were adrift. I think you are the anchor that keeps me who I am. I think that is why a liveship needs one of her own family aboard her."

Wintrow made no reply, but she hoped from his stillness he was listening. "I take from you," she admitted. "I take and I give you nothing."

He stirred slightly. His voice was oddly flat as he observed, "You've given me strength, and more than once."

"But only that I might keep you by me," she said carefully. "I strengthen you so I may keep you. So I can remain certain of who I am." She gathered her courage. "Wintrow. What was I, before I was a liveship?"

He shifted his fetters and rubbed his chafed ankles distractedly. He did not seem to understand the importance of her question. "A tree, I suppose. Actually, a number of trees, if wizardwood grows as other wood does. Why do you ask?"

"While you were gone, I could almost recall . . . something else. Like wind in my face, only stronger. Moving so swiftly, of my own free will. I could almost recall being . . . someone . . . who was not a Vestrit at all. Someone separate from all I have known in this life. It was very frightening. But." She halted, teetering on a thought she didn't want to acknowledge.

After a long silence, she admitted, "I think I liked it. Then. Now . . . I think I had what men would call nightmares . . . if live-ships could sleep. But I don't sleep, and so I could not wake from them completely. The serpents in the harbor, Wintrow." Now she spoke hurriedly in a low voice, trying to make him understand all of it at once. "No one else saw them in the harbor. All now admit of that white one that follows me. But there were others, many of them, in the bottom muck of the harbor. I tried to tell Gantry they were there, but he told me to ignore them. But I could not, because somehow they made the dreams that . . . Wintrow?"

He was dozing off in the warm sun on his skin. No one could blame him after the hardships he'd endured.

It still hurt her. She needed to talk to someone about these things, or she thought she would go mad. But no one was willing to truly listen to her. Even with Wintrow back on board, she still felt isolated. She suspected he was somehow holding himself back from her. Again, she could neither blame him, nor stop the hurt she felt at that. She felt an unfocused anger as well. The Vestrit family had made her what she was, created these needs in her. Yet since she had quickened, she had not had even a single day of ungrudging companionship. Kyle expected her to sail lively and well with a belly full of misery and no companion. It wasn't fair.

The thud of hasty footsteps on her deck broke her thoughts.

"Wintrow," she pitched urgency into her voice as she warned him, "Your father is headed this way."

"You're wide of the channel. Can't you hold a course?" Kyle barked at Comfrey.

Comfrey looked up at him, a hooded glance. "No, sir," he said evenly, as if he were not being insubordinate. "I can't seem to. Every time I correct, the ship goes wide."

"Don't blame this on the ship. I'm getting sick of every crew-member on board this vessel blaming their incompetency on the ship."

"No, sir," Comfrey agreed. He stared straight ahead, and once more turned the wheel in an attempt to correct. The *Vivacia* answered as sluggishly as if she were towing a sea anchor. As if in response to that thought, Kyle saw a serpent thrash to the surface in her wake. The ugly thing seemed to be looking right at him.

Kyle felt the slow burn of his anger begin to glow. It was too much. It was just too damn much. He was not a weak man; he could face whatever fate threw his way and stand up to it. Unfavorable weather, tricky cargoes, even simple bad luck could not break his calm. But this was different. This was the direct opposition of those he strove to benefit. And he didn't know how much more of it he could take.

Sa knew he had tried with the boy. What more could his son have asked of him? He'd offered him the whole damn ship, if he'd but be a man and step up and take her. But no. The boy had to run off and get himself tattooed as a slave in Jamaillia.

So he'd given up on the boy. He'd brought him back to the ship and put him completely at the ship's disposal. Wasn't that what she'd insisted she'd needed? He'd had the boy taken to the foredeck this morning, as soon as they were well out of the harbor. The ship should have been content. But no. She wallowed through the water, listing first to one side and then to another, constantly drifting out of the best channel. She shamed him with her sloppy gait, just as his own son had shamed him.

It all should have been so simple. Go to Jamaillia, pick up a load of slaves, take them up to Chalced, sell them at a profit. Bring prosperity to his family and pride to his name. He ran the crew well and maintained the ship. By all rights, she should sail splendidly. And Wintrow should have been a strong son to follow after him, a son proud to dream of taking the helm of his own liveship someday. Instead, at fourteen, Wintrow already had two slave tattoos on his face. And the larger one was the result of Kyle's own angry and impulsive reaction to a facetious suggestion from Torg. He wished to Sa that Gantry had been with him instead of Torg that day. Gantry would have talked him out of it. In contrast, Torg had acted immediately, much to Kyle's unspoken regret. If he had it to do over—

A movement off the starboard side caught his eye. It was the damn serpent again, slithering through the water, and watching him. It was a white serpent, uglier than a toad's belly, that trailed in their wake. It didn't seem much of a threat; the few glimpses of it he'd had, the thing had seemed old and fat. But the crew didn't like it, and the ship didn't like it. Looking down on it now, he realized just how much *he* didn't like it. It stared up at him, meeting his gaze as if it were not an animal at all. It looked like a man trying to read his mind.

He left the wheel to be away from it, striding toward the bow in agitation. His troubled chain of thought followed him.

The damn ship stank, much worse than Torg had said it would. Stank worse than an outhouse, more like a charnel house. They'd already had to put three deaders over the side, one of which had seemed to die by her own hand. They'd found her sprawled wide in her chains. She'd torn strips from the hem of her garment and stuffed them into her mouth until she choked on them. How could anyone do such a stupid thing to herself? It had rattled several of the men, though none of them had spoken to him directly about it.

He glanced starboard again. The damn serpent was pacing him, staring up at him all the while. He looked away from it.

Somehow it reminded him of the tattoo down the boy's face. It was just as inescapable. He shouldn't have done it. He regretted it, but there was no changing it, and he knew he'd never be forgiven for it, so there was no sense in apologizing. Not to the boy or his mother. They'd hate him for it to the end of his days. Never mind that it hadn't really hurt the boy; it wasn't as if he'd blinded him or cut off a hand. It was just a mark. A lot of sailors wore a tattoo of their ship or the ship's figurehead. Not on their faces, but it was the same thing. Still. Keffria was going to throw a fit when she saw it. Every time he looked at Wintrow, all he could imagine was his wife's horrified face. He couldn't even look forward to going home anymore. No matter how much coin he brought home, all they were going to see was the ship's tattoo on the boy's face.

Beside the ship, the serpent's head lifted out of the water and regarded him knowingly.

Kyle found his angry stride had carried him the length of the ship, up to the foredeck. His son huddled there. It shamed him to look at such a creature as his elder son. This was his heir. This was the boy he had envisioned taking over the helm someday. It was just too damn bad that Malta was a female. She'd have made a much better heir than Wintrow.

A sudden flash of anger jolted through him, clearing his thought. It was all Wintrow's fault. He saw that now. He'd brought the boy on board to keep the ship happy and make her sail right, and the little priest had only made her bitchy and sullen. Well, if she wasn't going to sail well with the boy aboard, then there was no reason he had to put up with the puling whiner. He took two strides and seized Wintrow by the collar of his shirt and hauled him to his feet. "I ought to feed you to the damn serpent!" he shouted at the startled boy who dangled in his grip.

Wintrow lifted shocked eyes to his father and met his gaze. He said nothing, setting his jaws firmly into silence.

He drew back his hand, and when Wintrow refused to cower, he backhanded his son with all the force he could muster, felt the sharp sting in his own fingers as they cracked across the boy's tattooed face. The boy flew backwards, his feet tangling in his clanking fetters, to fall hard on the deck. He lay where he had fallen, his defiance of his father perfect in his lack of resistance.

"Damn you, damn you!" he roared at Wintrow and charged down on the boy. He intended to heave him over the side and let him sink. It was not only the perfect solution, it was the only manly thing left to do. No one would blame him. The boy was an embarrassment, and bad luck besides. Get rid of the whimpering boy-priest before Wintrow could shame him anymore.

Beside the ship, a death-white head reared suddenly from the water, jaws gaping expectantly. The scarlet maw was shocking, as were the red eyes that glittered so hopefully. It was big, bigger far than Kyle had thought from his glimpses of it. It kept pace with the *Vivacia* easily, even as it reared such a great length of itself out of the water. It waited for its meal.

The tangle had been following its provider into what Shreever now recognized as one of its resting places when Maulkin suddenly arced himself in a hard loop and veered away. He drove himself through the Plenty as if chasing prey, yet Shreever saw nothing worthy of pursuit.

"Follow," she trumpeted to the others, and set out after him. Sessurea was not far behind her. In a few moments she became aware that the rest of the tangle had not complied. They had remained with the provider, thinking only of their bellies and the pleasures of growing and shedding and growing yet again. She thrust their betrayal from her mind and redoubled her efforts to overtake Maulkin.

She caught up with him only because he abruptly paused. Everything about his pose suggested fascination. His jaws were wide, gills flared and pumping as he stared.

"What is it?" she demanded, and then caught the tiniest flavor in the water. Shreever could not decide what it was she tasted, only that the sensation was a welcome and a fulfillment of a promise. She saw

Sessurea join them, marked the widening of his eyes as he, too, was seized by the taste.

"What is it?" he echoed her earlier question.

"It is She Who Remembers," Maulkin said in reverent awe. "Come. We must seek her." He did not seem to notice that of all his tangle, only two of his followers had joined him. He had thought only for the hanging scent that threatened to disperse before he could track it to the source. He drove himself onward with a force and speed that Shreever and Sessurea could not match. They trailed him desperately, trying to keep sight of his golden false-eyes as they flashed through the murk. The fragrance grew stronger as they followed him, almost overwhelming their senses.

When they again overtook Maulkin, he was hanging at the respectful distance from a provider who shone silver through the murky plenty. Her scent hung thick in the water, sating them with its sweetness. Hope was a part of that scent, and joy, but thickest was the promise of memories, memories for all to share, knowledge and wisdom for the asking. Yet Maulkin hung back, and did not ask.

"Something is wrong," he bugled quietly. His eyes were deep and thoughtful. A flickering of color ran the length of him and then faded. "This is not right. She Who Remembers is like to us. So all the holy lore says. I see only the silver-bellied provider. And yet, all my senses tell me that She is near. I do not understand."

In confused awe they watched the silver provider as she moved languidly before them. She had a single attendant, a heavy white serpent who followed her closely. He hovered at the top of the Plenty, lifting his head out into the Lack.

"He speaks to her," Maulkin blew out the thought softly. "He petitions her."

"For memories," Sessurea filled in. His ruff stood out in a shivering frill of anticipation.

"No!" Maulkin was suddenly incredulous, almost angry. "For food! He petitions only that she should bestow food upon him, food that she finds undesirable."

His tail lashed the atmosphere so suddenly and savagely that it thickened with bottom particles. "This is not right!" he trumpeted. "This is a lure and a cheat! Her fragrance is that of She Who Remembers, and yet she is not of our kind. And that one speaks to her, and yet not to her, for she does not answer, and it was promised, forever promised, that she would always answer one who petitioned her. It is not right!"

There was great pain in the depth of his fury. His mane stood out wide, welling toxins in a choking cloud. Shreever wove her head aside from it. "Maulkin," she besought quietly. "Maulkin, what must we do?"

"I do not know," he replied bitterly. "There is nothing of this in holy lore, nothing of this in my tattered memories. I do not know. For myself, I shall follow her, simply to try to understand." He bugled lower. "If you choose to return to the rest of the tangle, I will not fault you. Perhaps I have led you awry. Perhaps all my memories have been a deception of my own poisons." His mane went suddenly limp with disappointment. He did not even look to see if they followed him as he trailed after the silver provider and her white hanger-on.

"Kyle! Let him go!" Vivacia shrieked the words at him, but there was no command in them, only fear. She leaned wildly to swat at the white serpent. "Go away, you foul thing! Get away from me! You shall not have him, you shall never have him!"

Her motion set the entire ship to rocking. She unbalanced her hull, making the entire ship list suddenly and markedly. She flailed at the serpent, ineffectual slapping motions of her massive wooden arms that rocked the ship wildly. "Get away, get away!" she screamed at it, and then, "Wintrow! Kyle!"

As Kyle dragged Wintrow toward the rail and the expectant serpent, Vivacia threw back her head and shrieked, "Gantry! In Sa's name, get up here! GANTRY!"

Throughout the ship, other voices rose in a babel of confusion. Crew members shouted to one another, demanding to know what was going on, while in the holds slaves screamed wordlessly, terrified of anything—fire, shipwreck or storm—that might come upon them while they were chained down in the dark below the waterline. The fear and misery in the ship was suddenly palpable, a thick miasma that smelt of human waste and sweat and left a coppery taste in Kyle's mouth and a greasy sheen of hopelessness on his skin.

"Stop it! Stop it!" Kyle heard himself shouting hoarsely, but was unsure of whom he ordered. He gripped Wintrow by the front of his tattered robe. He shook the unresisting boy, yet it was not the boy he battled.

Gantry was suddenly on the deck, barefoot and shirtless, the pale confusion of interrupted sleep in his face. "What is it?" he demanded, and then at sight of the serpent head that reared up near deck-high, he cried out wordlessly. In as close to panic as Kyle had ever seen the man, he snatched up a polishing stone from the deck. Two-handed he gripped it, and then he reared back and threw it at the serpent with such force that Kyle heard the cracking of his muscles. The serpent evaded it lazily with a gentle sway of its neck, and then slowly sank back down out of sight beneath the water. It was visible only as an unevenness in the pattern of the waves.

As if awakening from a nightmare, all purpose and understanding of what he was doing suddenly left Kyle. He looked at the boy he gripped without any clear idea of what his intent had been. Strength suddenly forsook him. He let Wintrow fall to the deck at his feet.

Chest heaving, Gantry turned to Kyle. "What is it?" he demanded. "What set this off?"

Vivacia was now uttering short panting shrieks, answered by incoherent cries from the slaves in the hold. Wintrow still sprawled where Kyle had dropped him. Gantry took two steps and looked down on the boy, then looked up at Kyle incredulously. "You did this?" he asked. "Why? The boy is knocked senseless."

Kyle merely stared at him, speechless. Gantry shook his head and then glanced up at the sky as if imploring help from above. "Quiet down!" he snapped at the figurehead. "And I'll see to him. But quiet down, you're upsetting everyone. Mild! Mild, I want the medicine chest. And tell Torg I want the keys to these stupid chains, too. Easy. Easy, my lady, we'll soon have things put as right as I can make them. Please. Calm down. It's gone now, and I'll see to the boy." To a gaping sailor he shouted, "Evans. Go below, wake my watch. Have them go among the slaves and calm them, tell them there's nothing to fear."

"I touched it," Kyle heard Vivacia tell Gantry breathlessly. "I hit it, and when I hit it, it knew me. Only I wasn't me!"

"It's going to be all right," Gantry repeated doggedly.

The ship lurched again as Vivacia leaned far down to scrub her hands in the sea. She was still making small, frightened sounds.

Kyle forced himself to look down at his son. Wintrow was out cold. He massaged the puffy knuckles of his right hand and abruptly knew how hard he'd hit the boy. Hard enough to loosen teeth at least, possibly enough to break his face. Damn. He'd been going to feed the boy to the serpent. His own son. He knew he'd struck Wintrow, he recalled doing it. What he could not recall was why. What had goaded him into it? "He's all right," he told Gantry gruffly. "More than likely he's faking it."

"More than likely," Gantry agreed sarcastically. He took a breath as if to speak, then suddenly seemed to change his mind. A moment later he said in a low voice, "Sir, we should make some sort of a weapon. A pike or a spear. Something. For that monster."

"We'd probably just make it mad," Kyle said uneasily. "Serpents follow slavers all the time. I've never heard of them attacking the ship itself. It will be content with the dead slaves."

Gantry looked at him as if he hadn't heard him correctly. "What if we don't have any?" he said, speaking very clearly. "What if we're as smart and good as you said we'd be, and we don't kill half of them off on the way? What if it gets hungry? And what if the ship just plain doesn't like it? Shouldn't we try to get rid of it for her?" Belatedly his eyes roved over the idle sailors that were gathering to overhear this exchange. "Get back to your tasks!" he barked at them harshly. "If any man has nothing to do, let me know. I'll find him something." As the sailors dispersed, he swung his attention back to Wintrow. "I think he's just stunned," he muttered. "Mild!" he bellowed again, just as the young sailor bounded up with keys in hand and the medicine box under his arm.

Wintrow was stirring, and Gantry helped him sit up. He sat, hands braced wide on the deck behind him, and watched dazedly as Gantry unfastened the shackles on Wintrow's feet. "This is stupid," the man hissed angrily. He glared at the oozing sores on Wintrow's ankles, then barked an order over his shoulder. "Mild, haul him up a bucket of salt water." He turned his attention back to the boy before him. "Wintrow, wash those out good with salt water and then bandage them. Nothing like seawater for healing a cut. Leaves a good, tough scar. I should know, I got enough of them." He wrinkled his nose in distaste. "And wash yourself while you're at it. Those chained below have an excuse for stinking. You don't."

Gantry glanced up at Kyle, who still stood over them. He met his captain's eyes and dared to shake his head in disapproval. Kyle tightened his jaw but said nothing. Then Gantry stood and walked away from them, to where he could look down at Vivacia. She had craned her head over her shoulder to watch what was going on. Her eyes were very wide and she clutched her hands together at her breast. "Now," he said levelly. "I've had enough of this. Exactly what is it that you want to make you behave?"

Confronted so baldly, Vivacia almost recoiled from him. She was silent.

"Well?" Gantry demanded, indignation slipping into his voice. "You've tried the patience of every man aboard you. Just what in Sa's name do you want to make you happy? Music? Company? What?"

"I want . . ." She paused and seemed to lose her thought. "I touched it, Gantry. I touched it. And it knew me and it said I wasn't Vivacia nor was I of the Vestrits. It said I belonged to them." She was babbling now, Kyle thought in disgust. Babbling like an idiot.

"Vivacia," Gantry told her sternly. "Serpents don't talk. It said nothing, it just frightened you. It rattled us all, but it's over. No one's badly hurt. But you could have hurt us, with your wild behavior and—"

She didn't seem to be listening. Vivacia furrowed her wooden brow and frowned, then seemed to recall his first question. "What I want is to go back to the way it was before." It was a desperate plea.

"Before what?" Gantry demanded in despair. Kyle knew the man was already defeated. No sense in asking the ship what she wanted, she always wanted what no one could give her. She was spoiled, that was all, a spoiled female with vast ideas of her own importance. Trying to please her was the wrong tack. The more Gantry catered to her, the more she'd bully them all. It was the nature of women. Why hadn't they carved a man for a figurehead? A man could have understood reason.

"Before Kyle," Vivacia said slowly. She turned to glare at him. "I want Ephron Vestrit back at the helm. And Althea on board. And Brashen." She lifted her hands to cover her face and turned away from them. "I want to be sure of who I am again." Her voice shook like a child's.

"I can't give you that. No man can give you that." Gantry shook his head. "Come, ship. We're doing our best. Wintrow's out of the chains. I can't force him to be happy. I can't force the slaves to be happy. I'm doing the best I can." The man was close to pleading.

Vivacia shook her head slowly. "I just can't go on like this," she said, and there were tears in her muffled voice. "I feel it all, you know. I feel it all."

"Bilge," Kyle growled. Enough of this. He mastered the disgust he felt for his own unbridled anger. So he'd lost his temper. Well, Sa knew he'd been pushed hard enough lately. It was time to let them all know he'd tolerate no more nonsense. He stepped up to the railing beside his mate. "Gantry, don't encourage her to whine. Don't encourage her to be childish." He looked down on Vivacia and their eyes met. "Ship. You'll sail. That's all there is to it. You can sail willing or sail like a cow-hide raft, but we'll sail you. I don't give a rat's ass for whether you're happy or not. We've got a task to do and we'll do it. If you don't like having a hold full of slaves, why then, sail faster, damn you. The sooner we get to Chalced the sooner we're rid of them. As for Wintrow, there's no making him happy. He didn't want to behave as my son, he didn't want to be the ship's boy. He made himself a slave. So that is what he is now. That's your likeness needled into his face. He's yours, to do with as you will and you're welcome to him. If he doesn't please you, you can throw him over the side for all I care."

Kyle stopped. He was out of breath and they were all staring at him. He didn't like the look on Gantry's face. He was staring at Kyle as if he were mad. There was a deep uneasiness behind his eyes. Kyle didn't like it. "Gantry. Take the watch," he snapped at him. He glanced aloft. "Get her canvas up, every scrap of it, and see the men scramble lively. Move this tub along. If a seagull farts near us, I want the wind from it caught." He strode off to go back to his cabin. He'd bought incense in Jamaillia City, on the advice of one of the experienced slaver captains. He'd burn that and get away from the stink of slaves for a time. He'd get away from all of them for a time.

The ship had returned to near calm. A slaveship was never completely peaceful. Always, there were cries from somewhere in the hold. People cried out for water, for air, begging voices rose, pleading for the simple light of day. Fights broke out amongst the slaves. It was astounding, how much damage two closely chained men could work upon each other. The cramped quarters and the stench, the stingy rations of ship's bread and water made them turn on one another like rats in a rain barrel.

Not so different, Wintrow thought, from Vivacia and me. In their own way, they were like the slaves chained cheek by jowl below. They had no space to be separate from one another, not even in their thoughts and dreams. No friendship could survive such an enforced confinement. Especially not when guilt was an invisible third sandwiched between them. He had abandoned her, left her to her fate. And for her, the one whispered comment when she had first seen his marked face. "This falls upon me," she had said. "But for me, none of this would have befallen you."

"That is true," he had had to agree with her. "But that does not mean it is your fault."

By her stricken look, he had known that his words wounded her. But he had been too weary and despondent on his own behalf to try to soften them with yet more useless words.

That had been hours ago, back before his father had attacked him. Not a sound had she uttered since Gantry had left them. Wintrow had huddled in the angle of her prow, wondering what had possessed his father. He wondered if he would be suddenly attacked again. He had been too dispirited to speak. He had no idea what had stilled Vivacia's tongue but her silence was almost a relief.

When she finally did speak, her words were banal. "What are we going to do?"

The futility of the question jabbed him. He refolded the wet rag to find a cooler spot, then held it against his swollen face. The bitter words rose to his lips spontaneously. "Do? Why do you ask me? I no longer have any choices as to what I will do. Rather, you should tell your slave what you command."

"I have no slave," Vivacia replied with icy dignity. Outrage crept gradually into her voice. "If you wish to please your father by calling yourself a slave, say you belong to him. Not me."

His long frustration found a target. "Rather say my father is intent on pleasing you, with no regard to what it does to me. If it were not for your strange nature, he would never have forced me to serve aboard you."

"My strange nature? And whence did that come? Not from my will. I am what your family has made me. You spoke of choices a moment ago, saying you no longer had any. I have never had any. I am more truly a slave than any mark on your face can make you."

Wintrow snorted in disbelief. His anger was rising to match her own. "You a slave? Show me the tattoo on your face, the manacles on your wrists. Easy for you to flaunt such words about. Vivacia, this is not something I play act. This mark is on my face for the rest of my life." He forced the bitter words from his lips. "I'm a slave."

"Are you?" Her voice was hard. "Before, you said you were a priest, and that no man could take that from you. But that, of course, was before you ran away. Since you have been dragged back, you have shown me otherwise. I had believed you had more courage, Wintrow Vestrit. More determination to shape yourself."

Outrage at her words overtook him. He sat up, to look over his shoulder and out at her. "What would you know of courage, ship? What would you know about anything that is truly human? What can be more degrading than to have someone take all decision from you, to tell you that you are a 'thing' that 'belongs' to him? To no longer have a say in where you will go or what you will do? How can one keep any dignity, any faith, any belief in tomorrow? You speak to me of courage—"

"What can I know of courage? What can I know of such things?" The look she swung upon him was terrible to behold. "When have I ever known anything else than to be a 'thing', a possession?" Her eyes blazed. "How dare you throw such things up to me!"

Wintrow gaped at her. For a moment he felt stricken, and then he tried to recover himself. "It is not the same! It is more difficult for me. I was born a man and—"

"Silence!" her words slashed at him. "I never put my mark upon your face, but your family spent three generations putting your mark upon my soul. Yes, soul! This 'thing' dares to claim one!" She looked him up and down, and began to speak. Then she caught her breath; a strange look passed across her face, so that for an instant a stranger seemed to look out at him.

"We are quarreling," she observed in a sort of wonder. "We are at odds." She nodded her herself, seeming almost pleased. "If I can disagree with you, then I am not you."

"Of course not." For a moment he was confused by her foray into the obvious. Then his irritation with her came back. "I am not you and you are not me. We are separate beings, with separate desires and needs. If you have not realized that before now, then you need to. You need to start being yourself, Vivacia, and discover your own ambitions and desires and thoughts. Have you ever even stopped to think what you might truly want for yourself, other than possessing me?"

With a suddenness that shocked him, she suddenly separated herself from him. She looked away from him, but it was far more than that. He gasped as if deluged with cold water, and a shiver ran over him followed by giddiness. If he had not already been sitting, he might have fallen. He hugged himself for the wind seemed suddenly colder on his skin. In wonder he admitted, "I didn't realize how hard I was struggling to keep myself apart from you."

"Were you?" she asked almost gently. Her anger of a few moments ago was gone. Or was it? He could no longer feel what she felt. He stood to look over the railing and found himself trying to read her emotions from the set of her shoulders. She didn't look back at him.

"We are better parted," she said with great finality.

"But . . ." he faltered through the next question. "I thought a liveship had to have a partner, one of her own family."

"It didn't seem to concern you when you ran away. Don't let it concern you now." Her voice was brusque.

"I didn't mean to hurt your feelings," he ventured. His own anger was suddenly gone. Perhaps he had only been feeling hers? "Vivacia. I am here, whether I want to be or not. As long as I'm here anyway, there is no reason why . . ."

"The reason is that you have always held back from me. You admitted that, just now. And another reason is that perhaps it is time I discovered who I am without you."

"I don't understand."

"That is because when I was trying to tell you something important, earlier today, you were not listening." Her voice did not sound hurt. Instead there was a studied calm to it that suddenly reminded him of Berandol when his tutor tried to point out an obvious lesson.

"I suppose I wasn't," he admitted humbly. "I'll listen now, if you want me to."

"Now is too late," she said sharply. Then she amended it to, "I don't want to tell you about it now. Perhaps I want to puzzle it out for myself. Maybe it's time I did that for myself, instead of always having a Vestrit do it for me."

It was his turn to feel abandoned and shut out. "But . . . what shall I do?"

She turned to look back at him, and there was almost kindness in her green eyes. "A slave would ask such a question and wait to be told. A priest would know the answer for himself." She almost smiled. "Or have you forgotten who you are without me?" She asked the question, but desired no answer. She turned her back on him. Head up, she stared at the horizon. She had shut him out.

After a time, he heaved himself to his feet. He found the bucket Mild had brought earlier and lowered it over the side. The rope jerked hard against his grip as it filled. It was heavy as he dragged it up. He picked up the rag he had used earlier. She did not watch him go as he left her, taking his bucket and rag below into the slave holds.

I don't know if I can do this, she thought in despair. *I don't know how to be myself without help. What if I go mad?* She looked past the islands and rocks that dotted the wide channel, ahead to the horizon. She spread out her senses, tasting both wind and water. She became immediately aware of serpents. Not just the fat white one that trundled along in her wake like a fat dog on a leash, but others that shadowed her at a distance. Resolutely she shut them out of her thoughts. She wished she could do the same for the misery of the slaves within her and the confusion of her crew. But the humans were too close to her, they touched her wizardwood in too many places. Despite herself, she was aware of Wintrow as he went from slave to slave, wiping faces and hands with his cool wet rag, offering what small comforts he could. *Both priest and Vestrit*, she thought to herself. She felt oddly proud of the boy, as if he were hers somehow. But he was not. With each passing moment of this separateness, she realized more the truth of that. Humans and their emotions filled her, but they were not herself. She tried to accept them and encapsulate them and find herself as someone separate from them. Either she could not, or there was not much to herself.

After a time, she lifted her head and set her jaw. *If I am no more than a ship, then I shall be a proud ship.* She located the rush of the channel's current and edged herself into it. In tiny movements that were scarcely perceptible even to herself, she aligned her planking, trimming herself. Gantry was on the wheel now and she sensed his sudden pleasure in how well she ran before the wind. She could trust him. She closed her eyes to the rush of air past her face and tried to let the dreams come. *What do I want of my life?* she asked them.

"You lied to my captain." The *Ophelia* had a husky, courtesan's voice, sweet as dark honey. "Boy," she added belatedly. She gave Althea a sideways glance. Ophelia, like many figureheads of her day, had been arrayed upon the beakhead of the ship, rather than positioned below the bowsprit. The glance she gave Althea over her bare and ample shoulder was an arch warning against lying.

Althea didn't dare reply. She was sitting cross-legged on a small catwalk that had been built, she'd been told, solely that Ophelia might socialize more easily. Althea shook the large dice box in her hands. It was oversized, as were the dice within it. They were the property of the *Ophelia*. Upon discovering that there was an "extra" hand aboard the ship, she had immediately demanded that Althea would spend part of her watches amusing her. Ophelia was very fond of games of chance, but mostly, Althea suspected, because they gave her plenty of time to gossip. She also suspected that the ship routinely cheated, but this was something she had decided to over-look. Ophelia herself kept tally sticks of what each crew member owed her. Some of the sticks bore the notches of years. Althea's stick already bore a generous number of notches. She opened the box, looked within, and frowned at it. "Three gulls, two fish," she announced, and tilted the box for the figurehead's inspection. "You win again."

"So I do," Ophelia agreed. She smiled crookedly at Althea. "Shall we up the stakes this time?"

"I already owe you more than I have," Althea pointed out.

"Exactly. So, unless we change our wager, I have no chance of being paid. How about this: Let's play for your little secret."

"Why bother? I think you already know it." Althea prayed it was no more than her sex. If that was all Ophelia knew and all she could reveal, then she was still relatively safe. Violence aboard a liveship was not unheard of, but it was rare. The emotions that radiated from violence were too unsettling to the ship. Most of the ships themselves disdained violence, although it was rumored that the *Shaw* had a mean streak, and had once even called for the flogging of an incompetent hand who'd spilled paint on him. But the *Ophelia*, for all her blowzy airs, was a lady, and a kind-hearted one as well. Althea doubted she would be raped aboard such a ship, though the rough courtship of a sailor attempting to be gallant could be almost as fierce and bruising. *Consider Brashen, for instance*, she thought to herself, and then she wished she hadn't. Lately he popped into her mind at unguarded moments. She probably should have hunted him down in Candletown and bid him good-bye. That was all she was missing, putting a final close to things. Above all, she should never have let him have the last word.

"Well, you are right, I do know at least a part of it." The *Ophelia* laughed huskily. Her lips were painted scarlet, her own conceit. Her teeth were very white when she laughed. She lowered both her eyelashes and her voice as she said more softly, "And right now I'm the only one that knows it. As I'm sure you'd like it to remain."

"As I am sure it will," Althea replied sweetly, shaking the dice box soundly. "For a lady so grand as yourself could never be so petty as to give away another's secret."

"No?" She smiled with a corner of her mouth. "Do you not think I have a duty to reveal to my captain that one of his hands is not what he thinks him to be?"

"Mmm." It could be a very uncomfortable journey home, if Tenira decided to confine her. "So. What do you propose?"

"Three throws. For each one I win, I get to ask you a question, which you will answer truthfully."

"And if I win?"

"I keep your secret."

Althea shook her head. "Your stakes are not as high as mine."

"You can ask me a question."

"No. Still not enough."

"Well, what do you want then?"

Althea shook the dice box thoughtfully.

Despite the time of year, the day was almost warm, an effect of the hot swamps to the west of them. All this stretch of coast was swamp and tussocky islands and shifting sand bars that changed seasonally. The hot water that mingled with the brine here was terrible for ordinary ships; sea-worms and other pests throve in it. But it wouldn't bother the *Ophelia*'s wizardwood hull. An occasional whiff of sulfur was the only price they had to pay for it. The wind stirred the tendrils of hair that had pulled free of Althea's queue and warmed the ache of hard work from her joints. Despite her title of "extra" hand, Tenira had found plenty to keep her busy. But he was a fair man and Ophelia was a beautiful and sweet-tempered ship. And Althea suddenly realized just how content she had been the last week or so.

"I know what I want," she said quietly. "But I'm not sure even you can give it to me."

"You think very loud. Has anyone ever told you that? I think I like you almost as much as you like me." Ophelia's voice was warm with affection. "You want me to ask Tenira to keep you on, don't you?"

"There's more than that. I'd want him to know what I am, and still be willing to let me work for him."

"Ouch," Ophelia complained mockingly. "That is a high stake. And of course I couldn't promise it, only that I'd try for it." She winked at Althea. "Shake the box, girl."

Ophelia won the first round easily.

"So. Ask your question," Althea said quietly.

"Not yet. I want to know how many questions I have, before I start."

The next two rounds went to her as swiftly as the first. Althea still could not see how she was cheating; the figurehead's large hands all but overlapped on the dice box.

"Well," Ophelia purred as she handed the box to Althea for her to inspect her final winning throw. "Three questions. Let me see." She deliberated a moment. "What is your full true name?"

Althea sighed. "Althea Vestrit." She spoke very softly, knowing the ship would nonetheless hear her.

"No-o-o!" Ophelia breathed out in scandalized delight. "You are a Vestrit! A girl from an Old Trader family runs off to sea, and leaves her own liveship behind. Oh, how could you, you wicked thing, you heartless girl! Have you any idea what you put the *Vivacia* through? And her just a little slip of a thing, barely quickened and you leave her next to alone in the world! Heartless, wicked . . . tell me why, quickly, quickly, or I shall die of suspense!"

"It was not my choice." Althea took a breath. "I was forced off my family ship," she said quietly, and suddenly it all came back, the grief at her father's death, her outrage at her disinheritance, her hatred of Kyle. Without thinking, she reached up to put her palm flat against the great hand that Ophelia reached down to her in sympathy. Like a floodgate opening, she felt the sudden outflow of her feelings and thoughts. She took a long shuddering breath. She had not realized how much she had missed simply being able to share with someone.

The words spilled from her. Ophelia's features grew first agitated, then sympathetic as she listened to Althea's tale of her wrongs.

"Oh, my dear, my dear. How tragic! But why didn't you come to us? Why did you let them part you?"

"Come to who?" Althea asked dazedly.

"Why, the liveships. It was all the talk of Bingtown harbor, when you disappeared and Haven took Vivacia over. More than a few of us were upset by it. We had always assumed you would take the *Vivacia* over when your father's time was done. And she was so upset, poor thing. We could scarcely get a word out of her. Then that boy, um, Wintrow, came aboard, and we were so relieved for her. But even then she didn't seem truly content. And if Wintrow was brought aboard against his will, why, then, that explains so much! But I still don't see why you didn't come to us."

"I never thought of it," Althea admitted. "It seemed a family thing. Besides. I don't understand. What could the other liveships have done?"

"You give us very little credit, darling. There is much we could have done, but the final threat was that we would have refused to sail. All of us. Until the *Vivacia* was given a willing family member."

Althea was shocked. After a moment she managed, "You would have done that, for us?"

"Althea, honey, it would be for all of us. Perhaps you are too young to remember, but once there was a liveship called the *Paragon*. He was similarly abused, and driven mad by the abuse." Ophelia closed her eyes and shook her head. "At that time, we did not act. By our failure to aid one of our own, he was irreparably damaged. No liveship passes in or out of Bingtown harbor without seeing him, pulled out of the water and chained down, abandoned to his madness. . . . Ships talk, Althea. Oh, we gossip just as much as sailors, and no one gossips like sailors. The pact was made long ago. If we had but known, we would have spoken up for you. And if speaking did not work, then, yes, we would have refused to sail. There are not so many liveships that we can afford to ignore one of our own."

"I had no idea," Althea said quietly.

"Yes, well, and perhaps I have spoken too freely. You understand that if such a pact were well known, it might be . . . misconstrued. We are not mutinous by nature, nor would we ever enact such a rebellion if it were not needed. But neither would we stand by and see one of our own abused again." The drawling accents of a bawd had fallen from her voice. Althea now heard just as clearly the utterance of a Bingtown matriarch.

"Is it too late to ask for help?"

"Well, we're a long way from home. It's going to take time. Trust me to pass the word to other liveships as I encounter them. Don't you try to speak for yourself. We can't do much until the *Vivacia* herself comes into Bingtown harbor again. Oh, I do hope I'm there. I wouldn't miss this for the world. At that time, I—or one of us, I do hope I get to be the one—will ask her for her side of your story. If she feels as aggrieved as you do, and I am sure she will, for I can read you almost as clearly as my own kin, then we will act. There are always one or two liveships in Bingtown harbor. We will speak to our families, and as other ships come in, they will join us, petitioning their families to speak to the Vestrits as well. The concept, you see, is that we pressure our own families to put pressure on your family. The ultimate pressure, of course, would be if we all refused to sail. It is, frankly, a stance we hope we shall never have to take. But we will if we have to."

Althea was silent for a long time.

"What are you thinking?" Ophelia asked her at last.

"That I have wasted the better part of a year, away from my own ship. I have learned a great many things, and I do believe I am a better sailor than I was. But that I will never be able to regain the wonder of those first months of her life. You are right, Ophelia. Heartless and wicked. Or maybe just stupid and cowardly. I don't know how I could have left her alone to deal with Kyle."

"We all make mistakes, my dear," Ophelia assured her gently. "I wish all of them could be righted as easily as this. Of course we will get you back on board your own ship. Of course we will."

"I don't know how to thank you." It was like being able to take a deep breath again, or to stand up straight after bearing a heavy burden for a long time. She had never grasped that liveships might share such feelings for one another. Her individual bond with Vivacia had been all she had perceived. She had never paused to think that in time her ship might develop friendships with others like her. That she and Vivacia might have allies beyond each other.

Ophelia gave her throaty bawd's chuckle. "Well, you still have to answer one question for me."

Althea shook her head and smiled. "You have asked me far more than three questions."

"I think not!" Ophelia declared haughtily. "I recall only that I asked you your name. The rest just all came out freely. You spilled your guts, girl."

"Well, perhaps I did. No, wait. I clearly recall that you asked me why I hadn't come to the liveships for help."

"That was not a question, that was just a conversational gambit. But even if I give you that, you still owe me a question."

Althea was inclined to feel generous. "Ask away, then."

Ophelia smiled, and a bright spark of mischief came into her eyes. For a second she bit the tip of her tongue between her white teeth. Then she asked quickly, "Who is that dark-eyed man who gives you such . . . stimulating dreams?"

CHAPTER THIRTY-TWO

LET'S TRY THIS," WINTROW SUGGESTED. HE PUSHED HER FETTER AS FAR UP HER SKINNY SHANK AS IT WOULD GO. He took a strip of rag and lightly wrapped it around the girl's raw ankle. Then he slid her fetter back over the top of it. "Is that better?"

She didn't speak. The moment he took his hand away, she began working her ankle against the fetter again.

"No, no," he said quietly. He touched her ankle and she stopped. But she did not speak and she did not look at him. She never did. A day or so more, and she'd be permanently crippled. He had no herbs or oils, no real medicines or bandaging. All he had was seawater and rags. And she was gradually scoring her own tendons. She seemed unable to stop herself from working against the fetter.

"Give it up," a voice from the darkness suggested sourly. "She's crazy. She don't know what she's doing, and she's going to die before we get to Chalced anyway. You washing her and bandaging her is only going to make it take longer. Let her go, if that's her only way out of here."

Wintrow lifted up his candle and peered into the gloom. He could not decide who had spoken. In this part of the hold, he couldn't even stand up straight. The slaves chained here were even more restricted. Yet the rolling of the *Vivacia* as she cut through the heavy seas kept them in constant motion, flesh against wood. They averted their eyes from his dim candlelight, blinking as if they stared at the sun. He scooted farther down the line, trying to avoid the worst of the filth. Most of the slaves were silent and impassive to his passage, all of their strength invested in endurance. He saw a man half sitting up in his chains, blinking as he tried to meet Wintrow's eyes. "Can I help you?" he asked quietly.

"Do you have the key to these things?" one man to the side of him answered sarcastically, while another one demanded, "How come you get to move about?"

"So that I can keep you alive," Wintrow answered evasively. He was a coward. He feared that if they knew he was the captain's son, they'd try to kill him. "I've a bucket of seawater and rags, if you want to wash yourself."

"Give me the rag," the first man commanded him gruffly. Wintrow sopped it in water and passed it to him. Wintrow had expected him to wipe his face and hands. So many slaves seemed to take comfort from that bare ritual of cleanliness. Instead he shifted as far as he could to put the rag against the bared shoulder of an inert man next to him. "Here you go, rat-bait," he said, almost jokingly. He sponged tenderly at a raw and swollen lump on the man's shoulder. The man made no response.

"Rat-bait here got bitten hard a few nights ago. I caught the rat and we shared it. But he ain't been feeling well since." His eyes met Wintrow's for a glancing moment. "Think you could get him moved out of here?" he asked in a more genteel tone. "If he's got to die in chains, at least let him die in the light and air, on deck."

"It's night, right now," Wintrow heard himself say. Foolish words.

"Is it?" the man asked in wonder. "Still. The cool air."

"I'll ask," Wintrow said uncomfortably, but he wasn't sure he truly would. The crew left Wintrow to himself. He ate apart from them, he slept apart from them. Some of the men he had known earlier in the voyage would watch him sometimes, their faces a mixture of pity and disgust at what he had become. The newer hands picked up in Jamaillia treated him as they would any slave. If he came near them, they complained of his stench and kicked or pushed him away. No. The less attention he got from the crew, the simpler his life was. He had come to think of the deck and the rigging as "outside." Here "inside" was his new world. It was a place of thick smells, of chains caked with filth and humans meshed in them. The times when he went on deck to refill his bucket were like trips to a foreign world. There men moved freely, they shouted and sometimes laughed, and the wind and rain and sun touched their faces and bared arms. Never before had such things seemed so wondrous to Wintrow. He could have stayed abovedeck, he could have insinuated himself back into the routine as ship's boy. But he did not. Having been belowdecks, he could not forget or ignore what was there. So each day he rose as the sun went down, filled his bucket and got his washed-out rags, and went down into the slave holds. He offered them the small comfort of washing with seawater. Fresh water would have been far better, but there was precious little of that to spare. Seawater was better than nothing. He cleaned sores they could not reach. He did not get to every slave, every day. There were far too many of them for that. But he did what he could, and when he curled up to sleep by day, he slept deeply.

He touched the leg of the inert man. His skin was hot. It would not be long.

"Would you damp this again, please?"

Something in the man's tones and accent were oddly familiar. Wintrow pondered it as he sloshed the rag in the small amount of seawater remaining in his bucket. There was no pretending the rag and water were clean anymore. Only wet. The man took it, and wiped the brow and face of his neighbor. He folded the rag anew, and wiped his own face and hands. "My thanks to you," he said as he handed the rag back.

With a shivering up his back, Wintrow caught it. "You come from Marrow, don't you? Near Kelpiton Monastery?"

The man smiled oddly, as if Wintrow's words both warmed and pained him. "Yes," he said quietly. "Yes, I do." In a lower voice, he amended it to, "I did. Before I was sent to Jamaillia."

"I was there, at Kelpiton!" Wintrow whispered, but he felt the words as a cry. "I lived in the monastery, I was to be a priest. I worked in the orchards, sometimes." He moistened the rag and handed it back again.

"Ah, the orchards." The man's voice went far as he gently wiped his companion's hands. "In the spring, when the trees blossomed, they were like fountains of flowers. White and pink, the fragrance like a blessing."

"You could hear the bees, but it was as if the trees themselves were humming. Then, a week later when the blossoms fell, the ground was pink and white with them. . . ."

"And the trees fogged with green as the first leaves came out," the other man whispered. "Sa save me," he moaned suddenly. "Are you a demon come to torment me, or a messenger-spirit?"

"Neither," Wintrow said. He suddenly felt ashamed. "I'm only a boy with a bucket of water and a rag."

"Not a priest of Sa?"

"Not any longer."

"The road to the priesthood may wander, but once upon it, no man leaves it." The slave's voice had taken on a teaching cadence, and Wintrow knew he heard ancient scripture.

"But I have been taken away from the priesthood."

"No man can be taken away, no man can leave it. All lives lead towards Sa. All are called to a priesthood."

Some moments later, Wintrow realized he was sitting very still in the dark, breathing. The candle had guttered out, and he had not been aware of it. His mind had followed the man's words, questioning, wondering. All men called to a priesthood. Even Torg, even Kyle Haven? Not all calls were heeded, not all doors were opened.

He did not need to tell the other man he was back. He was aware of him. "Go, priest of Sa," the man said quietly in the darkness. "Work the small mercies you can, plead for us, beg comfort for us. And when you have the chance to do more, Sa will give you the courage. I know he will." Wintrow felt the rag pressed back into his hand.

"You were a priest, too," Wintrow asked softly.

"I am a priest. One who would not sway to false doctrine. No man is born to be a slave. That, I believe, is what Sa would never permit." He cleared his throat and asked quietly, "Do you believe that?"

"Of course."

In a conspiratorial voice, the man observed, "They bring us food and water but once a day. Other than that, and you, no one comes near us. If I had anything metal, I could work at these chains. It need not be a tool that would be missed. Anything metal you could find in any moment you are unwatched."

"But . . . even if you were out of your chains, what could you do? One man against so many?"

"If I can sever the long chain, many of us could move."

"But what would you do?" Wintrow asked in a sort of horror.

"I don't know. I'd trust to Sa. He brought you to me, didn't he?" He seemed to hear the boy's hesitation. "Don't think about it. Don't plan it. Don't worry. Sa will put opportunity in your path, and you will see it and act." He paused. "I only ask that you beg that Kelo here be allowed to die on deck. If you dare."

"I dare," Wintrow heard himself reply. Despite the darkness and stench all around him, he felt as if a tiny light had been re-kindled inside him. He would dare. He would ask. What could they do to him for asking? Nothing worse than what they'd already done. His courage, he thought wonderingly. He'd found his courage again.

He groped for his bucket and rag in the darkness. "I have to go. But I will come back."

"I know you will," the other man replied quietly.

"So. You wanted to see me?"

"Something's wrong. Something is very wrong."

"What?" Gantry demanded wearily. "Is it the serpents again? I've tried, Vivacia. Sa knows I've tried to drive them off. But throwing rocks at them in the morning does me no good if I have to dump bodies over the side in the afternoon. I can't make them go away. You'll have to just ignore them."

"They whisper to me," she confided uneasily.

"The serpents talk to you?"

"No. Not all of them. But the white one," she turned to look at him and her eyes were tormented. "Without words, without sound. He whispers to me, and he urges . . . unspeakable things."

Gantry felt a terrible urge to laugh. Unspeakable things uttered without words. He pushed it away from himself. It wasn't funny, not really. Sometimes it seemed to him that nothing had ever really been funny in his whole life.

"I can't do anything about them," he said. "I've tried and tried."

"I know. I know. I have to deal with it myself. I can. I shall. But tonight it's not the serpents. It's something else."

"What?" he asked patiently. She was mad. He was almost sure of it. Mad, and he had helped to make her that way. Sometimes he thought he should just ignore her when she spoke, as if she were one of the slaves begging him for simple mercy. At other times he thought he had a duty to listen to her ramblings and groundless fears. Because what he had come to call madness was her inability to ignore the contained misery caged within her holds. He had helped to put that misery there. He had installed the chains, he had brought out the slaves, with his own hands he had fettered men and women in the dark below the decks he trod. He could smell the stench of their entrapment and hear their cries. Perhaps he was the one who was truly mad, for a key hung at his belt and he did nothing.

"I don't know what it is. But it's something, something dangerous." She sounded like a child with a high fever, peopling the dark

with fearsome creatures. There was an unspoken plea in her words.
Make it go away.

"It's just the storm coming. We all feel it, the seas are getting
higher. But you'll be fine, you're a fine ship. A bit of weather isn't
going to bother you," he encouraged her.

"No. I'd welcome a storm, to wash some of the stench away. It's
not the storm I fear."

"I don't know what to do for you." He hesitated, and then asked
his usual question. "Do you want me to find Wintrow and bring him
to you?"

"No. No, leave him where he is." She sounded distracted when
she spoke of him, as if the topic pained her and she wished to get away
from it.

"Well. If you think of anything I can do for you, you let me
know." He started to turn away from her.

"Gantry!" she called hastily. "Gantry, wait!"

"Yes, what is it?"

"I told you to get on another ship. You remember that, don't you?
That I told you to get on another ship."

"I remember it," he assured her unwillingly. "I remember it."

Again he turned to go, only to have a slight form step out in front
of him suddenly. He startled back, suppressing a cry. A heartbeat later
he recognized Wintrow. The night had made him seem insubstantial
in his stained rags, almost like a wraith. The boy was gaunt, his face as
pale as any slave's save for the tattoo that crawled over his cheek. The
smell of the slave hold clung to him, so that Gantry stepped back from
him without thinking. He did not like to see Wintrow at any time, let
alone in the dark, alone. The boy himself had become an accusation to
him, a living reminder of all Gantry chose to ignore. "What do you
want?" he demanded gruffly, but he heard in his own voice a sort of
cry.

The boy spoke simply. "One of the slaves is dying. I'd like to
bring him out on the deck."

"What's the point of that, if he's dying anyway?" He spoke
harshly, to keep from speaking desperately.

"What's the point of not doing it?" Wintrow asked quietly.
"Once he's dead, you've got to bring him up on deck anyway to get
rid of his body. Why not do it now, and at least let him die where the
air is cool and clean?"

"Clean? Have you no nose left? There's nowhere on this ship that
smells clean anymore."

"Not to you, perhaps. But he might breathe easier up here."

"I can't just drag a slave up here on deck and dump him. I have no one to watch him."

"I'll watch him," Wintrow offered evenly. "He's no threat to anyone. His fever is so high that he's just going to lie there until he dies."

"Fever?" Gantry asked more sharply. "He's one of the map-faces, then?"

"No. He's in the forward hold."

"How'd he get fever? We've only had fever among the map-faces before this." He spoke angrily as if it were Wintrow's fault.

"A rat bit him. The man chained to him thinks that is what started it." Wintrow hesitated. "Perhaps we should remove him from the others, just in case."

Gantry snorted. "You play on my fears, to get me to do what you want."

Wintrow looked at him steadily. "Can you give me a real reason why we should not bring the poor wretch onto the deck to die?"

"I don't have the men to move him just now. The seas are heavy, a storm is brewing. I want my full watch on deck in case I need them. We've a tricky bit of channel coming up, and when a storm breaks here, a man has to be ready."

"If you give me the key, I'll bring him up on deck myself."

"You can't haul a grown man up from the forward hold by your-self."

"I'll have another slave help me."

"Wintrow . . ." Gantry began impatiently.

"Please," Vivacia interceded softly. "Please. Bring the man up here."

Gantry could not say why he didn't want to give in. A simple bit of mercy he could offer, but he wanted to hold it back. Why? Because if this small act of taking pity on a dying man was the right thing to do, then . . . He pushed the thought away from him. He was mate on this vessel, he had his job, and that was to run the ship as his captain saw fit. It wasn't his place to decide that all of it was wrong. Even if he faced that thought, even if he said aloud, 'this is wrong!' what could one man do about it?

"You said if there was anything you could do for me, I should let you know," the ship reminded him.

He glanced up at the night sky, shrouded in gathering clouds. If Vivacia decided to be obstinate, she could double their work through this storm. He didn't want to cross her just now.

"If the seas get any heavier, we'll be taking water over the deck," he warned them both.

"I don't think it will matter to him," Wintrow said.

"Sar!" Gantry declared with feeling. "I can't give you my keys, boy, nor permission to bring a healthy slave up on deck. Come on. If I have to do this to keep the ship happy, I'll do it myself. But let's be quick about it and get it over."

He raised his voice in a shout. "Comfrey! Keep an eye on things here, I'm going below. Sing out if you need me!"

"Aye, sir!"

"Lead the way," he told Wintrow gruffly. "If there's fever in the forward hold, I suppose I'd better see for myself."

Wintrow was silent as he led the way. Having made his request of Gantry, he could think of nothing more to say to the man. He was painfully conscious of the differences between them now. Gantry, his father's right hand and trusted advisor, was as far as could be from Wintrow, the slave and disgraced son. As he made his way into the crowded forward hold, he felt as if he led a stranger into his private nightmare.

Gantry had given him the lantern to carry. Its brighter light illuminated far more than the candles that Wintrow had become accustomed to. It enlarged the circle of misery, made clearer the extent of the filth and degradation. Wintrow breathed shallowly. It was a skill he had learned. Behind him, he heard Gantry cough from time to time, and once he thought the mate gagged. He did not turn to look back. As first mate, it was likely that Gantry had not had to venture far into the holds lately. He could command other men to do that. Wintrow doubted that his father had been belowdecks at all since they had left Jamaillia.

As they got closer to the dying man, they had to hunch over. The slaves were packed so tightly it was hard to avoid stepping on them. They shifted restlessly in the lantern light and muttered quietly to one another at the sight of Gantry's lantern. "Here he is," Wintrow announced needlessly. To the priest beside him, he said, "This is Gantry, the mate. He's letting me take your friend abovedeck."

The priest slave sat up, blinking in Gantry's lantern light. "Sa's mercy upon you," he greeted him quietly. "I am Sa'Adar."

Gantry said nothing to either the introduction or the slave's claim of priesthood. The mate seemed, Wintrow thought, uncomfortable at the idea of being introduced to a slave. He crouched and gingerly touched the dying slave's hot flesh. "Fever," he said, as if anyone could have doubted it. "Let's get him out of here before he spreads it."

Gantry sidled down to reach one of the heavy staples that had been driven into the *Vivacia*'s main timbers. Here was where the running chain was secured. The salt of the sea air and the sweaty humidity of the packed slaves had not favored the lock that fastened the running chain to the staple. Gantry struggled with it for a time before the key turned stiffly. He tugged at the lock until it opened. The running chain dropped free to the squalid deck. "Unhook him from the others," he ordered Wintrow brusquely. "Then re-secure them and let's get him up on deck. Quickly, now. I don't like the way the *Vivacia* is taking these waves."

Wintrow divined quickly that Gantry didn't want to touch the filth-encrusted chain that ran through the rings on each slave's ankle fetters. Human excrement and dried blood no longer bothered Wintrow much. He crawled down the row of slaves, lantern in hand, rattling the running chain through each ring until he reached the dying man. He freed him.

"One moment, before you take him," the priest slave begged. He leaned over to touch his friend's brow. "Sa bless you, his instrument. Peace take you."

Then quick as a snake Sa'Adar snatched up the lantern and threw it. His force was savage, his aim unerring. Wintrow clearly saw Gantry's eyes dilate in horror just as the heavy metal lantern struck him full in the brow. The glass chimney broke with the impact and Gantry went down with a groan. The lantern landed beside him, rolling as the ship was rolling now. Oil trailed from it in a crooked track. The flame had not gone out.

"Get the lantern!" the slave barked at Wintrow as he snatched the chain from his lax grip. "Quickly, now, before there's a fire!"

Preventing the fire was the most urgent thing to do, of that Wintrow had no doubt. But as he scrabbled towards it, he was aware of slaves stirring all around him. He heard the rattle of metal on metal as the running chain was tugged through ring after ring behind him. He snatched up the lantern, righting it and lifting it away from the spilled oil. He exclaimed as he cut his foot on the broken glass of the lantern, but that cry of pain turned to one of horror as he saw one of the freed slaves casually fasten throttling hands around the unconscious Gantry's neck.

"No!" he cried, but in that instant the slave had slammed the mate's skull down hard on the staple that had secured the running chain. Something in the way Gantry's skull bounced told Wintrow it was too late. The mate was dead and the slaves were freeing themselves from the running chain as fast as the chain could be dragged through the fetters. "Good work, boy," one slave congratulated him as Wintrow looked down on the mate's body. He watched the same slave claim the key from Gantry's belt. It was all happening so fast, and he was a part of it happening, and yet he could not say how he fitted in. He wanted no part of Gantry's death to be his.

"He was not a bad man!" he cried out suddenly. "You should not have killed him!"

"Quiet!" Sa'Adar said sharply. "You'll alert the others before we are ready." He glanced back at Gantry. "You cannot say he was a good man, to countenance what went on aboard this ship. And cruel things have to be done, to undo worse cruelty," he said quietly. It was no saying of Sa's that Wintrow had ever heard. His eyes came back to Wintrow's. "Think on it," he bade him. "Would you have refastened the chains that held us? You, with a tattoo of your own down your face?"

He did not wait for a reply. Wintrow was guiltily relieved at that, for he had no answer to the question. If by refastening the chain he could have saved Gantry's life, would he have done it? If by refastening the chain, he condemned all these men to a life of slavery, would he have done it? There were no answers to the questions. He stared down at Gantry's still face. He suspected the mate had not known the answer to such questions either.

The priest was moving swiftly through the hold, unlocking other running chains. The mutter of the freed slaves seemed part and parcel of the rising sounds of the storm outside the hull. "Check the bastard's pockets for the key to these fetters as well," someone suggested in a hoarse whisper, but Wintrow didn't move. He couldn't move. He watched in stunned detachment as two slaves rifled the mate's clothing. Gantry had carried no fetter key, but his belt knife and other small possessions were quickly appropriated. One slave spat on the body in passing. And still Wintrow stood, lantern in hand, and stared.

The priest was speaking quietly to those around him. "We're a long way from free, but we can make it if we're wise. No noise, now. Keep still. We need to free as many of ourselves as we can before anyone on deck is the wiser. We outnumber them, but our chains and our bodies are going to tell against us. On the other hand, the storm may be in our favor. It may keep them all occupied until it's too late for them."

The priest glanced at Wintrow. His smile was a hard one. "Come, boy, and bring the lantern. We've Sa's work to do." To the others he said quietly, "We have to leave you now, in the dark, while we go to free the others. Be patient. Be brave. Pray. And remember that if you move too soon, you condemn us all, and this brave boy's work will be for naught." To Wintrow he said, "Lead on. Hold by hold, we have to free them all, and then take the crew by surprise. It's the only chance we have."

Numbly, Wintrow led the way. Above him, he heard the first pattering of a hard rain falling on Vivacia's decks. Within and without, the long-brewing storm overtook the ship.

"I don't care about the weather. I want the ship."

"Aye, sir." Sorcor took a breath as if to speak further, but then changed his mind.

"Let's go after her." Kennit went on. He stood in the waist and stared out over the water, clutching the rail with both hands like a landsman. Ahead of them, the silvery hull of the liveship glistened as she cut the rising waves, and seemed to beckon him through the night. He spoke without looking away from her. "I've a feeling about this one. I think she's ours for the taking."

The bow of the *Marietta* bit deeper into an oncoming wave. Spray flew up suddenly, drenching them all. The blast of icy water almost felt good against his over-heated body, but even that splash was nearly enough to push him off balance. He managed to cling where he was and keep his leg under him. The ship fell off as she crested the wave and Kennit was hard put to keep from falling. His crutch hit the deck and washed away from him as the next wave rushed out through the scuppers. He was barely able to keep his foot under him by clinging tightly to the ship's rail. "Damn it, Sorcor, trim her up!" he roared to cover his shame.

He doubted the man heard him. Sorcor had already left his side and was shouting orders to deckhands on his way back to the helm.

"Let me take you back to the cabin," the ever-present whore said from behind his shoulder. He had just been about to tell her to do that. Now, of course, he could not. He'd have to wait until she believed it was his own idea, or until he could think of a good reason why he had to go there. Damn her! His good leg was beginning to tire, and the bad one just dangled there, a hot heavy weight of pain.

"Retrieve my stick," he ordered her. It pleased him to see her chase it across the wave-washed deck. At the same time, he noted that she definitely had her sea-legs now. There was nothing clumsy about her. Had she been a man, he'd have said she had the makings of a good sailor.

In that abrupt change so characteristic of these waters, the rain squall hit them. Torrents sheeted down over the ship, while the wind's direction seemed to switch almost constantly. He could hear Sorcor's bellowed commands to the deck crew. What had looked to be a simple little blow was now building up to something else entirely. There was always a current in Hawser Channel, and in some tides it could be difficult, but now the storm wind conspired with that current to send them racing. The liveship fled ahead of them. He watched her, expecting her to take in sail. Sorcor had their hands reefing canvas. Storm and current were driving them along swiftly enough without giving the treacherous winds anything extra to push on. Not far ahead was Crooked Island. To the east of the island was the better passage. The liveship would certainly take it. To the west of the island was how they would have to go. They'd use both storm and current to race ahead of the liveship and cut her off. It would be tricky, and no mistake there. He wasn't sure they'd make it. Well, he doubted he had long to live anyway. He might as well die on his own deck if he couldn't do it on the deck of a liveship.

Sorcor had taken the wheel himself; Kennit could tell it by the way the *Marietta* seemed suddenly to relish each challenging wave. He squinted his eyes against the downpour and tried to find their quarry again. For the space of three waves he could not see her. Then he spotted the liveship at the same time as he heard her distant scream.

She was taking the storm badly, her untended sails pushing her awkwardly against each wave. As Kennit watched in horror, she slid down the trough of a wave, disappeared, and then a moment later wallowed into view again. His straining eyes could pick out figures of men dashing about her dimly lit decks, lots of men, but no one seemed to be doing anything to save her. He gave a groan of despair. To get this close to capturing a liveship, only to see her go down right before his eyes because of her own crew's incompetency—it was too bitter to bear.

"Sorcor!" he bellowed through the storm's blast. He wouldn't be able to wait until they could cut her off. As she was going now, she'd end up on the rocks. "Sorcor! Catch her up and ready a boarding party of good seamen." The rain and wind snatched the words from his mouth. He tried to work his way aft, holding to the rail and hopping along on his good leg. Each jarring motion felt as if he'd plunged his stump into boiling oil. Suddenly he was shaking with cold as well. The waves were running taller. As each wave broke, he saw the salt water rushing towards him and could do nothing save clutch tighter to the rail. Eventually one swept his tired leg out from under him. For an interminable moment he clung desperately as the water washed over his body and out the scuppers again. Then Etta had him, carelessly seizing hold of him with no mind for his injured leg at all. She wrapped one of his arms around her shoulders and hoisted him up, gripping him around the chest.

"Let me take you inside!" she begged him.

"No! Help me get back to the wheel. I'll take the helm; I want Sorcor to lead the boarding party himself."

"You can't board another ship in this weather!"

"Just take me aft."

"Kennit, you should not even be out on the deck tonight. I can feel your fever burning you up. Please!"

His rage was instantaneous. "Do you completely discount me as a man? My liveship is out there, her capture is imminent, and you wish me to go lie down in my cabin like an invalid? Damn you, woman! Either help me to the helm, or get out of my way."

She helped him, a nightmarish trip across a deck that pitched with the fury of the storm. She hauled him up the short ladder as if he were a sack of potatoes. There was anger in her strength, and when his stump knocked against a rung, near stunning him with pain, she offered no apology. At the top she hauled on his arm as if it were a sheet, until she had it draped across her shoulders. Then she stood up under his weight and dragged him to the wheel. An incredulous Sorcor shook water from his eyes and stared at his captain.

"I'll take the helm. Our liveship's in trouble. Prepare a boarding party, as many sailors as raiders. We'll need to overtake her swiftly, before she gets too far into Hawser Channel."

Far ahead of them, they caught yet another glimpse of the liveship as the seas lifted her high. She sailed like a derelict now, wind and waves pushing her where they pleased. A trick of the wind brought her despairing shriek to their ears as she dived down into a trough of water.

She was headed to the west of Crooked Island.

Sorcor shook his head. He had to shout over the storm. "There's no catching up with her the way she's sailing. And even if we had the crew to spare, we couldn't board her in this storm. Give her up, sir! There'll be another one along. Let that one go to her fate."

"I am her fate!" Kennit roared back at him. A vast anger rose in him. All the world and everyone in it opposed him in his quest. "I'll take the wheel. I know that channel, I took us through there before. You work with the crew to put on a bit of sail so we can catch her up. Help me but overtake her and try to run her onto the shoals. And if nothing is to be done then, I'll give her up!"

They heard her cry out again, a long drawn-out scream of despair, haunting in its eeriness. The sound hung long in the air. "Oh," Etta exclaimed suddenly with a shudder as it finally died away. "Someone save her." The words were almost a prayer. She glanced from one man to the other. Rain had slicked her hair flat to her skull. The water ran like tears in streams down her face. "I'm strong enough to hold the wheel," she proclaimed. "If Kennit stands behind me and guides my hands, we can keep the *Marietta* on course."

"Done," Sorcor replied so promptly that Kennit instantly realized that had been the man's true objection all along. He didn't think Kennit could stand on one leg and still handle the ship's wheel.

Grudgingly he admitted Sorcor was probably right. "Exactly," he said, as if it had been his intent all along. Sorcor made room for them. It was an awkward transfer, but Etta eventually had her hands on the wheel. Kennit stood behind her. He set one hand on the wheel to aid her, and clasped her with his other arm to keep his balance. He could feel the tension in her, but was also aware of her pent excitement. For a moment, it was as if in clasping Etta he embraced the ship herself.

"Tell me what to do!" she called over her shoulder.

"Just hold it steady," he told her. "I'll tell you when you need to do anything else." His eyes followed the silvery liveship as she fled before the wind.

He clasped her close to him, and his weight against her back was not a burden, but a shelter from the wind and rain. His right arm wrapped her, his hand gripping her left shoulder. Still, she was frightened. Why had she ever said she would do this? Etta gripped the spokes of the ship's wheel tightly, so tightly her knuckles began to ache. She set her arms stiff to oppose any movement the ship might suddenly make. All around her there was only darkness and driving rain and rushing wind and water. Up ahead she could suddenly see flashes of silver-white water as waves dashed against barnacled rocks. She could not tell what she was doing; she could steer the ship directly into a rock and never know until they struck. She could kill them all, every man aboard.

Then Kennit's voice spoke softly by her left ear. Despite the storm, he did not shout. His low voice was little more than a whisper. "It's easy, really. Lift your eyes, look ahead. Now feel the ship through the wheel. There. Loosen your hands. You will never be able to react if you throttle the wood so. There. Now you can feel her. She speaks to you, does she not? Who is this, she wonders, who is this light new touch on the helm? So hold her steady and reassure her. Now then, now then, ease her over a bit, just a bit, not too much, and hold her steady there."

It was his lover's voice he spoke with, small and breathless, warm with encouragement. She had never felt closer to him than now, sharing his love of the ship that he guided through the storm. Never had she felt stronger, as she clasped the wooden spokes of the wheel and held the *Marietta*'s nose into the waves. Aloft, she could hear Sorcor calling to his deckhands. They were reefing in some sails in a pattern she still found incomprehensible, but which she suddenly found herself resolved to understand. For she could understand it. And she could do it. That was what Kennit's arm around her, his weight against her back, and his soft voice in her ear were telling her. She squinted her eyes against the driving rain. Suddenly the cold and the wet were simply a part of this, not pleasant, no, but not something to fear or avoid for their own sakes. They, like the wind, were a part of her life now. A life that was carrying her forward as swiftly as the current carried the ship, shaping her every day into a new person. A person she could respect.

"Why cannot it always be like this?" she asked him at one point.

He feigned surprise and asked in a louder voice, "What? You prefer the storm that sweeps us toward the Damned Rocks to easy sailing on peaceful waters?"

She laughed aloud, embraced by him and the storm and this new life he had plunged her into. "Kennit, you are the storm," she told him. In a quieter voice she added to herself, "And I prefer me as I am when I race before your winds."

CHAPTER THIRTY-THREE

DAY OF RECKONING

THERE WERE, WINTROW KNEW, SOME RELIGIONS THAT TAUGHT OF PLACES WHERE DEMONS REIGNED AND HAD the power to torture men endlessly. The ship, caught in the press of wind and rain, populated with two-legged creatures that shrieked and struggled with one another, seemed such a netherworld. The scriptures of Sa contained no belief in such a place. Men created their own torments, Wintrow believed, not the benevolent Parent of All, who only viewed such things with grief. This night on this ship, he had come to grasp in its fullness the truth of Sa's teaching. For here they were, one and all humans, each one a creature of Sa. Yet it was not the howling wind or the stabbing rain that raced through the ship shedding blood and tearing life free of bodies. No. Only the humans aboard the ship did that, and only to one another. This was not Sa's doing. There was nothing of Sa in this perdition.

From the moment Sa'Adar had thrown the lantern at Gantry, it had been out of Wintrow's hands. He had not started this carnage; this slaughter was not his doing. He could not even recall making a decision, only that he had followed Sa'Adar and helped him unshackle slaves. It was the right thing to do. More right than trying to warn his father and crew-mates? Don't ask that question, don't let that question exist. These deaths were not his fault. Over and over, Wintrow told himself that. Not his fault. What could one boy do to stop this torrent of hatred once it had broken loose? He was just a leaf caught up in a storm wind.

He wondered if Gantry had felt the same way.

He and Sa'Adar had been freeing the map-faces, deep in the bottom-most hold of the *Vivacia*, when they heard the yells from above. In their haste to join in the fray, the map-faces had literally trampled over him. Sa'Adar had led them with the lantern. Wintrow had been left behind in the pitch black, frightened and disoriented. Now he groped his way through the filthy holds, clambering over the bodies of slaves either too weakened or scared to join in the rebellion. Others milled in the confusion, calling to one another, demanding to know what was happening. He pushed his way through them and groped his way around them, and still he could not find the companionway up to the hatch. He knew every inch of this ship, he told himself. But suddenly the *Vivacia* had become a black maze of death and stench and frightened people. On the deck above him he heard running feet, and cries of both anger and fear. Screams of death, too.

Then another scream burst out, one that rang within the hold and wakened echoing cries of terrors in the churning slaves. "Vivacia," he gasped to himself, and then, "Vivacia!" he called out to her, praying she could hear him, and know he was coming to her. His groping hands suddenly met the ladder and he flung himself up it.

As he emerged onto the deck into a driving rain he stumbled over the first body of a crewman. Mild was trapped in a half-closed hatch. In the dimness he could not tell how he had been killed, only that he was dead. He knelt by him, hearing the sounds of fighting elsewhere in the ship, but capable of comprehending fully only this death. Mild's chest was still warm. The sluicing rain and flying spray had already chilled his hands and face, but his body gave up its warmth more slowly.

Others were dying now, slaves and crewmen. Vivacia lived it all, he suddenly recalled. She felt it all, and alone.

Wintrow was on his feet and stumbling towards her before he knew what he was doing. In the waist, some of the crewmen had been sleeping in crude canvas shelters. The wind and rain there had been preferable to the thick stink of the lower decks. Now the tent was collapsed, and wind and rain tore at it while men tore at each other. Manacle chains were suddenly weapons. Wintrow dodged through the blood-crazed fighters, shouting, "No! No! You have to stop this, the ship won't take it! You have to stop!" No one heeded him. There were men down on the deck, some squirming and some still. He jumped over them. He could do nothing for them. The only person he could possibly aid was the ship, who now screamed his name into the night. Wintrow tripped over what might have been a body. He scrabbled back to his feet, evaded a man who clutched at him, and groped his way forward through the rain and the dark of night until his hands found the ladder to the foredeck.

"Vivacia!" he called, his voice a thin and pitiful thing in the rising storm. But still she heard him.

"Wintrow! Wintrow!" she cried mindlessly, shrieking his name as a nightmare-plagued child calls for her mother. He clambered up on the foredeck, only to be driven back as the *Vivacia* plowed wildly through a sea. For a moment all he could do was grasp the rung of the ladder and fight for air. In the next space between waves, he was up and dashing foolishly forward. His hands grasped the forward rail. He could not feel her, could see her only as a shadow before him.

"Vivacia!" he cried to her.

For an instant she did not answer. He gripped the railing hard and reached for her with all his might. Like warm hands clasping on a cold night, her awareness joined gratefully with his. Then her horror and shock flowed into his mind as well.

"They've killed Comfrey! There's no one on the wheel!"

Figurehead and boy plunged into cold salt water. The wizardwood deck slid under his grasping fingers. In the dark he shared her knowledge and despair even as he fought for his own survival. He felt the widespread death throughout her, and knew, too, the lack of control she felt as the storm winds drove her forward into the towering waves. Her crew had been driven from their duties. Barricaded in the stern-castle were some who fought for their lives. Others were dying slowly on the decks they had manned. As lives winked out, it was as if Vivacia were losing pieces of herself. Never before had he sensed how immense was the water and how small the boat that preserved his life. As the storm waves ran off her decks, he managed to stand. "What should I do?" he demanded of her.

"Get to the wheel!" she cried to him through the wind. "Get control of the rudder." She raised her voice in a sudden roar. "Tell them to stop killing each other, or they'll all die. All of them, I swear it!"

He turned back toward the waist of the ship, and drawing as deep a breath as he was able, shouted at the men who struggled there. "You heard her. She'll kill us all if you don't stop the fighting now! Stop the fighting. Man her sails, those of you who know how, or not a one of us will survive this night! And let me through to the helm!"

They plunged again into a wave. The wall of water hit him from behind, and he was suddenly flying free with it, no deck, no rigging, nothing, only the water that offered a yielding resistance to his scrabbling hands. He might already be overboard and not even know it. He opened his mouth to scream and sucked in salt water instead. In the next instant the water slammed him against the port railing. He caught at it and held, despite the water's best efforts to carry him over the side. Right next to him a slave was not so lucky. He struck the railing, teetered and then went over the side.

The water ran off through the scuppers. On the deck, men thrashed like landed fish, choking and spitting seawater. The moment he could, Wintrow was back on his feet and struggling aft. Like an insect, he thought, in a puddle, struggling mindlessly only because live things always tried to stay alive. Most of the others who remained on the deck were clearly not sailors by the way they flung themselves at railings and ropes and grasped tight. They seemed just as shocked by the next dousing wave. A manacle key must have been found, for some were entirely free of chains, while others still wore their fetters as familiarly as their shirts. More faces peered up fearfully from the open hatches, shouting advice and questions to the groups on deck. As each mammoth wave passed, they ducked back to avoid the dousing, but seemed to take no care for how much water flooded down into the ship. Bodies of both slaves and crew washed back and forth in the waist with the wallowing of the ship. He stared at them incredulously. Had they fought for their freedom only to die by drowning? Had they killed all the crew for nothing?

He suddenly heard Sa'Adar's voice raised. "There he is, there's our lad. Boy, Wintrow, come here! They've barricaded themselves in there. Any way to smoke the rats out?" He mastered a band of triumphant map-faces outside the door to the officers' quarters in the sterncastle. Despite the storm and the tossing ship, they were still intent on their killing.

"This storm will take us down if I don't get to the wheel!" he shouted at them. He drew his voice from deep within him and tried to sound commanding, like a man. "Stop the killing, or the sea will finish it for all of us! Let the crew come out and man the ship as best they can, I beg you! We're taking on water with every wave!" He caught at the side of the aftercastle ladder as another wave hit. In horror he watched it pour down the open hatches like beer filling a mug. "Shut those hatches down tight!" he bellowed at them. "And put some men on the pumps, or everyone sick or hiding below is going to drown even before the rest of us!" He looked aloft. "We need to take in those sails, give the wind less to push on!"

"I'm not going up there," one slave declared loudly. "I didn't get out of chains just to kill myself another way!"

"Then you'll die when we all go under!" Wintrow shouted back at him. His voice broke on the words, going up into a boy's shrill timbre. Some of the slaves were making a faint-hearted attempt to shut the hatches, but no one was willing to let loose their secure holds to do so.

"Rocks!" screamed Vivacia. "Rocks! Wintrow, the helm, the helm!"

"Let the crew out. Promise them their lives if they'll save yours!" he roared at Sa'Adar. Then he scrabbled swiftly up the ladder.

Comfrey had died at the wheel, struck from behind. Whoever had killed him had left him as he fell, half tangled in the spokes. Only the weight of his fallen body had kept the rudder from slapping back and forth with every sea. "I'm sorry, I'm so sorry," Wintrow babbled apologetically as he pulled the lanky body free of its last post. He stepped up to the wheel and seized it, stopping its random turning with a wrench. He drew the deepest breath his lungs would hold. "TELL ME WHAT TO DO!" he bellowed, and prayed his voice would carry the length of the ship through the storm.

"HARD PORT!" Vivacia's cry came back to him. Her voice came not only through the wind but seemed to vibrate into him through his hands. The spokes of the ship's wheel, he realized, were of wizardwood. He set his hands to it more fully. Not sure whether he sinned or not, he reached not for Sa but for oneness with the ship. He abandoned his fear of losing himself in her.

"Steady," he whispered to her, and felt an almost frantic leaping of connection. With it came her fear, but also her courage. He shared her awareness of the storm and the current. Her wizardwood body became his greater self.

The wheel had been built with the assumption that a grown and well-muscled man would hold it. He had watched the ship steered, and taken a turn or two in milder weather, but never in a blow like this, and never without a man at his shoulder instructing him and catching at the wheel if it looked like it would overpower him. Wintrow put the full weight of his slight body to turning it. He felt every point he gained as a small victory but wondered if the ship could answer the rudder in time. It seemed to him that they hit the next wave more squarely, cutting through it rather than being nudged aside by it. He squinted through the driving rain, but could see nothing but blackness. They could have been out in the middle of the Wild Sea with emptiness all around them. It suddenly struck him as ridiculous; he and the ship were alone in their struggle to save them all. Everyone else on board was too intent on killing one another.

"You have to help me," he said quietly, forming aloud the words he knew she would sense. "You have to be your own lookout, for both waves and rocks. Reach for me with what you know."

In the waist he could hear men shouting to one another. Some of the voices were muffled and he guessed that the slaves negotiated with the captive crew. From the fury in the voices, he doubted if they would agree in time to save the ship. Forget about them, he counseled himself. "It's you and I, my lady," he said quietly to her. "You and I alone. Let's try to stay alive." He gripped the wheel tight in his hands.

He did not know if he felt her answer him or if his own determination lent him new strength. He stood, blinded by both water and darkness, and defied them both. He did not hear Vivacia call out to him again but he seemed to catch a feel for the ship. The sails overhead worked against him, but he could do nothing about them. A different sort of rain suddenly began to fall, just as insistent but lighter somehow. Yet even as the storm abated and the first graying of dawn tinged the sky, the wheel seemed to grow stiffer and heavier under his hands. "The current has us!" Vivacia's low cry carried back to him. "There are rocks ahead! I know this channel from long ago! We should not have come this way. I cannot stay clear of them by myself!"

He heard the clank of chain and then the fall of a heavy body to the deck. He spared a glance for a group of men making their way towards him. Several manacled and fettered man were shoved along in their midst. As they reached Wintrow, someone gave the front man a harder push. He went to his knees on the wet deck. Sa'Adar's voice boomed out. "He says he'll steer and steer true if we let him live." In a quieter voice he added, "He says we cannot get past those rocks without him. He alone knows this channel."

As the man struggled to his feet, Wintrow finally recognized Torg. He could make out little of his features in the dark. His shirt was torn away from his back; the pale rags of it fluttered in the wind. "You," Torg said. The low laugh he gave was disbelieving. "You did this to us? You?" He shook his head. "I don't believe it. You had the treachery, but not the guts. You stand there and hold the wheel like the ship is yours, but I don't believe you took her." Despite his chains and the snarling map-faces surrounding him, he spat to one side. "You didn't have the balls to take her when she was offered to you on a silver platter." The furious words poured from him like a pent-up flood. "Oh, yes, I knew all about your father's deal with you. I heard what he said that day. Your father was going to give you the mate's position on her when you turned fifteen. Never mind that I worked like a dog for him for the past seven years. Never mind old Torg. Give the captaincy to Gantry and the mate's position to a pink-cheeked boy. And you'd lord it over me."

He laughed. "Well, Gantry's dead, they tell us. And your father's not much better off." He crossed his arms on his chest. "You see that island off our starboard side? That's Crooked Island. You should have taken the ship on the other side of it. There's rocks and current ahead. So if you want a man at the helm of this tub, maybe you'd better talk nice to Torg. Maybe you'd better offer him something a bit more than his own life to get your sorry asses out of this fix." He smiled a toadish smile, confident suddenly that they needed him, that he could turn the whole situation to his profit. "Maybe you'd better talk nice and fast, for the rocks are just ahead." The men behind him, new hands taken on in Jamaillia, cast fearful glances ahead through the darkness.

"What should we do?" Sa'Adar asked him. "Can we trust him?"

The situation was laughable, it was so horrifying. They were asking him. They were putting the whole ship's survival in his hands. He glanced up at the lightening sky. Aloft were two slaves, struggling vainly to take in sail. Sa have mercy on them all. He tightened his grip on the wheel and looked at Torg's smug face. Was Torg capable of putting the ship on the rocks for the sake of vengeance? Could any man take revenge that far, to throw his own life away with it? The tattoo on Wintrow's face itched. "No," Wintrow said at last. "I don't trust him. And I'd kill him before I gave him the helm of my ship."

A map-face shrugged callously. "The useless die."

"Wait," Wintrow cried, but it was too late. In a movement as smooth as a longshoreman pitching bales, the map-face hefted the bulky sailor over his head, and then flung him over the stern with a force that sent the map-face to his knees as well. Torg was gone, as swiftly and simply as that. He hadn't even had time to scream. On his single word not to trust the man, Torg had died. The other sailors had fallen to their knees, crying out and begging him to spare them.

A terrible disgust welled up in him. It was not for the begging men. "Get those chains off them and send them aloft," he barked at Sa'Adar. "Reef the sails as best you can, and cry back to me if you see rocks." It was a stupid order, a useless order. Three men could not sail a ship this size. As Sa'Adar was unlocking their fetters, he heard himself ask, "Where's my father? Is he alive?"

They looked at him blankly, one and all. None of them knew, he realized. He supposed his father had forbidden the crew to speak of him among themselves. "Where's Captain Haven?" he demanded.

"He's down below with his head and ribs busted up," one of the deckhands volunteered.

Wintrow weighed it up and decided in favor of his ship. He pointed at Sa'Adar. "I need the ship's captain up here. And gently. He's no good to us if he's unconscious." And the useless die, he thought to himself as the priest dispatched men to fetch the captain. An overseer's threat to a slave became a credo to live by. To save the crew, he'd have to show the freed slaves their usefulness. "Unchain those two," he ordered. "Get every live sailor who can move aloft."

A map face shrugged. "There's only these two now."

Only two left alive. And his father. Sa forgive him. He looked at the man who had thrown Torg overboard. "You. You threw a sailor overboard, one we might have used. You take his place now. Get aloft, to the look-out's post. Cry down to me what you see." He glared around at the others standing around them. It suddenly infuriated him that they would stand about idly. "The rest of you make sure the hatches are down tight now. Get on the pumps, too. I can feel she's too heavy in the water. Sa only knows how much water we took on." His voice was quieter but just as hard as he added, "Clear the deck of bodies. And get those collapsed tents tidied away."

The first man's eyes went from Wintrow up to the tiny platform at the top of the main mast. "Up there? I can't go up there."

The current was like a living thing now, the tide speeding through the narrow channel like a mill race. Wintrow fought the wheel. "Get moving if you want to live," he barked. "There's no time for your fear. The ship is the only thing that matters now. Save her if you want to save yourselves."

"That's the only time you've ever sounded like a son to me."

Blood had darkened down the side of Kyle Haven's face. He moved with his body at a twist, trying not to jar the ribs that poked and grated inside him. He was paler than the gray sky overhead. He looked at his son holding the ship's wheel, at the scarred map-faces that lumbered hastily off to do his bidding, at the debris of the insurrection and shook his head slowly. "This is what it took for you to find your manhood?"

"It was never lost," he said flatly. "You simply couldn't recognize it, because I wasn't you. I wasn't big and strong and harsh. I was me."

"You never stepped up to the mark. You never cared about what I could give you." Kyle shook his head. "You and this ship. Spoiled children, both of you."

Wintrow gripped the wheel tightly. "We don't have time for this. The *Vivacia* can't steer herself. She's helping me, but I want your eyes, too. I want your knowledge." He could not keep the bitterness from his voice. "Advise me, father."

"He's truly your father?" Sa'Adar asked in consternation. "He enslaved his own son?"

Neither man answered him. Both peered ahead, into the storm. After a moment, the priest retreated to the stern of the ship, leaving them almost alone.

"What are you going to do with her?" his father demanded suddenly. "Even if you get safely through this channel, you haven't enough good men to sail her. These are treacherous waters, even for an experienced crew." He snorted. "You're going to lose her before you even had her."

"All I can do is the best I can," Wintrow said quietly. "I didn't choose this. But I believe Sa will provide."

"Sa!" Kyle shook his head in disgust. Then, "Keep her to the center of the channel. No, a couple more points to port. There. Hold her steady. Where's Torg? You should put him aloft to cry out what he sees."

Wintrow considered it an instant, combining his father's opinion with what he felt through Vivacia. Then he made the correction. "Torg's dead," he said after the brief silence. "He was put over the side. Because a slave considered him useless." He gestured with his chin to a man who clung, frozen, halfway up the mast. "He was supposed to take the look-out post."

An aghast silence followed his words. When his father spoke, his voice was strained.

"All of this . . . ." his father said in a low voice, pitched only for Wintrow's ears. "All of this, just so you could take the ship now, instead of a few years from now?"

The question measured the distance between them for Wintrow. The gulf between them was vast and uncrossable.

"None of this was about any of that." A stupid statement. But all the words he could utter in a lifetime would not make his father understand him. The only thing they would ever really share was the ship. "Let's just get her through these rocks," he suggested. "Let's speak of only that. It's the only thing we can agree on."

After a very long time, his father stepped up to stand beside him.

He set one hand lightly to the wheel beside his son's. He glanced up at the rigging, spotted one of his own men. "Calt! Leave off that and get to the look-out's post."

His father's eyes roved ahead. "Here we go," he warned Wintrow softly as the ship suddenly gained speed.

"You've sold me," Malta said dully. "You've sold me to a monster, to pay off a ship. So I can be dragged off to some swampy tree-camp to grow warts and make babies while you can all get rich off new trade contracts with the Khuprus family. Don't think I don't know how it works. Usually when a woman is given up to a Rain Wild husband, the family in Bingtown gets fat on the profits." They had wakened her early and called her down to the kitchen for this. Breakfast wasn't even ready.

"Malta, that's not how it is," her mother said in her "let's be reasonable" voice.

At least her grandmother was honest about how she felt. She finished filling the kettle, and then set it on the stove. She bent down and poked up the fire herself. "Actually, you sold yourself," she said in a deceptively pleasant voice. "For a scarf, a flame jewel and a dream-box. And don't claim you weren't smart enough to know what you were doing. You know a great deal more about everything than you let on."

Malta kept silent for a time. Then, "I have the things in my room. I can return them," she offered gruffly. The flame jewel. She hated to part with the flame jewel. But better that than to be pledged to a toadish Rain Wild man. She thought of the dream of kissing him and shuddered. In reality, behind his veil, his lips would be pebbled with warts. Even the thought of that kiss made her want to spit now. It wasn't fair, to send a dream in which he was so handsome when he was really a toad.

"It's a bit late for that," her mother said with asperity. "If you had been honest about the dream-box, things might have been mended. No. I take that back. You'd already accepted a scarf and a jewel, to say nothing of giving him a cup you had drunk from." She halted a moment, and when she went on her voice was kinder. "Malta. No one is going to force you into a marriage. All we have consented to is that the young man be allowed to see you. You won't be alone with him. Grandmother or I or Rache or Nana will always be there, too. You don't have to be afraid of him." She cleared her throat and when she went on her tone was unmistakably cooler. "On the other hand, I will permit no discourtesy. You will never be late, or rude to him. You will treat him as you would any honored visitor to our home. And that means no wild talk of warts, or swamps, or making babies."

Malta got up from the table and went and cut herself a slice of yesterday's bread. "Fine. I won't talk at all," she offered them. What could they do about that, really? How could they force her to talk to him or be nice to him? She wasn't going to pretend she actually liked him. He'd soon discover she found him disgusting and go away. She wondered if she'd be allowed to keep the scarf and the jewel if he said he didn't want to marry her. It probably wasn't a good time to ask that. But he could have the dream-box back anytime. It had turned an ugly, flat gray color after she had opened it, like ash in a fireplace. It still smelled pretty, but that was small reason to keep it.

"Malta, these are not people we can offend," her mother pointed out.

She looked very tired and worn of late. There were more lines in her face and she took even less care with her hair than she used to. Soon she would be as sour faced as Grandmother. And Grandmother was frowning now. "It is not a matter of who we can or cannot afford to offend. There are many ways of dealing with an unwelcome suitor. Rudeness is not one of them. Not for our family."

"When will my father be home?" Malta asked abruptly. "Do we have any peach preserves anywhere?"

"We don't expect him until late spring," her mother said wearily. "Why?"

"I just don't think he would make me do this. Pretend to like a man I don't even want to know . . . Isn't there anything good to eat in this house?"

"Put some butter on it instead. And no one asked you to pretend to like him!" Grandmother burst out. "You are not a prostitute, he has not paid you to smile while he leers at you. I am simply saying we expect you to treat him with courtesy. I am sure he will be a complete gentleman. I have Caolwn's word on that, and I have known her a very long time. All you need do is treat him with respect." In a lower voice she went on, "I am sure he will quickly decide you are not suitable, and cease his attentions." The way she said it, it was insulting. As if Malta weren't worthy of him.

"I'll try," Malta grudgingly conceded. She tossed the dry bread down onto the table in front of her. At least it would be something to tell Delo about. She was always subtly bragging about all the young men who came to her house. They were all Cerwin's friends, Malta knew that. But Delo knew their names, and they made teasing jokes with her, and sometimes brought her sweets and trinkets. Once, when she had been allowed to go to the spice market with Delo with Rache accompanying them, one of Cerwin's friends had recognized Delo, and made a big sweeping bow to her, with his cloak blowing out in the wind when he did it. He had offered to treat them to spice tea, but Rache had said they must hurry home. It had made Malta look like an infant. Just for once, it would be nice to tell Delo that a young man had come to her house, to see her. She didn't need to tell Delo he was probably covered with warts. Maybe she could make him seem mysterious and dangerous. . . . She smiled to herself and looked afar dreamily, practicing the look she'd wear when she told Delo about her young man. Her mother slammed a pot of honey down on the table in front of her.

"Thank you," Malta said absently as she helped herself to it.

Maybe Cerwin would be jealous.

"Are you going to let me live?" Kyle Haven asked softly as dawn began to tinge the sky. He tried to speak flatly, but harshness tinged with fear seeped into his words. Wintrow could hear weariness as well. The long night was nearly over, but it had taken both of them on the wheel and all Calt could see and all Vivacia could call back to them to get them through the channel. He had to admire his father for his tenacity. He had lasted it out. He still stood canted, sheltering the ribs on his left side, but he had helped bring the ship through. And now he asked for his life from his son. It had to be bitter.

"I will do all I can to see you live through this. This I promise you." He glanced from his father to Sa'Adar, who still leaned on the stern. Wintrow wondered how much he himself would have to say in any decision to come. "You don't believe me. But your death would grieve me. All the deaths on this ship have grieved me."

Kyle Haven stared straight ahead. "Another point to port," was all he said.

Around them the water suddenly spread and calmed. Crooked Island was falling behind them and Hawser Channel opened up.

His son corrected their course. Overhead, men shouted to one another in the rigging, arguing as to what they should do and how. His father was right. There was no way they could sail the ship with only two experienced and able hands. He gripped the wheel. There had to be some way. "Help me, ship," he breathed softly. "Help me know what to do." He felt her weary response. It was not one of confidence, only one of trust.

"There's another ship behind us," Sa'Adar observed aloud. "It's getting closer fast." He peered at it through the insistent gray rain.

"It's the Raven flag!" The joy in his voice was clear. "Sa has truly provided!" The man tore off his rag of a shirt and began waving it at the other ship.

"There's a boy at her helm!" Sorcor shouted down at him. The storm had died down, even the rain was ceasing, but still he pitched his voice to carry through it. "And a mess on her decks. I think they've had a mutiny."

"All the better . . . for us." Kennit shouted back. It took so much effort. He was so tired. He drew a long breath. "Make ready a boarding party. We'll take her as soon as she reaches the main channel."

"The kid seems to have a nice touch on the wheel, even with the sails set all wrong. Wait!" Disbelief was strong in Sorcor's voice. "Captain, they're hailing to us. It looks like the man is waving us alongside."

"Then let us oblige him. Boarders ready! No. Wait." He took a breath and tried to stand up straight. "I'll lead them myself. Gankis! Come take the wheel. Etta, where is my crutch?"

It was true. The ship was his for the taking, his luck had held. He had believed in it, he had persevered, and there it was, his beautiful liveship. As they gained her side, he thought he had never seen anything lovelier. From the castle of the *Marietta*, he could look down on her. There were bodies heaped upon a pile of fallen canvas, and her sails were hiked up like a bawd's skirts, but her silvery hull glistened and the clean lines of her were like music.

He swayed and Etta clutched at him. Gankis had the wheel now. The old sailor gave him an odd look, half of pity and half of fear.

"I don't know where your crutch is. Here. Let me get you to the railing." She grunted with effort as she tugged him along. He came with her in lurching hops until he could lean on it with both hands. "My love," she said very quietly. "I think you should go below and rest for a time. Let Sorcor secure the liveship for you."

"No," he said savagely. It was so damn hard to remain on his leg, and she had to waste his strength with stupid arguing. "No. She's mine and I'll be among the first on her decks. She's come to me by my luck."

"Please," Etta said, her voice breaking on the word. "My darling. My love. If you could see yourself just now . . ."

"Sar," Sorcor had joined them and he swore the word out on an exhalation. "Oh, Kennit, oh, sir . . ."

"I'll be leading the boarding party," he told Sorcor. His mate wouldn't argue with him. He'd make the damn woman stop arguing with him, too.

"Yes, sir," Sorcor confirmed very quietly.

"You can't mean it!" Etta cried out to Sorcor. "Look at him. He's exhausted, I never should have let him stay on the deck, if I had known what it would cost. . . ."

"Let him go." Sorcor spoke quietly. He had brought Kennit's crutch, but he set it carefully down on the deck. "I'll rig a bosun's chair for you, sir. And I'll see you safely to the deck of your liveship."

"But . . ." Etta began, but Sorcor cut her off. "I promised him," he said harshly. "Look at him, woman. Let me keep my promise to my captain." In a lower voice he added, "I think there's little else we can do now."

"But . . ." she said again. She looked at him and when he met her eyes, something in them seemed to go very still. She did not seem to breathe, only looked at him. Then she looked at Sorcor past him. "I'm going with him, then," she announced quietly.

"We both are," he confirmed it.

CHAPTER THIRTY-FOUR

RESTORATIONS

THE MATE ROUSED ALTHEA FROM A DEEP SLEEP WITH A CAUTIOUS TUG AT HER SLEEVE. "HEY," GRAG TENIRA said in an undertone. "Captain wants to see you now. He's on anchor watch, so meet him on deck. Roll out now." Grag turned and left without waiting to see if she would obey.

A scant second later, Althea's bare feet hit the deck. Around her, the forecastle was dark and quiet. The rest of the crew had liberty tonight. Without exception, they'd gone ashore to carouse. Althea, more eager for solitude than beer, had pleaded lack of coin and stayed aboard to idle and sleep.

The *Ophelia* was in port at a small island city called Rinstin. It was one of the few completely legitimate settlements in the islands of the Inside Passage. Originally founded near a tin deposit and possessing a good supply of fresh water, the town of prosperous tin miners was beginning to be a trade center as well. The inhabitants could afford a few of the Rain Wild goods that Tenira had to offer. He'd turn a nice profit selling off the casks of salt meat he'd taken on in Jamaillia as well, and depart with tinwares to sell in Bingtown. The man was a savvy trader. In her brief time with him, Althea had already grown to admire him.

As she emerged onto the deck and looked about for Captain Tenira, the oddness of the situation suddenly struck her. The captain was on wheel watch in port? And he'd sent the mate to fetch her? A terrible suspicion welled up in her. Ophelia had given away her secret. When Althea spotted the captain smoking his pipe up by the figurehead, her suspicion became certainty. The young sailor perched on the railing nearby would be Grag, waiting to witness her exposure. Her heart sank into her belly.

Althea paused a moment in the shadows, to smooth her hair back into its queue and rub the sleep from her face. She straightened her worn clothing as best she could. As bad as it had been to be thrown off the *Reaper*, this was going to be worse. These men knew her family, and would take this tale home with them. So. Head up. No tears, no anger, she promised herself. Dignity and pride. She wished her stomach would settle. She wished she'd had more warning.

As she walked forward, Ophelia's rich voice carried on the night air, almost as if she intended Althea to hear her words. "And you, Tomie Tenira, are turning into a cranky old curmudgeon, with no sense of adventure left to you."

"Ophelia," her captain warned her.

"No sense of humor either," Ophelia confided to Grag. The deck lantern left the mate's face in shadow, and he made no verbal response to her. Althea felt her mouth twist in an ironic smile. She wondered what Grag Tenira thought of his former dance partner now.

She smoothed the smile from her face. She kept her features dispassionate as she greeted Tenira with, "Reporting, sir."

"Indeed," Captain Tenira said heavily. He took his short pipe from his mouth. "You know what this is about, don't you?"

She tried not to wince. "I'm afraid so, sir."

Tenira leaned back on the railing with a heavy sigh. "We've discussed this, Grag and I. And Ophelia has had her say. And more than her say, as is usual. I intend this for your best, young woman. Gather all your things. Grag will give you some coin and escort you ashore. There's a rooming house on Clamshell Street. It's clean. He'll see you safely there."

"Sir," Althea conceded hopelessly. At least he wasn't shouting angrily at her. By keeping his dignity, he'd allowed her to keep hers. For that, she was grateful. But Ophelia's betrayal of her trust still stung. She looked past him to where Ophelia regarded her sheepishly over one round shoulder. "I asked you not to give me away," she rebuked her softly. She studied the figurehead's face. "I can't believe you did this to me."

"Oh, not fair, my dear! Not fair at all!" Ophelia protested earnestly. "I warned you that you couldn't expect me to keep such a secret from my captain. And I also told you I'd try to find a way for you to stay aboard, if you wished to, under your own name. Now how could I do that without telling him what your real name was?" Ophelia turned her attention to her captain. "Tomie, you're enjoying this. Shame on you! Tell her the rest, right now. The poor girl thinks you mean to maroon her here."

"This is Ophelia's idea, not mine," the captain observed grudgingly. "She's taken quite a shine to you." He took a draw from his pipe while Althea waited in suspense. "Grag'll give you enough coin to fix yourself up. A bath, the proper clothes and so on. Tomorrow afternoon, you'll come back aboard as Althea Vestrit. And we'll take you home."

"And," Ophelia cut in excitedly. "And, oh, this is the best part, my dear, and you can't imagine how hard it was for me to persuade Tomie. Grag was easy, of course, Grag's always easy, aren't you, my lamb?" She didn't wait for the mate's murmured assent. "You'll be acting as mate for the rest of the voyage home," she announced to Althea gleefully. "Because a day or so out of Rinstin, poor Grag's going to have such a horrible toothache that he'll take to his bunk. And Tomie's going to ask you to fill in, because he knows you sailed with your father."

Grag leaned forward to see her expression at this. At the shock on her face, he burst out laughing. His blue eyes darted to Ophelia, sharing his delight with her.

"Do you mean it?" Althea asked incredulously. "Oh, how can I thank you?"

Captain Tenira took the pipe out of his mouth. "You can thank me by doing a damn good job so that no one says I'm daft to have taken you on. And you can keep it to yourself, forever, that you ever shipped aboard the *Ophelia* as a boy and I didn't know it." He rounded abruptly on his figurehead. "And I expect you to keep your word on that as well, you old busy-body. Not a word of this to anyone, man or liveship."

"Why, Tomie, how can you doubt me?" Ophelia demanded. She rolled her eyes and laid a hand over her heart as if stricken. Then she tipped a showy wink to Althea.

Grag choked and the captain whirled on him. "Stop your sniggering, pup. You'll be as much a laughing-stock as I if this gets out."

"I'm not laughing, sir," Grag lied merrily. "I'm just looking forward to the prospect of reading and lazing all the way from here to Bingtown." His eyes darted to Althea's to share the joke. His gaze lingered on her face, and she was sure he was trying to see the girl he had known in her grubby boy's guise. She lowered her eyes uncomfortably as his father spoke to him.

"I'm sure. Well, be prepared to make a quick recovery if I decide I need you on the deck after all." Captain Tenira swung his gaze back to Althea and almost apologized as he added, "Not that I think I shall. I've heard you can scramble lively and with the best of them. Now. Do you anticipate any problem, ur, changing from boy to girl again?"

Althea shook her head thoughtfully. "I can go to the rooming house as a sailor lad and get cleaned up there. Tomorrow morning, I'll shop about town for 'gifts' for my sister. Then back to my room, change clothes, fix my hair, and whisk out the back. Unnoticed, I hope."

"Well. Let's hope it all goes that simply."

"I truly don't know how to thank you, sir. All of you," Althea's warm gaze included Ophelia.

"There *is* one other thing I'd ask of you," Captain Tenira said heavily.

Something in Althea braced at his tone. "And that is?" she asked.

"Ophelia has told us about your situation with your ship. If I may be bold, young lady, I advise you to keep it a family matter. Oh, I'll vouch for you, if you prove yourself to me. I'll give you a ship's ticket with a mate's stamp on it, if you perform well. I'll even stand beside you in Traders' Council and take your part if need be. But I'd rather not. Vestrit family business should be settled behind Vestrit doors. I knew your father, not well, but well enough to know that's how he'd prefer it."

"I will if I can, sir," Althea replied gravely. "I'd prefer it that way myself. But if it comes down to it, I'll do whatever I must to regain my ship."

"I knew she'd say that," Grag crowed. He and Ophelia exchanged triumphant glances.

"I knew your great-grandmother," Ophelia added. "You take a lot of your looks from her. And your spirit. She'd want you to have her ship. Now, there was a woman who knew how to sail. I remember the day she first brought the *Vivacia* into Bingtown Harbor. There's even a notation about it in my log for that day, if you'd ever care to see it. Anyway, the breeze was fresh and—"

"Not now," Captain Tenira chided Ophelia. He fixed Althea in his gaze. "I've my reasons for asking you to keep Vestrit family business in your family. Selfish reasons. I don't want to be seen as siding with one Trader against another." When Althea looked puzzled, Tenira shook his head. "You've been away from Bingtown for a while. Things are heating up there. It's no time for Trader against Trader problems."

"I know. We got enough problems with the New Traders," Althea agreed quietly.

"Would that were all," Tenira said fervently. "But I fear worse is to come. I got the word in Jamaillia City itself. You know what that fool of a boy-Satrap has done now? Hired Chalcedean mercenaries as privateers to patrol the Inside Passage. Word I got is that he's given them the right to stop in Bingtown for water and supplies. Free of charge. Says it's the least Bingtown should be willing to do to help clean out the pirates. When we left Jamaillia City, his messenger boat was already two days out. With papers authorizing the Satrap's revenue officer to see his Chalcedean hirelings are treated well. 'To collect contributions for their provisioning' was the pretty paper he wrapped it in."

"We've never allowed armed Chalcedean ships into Bingtown harbor, only trading vessels," Althea observed quietly.

"You catch on quick, girl. My guess is that we still won't. It will be interesting to see how the New Traders ally. I fear more will support the Satrap and his Chalcedean dogs than . . ."

"Tomie," Ophelia interrupted. "Save politics for later. You can bore her to tears with that at every meal from here to Bingtown. But first Athel has to become Althea again." Her eyes lifted to Althea's. "Go on, girl, go fetch your things. Grag will see you ashore and safely to the door of the rooming house." Her mouth widened in a bawdy grin and she suddenly winked at the mate. "And mind you behave yourself, Grag, for Althea will tell me all about it otherwise. Go along now, but be sure you stop at her door."

Althea found herself more flustered at the ship's humor than Grag did. He seemed accustomed to it. "Thank you, sir," she managed to Captain Tenira. "I do so appreciate this." Then she hastened away where the shadows could hide her face.

When she came back out on deck, Grag was waiting for her by the hatch. She shouldered her sea-bag, and was relieved when he had the sense not to offer to carry it for her. She followed him down the gangplank and then up into town. He set a good pace. She found herself without words, and he seemed as shy. The night was mild, and the roads lit with the light spilling out from the sailor taverns they passed. When they came to the door of the rooming house, Grag halted.

"Well. Here we are," he said awkwardly. He hesitated as if about to say more.

Althea resolved to put him at ease. "Can I buy you a beer?" she offered, gesturing to the tavern across the street.

He glanced at it, and his blue eyes were wide as they came back to hers. "I don't think I'd be comfortable," he said honestly. "Besides. My father would skin me if I took a lady in a place like that." After a moment, he added, "But thank you." He didn't move.

Althea ducked her head to hide her smile. "Well. Good night, then."

"Yes." He shuffled his feet, then hitched up his trousers. "Uh, I'm supposed to meet you tomorrow and bring you back to the ship. As if it's 'by chance,' as Ophelia put it." He looked down at his feet. "I don't want to look all over town for you. Shall we meet somewhere?" His eyes came up to her face again.

"That would be a good idea," she said quietly. "Where do you suggest?"

He looked away. "There's a place just down the street from here." He pointed through the darkness. "Eldoy's. They make chowder and fresh bread there. It's very good. We could meet there. I'd buy you dinner, and you could tell me your adventures. Since you left Bingtown." His eyes came back to her face and he managed a smile. "Or since we last danced together."

So he had recalled that. She returned his smile.

He had a good face, open and honest. She thought of what she had seen of him, especially him and his father and Ophelia together. The fondness and ease that existed among them made her suddenly hunger for such things as simple jokes and companionable times. When she smiled back at him, his grin widened before he looked away. "I'll meet you there tomorrow afternoon," she agreed easily.

"Good. Good, then, that's settled. Good night, then." Almost hastily, he turned away from her. He gave another hitch to his trousers and then shifted his cap to the back of his head. She smiled as she watched him walk away. He had a jaunty sailor's roll to his gait. She recalled now that he'd been a very good dancer.

"You know something?" Tarlock queried drunkenly. "I know you. I'm sure I know you."

"Not surprising. I'm only the mate on your ship," Brashen told him disgustedly. He swiveled in his seat so he didn't have to face the seaman. Tarlock didn't take the hint.

"No. No, I mean, yeah, that's true. That's true, you're mate on the *Springeve*. But I knew you before that. Way before that." With elaborate care, he sat down beside Brashen. His mug sloshed a bit over the lip as he set it down.

Brashen didn't turn to face him. Instead he lifted his own mug and drank from it as if he hadn't noticed Tarlock had joined him. He'd been alone at the tavern table before the grizzled old sot had sought him out. He'd wanted to be alone. This was the first port the *Springeve* had made since they'd left Candletown, and Brashen had wanted time to think.

His job was pretty much what he'd expected it to be. The day-to-day running of the shallow-draft vessel was not a large strain on his abilities. Most of the crew aboard her had been with her for some time and knew their tasks well enough. He'd had to back up his bark with his fists a few times, especially when he first came aboard, but that was something he'd expected. Men were bound to challenge a new mate, regardless of whether he came aboard fresh or rose up through their ranks. It was just how sailors were. Knowledge and ability weren't enough in a mate; he had to be able to back it up with his fists. Brashen could. That wasn't the problem.

It was his off-ship tasks that were bothering him. Initially the ship had followed the coast of Jamaillia north, skipping along its increasingly broken shoreline. Now it ventured from island to island, skirting and sometimes venturing into what was acknowledged as pirate territory. This little town was typical. It was little more than a wharf and a handful of warehouses on a scummy slough. A couple of taverns housed a few run-down whores. A scatter of hovels marred the hillside behind the taverns. The town had no reason to exist that Brashen could see.

Yet he'd spent the whole afternoon with a sword hanging at his belt and a truncheon in his hand. He'd been watching his captain's back, standing guard behind him as he sat at a table in one of those warehouses. Between his captain's feet was a chest of coins. Three of the most suspicious sea-dogs Brashen had ever encountered brought out merchandise samples, a bit at a time, and prices were negotiated. The variety and condition betrayed the source of their wares. Brashen had felt a surge of disgust with himself when the captain had turned to ask his opinion on some blood-spattered but heavily illustrated manuscripts. "How much are they worth?" Captain Finny had demanded.

Brashen had pushed aside a squirming memory. "Not worth dying for," he'd said dryly. Finny had laughed and named a price. When Brashen nodded, the pirates selling their loot had consulted one another briefly, then accepted it. He'd felt soiled by the transaction.

He'd suspected from the start that the *Springeve* would be trading in such goods. He just hadn't imagined himself inspecting merchandise with a dead man's blood on it.

"Tell ya what," Tarlock offered slyly. "I'll just say a name. You recall it, you tip me a wink and we'll say no more about it. No more at all."

Brashen spoke softly over his shoulder. "How about you shut up right now and stop bothering me, and I don't black both your eyes?"

"Now is that any way to talk to an old ship-mate?" Tarlock whined.

The man was too drunk for his own good. Too drunk to be effectively threatened. Not drunk enough to pass out. But that, perhaps, Brashen could remedy. He changed tactics and turned back to face him. He forced a smile to his face. "You know, you're right. Now I don't recall that I've shipped with you before, but what difference need that make? As we're ship-mates now, let's have a drink together. Boy! Let's have some rum here, the good dark stuff, not this piss-thin beer you've been serving us."

Tarlock's demeanor brightened considerably. "Well. That's a bit more like it," he observed approvingly. He raised his mug and hastily drank his beer down to be ready for the rum when it arrived. He wiped his mouth with the back of his hand, and grinned at Brashen, displaying what remained of his teeth. "Thought I recognized you when you first come aboard, I did. Been a long time, though. What's it been, let's see. Ten years? Ten years ago aboard the *Hope*?"

The *Despair*. Brashen took a pull from his own mug and appeared to consider. "Me, you mean? Ten years ago? You're mistaken, man, ten years ago I was just a lad. Just a lad."

"Right. That you were. That's what made me uncertain, at first. You didn't have a whisker to your chin then."

"No, that I didn't," Brashen agreed affably. The serving boy came with the bottle and two glasses. Brashen clenched his teeth and paid for the liquor. He grinned at Tarlock and elbowed the small glass aside. The rum gurgled happily as Brashen poured it into the sailor's emptied beer mug. Tarlock beamed. Brashen tipped a bit into his own glass, then lifted it in salute. "So here's to ship-mates, old and new."

They drank together. Tarlock took a hefty slug of the rum, gasped, then leaned back with a sigh. He scratched his nose and whiskery chin energetically. Then he pointed a single thick finger at Brashen. "*Child of the Wind*," he said, and grinned his gap-toothed smile. "I'm right, ain't I?"

"About what?" Brashen asked him lazily. He watched the man

through narrowed eyes as he took a slow sip of his own rum. Tarlock followed his example with another swallow of his.

"Aw, come on," Tarlock wheezed after a moment. "You were on *Child of the Wind* when we overtook her. Little whip of a kid you was, spitting and scratching like a cat when we hauled you out of the rigging. Didn't have so much as a knife to defend yourself, but you fought right up until you dropped."

"*Child of the Wind.* Can't say as I recall her, Tarlock." Brashen put a note of warning in his voice. "You're not going to tell me you were a pirate, are you?"

The man was either too stupid or too drunk to deny it. Instead he spewed a rummy laugh into his own mug and then sat back, to wipe his chin with his wrist. "Hey! Weren't we all? Look around you, man. Think there's a man in this room hasn't freebooted a bit? Naw!" He leaned forward across the table, suddenly confidential. "You wasn't too slow to sign the articles, once you had a blade at your ribs." He leaned back again. "But as I recall, the name you went by wasn't Brashen Trell of Bingtown." He rubbed his reddened nose, considering. "I bin trine to member," he slurred. He leaned heavily on the table, then set his head down on one of his arms. "Can't remember what you said it was. But I recall what we called you." Again the thick finger lifted, just from the tabletop, to wag at Brashen. "Weasel. Cuz you was so skinny and so fast." The man's eyes sagged shut. He drew a deep, heavy breath that emerged as a snore.

Brashen stood quietly. The merchandise would be nearly loaded by now. It wouldn't take much to speed up their departure. Perhaps when Tarlock awoke, he'd find his ship had sailed without him. He wouldn't be the first sailor to get drunk and be left behind. He looked down at the snoring Tarlock. The years had not been kind to him since the *Child of the Wind.* Brashen would never have recognized him if he hadn't revealed himself. He lifted the bottle of rum, then in a spirit of largesse, he re-corked it and nestled it in the crook of the old pirate's elbow. If he woke up too soon, he'd likely delay himself with another drink or two. And if he woke up too late, perhaps the rum would console him. He really had nothing against the man, except that he reminded Brashen of a time he'd sooner forget.

Weasel, he thought to himself as he left the tavern and emerged into the chill fog of the early evening. *I'm not Weasel anymore.* As if to convince himself, he took a stick of cindin from his pocket and snapped the end off in his mouth. As he tucked it in his cheek, the sharp bitterness of it almost made his eyes water. It was probably the best quality of the drug he'd ever known, and it had been a parting goodwill gift to him from the freebooters they'd dealt with earlier in the day. Free.

No, he wasn't Weasel anymore, he reflected wryly as he headed back toward the dock and the *Springeve*. Poor Weasel never had cindin like this.

CHAPTER THIRTY-FIVE

PIRATES AND CAPTIVES

"THEY'RE PIRATES, YOU DAMN FOOL!" KYLE SPAT AT SA'ADAR. "MUSTER YOUR MEN TO REPEL THEM. WE'VE still got a chance to get away. With Wintrow at the helm, Vivacia will . . ."

"Yes, they are pirates," Sa'Adar agreed triumphantly. "And they fly the Raven flag. They're the pirates that every slave in Jamaillia prays for. They capture slaveships and free the slaves. And they feed the crews to their own stinking serpents." The last he uttered in a low growl that was at odds with the joyous smile on his face. "Truly, Sa has provided," he added, and then he was striding away from them, to the waist of the ship where the gathered slaves were pointing at the Raven flag and shouting joyously to one another.

The word had spread through the ship like fire. As the *Marietta* came alongside, grapples were thrown. Wintrow felt Vivacia's apprehension as the sharpened hooks dragged across her decks to catch in her railing. "Steady, my lady," he breathed to her again. Her anxiety mingled with his own. They had no crew with which to resist the capture, even if he had had the stomach for more fighting and blood. He felt his exhaustion hung on him like a heavy, cold garment. He kept her wheel, even as the other ship hauled in tight to her. Like an outpouring of ants from a disturbed nest, gaudily dressed sailors were suddenly swarming over her sides. Someone in the waist was barking orders, to slaves as well as sailors. With a swiftness and order that was almost magical, men began to flow up the masts. The sails were quickly and neatly reefed. He heard the anchor chain rattle out. Someone was barking orders in a voice of authority that the slaves responded to as they crowded out of the way of the pirate crewmen.

Wintrow kept still, and he hoped, inconspicuous among the other slaves. A feeling of almost relief welled up in him. These pirates were taking over his ship, but at least they moved competently. She was in the hands of true seamen.

The relief was short lived as, a moment later, bodies began to splash overboard. The white serpent that Wintrow had supposed left far behind in the storm suddenly broke to the surface to gape eagerly for the corpses. Several others, more gaudily colored, lifted their heads at a distance to regard the ship both warily and curiously. One suddenly lifted a great crest around its neck and flourished its head with a challenging bellow.

Vivacia gave an incoherent cry at sight of them. "No! Get them away!" she cried out. Then, "Not Gantry, no! Do not give him to the foul things! Wintrow! Make them stop, make them stop!"

The only response was a terrible laughter.

He glanced at his father. His eyes looked dead. "I have to go to her," Wintrow apologized. "Stay here."

His father snorted. "There's no sense in bothering. You've already lost her. You listened to that priest and let the pirates just board her. You just stood here and let the pirates take her. Just as last night you did nothing to warn us when the slaves rose against us." He shook his head. "For a time, last night, I thought I had misjudged you. But I was right all along."

"Just as I stood by and did nothing as you changed my ship into a slaver," Wintrow pointed out bitterly. He looked his father up and down slowly. "I fear I was right, too," he said. He looped off the wheel and went forward without a glance back. *The ship*, he told himself. *I do it for the ship.* He did not leave the man there alone and injured because he hated his father. He did not leave him there half-hoping someone would kill him. He only did it because the ship needed him. He moved towards the foredeck. When he reached the waist, he tried to thread his way inconspicuously through the gathered slaves there.

By daylight, the released slaves were an even more ungodly sight than they had been in the dimness of the holds. Chafed by chains and the movement of the decks beneath them, their rag-draped hides showed scabby and pale. Privation had thinned many to near bones. Some few wore better clothes, stripped from the dead or salvaged from the crew's belongings. The map-faces seemed to have appropriated his father's wardrobe and seemed to be more at ease than some of the others. Many had the blinking, confused gaze of animals caged long in the dark and suddenly released. They had broken into the ship's stores. Barrels of biscuit had been dragged out onto the deck and stove open. Some of the slaves clutched handfuls of ship's biscuit, as if to promise themselves food readily available. Freed of chains, they looked as if they could not yet recall how to move freely or act as they wished. Most shuffled still, and looked at each other only with the dull recognition that cattle have for one another. Humanity had been stolen from them. It would take them time to regain it.

He tried to move as if he were truly one of the slaves, slipping from one huddled knot to another. Sa'Adar and his map-faces stood in the center of the ship's waist, apparently offering a welcome to the pirates. The priest was speaking to three of them. The few words that Wintrow overheard seemed to be a flowery speech of welcome and thanks. None of the three looked particularly impressed. The tall man looked sickened by it. Wintrow shared his feelings.

They were not his concern. Vivacia was. Her futile pleas had died away to small inarticulate sounds. Wintrow caught sight of two map-faces on the lee side of the ship. They were systematically throwing the stacked bodies of slain crewmen and slaves overboard. Their faces were detached, their only comments relating to the gluttony of the white serpent who seized them. Wintrow caught a glimpse of Mild as he went over, and would recall forever the image of bare feet dangling from ragged trousers as the white serpent seized his friend's body in an engulfing maw. "Sa forgive us," he prayed on a breath. He spun away from the sight and got his hands on the ladder to the foredeck. He had started up it when he heard Sa'Adar order a map-face, "Fetch Captain Haven here." Wintrow halted an instant, then swarmed up it and raced to the bow. "Vivacia. I'm here, I'm here." He pitched his voice low.

"Wintrow!" she gasped. She turned to him, reached up a hand. He leaned down to touch it. The face she turned up to him was devastated with both shock and fear. "So many are dead," she whispered. "So many died last night. And what will become of us now?"

"I don't know," he told her truthfully. "But I promise that of my own will, I will never leave you again. And I will do all I can to stop any further killing. But you have to help me. You must."

"How? No one listens to me. I'm nothing to them."

"You are everything to me. Be strong, be brave."

In the waist there was a sudden stir, a muttering that grew to an animalistic roar. Wintrow didn't need to look. "They have my father down there. We have to keep him alive."

"Why?" The sudden harshness in her voice was chilling.

"Because I promised him I would try. He helped me through the night, he stood by me. And you. Despite all that is between us, he helped me keep you off the rocks." Wintrow took a breath. "And because of what it would do to me if I just stood by and allowed them to kill my father. Because of who that would make me."

"There is nothing we can do," she said bitterly. "I could not save Gantry, I could not save Mild. Not even Findow for the sake of his fiddling could I save. For all these slaves have suffered, they have only learned to disregard suffering. Pain is the coin they use now in all their transactions. Nothing else reaches them, nothing else will satisfy them." An edge of hysteria was creeping into her voice. "And that is what they fill me with. Their own pain, and their hunger for pain and . . ."

"Vivacia," he said gently, and then more firmly, "Ship. Listen to me. You sent me below to recall who I was. I know you did. And you were right. You were right to do so. Now. Recall who you are, and who has sailed you. Recall all you know of courage. We will need it."

As if in response to his words, he heard Sa'Adar's voice raised in command. "Wintrow! Come forth. Your father claims you will speak for him."

A breath. Two. Three. Finding himself at the center of all things, finding Sa at the center of himself. Recalling that Sa was all and all was Sa.

"Do not think you can hide yourself!" Sa'Adar's voice boomed out. "Come out. Captain Kennit commands it!"

Wintrow pushed the hair back from his eyes and stood as tall as he could. He walked to the edge of the foredeck and looked down on them all. "No one commands me on the deck of my own ship!" He threw the words down at them and waited to see what would happen.

"Your ship? You, made a slave by your father's own hand, claim this ship as yours?" It was Sa'Adar who spoke, not one of the pirates. Wintrow took heart.

He did not look at Sa'Adar as he spoke but at the pirates who had turned to stare at him. "I claim this ship and this ship claims me. By right of blood. And if you think that true claim can be disputed, ask my father how well he succeeded at it." He took a deep breath and tried to bring his voice from the bottom of his lungs. "The liveship *Vivacia* is mine."

"Seize him and bring him here," Sa'Adar ordered his map-faces disgustedly.

"Touch him and you all die!" Vivacia's tone was no longer that of a frightened child, but that of an outraged matriarch. Even anchored and grappled as she was, she contrived to put a rock in her decks. "Doubt it not!" she roared out suddenly. "You have soaked me with your filth, and I have not complained. You have spilled blood on my decks, blood and deaths I must carry with me forever, and I have not stirred against you. But harm Wintrow and my vengeance will know no end. No end save your deaths!"

The rocking increased, a marked motion that the *Marietta* did not match. The anchor rope creaked complainingly. Most unnerving for Wintrow, the distant serpents lashed the surface of the sea, trumpeting questioningly. The ugly heads swayed back and forth, mouths gaping as if awaiting food. A smaller one darted forward suddenly, to dare an attack at the white one, who screamed and slashed at it with myriad teeth. Cries of fear arose from Vivacia's deck as slaves retreated from the railings and from the foredeck, to pack themselves tightly together. From the questioning tones of the cries, Wintrow surmised that few of them had any understanding of what the liveship was.

Suddenly a woman broke free of the pirate group, to race across the deck and then swarm up onto the foredeck. Wintrow had never seen anything like her. She was tall and lean, her hair cropped close. The rich fabric of her skirts and loose shirt were soaked to her body, as if she had stood watch on deck all night, yet she looked no more bedraggled than a wet tigress would. She landed with a thud before him. "Come down," she said to him, and her eyes made it more a command than her voice did. "Come down to him now. Don't make him wait."

He did not answer her. Instead he spoke to the ship. "Don't fear," he told her.

"We are not the ones who need to fear," Vivacia replied. He had the satisfaction of seeing the woman's face go blank with astonishment. It was one thing to hear the liveship speak, another to stand close enough to see the angry glints in her eyes. She glowered scornfully at the woman on her deck. The *Vivacia* gave a sudden shake to her head that tossed her carved tresses back from her face. It was a womanly display, a challenge from one man's female to another. The woman brushed back from her brow the short black strands that had fallen over her forehead and returned the figurehead's stare. For an instant it shocked Wintrow that the two could look so different and yet so frighteningly alike.

Wintrow did not wait any longer. He leaped lightly from the foredeck to the waist of the ship. Head up, he strode across the deck to confront the pirates. He did not even look at Sa'Adar. The more he saw of the man, the less he thought of him as a priest.

The pirate chief was a large, well-muscled man. Dark eyes glinted above the burn scar on his cheek. A former slave himself, then. His unruly hair was caught back in a queue and further confined in a bright gold kerchief. Like his woman, his opulent clothing was soaked to him. A man who worked his own deck, then, Wintrow thought, and felt a grudging respect for that.

He met the man's gaze. "I am Wintrow Vestrit, of the Bingtown Trader Vestrits. You stand on the decks of the liveship *Vivacia*, also of the Vestrit Family."

But it was a tall pale man next to the scarred man who replied to him. "I am Captain Kennit. You address my esteemed first mate, Sorcor. And the ship that was yours is now mine."

Wintrow looked him up and down, shocked beyond speech. Numbed as his nose was to the stench of humans, this man reeked of disease. He glanced down to where Kennit's leg stopped, and took note of the crutch he leaned on, on the swollen leg that distended the fabric of his trousers as a sausage stuffs a casing. When he met Kennit's pale eyes, he noted how large and fever-bright they were, how the man's flesh clung to his skull. When Wintrow replied, he spoke gently to the dying man. "This ship can never be yours. She is a liveship. She can only belong to one of the Vestrit family."

Kennit made a brief motion of his hand to indicate Kyle. "Yet this man claims he is the owner." Wintrow's father yet managed to stand, and almost straight. Neither fear nor his physical pain did he permit to show. He was a man who waited now. Kyle spoke not a word to his son.

Wintrow shaped his words with care. "He 'owns' her, yes, in the sense that one can own a thing. But she is mine. I do not claim to own her, any more than a father can claim to own his child."

Captain Kennit looked him up and down disdainfully. "You look a bit young of a pup to be claiming any kind of a child. And by the mark on your face, I would say the ship owned you. I take it your father married into a Trader family, then, but you are blood of that line."

"I am a Vestrit by blood, yes." Wintrow kept his voice even.

"Ah." Again the small gesture of his hand toward Kyle. "Then we don't need your father. Only you." Kennit turned back to Sa'Adar. "That one you may have, as you requested. And those other two."

There was a splash, and a trumpeting from one of the serpents. Wintrow looked starboard just in time to see two map-faces tip the other Jamaillian sailor over the edge. He went screaming until the white serpent cut his cry short with a snap. Wintrow's own cry of "Wait!" went unheeded. Vivacia gave a wordless cry of horror, and flailed at the serpents, but could not reach them. Map-faces were laying hold of his father. He sprang, not towards them, but at Sa'Adar. He gripped the man by the front of his shirt. "You promised them they would live! If they worked the ship for you through the storm, you promised them they would live!"

Sa'Adar shrugged and smiled down at him. "It's not my will, boy, but that of Captain Kennit. He does not have to keep my word for me."

"You spin your word so thin, I doubt anyone could be bound by it," Wintrow cried furiously. He whirled on the men who had seized his father. "Set him free."

They paid no attention to him as they forced his struggling father to the rail. Physically, Wintrow had no chance against them. He turned back to Captain Kennit, speaking quickly. "Set him free! You have seen how the ship is about the serpents! If you throw one of her own to them, she will be greatly angered."

"No doubt," the pirate captain replied lazily. "But he isn't truly one of her own. So she'll get over it."

"I won't," Wintrow told him furiously. "And you will soon discover that if you cut one of us, we both bleed." His father was struggling, but wordlessly and without much strength. Beside the ship, the white serpent trumpeted eagerly. Wintrow knew he had not the strength to prevail against those two men, let alone however many would muster to Kennit's command.

Kennit, however, was another matter. Swift as a snake striking, Wintrow seized the pirate captain by his shirt front. He jerked him forward, so that his crutch fell to the deck and he must depend on

Wintrow or fall also. The sudden motion wrung a low cry of pain from the man. The mate sprang forward with a snarl.

"Back!" Wintrow warned him. "And stop those men. Or I'll kick him in that leg and spatter his rotten flesh all over the deck."

"Wait! Release him!" The command came not from Sorcor, but the woman. The men halted uncertainly, looking from her to Sa'Adar. Wintrow did not waste time speaking to them. Kennit was all but fainting in Wintrow's grasp. Wintrow gave him another shake and growled up into the man's face. "You burn with fever and you stink of decay. As you stand here, on the one leg left to you, you may kill both my father and myself. But if you do, you will not possess my ship for more than a handful of days before you follow us down. And whoever you leave behind upon the *Vivacia*'s decks will perish, too. The ship will see to that. So I suggest we find a bargain between us."

Captain Kennit lifted his hands slowly, to clutch at Wintrow's wrists with both of his own. The boy didn't care. At the moment, he had it within his power to cause the man incredible pain, perhaps enough pain to kill him with the shock of it. The deep lines in the pirate's face told Wintrow that he, too, knew that. Beads of pain sweat shone on the pirate's brow. For a scant moment, Wintrow's eyes were caught by the odd wrist-brooch the man wore. A tiny face, like to the pirate's own, grinned up at him gleefully. It unsettled him. He looked up again at the man's face, met his eyes and stared deep into their coldness. They returned his gaze and seemed to look deep into the core of him. He refused to be cowed.

"Well? What say you?" Wintrow demanded, with the barest hint of a shake. "Do we bargain?"

The pirate's mouth scarcely moved as, in the softest whisper imaginable, Wintrow heard him say, "A likely urchin. Perhaps something useful can be made of him."

"What?" Wintrow demanded furiously. Savage anger rose in him at the man's mockery.

An extremely strange look had come over the pirate's face. Kennit stared down at him in a sort of fascination. For an instant, he seemed to recognize him, and Wintrow, too, felt an uncanny sense of having been here, done this and spoken these words before. There was something compelling in Kennit's gaze, something that demanded to be acknowledged. The silence between them seemed to bind them together.

Wintrow felt a sudden prick against his ribs. The woman with the knife said, "Take Kennit gently, Sorcor. Boy, you have missed your chance to die swiftly. All you have bought is that you and your father will die together, each praying to be the first to go."

"No. No, Etta, stand aside." The pirate managed his pain well, never losing his educated diction. He still had to take a breath to speak on. "What is your bargain, boy? What do you have left to offer? Your ship, freely given?" Kennit shook his head slowly. "I already have her, one way or another. So I am intrigued. Just what do you think you have to trade with?"

"A life for a life," Wintrow offered slowly. He spoke knowing that what he proposed was likely beyond his skill to perform. "I have been trained in healing, for I was once promised to Sa's priesthood." He glanced down at the pirate's leg. "You need the skills I have. You know you do. I'll keep you alive. If you allow my father to live."

"No doubt you'll want to cut more of my leg off for such a bet." His question was contemptuous.

Wintrow looked up, searching the older man's eyes for acceptance. "You already know that must be done," he pointed out to him. "You were simply waiting until the pain of the festering would make the pain of the removal seem like a relief." He glanced down at the stump again. "You have nearly waited too long. But I am still ready to honor the bargain. Your life for my father's."

Kennit swayed in his grasp and Wintrow found himself steadying the man. All about them, men were frozen in a tableau of watching and waiting. The map-faces had his father pressed up against the railing, that he might watch the serpent that waited so impatiently.

"It's a poor sort of bet," Kennit observed weakly. "Up the ante. Your life as well." He grinned a sickly grin. "So that if I win by dying, we all lose together."

"You have a strange idea of winning," said Wintrow.

"Then you include your crew in your wager," Vivacia suddenly pointed out. "For if you take Wintrow's life from me, I shall see every one of you to a watery grave." She paused. "And that is the only bargain I offer to any of you."

"High stakes," Wintrow observed quietly. "Nonetheless, I accept them if you do."

"I am scarcely in a position to shake hands upon it," the pirate pointed out. His tone was as cool and charming as ever, yet Wintrow could see the man's strength fading even as they spoke. A small smile bent his lips. "You do not try to make me agree that if I live, I give your ship back to you?"

It was Wintrow's turn to shake his head slowly. His smile was as small as Kennit's. "You cannot take her from me. Nor could I give her to you. That, I think, is something you must discover for yourself. But your word will suffice to bind me to the rest of our wager. And that of your mate and the woman," he added. He looked past Kennit to the woman as he added, "And if my father comes to ill from the slaves aboard this ship, I shall take it to cancel the bet."

"There are no slaves aboard this ship!" Sa'Adar declared pompously.

Wintrow ignored him. He waited until the woman gave a slow nod.

"If you have my captain's word, you have my word," Sorcor added gruffly.

"Fine," Wintrow declared. He turned his head and looked straight at Sa'Adar as he spoke. "Clear the way to my father's salon. I want the pirate captain in his bed there. And let my father go to Gantry's cabin and take some rest. I will be seeing to his ribs later."

For just an instant, Sa'Adar's eyes narrowed at the boy. Wintrow was not sure what passed through the man's mind. He knew he could not trust the priest to abide by anyone's word, not even his own. The man would bear watching.

Slaves milled apart to open a channel to the aftercastle. Some moved grudgingly and others impassively. Some few looked at him and seemed to remember a boy with a bucket of water and a cool, moist rag. Wintrow watched his father led away to Gantry's cabin. He never turned to look back at his son, nor spoke a word.

Wintrow decided he should press his power, to see how far it would extend. He glanced at the map-faces that flanked Sa'Adar. "This deck is still a shambles," he observed quietly. "I want the canvas and line cleared from it, and all mess scrubbed away. Then begin below decks. Free men have no excuse to live in squalor."

The map-faces looked from him to Sa'Adar and back again.

Sorcor broke the impasse. "You can obey the boy when he tells you to do it, or you can obey me. The point is, it gets done and promptly." He looked away from them to his own crew. The map-faces slowly moved away from Sa'Adar, to take up their directed tasks. The priest remained standing as he was. Sorcor was giving commands. ". . . and Cory on the wheel, Brig running the deck. I want anchor up and sail on as soon as you see the *Marietta* start to move. We'll all be heading back to Bull Creek. Move lively, now, show them how a sailor does his work." He glanced again at the slowly dispersing map-faces and included the priest, who stood with his arms crossed on his chest. "Lively. There's work for all of you. Don't make Brig find it for you."

Two steps brought him to Wintrow's side, where the boy more held than threatened the man anymore. As gently as if he were picking up a sleeping infant, the burly mate eased his arms about his captain. The smile he gave Wintrow showed him more teeth than a bulldog's snarl. "You lived through laying hands on the captain once. It won't happen again."

"No. I trust it won't need to," Wintrow replied, but it was the woman's cold black eyes on his back that made his belly cold.

"I'll see you to your room, sir," Sorcor suggested.

"After I have presented myself to the ship," Kennit countered. The man actually tried to smooth his shirt front.

Wintrow smiled. "I'll be pleased to introduce you to Vivacia."

The methodical slowness with which Kennit worked his way across the deck made Wintrow's heart sink. He was a man held together by sheer will and sense of self. Should either falter, he would die. As long as he was determined to live, Wintrow had a powerful ally in curing him. But if he gave it up, all the skill in the world would not prevail against the spreading infection.

The ladder to the foredeck was a major obstacle. Sorcor did his best to maintain Kennit's dignity as he helped him up it, while Etta, who had preceded them, turned to glare down at the gawking slaves. "Have you nothing better to do than stare?" she demanded of them, and then to Brig she suggested, "There are sick slaves below, no doubt. These ones could be employed in bringing them up for air." A moment later Kennit gained the foredeck. She tried to take his arm, but he waved her away. By the time Wintrow had gained the foredeck, Kennit had used his crutch to make his painful way to the bow.

Vivacia turned to look over her shoulder. Her eyes traveled up and down him before she said in a quietly reserved voice, "Captain Kennit."

"My lady Vivacia." He bowed to her, not as deeply as a healthy man might have, but more than a nod. When he straightened, he returned her inspection. Wintrow watched uneasily, for the man's nostrils widened and the smile that curved his mouth was both approval and avarice. His frank appraisal flustered Vivacia. In an almost girlish response, she drew back and lifted her arms to cross her wrists over her breasts. Kennit's smile only widened. Vivacia's eyes went very wide, but she could not seem to stop the smile that crept to her own face.

She broke the silence first. "I do not know what you want of me. Why have you attempted to claim me this way?"

Kennit took a step closer. "Ah, my lady of wood and wind, my swift one, my beauty. What I want could not be plainer. I wish to make you my own. So my first question must be, what do you wish of me? What must I do to win you?"

"I do not . . . No one has ever . . ." Obviously flustered, she turned to Wintrow. "Wintrow is mine and I am his. We have both discovered that nothing can change that. Certainly you cannot come between us."

"Can't I? So says the girl who speaks fondly of her brother, until her lover steals her heart away."

Wintrow found himself speechless. Perhaps the only other person as flabbergasted at this interplay was the woman who had come aboard with Kennit. Her eyes were narrowed, like a cat's when she stares down a hostile dog. Jealous, Wintrow thought. She is jealous of his sweet words to the ship. As I, he admitted to himself, am jealous at Vivacia's confusion and pleasure.

The fine grain of her cheeks had taken on a pink blush. The breath that moved her bare breasts behind her arms came more swiftly. "I am a ship, not a woman," she pointed out to him. "You cannot be my lover."

"Can't I? Shall not I drive you through seas no other man would dare, shall not we together see lands that are the stuff of legends? Shall not we venture together under skies where the stars have not been named yet? Shall not we, you and I, weave such a tale of our adventures that the whole world will be in awe of us? Ah, Vivacia, I tell you plainly that I shall win you to me. Without fear, I tell you that."

She looked from Kennit to Wintrow. Her confusion was pretty, as was the sweetness of her pleasure at his words. "You shall never take Wintrow's place with me, regardless of what you say," she managed. "He is family."

"Of course not!" Kennit told her warmly. "I do not wish it. If he makes you feel safe, then we shall keep him aboard forevermore." Again he smiled at her, a smile both wicked and wise. "*I* do not wish to make you feel safe, my lady." He crossed his arms on his chest, and despite his crutch and shortened leg, he managed to look both handsome and rakish. "I have no desire to be your little brother."

In the midst of this courtship, his leg must have pained him, for he suddenly faltered, losing his smile to a grimace of pain. He bowed his head forward with a gasp, and in an instant Sorcor was at his side.

"You are hurt! You must go and rest now!" the *Vivacia* exclaimed before anyone else could speak.

"I fear I must," Kennit concurred so humbly that Wintrow suddenly knew he was more than pleased at the ship's reaction. He even wondered if the man had deliberately sought it. "So I must leave you now. But I shall call again, shall I? As soon as I am able?"

"Yes. Please do." Her hands fell away from her chest. She extended one towards him, as if to invite him to touch palms with her.

The pirate managed another deep bow but made no move to touch her. "Until then," he told her, fondness already in his voice. He turned aside, to say in a huskier voice. "Sorcor. I shall require your assistance yet again."

As the brawny pirate took his captain's weight and began to help him aft, Wintrow caught sight of the look that the woman gave the ship. It was not pleasant.

"Sorcor!" All turned back to the *Vivacia*'s imperious command. "Be careful with him. And when you have finished there, I would borrow some of your archers. I'd like these serpents discouraged, if nothing else."

"Captain?" Sorcor asked doubtfully.

Kennit leaned on him heavily. His face was moist with sweat, but still he smiled. "Give the lady her due. A liveship under me. Court her for me, man, until I can charm her myself." With a sigh like death, he folded suddenly into his mate's arms. As Sorcor hefted the man and then bore him off to what had been his father's stateroom, Wintrow wondered at the strange smile Kennit yet wore. The woman walked behind them, her eyes never leaving Captain Kennit's face.

Wintrow turned and walked slowly to the bow, to the spot where Kennit had stood. No one, he marked, moved to stop him. He was as free aboard the ship as he had ever been.

"Vivacia," he said quietly.

She had been staring after Kennit. She broke from her bemusement to look up at Wintrow. Her eyes were wide with wonder. They sparkled.

She lifted a hand to him and he leaned to let their palms touch. No words were needed, yet he spoke them anyway. "Be careful."

"He is a dangerous man," she agreed. "Kennit." Her voice caressed the name.

He opened his eyes to a well-appointed room. The grain of the paneled walls had been carefully selected to match. The fixed lanterns were of brass that would gleam when properly polished again. Rolled charts graced the chart rack like fat hens in nesting boxes. They would be a treasure trove of information, the gathered wealth of a Bingtown Trader family's charts. There were other niceties, too. The washstand with its matching porcelain bowl and pitcher. The framed paintings fastened securely to the walls. The meticulously carved shutters for the thick glass windows. A tasteful and elegant room indeed. True, it had been recently rifled, and the captain's possessions scattered about, but Etta moved quietly about it, setting it to rights. There was an over-lying smell of cheap incense that could not disguise the under-lying stench of a slaver. Yet it was obvious to him that the *Vivacia* had not been so used for long; it should be possible to scrub it out of her. Once more she could be a bright and tidy vessel. And this was a room for a true captain.

He glanced down at himself. He had been undressed and a sheet draped his legs.

"And where is our boy-captain?" Kennit asked Etta.

She spun at the sound of his voice and then hurried to his side. "He has gone to tend his father's ribs and head. He said it would not take long, and he wished to have the chamber cleared of clutter before he tried to heal you." She looked at him and shook her head. "I do not understand how you can trust him. He must know that if you live this ship can never be his. Nor do I understand why you will allow a mere boy to do what you forbade three skilled healers even to think of in Bull Creek."

"Because he is a part of my luck," he said quietly. "The same luck that has given this ship to me so easily. You must see this is the ship I am meant to have. The boy is part and parcel of that."

He almost wanted to make her understand. But no one must know of the words the charm had spoken when the boy looked so deeply into his eyes. No one must know of the bond forged between them in that instant, a bond that frightened Kennit as much as it intrigued him. He spoke again to keep her from asking any more questions. "So. We are under weigh all ready?"

"Sorcor takes us back to Bull Creek. He has put Cory on the wheel and Brig in charge of the deck. We follow the *Marietta*."

"I see." He smiled to himself. "And what do you think of my liveship?"

She gave him a bittersweet smile. "She is lovely. And I am already jealous of her." Etta crossed her arms on her chest and gave him a sideways glance. "I do not think we shall get along easily. She is too strange a thing, neither woman nor wood nor ship. I do not like the pretty words you sprinkle so thickly before her, nor do I like the boy Wintrow."

"And as ever, I care little what you like or dislike," Kennit told her impatiently. "What can I give the ship to win her, save words? She is not a woman in the same way you are." When the whore still looked sulky, he added savagely, "And were not my leg so painful, I would put you on your back and remind you of what you are to me."

Her eyes changed suddenly from black ice to dark fire. "Would that you could," she said gently, and disgusted him with the warmth of the smile his rebuke earned him.

Kyle Haven lay on Gantry's bare bunk, facing the bulkhead. All that the ransacking slaves had left of the mate's possessions were scattered on the floor. There was not much. Wintrow stepped over a carved wooden chain and a single discarded sock. All else that had been Gantry's—his books, his clothes, his carving tools—had been taken or left in fragments, either by the slaves in their first rush of plundering, or by the pirates in their far more organized gathering of loot.

"It's Wintrow, Father," he told him as he shut the door behind him. It would not latch anymore; during the uprising, someone had kicked it open rather than simply trying the knob. But the door stayed shut, and the two map-faces that Sa'Adar had posted as sentries did not try to open it again.

The man on the bed did not stir.

Wintrow set the basin of water and the rags he'd salvaged down on the cracked remains of Gantry's desk and turned to the man in the bed. He hastily set his fingers to the pulsepoint in his throat, and felt his father jolt back to consciousness at his touch. The man shuddered away from him with an incoherent sound, then sat up hastily.

"It's all right," Wintrow said comfortingly. "It's only me."

His father showed his teeth in a mockery of a smile. "It's only you," he conceded. "But I'll damn well bet it isn't all right."

He looked terrible, worse than he had when the slaves were trying to feed him to the serpent. *Old*, Wintrow thought to himself. *He looks suddenly old.* Stubble stood on his cheeks and blood from his head wound was smeared through it. He had come in here intending to clean his father's wounds and bind them. Now he felt himself strangely reluctant to touch the man. It was not dismay at the blood, nor was he too proud to do such tasks. His time in the hold tending the slaves had eroded those things away long ago. This was a reluctance to touch because the man was his father. Touch might affirm that link.

Wintrow faced what he felt squarely. He wished with all his heart he had no bond to this man.

"I brought some wash water," he told him. "Not much. Fresh water supplies are very low just now. Are you hungry? Shall I try to get some hard-tack for you? It's about all that is left."

"I'm fine," his father said flatly, not answering his question. "Don't trouble yourself on my account. You've more important friends to pander to just now."

He ignored his father's choice of words. "Kennit's sleeping. If I'm to have any chance of healing him, he'll need all the rest he can get to strengthen him."

"So. You'll truly do it. You'll heal the man who's taken your ship from you."

"To keep you alive, yes."

His father snorted. "Bilge. You'd do it anyway, even if they'd fed me to that snake. It's what you do. Cower before whoever has the power."

Wintrow tried to consider it impartially. "You're probably right. But not because he has power. It would have nothing to do with who he is. It's life, father. Sa is life. While life exists, there is always the possibility of improvement. So, as a priest, I have a duty to preserve life. Even his."

His father gave a sour laugh. "Even mine, you mean."

Wintrow gave a single nod.

He turned the gashed side of his head toward his son. "May as well get to it, then, priest. As it's all you're good for."

He would not be baited. "Let's check your ribs first."

"As you will." Moving stiffly, his father drew off what remained of his shirt. The left side of his chest was black and blue. Wintrow winced at the clear imprint of a boot in his flesh. It had obviously been done after his father was already down. The rags and the water were the only supplies he had; the ship's medicine chest had completely disappeared. Doggedly, he set out to at least bind the ribs enough to give them some support. His father gasped at his touch, but did not jerk away. When Wintrow had tied the final knot, Kyle Haven spoke.

"You hate me, don't you, boy?"

"I don't know." Wintrow dipped a rag and started to dab blood from his face.

"I do," his father said after a moment. "It's in your face. You can scarcely stand to be in this room with me, let alone touch me."

"You did try to kill me," Wintrow heard himself say calmly.

"Yes. I did. I did at that." His father gave a baffled laugh, then gasped with the pain of it. "Damn me if I know why. But it certainly seemed like a good idea at the time."

Wintrow sensed he would get no more explanation than that. Perhaps he didn't want one. He was tired of trying to understand his father. He didn't want to hate him. He didn't want to feel anything for him at all. He found himself wishing his father had not existed in his life. "Why did it have to be this way?" he wondered aloud.

"You chose it," Kyle Haven asserted. "It didn't have to be this way. If you had just tried it my way . . . just done as you were told, without question, we'd all be fine. Couldn't you have, just once, trusted that someone else knew what was good for you?"

Wintrow glanced about the room as if looking about the entire ship. "I don't think any of this was good for anyone," he observed quietly.

"Only because you muddled it! You and the ship. If you both had cooperated, we'd be halfway to Chalced by now. And Gantry and Mild and . . . all of them would still be alive. You're to blame for this, not I! You chose this."

Wintrow tried to think of an answer to that, but none came. He began to bind his father's head wound as best as he could.

They worked her decks well, these brightly clad pirates. Not since Ephron had sailed her had she enjoyed a crew so swiftly responsive to her. She found herself in turn accepting their competent mastery of her sails and rigging in a sort of relief. Under Brig's direction, the former slaves moved in an orderly procession, drawing buckets of water and taking them below to clean her holds. Others pumped the filthy bilge out while still others worked with scrubbing stones on her deck. No matter how they abraded the blood stains, her wood would never release them. She knew that, but spoke no word of it. In time the humans would see the futility of it and give it up. The spilled food had been gathered and restowed. Some few worked at removing the chains and fetters that festooned her holds. Slowly they were restoring her to herself. It was the closest she had felt to content since the day she had been quickened.

Content. And there was something else she felt, something unsettling. Something much more fascinating than contentment.

She extended her awareness. In the mate's cabin, Kyle Haven sat on the edge of the narrow bunk while his son silently washed the blood from the gash on his head. His ribs were already wrapped.

There was a quiet in the room that went beyond silence, as if they did not even share a language. The silence ached. She pulled away from it.

In the captain's salon, the pirate dozed restlessly. She was not aware of him as keenly as she was of Wintrow. But she could sense the heat of his fever, feel the uneven rhythm of his breathing. Like a moth drawn to a candleflame, she approached him. Kennit. She tried the name on her tongue. A wicked man. And dangerous. A charming, wicked and dangerous man. She did not think she liked his woman. But Kennit himself . . . He had said he would win her to him. He could not, of course. He was not family. But she found that there was great pleasure in anticipating his attempts. My lady of wood and wind, he had called her. My beauty. My swift one. Such silly things for a man to say to a ship. She smoothed her hair back from her face and took a deep breath.

Perhaps Wintrow had been right. Perhaps it was time she discovered what she wanted for herself.

CHAPTER THIRTY-SIX

SHE WHO REMEMBERS

"I WAS WRONG. IT IS NOT SHE WHO REMEMBERS. COME AWAY."

"But . . . I do not understand," Shreever pleaded. She had a great gash down her shoulder where the white serpent had attacked her with his teeth. With his teeth, as if he were a shark instead of serpent. A thick green ichor was already closing the wound, but it stung sharply as she hurried to keep pace with Maulkin. Behind them, Sessurea trailed, as puzzled as she was.

"I do not understand either." Maulkin's mane streamed behind him in the speed of his flowing. Behind them the white serpent still trumpeted mindlessly, gorging endlessly. Faint as old memories, the scent of blood wafted through the atmosphere. "I recall her scent. I have no doubt of her fragrance. But that . . . thing . . . is not She Who Remembers."

Sessurea lashed his tail suddenly to draw even with them. "The white serpent," he asked suddenly, dread in his voice. "What was wrong with him?"

"Nothing," Maulkin said in a terribly soft voice. "I fear nothing was wrong with him, except that he is further along in the passage we all make now. Soon, I fear, we shall all be just like him."

"I don't understand," Shreever said again. But a cold dread was welling up in her, a sense that she would understand, if she chose to.

"He has forgotten. That is all." Maulkin's voice was devoid of any emotion.

"Forgotten . . . what?" Sessurea asked.

"Everything," Maulkin said. His mane suddenly drooped, his colors dulled. "Everything except feeding, and shedding and growing. All else, all that is real and significant, he has forgotten. As I fear we all shall forget, if She Who Remembers does not manifest herself to us soon." He turned abruptly, wrapping them both in his coiling embrace. They did not struggle, but took comfort in it. His touch sharpened their memories and cognizance. Together they settled slowly to the soft muck, sinking into it still entwined. "My tangle," he said fondly, and with a pang Shreever knew the truth of it. These three were all that was left of Maulkin's tangle.

They relaxed in their leader's embrace. Soon only their heads remained above the muck. They relaxed, their gills moved in unison. Slowly, comfortingly, Maulkin spoke the holy lore to them.

"After the first birth, we were Masters. We grew, we learned, we experienced. And all that we learned, we shared with one another, so that wisdom ever grew greater. But no bodies are made to last forever. So the time of mating came, and essences were exchanged and mixed and deposited. Our old bodies we laid down forever, knowing we would take up new ones, as new beings. And we did. Small and new we emerged. We fed, we shed, and we grew. But we did not all remember. Only some. Some guarded for us the memories of all. And when the time was right, those who remembered called to us with their fragrances. They led us back, and gave us our memories. And we emerged again as Masters, to roam both Plenty and Lack, amassing still more wisdom and experience, to mingle it yet again at the time of mating."

He paused in the familiar tale. "I do not recall, now, how many times that has come to pass," he confessed. "Cycle after cycle, we have survived. But this last time of shedding and growing . . . has not it been the longest ever? Do not more and more of us forget that we are meant to be Masters? I fear we decline, my tangle. Did I not once, long ago, recall far more than I do today? Did not you?"

His questions probed the uneasy place in Shreever's heart. She tangled her ruff against his, daring the toxins that she might feel the sting of his memories and beings. Her thoughts came sharper to her.

"Once, I remembered far more," she admitted. "Sometimes, I think all I remember clearly now is that you are the one to follow. The one with true memories."

His trumpeting was deep and soft as he spoke. "If She Who Remembers does not come to us soon, even I may forget that."

"Remember this, then, above all else. That we must continue to seek She Who Remembers."

ROBIN HOBB,
who also writes as Megan Lindholm,
lives in Washington State.